Memoirs
of a
Shape-Shifter

☙

Also by Thomas Kaplan-Maxfield

THE SCARAB CHASE

BROCKTON STORIES

HIDE & SEEK

THE GHOST OF HOLLOW PINE

THE POSTHUMOUS WRITINGS OF WITMAN DRUCKER

BLACK FOREST LOVE STORY

Memoirs
of a
Shape-Shifter

❧

Thomas Kaplan-Maxfield

KEPLER PRESS

CAMBRIDGE

KEPLER PRESS, PUBLISHERS (SAN 255-6014)
P.O. Box 400326
Cambridge, MA 02140 U.S.A.
http://www.KeplerPress.com

Library of Congress Control Number: 03 107938
ISBN 0-9713770-3-0, print ed.
Printed in the United States of America

Cover photograph of *Wraith Wrap*, © 2004 Leslie Wilcox
Original 25 ft. stainless steel sculpture by Leslie Wilcox installed at Forest Hills Cemetery, Boston, Massachusetts in 2004. For more information, contact www.LeslieWilcox.com or www.foresthillstrust.org.

Cover and book design by eProduction Services, www.eproduction.com

The author is grateful for permission to quote the line of the Druid poem on p. 285 from "Avalloch and the Tree Fairy: A Triptych," by Peg Aloi.

Celtic Ogham font "Beth-Luis-Fearn," © 1992-1998 Curtis Clark, jcclark@csupomona.edu

Publisher's Cataloging-in-Publication
(Provided by Quality Books, Inc.)

Kaplan-Maxfield, Thomas.
    Memoirs of a shape-shifter / Thomas Kaplan-Maxfield.
    p. cm.
    LCCN 2003107938
    ISBN 0-9713770-3-0

    1. Women--Social conditions--Fiction. 2. Man-woman relationships--Fiction. 3. Mothers and daughters--Fiction. 4. Religions--Fiction. 5. New England--Fiction. I. Title.

PS3611.A664M46 2005   813'.6
                    QBI05-800307

for E.

CONTENTS

INTRODUCTION

THE SOUL OF GLOUCESTER is split as the souls of its sons and daughters are split, as a rock may be split by chisel and mallet. The town clings by fingernails to one mass of jagged granite that is Cape Ann, surrounded on three sides by the northern manic sea. The sea throws itself at the rocky shore like a demon lover, caressing and fleeing, caressing and retreating. On the highest point of the Cape, originally the center of old Gloucester, lie deep woods moist with cleft life: pines, oaks, maples, firs; owls, bluebirds, robins, chickadees. Nearby down rambling old stone roads crumble the ruins of many a cellar hole—ancient foundations of houses that once lined the streets.

There Gloucester was first settled by English Puritans as a farming community in the 1600s. But when the granite proved too difficult to farm, the settlers moved downhill that their men might earn a living by the sea. Eventually the families established the town as the premier fishing village in New England. For day after relentless day every dogged Odysseus, leaving behind his woman, set sail on the salt-clean sea and returned boat heavy with the day's catch, heart hardened by the cold Goddess Atlantic. Drunk, knotted hands twitching on tables laden with fish-bought coin, their silent dinners served by stranger-women, the fishermen and lobstermen came to rage at the fixed course of their common fate.

Over time the men of Gloucester abandoned the decaying houses to the spinsters and whores, the healers, witches and Druids, and the woods up the hill became known as Dogtown, after the witch Hecate's totem. There the women suffered their own splintered lives, without men to mend roof or shingle, to balance the scales. Dogtown's women came to rage at their share of fate, splitting their bodies for the men below while spitting venom and curses, in their own dog-protected ways becoming as fearful as the men.

Devotees of a religion older than Christianity, some of those women tended to the discards of the spoils below: sacred knowledge of the earth, the use of herb and mineral, bark and fresh water. While heavenly, God-driven men tamed a world with reason and commerce, the witches and Druids of Dogtown huddled close to the trees, the earth's mantic, stone-clad root.

Two centuries later sturdy Finns arrived to mine the granite skeleton of Cape Ann, sending boxcar-sized blocks southward to build the mansions of the newly rich. Men worked land and sea until nature gave up her all, as she will for a time. The seas were finally emptied out while many a hidden rain-filled quarry was forgotten in the woods, for no longer is Gloucester a resource of stone, much less of fish. Yet still in the Dogtown air lingers the spirit of the first women arrrested in the Salem witch trials; the moist, piney woods, female smells where cleaves the mind of reason.

Nowadays down in the village harbor old sailors huddle on cracked wooden benches that line Rogers Street. They stare out to sea, lick salt-dried lips and remember, fists clenching warm beers. They totter home at midnight, drunk down narrow, pitched streets of crumpled vinyl-clad houses, mumbling snatches of sea shanties. Kicking at the emasculated dreams of lottery tickets, leering out of red-rimmed eyes for the next hit of heroin, they long to forget their fathers' dreams of faraway tropical isles teeming with soft brown women and dangling fruit; to forget the hounding.

Out of the long line of woodland Druid mothers and seafaring, stone-cutting fathers, Gloucester contrived to give birth to a daughter, Nikki Helmik, who was made to carve out the town's divided nature, bearing the land's fault line within.

1.

NIKKI'S FALL

NIKKI HELMIK, forty years old, huddled her face in her coat collar, far enough away from the black-clad mourners gathered in a dark clutch near the pit of the grave so they wouldn't notice her. She lowered her umbrella until her view of the burial was compressed. Her nose and mouth were red-lined with grief as she clutched in her pocket the stump of a dried rose the dead man had once given her. As an unusually warm January mist was veiling softly, the mourners held their umbrellas uncertainly, some aloft, some folded at their sides. A great wintery oak clawed the massive air above the grave, blasted grey, its bark slick as a seal in the mist. Nikki watched Rose, Ernest Eveless' widow, head bowed, toss a red rose into the grave on top of the descending casket. It was the most ornate—gaudy, in fact— casket Nikki had ever seen, made of cherry wood with curlicued, solid-brass handles, hinges, and medallions all over it. But that was Rose all over—ostentation. Let every-one in Gloucester know you are rich, even if (assuming the rumors were true) your dead husband had lost most of his money when his fishing business went under and left you with only that huge granite house on the hill.

Even with her face stained—*was it the rain or sadness?* Nikki wondered—even so, Rose was beautiful, her dark mass of Portuguese hair pulled back, eyes deeply high-lighted, lips blood red. Tiny droplets of rain glistened in her hair—she was aware of the effect she produced, Nikki could see. She knew her friend, her enemy, intimately.

Beside Rose stood a younger man whom Nikki knew immediately as Rose and Ernest's only child, Philip, lately home from France. The winch rumbled softly as the casket disappeared into the wet ground; Nikki thought of her own father's burial, a short month ago, in this same cemetery not far from Portuguese Hill, on a bluff overlooking the slaty, brooding waters of the restive Atlantic. His casket was almost the cheapest one they could find, even though her sister Cynthia, concerned with appearances, insisted they spend money on a pricey one. When Nikki and her other sisters suggested Cynthia spend her own money on a more expensive one, Cynthia had suddenly agreed it was a waste of money.

Should she speak to Rose? *No!* Pursing her lips, Nikki kept her eyes on Philip, his lean face and bowed head making him look, in profile, very much like his father,

3

even to the glasses his father had worn. The sight of him sent a thrill through her. She had not spoken to Philip since they were fifth-grade classmates, when he was sent away abruptly to boarding school in Europe. She hadn't known him well then, but he had grown now into a beautiful man, beautiful like his mother, the great beauty of Gloucester, yet stern with the thin, set mouth of his father. His face like his father's was long and pronounced, strong-boned especially in the jaw and cheek, his Adam's apple prominent and narrowly vulnerable. His hard, intense expression was markedly like his father's as well. Even from a distance she was struck by his brooding air, which intimidated and attracted her.

The priceless casket sank, and a sigh rose from the little knot of people. The great Ernest Eveless dead! By his own hand, according to gossip, although Nikki was too frightened of Rose after their recent fight to ask her the truth. How terrible that the one woman who had been mentor to Nikki, teaching her everything, now was her enemy!

Nikki watched Rose solemnly close her prayer book with voluptuous fingers, red-tipped nails moving like soft snakes. Rose looked up, tears carefully staining her eyes; everything she did was rehearsed, Nikki knew. Rose had instructed Nikki carefully: "Every move you make as a woman, if you want power, must be calculated and directed. The men of power are always watching." And power was what Nikki had always wanted, like her heroine Rose. Nikki shivered; she was still overawed by Rose, still afraid of her, still seeing her as all of Gloucester did, as the great and powerful beauty of the town. And there was Philip beside his mother; Nikki would have to talk to him some time. Not today, but soon. She was patient, for she, too, was confident of her own power with men. Hadn't she hooked any man she ever wanted? Rose had taught her well—Rose, who had climbed to power in Gloucester not only by means of her husband's wealth but by her own steel heart and willingness to use her sex to make men tremble. There was an edge to everything she did, a hint of desperation that drove men mad. In fact, insanity lay in Rose's Portuguese family; her uncle had long been institutionalized as schizophrenic, and her father like Nikki's had been a hopeless drunk.

The gravediggers were sopping wet, leaning over in their heavy, dark coats to dismantle the winch, hauling the straps up and out of the pit. Nikki did not dare move closer.

Ernest! The thought that he might have killed himself terrified Nikki. Could it have been over her? So soon after the wrenching fight between Nikki and Rose, when Rose had accused Nikki of sleeping with her husband?

Nikki bowed her head as the rain slid down her cheeks. No, it wasn't true, though how often had she wished it were! Ernest, the man she had grown up around, idealizing him for his strength as she had idolized Rose. The richest man in Gloucester, owner of the largest fleet of fishing boats anywhere on Boston's North Shore. Nikki had spent her youth in the Eveless house as Rose's assistant and companion, sitting many evenings with Ernest. She saw how cruelly Rose treated her husband, Nikki's heart going out to him. He was so silent, so powerful in his own grim way, with his set jawbone and piercing stare, such an anodyne to Rose's wildly passionate Mediterranean nature. Rock-hard, self-contained, he was a Puritan Yankee fisherman from a poor family who through force of will had bested the sea. His knack for finding the fish was legendary; no one in Gloucester was ignorant of the stories of Ernest at the bow, staring ahead, motioning back at the helmsman, two points to starboard, one to larboard, a quick nod with never a smile. He always navigated with a sixth sense to the exact spot where the cod were running.

How had Rose and Ernest ever loved each other enough to marry? Nikki stood musing. She recalled the thrill it had given her as a girl to be in Ernest's presence, bringing him a message from Rose in his high-ceilinged library, standing shyly by his leather chair and watching his craggy face as he spoke slowly and carefully to her, peering through her with bright, hard blue eyes behind his glasses. Then she would hurry back to Rose. How she had loved Rose, those years growing up! And how much Rose had given her, teaching her all the secrets of how to be a powerful woman, to disdain men but for their usefulness—for sex, money, and power. But Nikki had secretly loved Ernest too.

For no matter how gruff his manner, his eyes invariably sparkled at her with a flame of recognition. Nikki felt, as she grew to be a woman, that they naturally understood one another. When Rose was out or in bed with a headache, as was often the case, Nikki as she got older sat with Ernest in his library talking over love and the sea and life. Many nights at home Nikki lay in her narrow bed weaving stories of Ernest and herself, which as she matured descended from fairy-clouded castles to increasingly take on dark sexual shadings. Then when her father climbed into bed with her, first touching her as she pretended to sleep, staying until she shoved him off her at the end, she imagined him as Ernest come to love her, and so had found a path to follow that made it not hurt. For Ernest had been protective of her, soothing her and taking her side whenever she caught the storm front of one of Rose's infamous tantrums, joking that at least she didn't have to live with Rose. But for all that, Nikki adored Rose so much that life apart from her was bleak and colorless. Ernest patted her and protected her through it all.

After all, nothing came of her crush on Ernest. Nearly nothing—Rose had a witch sense about her; how else could she have known of the one embrace between Nikki and Ernest, a short two months before the funeral? He had grabbed her in the library and held her close, pressing his hard lips against her softer ones. *Too late!* she had cried, for she was now too old. Years had passed since her girlhood crush; she had traveled, gone to school in Boston, become a lawyer, rarely returning to her hometown. Except when her mother had died, two years before. And then again when her father was dying two months ago. She had been stuck without any help from her sisters to care for the man she despised with all her heart. Her father was dying of alcoholism—a bad heart, they said.

While she waited for her father to die, Nikki had gone to see Rose to catch up on old times and renew their affection. Seeing Ernest looking so old and haggard at first did nothing to stir her heart, but as the weeks passed and Nikki's father sundered and floundered closer to death, Nikki realized that she still loved Ernest.

She found out on the day her father died. Nikki had entered the kitchen at the back of her father's yellow-shingled house, as she always did. She peered through the dining room into the living room, where she could see her father's huge white tee-shirted back blocking a blaring TV. His scotch sat untouched on the armrest.

"Father?" she called, but there was no answer. Perceiving a shudder pass through him, she drew slowly closer. "Father?"

Her entire life she had been terrified of the enormous, cruel tyrant, afraid of his clutching hands, afraid of his temper that rose and fell like the wind. Afraid of his bellowing, the traps that he laid for all four of his daughters and his wife.

"Father?" she repeated; again no answer. She slowly drew parallel with the green overstuffed chair. Her father was slumped over, breathing stertorously like a beached whale. His bloated body shook with horrible spasms, one fat hand clutching at his heart. Oddly, she thought of how clean he had always been, going like a good Finn to the steam baths nearly every day. How clean and what a monster! The house roared with the echoes of his rages.

As his eyes looked up at her, Nikki backed away, stumbling on the braided rug, turning, racing from the house. She plunged into the dark wooded paths of Dogtown, the deep woods that lay behind the Helmik house. She pressed her hands over her ears, hooting and whistling to herself so as not to hear the echoes of her father's alcoholic rage. It was early evening; the wind was coming up snapping and lashing through the tall maples and oaks. Hurrying deeper into the dark thatched forest, she was unable to return to do what she should: call an ambulance. *There is still time,* a voice called out to her. *Leave him to hell!* cried another. Clamping her hands over her ears while crying out, she fled right through the forest until she found herself on the doorstep of Rose and Ernest's mansion.

Shaking, she raced into the library where Ernest sat turning the pages of a history book, drink in hand. Turning a lined face to her, he smiled with his eyes.

"Rose is out," he explained softly. In such contrast with his salt-creased face, Ernest's voice always caught Nikki off guard. His Adam's apple bobbed.

"You look a sight," he observed, rising and going to greet her. When she shied, he stopped, then indicated a seat across from him. He rang for a servant to bring her a snifter of brandy.

"A cold November night to be out without a jacket, Nikki," he remarked, laying his book aside to study her.

"I—it's my father," she mumbled, gulping hotly at the brandy. It went up her nose, burning briefly like a brazier.

"What is?"

Nikki stared wide-eyed in horror. "I've killed him!" she whispered, as a thrill rang through her.

"More slowly," Ernest insisted, holding her steady with his eyes.

"He's dying—I should help," she coughed. "I have to help, but it's probably too late now. I went to the house—he was in his chair, wheezing—heart attack—I know it!" She looked up at him pleadingly. "Do you know that fear? When it's too late for anything?"

Nodding, he set his mouth. "My entire life has been too late." Putting his drink down, he stood and came over to her. "Your father will die with or without you, when he wants."

"How would you know? You don't even know him."

Ernest said nothing, studying her. As he offered her a horned hand, she accepted it and stood up close enough to him to smell the alcohol as he breathed. He took her in his arms while she cried like a child, mumbling, "I'm forty years old, forty years old." He kissed her softly over and over as she sagged in his arms. He tilted her soft head back, pressing his lips against hers. She instinctively wrapped her arms around him.

Abruptly she pulled away. "Too late!" she cried, fleeing the room. Running, she reached the yellow-shingled house in time to see medics heaving the whale body through the double doors of a waiting ambulance. When she approached a medic to ask, he looked up in surprise, looked into her eyes, decided she could take it, and shook his head.

"An hour ago, maybe," he murmured.

A thrill of panic flashed in her wide eyes. Waiting only long enough to see she wasn't going to faint, the medic hopped lightly into the back of the ambulance as it wailed away into the gloaming, down the hill to Addison Hospital. The same hospital in which her mother had died.

Not long after her father's funeral, Nikki received a call from Rose inviting her to tea. Ever since Nikki was a young girl, she and Rose had a tradition of taking tea together, like proper ladies, so Nikki didn't suspect a trap. They sat on Rose's great stone balcony overlooking the Dogtown woods. Rose would not live in a room that faced the sea. Bees swarmed in the cool November air and made small talk.

"So coming full circle you now want to steal my husband?" Rose casually dropped the words while looking out over the woods. Classic Rose, Nikki thought. Never direct but always hard, demanding her needs be met, putting her audience on the spot. Yet what did Rose mean by "full circle"?

"I—" she began, as Rose held up a gold-ringed hand.

"It's all the worse that you betray me in my own home, Nikki. I understand that is your fate, but it does not excuse your conduct."

"Nothing happened," Nikki mumbled, sitting with head bowed. Rose was beginning to rant, her voice rising; Nikki cowered in her chair. Then unexpectedly, deep down in herself, Nikki felt a flame—and smiled. She was in love with Ernest still after all these years!

"You don't love him," Nikki cut in.

Rose stopped, fixing the younger woman with a long stare. "You will not cross swords with me, my child," Rose threatened, her voice husky. "You have no idea of my power," she intoned, softly scraping the arm of her lion-headed chair with her sharp red nails. In the stately quiet the soft rasp was sinister and persistent, like the conqueror worm eating slowly at the armor of life to let death in. Nikki caught the gesture and the intonation; she had never heard Rose use such a dark tone with her, threatening doom. It frightened and bewildered her.

Rose's power was real. The insinuating stories with vague details that Rose used to relate with such relish to Nikki—real estate deals she had closed by bringing her adversary, usually a male real-estate magnate in Gloucester, to his knees. "Strapped his balls to his back" was her crude expression. She had always been crude—no amount of expensive clothes and elegant perfume could completely hide the peasant Portuguese behind the Gloucester veneer.

Armed with her rediscovered love for Ernest, Nikki felt strong even if afraid of Rose's revenge. She stood suddenly and left the balcony, hurrying for the door. Rose screamed after her.

"Come back! I haven't given you leave! I'll pay you—" the voice was muffled. Nikki silently closed the French doors and exited the sumptuous room.

Nikki went straight to the library but found it empty. She left the house—for the last time, she felt certain. As she pulled away from the house in her red Miata, Ernest walked stiffly past, hands in his pockets, looking much older than sixty.

She gave him a smile that said, "Perhaps it's not too late after all."

She drove to the yellow-shingled house, there to indulge in the luxury of remorse and regret. What had she been thinking when she and Ernest kissed? What was she thinking now? Of a love affair with a married man? Her torture was voluptuous and deep.

They did not meet, the two lovers, for Ernest soon sailed off on his boat for a long trip around Cape Cod and down to Martha's Vineyard. Nikki read New Age self-help books about actualizing her potential and waited. He would return, she knew—and he knew she was waiting.

Six weeks later the media reported Ernest's body found dragging on the end of a long line that drifted astern of his sailboat, the *Lamia Claire.*

NOW AS THE gravediggers pitched dirt into the hole, Rose nodded to Father O'Malley and turned away. Nikki had positioned herself so she could not be seen by Rose, but Philip, looking bewildered and young, caught Nikki's eye as he adjusted his glasses nearsightedly. He glanced puzzledly at her. As she returned his look, a dark flame shot up through her from womb to throat. *Yes,* a voice whispered in her, so that her umbrella slipped. The drizzle wetted her blond hair, and it clung to her forehead.

The little mourning party dispersed, staggering down the muddy slope to the waiting limousines—first Rose holding her son's arm, then Rose's ancient parents, the cousins, nieces and nephews all trundling awkwardly behind, all with the same secret hope for the reading of the will. At the end went the haggard, smug priest followed by an altar boy with a tattoo on his right forearm, swinging the incense censer as he walked, which sent damp clouds of white smoke rolling over the muddy hillside.

The late afternoon sky already darkening, the gravediggers hurried to finish and get out of the rain. Nikki huddled again under her umbrella watching them, the impact of the clods hitting the casket thumping in her chest. She was feeling girlishly sentimental; forever after there in the ground lay her pure love, the man whom she had at last found, after all her years wandering through brief affairs with men old and young, countless dark meetings in bars that ended in drunken beds where she awoke a stranger. She had found Ernest only to lose him to a darkness where the frightening questions crowded in on her. Were the rumors true—did Ernest kill himself? For her? The papers called it an unfortunate accident.

Spades of dirt piled up over Ernest until it was done. The two diggers gathered their tools and rolled up the tarp, clambering downhill. Through the falling rain Nikki watched the dead mound, her mind dull. She stared a long time, then walked to the grave, looking downward at the muddy mound. Suddenly she felt sure the grave was empty, a vast yawning maw of nothingness. Ernest was not there, she was certain. Something was terribly wrong; she began to breathe hard. It seemed so clear to her: The ornate coffin was empty. Nikki dropped her umbrella and fled panicked, slipping and staggering down the hill, digging wildly in her purse for her keys, hands shaking as she fumbled and ran. Breathlessly reaching her car, she jabbed the key in the lock, flipped the door open and dove inside.

There she stopped, feeling her heart thudding behind her eyes. The windshield was smeared with rain. She started the car and swerved away, desperate to find someone living, desperate not to be alone.

THE APRIL EVENING three months later was unusually warm when Nikki Helmik pulled the red sports car up to her friend Claire's house for a party. She twisted the steering wheel easily in her long-fingered hands, flicked the key off and, flipping the overhead light on, leaned close to the rearview mirror to examine her face. Her friend Alexandra brushed her dark hair and waited.

In repose Nikki's face had a serious, intent expression, her jaw line slightly jowly, an effect that was accentuated when she frowned over her reading bifocals. She was a child of Gloucester, half granite hardness, half fire. Her temperament was given to outbursts of anger, which nevertheless were as controlled and delimited as a fire in a glacier. Yet like all people who live fundamentally by their emotions, Nikki was often swept away, her feelings calving off her as if from an iceberg, to float away from her control. Even while she trusted her feelings, she was frightened of them. In love she gave herself always with a slight turn of self-conscious hesitation, as if her desires might not be met; but she had steeled herself against love, for it, above all feelings, threatened to take her wholly out of herself.

"Think there'll be guys?" Alex asked, looking at Claire's door.

Nikki was wearing a red-flowered summer dress of light cotton with narrow straps that left her shapely shoulders whitely exposed.

They glided to the front door, walking in the slender moonlight across the scraggly seaside lawn. Nikki paused and looked up.

"Look at the moon!" she exclaimed, pointing at the fingernail moon hovering and watchful as a cat above them. She smiled and said a silent prayer, as if the moon were waxing for her, for she was an idealist and in the way of all idealists believed that the world would give her perfection. She had always believed it was possible to find the perfect man, although her search had led her to hate anyone who fell short. And they all had, except Ernest.

A breeze brushed the bangs from her eyes. They pushed the door open, swam into a sea of pulsing sound, dancers, and conversation, and there stood gazing and stunned like everyone who enters a noisy party.

Nikki had washed her hair, and it sparkled golden in the party lights and looked like fine, flat threads of gold flax. She was made-up but not too dramatically, with little curls of blue shadow at the corners of her eyes and mascara with clots you could see only if you were staring into her eyes, and then you would miss them staring at the expressive roundness of the eyes themselves. A tiny bit of color on her full mouth and a hint of pink shadow along the underside of her high cheekbones was all.

To Philip, glancing up from the far side of the room and who saw her from a distance, she was beautiful and the familiar someone he had once known. *Yes, Nikki Helmik,* he whispered, and his heart was as pierced as when for a moment he had observed her from a distance at his father's funeral. This depression brings its own beauty, he mused.

Her blond hair shone in an arc like a halo, and she had deep-set eyes blue-green like the sea, always in motion. She wore a wry smile with enough mystery in it to rival Philip's new love, the ocean. It hurt to look at her, he reflected as he stood talking to one of Claire's friends, a lanky woman named Geraldine who was studying world religions at Harvard Divinity School. But then, everything hurt since his father had died. He was amazed at this new land, America.

Born in Gloucester, he had been sent to Europe for school and lived there ever since. Returning for his father's death made Gloucester seem melancholy and beautiful, and this golden-haired woman seemed to him to be standing at the heart of the heart-aching beauty he had so recently found in dark Gloucester. Where had all this feeling come from? he wondered. In the past weeks he had been wandering the streets of Gloucester, marveling at the old brick buildings, standing in silent recognition of the old waterfront while the ancient seamen, sitting in chairs, in turn pointed recognition at him. He had relived his boyhood adventures, finding the old paths through the deep woods of Dogtown, nosing out the wharves where his father's vast fleet of fishing trawlers once lay, now all sold and gone. It was all ghosts after all, he thought as he walked, all the ships gone, the childhood hiding places built over with new houses, trees cut down. The people themselves were ghosts of those he had known as a child. When they uttered exclamations of amazement and fright as he introduced himself, he wondered whether he too seemed a ghost to them.

But she had come, this woman who at once coalesced all his disparate feelings, as if knitting together in one person his frayed heart! Such a small town; where had she been hiding all these weeks? He had almost missed Claire's party, but he happened to have called a few people he once knew in school, Claire one of them. How was he to know that Claire and Nikki were great friends? He knew Nikki, of course—he remembered her from his childhood, for they were the same age.

Over his glass of beer he kept up his stories about Europe to Geraldine. But he was watching Nikki. Her face had been in him since the funeral, and he had asked his mother about her.

His mother's answer was so fraught with complex emotion—her eyes darting in their familiar way, her voice growing husky with feeling—that instead of his staying away from Nikki, which had been his mother's intent, he looked for the beautiful blond woman in long walks along the harbor and up and down the cobblestoned, slanting streets of the seaport. Thirty years he had been away!

Yes, it hurt to look at Nikki in the flesh after carrying an image of her around. As if she were too large for his eyes, or too present. As if her hair, reflecting the party lights, was shooting back a crown of sharp-pointed lights, glass shards of stars that pierced his knowing like a sudden, hurtful realization. He felt dismayed, and confusedly tried to attend to the tall minister's disquisition on the relevance of Wicca to a feminist view of Christianity.

No, it couldn't be love; he was married and loved Françoise deeply. It was just one more manifestation of his old attachment to Gloucester, nostalgia and her soft contours that turned perception into vague longing and indiscriminate, searching feeling. This woman was but the latest in his weeks-long encounter with the lovely ghosts of his past; an infatuation, and why shouldn't he feel seduced by his old home? It was his mother's doing, talking with such animation about Nikki. That propelled him to find out who she was, what had brought her back home to Gloucester.

Nikki did not let him catch her eye, giving him only the briefest of glances and turning to look for Claire. She smiled and laughed at the music and hubbub in Claire's living room as she spied her friend across the crowded, noisy room, then took one of the proffered glasses of white wine that Claire knowingly carried to her and to Alex, over the heads of talking and dancing friends.

"Nice party," Nikki said happily, smiling and speaking over the throbbing music, her eyebrows dancing.

"You saw him too," Claire replied, leaning close to Nikki and flicking a glance at the dark-haired Philip, still in conversation with their friend Geraldine and three other women. "He's got them all entranced by his stories. You should hear him talk!"

Look at them—like groupies," she laughed. "Remember him from—" Claire began, but Nikki hushed her with a nod that shook her blond bangs. Claire reached a platter from an end table and held it before Nikki and Alex. One end of the oval held brownies, the other strawberries and grapes. Claire rotated it so the fruit was in front of Nikki, who frowned, took a strawberry, and began to make her way across the room toward Philip, stopping and chatting with friends along the way. All the while she had her eye on the man, though, regarding him with sideways, quick glances. He was talking, but not concentrating on what he was saying. Her forehead felt warm.

What she saw was this: A man as tall as she, perhaps an inch taller—? Dressed all in black, he stood with slightly hunched shoulders. Black shirt—of silk, was it?—open at the collar and showing dark chest hair; his hair brown and straight and worn longish, just like she imagined they wore it in Europe. He was beginning to grey at the temples and wore an intent, slightly intellectual frown. She could see the bones in his jaw flexing as he spoke and his Adam's apple bob. Looking slightly Italian, he had a thin, intelligent face with a look of high seriousness and intentness, especially in the creased brow between his eyes. His eyes were set close together, an aspect heightened by his black thin-rimmed glasses. The effect was of a casually elegant, educated man, comfortable, sophisticated.

Yes, this was Rose's son all right; he had the mark of Europe all over him—she could almost smell that wonderful indefinable perfume of the continent. Nikki had never been to Europe, but she had had European lovers, and she remembered their ineffable scent, their fine clothes, how their jackets slid easily over their shoulders, their particular way of loosening their ties with a short, slow pull to the side and then down. Stylish.

Philip had his mother's beauty, too—pursed, thoughtful lips and narrow, well-shaped chin. Nikki fingered her own small, rounded chin as she nodded a greeting to her friend Dawn.

She looked intently at Dawn's frail frame that showed through her long sleeves and pants. Her body was merely a coat hanger. Her face was one longish bone, her eyes enlarged like a child's. Big blue rivers ran engorged along the back of Dawn's narrow hands, which she fluttered like starving birds as she spoke.

"You should have the brownies, Nikki, they're great!" Dawn was beaming up at her. Nikki stared.

"Well, ok, I didn't taste any," she continued defensively, "but I can smell them from here! They smell heavenly!" Dawn waved her hands around. She had lost more weight since Nikki last saw her. Nothing any of their friends said to her worked. They tried to get her to eat; it was no use. Dawn always insisted that she was full after one bite, then got bitchy if they pressed her too hard. And now she had become a walking corpse. Nikki looked with pity at her friend.

"How are you feeling?" Nikki asked seriously. She wanted to get away from Dawn as soon as possible, although really she was quite pleasant to be around, for the most part, if you could ignore her always talking about food.

"Fine, fine," Dawn smiled at her. She waited, then nodded. "Yes, I've lost more weight. I don't know, I just feel better without it. It drags me down," she finished in an almost pleading voice.

"Anyway, my art's going good," she pouted.

Nikki looked down at her friend. "Yes? What are you working on?"

"Oils—you can scrape them off to get them just right. Start over and over if you want. You should come visit. The water's right there, lapping at the door."

Nikki hadn't been to Dawn's studio in East Gloucester in years. It was too depressing: everything neatly in place, all the brushes clean and a clean white canvas clamped to the easel, waiting for nothing. And Dawn standing in the middle like a hesitant reed, looking like a starving child in a grown-up smock, about to collapse. It was a perfect spot, and Nikki was vaguely jealous that Dawn's mother had the money to buy such a studio for her, right on the old East Harbor. A perfect spot where everything was waiting in white for something to happen. And it made Nikki self-conscious of how bad a housekeeper she was herself; the dirt and mess had to become monstrous before she was moved to clean.

"You've got to eat," Nikki insisted. "How's your mother?"

Dawn frowned suddenly. "I'd rather not talk about her," she said abruptly, looking around. *Good,* thought Nikki, just what she wanted. She was sure that mentioning Dawn's mother, Boston district attorney and great friend of Rose Eveless, would shut Dawn up.

"Go look at the moon—it's huge!" Nikki said, not quite knowing what she meant by it. But she was smiling and listening now to Philip, who stood just to her left.

"…it's the same old thing, isn't it?" Philip was remarking to Geraldine. "More monotheism, which is the problem no matter how you dress it up. It's laudable you incorporate these feminist ideas into your understanding of Christianism, but do you think the pope will OK making women into priests?"

"Christianism—?" she asked.

This was Nikki's chance, and she smiled a goodbye to Dawn and bowed toward Geraldine's side.

"I have an aunt in Salem who's a priestess," Nikki smiled, looking at Philip. Could this be the little boy she remembered from fifth grade?

"Philip, this is my friend Nikki," Geraldine began. "Nikki, this is—"

"Philip," Nikki nodded once, still smiling. "Rose's son; I know. You haven't changed much," she observed, letting a glance of hers flash in his eyes.

"Nikki—yes," Philip said, the crease between his eyes narrowing slightly. "Nikki Helmik—I knew you in fifth grade." His Adam's apple bobbed as he swallowed.

There was a brief pause as both recalled their past, and Philip smiled in silent recognition as Nikki nodded at his smile. They shook and the touch of her long fingers was cool and expressive, like an artist's. She was expecting the soft, cushioned hands of the pampered rich boy who had gone to private school in Switzerland. Instead she was surprised to feel that his hands were hard and full of calluses.

"Haven't changed much! That must be the understatement of the new millennium. It's been thirty years," he observed dryly. His voice was curiously high for a man, and he spoke with a slight accent. Altogether there was something effeminate about him, Nikki thought. Yet that made him seem more mysterious and attractive.

"Yes, but I recognized you immediately. You have the same intellectual look you had in fifth grade. You had glasses then, too."

Philip cleared his throat diffidently. "My mother told me about you."

Nikki did not let the jet of fear play on her face.

"Good things, of course," she said wryly, pulling her mouth up at the corner.

"Only," Philip smiled, showing white teeth. But he was troubled by Nikki's look of fear and by the recollection of his mother. Why had his mother been so emotional when he asked about Nikki?

"Welcome back to Gloucester." *She would take him to bed tonight,* a voice in her spoke. She wanted to hurt him, and she didn't know why. Because of Rose? Because he looked so much like Ernest? And she did not know that she already had hurt him. A great anger and fear welled up in her, the desire of her heart for love and the fear of loss. The welter of feelings made her talk.

"Gloucester!" she exclaimed in a girlish, singsong voice, waving her hands around. "And the moon!" she sang, as if it were a child's song.

"Thanks—I'm glad to be home," Philip said hesitantly. "Although I can't really say it's home—or can I?" he asked, looking at Nikki.

"You said thirty years, right? Thirty years. Can it be thirty years?" Nikki asked. She turned to Geraldine. "Since you're not from here, Gerry, you don't know the story that everyone knows in small-town Gloucester, about how poor little Philip was suddenly packed off one day by his parents and sent away to Switzerland."

"And your parents are—" Geraldine inquired.

"Rose Eveless," Philip answered, keeping his eyes on Geraldine.

"Oh," Geraldine said, recalling the rumors of Ernest Eveless' suicide. "I'm so sorry about your father," she frowned, switching into the comforting minister's tone she was working on perfecting, using every chance she could get to practice.

"Thank you," Philip bowed slightly, which Nikki found charming and so European. Her girlish heart fluttered. She wanted to reach and touch him softly, and she felt as if an invisible hand of hers did. She was certain of her power as a woman. Yet there was something held back in him, kept in reserve, that he didn't show. It troubled her. He smiled with his mouth, but his eyes were watching all the time. Nikki shivered; it was what Philip's father used to do: always watch from behind his round glasses.

"Philip and I need to catch up on all the years," Nikki explained, glancing at Geraldine, who excused herself.

"Very smooth," Philip smiled, speaking softly so that Nikki barely heard him over the music. Still, she had good ears and caught the inflection.

"Let's go into the kitchen," he motioned with his beer. He followed her, and they found a quiet corner where the din was not at their elbows.

"I lied—you have changed," Nikki corrected, as Philip leaned against the wall and looked at her.

"Indeed! And you!" he smiled and clinked his beer against her wine glass.

"Beer? You?" she asked.

"It's a bad habit I picked up in Germany," he admitted. "I drink wine with dinner; I used to have such a good time at Oktoberfest that I guess every party reminds me of it."

"I'm so sorry about your father," Nikki murmured. "It was sudden, wasn't it? He had a heart attack?"

Philip frowned and nodded finally. "I saw you at the funeral—it was kind of you to attend."

"Biggest event in Gloucester in years!" she exclaimed, then regretted it when she saw the pained look in his eyes.

"I'm sorry. You must be very upset. How can you be at a party?"

"Quite all right—although it is strange," he smiled. "I never saw my father much all these years. I'm not sure who I'm missing now, or brooding over. My mother told me your father died just a few months before mine," he added.

Nikki felt the old fear snake through her. *Murderer!* a voice shouted in her head. She shook her head. "I was never close to him."

He nodded. "It hurts anyway. And then you learn one of those distillations of life when someone dies."

"What did you learn?"

"To speak your mind when you think of it. Otherwise the opportunity is gone—forever, usually. It sounds like a cliché, but it's a complex thought, like most true things."

"Don't miss your chance," she mused. "A good idea. Are you going to take over your father's business?"

"Maybe," Philip evaded. "I don't want to talk about that, though. Tell me about yourself—what have you been doing all these years?"

"I got out of Gloucester as fast as possible after high school—"

"Good move," Philip acknowledged.

"—though I didn't go as far as you."

"You weren't sent away—or were you?"

She smiled at him and raised her glass to his questioning glance. "Take a walk?" she asked. He smiled back.

They scooped brownies and strawberries from nearby platters, wrapped them in napkins, and with their drinks left through the back door. The evening was warm and humid still, the crescent moon riding high overhead. They went through the backyard, the noise of the party dimming behind them. The wind was coming up through the grass, a warm breeze from the land kissing the ocean. They came to the causeway and hurried across it, then ducked past the statue of the mariner looking out to sea, leaning heavily on his stone wheel. They hopped off the low stone breakwater and walked in the sand and sat upon a pile of granite rocks at the edge of the beach, setting out their booty.

Before them lay the great ocean growling softly in the dim moonlight. Concentric ranks of breakers hurried like soldiers toward shore. Overhead the curved bowl of stars was a spangled geode, and the crusted jewels winked and nodded in quiet and self-absorbed conversation. The queen moon rode ankled in the dim, her twin horns charging smoothly through the black cloth of heaven, and the dark oriental carpet of the sea lay rippling at their feet.

Nikki wondered at the indifferent miracle and smiled up, leaning and giving her face to the moon. A long time she sat, eyes closed, smiling and sighing deeply, feeling the pulse of the white goddess upon her cheeks, and she was far away and whole for a spell, neck arched back like a feeding chick.

Then she recovered and her soul split again into life's unmanaged pieces; she opened her eyes and caught Philip staring at her. He looked away and straightened his glasses. She leaned with a secret smile and took a strawberry, red as a planet, and bit the crimson, bloody fruit. Cars passed from time to time behind them, but otherwise they were alone with the crescent beach dancing with the moon. The tide was coming slowly in, long curls of waves crackling along the shore and spilling foam in softly blown cotton webs about the moonlit sand.

"Are you back for a while?" she heard herself ask, then regretted it. No, she mustn't second guess herself, she thought. "Is it possible I'm drunk after one glass?" she wondered out loud.

He smiled at her, understanding she wasn't looking for an answer. "For a while… I don't know what I'm doing. My father's death—my mother—" he groped for the thought, frowning.

"Your mother," Nikki nodded.

"You've known her a long time, she says," Philip remarked, looking at her.

"A long time. I always loved her—everyone here does. You know that," she stopped. "Or is afraid of her. The same thing, after all."

"Do you think so?" he peered at her. "Fear and love—aren't they supposed to be opposites?"

"Not in my experience," she said.

They were silent a moment, both digesting the thought.

"I know very little about Gloucester because I've been away so long. When they sent me away—it was my father—I was eleven and loved it here. But Europe became my home, and I only remembered the sea and the smell of salt. Whenever I got homesick one of my parents would come and we'd go for a holiday on the Italian coast, then later the Côte d'Azur. But it was bluer there than here—I remember the whiteness of the sea here in Gloucester. And you can tell it's bigger than the Med."

"You never came for a visit in all those years?"

"Hardly."

"You weren't allowed?"

He laughed. "It's not as insidious as you make it sound. They made it seem normal for me to stay over there, and they came so often and said such great things about Europe. I came here sometimes for holidays, but then we never spent much time in the old house up on the hill. We were always running off to New York or the West Coast to spend holidays with relatives or friends of theirs. I think my father wanted to keep me away from my mother's adventures in the demimonde, and my mother wanted to keep me away from my father's hatred of her. So I grew up in Geneva and later in Marseilles, and I made friends and fell in love..."

"That changes things," she agreed.

"That changes things. So now I'm here because my father decided after all this time that my mother's affairs had finally become too much for him, so he said farewell—"

She gasped. "Said farewell? Affairs?" The thoughts piled into one another like cars on the freeway. She was confused with the wreckage.

He studied her in the half-light. She was so charming, with her hand over her mouth, staring wide-eyed out at the sea! Yet as he watched he felt a thrill of fear shoot through his heart. He did not know why, but he knew she was dangerous. He smelled it with his mind.

"It's true, anyway," he said finally, looking away. My father killed himself. I think it was because of my mother's—life, her lovers. She really was throwing it in his face toward the end, if I can believe his letters."

"That's a cruel thing to think of your mother."

"About her having affairs? She was the cruel one. That's what bothered my father. Did you see her cruelty? Or was it reserved for him?"

She glanced once at him. Yes, it was a real question. And she was caught now between the two, her loyalty split between Rose and Ernest, even in death. Yes, even in death she loved Ernest, and now that he was dead, she could dream freely of the love she wished they had risked.

Despite her fight with Rose, she had some lingering loyalty to her, too, and Philip's criticism of his mother was an implied criticism of her, wasn't it? When she was in high school, she had modeled herself on Rose, taking lovers old and young with the whim of the virgin huntress. Yet the whole world of men made her lungs heave, as if she could not catch her breath. She felt suddenly ready to run, fast and far. She could not think about her lovers, her secret, dark life of men found in bars, of men.

Another thought clouded her mind: Philip knew nothing of her connection with his father. It was a odd combination of relief and disappointment she felt, that Philip did not even consider his father might have died because of her. Because, after all, she was certain that he had, and had been strangely satisfied when Rose accused her of his death. It meant she was as powerful as Rose, if she could be the cause of Ernest's death.

"I—feel loyal to your mother," she said at last, looking at the waves. She was wondering whether she had loved even that in Ernest…the critical, discerning lines in his forehead. Had she loved that Ernest hated Rose? Didn't she have to love his hatred of Rose in order to draw close to him? Nikki breathed hard with the dangerous thought, and shivered.

"So you stand by her," Philip commented. "That's admirable."

"You don't get along with her?"

"In my own fashion—or should I say, in the fashion that she allows."

Nikki laughed shortly.

"So you do admit that about her," he observed wryly. They were silent.

"We're both fatherless now," Philip said sadly to the waves.

Nikki looked at him, and he looked so much like his father in the moonlight profile! Her excitement and fear grew, and her ears pricked up to distant sounds around them. Was someone coming? She glanced quickly behind them in the dark, but the beach was empty. Yet she was sure someone was there!

"Do you miss him?" she asked.

"I didn't know him well. My mother insists I'm nothing like him. I don't know—they say fathers and sons compete for the mother. I don't know about that, but it's true my father and I competed, maybe not for her, but for some other female."

"Other?"

"The blue-robed one," Philip explained. "Men are close to their mothers, or lovers. They're in search of the original one behind them all; yes, even those ineffectual boys who come home to help their mothers…" He arched an eyebrow at her.

Nikki looked at him curiously.

"I can't even tell whether there's still the old competition, now he's dead. I hear him still. He used to call my mother and me 'the procrastinators.' He referred to us as 'you people.' Odd, eh?" Philip looked at her. "There was nothing I could do to keep up with him, was the clear message I received. Even when he decided to open a branch of his export business in France, and put me at the head of it, he always made it clear to me that he could have done better. When the business began to go to hell, it was as much my fault as the fact that the seas were drying up, according to him."

Now Nikki's loyalties were strained in another direction. As a fellow child of a tyrant father, she felt on Philip's side. But this was Ernest, after all!

"…so I came back, to help my mother," Philip was going on. "It's like returning to a lover you had when you were twenty. There's something so sadly familiar, and so distant about the place—maybe that's the sadness, too. Gloucester is so beautiful in the moonlight, the waves rocking and wearing away, patiently, working and working the ground out from underneath us…as if, as if I can't quite grasp the spirit of this place, even while it's in my bones and my blood."

He stood up and the flat waves gabbled near his feet like little hungry animals. Nikki watched him, fascinated. Might he walk right out into the sea? But he merely stood and gestured out at the expanse of white-lined foam waves.

"As if it were some sea nymph staying just out of my reach," he waved vaguely, his voice growing huskier with feeling. "I've been back only a few weeks, and the sea-remembering has taken me over. I'm filled with an ineffable longing for some beautiful maid who lives far out there, a mermaid or a silkie, I don't even know her name…"

It crept in on him like the foamy tide coming in at his feet that he was speaking of Nikki, of her beauty, of her taking the ground out from underneath him, and he turned to look at her. How could this be? Her golden hair and deep-set eyes, so thoughtful, so hard and cold, too. Her voice was like a little girl's, but she was an old love of his, wasn't she?

"Do you remember me?" he asked suddenly and softly, tilting his head.

She recovered herself, for she had been floating on the tide of his words. She knew, too, and shivered feeling the power of this man, his self-possession, his worldliness, the wings in his words. But this was not the son, this was the father! her voice cried, and she looked with fearful eyes at Philip.

"Yes!" she blurted finally. "Yes," she repeated more softly. She was panting a bit, and patted the rock so Philip would sit and look less like his father, standing and squinting slightly through his glasses at her. She flung herself at a random memory. "Um—we were in fifth grade together, in Miss Heasley's class. Remember her?"

"I do," he responded. "With her horn-rimmed glasses and those little clasps with the chain that held the sweater together at the collar. I found out all sorts of things in fifth grade—Charlie somebody…"

"Luntzel," she put in.

"Charlie Luntzel, hmm. Charlie Luntzel. He was the smartest kid in class—and he got hold of some book and showed me pictures about sex. I couldn't believe it. I thought my parents would never do something like that. Although that was the year I kissed my first girl, on her hand. Peggy somebody."

"Pekkala," Nikki noted. She remembered it all, even little Peggy giggling and telling Nikki how Philip had bowed in front of her just like a knight of the round table, then kissed her dainty little hand. And Peggy was Finnish like her.

"I was the tallest one in class, including you," Nikki declared.

He looked at her again. A picture was beginning to form; he could half see her at the edge of his memory, standing a long way off and watching, it seemed. A tall girl, awkwardly self-conscious, standing slumped at the shoulders with arms folded. She had golden hair and was beautiful, even as a twelve-year-old. Like an Amazon, Philip was thinking. He recalled distantly feeling threatened by her size and her beauty, like there could never be enough of him to hold her. He frowned.

"Anyway, you got taller finally," she stated, as if reading his thought. "Do you remember the picnic?" Nikki asked, wanting to save him from whatever dark-winged bird had flown into his heart. She liked gay, powerful men with broad-spread wings. This man, so serious and self-possessed, was a vague threat to her, and so her thought was to vanquish him, to have him as soon as possible, tonight if it could be done, and then be done with him. And why shouldn't she have him? If he was Ernest come to her in a different guise, then why not? Was it not fate?

"At Halibut Point?" he asked.

"Sally fell in the water, and then Johnny Sparrow jumped in to save her." She stopped suddenly, her face flushing in the dark. She remembered what she had done, sneaked off with the older boys into the woods...

But Philip was laughing now. "And Miss Heasley yelling and snapping like a dog until she slipped on the rock when a wave came in, and in she went too!" He stopped and grew serious. "And that's where poor Charlie fell off the rocks and nearly killed himself. I remember we were at the top and fooling around. We had been talking about love, girlfriends, all that stuff we knew nothing about. It was weird—he got dizzy and just fell." He was meditative. "Wonder what happened to Charlie."

"He's in the same cemetery as our fathers," Nikki intoned.

"Oh my god!"

"Drugs," Nikki nodded. "I remember you from then," she said, because it was the truth and to change the subject. Even then she had known about Rose, and this was Rose's son. She had tried to talk to him, but he was one of the smart kids who always spoke up in class, who didn't talk to her. And anyway, she was beginning her wild life, playing hooky and running around with the older boys, smoking and driving to secluded places with them.... The more fearful she became, the more fiercely she adventured with the boys, all the while hating her tyrant of a father, his great wagging head in the background spitting at her that she was a whore...

"What do you remember?" he asked, looking at her and smiling.

Nikki recovered herself. "You were kind of—pretentious," she observed, whereupon he coughed. She looked at him and smiled. "I felt inferior to you—all that money and your mother and her beauty. You were so smart—won the prizes—and you had your best friend, Charlie. You two used to have all these private jokes and make fun of everyone."

"We did? I was that bad?" he was genuinely mortified.

"Kid stuff," she shrugged. And felt a certain satisfaction recalling that she knew what had happened to Charlie. She had had sex with him a few years later, after Philip went away. That had brought him down a few notches, to get him to do that, to let her teach him what she knew and let him make a fool of himself in his inexperience. It was in the basement of Charlie's parents' house, in the pine-paneled game room, underneath the pool table that smelled of lemon furniture polish. Charlie had known nothing, she now thought with sudden venom, and her mouth curled as she recalled the lost years. With his limp and his ignorance. And his death that she had predicted to him and to everyone else for years, and then felt such satisfaction to be proven right when he died in an abandoned house down near the docks, a needle in his arm and his bloodshot eyes staring at nothing...

Now she remembered as well her conviction that she would sleep with Philip and felt the seed of her power seeping back into her.

"Well," he began, "I hope I've outgrown my youthful rudeness—I suppose it was just self-conscious clumsiness."

"No trace of clumsiness left," Nikki said.

He smiled as a light danced in his eyes. "Tell me about yourself—what have you done? What are you doing in Gloucester? Or are you not living in Gloucester now?"

"As a matter of fact, I moved back only a few months ago, into my parent's old house. My mother died two years ago, then my father in late fall. None of my sisters wanted the house, and I was sick of my job, so I quit it and moved back."

"What were you doing?"

"Lawyering in Boston," she replied.

"A lawyer!" he whistled.

"A corporate lawyer—even worse," she laughed, and her face lit up. "I hated it—it was soul-sucking."

"What a wonderful phrase!" he exclaimed.

She felt vaguely annoyed and pleased with herself. "Well, it was. I worked for an insurance company, with doctors."

"Why a lawyer?"

"I could make money at it, and get out of here, and then I had my daughter Alice," she explained, and felt a little sad.

"Really! How old?"

"Nineteen. She just moved in with her boyfriend." She sighed.

"And he's not good enough for her," Philip guessed, raising a shrewd eyebrow.

Nikki looked at him. "It's that—but more. A fundamental connection between us has changed. It's sad. It's just happened, so I'm not over it yet—guess it's empty nest syndrome."

"And your husband is with you?"

Nikki laughed. "What a thought! Husband!" She shook her head and twisted a smile. "We were never married, Alice's father and I. No, he's married in Vermont now, with kids of his own. He never visits or calls Alice."

"That's terrible!" Philip said, so that Nikki turned suddenly to see whether he was serious. She was touched to see that he was, and yet she remained cautious and skeptical. What man ever had stood by a woman for all time? Yet hadn't Ernest stood by Rose?

"Do you—have kids?" she asked hesitantly.

"No kids. Married fifteen years, no kids."

Nikki felt a pang. "Your wife is European?"

"French—Françoise is her name. She's in Marseilles."

They were silent a moment, Nikki thinking what did it matter, she only wanted to sleep with him, not marry him.

"So you're going back soon—to France."

He frowned at the sea. "Not soon..." he glanced at her. "Françoise and I live apart some of the time—she travels—we go our own way. So I plan to stay for a while—I can't tell."

"What are you doing living back here?" he asked suddenly.

"You mean, why did I come back?"

"Yes—and more. You're looking for something."

She regarded him and his dark look, as if he were looking through her. "I—was tired of that fast life. Cell phone, beeper, faxes, long days, everything hyped and speeded up. Drinks after work, home late. Life was seeming unreal the faster it went. Five years of therapy didn't help, nor did all my trips to the Southwest; I did it all—hypnotism, chanting, meditation, the whole works. Nothing really slowed life down for me."

"I understand. Even in Europe everything's speeding up, as if hurrying to its doom before the end of the century. It will come anyway," he murmured, looking out to sea.

"And Gloucester seems more real," she declared. "Something after my father died. The house sort of landed in my lap, and I was ready, I guess. It's quiet here; a different life."

"A different life!" he exclaimed softly. "But the old anger accompanies you even here, eh?" He observed her; she started, then looked away.

They were silent while Nikki munched a strawberry, then picked at a brownie. She looked at the small pile of them, wanting to devour them all, suddenly angry at her appetite, wanting to pitch the plate into the sea.

"I was feeling powerless in my job—working for doctors who were callous, selfish little boys. Men in charge of everything; I was supposed to do some good, get bills passed in the state legislature. The doctors thought I was helping them—that was my job, anyway. But really I was undermining their power, as much as I could."

"How so?"

"Making them accountable," Nikki said with finality.

"What did they do to you?"

"Killed my mother. Oh—what does it matter?—they're boys in their little kingdoms. Isn't that enough?"

Philip looked thoughtful. "Killed your mother—?"

"She had cancer, and they wouldn't tell her, wouldn't give her the option of choosing what to do with her life. Cavalier and imperious—and I tried to make them pay."

"But it didn't work."

"I got exhausted, burned out on that whole manic world. You asked what I came back for—I think it's to find my power center again. I have a feeling it's here somehow, somewhere, that I'll find it. Like things fell into place for me, and I ended up here again."

"Power…" Philip mused. They sat in silence.

"Tell me about everyone else—the old gang," he said finally.

"Well, you've seen Claire," Nikki hurried on, glad to be smothering her feeling with talk. Talk usually worked best. Yet every time she looked at him, Philip seemed to be his father, and a thrill ran through her. She reached and touched his jacketed arm softly, as if to reassure herself. He glanced at her quickly, and she hurriedly took another strawberry.

"Claire's father left when she was a kid, remember?"

"I do, now that I think of it. He just walked out one day?"

"Right, and never a word since, leaving Claire's mother and her brothers in that little dumpy house down near Pavilion Beach."

"So what's she do now?"

"She's a nurse. Funny, huh? There was a report that her father was killed boar hunting in Vermont. Claire never got over it, even though the story was never proved. I don't think she even remembered what he looked like, she was so little when he left. And for a long time she would only go out with men old enough to be her father. She even went to Vermont once and got a couple of boyfriends there."

"Hmm!"

Nikki nodded. "She spread out after a while," Nikki mused, thinking of how many times she had warned Claire to get her lovers in Boston, which was far enough away so no one at home could find out. That's what Nikki had done, from the time she was in high school. Taken the train with girlfriends down into Boston to the rock concerts on the Common. Plenty of boys there who had cars or houses empty of parents.... Later she moved to Cambridge, and that was far enough away from Gloucester that she didn't even have to think about anyone finding out. And the singles' bars were all anonymous faces and lives, flesh-and-blood ciphers of desire. Their faces and bodies remained in her only as long as their seed, drying slowly or absorbed into her soul until their images faded and she was left with only herself again.

"She still dates strange guys, though—cops and army guys."

"And you—did you date them?" Philip asked, displeased with himself for asking.

"A long time ago I went through that phase," she said abstractedly. "You know—protesting the war, dating army guys."

"You were against the war and yet went out with men in the army?"

"Well, they were officers!" she exclaimed, then fell back into thoughtfulness.

"So you got out of Gloucester to become a lawyer and have a child, and then came back to this small town," Philip continued.

Nikki looked up from the food, relieved to have something to say, to get herself out of brooding. "It's small, but once you're older you can see it's beautiful and unusual in its way. I love it here."

"I think I love it here, too," he agreed. "Though it feels presumptuous to say."

"Why? It's your home, too." She wanted it to be his home, she thought. She was disturbed by these gentle feelings. They felt unfamiliar, but she felt them. Was it because this was Rose's son? She felt vaguely incapable of playing the seduction game;

or at least she could not play it easily. Then there was the business of his wife; deeply disturbing.

"Thank you for the welcome," he bowed his head slightly, and again she thought how European he seemed, so cultured. She was a little intimidated by his manner, by his self-containment, even as she felt a tug toward him. She wondered what the source of his power was. Well, it was all right to be attracted to his power. Yet she shivered. Of course she knew the source! She could see Rose in the soft curl of his underlip.

"And how did you get to know my mother? She spoke of you with some passion when she was filling me in on people and events in Gloucester."

"It's—a long story," Nikki sighed. "What did she say about me?"

"That I should watch out. That you had magic you didn't know," he said evenly.

Nikki laughed in spite of herself, frowning at the absurdity. "That's your mother."

"Of course," he observed wryly. "There's something going on here I don't know about, but I wonder if it could be as simple and complex as that she feels jealous of your looks. My mother is getting older, you know, and afraid." He stood up and straightened, then stooped and picked up a handful of stones and proceeded to skim them in the surf.

"Of what?"

"Losing her beauty. She's quite vain, but you know that, of course. I suppose you could say she has had reason to be." He aimed and threw a stone, watching it disappear skimming into darkness. "Except that now with my father dead and most of the money gone, she's feeling terribly vulnerable. That's why she insists I stay here. That and with the business gone to hell, there was eventually nothing left for me to manage in Marseilles. No money; I closed the office and came back." He had been thinking out loud and now turned to Nikki.

"But this comes after whatever it was that brought you two to part, so your argument couldn't be due to my father and money." He sat again, silently watching her, waiting politely. She stared at the black surging waters.

"OK," she said finally, taking a deep breath. "I'll tell you. I guess I trust you enough to tell you about your mother and me. Of course, it's just my side of the story; you'll have to get the rest from your mother. Loyalty is important to her."

He pursed his lips and nodded, straightening his glasses.

"Your mother was always a heroine of mine—I guess for her looks and the way she asserts herself. I admire her style—I did when I was a kid. Who didn't know her? You must have felt that—the whole town is aware of her."

"I knew…" he said quietly.

"She dresses well and looks exotic and has—class. When I was a girl—when we were all girls—we used to play at being her, like dress-up."

"I remember," he said. "It was embarrassing, and I couldn't understand it."

"It made you popular—and feared. The game was ridiculous—all of us white girls, white skin! Then there's your mother—her dark skin, dark eyes, dark hair. Most of the Portuguese here are ugly, but your mother—she was to all of us just so beautiful. With all that money and her flair, her picture was in the paper everyday. She is Gloucester's Princess Di and Jackie O all in one. So I dressed like her one Halloween—Gloucester's probably the only place on earth where a little girl could dress up as a local character and be recognized."

"What did you do?" Philip asked, smiling puzzledly. "Wear a black wig?"

Nikki nodded. "It drove my mother crazy. She worked at Michelle's, the salon where your mother gets her hair done, so even though she complained the whole time, she did a great job. I was a miniature version of Rose."

"Lots of jewelry," Philip added.

"Tons! And a red ball gown and rouge and eyeshadow."

"You must have looked like a little vixen." They both were silent a moment at the pregnant thought.

"I kept a scrapbook," Nikki went on, a little sadly now. "Full of pictures of your mother. Rose at the Fishermen's Ball, Rose at the governor's for dinner, Rose with the Kennedys. We were all crazy about her, but I was especially so; as if I knew that somehow my fate was bound up with hers. I began to dream about her as my fairy godmother. I made up stories while I walked in the woods in Dogtown, about how one day she would come to see me and take me to live in that big house on the hill, and I would be a princess and have clothes and cars and lots of boyfriends…"

"Was it her beauty?"

Nikki thought. Rose had been such an assumed part of her life for so long that she no longer knew, if she ever had. "I guess so—her beauty, and other things. She was independent. She went her own way, had her own friends. Your parents seemed to have an unusual relationship. All I knew about men and women came from observing my parents and my friends' parents. Father out of the house all day, mother doing housework and cooking and raising kids."

"Your mother worked."

"That was later, after I was eight or nine. I'm the youngest; when my sisters were little, she stayed home. And my father was a horrible drunk and used to beat her and have terrible fits. He controlled her, gave her money to buy food for the household. Some weeks he wouldn't give her money, and she would be frantic…. Anyway, your parents seemed different. They had their own lives, and your mother had her own business. She was the head of all the important clubs and committees in town, and was a friend of the mayor. She used to advise him, you know." Nikki looked at him, wondering how much he did know.

Philip was thoughtful. "So how did you finally meet?"

"It was while my mother was working at Michelle's. My father was home that day getting drunk, and he suddenly insisted that she come home. He wanted her to bake him some *nisu*—some Finnish bread. That was my father, the old tyrant," she said, shaking her head. "Up one day, happy and spending money like there was no tomorrow. Piling all the neighborhood kids into the car and driving all the way down to Fenway to see the Sox play. Then the next day mean and angry, throwing things and having a fit." She stopped and thought. "The worst part was that I believed him for years, every time he was in a good mood. I loved him like that, and I'd sit on his lap and memorize all the batting averages of the Red Sox players just to please him. I fell for it," she shook her head, staring at the black water.

"Then he'd change, every time, and I'd feel like a fool. The day I met your mother was one of his mean days, when we all knew to stay clear of him. He had these huge hands like mitts and he'd sit and sit in front of the TV, one big mitt around his scotch, grabbing at us with his free hand as we went by. My sisters and I avoided him as much as we could."

Nikki mused. "The old man. Such a tyrant! He was so easy to fool," she giggled.

"I happened to be home—it was a Saturday, and he grabbed at me and screamed at me to go get my mother and tell her to come home."

"You obeyed him?"

"I wasn't going to—" She shook her head, and her gold bangs coruscated in the wan moonlight. "I didn't care what he wanted. He used to make all sorts of wild demands on us, jealous as anything, and my sisters and I always tricked him. We usually got our own way. I just put on a coat and left." She shrugged. "I stopped at Michelle's just to let my mother know that Father was about to wreck the house again. When I got there they told me my mother was up the hill at your house, doing your mother's hair. Your mother always had Michelle herself do her hair—you know they were girlhood friends?"

"Aunt Michelle—yes, I knew."

"Michelle was sick that day, or something. She used to walk up the hill from the shop downtown, and cut your mother's hair and get it ready for Saturday night. This time my mother was doing it, and so I went up the hill, my heart pounding."

"And you were how old?"

"Twelve—same year you left. I was terrified—this was my big chance. But I was ashamed, too. What was I going to say, in front of your mother? That my father was drunk again, and going crazy at home? That would pretty much seal any chance of making a connection with your mother. And that's what I wanted so badly, what I had dreamed about. For years I begged my mother to take me to meet your mother, but my mother was a little mouse, and she never would. I went up and knocked on the huge door with that big anchor door knocker. I was nearly as tall then as I am now, but I felt about two feet tall standing there waiting for someone to open—a bearded giant with a sword, I thought.

"Instead, this little hunched-over Hispanic woman opened the door and motioned me in, hardly looking at me, and turned and led me upstairs. I guess she assumed I was from Michelle's. And then, with my heart in my mouth, I went into your mother's bedroom, the big one at the back of the house that looks over the fields and down toward the forests in Dogtown. She kept the room the same for years—up to the last time I saw her there, six months ago or so..."

"When your fight broke out."

"Right." Nikki paused. "I'll get to that eventually. I think I should tell you the background, so it will make sense."

"Yes."

"It's a great room, with the tall windows looking out on the woods, those window seats where I sat and talked with your mother for hours on end. The biggest four-poster bed in the state, I'm sure, and with those huge damask curtains all around it. The fireplace—I've always wanted a fireplace in the bedroom, and with the same carved lions. And those mirrors! Tall mirrors reaching to the ceiling, with rose cherubs etched all around the edges, so when you look in them you're surrounded by adoring angels holding rosy mirrors and playing flutes. Mirrors within mirrors! So many mirrors it makes you dizzy to be in the room. That great balcony; she used to sit out on her stone balcony when the weather was good, leaving the big casement doors open. There were always lots of bees buzzing around. Does she still keep them?"

"The apiary is still functioning, yes."

"She said they kept the flowers blooming brightly, the trumpet vine and the hibiscus, all of them creeping around the balcony and growing right into the room, laying their long tendrils along the carpet like lovers in a faint."

"That's quite poetic. You're making a fist," he remarked casually, indicating her left hand in repose on her lap.

She looked down quickly, surprised to see her hand indeed making a fist. She unfolded it slowly and finished her wine, set the glass down carefully beside her and nudged herself a little closer to Philip. He adjusted himself, sitting next to her and looking at her. She looked out to sea.

"It was my favorite room in the world, from that first time I saw it. I could barely speak when I first went in; it was too big, and Rose—your mother—was too large a presence. Even though I saw her from time to time in town, I was a little thing, and the pictures of her I kept were more real than she was. And I was scared, I guess. I heard a story from Michelle, who never minded gossiping. She was the one I used to visit to keep my connection to your mother. Michelle told me a story that years ago your mother's gardener fell in love with your mother—she used to keep those balcony doors open when it was warm, even when she was dressing. I guess he caught a glimpse of her, and wanted her. So he snuck into her room when the house was empty, climbing up the vines, and he later caught her naked by her dressing table near the balcony. The way Michelle tells it, he went to grab her, but right then a whole swarm of bees came in and stung him in his eyes, and it made him blind."

"This is a factual story?" he asked, looking at her as if she were telling him something important. As if it had to do with her. A fleeting thought of what he was thinking made Nikki uncomfortable, and she hurried on.

"Well, one of the gardeners was blind—I remember that. Anyway, when I first saw her, she was sitting in her favorite chair on the balcony, looking out over the woods and the vines and those bees buzzing around her. Her black hair was all piled up, and my mother was leaning over her with a comb in her mouth, pinning your mother's hair and snipping at it. I stopped and couldn't breathe. I wanted to rush over and collect the little black curls that had floated to the floor. Your mother turned to me and called me over to her. I stood in front of her and my mother introduced me, and then poked me with the comb when I didn't say anything."

" 'She's a real beauty!' your mother said, looking at me with those huge, dark eyes of hers. Then she jumped up—she can't sit still—and went to one of her tall mirrors and examined herself closely, looking her hair over, I guess to make sure my mother was doing it right. Then she raced to her end table, grabbed a cigarette, lit it and ran back and plopped in her chair, talking the whole time while she ran around. I couldn't understand what she was saying, just stood there like a stump."

"Frightened of my mother!" Philip exclaimed softly.

"Everyone's afraid of your mother!" Nikki explained, turning to him. "She's such a—force—something elemental, out of the earth, or heaven. Her dark face! And those eyes! They just radiate power!"

"She can be disarming."

"That's an understatement! Well, but I worshiped her, so that was that. For some reason she took a liking to me and invited me to tea the next day at four, if my mother would allow it. Of course my mother said yes. Then I gave my mother the message from my father, that he was yelling for her to come home and cook him supper. That's when your mother spoke up."

" 'Leave the bastard, or kill him!' she insisted, flicking her cigarette out the window. And then my mother just stood there like me, mouth open, unable to speak. I mean, my sisters and I always fooled our father and kept out of his way, but our mother was a martyr. She doted on my father. Now your mother kept talking, telling my mother what she would do if any man mistreated her. She jumped up and went back to one of the mirrors and continued muttering, half to herself while she examined her pores. 'Men are brutes, and it's up to us women to stick together and tell the little shits when to go to hell!' she yelled in that throaty voice of hers. My mother was scandalized hearing Rose swear. It was wonderful! I broke out in a grin, and my mother swatted at me with her comb, but I dodged away. I knew my mother would never have allowed me in the company of anyone who swore, but she didn't dare stand up to your mother.

"I could see my mother considering how to refuse letting me go the next day, so I excused myself quickly and ran out of the room, knowing I'd be back. As I ran back down the hill I kept saying to myself, 'the little shit,' 'the little shit.' It was so funny and naughty. Awful, really. But true, to the point, like fresh sea air."

Nikki stopped and breathed. She lifted her glass and tilted it, saw it was empty, and set it back down. Philip reached in his jacket pocket and pulled out a bottle of Sauvignon Blanc.

"Where did that come from?" she asked, delighted. He bowed and poured for her, pulled an unopened bottle of beer from his other pocket, opened and drank.

"So anyway, that was the beginning. Tea was awkward—well, I was awkward. You've got your mother's manners. Well, sort of. You do everything with ease."

"*Sprezzatura,* the Italians call it," Philip observed. "It means something like 'effortlessness.' The idea is to do something difficult, like ballet, and make it look easy. Anyone can make it look difficult. I believe my mother taught me the meaning of the word after I read it in a book," he said wryly.

"I guess it was important for her," Nikki nodded.

"How do you mean?"

"Well—she grew up poor—" Nikki glanced at Philip, hesitant.

"It's all right, go on, speak," he said mildly.

Still, she hesitated. "I don't know—I'm sure I could be wrong, but sometimes I get the feeling your mother is still trying to get away from her roots."

"Appearance," Philip nodded.

"I didn't mean anything negative!" Nikki blurted.

Philip looked at her and smiled, nodding. "Well, go on. This is all quite fascinating."

Nikki looked at him, startled. That was exactly the expression Ernest used to make when they talked. Her heart raced. But that was to be expected, wasn't it? He was his father's son, wasn't he? She gathered herself back into her story. "Tea the next day was like being in heaven. We sat on the balcony with the bees buzzing around. I remember the table loaded with all sorts of cakes and pastries, all this rich food! She has always seemed to eat like that—it's been a wonder to me all these years how she can eat so much fat and stay the same."

"Maybe she has a thin soul."

"No—not thin—womanly. I was jealous for years of her womanly figure—but she's Mediterranean."

"With the Mediterranean temper to go with it," he observed.

"What a tongue on that woman!" Nikki nodded. "I learned all sorts of curse words I never knew before. And she carries a gun, did you know? This little pearl-handled thing your father gave her, after the incident with the gardener. She used to wave it around when she was talking about getting revenge on someone for a bad business deal. Scary."

He frowned. "Go on."

"After tea I was invited back again, then again, and soon hired as your mother's sort of personal child. I thought at first that she was using me as a substitute for you, but later I didn't think so. Or maybe I was; I don't know. I didn't care, I loved her so desperately. Then she caught me in front of her mirror one day, trying on her lipstick. I nearly fainted! I thought she had gone out for the day. But she sat me down and looked me over carefully, then told me she was going to bring out my real beauty. I was going to your house every day by then, working in the hothouse or with the bees, doing small errands for your mother, and now I began a course under her instruction on how to be beautiful."

"You graduated summa," Philip said simply. It was good not to make too much of women's beauty. Leave that to everyone else. He did not feel cutting; rather that compliments were unnecessary beyond the obvious. Nikki's beauty came from a place strange and familiar to him; it spoke a different language and it worshiped a red-sulfur goddess. It was like his mother's, but went deeper.

"You're very kind," Nikki bowed. "That's something an old lover taught me to say at compliments."

"How's that?"

"It's a line from *Casablanca*. Ingrid Bergman is told by Claude Raines that she is the most beautiful woman in the city, and she simply replies, 'You're very kind.' Instead of making a protest in the face of the compliment."

"I see. A smart man, this old lover." Was he feeling jealous? he wondered. What a fool! He coughed once. "So you grew up at my mother's knee."

"Oh, I didn't mean it like that," Nikki hurried to explain.

He smiled openly and shook his head, gesturing for her to continue.

"So I grew up a kind of protégée to her, and I learned all sorts of things about her, about where she went, who she saw. I tried to carry myself like her, and as I grew she gave me her old clothes, so that overnight I was dressed in all these expensive clothes I had absolutely no use for. But it impressed my girlfriends, and I was seen as becoming like your mother. I spent most of my time at the house, and it used to make my father furious and my mother sad, but I didn't care. I was in heaven. And when it came time to go to college, she paid."

"Good!"

Nikki looked at Philip. Was he serious? "Well, it's not like I assumed—it was a complete shock, and I never took money from her again. I paid for law school myself."

"What about my father, what did he think?"

Nikki hesitated. "I never saw him much, at first. He went to sea a lot, and your mother and I ate meals in her room, in the little alcove near the fireplace when it was cold, where I would sit and pet the stone lions. Or we'd eat out on the stone balcony when it was warm. I loved her like a mother—I loved her more than my mother, because she wasn't afraid to use her power."

"Is that what caused your break with her?"

Nikki thought a moment. She breathed deeply again and held her glass out as Philip reached and poured. She was feeling dizzy, full of wine and Philip's warm, strong presence, and full of memories of Rose.

"I moved back here, as I said, just this year after my father died."

"How did he die?"

"Alcoholism—actually, a heart attack, but it's the same. I found him when I came for one of my visits." She was suddenly back in the house, and her father was wheezing horribly. She breathed heavily, staring out to sea.

"That's the house I live in now, with my dog. It's a little yellow cottage perched on the side of the hill on the other side of Dogtown."

"Yes, Dogtown," Philip mused. "I went walking there with my mother the other day. She said she was thinking of doing some building down along the side of it. I hadn't been in those woods for thirty years—I would have gotten lost by myself."

"Your mother—?" Nikki asked, suddenly stiffening.

"Did you know my mother was involved in developing?"

"Yes, she's had a company for years—Cleavage Builders."

Philip laughed out loud.

"It is kind of funny, though I laughed so long ago the joke is almost lost on me," Nikki said. "It's your mother all the way—right out there. She's always worn the most provocative dresses, really made a few scenes. I could never wear those dresses she gave me—not those. She looked like the women in the magazines—well, more voluptuous, but just as elegant. She was crazy about magazines, and owned more makeup and hair spray and gel and every sort of beauty product."

"She has even more these days. But you were telling me about your house and what happened to your father."

"The old house—yes." She was thinking again of Rose building in Dogtown. She was afraid to think of her father.

"After my mother died—are you sure you want to hear all this?—I feel like I'm jabbering."

"It's delightful," Philip said, pouring wine for her.

"OK—but stop me if I get boring. Wine makes me talk and talk. OK, so the house—right! My mother died two years ago, and my father went downhill fast after that, sitting around and drinking harder, quit his job, never went out. I used to drive up from Cambridge to make his meals and clean the place."

"What about your sisters?"

"They all live far away—Florida, Chicago, West Virginia. It was all left to me, the youngest. Guess that's what happens. So I came, and it was horrible, watching that big whale, all blubbery, sitting there in front of the TV. Every once in a while my brother-in-law was there—he would fly in from Chicago to work on my father's will."

"He is a lawyer too?"

"No!" Nikki exploded, as the old anger filled her as if being pumped into her. "He wasn't a lawyer; I'm the lawyer. It's because he was a male, and also not in the family. You have to understand my family—my father, in particular. He hated women; well, he was threatened by them, by us. Then he had four girls—what a laugh! He never trusted us. No—my job was to fill in for my mother—cook, clean, bring him bottles of scotch. He got pretty wild talking in those last days. Used to talk about ghosts in the house—mainly my mother's and my grandmother's. He was really crazy!" She breathed heavily. "Then one day he died. But he was such a large presence, overwhelming our little house, controlling everything. How could he die?" She shivered.

"People do," Philip said quietly.

"Not someone that big," Nikki snorted. She looked at Philip. "Oh, I'm sorry! You had a different relationship with your father."

"So then you moved into the house?" Philip asked, moving on.

"Yes, no one wanted it. I was sick of lawyering and ready to quit. Actually, they didn't renew my contract, but that's another story. I broke up with the man I was seeing and moved here, back home where I never thought I'd ever come back to."

She slumped her shoulders, and Philip looked at her. It was getting late.

"Are you cold?" he asked.

"A little," she said, distracted with the wine. It was like all the other times, she thought vaguely. Getting slowly drunk. What was she doing talking so much? She never talked like this—not about herself. Philip's wonderful aroma of Europe enveloped her like a warm fog. Then he was sitting right next to her, lifting the food and drink away, putting his arm around her shoulder, rubbing her upper arm softly. She snuggled against him and leaned her wagging head on his shoulder.

Her perfume wafted into his nostrils, and it was a scent of smooth cream and gliding. Stretching limbs flashed rainbows before him like glittering salmon in the stream, and then they were gone, leaving only the wake of the dark, emotional sea.

"You didn't tell me how you and my mother fought," he murmured, not really wanting to disturb her, wanting to disturb her.

She sat up, and her eyes were blurry. Philip kept his arm about her shoulder. She might as well tell him, she thought, and get it over with.

"We fought—over your father."

"What?" Philip sat up.

"It's not what you think," Nikki said hurriedly. "Or what your mother thought—that's the problem. She thought your father and I—"

He looked at her wide-eyed.

"But it's not true!" she cried.

"Then—why did my mother think that?" he frowned.

"Because she knew—with that witch sense of hers—that I did have a lot of affection for him. I guess I had a crush on him when I was a girl. I didn't tell you—actually your father and I became friends through the years, and he would listen to my stories while we sat in his library. I loved him, like a father, I guess. Then the day my father died, I went to your parents' house, and saw your father, and he was a comfort to me—but that's all!" she finished quickly, seeing Philip's eyes widen again.

He laughed softly at last. "Well, I can see my mother reacting, if she had any inkling at all. What did she do—threaten to kill you?"

"Not exactly, but we fought horribly. I'm so sorry."

"That nothing happened?" Philip jabbed. Again! The old competition.

"No!" she pleaded, and he looked in her eyes and believed her. Yet there was something else in her he could just discern over the horizon of her consciousness, some secret she was keeping, and it made him wonder.

He reached his arm around her, and she slumped against him. "My mother is the wrong person to tangle with, that's for sure," he murmured, rubbing her shoulder. "Still, you may be better off now. My parents—both devourers."

She waited, glancing at him.

He was thinking out loud. "I came back because my father's business failed. He swallowed the ocean. It's not just that he's dead; the fishing industry is dying."

"The fishermen are all getting laid off," she said.

"Even before his death, the business was going downhill. Oh, if it was my mother who drove him to it, it wasn't only my mother! Too much greed; too many fishermen vacuuming the ocean floor."

"Your father was the biggest."

Philip looked at the top of her golden head. "Yes, he was. He made it a point to be. And so he was the hardest hit. He left no note; maybe it wasn't my mother after all; maybe it was the seas drying up, and he had no idea what to do about that. He opened up to me, in his gruff way, when he came to visit in France. He used to tell me that no matter how bad he felt about my mother, he always had the sea."

"So now what happens?"

"The fleet is all sold, did you know?"

"So I heard."

"The business dying has made my mother frantic. She's feeling her age; and now with the money gone, there's no cushion."

"She's still got her looks."

"Not as she sees it. You know, the American ideal—the young woman is the ideal of beauty here. Past twenty you're over the hill. That's what I meant when I wondered if you were just too much competition for her," he said, smiling at her and arching an eyebrow. "So the poor thing is working harder than ever to rebuild the family fortune. The other day, as I said, she walked me through Dogtown—it must not have been very far from your own back door—and told me how she planned to build houses there. She's trying to drag me into the business."

Nikki sat up and looked at him. "Dogtown is protected land."

"When did that ever stop my mother?"

Nikki nodded. "But—it's the green heart of the town. Where the witches and prostitutes used to live, you know. I grew up playing games there, imitating the old women who had lived there. I remember their names," she said wistfully. "Judy Rhines was one... What's your mother's plan? I used to help her out when I was first a lawyer, and some of her tactics put me off, so I made an excuse not to do any work for her."

"That was smart. And I don't know what her plan is. But it scared me to walk along with her and listen to her talk and talk—one minute about how ugly and old she is getting, the next swearing to squash anyone in Gloucester who tries to prevent her from building houses in Dogtown. She kept muttering and railing in that way she has, half to herself, as if the world doesn't exist around her until she admits it to her presence. She was swearing that she would find something."

"What?"

"I have no idea—and she clammed up when I asked."

Nikki shivered, and something deep in her quailed. She was not finished with Rose, the voice said. But she would think about that later.

She looked at him and then slumped back against his shoulder, partly hiding her face. Men had always seemed weak to her, little boys when it came down to it. So easy to manipulate, to seduce, to get rid of. But Philip had a power about him; he knew things, and even though it was clear he was attracted to her, he wasn't acting in any way she could predict or work with. She had been trying things all evening with him, and nothing was working. When she spoke in her little-girl, spacey voice, he just looked at her as if she were an alien. Even now, leaning against him, him stroking her hair, she felt that he could take or leave her. Not indifference, yet. Something else; a quality of distance about him. It began to make her angry, and again she resolved to take him to bed and so make him vulnerable.

But Nikki was unwilling or unable to see how like paper his heart was. Philip sat stroking her beautiful flaxen hair, hair like beaten gold, the long strands coursing over her shoulder like sea currents. His jacket was around her, close to her. He trembled a little.

She sat up abruptly, her eyes bleary. "You're cold," she said.

He looked closely at her and then leaned and put his face next to hers and their lips touched. He felt about to faint, and the miracle of touch was upon him faster than he could think, and everything was lost, a catastrophe flowing over him and taking him. The world turned slowly over on its axis, and everything was changed in an instant. She felt the great presence as his face swarmed up to hers, and she smiled and murmured as they kissed.

But a strange, deep sadness overcame Philip, and he cried out, "Too late!"

Nikki drew sharply back, for in looking at Philip she had looked over his shoulder, back toward the causeway. A dark figure walking toward them at the water's edge.… Her eye was certain in an instant; it was Ernest. She clutched Philip's arm and stared over his shoulder in horror.

He turned to look as the wind came up and blew sand in their faces, and he ducked and turned back to her. Nikki ducked her head, too, and bowed toward Philip's chest. Her heart was racing in terror. In a moment Ernest's ghost would be upon them!

Yet when the wind died down, Nikki looked, and there was no one. She was spellbound, again at the graveside, witnessing that awful heave in the ground. She stared blind; what had she seen? Had it been real? It could not have been; she had pushed the image out of her mind for months, had nearly forgotten.

"No, it's not too late!" she whispered, grabbing at Philip, and they left their glasses and the half-eaten brownies and strawberries to the tide, rushing away arm in arm across the causeway and back to the safety of Nikki's red Miata, parked in front of the party still going on.

She shivered and they kissed, and he wondered that she was all business.

"Your house?" he asked, eyeing her closely.

"Can't—my dog hates men."

He smiled grimly, and remembered his feeling that she was dangerous.

In the end they drove to the Wingaersheek Motel, just off Route 128 on the out-skirts of town, and all night the intermittent sounds of highway traffic accompanied them. A flare of fear shot through her as they approached, but it had been her idea; and the old time she remembered, that was years ago.

PHILIP PUT his hand on her stomach, and Nikki groaned with the weight of desire. They had gotten their room from the tee-shirted manager who came out of the back room, TV blaring, scratching his big belly. Together, silently, they found their room upstairs around the back, then locking the door they fell into the bed as soft and lumpy as an old lady.

Philip put his hand on her stomach and leaned and brushed his lips against the left side of her neck, and her mouth fell open a little.

"Only if you mean business," Nikki whispered, her voice going raspy. He pushed her hair back away from her forehead and ran kisses along the curve of her neck, and now she arched her body to him, and he put his hand behind her, fully clothed, and pulled, softly and steadily, her back to him, then moved his hand and pressed her hip, then pressed her stomach with his palm. Her body was coming apart; he unbuttoned the front of her dress with the exploding flowers and, spreading the seams, brushed her stomach with his fingertips. He leaned and kissed her belly, but it was far too much, and she clutched his dark hair and pulled his face up to her lips, where they kissed and touched, whispering to one another in fragments of a secret language.

She was rising to him now; kneeling before her, he pulled her dress up and over her hips, and she closed her eyes and let him look at her; even the little quiver of loose flesh on her stomach. He lifted the red-flowered dress over her head slowly, as if enacting a sacred ritual, and unhooked her bra, she sitting up now and pulling half attentive at his shirt, at his belt; dazed with desire and waterlogged with wine. She could not undo it. But miraculously Philip stood up and was naked in a flash, the muscles in his chest and arms rising over her like a wave.

He lay softly upon her and she felt his sex press softly against her belly, and she stretched her legs and he lay between them, stroking her long blond hair and taking her head in his hands and kissing her gently, as if he were weeping into a flower of delicate beauty. She never cried except now, soft and her whole being thinned into a rose-hued petal. He kissed her tiny pooled eyes, and she knew he would not tease her for the tears.

Flames licked her, and she wanted him. She was a warm spring waiting and he plunged his muscle into her so that she jerked and arched her back, groaning and opening her mouth, her eyes closed. Far, impossibly far inside of her, into her far, distant darkness he pressed, until she felt he would touch her heart, and he gathered her up and raised her to him, and she felt as if they were clenched hard around an excruciating softness, so soft, so rising that she panted and began to cry out. He patted her head softly, brushing strands of her gold hair back from her face. Tiny droplets of sweat gathering on her brow and lip, and he looked long at her, and together they moved up and up and up and up in the eternal rocking of the cosmos, as he lay back down upon her.

God, how he pressed her! Her hands were confettied birds and her mind was going, scattered in fragments like her body, the wonder too great to bear straight on. She flung her arms out and he caught them at the wrists and pressed his arms around them, holding her as they rocked. Her head arced back over the edge of the bed and still he drove her on and on, her desire rising and she crying out like a child, like Wise Woman herself, until the cries caught themselves and she split herself upon his rock and went tumbling down in jagged echoes into the dark sea, dark sea...

Very soon he raced after her, methodical, crouched like a cat, stroking her, his hardness growing and overmastering him; she could feel him grow harder than he was capable of growing on his own, as if a mountain were emerging from inside his body. And then she knew it was time, and she smiled from a long way off, seeing in closed eyes his own open mouth, open in surprise and awe at the miracle of being taken, though he was never taken, she knew, taken now by her and he was dragged along the edge of the rocky cataract until he was plummeted over and fell spuming into her earth, her body, her womb. She smiled sadly, triumphantly glistening along the starry curve of birth and death, and there they lay like gods splayed across the heavens.

She smiled through closed eyes as he whispered to her and his voice was soft and the words were good medicine. She caught them leaning back and away, in her left ear, feeling still the warmth of his silken thread pulsing like a newborn nebula deep in the space within her.

For a time they lay quietly, Nikki listening to the thud of a loose shutter in the night wind.... She felt very close to Philip, but now in the dark and quiet he seemed to sleep, and everything came back to her. He lay with his arm draped over her, pressing down on her, pressing on her heart. She was suddenly afraid in the dark. Who was this man? Always in the past she had gotten so drunk that it hadn't mattered which man it was. Tonight she was not drunk, only her heart was stirred, and she was frightened. Images of Rose in a fury pursuing her floated over the bed; then Ernest came as a flash of red, pointing an accusing finger. Her father looked at her with one great fish eye from the dark corner, and her heart raced as she stared at the shadowy image.

Philip was unconscious of it all. Where was a safe place? Nikki wondered. There was a great danger before her, and it was Philip, she knew.

Yet she knew she was already caught under his weight; she wanted to ease herself out of the bed and, dressing quietly, hurry home to be safe. Home! Where the ghost of her father roamed, looking for her? Where could she go? Could Philip save her? Or was he the culmination of all the dead and threatening living come to capture her at last?

For hours Nikki lay under Philip's heavy arm, miserable with fright and worry, while the lonely window shutter, crusted in the salt air of Gloucester, banged forlornly in the dark.

2.

A BARGAIN WITh BEAUTY

Nikki moved about the yellow-shingled house in a half dream as the days passed. Although she had been living there already four months, it had lost none of its strangeness. How curious to be walking about like a ghost through the house you grew up in! She creaked over boards and ducked her head going up the low-ceilinged stairway. She had taken her old room, not her parents' bedroom, at the end of the upstairs hall. Her dog, Guy, slept next to her in bed, waking in the night at the house creaking and groaning with age. An odor of musk and old alcohol permeated the house; near the kitchen the smell of her mother's paints lingered, closed up in their little room adjacent to the back door. The kitchen smelled of cooking herbs, as it always had, for Nikki's mother had forever been brewing cinnamon tea or an herb salve for one of her daughters' sore throats. They left a clean, earthy smell.

Gloucester was so much quieter than Cambridge, even compared to the side street Nikki had lived on in the city. Her family house was on Grove Street, which narrowly wound and jagged drunkenly up- and downhill alongside the woods of Dogtown. The house was backed up to the woods. Nikki had but to walk through her backyard, up a small incline, and through an unmown field of high weeds to be under the maples and oaks of the old wood where the witches once lived. But when she moved back she didn't give a thought to the deep woods or to the witches, nor to the Druids who supposedly had lived there as well.

She took instead to wandering the narrow tilted streets of Gloucester. Throughout her years living in Boston and traveling she had carried a mental image of her hometown that now, she realized, did not quite correspond to outer reality. Yes, there was the old Mariner's house, with the same archetypal old salts sitting sunning themselves while exhaling sad, desultory smoke rings. There the harbor with its lines of salt-whitened boats, a porcupine field of masts. There the statue of Saint Peter in the storefront window, awaiting the summer festival. Yet Gloucester was all different, so much *smaller,* that her heart was struck as she sauntered through town, reacquainting herself as with an aged aunt from whom one half expects an inheritance. The light on the harbor was magnificent and broken.

The town, as indeed her childhood home, seemed somewhat countrified and so dirty, as if closer to the earth than Boston. In the yellow house that was now hers, cobwebs gathered along the upper walls of the quiet rooms, spiders spun their webs in all the low corners and narrow places, husks of moths and bees hung suspended between toilet and wall. Nikki heard mice skittering neurotically in the wall cavities, sparrows and starlings fluttering in the trees and the bushes out back who woke her up before dawn.

With no job and time on her hands, she sank slowly into the spirit of her family, the spirit of the old, sad yellow-shingled house, reconfiguring herself in its timeless pattern. On the narrow dark wood mantel she set her incense burner and carved stone goddess, next to dusty portraits of her parents and her sisters. She took down her mother's crucifixes and pictures of Mary and set over the vividly unbleached ghost squares on the wallpaper her own pictures: the goddess of dreams, gliding in blue stars across a golden heaven, finger upraised to her lips; landscapes of Monument Valley, mystical rock formations of ochre and dried blood. It was as if she were quietly, with no one there to witness, asserting her youngest-child presence. She smiled absurdly at her belated triumph, now that only ghosts were present.

During the cool spring evenings she sat in a rusted iron chair in the backyard musing on the dense forest wall of Dogtown, inhaling the smell of melting earth, mud, quickening, the faint spice of anticipation. Later, partly for lack of anything else to occupy her time, she took up the gardening she had once loved as a child. The beds were all overgrown, bushes needing trimming and pruning. As the weeks passed Nikki worked with more purpose and attention. She began to walk Guy deeper into the Dogtown woods instead of just taking him far enough to relieve himself in the underbrush. She found she knew the old paths still; they were changed, more sober and quiet than she remembered; but they were there, leading her to follow them more and more deeply into the wood.

At home again she cleaned and cleaned, as if to clean away the spirit of her family; futile. She set her slightly jowly face and pursed lips to the task, her blue eyes flashing in ironic awareness of what she was about. The kitchen for one had never been finished—a project of her father in one of his active moods. The countertops were new but one end was uncut and unfinished, hanging out in space like an abandoned lover. The same old red linoleum floor, same stained cast-iron sink her father kept saying he was going to get rid of. The kitchen was in the rear of the house, reached through the back door that everyone used to enter. There was a small mudroom off the kitchen, really its own closet-like room, in which Nikki's mother had set up her painting things.

Meanwhile her connection to Philip took root, just as Nikki did not want it to; as part of her said she did not want it to happen. She had wanted only to sleep with him that first night, then be done with him, as she had been done with all her men over the years. But from the start his presence frightened and overwhelmed her. So like his father he seemed that Nikki felt haunted and then confused, not knowing whether it was Ernest's ghost come to berate her, or to comfort her; whether it was Ernest at all, or just Philip and her fear of being deeply touched and made open to him.

Because for all his darkness, Philip was a comfort to Nikki. Clinging at first to him with her petals, tentatively, she soon thought of nothing but him for days on end. Finally she threw herself at him with near complete abandon, giving herself up to her feelings when they passed through her. Yet Philip detected in her a barely perceptible hesitation, as if she were watching him with one eye to see whether he should accept her (she had the native self-consciousness of tall women). In love she gave herself without restraint, her long arms flying and writhing, as if the hysteria were splitting her body apart. Then Philip grew charmed, a little afraid of how deeply and strongly she was taken away. He learned quickly enough that her fires burned her ideals, too, and left her fiery and red and disillusioned in her love for him.

When Philip held her, Nikki felt sometimes as if Ernest himself were holding her, caressing her, his firm fatherliness keeping her safe and warm and secure. But then with a shock Nikki woke to the fact of Ernest's death, suddenly feeling a corpse was holding her. She then became frightened of needing this man and would call Philip to insist they stop seeing each other, half in panicked fear, half in resentment. Yet for all Nikki's fears, they came slowly to spend nearly every day together.

"There are too many stress factors in my life right now," Nikki insisted to Philip, who listened quietly on the other end of the phone. "We have to stop. Anyway, you're married."

"You're acting the tyrant," Philip once replied. "You dictate when I come and go, when we'll be together."

"It's you who controls everything—puts the limits on our connection," Nikki argued tiredly. "We can't go on."

And for a week or so they would have no contact. But Philip would invariably call to suggest an unthreatening lunch downtown, and Nikki would go. The afternoon turned into evening with a bottle or two of good champagne and a quiet party, then Philip would be climbing the narrow staircase in the little yellow-shingled house, following behind Nikki, heavy with wine and desire; both of them afraid to speak, lest they break the spell.

She could not seem to untangle him, and that was what frightened her. Philip remained secretive and aloof, disappearing for days at a time off sailing his father's sailboat, leaving Nikki to worry, then to grow resentful at her worry, then to fill with loathing for him.

So they went, as April tipped into May and May fell into the arms of June. Nikki felt caught in a passion beyond love, infuriating and tantalizing. For Ernest had been there from the beginning, looking over Philip's shoulder, sometimes even speaking through Philip. A casual expression Philip used would have the exact words and intonation of his father, and Nikki would hearken suddenly, eyebrows raised in wonder and fear.

She continued to busy herself in the house, cleaning out the basement and carting boxes of junk to the trash. Her sisters had come and carried off the treasures they wanted, leaving most of the old furniture, except for the dining room table, which Jane took.

It was one dusty afternoon when Nikki was pulling boxes out of a lost corner of the basement that she first saw her father's ghost. She had put the Beatles' *Revolver* on upstairs, faint sounds of "Eleanor Rigby" floating down the narrow, steep stairs.

She was bent over a box, flipping its top open and examining the contents, which this time turned out to be old photo albums.

She sat and opened a dusty black folder, pages half falling out. Guy lay beside her, head on paws, bored. Her parents' wedding pictures drew Nikki into a reverie. But, as always, she skirted her father's death. She could not think of it without his voice beginning in her head like a weight descending on her. She was thinking again of her father's hands, always reaching out to grab her or one of her sisters as they ran past his old green chair.

Guy sat up growling, as Nikki turned absently. Guy was given to growling suddenly at some noise three blocks away, then settling back down into lethargy. This time he did not settle back but sat up stiff and staring.

Nikki peered into the dim corner of the basement where Guy faced, his ears pricked. A hulking shadow brooded restlessly in the dim. Nikki stood up, shaking and staring. Out from the shadows staggered her father, fat as a whale, his great flabby cheeks sagging as if full of water, staring through her.

Her heart raced; she thought to bolt for the stairway. Guy was barking in a motionless frenzy. Nikki could not move either, as she stared and waited. The figure stood wavering, then raised an arm and pointed in her direction. At first Nikki thought it was pointing at her, then saw that it was indicating something behind her. She did not dare turn. Then it disappeared, fading slowly into the must and dust of the basement shadows.

Nikki stood shaking to her bones. Guy stopped barking abruptly, though he growled as he crept to the spot where the shadow had appeared. Snarling once or twice, he sniffed the dirt floor and trotted back to Nikki's side.

When her heart slowed enough for her to breathe, she sat staggering on a box, setting down the photo album she still clutched to her side.

Although she hesitated, she at last called Philip once she made it upstairs. He came immediately, of course, but before he arrived Nikki thought better of telling him everything. Wasn't he a threat, too? Yet she confided in him more than in any of her girlfriends now. Could he help her? But what could he do?

While Nikki was arguing with herself, Philip knocked softly, letting himself in through the kitchen door. Guy barked happily. In the weeks since Philip had been coming to the house, he and Guy had become friends, much to the awkward delight and rising fear of Nikki. Guy was supposed to be her protection against men, but here he was befriending the most dangerous of them. Usually he was a snarling mutt who attacked any man who came to the house. Nikki had to lock him in a room just to let the phone man in. He was her protection, her excuse when she didn't want a man coming home with her. But Philip had moved through Guy's barrier as he had slipped past her own, with charming ease and with a certain presumption.

Philip bent down to ruffle Guy's ears, then went to Nikki with a worried look.

"You sounded so upset," he remarked, looking at her closely after sitting beside her at the round kitchen table.

"Oh, it's nothing."

He sat quietly, watching her.

"Really," she insisted, laughing self-consciously. "This old house gives me the creeps. I feel like I'm being sucked down into my family—what I tried to get away from for years. Now it's all coming back."

"Can I help?" he asked.

"Oh—no!" she said, smiling now. "I'm under a lot of stress. The house feels alive, somehow."

"Your family," he nodded. "Both of your parents dead—you saw something," he said evenly, still eyeing her.

"Well—I thought I saw something. Guess I was imagining it."

"Where?"

"Basement." Now completely self-conscious, she shifted nervously in her seat.

He went immediately, as was his way, clattering down the narrow, steep stairs fearlessly, or else indifferent, or else too full of knowing. Nikki stood waiting at the top, breathless. Guy padded downstairs after Philip, and she heard the two of them snuffling around. Philip called up to her.

"There's nothing here. What did you see—a ghost?"

Shivering, she said nothing. When he tramped back upstairs and turned into the kitchen, she was sitting reading the paper. He looked at her.

"Do you have a gift for seeing things?" he asked abruptly, tilting his head slightly.

"What?" she jerked the paper away. She smiled. "Why do you say that?"

"You won't tell me what you saw, so I assume it was a ghost. You said your mother's mother lived here with you?" He sat at the table with her, pouring himself coffee.

"Grandma Grace," Nikki replied, looking up. "This was her house; my parents moved in before I was born. Grandma stayed in the back room upstairs that's mine now. I remember her in black, tall and severe. She and my father used to fight all the time, but he fought with everyone. My mother and grandmother had a secret—some way of dealing with my father that I never understood."

"Did your mother grow up in this house?" Philip asked.

"Oh, yes! She and her sister, my Aunt Meg who lives in Salem, were both born here. My grandfather died in World War II—I guess he was kind of old to go to war, but he did. I never knew him."

"You had many women around you."

She looked at him oddly. "That's not the way I think of it. Grandma lived in her room most of the time, but whenever she did come out, she and my father used to go at it. My mother martyred herself to my father." Nikki rose suddenly. "Want to sit in the living room?" she asked, taking her coffee, walking through the dining room and sitting on the couch. Philip followed and sat next to her, picking up a framed photo of Nikki's parents.

"It's funny, I can't visualize my father's face, even looking at that picture," Nikki frowned. "That was taken when he still looked good. These past years he turned all huge and bloated. Ugh." She made a face.

"He's very handsome in the picture," Philip noted, studying the framed photo enlargement of the newlyweds. Nikki's father smiled at the camera, aware of his beauty, the sly, satisfied look in his eye. He towered over his wife who looked up at him with surprise in her eyes, as if she had never expected such good fortune to befall her.

"What were their names?"

"Pekka," Nikki answered.

"What?"

"A Finnish name. My father's brothers were Keijo and Heikke; their father's name was Manne Helmik. He came from the old country around 1900. They came to quarry stone. Big men with huge hands. It's what I remember about my father." She turned her own hands over, seeing her father's. They were big and hard on the back and had soft palms.

"But he had an insurance office downtown?"

Nikki nodded. "His father never forgave him for it. My uncles both died when we were little kids. A big slab of granite fell on them while they were setting stone for one of the mansions."

Abashed, Philip shook his head silently. They both knew how many men had died building houses like the one Ernest Eveless had built up on the hill.

"Your father's handsome," he remarked.

"You said that already," she replied.

"I can see where you got your looks. Same high cheekbones, same round chin, big eyes—"

"Stop!" she cried, raising her hands in front of her face.

He turned to her with his dark eyes, straightening his glasses.

"I can't stand thinking I look like him. My mother and my sisters all used to say I resembled him the most. I'm the youngest, you know, after four girls. I was supposed to be the boy, to save him."

"A lot of pressure," Philip nodded.

"Worse than that. He was a tyrant. One day sweet and loving, the next a complete switch, yelling and having a fit, driving us all out of the house." She giggled.

"What's funny?"

"He was so easy to fool. He used to call me his 'little whore.'"

"My god!" Philip whispered quietly, misery in his voice.

She laughed. "Nice guy, huh?"

"What was he so angry about?"

"I don't know," she shrugged. "But we fooled him, all right. We all used to climb out our windows at night, sneaking off to meet our boyfriends. I had a different one every week."

"Of course," Philip replied, stiffening slightly.

Nikki shot him a quick look. Well, what did it matter? she asked herself vehemently. Who was he to want to possess her? A flare of red anger seared her as she looked away. But her inward gaze was met by the flashing images of her many lovers, reminding her that each time she ever lay with one she heard her father's voice calling her whore, as if her father's curse lay upon her like the heavy men's bodies. She remained drunkenly silent with the stranger men, yet in the dark they swore "Whore!" in her ear from the chill depths of her father's voice.

"What about your mother?" Philip continued.

"My mother the mouse!" Nikki exclaimed. "She was from an old family in Gloucester; she knew nothing about Finland or the Finns. I don't know how the two of them got together. But she dutifully learned to cook Finnish food for the old tyrant—*pulla, nisu,* all his favorites."

"Your sisters all moved away, you said?"

"I was the only one to come back..." she mused. "This house feels so strange—like it's calling me to some unfinished business. While I was cleaning out the basement and the attic, I discovered these old albums and papers. In his last days my father used to rage about spells on the house—ghosts and things."

"Ghosts?"

"I think he was afraid."

"Of your grandmother?"

"Of her, maybe. Women in general." She shrugged, leaning for him to kiss her. It was easier not to think.

Surprised by her sudden move toward him, he drew back. "So it was your grandmother you saw in the basement?"

She pulled away slightly. He noted the minute meaning in her move but persisted, not yet leaning to take her in his arms.

"I'm so tired," she sighed. When she saw him looking steadily at her, she continued abruptly. "My father. I feel like an idiot. I think I saw his ghost!"

His seriousness frightened her. He nodded. "I've seen my own father—I thought I saw him walking down the hallway in my mother's house the other night." He laughed, almost scornfully. "I suppose even death doesn't just happen."

"What do you mean?"

"It's as if the dead have to learn to be dead. Our fathers don't seem to know that yet."

"What a strange idea... but you're right. And why should we know we're dead?"

"They say that's what ghosts are—dead people who haven't yet learned. They need something from us." Although he dared not say it out loud, when Nikki spoke of her father's unpredictability he was reminded of her penchant for driving him suddenly away. He did not say, because he wanted her warm and near. If he spoke his mind she would grow cold.

She snuggled close to him, letting the image of her father dissolve.

Now that the blossom was opening, each wondered secretly whether all the glory that was theirs for a time was worth the storms to come. Or was their budding tenderness a *fleur du mal?* Yet, there was something of friendship and abiding between them that made them pause, as if they were standing amazed and hesitant before a rare African blossom of complex beauty, its huge red fronds and electric green fuse pulsing, pistils of virgin white and stamen of crimson emerging from blue depths.

They were two explorers standing before this cruel, beautiful flower garlanded with lianas licking and curling at their feet. Even while enthralled Philip seemed to observe from a distance. The flower's strangeness made Nikki angry, when she was not leaning over the brooding blossom to slake her thirst.

And so into June the two wrestled their way. Lying in his bed in his stately, high-ceilinged room in his mother's house on the hill, Philip brooded on Nikki, not daring to tell his mother about her. He was exhausted from long days at the offices of Eveless Fisheries, where day after day he strove to salvage something from the wreck of his father's business. He did it for his mother because he could not bear to see, close behind her bravado, how pathetic and frightened she was. But the books were a mess; his father had been taking money out of the business even as it was sinking. There was not much left besides papers and the *Lamia Claire.*

Finally he roused himself from his half stupor of exhaustion to call Françoise in Marseilles, telling her about Nikki. She was understanding and thoughtful as the two talked at length. His heart was splitting and thoughts of leaving Françoise were inevitable. But to leave her for a woman who hated him as much as desired him? He was not certain Nikki knew what love was, not certain it was not simply desire for the red apple of his being. How was it possible to gain a foothold even as the avalanche sucked the ground from under him and he fell down and down and down, tumbling head over heels to his death? He set the phone down, feeling that Françoise's low voice dragged like a lost anchor far away from him, out along the infinite transatlantic line of the telephone, and then gone.

A foothold on the doorstep of death, he mused grimly, lying once again on his bed, listening to the muffled sounds of his mother returning from another night out, all screams and cries of horrid triumph at her latest conquest. Piled around him were the labyrinthine accounts of his father. Precise numbers on long ledgers, all adding up to nothing. She was like Nikki, he reflected: never admitting the hurt. His father had been his mother's sobering, necessary counterweight. Without him she threatened to fly away shrieking, like a terrified pterodactyl.

AS SUMMER BEAT its bright golden gong, the couple took long walks in Dogtown, Nikki showing Philip all the places she had played as a child: the old crumbling cellar holes where the witches used to live; the dark parts of the forest where no hikers or mountain bikers went. Donning mosquito helmets and boots, they trudged into the forgotten swamps, stopping and standing ankle-deep in sucking grey-brown mud, standing silently as trees waiting for the hiccup of a frog or the rare screech of a bluebird in the underbrush.

They walked along the beach at Halibut Point, climbing up onto massive blocks of tumbled granite that spilled like fallen soldiers down a steep cliff right into the sea. Even while waves slapped and shook the blocks as if trying to awaken them, they sat sunken in their stony meditations, unmoved by all the activity of the waves and the gulls screaming and pitching overhead.

Philip was a long-legged mountain goat, scrambling quickly up the long, steep cliff of gargantuan blocks, finding footholds and sneaker ledges hidden from below. Nikki watched, fascinated by this strange man, half European sophisticate, half little boy still adventuring in Gloucester. She took the longer way up to the top of the cliff, winding her way on the path made of stones set in a stairway.

At the top the two joined hands, gazing down into the frothing surf.

She looked into his eyes. "Don't scare me like that."

Smiling, he leaned away from her. "Jumping up the rocks?"

"That's where Miss Heasley fell in the water," Nikki nodded, pointing to their right where the granite avalanche converged in a narrow, wave-bitten cove.

"Behind us is the quarry where Charlie and I used to swim," Philip pointed out, turning toward the great pit through the trees. "Did you ever swim there?"

"Sometimes," she answered vaguely. She had by then seen enough of Philip's look when she told him about her old boyfriends. Now she was on guard.

They stood staring out over the Atlantic, leaning slightly into the stiff breeze.

"Over there is France," he said gaily. Both were silent reflecting on what that meant.

"Are you leaving soon?" she asked. Was it her fault she had fallen so in love with him? As a flare of anger bubbled up like lava, her mind spattered and heaved in red viscous lumps. She was seared and wanted to hurt him.

"Going back to your wife?"

"I don't know what I'm doing," he stuttered, turning his head as if struck by her bluntness. "I'm happy when I'm with you—you know that. I love you," he said, turning to her. "I don't know what any of this means—do you?"

"Me? No!" she cried in the stiffening breeze, as if it had nothing to do with her, it was his problem to figure out.

He heard her tone. "Don't you want to know?"

She looked at him as her anger passed. Leaning her face to his, she murmured, "I just want to enjoy you and bless—this," she finished, kissing him. He loved her kiss and it disturbed him. She seemed able to forget things so easily, while all of it, all the time, the good and the bad, simmered in solution in a cauldron of his heart, leaving him brooding and guarded.

Turning away from the sea, they wandered into the woods, skirting the great cliffed lake filled with rain water, the old quarry.

"My mother painted all sorts of pictures of this place. Did you see the paintings?"

"The one over the mantel?"

"And others in the back hall and upstairs. I don't know why she focused so on Halibut Point. The other day I looked at the one over the mantel and was amazed. There's this splotch of red in it I'd never seen."

"Sunrise?" he asked.

"No, more like—anger, or something," she giggled.

"What's funny?"

"Thinking of her as angry."

"She was quiet, you said."

"Her mother was the angry one."

"Maybe your mother was, too. She never yelled back at your father?"

"Not even once. I remember the time I burned my hand in her kitchen. I was in my twenties, home visiting.

"You burned your hand, and your mother fixed it?"

"Yes, she kept an aloe plant on the kitchen windowsill and had lots of herbal cures she used to mix up and use on us—I never paid much attention. There are some left, though most of her jars are empty now. She grew and dried herbs and rare plants in the backyard. She was one of the original herbalists, long before the New Age. These are probably some of the plants," Nikki laughed, pointing at the little shoots growing along the path.

"I thought of the burn because one day I finally said something to her about my father. She was rolling out dough for *nisu* and baking coffee cake, which had just come out of the oven and smelled heavenly. I got angry and asked her why she made it for him, since she never ate it herself. She looked at me with her little bird's eyes, like she could take in a whole room in a second, cocking her head to the side as if hearing something. She smiled, which made me madder. I started going on about how mean he always was to her, how could she put up with it, the whole thing.

"She spoke very softly, like she always did, and said that my father was restless, that he had a rootless spirit and that maybe it was her life's work to take care of him. You know, he used to stand in the kitchen door with his huge white bulk, just stand there like a ghost, never coming into the room. He was afraid of it. He only wanted familiar food to come out of it.

"Meanwhile, as I was yelling at my mother I put my hand on the coffee cake tray and burned it. I yelled, and my mother was there breaking a stem and smearing the juice on my palm. She said the house was going to be mine one day, she could see that. That made me madder, as if she were giving up on her own life and instead handing it off to me. I didn't want the pressure, so I got mad again and continued yelling.

"She shushed me by saying something very strange. That I was angry like my father, who drank because he was angry. But she said maybe my anger would teach me what I needed to learn."

"What's that?" Philip asked, rapt.

She looked at him and groaned.

"An interesting woman."

"Interesting!" Nikki snorted. "I should have had my grandmother as my mother."

"So you picked my mother instead."

She looked at him, shocked and relieved by his bluntness. For all the things she would not let herself trust in him, she could trust that at least.

"How did she die?"

"The doctors got her. It was cancer, but no one told her, and she went along passively, the way she did everything. Ended up in intensive care with all the tubes and IVs."

"Grim."

"I sat watch. My sisters came and went; they all had families. My father was too broken up and drunker than ever. So I sat and watched her die, hating the doctors and what they did to her, the men, my father!" Seeing blood in her eyes, Philip flinched.

Nikki sighed deeply. "So, of course, I ended up lawyering for doctors. Why am I telling you all this family stuff? I never talk about it to anyone."

"Because I asked, and I'm interested. So she died last year?"

"Two years ago, and then my father died, as you know."

"And he left you the house in the will?"

Nikki laughed out loud. "*Right!* I bought it from the estate because no one else wanted it. I had a feeling. It was the right thing to do. I lost my job at the same time, so I moved back, and here I am."

He reached and took her in his arms, his touch like heaven to her, electric and smooth and so very present that his body threatened to smother her. And she desired to be smothered. Taking his hand after their kiss, she led him back to the car. They drove quietly, like two meditating poets possessed of a single thought, back to the little yellow-shingled house on Grove Street. But her last thought before the warm darkness was of his caution, how cleverly he turned every question about himself into a discussion of her, her life, her family. She would have to be on her guard. Like he was.

BECAUSE NIKKI had no present job and Philip's work at Eveless Fisheries was limited, they had time to spend together. Of his father's fleet, only the *Lamia*

Claire remained—the boat Philip's father had built for himself at the height of his powers and wealth. A sleek forty-two foot schooner with a mahogany mainmast and lovely dark-teak decking; Philip and Nikki went out on it often. She was impressed; it was the small sailing boat of a rich man, with shiny brass fittings everywhere and a magnificent wheel with turned spokes good to the touch. She felt the power as the boat surged white-sailed through the swells, sending sprays up that doused the two in salt.

Nikki had grown up on the beach but rarely gone sailing. Philip, on the other hand, was practiced and smooth in his movements, handling the *Lamia Claire* as if it were an extension of his body. Sometimes he went out by himself, staying for a day or two.

The first time it happened Nikki was frantic, meeting Philip at the dock as soon as he came in.

"Where have you been?" she asked, angry at herself for not keeping away.

He leaped off the boat and caught her up in his arms, but she pushed him away. "I went out—"

"I was so worried!"

"I'm sorry!" he cried, hugging her close to him. "I wanted to be alone—on my father's boat."

"Your mother didn't even know," she said angrily, moving away.

"You talked to my mother?"

"I didn't talk to your mother. I had Michelle ask. According to Michelle, you didn't even tell your mother. Philip, what were you thinking?"

"My mother," he echoed grimly, furrowing his brow. "I'm sorry I didn't tell you, Nikki. I won't do that again. As for my mother—I wouldn't tell her."

Nikki eyed him silently. Her clinging need of him frightened her. When they were making love that night she heard herself whisper, "I don't want to live without you," and his sweet reply, "Nor I." But still he kept himself apart from her.

For weeks they lived and loved, Nikki time after time falling into depression over the senselessness of being involved with a married man. *Married man,* she mentally repeated. The words were so large, the reality so unmovable that she grew frightened, hiding the fear inside anger. She sent Philip home a few times, telling him to go back to his wife. But he always called, or else he didn't call, which was worse.

June wended its way onward. On the Feast of Saint Peter they met downtown amid the crowds, eating fried clams from carts served by old Portuguese men who smiled knowingly at Philip. They knew from knowing Rose who the man was. They smiled warmly at Nikki and would have blown kisses at her had she not been with Philip. Wearing her red sun dress with the exploding flowers, her gold hair blowing in the breeze, Nikki looked like a blond Aphrodite recently ridden in on the foam.

They walked down past the gathering site, an arc of bleachers to the left, food booths selling fried dough and clams to the right. In the center, backed up to the harbor, a makeshift altar with a tremendous colorful backdrop had been erected, on which stood the cardinal of Boston along with his acolytes. In his ecclesiastical vestments he looked like the rainbow dove of terrible justice, hands raised over the crowd in stern and benign blessing.

He was one of the new order of Catholic priests ready with a joke and a smile, and just as ready to politick with the fishermen and their wives.

"The thirty-pound catch limit is too low," he declaimed to a cheering crowd. "We feel it should be raised to one hundred pounds, and we're going to work for that." The old priest was referring to the recently enacted daily cod catch limit for fishermen. There were banners flying in the air and young boys dressed as the four evangelists, though the most important boy was the fifth, dressed as Saint Peter, the patron of Gloucester and a fisherman in his own right. The young actor knew that he played the most important character in the drama; it showed in his swagger and in the smirk of power on his face.

Nikki and Philip strolled past the faithful bathing-suited worshipers as the Mass proper began, complete with electric piano singing while Mediterranean mothers loudly scolded their children. Tourists stood on the bleachers taking pictures.

Leaving the noisy praying, they sauntered along the harbor under the June sun flashing in the waves, which splashed oilily against the concrete piers. About them fussed broods of pigeons bustling together and scurrying apart, gurgling their gossip unaware of the humans skirting them. Overhead, black crows prophesied in the breeze, their voices screeching like winged sibyls.

"The gulls are as grating as sandpaper," Philip remarked, looking up while looping Nikki's arm through his. "I guess it has to be so, in order to corrode our delusions and leave the truth."

"What truth is that?" she asked, frightened.

Philip glanced at her. The hidden truth of their guilty love was as near as the gulls, aloft just beyond their reach yet within sight. Would he say what he was thinking? No, he would counter her again, for that was his role. "I don't speak Crow," he smiled at last, and she laughed with relief as they walked on.

They soon reached the dock where the *Lamia Claire* lay, riding like a soft sigh at anchor, nudging the dock like a cat. Philip looked up: a single pennon floated at the masthead, staggering against the sky.

"We going aboard?" Nikki asked.

Philip regarded the boat. "He built it himself—in the boathouse up the coast where the fleet was serviced. It's all that's left," Philip said sadly, stuffing his hands in his pockets.

"I never asked—what's the name mean? Is it his mother?"

Philip let out a peal of laughter. "No! It's a joke, I think. *Lamia* is Greek and means something like 'Devourer.' 'Claire' is just a name he liked, I guess."

"It's named after your mother?" Nikki asked, a bit shyly.

He strode over to the boat, stepping lightly onto the deck. Nikki following him, they walked to the stern, sitting down on either side of the wheel. The boat rocked as the remains of some distant wake sloshed quietly against the hull.

"You have judgment in your voice," he noted.

She demurred.

"You do, though. It's not as easy as that, as usual. Lamia was a sea nymph whom Zeus loved. Legend says she was one face of the original earth goddess—the first, most ancient one." He paused. "But I do think my father was devoured by my mother. It's the age-old problem of men and women and love; women with their secret, dark doorways are the entrance to the underworld."

"That's a bunch of sexist crap," she said flatly.

He smiled merrily at her. "Even if it's the truth?"

"It's a projection—typical male stuff."

"Arche-typ-typ-typical. My father's story is almost mythic. When they were in high school, he was absolutely possessed by my mother, he used to tell me. Of course, everyone was—the great beauty of Gloucester. My father was skinny and ugly and saw himself as having nothing except his love for my mother.

"She's very hot-blooded, but you know that," he went on. "She was the daughter of a fisherman. My father was not quite as poor, but he lacked the power of her beauty. He always had that gaunt look. He kept to himself, although once he set his mind on something, he went after it in a cold fury. The most powerful man I've ever known," Philip mused. "That's the way he wooed my mother. He persisted, and in high school he already owned his own lobster boat. I know my mother knew him, but she never talked to him in school; at least that's what my father says. My mother says he's lying, as usual.

"They were both Catholic, so there was no problem there, but my mother—well, you know how ambitious she is. My father was determined to become the most powerful and richest fisherman in Gloucester. And he succeeded. But there was always something eating at him. Whenever he visited me at school in Geneva he would get a wistful tone in his voice, leafing through my books and walking with me over the school grounds. Having dropped out of high school, he felt that unfortunate inferiority. He used to pick my brains about my studies, which I think is how he came up with the name for this boat—the same year I studied Greek mythology, he was building the *Lamia*.

"In that gruff, choked-up voice of his, he used to vow to keep up with me by reading the same books I was reading. In fact, he was going to best me."

"Strange."

"Not to my adult ears, but as a child it made me awfully embarrassed. It was like my father was in school with me. At the time I couldn't appreciate his wanting to learn. All it did was remind me of how unschooled he was. Then, of course, he saw me looking at him condescendingly, and I watched the cold fury grow in him. That was one of the first times I understood how powerful he was and what had attracted my mother to him. That year he actually got books on Greek mythology, writing me letters full of stories I already knew about the gods and goddesses."

"So he named this boat."

"I believe he was determined to become rich just to win my mother. After rousing himself to win her, he subsided back into his usual taciturn self. It was then she realized she had married a man who didn't share her dreams. She felt deceived and became terribly angry; she never forgave him. Perhaps that's when they worked out their unspoken agreement. He would make lots of money for her to spend, and she would leave him alone. So he did, and they went their separate ways, she to her committees and politics and building projects—and to her lovers; he to his business and out to sea by himself.

"He would go sailing in this boat for days at a time, which made my mother furious. When I became old enough we two went together—then she'd really throw a fit! We'd be gone for two or three days, the two of us out on the waves fishing, my father telling stories of the sea, teaching me sailing songs. When we got back my mother was always in a fury. She would come down to the dock and snatch me out of the boat, screaming at my father, which made the other fishermen laugh. That, of course, only made her madder. I remember once when yelling at him she demanded to know whether he was a man or a fish." Philip smiled in memory. "That made me laugh, too, until she grew livid.

"Dragging me home by an ear, she slapped me into bed after making me bathe, and scrubbing me so hard I concluded she was trying to wash my father out of me.

"Other times she would murmur over me when I was tucked up tight in bed, 'Mine, mine, mine,' in a weird kind of croon. I quickly became a marker in their board game, and so as a compromise was sent away to Europe."

"What did he love about her? They seem so unmatched."

"They do, don't they?" Philip paused. "But actually, only their outer styles differed. My father's fires burned just as deeply, except he contained and hid them. Look, he spent his high school years working every minute he wasn't in school, eventually dropping out to build his fleet while other kids were out at dances and movies. He had a lonely anger to him; very few friends, spoke little, except when we were out on the *Lamia*. He never went into the service during Korea because he was more valuable to Uncle Sam as provider of fish for the country.

"He was a gifted lobster man—it used to scare his men, some of them told me. They called him 'Golden Eveless' because his traps were always full, and when he branched out into cod fishing he always seemed to know just where to drop the nets. They used to say he had some magic charm, and that one day the devil would come to claim him. Old New England devil stories! At his funeral a few of the old salts took me aside and muttered that was what had happened!"

"You don't believe it?"

"What—the devil business?"

"No—the magic charm."

"You believe my father was using magic?"

"Of course," Nikki answered matter-of-factly. "It's not so unusual. Besides, you don't know, do you? He might have had magical powers."

Philip observed her closely. "You're still infatuated with the old coot."

"Don't call him that!" she cried.

"Magic or no, he worked hard to become a success, just to win my mother. Since I've been back, I've read a diary from his high school days in which he wrote: 'I will have Rose. I have no beauty like those Portuguese punks, but I'll have money, and I'll marry her. This I promise myself and my dark god.' Something in that vein."

Nikki shivered. "Scary."

Philip nodded. "Once when we two were out on the *Lamia,* I went to bed and he stayed up to brood, like he always did, telling me he wanted to read on deck. During the night I woke and walked quietly up the ladder to find him leaning out over the gunwales, his face nearly flat against the calm ocean. He was murmuring something, and I moved closer to hear. 'Some day,' he was chanting. 'Some day!' I crept back down to my berth fast!"

"What did he mean?"

"I think he meant his death—going to it, meeting his dark god. So when last winter he went out on the *Lamia* and stayed out, no one took any notice, certainly not my mother. Then the *Lamia* washed up on shore in Rockport. He wasn't with it."

Nikki stared wide-eyed. "But the funeral—I saw the coffin—and the papers said he was found with the boat."

Philip shrugged and nodded. "There was no body. In the sea business, we say the harpies got him."

"So what happened?"

"Who knows? I think the 'some day' finally came to pass. I think he made some bargain with the sea nymphs, but once he got his prize and found he was miserable with it, he gave it up."

Nikki considered him with a half smile of wonder. "Nymphs? I may believe that, but you don't—what do you really think?"

"I think he went into the sea," Philip answered evenly, looking at her.

"You said the harpies got him—you mean your mother, don't you?"

"Why?"

"It's not the picture I gathered from your mother. About him, I mean. I don't mean to pry."

"Why not? You're like one of the family. I've given you my father's side, of course. I assume my mother has something different to say. She must have told you how cruel and unfeeling he was, how stupid and not of her class," he said ironically.

Nikki colored slightly.

"It's all right; it's nothing I'm not aware of," Philip remarked. "When my parents used to visit me separately, they would each tell their side of the story. I think they were a lot more alike than they thought, and it frightened them to think that.

He acted completely unlike her. Maybe that's what love is. Experiencing the great, fearful realization that you really are more like the person you love than you'd like to think. He told me the story of when he finally got her to notice him—he used to send her notes in high school, which she would show to friends and laugh over. But once he was twenty or so and had a few boats, he made his move and asked her to marry him. She laughed, but he persisted, wouldn't let her say no. Eventually she saw how much money he was making and said yes."

"Not a very romantic story."

"Only if you don't think that money and power are aphrodisiacs," he responded, as she looked at him. "There's as much magic in money as in spells or charms," he added, looking up the street in anticipation of the parade.

"Want something to drink?" he asked suddenly. Standing up to pull a key from his pocket, he unlocked the hatch and went below, returning in a few minutes with a bottle of red wine and two glasses.

"There's nothing to eat on board," he apologized.

She shook her head, holding her glass while he poured. "I shouldn't have eaten those fried clams." He poured for himself, then settled next to her in the stern.

The muffled blaring of parade trumpets grew louder, the jumbled music ricocheting off the narrow brick streets and spreading out over the cobblestoned pier. Finally the parade rounded the corner in full array, trumpets leading a jostled statue of the Rock of the Church carried on high. Following behind marched Father Peter, his face indeed a rock, grimly set and frowning even on this happy day of the blessing of the fleet. The crowd walking alongside made sure not to touch the stern priest, while the nods and signs of the cross he bestowed on his flock as he passed were received with suddenly quiet fearfulness, heads ducked as if to ward off a blow. The ceremonial blessing of the fleet was to be held at the end of the dock facing out to sea. As the chaotic parade marched along, Father Peter gave out his preliminary individual blessings, the lean, hard priest firing away with vertical and then horizontal cuts of his pious hand, index and middle fingers curved outward in correct sacred fashion.

The ragged band marched boisterously past the *Lamia,* one or two of the hearty musicians winking surreptitiously at Nikki. The teetering statue of Saint Peter followed, dollar bills stuck to long streamers extending from all parts of a body made of plaster rather than stone.

The sight made Nikki and Philip laugh out loud.

Father Peter stalked behind the statue. When he arrived at the *Lamia,* Philip and Nikki looked up at him. The curious stared amazedly at the fateful boat and its occupants, while others went off with the band. The priest clenched his jaw as if to pronounce judgment on the mortal sin of suicide, but he hesitated, his horned hand borne aloft and still, frozen in mid-blessing. Everyone around the old priest grew quiet in anticipation.

To himself the old priest reasoned: "Yet this is not Ernest himself; this is but his son and little Nikki Helmik." All the while holding his chasubled arm at hesitant half-mast, he briefly made a half-hearted motion in the air and quickly stalked wordlessly off, surging back into the crowd, which was only too happy to hurry the priest along to the main event. For following upon the great event of the blessing of the fleet began the real festivities—feasting and drinking, dancing and lovemaking.

"A *mudra*," Philip humphed when the noise had passed. "Better than the sign of the damn cross."

They were silent as the noise subsided.

"The old priest can go on blessing the hell out of the boats—God's not listening, or he has something else in mind for the sea and the fishermen."

"So is your mother—are you—is the money really gone?" Nikki asked.

"There's money in the bank—some, but not like in the old days. My father's heart was broken—fishing was his one love. No, that's not right. Fishing was an acquired love that mirrored his primary love for my mother. For him the sea and my mother were somehow the same. Running away to sea for days was running into her arms after all."

"What did she do that was so bad?"

"Her wildness, I suppose. Her men, her—not caring what anyone thought. You know yourself the way she gets it in her mind to do something and does it, to hell with the consequences. He loved her, certainly, but once he married her, he perhaps thought she would settle down. She did just the opposite. He was from the old school— woman in the home. He adjusted to her wanting to work, even providing money for her to start her business. But beyond that he just couldn't understand."

She had a right to her own life, Nikki was thinking, although she stayed silent.

LATER THAT EVENING they walked in Dogtown, as they often did, talking quietly, Guy towing them along. They rounded a corner by a rough and narrow unpaved road and came upon a square stake stuck in the ground, a red ribbon fluttering from it. Nikki went up to the stake and bent while lifting the ribbon. The sign of Cleavage Builders, she well knew; two lines intersecting in a visual pun of hills or breasts:

She lifted her head to beckon Philip near, as Guy barked at the stake.

"It's like I said," he yelled, yanking on Guy's leash to quiet him.

"Is someone there?" she asked suddenly, whirling around. Sensing a large, dark presence, she rose to huddle near Philip.

"No one," he answered, looking around in the gloaming. Under the trees it was dark already, but only a soft breeze stirred.

"It's impossible," Nikki panted, breathing hard and looking at the ribbon. "I'm frightened. She's relentless. But she can't—not here."

"I told you weeks ago about this plan of hers."

"I didn't want to believe it. It means I have to go see your mother. I'm scared to."

"I'll go with you."

"You're on my side, against her?"

"I have to stand up to her sometime," he smiled ruefully.

They turned for home. Later in her deep bed she sat propped against pillows, like a sibyl in the dark, listening to Philip's snoring while reflecting on her life. A strange, heavy woman draped in shadow, garbed in a long black cloak and deep hood, came and sat at the end of the bed. She stared at Nikki; Nikki was filled with the woman's atmosphere of depressed dullness. Her eyes were hooded but they glowed like suffering coals in a dying fire. Distant and glittering like a cobra's eyes they were, as Nikki sat heavily rooted on the bed, unable to move or to look away from the ancient, ageless woman.

The figure held three fingers out while tracing an indefinite pattern on the comforter. Was it Nikki's mother? No. Mary? No. Rose? The figure looked up at her wistfully, then turned away, melting into shadow at the end of the bed. Nikki waited a moment, then flicked the bedside lamp on as the shadows snapped off. She stared a long while where the figure had been. Philip turned heavily, as if wrestling with sleep. The air was heavy and fetid. Unable to breathe in the low-ceilinged room, she rose softly to push the window sash further up. Crawling back under the sheets, she shivered and turned the light off.

RETURNING FROM running errands the next day, Nikki found a phone message from Rose commanding her to pay a visit at once. At first angry, Nikki stopped to think; something seemed operating beyond her, nudging her in a direction. The notion puzzled her and made her thoughtful. She dressed carefully, doing her hair and applying makeup more artfully than she had done since quitting her job, and drove to the Eveless' house, shaking inside.

She drove slowly up the curving drive and parked behind Rose's gigantic black Mercedes. Somber even in the bright sunlight, the mansion brooded like a massive and ornate jewel set atop a mound of rocks; the barroom town of Gloucester.

The maid ushered her into Rose's room, then retired to a corner near the bed to await Rose's next command. Immediately two sleek Afghans trotted silently up to Nikki, reaching out elegant elongated snouts to sniff her. They looked like royalty, these two, with silvery hair and dark, intent eyes. Not just pedigree dogs but champions of beauty and grace. Delighted, Nikki reached and petted their heads, glancing at Rose sitting at her desk, absorbed for the moment signing papers put before her by her secretary. Nikki found it endearing that Rose had bought the dogs, then realized Rose acquired them for show, literally, not for themselves.

Rose turned once, frowning at the dogs over the top of her reading glasses. "Borgia! Antique! Sit down!" she commanded. The twin princes trotted back to the hearth where they lay down side by side—alert, poised, watchful. Rose returned to signing papers. Typical Rose tactic, Nikki sighed, regarding the room while she waited.

It had been redecorated since Nikki had last seen it. Gone were the heavy red velvet drapes over the tremendous windows. In their place were gossamer lime angels' wings that wisped along the floor. Rose had had the room repainted as well; the walls had been treated to look like distant clouds aswirl in faint blues and golds.

The effect was pleasant and airy, although the old fragrance lingered. Rose's room had always smelled the same to Nikki, cinnamon and a distant scent of cedar. Aromatic, with traces of Rose's signature perfume, mixed especially for her in a perfumery in Provence, Nikki knew. Rose's smell was like the room, part honeysuckle vine on the balcony and part...something fleeting. Not a scent to grab you, rather to evoke and tease.

Despite the changes, all of Rose's favorite things were there: the little writing book covered in Moroccan leather from which a gold tassel hung, kept on her end table; the rainbow-swirled reading glasses that were like Nikki's—bought at the local drug store off the rack; an ivory-handled set of hair brushes, which had once belonged to Rose's great-grandmother in Portugal.

Nikki trembled a little in anticipation.

"I've come," she announced uncertainly, watching Rose at her writing desk. Rose glanced once at her, then turned back to her papers. Her secretary was a waifish young woman of twenty, dressed primly in a plain dark-green cotton skirt and white blouse. Noticing the woman's arms like sticks, Nikki mentally flinched thinking of Dawn.

"Thank you for coming, my dear," Rose replied at last. She still looked stunning, Nikki observed. Even in her grieving black and in the middle of the day, she looked like she was going out for a night on the town. Not Gloucester but New York.

Invited or not, Nikki decided quickly not to let Rose have the advantage.

"I wanted to talk to you about something," she said haltingly. Rose nodded to the secretary who thereby withdrew, glancing nervously at Nikki as she closed the ten-foot door.

"What is it?" Rose demanded peremptorily, turning back to her papers.

"I found one of your company stakes in Dogtown when I was walking there." "Yes?"

"It's just that—Dogtown is protected land—I don't think you should build in Dogtown," Nikki heard herself say, voice shaking.

Rose turned her head, looking up from her paperwork. She was dressed in an expensive French-designed black silk dress, its décolletage revealing her cleavage. Reading glasses on a gold chain sat low on her nose. Her black hair was piled up in magnificence on her well-shaped head. Her dark eyes flashed and then settled into narrowing slightly, peering intently at Nikki. Nikki had seen the look a million times before; this was all part of the woman's style. She had grown up observing Rose, noting how she intimidated anyone, man or woman, who stood in her way. And Rose always got her way. If her beauty did not do the trick, if smiling wiles and soft pleasures did not win, then she turned to her harder strengths. Those who could withstand Rose's beauty wilted before her wrath. Rose knew that well.

She stared a long moment at Nikki, smiling through those gorgeous narrowed eyes, pursing her red lips slightly, looking over the top of her glasses. Then she lowered the glasses carefully.

"You know, Nikki, you and I are fundamentally different. You are cold and I am hot. Our temperatures are from the opposite ends," she said with that hint of Portuguese accent Nikki had always considered an affectation. But Rose never dropped it, not even talking with her in private.

"You used to say how alike we were," Nikki countered. Her heart was thudding against the sides of her head.

"Have you turned into the Ghost of Christmas Past? I don't need you to remind me of my words—I don't need anyone to remind me. But look, let's be friends," Rose smiled, her white teeth dazzling. "I only meant that if it were I who was upset about Dogtown, I would have come in here like a banshee, screaming my head off."

"I know—I've seen you work."

"Why wouldn't you ever come to work for me as my personal attorney?" Rose asked.

"I told you—I was very flattered you asked, but it would have been too compromised for me. Conflict of interest."

"So you admit you are on my side?"

Nikki paused. "Yes."

"Then what's the trouble with Dogtown?"

"I found your surveying stakes in the woods."

"But they are on the other side of the woods from your little house, my dear. What's the problem?"

"It's public land."

"You never objected before—for years I've built in places where no one else could get permission." Rose smiled conspiratorially.

"I know. I—it's something. I just feel that this time it's very wrong. And you have plenty of other places to build."

"Oh, but I don't!" Rose said, raising her voice. "And even if I did, why should I listen to you?"

"For our friendship."

Rose considered, shifting her weight in the chair. "My dear Nikki, would you say you have received benefits from me over the years?"

"Of course I have," she answered softly.

"Then suppose I said, 'Nikki, for you I will not build there, but because it costs me so much, it goes against my principles and will mean the end of our friendship.' What would you say to that?"

Nikki was silent.

Rose continued. "What if I told you this was not merely a case of building, but of protecting myself?"

"What does that mean?"

"Look at me," Rose invited, rising and going to her vanity. Sitting down before it, she gazed at herself in the mirror. Nikki moved closer to stand behind her, observing Rose's reflection. She remembered all the years she had stood thus, watching from the shadows while Rose made herself up, dressed, selected and adorned herself with jewels. Rose had a perfect eye for what looked beautiful on her, and she was unfailing in using her hair and makeup and dress until her beauty blossomed into a flower of grand and unsurpassed magnificence. Watching her had been breathtaking for young Nikki.

First Rose after her bath sat naked before the vanity, completely unself-conscious the way the powerful are amid their servants, and let Nikki drink in her body. The supple, womanly lines of her soft shoulders and rounded breasts, like the curve of the earth, Nikki imagined. Her small, rounded tummy and hips not too wide, yet warm and generous, and her legs, smooth skinned with feet delicately pointed. Rose's skin was tawny like satiny caramel, perfect over her whole body, even her thighs. She had no cellulite or wrinkles, no moles or pimples.

Nikki would compare her own body, with its bumps and swirls; its stocky, thick legs; her small breasts and too wide hips; her broad Finnish feet and white skin. How ugly she felt next to her goddess! She never let Rose see her naked, not even when Rose playfully prodded her.

Next Rose put on her makeup, leaning well into the mirror and touching her cheeks, eyes, nose and mouth with delicate strokes and pats, using a light foundation and subtle eyeshadow. She went wild, though, on mascara, painting it over her long lashes in thick, repeated coats, building up the hairs until they stood out like the tines of black forks. Her large mouth, with its voluptuous lips, was always painted red, the deep red that men call the color of suffering over women. She was extravagant, she was cruel, she was as uncaring and as centered on death as nature herself.

Then Rose would slip on her silk lingerie as if it were part of her skin, completely unconcerned by Nikki staring at her. Her maid silently brought over her accessories, silently accommodating her changes of mind. Gliding to her great four-poster bed, Rose would lift her dress from the bed, something silk or linen, very chic and very dramatic, flowing skirts in shades of red or royal blue; plunging necklines that showed off her cleavage like the proud figurehead of a ship; high collars with long lapels, or flat, rounded collars and puffed sleeves. She loved especially to dress in costume for balls, and went as Aphrodite or as Joan of Arc or as a Spanish dancer in a jangled silk dress the color of dried blood with black fringe, surmounted by a silk diaphanous chemise, sometimes with no bra, which made Nikki gasp and blush.

BUT THAT WAS years ago. Nikki had not watched Rose dress in a long time.

"Look at me," Rose insisted, leaning toward the mirror and touching her face. She intoned, "At my back I always hear time's winged chariot hurrying near...." She stared at her face, reciting like a sibyl, "Thy beauty shall no more be found."

Rose stopped and sighed. "Look at me. The ravages of time."

"You're not old," Nikki declared.

"I'm fifty-eight," Rose replied to her reflection. "Fifty-eight! How am I supposed to come to terms with that?"

Rose leaned back, looking in the mirror at Nikki's reflection. "You are looking very beautiful," she judged. "Very beautiful, my cold beauty, Nikki! We make a pair; one hot, the other cold. One beautiful and young, the other—"

"I'm forty," Nikki explained. "Not exactly young." And it was true. She had been feeling her own beauty slowly departing. Already she felt the pull in her stomach, the clenched attempt to hold on as you tipped slowly over the cliff of time.

"Forty," Rose reflected. "You still have no idea what it is like at nearly sixty. At forty I was still young and beautiful. I had men—oh, the men! There were endless men, and dancing and parties! Oh—the parties where I brought my beauty like a present!"

"You are the most beautiful woman in Gloucester," Nikki insisted.

"No! I am not!" Rose suddenly screamed, rising and rushing at Nikki, arms outstretched and long red claws lunging at Nikki's face. The dogs stood up, barking.

Nikki moved back. She knew it was not serious; she had seen Rose have such fits. They passed quickly, leaving no residue of blame or guilt.

Indeed, Rose stopped to look at her hands, returned to her vanity and slumped down on the embroidered seat. The dogs circled themselves and sat, watching Nikki. Rose did look suddenly old and tired, Nikki realized with a start. How could that be? The magnificent Rose.

"So now it's you, my little angel," Rose said with a gleam in her eye, looking at Nikki through the mirror. "It's you who are the beauty now. I taught you everything—and look how you repay me!" Rose was beginning to yell again. Nikki sighed. No sense arguing with her. Yet Rose's palpable fear was new to Nikki.

"Yours is a different kind of beauty," Nikki explained. She was aware of not being able to insist that Rose was wrong. In her deep heart, with the ear that heard things accurately, she knew Rose was right. Youthful beauty is the true oak of beauty.

"Oh, don't patronize!" Rose screamed. Stopping again in mid-rant, she shook her head. "I am not finished yet, my little beauty, my Nikki the betrayer!"

"Are you saying you're building in Dogtown as a way of getting back at me? For something I don't have any control over?" Nikki asked, her own voice rising.

"I'm angry with you—yes!—for taking everything I've taught you and turning it against me."

"But you wanted me to learn, letting me stand behind you year after year, watching you dress, studying how to be just like you."

"Yes! I wanted you to learn to be like me, to be my daughter, to worship me, yes! I wanted your love and admiration because it made me feel my beauty all the more. It's one thing to have the adoration of handsome men, but what do they know of beauty? Another woman—another beautiful woman—only she knows what real beauty is. I wanted that recognition from you, but not that you should take it from me."

"I never took—"

"You took! You took! You thieved my only gift!" Rose screamed, pulling at her own mass of dark hair. "Look at this! Look! I am ugly now, ugly by contrast with you!" Rose wailed loudly. "First you stole my beauty in order to take my own husband—"

"I told you, Rose—" Nikki began, her own voice rising, but Rose cut her off.

"And now—" her voice trembled with histrionic emotion. "And now you will take my Philip away from me, the only comfort I have left in this disaster of my old age!"

"Philip! I don't even—"

"Don't argue with me!" Rose screeched, throwing herself back against the chair. "I see through you—Ernest killed himself because of you, and you are happy with that fact. You can't hide from me—you are my creation. You have my beauty, and I know how beauty operates," she said in a voice from the depths. Nikki was rooted to the floor.

Rose was screaming in earnest now, pulling at her hair, then rising and throwing herself upon the great bed.

Nikki glanced at the maid, who kept her head down and remained silent, still standing near the bed. The two had seen Rose's histrionics many times.

"Those are just fears—and what has that to do with Dogtown anyway?" Nikki persisted quietly, after Rose's cries had subsided. The older woman's face was streaked with real tears, her mascara running in black rivers down her face.

But Rose would have none of it. Half lying across her bed, she raised her head and regarded Nikki.

"My son spends all his time with you, you whore!" she spat. Nikki flinched as if slapped. Her heart was wounded, but it sunk quickly into the old depression. How many times did she have to hear her father's curse? She felt suddenly very tired.

"You have bewitched him. He pleads with me—actually pleads with me, to be friends with you."

"Rose, your son is married, the last I heard."

"Yes, and you dare—"

"No, I don't! You want me to have nothing to do with him—then fine! It should never have happened!" Nikki stopped, panting. As a vision of Philip flashed, a pang shot through her. But could she do it? Give him up utterly? And for Rose, who hated her?

"Hah! I see it in your eyes, liar!" Rose shouted, flinging herself from the bed. Nikki moved away to stand by the door. The maid jostled her out of the way and exited.

"Rose, I think it's wrong to be involved with your son. I came because you called me, and if that's all you have to say, I've heard enough. I'm still waiting for an answer to what gives you the right to build in Dogtown. What do you mean about protecting yourself?"

Rose slumped before her vanity again, pulling at her sagging cheeks. "Without my beauty, I am nothing. This is why I must find the secret of remaining beautiful. My son sees that I am ugly and prefers your beauty to mine; I must keep him here with me. Otherwise, I will die."

Nikki straightened herself. Confused by Rose's meandering thought, she turned to her own motives. Why did she suddenly care so much about Dogtown? What was it really to her? Yet something made her speak. "If I agree never to see your son again, will you give up building in Dogtown?"

Rose turned to her, a sly smile on her face. For a long moment she studied Nikki. Even after all these years, Nikki realized, she still could not read Rose's thoughts from her expression.

"Yes, I will do that—as my part of the bargain."

"You've never kept a bargain in your life," Nikki pointed out.

"You have no choice, my dear," Rose said softly, her voice a cobra. "You cannot trust me, but if you do not, I will take my revenge on you. I will thieve your beauty—my beauty—back from you, and you will turn into a hag."

Nikki gaped at her old friend. Had she cracked? She smiled slightly. "OK then," she said, her eyes brightening.

Rose saw Nikki's sudden lightness and sprang to her feet. "Go!" she shrieked, pointing a long-fingered nail at the door. "Go! You whore, slut, thief! Devourer of men! Ungrateful child! You have ruined me, but I will have my revenge! Go!" she screamed. Taking her seriously, Nikki left silently, closing the door behind her, her hand trembling as if salted.

AND THOUGH Nikki desperately wanted to break her love for Philip as one breaks a flower in full bloom, she could not say goodbye when they met soon afterward for dinner. Philip chattered away gaily, telling her stories of Europe that any other time would have fascinated her. As they sat at a window table at Jalapeño's, Nikki barely touched her spicy fish. But by the time she finished drinking three margaritas, the clouds descended and she didn't have to think, only to feel that Philip was beautiful and she was frightened.

Nikki woke in the middle of the night; leaving Philip snoring under the covers, she descended the narrow staircase and went into the kitchen, where she made a cup of herbal tea. Sitting down at the peeling round table, she drew a compact from her purse and, flipping open the mirror, scrutinized herself in the glare of the overhead light. Unable to view her entire face in the small mirror, she flicked on the light in the living room and went to the mirror on the wall by the front door.

Setting down her mug of tea, she raised her hands to her face. What was beauty?

The skin at her jowls was already sagging. Already? She smiled. "Forty," she said softly aloud. What did she expect? She pressed the skin back from her chin, smoothing the jowly lines out and up. All the character went out of her face, replaced in a single move by youthful smoothness. She let her skin go and pulled her hair up on both sides of her head, holding it on top with one hand. Her eyes were a little watery, her skin not nearly as smooth as when she was younger.

She thought of Philip. If he thought she was beautiful now, too bad he hadn't seen her when she was really beautiful, she mused. She thought of all the men who had seen her young body. How she loved Philip! A pang shot through her. But how much longer would he love her? He would return to France, leaving her at last...

The thought made her spirits drop. Instinctively she greeted the arrival of sadness the way she always did, with a surge of anger. Looking in the mirror, she smiled horribly, her mouth curling up on the side, a glint showing in her eye. She was beautiful in her anger, she nodded. Beautiful! Strength and force in her eye and in the set of her jaw fascinated and appealed to her.

In anger there is truth, she concluded. She would not let Philip get away with taking advantage of her. Instantly hit by a wave of exhaustion, she pulled a blanket from the front hall closet and, spreading it over herself, lay down on the couch and fell asleep. Without Philip's snores to awaken her, she slept until the sun was high and the smell of coffee that Philip had made came wafting to her from her own kitchen. She woke from troubled dreams of storms on the ocean.

She staggered into the kitchen, deeply depressed. Philip began by smiling at her, and Guy wagged his tail expectantly, but immediately the two became serious. Both could smell what was in the air. Philip poured her coffee and leaned against the counter, observing her.

Nikki sat down heavily, set an elbow on either side of the steaming coffee cup, and put her head in her hands, rubbing her hair into more of a mess. She sensed that Philip had already fed Guy and taken him for his morning walk. So much for protection, she thought.

"Something has to change," she said from inside her hands. Philip immediately heard the tone of urgency and fear.

"Yes," he responded, sipping coffee. "But how? Life rarely takes us up all in an instant. It's not often that you get the call one day to put down your book or fork, stop talking to your lover, and simply rise and walk out the door. Once you've done that, it's easier, of course, to continue. It's the beginning that's difficult. First law of thermodynamics."

"I don't care about science right now," she retorted.

"I was taken up when I fell in love with you," he said simply.

"Maybe that was a mistake."

"Do you think so?"

"Yes—sometimes." She was determined to go ahead, yet unable to make the thrust a clean one. She was waiting for him to say something to make her angry.

"You're speaking of your own needs, rather than what's good for us."

"I think we've worn out a path between us," she replied, sipping.

"I listened to the tape of Carol Harker, that psychic you saw."

"What did you think?" Nikki asked.

"It's strange that they let you tape these psychic readings. Kind of ruins the privacy." When she said nothing, Philip continued. "We never talked about it when you went two weeks ago. What did you think?"

"I asked you."

"She says this is a time where logic doesn't make any sense. That you've got to trust."

"Unless what's going on is self-destructive and dangerous."

"Maybe that's especially the time to trust. How can you tell the difference?"

"I trust my instincts."

"Maybe they're wrong."

Now she stared him fully in the face, rising to her anger. "It's always that, isn't it? You want me to suffer, that's all. You don't care; you don't care what I'm feeling. You say you love me. You don't love me, you just want me; you want your wife, you want me. You won't ever decide; you just have to have multiple relationships," she finished bitterly.

Philip was deeply stung, but he had heard this before from her. He felt horribly guilty and caught. Yes, he loved her, but he suffered as much as she. Maybe the simple truth was the one she kept mouthing, that the main thing was their suffering. Her suffering, his suffering. Yet that word meant such different things to each of them!

"My sister says her rule in life is if something feels good, do it. If it doesn't, don't. This doesn't feel good, Philip."

He stood silent, gulping coffee. What could he say? If he made any effort to shift the understanding of why they were together, she took it as a personal attack, or as indifference on his part to her suffering. Was he indifferent? He knew how much he asked of her. He asked for everything. Was that fair?

"We have to stop, Philip. We can't go on. I can't do this—it's not good for me, and I've got all these other stress factors in my life right now. I don't need this."

Now *he* was angry and wanted to revile her, her weakness, her selfish focus on her own suffering. Didn't she see on what verge they stood? Couldn't she see the view from the cliff, into a new and glorious land? Didn't she know that every profound change brought grief and destruction and pain?

"It always hurts to realize," he said softly.

"Oh, that's so cold and intellectual! Don't you see how you are? Can't you see how distancing you make things? You compartmentalize; it's in your family, that way of thinking instead of feeling. You've started acting like your father, going out on the boat for days, not telling me—"

"I told you!"

"Only that you were going, that's all. Philip, what am I supposed to think? I don't know where you are—with another woman for all I know. You don't tell me," she ended in an exhausted voice.

"I'm alone—I told you. Are you jealous of my time on the boat?" he asked, incredulous.

"You know it's not that. But you don't care. You just go off without thinking. I can't take my guilt, your betrayals. All this insecurity. I'm depressed all the time. No— I'm coming to understand you and your family. Ha!" she snorted a sarcastic laugh. "To think I spent all those years with your mother and never really saw what was in front of me. I thought she loved me—she didn't love me, she loved herself. You're the same—it's in your family, your screwed-up relationship with your mother—"

"Enough!" he cried.

"I have spent my life hearing your mother's voice inside of me. For years I couldn't make a move without consulting her, and if she wasn't there, I heard her voice in my head. Now it's you—your voice. I go food shopping and I hear you judging the food, telling me what to choose. It's too much."

"I hear your voice," he murmured, furrowing his brow. "I thought that's what happens when you love someone."

"Not like this—so that I don't even know what I think or who I am."

He was silent, brooding on her past admission that what had attracted her to him at the start was his power.

"Philip, I can't rely on you."

"What do you mean? I'm here!" his voice rose in protest.

"Philip—you're married. You love someone else, ok? And you say I either have to live with that, or too bad."

"When did I say that?"

"You don't have to say it," she replied tiredly. "It's just—dirty, and wrong. Awful."

"Do you have to make everything ugly, too?"

"It *is* ugly," Nikki said in a voice out of the icy depths of her knowing. "I feel degraded—and don't want you taking us down into those places anymore."

Philip's mouth fell open; his eyes widening. There was nothing further to say; they had hit rock bottom. He could feel his heart begin racing, first far off, then galloping closer and rapidly closer with the speed of a stallion, until it was on him. With a groan, he tore his eyes from her and rushed out the back door while Guy snapped at his heels, barking at the door for a long time afterward.

3.

AT THE CLIFF'S EDGE

For TWO WEEKS Nikki wandered around her house and the back pathways of Dogtown, hearing nothing from Philip. The first few days she was relieved, even if distressed when he ran out. Let him go! she insisted. Let the little boy run away. Why did they have to fall in love? Why not have a quick affair and get it over with? It was what she had wanted at the beginning. Now maybe she could get on with her life and forget all this self-destructive behavior. True, she was not happy that by not seeing Philip, she was inadvertently obeying Rose's command. She tried not to think about that.

These were her thoughts as she moved through the little yellow-shingled house. She picked up Virginia Woolf but had a hard time concentrating. She called Claire and met Geraldine in Cambridge for coffee. She stayed for hours on the phone with Dawn, mostly listening to her talk about food. She decided she had been neglecting her friends and resolved to have that housewarming party she had been intending to throw for months. She called her women friends and set the date for late June.

Nikki cleaned the house and straightened things up, chores she had neglected in order to spend time with Philip. The memory made her jam the vacuum into corners and brush Guy rudely out of the way. She puttered around the house, picking things up and rearranging them, dusting and putting dishes away. Once she found herself staring morosely at her mother's painting of Halibut Point. The inexplicable red splash of paint fascinated her. They were all over the house, these little oil paintings by her mother.

She thought again of her mother and father, and of how lucky she was to have escaped a man's tyranny. She was resolved never to be her mother, silent and quiet for a man, for any man, especially not a strong man, especially not Philip. Especially not a married man! she reminded herself. A married man! What had she been thinking?

For nearly three weeks Nikki filled her days with cleaning and talking on the phone, getting together with women friends in Cambridge, gardening at home, cleaning out the attic, calling her sisters and mailing them household belongings each had claimed. The time went quickly, as if she were in a daze, and though she thought often of Philip, she never considered calling him. Let him call her, she argued. Besides, she got news from Claire who gossiped about everyone. Claire, of course, had known about Nikki and Philip, and she actually saw him from time to time downtown.

Claire relayed to Nikki how miserable Philip looked.

"Mostly he just seems to wander the docks wearing black clothes in the middle of summer," she laughed. Nikki was satisfied; hearing about Philip took any pressure off she might otherwise have felt to call him. But it was a grief to her that now she was feuding with both Evelesses.

The gang arrived for the party one Sunday night. Guy was exiled to the basement since he wasn't familiar with everyone coming: Sukie and Carol, her gay friends; dark-haired, opinionated and smart Leah; Antonia, a professor of English with a doctorate and less opinionated than Leah; Gerry the minister; Jess, her old friend and drinking buddy from law school; Katrin (there had to be a token married friend); Ruth who was always fun; Gabby, slow and good-natured; Claire; and the anorexic Dawn, who came to drool over the food and eat only a very red apple. Ruth brought a friend, a Finnish woman whom Nikki had met the year before.

"I'm so sorry!" Ruth whispered to Nikki in the kitchen. She busied herself helping with the glasses and dishes of food, moving her short, heavy body gracefully. She owned a catering company and knew how to move in a kitchen. "I hope it's OK—I thought this was an open party. But you're going to love her—she's Finnish too! And guess what, Nikki? She's a shaman!" Ruth's eyes opened wide. "I met her at Interface last month—remember, I called you? At the *Coping* workshop she sat beside me. She gives her own workshops, and is actually from Finland."

"I know," Nikki frowned. She had attended one of Erika's workshops, casually introducing herself to the shaman afterward, secretly hoping for a connection through their heritage. But Erika just nodded absently, gathered in a whirl of other women who were clamoring for her attention, holding her book out for autographs, begging advice for personal problems. Nikki hadn't known what she herself wanted or expected. An answer; some hope, perhaps.

That was last year. Now Nikki was cautious—and jealous. She looked around Ruth into the living room, where she spotted a short blond woman chatting animatedly with Carol and Sukie. Same Finnish shaman, she noted. Broad cheekbones, high forehead, blue eyes, pale skin. Just like her own. She could just distinguish her voice amid the others; Nikki recalled that she hadn't liked it. Too high and spacey, she thought, pouring wine. She nudged Ruth to take the indicated tray and follow her into the living room.

"...it's a matter of channeling properly all your energies, in combination with the necessary herbs," the Finn was explaining to Sukie. Carol had wandered off to talk to others. Sukie was a graceful giraffe of a woman, studying with various local healers to become a naturopath. She had already undergone the rigorous six-year training to become a chiropractor and had a thriving practice in Cambridge. She stood with bowed narrow head, dark-eyed and dark-haired, nodding and listening intently as she did with everyone, considering for a long while before speaking. She had an air about her of thoughtfulness; everyone trusted her opinions. As sometimes happens with humans, however, her grave demeanor and large frame contrasted sharply with her surprisingly high and piping voice.

"Then you can accomplish even more—oh!" Erika exclaimed, waving arms in the air. "I am able to accomplish everything I wish for, all by the sacred methods of journeying taught me by the oldest shaman in Finland. Dead now for many years, unfortunately." She wagged her head, tossing her bangs about.

Nikki stood by with a bottle of white wine and filled when Erika leaned her glass. She beamed at Nikki as Nikki introduced herself, and they shook hands. "But I am told you have a love for shamanism and, of course, are Finnish, too!" she chirped. Her high voice was too singsong for Nikki, who mentally pulled back. Then she felt self-conscious; if Erika were for real, the woman would know immediately. Even if not, perhaps.

"We must get together to talk, and I can tell you so many things about my father-land, about all the spirits and magic spells!" Erika insisted, reaching up to pat Nikki on the shoulder. But that voice! As if everything were magical in the world, nothing serious, everything remarkable! Nikki smiled and raised her eyebrows, pouring and then handing the bottle away.

"How did you know—"

"—you are Finn? I see the shaman in your eyes, you! But we two must be soul-mates, I just knew!" she singsonged, her eyes turning into blissful slits.

"Yes, we'll have to get together," Nikki assented vaguely, her own voice sounding low and grave to her ears.

Nikki moved away to talk to the others, passing Ruth and muttering out of the corner of her mouth, just below the sound of the music, "Who is this woman?"

Ruth smiled puzzledly and passed. Nikki sat down in her father's chair across from Antonia and Leah, who were talking animatedly about Deborah DeNicola, a local poet who had been giving readings lately in Boston, having received a major grant from the NEA.

"It's the juxtaposition of the images, and the—curiously exact voluptuousness, as it were, that makes a coherent whole of her pieces," Leah frowned. "For example, her poem 'Starving Eros,' in which the man appears above her bed as if with wings on—"

"I just like her stuff—it's sexy," Antonia winked, regarding Nikki with her cow-warm eyes.

"I see you met our shaman," Antonia interrupted herself, speaking in the voice that Nikki loved to listen to. Antonia was from Mississippi originally but had lived in Cambridge for years, schooling herself in an accent that had just a hint of the old aristocratic South. She was a poet and scholar, the only woman—the only person—Nikki knew who was tenured at two colleges. Now she was at Tufts and corresponded regularly with Mary Oliver. Nikki loved Antonia's poems for their sweet irony, the "always-longing," as the poet called it, of the here and now.

Leah—Leah was harder for Nikki to take. She was always arguing, always articulating, pressing home a point. And at bottom such a shy person! With her jet-black hair, all-black wardrobe, ankle-high soft leather black boots with pointed toes to look sharp and sound sharp. Nikki was disturbed by an inchoate awareness of underlying similarity between Leah and herself. She remembered Philip noting that she had an "insistent independence." She shook the thought away.

Antonia looked past Nikki at Erika, arching her eyebrows at Nikki and smiling, which brought out the elegant and thin lines curving around her mouth. She brushed her boyishly cropped bangs back as Nikki fidgeted and then brightened.

"Shamans everywhere!" Nikki lilted, springing up and down on the chair as in a two-year-old's game. She bobbed her head from side to side, then stopped suddenly, seeing Antonia raise an eyebrow at her.

"So—how are you?" Nikki asked.

"Not bad. A new poem or two—I think!" Antonia finished in her light and learned Southern accent, then chuckled deeply, which made her bright eyes twinkle. "God! If I could build poems the way my contractor constructs my house, I'd be on Olympus! But tell me—what a lovely old house, Nikki. Do you like living up here, away from all of us?"

"It's so bucolic," Leah said softly, leaning forward.

"I do like it," Nikki replied quietly. To her annoyance, she couldn't concentrate. She could hear Erika in the background talking nonstop, a mile a minute, in that little-girl singsong voice of hers. Hearing her made Nikki feel very grave, and slightly embarrassed.

"There is something to do here—that I have to," she said indefinitely. She sipped wine.

"Oh? What?" Antonia asked.

"Something to do with my family—I'm not sure." Able to listen to two conversations at once, she was still half listening to Erika. Now Erika was telling Claire about Finland and all the magic she performed there. Of course, Claire was a captive audience—she didn't know how to extricate herself from boring people, Nikki thought. She was always being pushed around. Dawn wandered over and was promptly caught in Erika's net.

"Oh, you poor thing!" Erika said to Dawn, who shied from her. But Erika was having none of it and grabbed Dawn's arm to hold her near.

"And look how thin!" she exclaimed. While Claire said nothing, Dawn stood stock still, staring at Erika with the wide eyes of a starving child. "Your poor arm is like a toothpick!"

"I have just the thing for you, my starving sister!" Erika chattered on. "You are down there with Persephone, it's true! Down in the underworld, and it's a good thing! A good thing to remind all of us!" Erika turned to the rest of the women scattered in groups talking. "Isn't it true, everyone? We all have eating disorders, no? Maybe not so much in my country, but here! America has destroyed women!"

"God, I'm PM-ESSY!" Jess groaned, slumping down on the couch next to Ruth. "Dawn and all this talk is making me hungry!" She was slurping at her fourth glass of wine and already looked a mess. On a small plate she held a slice of fruit tart that Dawn had brought. The tart was drooled in red strawberries and emerald kiwi slices, orange peaches and creamy bananas, the whole drenched in a thick syrup that made the jeweled tart glisten. Jess bit hungrily into it, taking no notice of anyone around her. She smacked her lips, smiling dreamily.

Jess was a wreck of a beautiful woman, Nikki observed. They had been in law school together, gone out to bars together, had adventures. But Jess seemed to have learned nothing from life to give her weight. When Nikki had her daughter Alice to look after, Jess had no one but herself; she looked after herself in bars. Her voice had grown husky from drinking, the thousand curls in her brown hair gone limp and thin, her skin faded to sallow. But she was good-natured for all that, even while clients slipped through her fingers time and again and her business went to hell. They met with her once, sniffed the fetid atmosphere of her office, and never returned. How long could she hold on? Nikki wondered. Nevertheless Jess was cheerful, a happy drunk.

"Look at me," Jess mumbled, plucking at her blue silk blouse and munching on the tart. "Stained already. How'm I supposed to go out to bars afterward for some real drinking looking like this?" she guffawed and fell into coughing, covering her mouth with a napkin. Antonia blinked at her.

"Nobody notices," Nikki remarked quietly, thinking: *No, the men didn't notice.*

"What are you doing up here in the 'burbs?" Jess pursued, emptying her glass into her mouth. "Seems pretty quiet." She pulled a mashed pack of cigarettes from her purse and lit, inhaling and blowing a long plume upward.

"That's what I want," Nikki remarked.

"Who's the chick?" Jess motioned with the cigarette.

"Erika—Finnish," Nikki said quietly.

"Oh, right! What a voice!" Jess laughed. Nikki frowned, feeling anything but light and airy the way she always did at her own parties. Everyone would notice. She saw Sukie nod and end a conversation with Erika. Sukie caught Carol's eye and took her hand. The two went into the kitchen. Nikki caught Sukie's eye; Sukie nodded that everything was fine, as Katrin pulled up a chair near Nikki.

"May I have one?" she asked Jess.

"You don't smoke," Jess replied gruffly, though she pushed her pack at Katrin.

Katrin lit up; she only smoked at parties. She was one of those smokers, Nikki marveled, who could smoke a single cigarette a day, maybe two, for years on end without ever succumbing to addiction. Yet she smoked like a pro, gracefully, elegantly. That's because she's an actress, Nikki thought.

"Let's talk about men!" Katrin giggled. She was the most exotic woman Nikki had ever seen, with a broad, voluptuously lipped, expressive mouth, wide cheekbones, high forehead and dark-brown eyes. She looked like a female Yul Brynner or a pale-skinned Tina Turner, her hair a gorgeous mahogany that shimmered in the candlelight from a nearby end table. The face of an actress, de trope for normal life yet on stage full of dramatic presence. There was something womanly and self-possessed about her that Nikki envied, but Katrin was usually so gregariously friendly that you couldn't really be jealous of her life. A touch self-centered, though that seemed to go with the territory for actors. Married for more than twenty years, she had two children and was the director of a local theater.

"OK, why is it that the conversation always changes when a man comes in the room?" Nikki asked with bright, smiling anger.

Everyone stopped and looked at her. Ruth pulled up a folding chair to join in. "Yeah, what's wrong with men? Or is it us?" she grinned wickedly.

Across the way Erika was still bending Claire's ear; Gabby had been sucked in, too. Nikki could hear Erika talking about music, exclaiming how wonderful it was that Gabby was a flutist, how important music was to the shamans, and so on. At least she was leaving poor Dawn alone. Nikki pressed on. "Everyone stops and pays attention to him," she insisted, feeling foolish and therefore more determined to make her point.

"Yeah…" Jess said vaguely, lighting another cigarette.

Cocking her head at Nikki, Antonia drew her into conversation. "How's Philip?" she asked.

"I don't know. Haven't seen him in a while," Nikki retorted, glancing at Erika blabbering away at Claire and Gabby.

"I thought you two were madly in love," Antonia remarked. Nikki didn't like the way Antonia was looking at her.

"Yeah, well—you know love," Nikki shrugged.

"Have you fallen out of love?" Antonia pursued.

"Oh, love! Who ever came up with that idea!" Katrin pealed. "No—love's fine. Just don't expect anything from it. Live with low expectations—that's the key to a successful relationship. And life." She winked over her glass, smiling gaily.

"Cynical!" observed Leah, her dark eyes flashing.

"No—realistic. It's not that I expect nothing from Dan—of course I do. From myself, too. But as my friend Tim said once, 'Every life is a failure.'" Katrin shrugged.

"More cynicism!" Leah replied.

"Not at all," Katrin shook her head. "I find that attitude a relief. I mean, come on! All that idealizing, expecting your lover to be the white knight, expecting yourself to be a queen! All that pressure for love to succeed—who needs it?"

"But you're a success," Antonia noted mildly.

"Probably because I gave up my high expectations. I work like a demon—it's not about giving up. It's about focusing on what's in front of you."

"And you don't expect anything from Dan?" Jess asked.

"Yes and no. I just go on with my life—we each do. It works that way. You both have jobs; you see each other once in a while. Life goes too fast—you barely have time. But I wonder whether you're right, Nikki—do I change when Dan's around? I guess I do—in some ways," Katrin mused.

"That's what I mean," Nikki nodded.

"It depends on the man," Ruth observed.

"Oh, I've never seen a man defer to a woman, unless he's being patronizing," Nikki insisted.

"Let 'em patronize," Jess slurred. "Whatever it takes."

"See, that's our problem—we defer to them." Nikki shook her head.

"Sounds like you're setting yourself up for a war," Katrin smiled wryly, looking sideways at Nikki.

"Remember Clinton."

"Yeah, he must have been irresistible," Jess smiled.

"Isn't that the problem?" Nikki asked.

"Oh, brother! Why couldn't they let him alone?" Katrin shook her head. "All of his women—who cares!"

"I agree it was never really any of our business," Antonia said. "But it didn't say much for his powers of discrimination, did it? I mean, his choice in women!"

"Boy-man," Nikki declared. "Of course, it's expected that he had affairs. Men in power—they're all like that—it's what the old-boy network presumes is the right way to approach women."

"Or to approach anyone," Leah proclaimed. "Power relationships. It's not just the men—I've known women guilty of the same thing. Where's their taste? I hate to sound unsisterly but, really, these coeds!"

"Precisely, Leah," Antonia nodded. "Can't we expect of our leaders a little leadership in the arena of love?"

Everyone laughed, Nikki the loudest. Then she straightened. "But that poor little girl—Monica. What he did to her," she muttered.

"Poor Monica!" Katrin and Antonia exclaimed together.

"You think she's a victim?" Antonia asked incredulously. "With her TV show?"

"Well—he was the President, the most powerful leader on the face of the earth. How could you think otherwise?" Nikki asked rhetorically.

"You're not giving much acknowledgment to Monica's ability to make her own decisions," Antonia continued.

"How was she supposed to?"

"I think she made a choice—she said so herself," Katrin added.

"Yeah, didn't she say she wanted the affair, that she tried to keep it going?" Jess asked.

"It's crazy—I remember one of the conservative commentators calling it borderline child abuse," Katrin laughed.

"It was," Nikki insisted, setting her chin. No one spoke.

"Well, Hillary didn't seem to mind enough to divorce him," Katrin put in at last.

"Isn't that what matters? Don't two people have the right to determine for themselves what works?"

"So anything goes?" Nikki challenged. Her heart was beginning to pound in indignation.

Katrin looked at her evenly. "Yes, I think so."

"How 'bout abuse?" Jess wondered. "OK for the man to beat up his woman? Do we say she asked for it, that it was an unspoken agreement?"

"How do you get a woman—or anyone—to leave an abusive relationship until you admit there's something attractive about abuse?" Leah asked seriously. "That's the real problem."

"As long as women believe they bring it on themselves, there is no solution," Nikki stated flatly. "Presuming some women ask for abuse is just the patriarchy determining the whole agenda, once again."

"So Monica was brainwashed?" Leah asked archly.

"Does the patriarchy have the corner on the pleasures of suffering?" Antonia asked. "Goethe thought the best place to be was in-between, full of longing for somebody but not possessing him. Unfulfilled desire can be a kind of pleasurable suffering."

"Suffering is pleasurable? Isn't that just what abusive men want us to think?" Nikki asked, her voice rising.

"Read Camille Paglia," Leah remarked dryly.

"I have," Nikki shot back. "I have, and I say she's sold out."

Sukie and Gerry wandered in from the kitchen, picking up the gist of the discussion. "What about a woman who abuses another woman?" Gerry asked. "Is that the patriarchy?"

"No, the patriarchy doesn't have a corner on abuse," Nikki responded quickly. "Abuse is abuse, whoever inflicts it."

"And it's always wrong?" Leah challenged.

"Otherwise you open the floodgates to—anything," Nikki declared.

"I don't know how you keep them closed," Katrin remarked mysteriously, drawing on her cigarette.

"By keeping your sense of authority," Nikki said. "Know what makes me mad? I keep hearing Philip's voice in my head. He has all these strong opinions, so when I go food shopping or for clothes, anything, I keep hearing him complaining or spouting some opinion."

"Sounds like he's very close to you—or you to him," Antonia observed mildly.

"Sure, that's what happens in love," Katrin remarked. "You lose those clear-cut boundaries. What else is love?" she asked the group.

"I think Philip's great!" Gerry noted, sitting with a glass of wine.

"Yeah, well, you don't know the other side of him," Nikki observed.

"No, I guess I don't."

"I want to make my own decisions, think for myself!" Nikki replied vehemently.

Carol came in from the kitchen carrying vegetables, setting the tray on the coffee table. She looked seriously at Nikki. "I hear Sukie's voice everywhere I go. I guess I must not have your sense of propriety. Or maybe I'm naturally more independent than you," she considered aloud.

Nikki felt herself bristle.

"Hearing the voice of someone you are close to does seem to be a condition of love," Antonia continued. "I hear my father's voice all the time. But your remark was about autonomy, wasn't it?"

"Right, having your own thoughts without interference."

"That sort of goes out the window when you fall in love," Katrin explained.

"And if I may bring the notion of God or Goddess or the Great Spirit in at this point," Gerry offered, "that voice should be with you all the time. Otherwise you're lost."

"Unless you can keep yourself a deaf virgin," Leah suggested.

Antonia picked up the thought. "What an image—losing your virginity through your ear! I read a wonderful essay on Hamlet by Patricia Berry on just that subject."

"That's a different form of loss of virginity," Katrin uttered frankly. "Hamlet dies."

"Every loss is a little death, isn't it?" Leah asked rhetorically. "So aren't they connected?"

"One way or another, though, it's absolutely necessary to lose your virginity," Jess affirmed, waving her glass. "Or you can try keeping yourself untouched and see where that gets you," she added. "We know where that got both of us," she said pointedly to Nikki. They exchanged a glance, Nikki recalling suddenly a casual remark Jess made years ago, as they sat at a bar waiting for the men to approach one more time.

"Is it possible we're keeping ourselves virgins?" Jess had asked.

"What?" the younger Nikki frowned half-drunkenly.

"I mean all this sporting around, never a real relationship—all this complaining about where are the real men," Jess lamented, waving her cigarette in the general direction of the men in the bar.

"I just read a story by Washington Irving called 'The Specter Bridegroom.' You know I'm taking this workshop for women on the *Virgin,* and that was our homework. They were talking about how girls fall in love with a ghostly lover. The problem comes when we never get over it. He's too perfect. And dead."

But two actual men approached then to put an end to the fledgling thought, which drowned in wine and flirtation and later in the tangled sheets of immediate flesh and smothered spirit.

"I think some women ask for trouble," Leah now ventured. "I've seen it. It's what men are good for. When we are too virginal, we're asking to be raped. When we don't admit our own violence—"

"What?" Nikki cried out, startled out of her daydream.

"I know it sounds outrageous if misinterpreted, but I don't mean it physically. Although in some cases maybe it is also true physically."

"Women ask to be raped?" Nikki was incredulous. "You're mouthing the words of the worst kind of fascist male sentiment!"

"Carol," Gerry inquired, "you still work at the clinic for abused women, don't you?"

"Yes," Carol nodded, "I see where you're headed. It's true—the first and most crucial thing we work on with these poor women is why they want to get beaten up."

"My god!" Nikki exclaimed.

"That goes for any addictive behavior, of course. As far as your assertion that men are the ones who administer violence, Leah," Carol continued, "I've seen women beaten up by their women lovers. It doesn't take a man to be cruel."

"Yet if we understand these attacks as unprovoked, then we're making those who bear the brunt of them—usually women—out to be merely passive victims," Leah went on.

"That's the difficulty I mean," Carol explained, "in working with these abused women. How do you recognize possibly deep-seated needs on their part for self-destructive patterns of involvement—while at the same time making no allowance for the perpetrators of violent behavior?"

"This is dangerous territory," Nikki warned. "You leave yourself open to thinking along the same lines as abusive men—at the risk of excusing them."

"Well, we've got to understand more deeply what's going on, if these women are to change their lives for good. Things don't seem to be changing for many of them. We have to admit that some women do ask for violence," Carol murmured. "It's clear from their behavior. We get them to swear out warrants to have their boyfriend or husband arrested, and the next month the man is out on bail and the woman back with him."

"Lot of charm," Jess raised an ironic glass. "Nikki, you know I've had some abused women as clients. They come to me, and it breaks my heart. Ready to go to court, to end the whole thing once and for all, to take their lovers to the bar for what they've done. 'Good!' I say to them. 'Good for you!' OK. Now we're ready to work; I stay up researching cases, filing a complaint, compiling a brief. Put away the bottle; days and days I work late till I've got it all memorized. And behind it all is this image of the man with his swinging fist, and the sight of the bruises on the woman's face. A week later she returns, all sheepish. 'I'd like to forget all about it.' Done! No more! Happy again!"

"Then you have to insist," Nikki said quietly. She set her glass down and took a cracker on a napkin, breaking it slowly into a million pieces in her lap.

"It's like heroin," Carol commented. "You'll never get at the problem until you understand that the desire to be hurt is human, and therefore not despicable."

"It is despicable!" Nikki exploded, knocking the crackers to the floor. "Oh!" she cried. She leaned and brushed the pile onto the napkin, setting the offal in a nearby ashtray.

"Painful, surely. But is it a moral problem?" Antonia asked.

"Most certainly, if you ask them at the div school," Gerry stated. "It's so easy to say 'Be good,' 'Do good,' and yes, we all have impulses that lead us to God and goodness. But any religion—any system at all—that doesn't recognize the deep human need for suffering is doomed."

"Voluptuous, even," Leah added. "I once read an essay comparing makeup and torture devices. Very interesting."

"I've got an announcement," Ruth broke in, shoving her chair closer. She glanced at the women. "Although maybe with the way the conversation is going, it's a bad time."

"No, tell us please," Antonia begged.

"Tell us something juicy!" Katrin insisted gaily.

Now that she had center stage, Ruth was shy. She and Katrin had both been actors, but Ruth left the stage. She shifted her eyes right and left.

"OK—I'm getting married," she laughed nervously.

"Oh, no!" laughed Katrin.

"Wonderful!" said Antonia.

"How much money does he have?" Jess wondered.

"I was wondering about your ring," Nikki remarked quietly.

Ruth spun it on her left finger, then held it out suddenly, everyone leaning to look at it. A thin, elegant band embedded with tiny diamonds. She blushed.

"So who is it?" Katrin asked. "God, Ruth—I never thought—you?"

Ruth stammered. "I know—that's what I thought—me? With my luck?"

Nikki wondered herself. Ruth was the most gloriously neurotic person she had ever known. Talented, with the biggest heart in the world, funny, familiar, comfortable. A body like one of those earth mother figurines from ancient times, all breasts and hips. But with an edge to her personality that was forever turning friends into enemies, discovering insults to herself that were usually unintentional, holding grudges for years. She couldn't get along for long with anyone. She had always been that way. To think her capable of keeping up any sort of relationship, casual or romantic, long enough to lead to marriage—out of the question!

"Tell!" Antonia insisted kindly.

"Since we're talking about men…" Ruth continued. "His name is Derrick, and he's black. I think he's a soulmate."

"Good line," Katrin nodded.

Ruth laughed. "There's more to it. Remember when I was involved with Robert, five years ago or so?" Ruth looked at Katrin, her best friend there, but they all knew. News traveled around their group like mercury.

"It was horrible," Katrin nodded.

Nikki remembered clearly all the nights she had spent on the phone with Ruth, commiserating with her about men, what little boys they were, how unreliable, how they all wanted to have their cake and eat it. Nikki felt their strong bond of sisterhood over this. Now what?

"Some of it *was* horrible," Ruth admitted, glancing at Nikki. "Maybe it took some time—maybe I wasn't ready to love when I was with him. But he badgered me enough to make me open up."

"What?" Nikki frowned.

"I heard about the fights," Antonia put in. "You poor thing! It sounded like you were being tortured."

"It was torture," Ruth nodded. "But I learned something. About love, I guess—from Robert. And now I feel like a queen. He used to say I was a princess, and one day I'd be a queen."

"Oh, come on!" Nikki exploded. "And you believed him!"

"It's mythic," Leah declared, observing Ruth closely. "This is what I was talking about earlier. In all the myths and stories, the female character often undergoes some remarkable transformation through the sufferings of love."

"That was my life!" Ruth nodded, growing animated. "Look," she indicated, presenting her profile, "Cleopatra's nose!" She touched its fine tip, then resumed. "I'm not pretending being with Robert was a fairy tale—I know it wasn't. But I learned things from him. The suffering led me to learn things. And I used them with Derrick. It works! I feel like a queen now!"

"She done got her man!" Jess slurred, bowing her head in mock honor.

"What's all this queen fantasy?" Katrin asked. "Sure, love, but what's this about?"

"Robert used to say that love educates, and he was right! I really do understand all sorts of things that I never understood before."

"And you had to learn these things from a man who made you suffer, who hurt you?" Nikki asked pointedly.

Ruth stopped, cocking her head. "We hurt each other."

"Wait a minute—he was married, remember?" Nikki asked.

"Yes," Ruth replied hesitantly. "You should talk," she added more softly.

"You learned how to love from a married man," Nikki remarked dryly. "That's my point—how could you learn anything good from such an awful situation? It's what's all wrong with Philip."

"Everyone should study with Robert," Ruth replied simply.

Everyone guffawed.

"I only mean that being involved with him changed my life."

"You wouldn't be getting married if you hadn't had that affair?" Nikki asked.

"That experience happened, and then this," Ruth stated, raising her ring again.

Erika floated up to them, having released Claire and Gabby. She was holding a glass of wine delicately at the tips of clear-polished nails. Her face gleamed. "I heard you talking about men—can I join in the fun?" She sat down in a chair near Nikki.

"Nikki wonders what you can learn from them," Katrin explained.

"But aren't they wonderful creatures!" Erika exclaimed. Her free hand floated in the air, bouncing on a magical current. "So big and—different," she giggled.

"Wonderful!" Nikki snorted, her voice low.

"That's how we're alike, Nikki," Erika insisted.

"What's that?"

"We both adore men, like good Finnish women!" Erika pealed. "Such wonderful little boys! We'll have to get together and talk over our love lives, yes?"

Nikki stood quickly, picked up an empty plate and stalked into the kitchen, where she bumped into Claire doing dishes.

"What are you doing?" Nikki snapped.

Claire turned with a hurt expression, then went back to washing. "That Erika—she's a character. So full of stories. She reminds me so much of you—"

Nikki dropped the plate she was carrying. It clattered once before breaking into splinters. Talk ceased in the living room as faces peered toward the kitchen. Nikki was on the floor cleaning up, talking to herself in a singsong voice. "'We'll have to get together, no? You and I are the same, yes?'" She threw the pieces in the trash.

"Stop doing dishes!" she barked, as Claire shied.

"I like to," she said apologetically. And then, "I haven't seen Philip around for weeks."

"So?"

"What is the attraction?" Claire asked, suddenly and unexpectedly direct. The question caught Nikki off guard. "I know he looks nice and has nice manners, but really, it's so unlike you, Nikki. To be so stuck on a man."

"I'm not stuck on him!" Nikki screamed.

"All right. Just curious. Sorry." She lowered her head.

HER FRIENDS LEFT finally, the last of them Erica, who insisted the two of them get together the following week; Nikki nodded curtly at the invitation. Freeing Guy from his basement captivity, she finished clearing and washing, putting all the dishes away, then sat at the table stewing. Guy had fallen asleep in his corner. What *was* the attraction to Philip? When she thought of him, she thought of his power. He seemed to carry in him a dark distance that frightened and attracted her. Yes, it made her angry, too, for she could not understand it, and did not know that a man's strength cannot be given or taken over by a woman, nor a woman's by a man.

A storm was coming up with some determination by then, the wind blowing harder, rain just beginning to fall. She was not tired and was enjoying feeling high from the wine, her perceptions at once sharpened and coated in wool. Now that the insufferable Finnish woman was gone, she could breathe easily. She was glad of the coming storm. What to do?

Shaking herself, Nikki clambered downstairs to continue cleaning out the basement. Guy awoke to trot down the rickety wood steps after her and sit in a corner, eyeing her quizzically. She was relieved Philip was gone for good, she told herself. No two-hour conversations on the phone, no sudden need to meet at the Glass Moon Café downtown for cappuccino and conversation, no sudden appearances at her back door, his self-conscious smile anyway never lowering the bar on the door of his self-possession. Only, she was angry she had to hear his voice, its occasional catch, hear it in her so loudly with all his opinions and expressions. It was as if he inhabited her, as if he were thrust deep inside of her even when he was gone. Why should she have to suffer that?

She grabbed old dusty boxes and yanked them open, threw trash aside, sorting out the old books and papers that seemed to have some value. In a dark corner of the original circular stone basement she found a cracked wooden crate with a rusty lock, the name "Cleves" cut rudely in the cover. It gave her pause, it was so old. Nikki hoisted it up the stairs and dropped it on the kitchen floor, musing on the strange name carved into the top. She went back downstairs.

Four weeks since she had heard from him. Probably out on his boat, she imagined, and suddenly she could see him clearly standing at the wheel, silent, a grim look on his face, unshaven, staring, staring like she was staring.

"Well, what does he want from me?" she asked Guy, passing him on her way upstairs, carrying a heavy box of trash. Entering the kitchen again, she regarded the ancient box. She looked at the clock: half past midnight; sat down at the table, suddenly exhausted. It was very quiet, even with the radio playing soft classical music in the background. Guy joined her and lay down on his blanket in the corner near the fridge, raising first one eyebrow and then the other as he watched her with a look of forlorn dejection.

Nikki studied the box: it was smallish, about two feet long by a foot wide and as much deep, with cracks in its worn wood. The padlock looked forbidding, but Nikki rummaged through a drawer and, finding a pair of pliers, hefted the box onto the table, working at the old lock. Finally she pried open the lock, its rusty metal squealing. Guy looked up once before lowering his head, uninterested.

Nikki pulled the hasp back slowly, opening the lid. Inside lay a thin sheaf of papers. An upside-down family tree with the name "Anne Cleves" at the top, then branches extending down and out, down to where they indicated Grace Carter marrying Stephen Keefe. These were Nikki's grandparents on her mother's side. Interesting, Nikki noted: The family tree was matrilineal, tracing none of her father's family line, the Helmiks. The tree showed a direct line from Anne Cleves down to the generation of Nikki's mother, where it stopped with Megan and Carol, Nikki's aunt and mother—the children of Grace and Stephen.

She folded the document carefully, stowing it back in the box, then rooted around in the bottom and came up with a small leather pouch tied with a dark red string, stiffened with age. When she opened the little bag and dumped the contents into her palm, out tumbled an antique emerald brooch in the shape of a five-pointed star, one of whose points was missing. But for its broken piece the brooch was intact, the pin still functional, the gold filigree glistening darkly under the glow of the fluorescent kitchen light.

Nikki nestled the brooch back into the sack and lowered it into the box. She studied the other papers; they were legal in nature: deeds for land, sales and purchases, miscellaneous agreements on the use of land for grazing and farming, signed with scrawls of names unknown to Nikki.

She marveled at the treasure, though, feeling deep satisfaction. "My mother must have left this," she said in wonder to Guy, who again raised an eyebrow at her.

"What do you care? You're a male," she finished, setting the box aside. Memories of her mother and father darted before her.

She saw images of her father again, her mind contorting in anger. She saw his great grabbing mitts, the hands whose range she stayed out of as a girl. She again saw him dead in his chair, vivid as if it were now. She felt heavy and sodden with wine.

Nikki looked through the darkened dining room and into the living room beyond, at the back of her father's green brocade easy chair where he had spent all his time watching TV. She thought of his funeral and stood very still, suddenly back at the cemetery last November…

FATHER OWEN finished praying over the sealed coffin and smilingly sniffed his red nose. Joyously humbled before the mighty power of death, he was surprised and amazed there really could be a Judgment Day. He looked around at everyone as if to say, "See, I told you so." But no one hearkened, and so with a sigh he nodded to the man from the funeral parlor, looking out of place in a frayed black tuxedo too small for him. The portly man nodded in turn to his assistant, a teenager also in a black tux, shaved head and goatee, tattoos on the back of both hands. The boy slid the two-by-fours from beneath the coffin, his boss bent and flipped a switch, and the winch began shuddering the casket into the ground, as excruciatingly slowly as an old-old man trying to walk. Father Owen found a new page in his book of prayer to begin all over, his voice matching in volume the screech of the winch, so no one could understand his words. Nikki smiled, about to laugh. The casket disappearing so slowly in jerky movements was the funniest thing she had seen in years. Like a malfunctioning prop. She had to bite her cheek to keep the laughter in, but her eyes were merry. Rachel was looking across the casket at her sister with a curled half smile of her own. Nikki began to shake with suppressed laughter.

She had to turn away and so turned to look behind her at her mother's marker, after only two years its bronzed lettering filling with dirt. The marker was set flat on the ground, so low that the grass crowded in, waving above the plaque in indifferent immortality. Picking up a twig, Nikki stooped and carefully scraped out the grooves until the name and dates were legible:

Carol Keefe Helmik
1930-1994

Well then. She had determined not to live like her mother, and she had not. She had started off as a welfare mother: protecting Alice against the world. By sheer effort, struggling along the upward curve, she finished law school and landed a lucrative job at DeVague Insurance. Never would she cower before any man, come when he called—as her mother used to do whenever Nikki's father bellowed—speak softly, subsume her life to his. Men! Tyrants—or irrelevant and unwanted presences.

Not much of a life, Nikki concluded of her mother, rising and dusting off her pants. Her right shoulder ached. She looked at the others standing around the black hole in which the coffin was quietly testing its new home in eternity. The priest closed his black book, turning to comfort the sisters. None of them were having it. Jane was busy with her children, Cynthia speaking softly to Todd, touching his shoulder. Todd seemed to be taking it harder than she, for he shook his face into a handkerchief. It looked like laughing to Nikki. Father Owen turned to her father's old friends. Her Aunt Meg, her mother's sister, stood by herself, staring down into the hole. Then, as Nikki watched, Meg did a curious thing. She lifted her black skirt and exposed herself to the hole. She wore no underwear, and her dark thatch seemed like the first real thing Nikki had seen in days. The startling immediacy made Nikki laugh out loud.

Aunt Meg looked up, cocking her mouth at Nikki. Cynthia and Father Owen turned, but Meg's skirt was down.

Returning to the cottage after the funeral, the four sisters set out food to welcome their parents' few friends for drinks and small talk. While the children played upstairs and down, Jane plopped herself unceremoniously in their father's chair and lit a cigarette. She was wearing a dark-blue polyester skirt too short for her heavy legs and a mismatched black jacket with frayed collar. She made no move to take the jacket off even as tiny beads of sweat threaded her upper lip. Her kids ran outside screaming at each other, chasing each other around and around the house.

Nikki's daughter, eighteen-year-old Alice, sat by herself on the end of the couch, distractedly watching the old TV. Every so often jumping up to primp in the hall mirror, sighing loudly, she was clearly impatient to leave. Nikki caught all this with a glance out of the corner of her eye while standing in the doorway to the kitchen, half listening to an obscure story one of her father's friends was telling. Alice caught her mother looking and went up to her.

"I'm moving in with Stephen next week," she interrupted bluntly, prompting her mother to excuse herself from the man, who swallowed his drink and muttered apologies. The news hit Nikki like a bomb, although like a good Helmik she didn't show it.

"Sure you're ready for this?" she murmured, as Rachel passed on her way into the living room.

"More ready than you are," Alice smirked, then returned to her TV.

So that was that, Nikki sighed, taking a deep breath and straightening herself. She carried a chair into the living room to sit beside Jane. It was powwow time.

The news that their father had named Todd the executor stung Nikki sharply. She was the lawyer in the family, after all! And Todd, who was he? A nice little man with a thin nose and thinning hair, good suits, a quiet manner, a stockbroker! Someone Cynthia had married so she could push him around. Nikki recalled Todd flying in from Chicago from time to time to sit down with her father and talk over the estate, Todd obsequious, speaking in that hesitant, careful voice. How could such a guy be a stockbroker and make a success of it? She took some comfort in knowing that her father despised Todd for his weakness, for his servile attitude around Cynthia. Nikki could see her father picking up on that, all right. He was a quick study, as was she. But on any of the occasions she visited him before he died, he never said a word about meeting with Todd. Nikki had found out from Cynthia.

Dragging a second chair in from the dining room, Rachel set it next to Nikki's and touched her sister's shoulder. "It's because Todd's not in the family—typical Dad stuff," she whispered with a smile, her brown eyes warm in her tanned face. "Anyway, he's a geek—don't let it bother you."

"It doesn't bother me," Nikki insisted flatly.

"He's still manipulating us from the other side." Rachel shook her head and drank off her glass of orange juice. Nikki looked at her own white wine, swirling it a bit in the glass. She looked down. Her free hand formed a fist in her lap. She bit her lip.

In the kitchen Cynthia and Todd were saying goodbye to their parents' old friends, who slumped out the sagging back door even infrequent visitors used. Cynthia came into the living room, sitting on the couch. Nikki shot a fierce glance at Alice, still watching TV. Alice sighed, flung herself upright, slapped the TV off button and stomped out of the room. Jane looked at Nikki, then shrugged her heavy shoulders sympathetically, as if to say, "Kids—can't do anything with 'em." Nikki's face was a mask.

Todd entered at last and sat beside Cynthia on the couch, lowering his narrow haunches delicately beside her. Patting the dusty arm of the couch, he cleared his throat. The four sisters waited.

"I have been named executor, as all of you know," he began, his voice faltering a little, as he glanced at Nikki, then at Cynthia, who smiled and patted his arm. She wore a black silk pantsuit, very chic, and real pearls. Her hair was swept up in the back, not just pulled up, Nikki caught with a glance, but carefully done up off her sleek neck, pearl earrings bobbing softly against the faint blush of her carefully-tended skin.

"When your father and I spoke about the estate, I offered some suggestions. He chose me, instead of one of you, because, well—because for one thing, I was the executor of my parents' estate, so I have some experience in these matters. Second, he indicated to me that he thought this would be a good way of avoiding any—unnecessary conflicts." Todd smiled and blushed.

"Conflicts he was responsible for," Rachel said flatly. Jane chortled, folding her hands under her ample bosom, then unfolding them; lifting a pack of cigarettes out of her jacket pocket, she lit a Camel Light. She was wholly concentrated on the flame two inches away from her nose. Nikki caught Cynthia wrinkling her nose. Rachel rose and opened a window behind the couch.

"You were chosen because you're a man, the stable one in the family," Nikki declared, unconcerned whether they all heard the irony or not.

"It's true Dad never trusted women," Rachel nodded, sitting down.

Todd searched Nikki a long moment, but Nikki was drinking her wine. "Well. He has left each of you bequests for small amounts of money. Jane, as the oldest, you are granted certain preferences. The furniture and effects are to be divided by equal choice. As for the house—your father would never discuss the house."

"What does that mean?" Nikki asked, staring at Todd. He looked away.

"I asked him what he wanted to do with it, but he never gave me a clear answer."

"He was too frightened," Cynthia nodded simply.

"Dad?" Nikki inquired.

"Afraid of dying?" Jane offered.

"About time he was afraid of something. It took death," Rachel snorted, pushing her long dark hair back away from her face.

"Actually, I don't know whether he was afraid," Todd continued, acutely aware he was privy to information from conversations with their father they had never had. Yet he understood only vaguely what each of them had long known: the women their father's life so revolved around were the very ones he could never bring himself to trust. And the very love he most craved, from a wife who loved him and from daughters who would have adored him, he was too terrified to receive. Now each of his daughters sat in the living room considering that paradox, the particular way it had shaped her life and character.

"I never saw him afraid," Nikki testified. "He was always too mad."

"He didn't seem afraid—of dying," Todd went on after a minute. "It was something different." There was a tremor in his voice.

"Something else?" Nikki looked quickly at Todd, who looked away again.

"What's this, dear?" Cynthia asked, smiling, though clearly she was growing angry, as she often did—especially when Todd did not confide in her. It left her at a disadvantage with her sisters. "What's this?" she repeated, her lips thinning. She leaned forward and rested her glass of white wine carefully on the coffee table, then turned all her attention on her husband, interlocking her well-manicured fingers on her waiting lap.

Nikki watched the little interplay. That was why she would never marry. She glanced at her own fingers. How was it that her fingers were so much larger than Cynthia's? Though her sensitive, spatulated fingers ended like her sister's in shapely nails, she liked to dig in the earth with them. She still had the Finnish peasant in her. Nikki couldn't imagine Cynthia digging with her nails, except into Todd. "And look at her," her little voice said. "Cynthia doesn't even have blond hair like a good Finn should. I'm the only one of the four of us with blond hair."

"Uh—hard to describe," Todd answered his wife. "When I asked him about the house—and you know he was a hard man to approach directly with any question, especially when he didn't want to talk about it..." Todd touched his glasses. "So when I asked him, carefully, he said something about there going to be something to happen to it."

"Sounds like Dad turned psychic at the end," Rachel remarked.

"What does it mean, Todd?" Jane asked, blowing a plume in Cynthia's direction. "Did he have something else in mind for the house?"

"No, I don't think so—at least he never said anything to me about any other plans for the house. It was just this one phrase that he would repeat, using different words."

"What phrase?" Nikki inquired.

"'Something is going to happen to the house,' or maybe 'in this house'—it varied."

"And he'd be three sheets to the wind," Rachel nodded, waving away the smoke drifting over from her sister.

Todd sighed. "Well... We all knew about your father's—problem," he ventured.

"Oh, it's a problem?" Nikki challenged, her eyebrows rising.

"I—didn't mean that," Todd equivocated.

"Oh, for chrissakes, Nikki," Cynthia chided, her voice sharpening.

"Leave her alone," Rachel snapped at Cynthia. Cynthia bristled at Rachel, pursing her lips.

"Dad was an alcoholic," Jane said simply, pausing to light a new cigarette. "What's the big deal?" she growled around the cigarette, giving a low chuckle.

Cynthia settled back in her seat, glaring at Nikki. Nikki ignored her.

"I didn't mean any insult, of course," Todd continued, as Cynthia patted his arm and smiled frostily. He looked at her a bit hesitantly, as if wondering which had been meant for him—the frostiness or the smile.

And that's why I'll never marry, Nikki silently affirmed.

"He was less than direct about the house, that's all," Todd said hurriedly, relieved to get the words out at last.

"So what do we do about it?" Jane asked, blowing another long purple plume across the room. Rachel sighed dramatically and shifted her seat.

"There are several options, of course," Todd explained, leaning forward and touching his glasses again. "You could decide to sell it, or one of you could buy it, or you could keep it as a family house, a vacation home—although that would take upkeep, repairs, all that..." he added uncertainly, looking around at the dilapidated, comfortable, sagging house.

"I say sell it," Rachel declared, putting both hands on her knees. "I'm not coming all the way from West Virginia to vacation here. God knows none of us has any sentimental feeling for this house of horrors." She looked at her sisters. "Unless someone really wants it—?"

"I agree," Cynthia said softly, straightening her legs and lowering her eyes discreetly, as if selling the family home required the proper degree of regret, which she was now dutifully enacting.

" 'House of horrors'? Sure we had hellish times, but I've always liked this place," Jane commented, her eyes sweeping the room. "Though it's clear you and Todd don't," she said to Cynthia. Her sister shrugged.

"What do you want to do with it?" Nikki asked Jane.

"I might like to buy it from the estate and live in it—you know, move the whole crowd up here and settle in Gloucester again. Get the hell out of Florida and that damned heat. Hell, I've still got friends here," she chortled, coughing hoarsely.

"And there's always good drinking," Nikki said, raising her glass.

"There's always good drinking in Gloucester," Jane nodded, uncertain fleetingly whether Nikki had intended irony. "Or do you want it?" she asked.

"Me? No—the thought hadn't occurred to me. I mean, I hadn't even considered it." Nikki frowned.

"Does that mean you don't want it?" Rachel pressed.

"I don't know—I hadn't thought about it." Nikki looked around the room. "I like this old house. It was tough growing up here—maybe that's why I like it. I don't know about 'wanting it.' "

"Well, maybe you should think about it," Cynthia said stiffly. She hated messes, and not selling the house outright was going to be a mess, she could already see.

But Nikki did not hear her sister. She had suddenly gone into a vision:

Todd is sitting beside her father, the one man younger, small-framed, polite, the other heavy, passionate, large. One balances a sheaf of papers unsteadily on his narrow lap. The other has a scotch at his elbow, and he drinks often, rattling the ice cubes, shifting in his chair like a massive, old, restless reindeer, bowing his head, shaking his horns. They finish talking about all the details of the furniture and the little money the elder one has stashed away. Todd asks about the house; her father nods his head and raises eyes to the ceiling, then looks down. He takes a long drink, his voice thick with the alcohol.

"There's something to this house. There's something in it. Something is going to happen in it. I can see that."

Todd studies the old drunkard, puzzled, half frightened, and, mumbling something himself, drops the matter.

Suddenly the old man reaches over and with his big mitt grabs Todd by the shirt front, the papers spilling onto the floor. He leans his jowly, heavy face close to the younger man, who nearly faints from the smell of alcohol and the man's looming largeness.

"It's in this house!" he yells. "Something is in the house! I know it, dammit! I know it! Godammit, it's here!"

He throws the little man back in disgust, slumps back in his chair and upends his glass, his eyes turning up into oblivion.…

"Nikki, maybe you should think about it," Cynthia repeated, her voice a little louder. She sighed at Nikki—the youngest, the space cadet, the dreamer in the family.

"Nikki? Yoo-hoo! Nik!" Cynthia cooed at her sister, smiling at the others while waving her hand.

Nikki shook herself. She had seen her sister waving her hands around, looking like a fool. She hated being called "Nik," except sometimes by her father. She hadn't been gone completely. It was the way it always had been with her, ever since she was a little girl. She would suddenly fall into daydreaming, falling out of the present as far as her watching family could tell. But, in fact, even while held in her vision she saw two worlds simultaneously. She sometimes confided in Rachel or her mother, at least when she was a little girl, what she saw when she daydreamed since it happened so often. Yet what she never told anyone was that she saw both worlds at the same time. "Space cadet," they had called her, and she resented the name while simultaneously wrapping herself up in it, having found a way out of her father's reach.

"What did our father say about something being in the house?" Nikki blurted out to Todd, surprising even herself.

Taken unawares, Todd responded quickly. "That there was something in it," he gulped.

"Yes—what did he mean? A treasure?"

"No—nothing like that. I mean—I don't think. It sounded more like a spirit, or something of that kind." Todd was breathing shallowly, slightly panting.

"A ghost?" Nikki asked pointedly.

But now that Todd had caught up with her train of thought, he was more cautious. He waited a few moments before answering, touching his glasses. "No ghosts, no treasures. He never said anything to me about that. No—nothing about a ghost."

"Really, Nikki, this is absurd," Rachel interjected.

"It's remarkable, isn't it?" Nikki reflected, ignoring her sister. "We all know that Dad was a Catholic, and Mom wasn't. He made her convert when he married her, then he stopped practicing himself, stopped going to church. But Mom kept going—remember her taking us to Mass? It made Dad furious—as if somehow she had outdone him in the spirit world."

"He certainly imbibed them," Rachel snorted. "What's Catholicism got to do with it?"

"It's true," Jane picked up the thought. "Dad did hate that Mom went to church, remember? Rachel and Nikki are too young, but Cynthia, you remember, don't you? I do. All those fits on Sunday morning, throwing things—Grandma disgusted with Mom, slamming the door to her room…"

"What's this all about?" Cynthia asked, her voice shaking slightly. "Why are we talking about Mother?"

"...talking about something being in the house, near his death," Nikki said. "I think it's important."

"Do you think there's a ghost in the house?" Jane asked, looking around wide-eyed.

"I think—his ghost is here," Nikki replied simply. An odd affection for the house stirred in her. She felt surprisingly sad to let go of so much history—a connection back through the generations. Although Nikki and her sisters had grown up well-aware of their father as second-generation Finnish, details of their mother's ancestry seemed lost to an obscure past. Nikki knew only that her mother's family, originally of Irish descent, had lived in Gloucester for centuries.

"Whose ghost?" Rachel asked, leaning close to her sister.

The house had in fact belonged to their mother's parents, passed down to their mother after her own mother died. Nikki had imagined being haunted by her father—his presence was so large. But her mother? Was that what her father had sensed in the house—his wife's ghost?

"Well!" concluded Cynthia. "A ghost won't help the house sell, but if there's no objection, I know of a reliable broker who can come in and give us a good idea of what the house is worth, including any of the contents we might not want."

Everyone looked at her. She did not blush but looked at Todd, who blushed and stammered for her....

BACK IN HER KITCHEN a half year later, Nikki recovered her presence as Guy rose suddenly and came to her side, barking sharply once. She looked strangely at him, then reflexively retrieved Guy's leash from a hook near the back door and, clipping it to his collar, took the excited animal out for a walk.

By now the wind was coming up high, whipping the pines and oaks in the backyard. A warm June night with a bright moon nearly full, dark clouds passed and repassed, making night shadows on the lawn. She stumbled up the short hill into Dogtown, Guy straining at the leash, yanking her into the depths under the trees. Walking without taking notice, she let Guy take the lead. When he wanted to stop she stopped, not seeing, hearing the whistling in the trees and feeling prickles along her upper arms where the wind blew across.

Despite the balmy air, she shivered as Guy led her deep into the woods, ending up in the rolling wooded hills of Dogtown whose massive granite boulders lay strewn about like blocks, giant children having left them where they fell from their game.

Before her mind's eye appeared a vision of the *Lamia Claire* pitching in the whistling wind, Philip standing before the wind-whipped sails and smiling with that set look. The vision was starkly vivid. She shook herself and hurried on.

Then the rain fell hard, and Guy dragged her home. She was soaked by the time they jostled one another through the back door. Nikki went upstairs to change while Guy shook himself, took a few laps of water from his bowl, and lay down on his snug blanket to snooze.

Wrapped in a white bathrobe, Nikki descended, skirted her father's chair and returned to the kitchen, where she reached for an opened bottle of Sauvignon Blanc from the fridge and poured herself a glass. She sat and pulled her Moroccan leather-bound journal toward herself, flipping it open and writing what came to mind:

Anger = truth. What does he want? Philip-magic, day full of too many thoughts. Vivid dreams and daydreams. Have to speak to Rose again.

Intentions: Speak to Rose re Dogtown. Make friends. Help Dawn. Work with Claire on her divorce. Stop procrastinating! Journeying. Collect some rocks from Dogtown. Call Gerry about that guy she mentioned. Forgot his name. Get on with my life!!!

She flipped her wolf pen in her hand, then wrote again:

Go see wolves at Wolf Hollow; ask about volunteering.

She lowered the pen and looked up, her eyes falling on the window in the back door. Seeing a face there, she gasped and jumped out of her chair, spilling her wine over her journal, her heart pounding furiously. Guy rose and barked once at her commotion, then, whimpering, retreated to his blanket.

Nikki could not take her eyes off the face. It was Ernest, his sharply-lined, heavy-lidded face staring passively through the window at—her? At nothing. The eyes were listless, dull, unseeing, but his face was still beautiful. The rain beating furiously against the pane cut right through his face. Nikki breathed heavily. She stood riveted to the vision, which made no eye contact with her.

She glanced at the clock: two in the morning. When she looked back, the face was gone; only the rain. Standing for some time in utter silence, hearing her heart clash like kettles, she watched the rain spatter dark drops on the smeared glass. She flicked glances at the other windows, but they were empty. She had a sudden impulse to cover all of them with heavy curtains. She felt cold and vulnerable.

Finally she sat down again, righting the overturned glass. She wiped up the spill, refilled her glass and sat wiping the damp pages of her journal thoughtfully, her hand trembling. She glanced again quickly at the back door. Nothing. She stared, as if staring might make him come back. Her eyes pierced the glass and fell into the darkness without. She could not help staring, afraid of calling him back even as she tried.

Now that her heart was slowing, she was able to think. She was glad he had shown himself to her; it meant that he was still around, hovering over her. "Maybe he's my protection," she said to Guy, who barked once jealously. "In the other world," she reassured him.

All at once a vision hit her like a tidal wave, capsizing her psyche into passive acquiescence as her body floundered. She sat very still; there was no time; the heavy earth hesitated on its axis. Philip stood at the wheel of the *Lamia Claire,* facing the storm. The certainty of the vision overwhelmed her; she knew it to be true just as she knew she was in her own kitchen. She watched as if possessed while Philip fought the waves crashing over the gunwales of the boat, the *Lamia Claire* listing heavily from side to side as he strove to keep the boat headed into the gale-force wind. He was not far offshore but blinded by the rain and unable to see any lights. The light winked out in the mahogany binnacle; he could not see the compass but two feet in front of him. He was trapped in a moving mountain range of white waves that battered the boat, as the crests rose higher than the top of the mainmast.

The boat could not sink, could it? Nikki wondered as she watched, the little hairs on the back of her neck standing up. *Wasn't it one of those boats with air pockets?* She didn't know. How it pitched and rolled, with the huge seas crashing over the bows running torrents down the deck! The mainsail was blown into shreds. Nikki, wholly swept up in the drama, watched Philip make the boom fast, hauling hard on the sheet and twisting it around a cleat. But the wind tore cleat and bolts clean out of the deck, Philip ducking as the boom arced toward him like a raging bull, the cleat blown like shrapnel whistling past his head. It swung back, flung in a great snapping arc by the fury of the wind, raking his cheek as it passed. He fell with a cry, then rose and, staggering back to the wheel, made it fast with a line and held on for dear life.

Navigating blindly, he struggled to bring the *Lamia Claire* into port, his cheek streaming blood. He was sailing by the jib alone, the only sail left, which filled and luffed in quick succession as the boat pitched back and forth, switching its head in the wind. The gale was out of the north-northeast; only by means of a long reach might he find land. But the wind was so strong that he was forced to tack back and forth, facing nearly into the gale, the little boat heeling dangerously, threatening to throw Philip overboard each time a stronger gust blew up.

Up, up a nearly vertical behemoth of a wave the *Lamia Claire* climbed, up an endlessly long arc, heeling hard to port, bow cresting through the blowing peak. The wind ripped the boat nearly free of the water so that its great keel knifed above the water to clear space, then the *Lamia Claire* pitched vertically down into the next trough, plummeting so steeply that the door of the cabin lay below Philip's feet. He grabbed a sheet and hung on, then wrapped a line around his waist, making himself fast to the wheel. The wind was howling past his ears, and he began to howl in unison, eyes blaring and hair flying.

Nikki was panting softly, still dizzy with the vision when hours later she broke the surface of the water. She looked around, flexed her fingers and squinted at the clock. Five o'clock. The wind was rattling the windows like mad tambourines. She raced upstairs, yanked on jeans and sweatshirt and rattled back down the narrow staircase. Grabbing her raincoat from the hook near the back door, she glanced blindly at Guy as she rushed out.

The wind shoved her down the driveway to her little red car; she pulled the door open and drove through the howling streets to Halibut Point. Her hair was streaming in her eyes. Leaves and maple branches skittered wildly past the car or slapped it as she drove slowly by, passing through a roaring gauntlet with no end. She took the winding road through Lanesville, circling cautiously through the little town, empty as if abandoned, crept along through the woods to come out along the water, past Pigeon Cove, then wound around the rocky shore until she reached the turn-off at Halibut Point.

She pulled into the parking lot. Wrapping her slicker around her, she headed through the pine woods for the water. The rain was tapering off now in the morning gloaming, dark trees emerging from shadow. But the path through the woods turned into a long and scary walk, full of voices calling *Away! Away!* as spirits whistled by, branches that caught in her hair and lashed her slicker. Finally she emerged from the trees and found her way to a cliff of gargantuan boulders piled high along the sea. It was a place of primordial instance; atop the cliff overlooking the roiling ocean, tremendous piles of granite boulders plunged vertically to the surging sea below.

The sky was aswirl in dark greys and streaky, smeared blues, the sun coming up somewhere far out over the sea in the middle of that mess. Churning and frothing forty feet below Nikki, waves smashed their psychotic heads against the tumbled boulders, again and again in a delirium of rage. The wind blew in an endless screaming howl so deafening that Nikki pressed her hands over her ears, and though the rain was only spattering now, the tiny drops stung her face like acid.

As dawn spread apace, she spied the *Lamia Claire* pitching about like a cork, half a mile offshore. She was not surprised; she had seen it here in her vision. Philip was not visible on-board; her teeth chattered in fear and anticipation as she strained to see, helpless. She looked down the cliff: no use climbing down; she would see even less at sea level. The boat looked whole, but it pitched heavily in the waves, the jib flapping loosely, the boat listing to starboard, then to port. *All is well, all is well,* she repeated to herself. *Just come home to me. Just come home.* She knotted her fists and waited, the wind pushing her about like a doll on the granite boulder cliff, so that she had to strain to keep her sneakered footing.

The wind was pushing the boat to shore; soon the *Lamia* was a hundred yards out and nearing quickly. Still seeing no sign of Philip, Nikki picked her way carefully down the giant steps of the rock wall, down close to where the great waves drove themselves against the rocks, filling the air with a dense spray of saltwater.

She stood on a granite ledge in a small cove where the water was deep, she knew. The *Lamia* would be blown right against the rocks here. This was where the kids (the brave ones) jumped off the rocks above to land in the sea below. They jumped from partway up the cliff; no one she knew had ever tried it from the top. It was too far—you would kill yourself.

She was drenched, although not cold. The morning was warm in spite of the storm, the water and the humid air making her clammy inside her slicker. She loosened the knotted belt, securing herself in a cleft in the rock where she could still spy the *Lamia* but was half out of the wind and water spray.

Soon the boat drew near, drifting into the boulder-lined cove where Nikki waited; as if it were coming to her. But where was Philip? The boat came close, the waves pitching it near and nearer the rocks. It would wreck itself if something wasn't done. But Nikki had neither pole nor line.

Now the *Lamia* rolled but twenty feet from the granite ledge, and when it pitched into a trough Nikki could see Philip at last, lying in a long heap behind the wheel, face down against the bulkhead.

"Philip!" she cried out to him. He didn't stir. She reached out; she could nearly touch the gunwales, but the boat was pitching heavily, one moment surging tantalizingly within reach, the next pulling away just beyond her extended fingertips. She poised herself without thought, and when the *Lamia* fell deep into a trough, she leaped as far as she could, out into the air, felt one long moment of exhilaration and then came down hard on the deck, falling over and hurting her leg. She crawled to Philip, pulling at him, calling him over and over.

He groaned and moved, and Nikki hauled him into a sitting position, untying the line around his waist. She froze seeing his face; a long gash had torn his unshaven left cheek, though the whitened lips of the gash had been washed clean by the salt water. Nikki reached her long fingertips to touch it, but the *Lamia* was knocking against the rocks, shoving Nikki from side to side. The boat crunched and banged with a sickening thud each time a wave pitched her against the granite, then groaned loudly as her sides slid down the rock. Nikki, half falling with the waves but pulling herself upright, slapped Philip on his right cheek until he wagged his head in half-consciousness.

Opening puffy eyes, he looked at her bleary-eyed; his glasses were gone.

"We have to get off!" she cried, pointing at the looming cliffs now at their elbows.

Philip breathed deeply and got up shakily, leaning on Nikki. They stood holding onto the wheel.

"The *Lamia*," he gestured, but she shook her head. Already the boat was breaking up on the rocks.

"We'll drown or get smashed," she yelled, pulling him to the side, pointing at the shelf of granite. When the boat came nearly level, Nikki reached over the side, feeling for a finger hold. She couldn't possibly hold the boat, but perhaps for a second or two...

"You go!" he yelled. He righted her and pushed her to the edge, as she looked at him and grabbed his hand.

"Together!"

Waiting a split second, they leaped as one, landing on the slick rock before sliding together into a heap. They turned to crawl up the rocks. The sun was up now, oc-cluded in sickly clouds but casting a grey light over the ocean. Slowly they climbed, puffing all the while, achingly finding finger holds and footholds, ten, then twenty feet above the spray. Philip stopped often to look down at the *Lamia,* now being ground to pieces by the narrow boulders at the rear of the little cove.

At last pulling themselves up to the top of the cliff, they found a narrow cleft to lie in, both panting. For a long while they lay there. Then Philip turned, his eyes open fully, and gazed at Nikki, their faces very close. He took her from under the chin, pulling her face to him, kissing her softly for a long time. Soon they were fum-bling with their sticky clothes as once again he was kissing the vulnerable left side of her neck. She wanted him more certainly than she wanted her life. As he lay upon her in the rock cleft, their wet clothes for a bed, she whispered, "I don't want to live without you." Smiling myopically, he shook the water out of his hair. It splattered her face, and she was happy feeling him as they whispered love to each other while the wind blew outside the cleft.

She was very close, giving herself sweetly, which touched and amazed Philip, for she had always, even in the middle of passion, kept to herself. Or was it he who had kept to himself? Philip lay on her, feeling he could put his two hands right around her heart and caress it to him like a delicate child.

As for Nikki, she was wrapped in gold and there had never been another time in the world.

AFTERWARD THEY LAY in shipwrecked bliss, not speaking, listening to the sickening sounds of the *Lamia* being ground to pieces far below. Nikki reached to touch Philip's cheek with trembling fingers, lightly, as if touch might heal the gaping wound there.

"Damaged goods," he laughed shortly, raising himself on an elbow. He seemed utterly spent, the last of his energy sacrificed to the god of love. He panted softly.

Nikki shook her head as tears came into her eyes.

He looked at her triumphantly. *Yes,* this was what he wanted.

"You're perfect," she said softly.

"Not since I was in the cradle," Philip said, falling slowly to lie back down. "I feel like a planet warped out of its orbit. By you. I used to know where I was in life. Now I'm damaged. And god I'm dizzy!"

"It's your father," she steered, wanting it to be her. "You're upset about him."

Philip was silent. The wind was dying down, but the grinding and groaning went on. They lay quiet, listening to the death rattle of the *Lamia.* Finally Philip could stand it no longer.

"I'm a stand-in for my father. Isn't that so?" He sat up and hunched over.

She let out a peal of laughter. "Men are such little boys!" she exclaimed, although deep inside her something quaked. She pulled on her clothes.

"We're in this together now, Nikki. Both fighting to get away from our fathers—and the more we fight, the more entangled we become."

"Not me," Nikki said lightly, as if it were wholly his problem.

"Except that for you it's different," he went on as if not hearing her. "Because you're a daughter and I'm a son. It's different."

"Should we go to the car?" Nikki asked suddenly.

"I want to wait until it's over," he said grimly, straightening himself. They pulled their clothes on slowly, falling into deep meditation listening to the groans of the boat, like an animal slowly dying. They reached and put their wet sneakers on, the warmth in their blood spreading out into their wet clothes and shoes, making them more comfortable.

"I found something," Philip said, taking a plastic-sealed envelope out of his shirt pocket. "On the *Lamia*—I should have thought of looking there before. It was hidden in a secret compartment that I knew my father kept in the cabin. I wasn't supposed to know about the compartment, but the note is written to me. Which means he knew I knew. Which means he wanted me to find it."

"What is it?"

"Do you want to know where I've been?" he asked.

She shook her head. "I just want to feel us right now. Nothing else. I know anyway. I saw it."

"Saw?"

She grew more animated. "Last night—it was so vivid. Some friends were over, and afterward I was sitting up with the storm drinking wine. Suddenly I saw you—I mean, saw you in the *Lamia* with the storm. That's how I knew to come here."

He squinted at her curiously, even while he was moved utterly. When he didn't speak immediately, she knew, it always meant he was moved. All the same, he seemed to be weighing something.

"Nikki, who is Clarissa Barrow?"

"I don't know—did your father write that?"

"In his note, yes. It's odd—he said to ask you about Clarissa Barrow."

"Me?"

"Those words are all that's left of him—he said that's why he is going overboard."

"All that's left—?" Nikki frowned.

"I told you there was no body in the casket. Which only a few of us knew about, including his old first mate, Gene Greco. Gene towed the empty *Lamia* back to port and never said anything about it. You know the man? That craggy old guy, old enough to have fished from dories in the old days. Always wore his redjacks, even in town. He told my mother, of course. And she knew right away my father had gone overboard."

"In a storm?"

Philip shook his head. "Intentionally."

"I wondered what you meant when you said your father might have died because of your mother's alleged affairs," she recalled.

"Alleged," Philip echoed with a small curl. He rooted in the envelope, his fingers playing with an object.

"So—he was never found?"

"No—it was only on Gene's word that we knew he was dead and not just run away." Philip drew from the envelope a small piece of emerald gemstone, turning it in his fingers.

"Gene saw your father—kill himself?"

"No, he just followed orders my father had given him to go pick up the *Lamia* at a certain place at a certain time. My father had dropped a tow anchor—in a clear, flat sea."

"But—you just said yourself that he killed himself," Nikki said confusedly.

"That's the story he gave Gene, though not in those words. He told Gene one day that he was leaving 'for good.' That's all Gene would tell us."

Nikki paused. "And you think I know something about all this?"

"His note says you do."

"But I don't!" she exclaimed, then touched his hand. "What's that?"

He held up the bit of green gem. "I don't know. It was in the envelope." He shook his head, turning to her. "So you don't know anything about this?"

"I—it looks like the missing piece—" she began.

"Of what?"

"I mean—a missing piece—of—" Nikki laughed. "It's funny, it's like I recognized it for a second. I thought—" she stopped and laughed again, shaking her head.

"What did you think?" he pressed.

"That—it wouldn't make any sense."

"Say it."

"Well—all right. I just thought—you can see clearly it's a piece of jewelry, the way it's pointed, like the point of a star. An emerald star. So I just imagined the rest of it—and all of a sudden, I saw a brooch." She laughed again. "I don't know what I'm talking about."

Philip looked at her closely. "You recognize this. It makes sense to you—"

"I said it doesn't make sense!" she insisted.

"But it did for a second. Maybe you can, like my father implied, answer the question of his death."

"Just because I imagined some association, it doesn't mean I understand anything about this," she demurred.

He studied her, then shrugged. "Then it's a mystery. But I think you know more than you think you know. It never occurred to me that this was part of a brooch—certainly not part of a star."

"What's the difference?" She took the emerald piece and dropped it in the envelope, then pulled his face carefully to her, kissing him. "I love you."

He drew back, studying her for a long moment silently. She returned his look with a question in her eyes, then a wondering smile, a tilt of her head. At last she could stand his silence no longer.

"What is it?" she smiled.

"I love you, Nikki. We are bound up together—in some way."

She nodded.

"No—it's worse than that. I am going to leave Françoise, and I'd like to know if you will marry me." He looked at her steadily, blinking nearsightedly.

It was too much for her. She sat stunned, staring at Philip, staring at nothing, turning toward the wrinkled granite walls of their little rock cave. The groans of the *Lamia* echoed up at them from below. She looked back at him, seeing only the long cut in his cheek. It was horrible, but she didn't know what it meant.

"You don't want to," he concluded at length.

"No! It's not that—it's too much to think about right now, that's all. I'm over-whelmed."

"You don't want to."

"I didn't say that—I'm in shock."

"But you hesitate! I thought this was what you wanted—what's been making you angry and insecure all this time. The matter you always return to with me, remember? That because I'm married, our being together has been crazy and unhealthy for you—?" He searched her face as a troubled look came into his eyes.

She was touched, reaching her long fingers to stroke his left cheek again. He was right. Why was she hesitant? A moment before their two souls had been wrapped tightly around one another. The deep ache of longing—having to accept that Philip would never be hers completely—had given an edge to her passion. Now out of the blue he was changing course!

She should be ecstatic, she knew. And there was Philip looking at her, waiting.

"I—I can't live with you as long as you're married," she stammered. "It wouldn't feel right."

"Nikki, are you playing for time? What is it? It's not what you want after all, is it?" he cried, standing up suddenly. The death throes of the *Lamia* were loud in their ears. Philip stepped out of the cleft and stood on the slick granite, looking down the cliff.

Rising, Nikki went to him. But how curiously dizzy she felt! It was the weight of Philip, his presence. He was so heavy, how could she ever carry him, how ever bear him up, if he were to continue throwing himself on her as he was doing now? Since she had fallen in love with him, she had fretted that she could never give him what he needed. Nevertheless she could live with that, the pressure was not too great, since behind it all lay the certainty that he would go back to his wife. And she could use it against him, she knew. Yes, and then feel justified hating him for it.

But now, there he was. No one else there to help him and hold him but her. And she feared she could not hold him, never guessing that he did not want that from her. It made her angry that he was throwing himself at her like this—so vulnerable!

She spoke soothingly. "Look, Philip. You know I love you. It's just that—you've just been through a lot, with your father and now finding the note. And look at the poor *Lamia!*" They looked down while the wind swirled around them. The boat was in pieces, long, torn gashes of planking and hull cracking horribly against the grim rocks. She was going down between the massive granite boulders, the sea rocking and swelling, pitching the boat again and again against the rocks like some mad boxer, beating his opponent senseless against the ropes.

She went on. "Give it some time."

"You don't really love me," he said flatly, not looking at her.

She laughed merrily, though worry flickered in her eyes. "Of course I do! You're being a little boy!"

He looked at her seriously. "No. You think I am, but you misjudge me. I'm not looking for sympathy, I'm stating a simple fact." He laughed grimly. "It's suddenly clear to me. I spent the better part of two weeks with my soul on the rack, twisting and turning, not knowing what to do with myself, what to do with this passion I feel for you. I couldn't decide; days and days I spent sailing up and down the coast, going out to the Grand Banks.... Then I found the note from my father, and that tipped the scales.

"Imagine! I was all alone, brooding on you for days, when this note appears—and who does my father mention, but you! There was his voice whispering to me, all but revealing the connection between you and me as fated! It was a turning point; my decision was made. Although I didn't love Françoise less, my fate lay with you now. From then on the thought that I could give you what you wanted—what you led me to believe you wanted—filled me with happiness. And when the storm came up, my worst fear throughout the entire ordeal was that I might not see you again. Not Françoise, but you, Nikki."

He peered down at the *Lamia* sinking below the waves. "I can see now the lie you've been telling all these weeks. You never did want me. You just wanted someone to be angry at, so you could go on hating me—really all men, I suppose, like you always have."

This time she let out a genuine peal of laughter, but he did not smile. She pulled him close. "Oh, you're so upset about your father, and now you've found this note of his, and you think I have the answer. You're all upset—look, you just said it yourself—your father's note was what made you decide."

"What does that matter? I decided."

"I would prefer that you did it on your own, because you wanted to," she said quietly, as if it were a lesson.

He looked at her with raised eyebrows. "Are you taking issue with the way I came to my decision?"

"You're under a lot of pressure, Philip," she said, speaking more quickly. "I'm just saying wait a bit until things get worked out. You have this whole business of your father to deal with. Maybe now isn't the time to make such a big decision about your life. You've got your father's business, and your mother to worry about. Maybe you and I should wait a bit."

He grabbed her shoulders. "Why can't you just say yes? What do all these things matter? Why can't you help me?"

"I'll help you!" she cried. "I'll help you all you want! Only I can't be some sort of medicine woman with the big answer you're looking for!" She pulled herself away from him, feeling sick and heavy. His crack about her hating men she would slap him with later after this all blew over. But what *was* her hesitation? she wondered. Why was she not able to leap into his arms and say, *Yes, yes, I love you! I'll marry you today!* Wasn't that always what she wanted, more with Philip than with any other man she had loved?

"What are you talking about—what big answer?" he asked.

"I don't know who this woman is your father is talking about. Look at you— you're desperate and suffering terribly. You poor thing—I'm sure you haven't eaten for days—you look starved! But because I can't give you a magic answer about your father, you think I don't love you. Your father must have been making some kind of joke about me and this woman."

"When he's about to kill himself?" Philip was incredulous. Who was this woman? Shivering in the breeze, he felt weak and sick at heart. He looked down at the poor *Lamia*. The toes of his wet sneakers pointed over the edge of the cliff.

Now Nikki leaned toward him, looping her arm through his, pulling him to her. "Come on, little boy," she smiled. "Time to go home," she said in a singsong voice. "I think we've had enough for today. We'll talk about this later. Especially this nonsense about my hating men," she laughed.

But Philip pulled away from her, and in wrenching himself from her arm his sneaker slipped on the flat, wet granite, and in the blink of an eye he pitched headlong over the cliff. How fast he fell!—hitting the rocks halfway down, twisting and turning over sickeningly, falling again as Nikki gaped, horrified, his body falling down and down as if in slow motion as she watched, wide-eyed in horror.

She leaped down the rocks, catching her breath, tears streaming down her face, until breathing hard she reached him on the flat rock where the *Lamia Claire* was even now splitting her beams and sinking under the crashing waves. Its mainmast was leaning over Philip's inert form, nearly touching him, softly as if in farewell. Nikki clattered down next to Philip and knelt beside him, putting a hand under his head, smeared in blood. His eyes were closed; she leaned close. There was no breath she could sense.

She stood up in anguish and with shaking limbs hurried up the cliff. *She must find help; she must find help,* her panicked mind shouted. *Find help, find help,* she whispered as she panted up the boulders, gaining the top again. *Find help.*

NIKKI AGONIZED in the little yellow-shingled house, waiting for news of Philip as she pieced together in her grogginess all that had happened.

Fortunately she had never returned her cell phone to work after quitting her job, and so she was able to call the ambulance from her car not two minutes after Philip fell. Nikki was not surprised when Rose showed up with a police escort, right on the heels of the emergency crew. Philip, unconscious, was strapped to a stretcher and hoisted up, slid into the back of the ambulance, and whisked away. Even though Nikki and Rose did not speak, the grande dame's look left Nikki shivering.

The police were kinder, asking once Rose was busy looking over Philip whether Nikki was all right. She was trembling badly. The medic gave her a pill to take, on condition she wait until she got home. The pill put her out for fifteen hours, after which she awoke in a stupor of half remembrance, Guy whimpering for food. It was nearly midnight, the red-numbered bedside clock said. *But what day?* she wondered dizzily as she struggled out of bed. Pulling on clean clothes, she hobbled downstairs, fed Guy and in a daze cleaned up his accident on the kitchen floor.

What day *was* it? She looked at the clock. Was it the same day that she and Philip had—? But that was aeons ago, another life. She opened a can of vegetable soup, splashing it into a bowl. Then she set it in the radar-range and leaned on the counter with her head in her hands. When the beep came she sat at the table, spooning the soup tastelessly down. She took Guy out for the shortest walk of his life, then plunked down on the couch. She turned on the TV to the local access channel, and there was Philip being taken into the hospital. There was Rose, looking worried but still powerful in her fur coat, never mind the warm weather, and perfectly made-up, as always.

Fumbling the phone to her ear, Nikki called Addison Hospital, the same place her mother had died in two years before. The nurse on duty in the emergency ward could only confirm that Philip was alive. A nurse in intensive care told her she wasn't supposed to talk about it, and how did she know Nikki wasn't the press calling?

Nikki was good at making it seem like the nurse's idea to tell her the whole story. Yes, Philip had been admitted; he had suffered broken ribs, and his face was a mess. He had a cracked skull and was still unconscious. They did not yet know whether there was any brain damage. A lung was punctured, and there was a crack in one of his vertebrae, but nothing life-threatening. However, it would be months—if ever— before he would be up and about. No way to know yet whether there was paralysis, but they didn't think so. The last time she checked, he was comatose. No, she had no further information, because Rose Eveless had swooped down with her doctor from Boston and taken Philip to her home. She was told, of course, that the hospital could not take responsibility. No trouble at all.

Nikki set the phone down. Rose's assertion of complete control was all too pre-dictable. So now what? She had to see Philip somehow, but Rose would never let her, not with their falling out and now this—she knew Rose blamed Philip's fall on her. The circumstances wouldn't matter; once Rose was struck with a notion it lodged itself in her brain like an axe in soft wood.

Nikki fell asleep again and slept until morning, then rose and tried to read. She called Claire though found out nothing more than she already knew. She waited another day, then another, then another. The nurse she had spoken to was off duty, and she could get no more information from the hospital. She began to daydream about Philip. She saw him in his bed in the big stone house, Rose and a team of nurses tending to him. But he was so pale, and his eyes were closed!

She could contain herself no longer. A week after the wreck she put on the first business suit she had worn since quitting her job, did herself up in the manner she had been taught by Rose, and drove slowly over to the granite mansion.

She was ushered into the library, downstairs. This is bad, Nikki thought, sitting on the Chesterfield as the maid withdrew. The high coffered-ceiling room was cold, even on a hot day, as the tall banks of books encased in glass stared morosely down at her. The shutters had not been pulled back, a deep gloom lingering in the room like a half-remembered bad dream. It sat like a gargoyle up in the high shelves, looking down at her with baleful eyes. This had been Ernest's favorite room; his ghost was padding about still. There were books open on the tables and chairs, piles of books at the foot of the tall bookcases, some bookmarked with slips of paper. Nikki could see Philip's father here, reading to keep up with his son.

Soon Rose appeared, dressed in sky-blue silk, her dark hair writhing across her broad peasant shoulders like snakes. Nikki took one look in her eyes and knew it was trouble. Rose did not smile—and who was Rose without a smile? She always wore a smile, making sure to put on a good face for "her people," as she called them. Perhaps because she wasn't smiling she looked older, Nikki observed, noticing that the mask of pride Rose was wearing gave an even more willful set to her mouth than usual, highlighting the creases at the corners. Nikki set her own mouth and stood up, extending her hand.

"Rose, I'm so sorry about Philip. Is he all right?"

Glancing at the hand as if it were made of marble, Rose sat regally in a high-backed chair of burnished calfskin with carved lion armrests. She set one shapely arm on each lion before speaking. "He almost died, thanks to you," she replied in her hard, throaty voice, the words echoing harshly in the canyon of air.

"I know you don't believe me, but I had nothing to do with it," Nikki said firmly, sitting again. She knew not to let Rose get the better of her. Then she would have no hope of seeing Philip.

"Hah!" Rose shouted. Unable to hold her pose after all, she leaped up and paced the room, touching books left lying open on chair arms and end tables. "Françoise is not here because my son is estranged from his wife—thanks to you."

"May I see him?" Nikki asked, trying to keep the quaver out of her voice.

Rose looked at her face for the first time. "You're looking very beautiful, Nikki," she pronounced.

"Rose—Philip. I'd like to see him."

"Do you love him? He loves you."

"I—yes, I guess," she stammered.

"But you don't know. Bad time for that."

"No—yes," Nikki said softly.

"He's about to die, and you can't tell if you love him."

"But he'll be OK, won't he?" she asked anxiously.

"Nikki, I want you to do something for me."

"Rose, I came to see Philip. Are you keeping him locked up?"

"Concerned about your victim? You know, I thought I taught you more than how to dress and do your hair and makeup, Nikki. I thought I had given you the better stuff—how when you've got someone down, you strap his balls to his back."

"He's not my victim, Rose!" Nikki cried.

"Shit!" she screamed, running at Nikki. Nikki jerked away as Rose stopped short, hands like claws stretched out. Nikki was alarmed, the more so for seeing the tears in Rose's eyes. The older woman stopped, hesitating as if uncertain what she could have had in mind, and returned to her throne. Nikki could hear her panting softly, and she seemed frightened, uncertain.

"He was beautiful, my son. Now, who knows?" she wagged her head. "Beauty is what is most important, you know. You think you've won, but watch out! First Ernest, and now my son—I won't stand for it!"

"Am I going to be allowed to see Philip?"

"If you do something for me," Rose smiled strangely.

"You don't want me to see Philip again," Nikki nodded.

Rose chuckled deliciously, lifting a well-manicured hand to her mouth, her eyes dancing. "No, I don't—but I'm willing to make a deal with you. You ignored your part of the bargain we made. You weren't to see my son, and you lied to me. Why should I keep any part of my end?" Rose smiled devilishly. "But look—I am generous. I will forgive all your betrayals. There is something I want you to do for me. Find something for me, then you may see him."

"Find what?" Nikki asked uneasily.

"A certain book—a journal—written by an ancestor of yours. I know a story that concerns you, a secret that was kept from you but that I know. You come from a long line of—some sort of magicians—I'm not sure what they called themselves—Druids of some sort."

Nikki sat very still, trying not to smile. Rose was cracked, it was clear. Nikki was wondering how to humor her so she could get to see Philip. Druids!

"Um, how do you know that?" Nikki asked amiably.

"It's a long story you don't need to know all of. Philip's father had a—friend, who knew, and she told him. He told me. Men are so bad at keeping secrets."

"And this will make it so I can see Philip?"

"Provided you find the journal."

"It's lost?" Nikki asked.

"For centuries. Written by an ancestor of yours named Anne Cleves who lived somewhere around here, in Dogtown, I believe."

Nikki sat up with a jolt. It was the name at the top of the family tree! Her eyes widened.

Rose went on. "They say the book contains magic spells, one of them how to keep your beauty."

Nikki could not help smiling. "I'm a descendant of some sort of magicians, one of whom wrote down a magic spell in a book, which you want for yourself."

"That's about it," Rose nodded.

"And if I refuse?"

"You won't see Philip. And you'll never reconnect to your past, if that matters."

"My mother was a Christian of English and Irish descent."

"I have offered you a deal, Nikki," Rose said, rising. "You have your choice. If Philip means nothing to you, not even after allowing him to fall from that cliff, then you can forget my offer. I'm a vain woman—why shouldn't I be?" she asked, her voice beginning to thunder in the lofty room. Her temper was about to erupt. Nikki winced.

Rose began pacing the room again, picking up books, now throwing them down on the table with a bang, turning, pivoting suddenly on Nikki. "My beauty, like yours, is a gift in need of protection. Ever since I found out about it forty years ago, I have been looking for the lost journal of Anne Cleves. I will find it and possess its secret."

"Why didn't you ever tell me any of this?" Nikki asked, inwardly feeling a depression settle over her. Was this why Rose had befriended her those many years ago?

"I thought I could find it myself. But any number of others have looked for it, and they say some magic protects it so that it can only be found when it wants to be found. Or that it's dangerous to anyone finding it who isn't supposed to. Maybe it will want to be found by you," Rose shrugged. "I've searched every place that made sense. All these years Cleavage Builders has been my digging arm. I only built in places where the journal might have been buried. Now that I've finished with all the places I can think of, I'm going to build in Dogtown as a cover for my digging there."

"This is crazy," Nikki whispered, rising.

"I don't argue—I merely offer you a deal. It's now in your hands." Rose turned and walked out the door, leaving it slightly ajar. The maid slipped through the opening and stood waiting.

Nikki sat for a long time musing, then wandered distractedly out of the house, stepping thoughtfully down the stone steps to her car, parked in the circular driveway. Closing the door, she peered through the windshield up at the blank windows of the house. Could Philip even now be looking down at her through one of them? Could Rose's story be true? She shivered as she regarded the grey granite stones of the old mansion. Inside lived a madwoman and an invalid whom Nikki wasn't sure if she hated or loved.

Backing her car out of its space, she drove slowly around the curved drive. From the corner of her right eye she spied someone standing in the shadow of the house near a hedge, gesturing to her. She looked quickly over, slowing the car.

Ernest stood darkly still, his left hand out as if signaling to her. Nikki's eyes widened in horror, and she sped off, her heart thudding like lead in her chest. She did not look back.

4.

a ÐRUIÐ AUNT

NIKKI DECIDED to phone her Aunt Meg in Salem. She hadn't spoken with her since the funeral, when Meg ran off immediately following the little scene with her skirt. Not that Nikki had ever been close to her mother's sister, but she needed a woman friend now, someone older who could help her. She sat at the kitchen table feeling her heart pounding. What was the implied threat that Rose had made? Was Nikki guilty of hurting Philip, of somehow provoking his fall from the cliff? She knew it was nonsense, but her heart pounded and she could not sit still.

She had been thinking of religion, remembering how much when she was a little girl the Catholic Mass had meant to her—the stained glass, the incense, the strange and wonderful music. How she had hated that boys could serve Mass and not girls! Nikki remembered visiting her Aunt Meg in Salem on a Sunday afternoon once when she was little. Her aunt had not been to Mass and said that she did not go. Nikki was girlishly shocked—didn't all Catholics go to church, unless they wanted to commit a mortal sin?

"I'm not a Catholic," Aunt Meg had answered with a fling of her proud head. "It's the damn Catholics who have ruined everything—nasty Catholics, violent, intolerant!" Meg spat.

"Meg!" Nikki's mother cried.

"It's only the truth, Carol. Tell her the truth. About the Inquisition, the witch burnings, the pope and his destructive ways! It's really monotheism, Nikki, not just the Catholics but the Christians, the Jews, the Muslims—monotheism! Nikki, do you know what the word 'monotheism' means?" her aunt asked.

Nikki, three feet tall with hair nearly as long, stared at this strange, exotic creature, her mother's sister, who was uttering words as bad as curses.

"Now, Meg," her mother warned, but Nikki's aunt persisted.

"She has to be given some explanation, Carol," her aunt replied, turning back to Nikki. "Monotheism is the belief in one God only, and it messes everything up because you then judge yourself and all of life by only one standard. In believing in one God, you try to follow the one correct way of living and consider one ideal for behavior as superior to all others. Understand? You don't understand."

Nikki shook her head.

"OK, what's the worst sin you can think of?"

Nikki hesitated, undecided whether disobeying her parents or lying was worse. "Telling a lie," she said at last.

"OK, telling a lie is a sin, according to the Ten Commandments. But what if there is a right time to tell a lie, a good time, when telling a lie will save someone's life or do some good? What about keeping a secret? That's a kind of lie, isn't it? If I tell you a secret that you promise not to tell, and then your mother or father asks you to tell, what do you do?"

Nikki glanced at her mother, who looked distressed. "This is why Pekka doesn't like me coming here," she started, but Nikki's aunt shushed her again.

"You see, Nikki, if you have one God, he rules like a king. He demands we do things his way, and only his way. It's undemocratic, when you think about it. Other religions recognize more than one divine power at work in the world, like the ancient Greeks with all their gods and goddesses, nymphs, demigods, daimons—they imagined a whole world of spirit beings! If different gods can determine what is good, you can have secrets and tell lies when it's the right thing to do, and in that case telling a lie can be holy. Do you understand? I could tell you secrets, now, about your mother—"

"All right, Meg!" her mother had interrupted, and her aunt stopped, only patting Nikki on the head and giving her such a look.

Now with her new eyes Nikki looked back. Had Meg's words portended the secret Rose hinted of? The notion that monotheism was only one way of imagining spirit was one more feather on the scale; she had always remembered those words. As she grew she read more, until she felt the weight on her, tipping her into understanding at last that the problem with Christianity was not that it was wrong, but that it said everyone else was.

Another childhood memory came back to her: Once she had brought home a book of wonderful stories of gods and goddesses, half-human, half-animal creatures full of magic and power. Her mother took the thin picture book from her and turned it over, examining the title.

"I wonder why it says 'gods,'" her mother remarked. "There's only one God."

And Nikki, all of ten years old, catching a glimpse of her mother's quickly averted eyes, heard her saying words that in her heart she did not believe. Yet while her own mother had to be tricked into revealing those truths she actually believed (Nikki was later to learn), Aunt Meg was strong-willed, upsetting her sister Carol by swirling other perspectives like a wand trailing colored streams before Nikki's amazed eyes. Meg had dyed her hair red and kept a small bookshop where she told fortunes and gave tarot readings. The shop was filled with curiosities and strange smells; the few times she visited, Nikki found herself falling into a walking daze in her aunt's shop. Tasseled shawls and wall hangings of brocade covered the narrow space; overhead a pink bulb behind a leaded-glass shade glowed like rosy flesh.

Slanting wood bookcases held dusty books against the walls, and tables were piled with various occult paraphernalia for sale: tarot decks and Ouija boards; figurines of witches and Merlins; a bowl of multicolored glass beads; silver earrings in the shape of tiny animal figures; masks and scarves and long capes of dark-blue velvet.

On a broad, flat table made of worn pine planks lay a black runner on which sat a crystal ball. Nikki was fascinated with the orb, always hoping to see something like her future life inside, but any time she drew close (when no one else was looking) she saw only a distorted reflection of herself in curved space.

A creased old tarot deck waited mutely beside the ball, and there sat a small bowl where her aunt burned herbs and spices, an act that used to puzzle and intrigue Nikki; aromatherapy, she now knew.

And there was Fergus the parrot quietly sitting on his perch, colors all adazzle while he lived unconscious of his gorgeous beauty, like a mute sunset. Fergus talked from time to time, although not when spoken to but when he felt like it. Rocking back and forth, clamping and unclamping his talons on the wood perch, he exuded an endearing nervousness, as if frightened no one would like him. "Cards!" he screeched and "Ball!" he cried from his perch, set between two tall bookcases. He was half-hidden and so quiet most of the time in the shadows, a dark green smudge on the wall, that when he did speak new customers would jump a mile. Sometimes he exploded with words he seemed to have made up, like "Ganch!" and "Athane!"

The phone rang and rang; still no answer. Nikki was restless, prowling the house for a time, going to the refrigerator and standing at it, staring at nothing. Nothing to eat. She reached and poured herself another glass of wine, carried it around the house. She realized she had been standing once again for a long time at the fireplace, in front of her mother's painting of Halibut Point. She shook herself and drank off her wine, then in a flurry of sudden activity grabbed her purse and swished out the back door.

She drove slowly down winding Route 1A along the coast fifteen miles south of Gloucester, finally into the old New England witch town. Nikki hadn't been to downtown Salem in years. The old place had been spruced up, Main Street lined with cute stores. Nikki drove past the witch museum and Laurie Cabot's storefront, past the tourist shops advertising Salem as the "Witch Capital of the World," past the endless silhouettes of conical-hatted crones riding broomsticks across the face of the moon. It was big business. How could it be dangerous to be a witch these days? The revolution had been institutionalized, Nikki thought, corporate America had taken Wicca over, making it into a tee-shirt slogan to lure Sunday afternoon suburbanites looking for a safe thrill.

But somewhere behind the safe wall there must lie a truth. Nikki drove two more blocks and turned left, keeping her eye out for her aunt's store. Parking between a Mercedes and a Volvo, she got out and stood scanning up and down the street for her aunt's shop.

Up—no, down to the right, she remembered now. No sign except the small painted letters on the glass front announcing her Aunt Meg's fortunetelling. Spotting the green glass reflecting pedestrians, she walked toward it. She stopped before the door to look it over; same as it had always been. Same lettering proclaiming:

MADAME CLEVES' PALM READING

Other lines announced:

FORTUNES TOLD
TAROT, ASTRAL READINGS
HERBAL POTIONS

Of course—the name!—she had forgotten! The chest in the basement—maybe it was Aunt Meg's. Was it possible her aunt really was a Druid, and there was something to what Rose had said? Nikki realized she had no idea what a Druid was, except for a vague recollection from Caesar's *Commentaries*. "Simulacra," she mouthed the word. Burning human sacrifices in wicker simulacra. And something about oak trees. Was Merlin a Druid? Or had Rose gotten it all wrong? She was tough but not always smart. Could she have meant "witch" instead?

Nikki turned the pitted door knob as the door squealed open. No need for a bell. She held her bag close to her body, stepping into the cool, dark interior. Black curtains hung across the glass front; a dim amber light glowed from somewhere up high, near the torn and rusted tin ceiling.

The store was much as Nikki remembered—only dustier. You could tell it was an old person's room, for things had not been moved in a long time. Everything had settled into its place, like a house settling into the ground. The same crystal ball, same deck of tarot cards lay upon the same black cloth. The glass cases were the same, and the top of one of them, where the old cash register still sat, was cracked and badly taped with beige strapping tape. The same bundle of blackbird feathers hung high up on the rear wall, bound with a leather thong.

Above the register was a newer sign that read:

EAR AND BODY PIERCING

Time invaded—even here!

From the rear came a shuffling, as Nikki turned to wait for her aunt to appear through the limp dark curtain that separated the front of the store from the private area. Behind a beaded curtain her aunt lived with her microwave, hot plate, and single bed. Back there, Nikki recalled, shelves ran floor to ceiling filled with jars of various sizes and shapes. Some of them held strange green liquids; others, hardened and blackened things that made Nikki shudder.

It was a little like her mother's pantry, Nikki reminisced, full of jars of herbs and potions. Except that her mother's jars had seemed more domestic, less threatening.

The curtain was pushed back by a long-fingered, black-nailed hand that trembled slightly, and Nikki's Aunt Meg appeared in the doorway, dressed in a black shift and black soft slippers. Long strands of red and silver beads hung from the old woman's neck, clicking softly against her ample belly and hard, full hips. Meg pushed her straggly red hair back, squinting.

"Hello, Aunt Meg," Nikki said, trying to sound light. Her words echoed dully in the thick room. "It's Nikki."

For a moment Meg stood still. She bore the remains of a strong, clear face, her brow high, eyes set wide, nose prominent without being long. A mole just above the left side of her mouth gave her a rakish expression. Her jaw line was jowly, coming to a delicate curve under her small chin. Her tired violet eyes gazed from far back in her head.

Actually, Meg's features carried the remnants of Nikki's mother's looks—the same large eyes and rounded cheekbones. The same soft mouth with its expressively curved lips, although her aunt's mouth hung open a bit at the bottom in expectation. Nikki wondered whether she had awakened the old woman.

But as Meg shook herself her eyes cleared, their violet focusing a bright beam on Nikki. Her mouth tightened a bit into a wry smile, not without warmth.

"Nikki," she replied, and her voice was a croak in the silent, dusty room.

"How are you, Auntie?" Nikki asked, leaning forward.

Meg breathed deeply. "Fine, fine. What a funeral, eh?—the old bastard!" she muttered, chuckling hoarsely.

"Want a cup of tea? How are you?" Meg continued, coughing to clear her throat. She turned and dropped the curtain.

Knowing it was the signal to follow, Nikki skirted the long table, glancing once at the crystal ball before lifting the curtain and passing into the back room.

It, too, was the same as she remembered, although now plaster was falling from cracks in the walls. The place looked like an old person, in slow decline toward death, little fissures showing here and there. It needed a sprucing up.

Nikki looked through the same old beaded curtain into the rear of the room at the pathetic single bed, made but not neatly. There were beads missing from some of the curtain strands.

Meg went over to the stained cast iron sink, filling two mugs she took from a rusty metal shelf overhead. Her hands shook slightly as she set each mug in the microwave and, flicking the timer to two minutes, she pulled down a jar and unscrewed the top. The scent of tea filled the room, jostling the smell of stale Camels.

"Your damn father dead at last! Pekka and his drinking! Pekka and his drinking!" Meg said loudly in a half singsong voice.

"Well, he's gone," Nikki said hesitantly. "At the end he only talked about ghosts in the house—"

"He should have!" Meg cackled. "He should have," she repeated more softly. "What with my mother and your mother haunting the place! That house—get sold?"

Reaching into the hip pocket of her black shift, Meg pulled out a crumpled pack of Camels and a long black lighter in the shape of a bat with indrawn wings. She pulled a cigarette from the pack and stuffed the crumpled wad back in her pocket, flicked the wing of the bat so that its mouth spat flame, touched and drew deeply, holding the cigarette between yellow-stained fingers.

"No—I mean, yes. To me."

Meg turned to her. "To you?" A smile crept over her wrinkled face, a dim echo of Nikki's mother. Meg's was shrewder, with a glint of much knowing in her eyes and a hard worn smile that twisted around a sardonic sense of the follies of humankind.

"Well, there's something in you, then," Meg declared softly, taking a long pull from her cigarette.

When the microwave chimed, Meg went about making tea, cigarette hanging from her mouth, blinking in the smoke like a jazz pianist. Nikki cleared her throat quietly, sitting down at the round table that stood between the bed alcove and the sink. The ceiling-high shelves were the same, still crammed with old jars with strange dried-out potions. The old wood chair creaked beneath her.

"Ball!" cried a voice from the corner, making Nikki jump. As Meg croaked a laugh, Nikki peered into the gloomy corner where a splendid plumed parrot rocked self-consciously on his perch.

Meg brought the two steaming mugs to the table. "Fergus Jr.—I think," she explained, nodding at the bird. "Milk or sugar?" Nikki shook her head as Meg sat opposite, regarding her niece through narrowed eyes.

"You know that house should have come to me," Meg explained, sipping while keeping her eyes on Nikki. She rested her cigarette in a purple glass ashtray. "It's been in the family—I mean our family, the women—for a long time. Did you know that?"

Nikki nodded. "I found that out," she agreed slowly. "I discovered a box with the name 'Cleves' carved on it, along with a family tree that shows this woman 'Anne Cleves' as our ancestor."

Meg nodded. "And the brooch?"

"You know about that?"

"Oh, sure. It belonged to Anne, they say."

Nikki bent to sip the jasmine tea, scalding her tongue. She breathed in the perfume, and it made her feel good.

Meg studied Nikki, then sat back shaking her head, brushing her stringy red hair off her face. "I look like an old fool, I know." She sighed, picked up her cigarette and drew again. "It's been too long. Even—even fortunetellers get old," she concluded, slapping her knee and getting up. "Think I'll have some sugar."

Going to the shelves, she pulled down a small yellow porcelain sugar bowl with a bent spoon sticking out, brought it to the table and sat.

"How are your sisters?" she asked, spooning sugar and stirring.

"Fine. Cynthia is back in Chicago with Todd and their daughter. Rachel is still on her mountain in West Virginia. Jane threatened to move back, but she stayed in Florida with her twenty kids and five husbands. They were thinking of moving to the house."

"How did you get it?"

"What did you mean that there's something in me?" Nikki countered.

"I asked first." Meg's eyes were thoughtful.

"No one else wanted it. I didn't know you felt you had a claim—"

"Hell! A claim! You're a lawyer—you know how much legal status a feeling has. Tradition, heritage—what do they count these days? I wasn't named in the will, that's all. So much for a claim. Your father certainly wasn't going to leave the house to me."

"But you feel it's rightfully yours?"

"Why are you here?" Meg asked suddenly, squinting at her.

Nikki hesitated. "I asked you first." She regarded her old auntie, remembering how much fear and fascination she used to experience coming here as a girl. She never visited alone, always with her mother, and it wasn't often they came. Three or four times the whole time she was growing up. Each time Nikki played in the front room with Rachel, their quiet games playing fortuneteller and bookseller punctuated by Fergus' squawks. Their mother went into the back to talk with Aunt Meg. Grateful for her mother's protection, Nikki had preferred that her aunt stay in the back. And yet her fascination for her aunt had been strong. An independent woman, living on her own, running her own business, smoking, drinking when she wanted, traveling. Her world was at once faintly threatening and faintly inspiring to young Nikki.

Her aunt had grown less threatening as Nikki had grown, until Nikki came to like Meg's hard-edged independence. In a way, Nikki discovered, she resembled her aunt more than her own mother, particularly now that she could stand up to Meg and not be intimidated.

"I asked you first, Aunt Meg," Nikki repeated. "Do you feel the house is yours?"

Meg wrinkled her mouth, shaking her head. "I'm just talking. It's only an empty shell. It's all gone now, anyway—all the history."

"What history?"

"Of our family home. The house belonged to your grandmother's grandmother—did you know that? No, of course not. Your little fool of a mother wouldn't have told you girls that."

Nikki winced and Meg saw.

"She had promise, that girl. My own younger sister. The three of us—we were fine in the house. Until your father came along—"

"But—I always thought—you never liked my mother," Nikki interjected confusedly.

Meg leaned close. "Didn't like?" she snorted. "She was my sister. Of course we were completely unlike. I was embarrassed by her slowness and the way she was always creeping about like a mouse. Her unwillingness to embrace her own strength, to live the life she was supposed to live—"

"As a Druid—or a witch?" Nikki asked. A clock stopped in the room as the two women regarded each other.

"Ball!" cried Fergus Jr.

Nikki was frozen, but Meg was the first to crack. She smiled slowly, a gleam sparkling in her tired eyes. She reached for her cigarette and drew deeply, blowing a long stream of smoke.

"Did your mother ever tell you about the time when she was twelve and I was fifteen? We were different—very different—from the other schoolgirls. Your mother couldn't stand being different—that's why she married your father. He seemed so normal to her, at least at first. Rumors always surrounded us girls—especially about our mother. Everyone in Gloucester thought she was strange. In fact, most people called her a witch, although they had no idea what they were saying. I liked it being different. It meant I didn't have to abide by all the stupid rules everyone else thought applied to us all. I was willing to put up with whispers and snickers as the price of being able to make my own rules. It was harder for your mother, though.

"We both used to get harassed, but your mother was smaller and prettier than I, so she attracted more attention—especially from the bullies. Some of the boys who lived near the quarries started following her one day as she was walking home from school. She was such a little thing, and didn't feel she had the right to protect herself. We never walked home together, but I happened to come along and saw the whole thing unfold. They were big boys, four of them, with their rough clothes and rough hands. They had waited for your mother where she and I walked on the way home, near the woods that are all cut down now, up toward Dogtown. One minute I could see them horsing around—teasing your mother, grabbing at her, pulling her hair—and the next minute they surrounded her and hustled her off deep into the Dogtown woods.

"So I followed them," Meg shrugged, setting her cigarette down. "They had put their hands over your mother's mouth and held her fast so she couldn't escape. They took your mother to a place where no one went, except your grandmother and your mother and I used to go there to collect herbs. They threw her down on the ground and started to go after her. There were four of them! Four! They pushed her dress up, and the biggest one started to climb on top of her. Can you imagine!" Meg demanded, her eyes boring into Nikki's.

"Why are you making me imagine?" Nikki asked, breathlessly horrified by the image.

"Because it's important—it's what men do," Meg said grimly. She picked up her cigarette, clamped it between her teeth and drew.

"What did you do?"

Meg shrugged. "I grabbed a thick branch while I was following, uttering some prayers your grandmother had taught me for bringing strength into my arms. I took care of them, and your mother and I ran home."

"How did you do that?" Nikki's eyes widened. She remembered when growing up the boys, the rough hands of the boys and their smoky breaths, their tongues burning in her mouth, in the back seat of dark cars parked out near the rocks where the waves thundered in the summer nights. She wanted them to; she didn't want them to! How she had wanted to shout "Stop!" Listening intently, Nikki breathed hard.

"I beat them, of course," Meg said simply, stubbing her cigarette out. She smiled. "Beat them good, too. Beat the shit out of them. I cracked the big one who was on top of your mother right in his thick skull. He fell like a stone. I went after the others, breaking an arm or two. They ran like mice. We ran the other way, me pulling your mother to her feet and dragging her along, her crying and hitting at me like I had been the one attacking her. They never bothered her again."

"Then if you loved my mother, why did you always act like you hated her?"

"She told you that?"

"It's the impression all of us got."

Meg thought a moment. "On the way home your mother said something. She had been panting but stopped crying finally and spoke. 'It's because we're different,' she said. 'It will always be this way.' I slapped her, hard, making a dark red mark on her cheek. She was wrong, of course, but she believed that. I hated her then, because she was weak—and wrong. Wrong!"

Nikki took a breath. "Was she attacked because you were witches?"

"We weren't witches," Meg shook her head. "It was because we were girls," she finished, a hard edge to her voice.

"But later you hated her for marrying."

"I didn't hate her for marrying! I thought she was weak, that's all. She never fought back. Even with that boy on top of her, she just lay there, passive as a scared rabbit in a trap."

"But my father—before he became an alcoholic. From what my mother used to say, he was very sweet."

"Nikki—two of those boys were his brothers."

Nikki sat up.

"Now what's this about Druids and witches?" Meg asked, smiling wryly.

Nikki's head swirled—she needed time to think! Were those boys her own two uncles who had died young?

Meg leaned over and patted her hand. "You think I'm mean and hard, I know—all of you girls were afraid of me. I am tough," Meg smiled. "Had to be, to live in my world on my own. Maybe I was jealous your mother had your father, even though in some ways that made it harder for her. Your mother—she just wanted a normal life, had a passion for it. When she married, she submerged the better part of her nature—out of fear. Me, I wanted the moon—demanded the moon and nothing less! Now look at me," she shrugged, indicating the room. "Maybe your mother was right after all. *This* is my house, Nikki. Not the one you live in now. That hasn't been mine since I was a girl."

"You are a witch, then," Nikki spoke slowly, her head foggy and confused.

Meg shook her head, smiling. "I know the shop makes it look like I am—but actually, no. Nowadays the term 'witch' is used as a catchall, and it doesn't apply correctly to what I am—or what your mother was." She thought a minute, drawing on her cigarette. "Remember that time you came here with your little friend? I caught the pride—as well as the fear—in your eyes, heard it in your voice. Your aunt a real witch in Salem!" Meg chuckled.

"No—I mean something different—more," Nikki struggled for the words.

As Meg studied her for a long moment, Nikki noticed the gleam return to her old aunt's eye. Nikki had always thought of it as the Keefe gleam, from her mother's family. She started. Or was it the Cleves gleam?

"What made you come?" Meg asked softly.

"Rose Eveless," Nikki said.

"Ah," Meg sighed deeply, her whole body relaxing. The room was very still. "And just what could that old hag want now? Is she still trying to find Anne's journal?"

"She insists I have to find it for her—if I want to see—her son again."

"Yes, her son," Meg smiled, tapping her cigarette ash and eyeing Nikki.

Nikki squirmed. "He—got hurt."

"So I heard."

"You know about that?" Nikki was startled.

"The crystal ball reveals all," Meg intoned, gesturing toward the front room. Her voice shifted. "What's going on between you and Rose's son?"

"I don't want to talk about that," Nikki shook her head. "I can't believe what I've done."

"So I'm gathering. Hurt bad?"

Nikki hesitated. "I'll work that out. I came to see you about Rose's story. Is she right that there is a journal?"

Meg nodded, pulling on her cigarette. "There is a journal—so the legend says. Buried somewhere—we believe—in Gloucester, where Anne Cleves lived in the late 1600s. Everyone's searched for it—I spent time myself trying to find it. Guess I'm not the one to discover it," she said wistfully.

"Then it's true... But what do you mean when you say you're not a witch?"

"The truth is that your mother and I—and you, thereby—are descended from a long line of members of a tribe originally from Ireland known as the Raven clan. Not witches—rather, a group of healers, seers, and shape-shifters descended from Druids. Not Druids exactly, but something of our own. We share certain traditions with Druids, but we're too far descended to uphold the same practices. I have friendships with witches who belong to covens and so forth, but we're a more underground clan."

"So I'm a member of this—Raven tribe?" Nikki could hardly believe it.

"I suppose," Meg puffed. "Fourteen generations back we can count to Anne Cleves. Not every generation learned our traditions and practiced them. It's more like a family tradition," she chuckled hoarsely. "Some generations—both women and men practiced. Others—*pfft!*" She made a small explosion with her free hand. "Members have been homemakers, merchants, fishermen, some even able to do magic."

"Magic?" Nikki echoed doubtfully. "Why did my mother keep this from my sisters and me?"

Peering long into her niece's face, Meg at last stood up heavily and went into the sleeping alcove. Nikki heard the jingle of keys and the turn of a lock. Emerging from the alcove, Meg set a thick, dusty envelope in front of Nikki.

"Open it," Meg nodded, sitting.

Nikki looked at her, opened the flap and took out a thin journal of cheap red cardboard. Turning to the first page and recognizing at once her mother's fine, neat handwriting, she began to read:

March 21, 1983

My dear, darling daughters,

I begin this work that I should have begun many years ago. I can find no excuses. When the blue-faced goddess comes for me to ask what I have done with my time as a mortal, whether I fulfilled my task, I will have to hide.

Nikki choked. *"Goddess?"* She looked up at her aunt, who sat with a Cheshire smile observing her over a smouldering cigarette.

"She left it for whoever came for it," Meg declared. She shrugged. "You've come."

Nikki flipped the book closed, regarded the cover, turned it over and looked at the back, as if by tilting the thing back and forth she might divine its origins. Could it really be from her mother? She opened it again softly and read.

No, such thoughts only deepen my regrets. Down to work, then…

I confess to having been afraid. It is ironic and without any excuse that I who have been given so many daughters should have concealed from you the truths of your heritage.

So now after all these years of having raised you four without revealing my secret, I trust that you will go to your Aunt Meg and receive this record of what I should have been teaching you and telling you all these years. This journal of mine is for you, my daughters Jane, Cynthia, Rachel and, lastly, my own Nikki. I hope you will forgive me after you read it, and that it will help you to decide about your lives.

I can tell now that I will die before your father. Hateful man, whom I love so much! It is his fault that—but no, I can't blame him. I must bear this cross myself since it was I who decided, by not deciding, never to reveal your history to you. Perhaps your father is only the outer expression of my soul, and so is the visible indication of my own cowardice.

An old saying of our tribe goes that the person you love, you give part of your soul to for keeping. Powerful healers hide their souls in many places in order not to be overcome. It is a dangerous thing to love, for that is one of the few areas of life, or of the soul, where humans have little power. It is a rule of magic that you must keep the effects away from yourself. If you give the essential part of yourself to someone for safekeeping, there is no guarantee that person will care for it well. The old goddess of love is more powerful, I think, than any potion. The ancient goddesses Hecate and Aphrodite were sisters. We may invoke them, but once they arrive they cannot be controlled nor their effects predicted. The Morrigan is goddess of love and war in our ancient tradition and so in a sense unites Hecate and Aphrodite.

Perhaps the goddess has preserved me thus far that I might explain further. May Father Owen and Jesus forgive me.

In our basement is a box carved with the name "Cleves" containing useful information. It holds as well an object of mystery that has been passed down from mother to daughter for fourteen generations. That is the emerald star brooch, with one point broken off. Legend has it that it belonged to our ancestor Anne Cleves and that one day her lover will return with the missing piece, so that the brooch may be made whole again.

You know, of course, that our house belonged originally to my mother, but you don't know that it had belonged earlier to her own mother—and to her mother's mother before that. Your grandmother's grandmother built this house with money left her by her husband, Jeremiah Spooner. Although she went by the name "Edith Clinton," her real name—as is my real name and yours—was Cleves. Remember this name; it is your true name.

The box contains the family tree on the matrilineal side, going back to the 17th century when your ancestor Anne Cleves first bore the name. She was not born to the name—no women in our family were born to it—but she carried it within herself as we all must, for it is the name that links us down through the centuries. Her name appears at the top of the family tree. In actuality we do not know the name she legally bore; hence, her daughter is listed only by her first name "Diana." From her onwards the tree records the legal names of our ancestors. For Diana married Samuel Hawkins, and her daughter Rebecca bears the name "Hawkins."

Yet through all these generations the name of Cleves has stayed with us, cleaving to us, in a sense, and giving us our identity.

And what identity is that?

Your ancestor Anne Cleves was a shape-shifter, a healer, and a seer,

descended from Irish Druids and taught by them, as am I, in my own way—
and thereby might each of you be, in your own ways, if you so wish.

Nikki drew a sharp breath, looking back at Meg. "So the story is true," she said
with wonder and awe.

Meg nodded.

"Then I, too—?"

"You, too," answered her aunt. "If you choose, that is."

Nikki was pleased and angered, elated and maddened. She was a member of a
tribe—the Raven tribe. The sound, the sense of it, the belonging—she felt a power
seeping into her that thrilled in her veins. Never again to be weak, she vowed, never
again to bow to powers she hated and warred with—to men, to the patriarchy, to the
dark powers. Never again! She would inhale the new power and grow strong. Already
she felt her lungs expanding with the spirit.

Yet her mother had been anything but powerful, her other mind reminded her.
Her mother? Powerful? A magician? Impossible! Out of the question! That chubby
little woman? That little nothing, cowering and martyring herself to her tyrant husband? That short lady, forever baking Finnish coffee cake for her husband even though
she never touched the stuff herself? The one who never made a peep about all the
abuse she suffered? How could she have had even hidden power?

Nikki continued reading silently.

We are not witches, even though it is said that Anne was tried and
possibly burned as a witch. Her story, too, is part of the mystery; we do
not know what became of her. We believe she kept a record, for she could
write, but any such history has never been found. We know she lived in
Dogtown long before it was called Dogtown, when all of Gloucester fit in
the area now called Dogtown.

Mother told me that Anne's journal has been lost for hundreds of years,
and that it was most likely buried somewhere in Dogtown, protected by
spells.

The magic your ancestors practiced was natural magic, conducted by
means of herbs and intuition. They were doctors, midwives, even dentists on
occasion, providing remedies for premenstrual symptoms and for the pains
of childbirth. My mother spoke frequently of an "Otherworld," as the Raven
tribe called it, but I never saw it, and so I cannot speak about it—unless it
is, as I think, the world that exists alongside this visible one.

Much of our lore has been lost with Anne Cleves' testimony, which
would reconnect us with our past; perhaps one of you will find her lost
journal. I cannot help you from where I am now, I do not think. For the
afterlife I have never put much faith in, even though I have been a practicing Catholic and a believer in Jesus. Maybe I am wrong, and you will feel

my presence. Certainly I have felt my own mother's presence in this house. And my grandmother's.

If you wonder how I was able to become a Catholic and raise you girls Catholic, yet still be a member of our tribe, the answer is mixed: I decided after you were born, Jane, not to practice magic anymore. And there never seemed, in my mind, to be much difference between the original Father God our Raven tribe honored and the Christian God, nor between the Great Mother and Mary.

You girls think of me, I know, as a horrible model of a wife and mother for never speaking up to your father. Remember when you used to ask me what I wanted for my birthday or anniversary, how I would answer, "Just some peace"?

You must forgive me for my passivity—I ask only that you now understand the words that follow as my true voice. Because there is a more important reason why the Cleves' descendants write their journals than simply to transfer information from one generation to the next. What is more vital is that we may allow our own voices to speak, and so to enter the story.

By writing you write a story, becoming a character in that story. It alters you fundamentally, changing your nature—and this just may be the magic that we practice.

As you know, I was born in our house. Although you girls were born in Addison Hospital down the road, I brought you home right away. Because the doctors didn't want new mothers to breast-feed, I refused to stay in the hospital. They forced formula on our babies, telling us that breast milk was bad for babies. Can you imagine? Mother thought I was a fool to go into the hospital in the first place, insisting she knew better than any male doctor how to deliver a baby. I did at least have a midwife for each delivery.

Mother repeatedly accused me of denying her powers. Maybe she was right. From the moment she told me when I was eight that she was a magician, which meant I could be, too, as her daughter, I have always had a resistance to the idea. I guess my rebelliousness came out by having my babies in the hospital. How angry she used to get with me! Accusing me of making the mistake of rebelling against her instead of your father, as I should have.

"You'll never get anywhere or amount to anything," she used to yell at me. "Look at you, you're no Cleves. You don't believe. You're the slave of some slob of a Finn who drinks all day long."

But your grandmother didn't know how much I loved your father; she had forgotten how handsome and charming he was at first. She never understood that after he began drinking heavily, it was my fault as much as his, and I felt I owed him something for that. Besides, any advice my mother gave me regarding your father always led me to do the opposite.

I suppose that's why I never gave you girls much guidance. Maybe that's why I've waited until now to tell you about your occult family heritage, for I never wanted to interfere or to impose my will. You see, my own mother was so good at that, I vowed not to be like her. She pushed your grandfather around, and he padded around after her carrying her purse, afraid of her—how I hated that! Mother was always independent, sure of herself, very articulate. She had mapped a plan for her life and a plan for raising her two daughters, which she stuck to. No one I knew dared argue with her, she was so smart and so quick. She could be mean with her tongue—and often had sharp words for me. So I went in the opposite direction from her. Maybe I went too far.

My paternal grandparents who came from Ireland both died young, leaving my father, Stephen Keefe, to grow up an only child. After he married Mother they had my older sister Meg and me. In those days—at least where we came from—you pretty much had as many children as you could. Even though having girls seemed to run on my mother's side, Father wanted a son.

"Do you think we'll have more children?" I remember him asking Mother one day. In the middle of sweeping the kitchen floor, he had suddenly stopped and looked up at my mother. I was about ten at the time, holding the dustpan for him. It was as if he had suddenly figured out how to say what was on his mind.

I looked quickly at her. I was close to my father, and I already was feeling sorry for him for even asking my mother—the queen—about having more children.

She raised her eyebrows a bit as she always did when she was displeased. Maybe you girls remember when she lived in the upstairs bedroom at the back. Since she never wasted words, when she spoke, you listened. She looked at Father for a minute, as he and I held our breaths, then replied, "That's my concern."

That was all she said.

Father laughed weakly, trying to make a joke out of it while flicking a smile at me. "Don't you think I have something to do with having children?" he asked her.

I watched her hard face. "Not anymore," she answered.

The year before she had told my sister and me that she was a member of the Raven tribe, explaining that we could join too, if we wanted. For some time, then, in my childish way I had been trying to figure out what it meant to be a Cleves, which meant joining the Raven tribe. Suddenly it all was clear to me, listening to Mother reply to Father that day in the kitchen.

I knew vaguely she had done something to her body so she would never have any more children, no matter how many years she and my father might sleep in the same bed.

Wondering what she had done without actually knowing scared me. Explaining to us when we were young the facts of life—I was not yet eight— Mother had been very frank with my sister and me. But for a child, having information she doesn't understand is very different from understanding something she can experience directly in her own body.

Though I was curious, I didn't dare ask. I never asked Mother about anything, waiting instead for her to tell me whatever she thought important. I wondered whether she had made a potion out of the herbs she grew in the back yard. Or had she taken her little knife that she carried about and cut something out of herself, maybe even her own womb? My heart raced to imagine such a possibility.

Amazement flared in me to realize I might exercise the same control over myself when the time came. The idea that such matters could be taken care of was an opening into a mysterious world.

Meanwhile, my father was replying.

"Maybe it was a difficult experience having the girls," he offered. I could see he was completely outside the circle. Mother had told us that only females could be members of the circle. I believed it then, although I know now that's not true.

As Mother looked at Father again, suddenly I could see so much in her face! I saw her anger and her condescension toward him. It made me hate her to see her treat my father like a child.

"Having my daughters was quite easy," she said matter-of-factly. I felt she was on the verge of screaming—strange, considering I had never heard her scream before. She was a cold woman.

"Why did you insist on having only a midwife here with you?" he asked, treading on thin ice. "And why did you send me away?"

"Because it made it easier to bear them. Your male doctors would have hurt me, and I did not want that."

"Why not try to have a boy? I would love a son," my father asked.

"Because I will not have a son," she answered. "I will not," she finished, in such a way that my father dropped the subject and went back to his sweeping.

As I said, it was the year before that I had my initiation into the Raven tribe, which meant accepting what it meant to be a Cleves. Father was away visiting relatives in Boston for a few days. I now think my mother sent him off intentionally. Mother sat Meg and me down in the living room and stood in front of us.

"I have something to tell you girls, but I don't want any nonsense from you," she began. "Does either one of you know what magicians and herbalists are?"

Meg said nothing. I glanced at her, waiting. She was nearly four years older, much taller and bigger than I. She wouldn't say a word, just sat there sullenly like she always did. I was always the one making a joke, trying to lighten things up. I couldn't stand for there to be tension, and so I spoke up.

"They are ugly old women witches from Dogtown who make potions and put curses on little boys and girls walking by their houses." I smiled hopefully, thinking I had answered the question right.

Looking down at me, Mother nodded, lips tight; I could hear her breathe through her nostrils. The smell of boiled vegetables and beef wafting in from the kitchen made me think more of dinner than of her question.

You see, I used to play witches and dragons with my girlfriends up in Dogtown. We ran around, much as you girls did, up and down the old roads that run through the forest, hiding from each other, scaring each other with stories of the old women who used to live there—Thomasine Younger, Luce George, Judy Rhines.

We would find the ruins of their houses and walk carefully down into the old cellar holes, now marked out along Dogtown Road, expecting to find treasure. We had all heard stories of the old women who lived up there after the town of Gloucester moved to where it is now, down in the harbor. The center of Gloucester used to be right behind our house along Dogtown Road, up on the hill where there was good land for farming. Some time around 1800 the town was moved down to the harbor, for the fishermen's sake. The poor people left behind, mostly widows and single women, became inhabitants of Dogtown—called "Dogtown" because the women left behind often kept dogs for protection.

These women whose names we knew were our invisible companions. In the way of children, we imagined them as powerful and cruel magicians rather than as actual humans possessing knowledge of healing and spells. Just as the judges and good people of Salem were possessed when they saw innocent girls and women as dangerous demons.

So I assumed I knew perfectly well what a magician was.

"You're a little fool, Carol," Mother retorted, so that I nearly started crying. "A well-intentioned little idiot, just like your father. Meg, do you have any idea?"

Not only was Meg more cautious than I, but with her dark hair and eyes she looked a lot like our mother. I was the fair one, taking after our father.

"You're a magician because you're a Cleves," Meg answered slowly, staring steadily into our mother's eyes.

Thinking that now Meg was going to catch it, I leaned away. Neither Meg nor I much liked Mother, although each of us for different reasons. Meg behaved toward her with a kind of surliness that scared me. I was always afraid Meg was going to catch a licking from Mother. Strangely enough, Mother never did spank Meg, at least not that I saw. She spanked me often enough. When I was little I thought it was because she liked Meg better, that they were closer. Now I know otherwise.

Towering over us girls while standing with hands on her hips, dressed in an elegant black dress like always, Mother actually smiled at Meg! This was a woman who almost never smiled. But she smiled! It had a kind of secret to it, that smile, and I never saw her smile that way again after that day, not ever.

"How do you know that, Meg?" Mother asked.

"I've read. You're a Druid. Carol's got no idea what's going on. But I can tell—I've known for a long time," she finished with a combination of pride and a little disdain in her voice. I was amazed. Meg was eleven at the time.

"What have you read?" Mother again asked.

"Books at the library and from the historical society," Meg shrugged, as if gleaning such knowledge were natural. I stared wide-eyed at her. She was always the smartest person in her class at school—far smarter than I ever was—and I had no idea what she was talking about.

Mother kept her smile. "That's very good. What have you learned?"

"There is a mysterious family from Gloucester named 'Cleves.' I think they have nothing to do with those old women who used to live in Dogtown," she sneered at me.

"What made you want to read up on this?" Mother pursued.

"You're a Druid," Meg answered.

"Yes, but what makes you think I am one?"

"Your herbs. The way you mix them. How you've always given us herbal remedies for colds and flu. I used to show the kids at school the little hard candies you make for us, but I stopped when they got suspicious. Just their suspicions of the kind of medicine I was taking made me realize you were different. You only have certain kinds of friends, all women, who are odd. I know you've decided not to have more children, and that somehow you can control that."

"How do you know that?" our mother asked mildly.

"Because you haven't had any more. Other mothers just keep having children."

"Not all of them," Mother countered.

Meg shrugged. Mother sat down across from us. "It's true that I am what you say. Both of you, because you are my daughters, are likewise descendants of Anne Cleves, who was a shape-shifter. According to family legend, she was able to change herself into an animal. I belong to a tribe, the Raven tribe, which you can both join if you choose. We are descended from Druids, though strictly speaking we are not Druids. I can teach you all the arts I learned from my mother, which she in turn learned from her mother. I can tell you the story of Anne Cleves, the first of our line, who lived here in Gloucester three hundred years ago. I can teach you how to make drops, liquids, and potions to heal illnesses."

"So we won't need doctors?" I asked.

"When have you ever gone to the doctor?" Mother countered.

She was right—we never had. Our father went in the face of Mother's ridicule. She referred to his faith in doctors as believing in a different religion, even though once I heard him reply that such doctors practiced science.

"Will you teach us the dark arts?" Meg asked.

Our mother stopped. "What do you know of them?"

"Only what I've read in books. They don't tell anything. I want to learn how to put spells on people, how to take revenge, how to protect myself so I'll never be in danger."

Mother looked uncomfortable for a moment. "I don't practice the dark arts. We Cleves are not witches—and I have no idea whether witches practice such things."

"But you can teach us, can't you?" my sister persisted.

"No—I don't know them, actually."

"Then Aunt Hannah will teach me," Meg answered confidently. Our mother's sister lived in Essex, alone in a house out on the marsh. I remember her as an exotic woman with long hair, very tall, taller than my mother, who wore robes and long beads of dark purple stones around her thick neck. She made my mother look conservative. Where my mother was quiet and firm, Hannah was emotional and vivid—you could never tell what she would do next. Her husband had died and left her money, she had no children and didn't work, instead traveled the world several times. Each time she returned, she would bring us girls presents from strange places.

"Your Aunt Hannah might tell you," Mother responded, "if you ask and she is willing. But you'll never learn all the knowledge you need from her. She's too inconsistent to make a good Cleves."

"Are you a good Cleves?" I asked, still stunned at hearing our mother was a magician.

"I'm not a bad one, though no one knows all the lore," our mother answered. "Except perhaps your great-grandmother Emer, who died long before either of you was born. And perhaps Anne Cleves—except no one knows what became of her journal, which could fill in the secrets we have lost."

"Can't you learn the secrets from other Cleves or from some old books?" Meg asked impatiently.

"Meg, you're rather insistent," Mother observed.

"Well, here you tell us you're a Druid descendant who can do magic, but then you say you don't know the dark arts and aren't interested in using those sorts of powers. If I'm going to join, I want to know it all—the spells and powers, including how to practice them." Seeing the determined pout on Meg's dark face, I was afraid of her then, of what she would become when she grew up. Already I could see her flying on a broomstick across the moon!

"Everything in time," Mother cautioned. "You must study, and it takes time to learn. As far as possessing certain powers, being a member of the Raven clan is not defined by using your powers but rather by choosing which powers to use. That is the key. I will teach you the Cleves code, handed down for centuries."

"Teach us now," Meg insisted, leaning forward.

Mother cleared her throat. "This involves sacred and secret words that must never be repeated to anyone, except to another Cleves. Before we begin, you must both swear that you will never tell." Mother looked darkly at us; we both nodded.

Then she rose and went into the kitchen. We could see her opening a drawer, taking out a box and opening it. She took from the box some herbs and cut them on a cutting board, placing them in a saucepan of water and striking a match to the gas. In a few moments the room was filled with an aromatic scent I had never smelled before, completely overwhelming the smell of cooking meat and vegetables. It was a strangely pleasant fragrance, making me think of dusty attics, and for some reason I imagined a crescent moon. The aroma filled me with a sense of relaxed well-being, sitting in the living room next to my sister. I now know this herbal scent as moonbane.

Soon Mother returned carrying the saucepan and her favorite small knife, a cloth draped over her forearm. She set the pan on our coffee table.

"Meg, come here," she called, as Meg immediately, eagerly, went to her. Already grown tall, Meg managed to hold her own while standing beside Mother, who held the knife. "Lean your head to the left," Mother directed; Meg did so without hesitation. Mother took the knife and with her free hand brushed Meg's long dark hair back away from her throat, raising the knife. I jumped up involuntarily, about to scream, but Mother glared at me. My heart pounding, I sat down again.

With a quick movement, my mother cut my sister below her right ear. She set the knife down, still holding Meg's hair back, dipped the cloth in the pan with her free hand, then applied the cloth to the fresh wound. During the entire ritual Meg didn't flinch, didn't move, didn't show she felt any pain. I saw her blink once, seeming to me to be glimpsing another world. She was calm, like she had been waiting a long time for this.

When Mother finished stanching the wound, she smiled that strange smile again and, leaning over, kissed Meg on the forehead. Meg turned to sit down next to me, a strange glistening look of knowing in her smiling eyes.

"Carol," Mother was saying. I turned to her with a shock, my face going white.

I began to shake my head, terrified.

"Do you not wish to join?" she asked, her voice soft and distant, as if she were chanting.

"Baby!" Meg taunted, turning to me. Her eyes were dark as coals all of a sudden.

"I don't know," I stammered. "I don't understand."

"This is but the first step," Mother replied. "Don't be a bigger fool than you already are. Becoming one of us is the way to overcome your natural passivity."

"I like being passive," I muttered, not at all sure what I was saying.

"Carol, joining means you never have to be beholden to a man. You can control them if you have a mind to, bend them to your will. Men cannot do this, only women can, and only Cleves women possess such power over men."

I stared at Mother, unable to answer. The only man in my life was my father, whom I adored and whom I had no thought of dominating, having no desire to become like Mother. Only many years later did I realize that she was wrong in wanting to dominate men. I now think that our greatest duty is to love, which means giving up the idea of dominating.

"I'M GOING OUT for some cigarettes," Meg exclaimed suddenly, rising. "You go on reading, and I'll be back later to answer your questions," she smiled.

"Aunt Meg," Nikki said softly and shyly. "Mother writes about you receiving some sort of cut from your mother as an initiation."

With a grunt Meg leaned toward Nikki, pulling her red hair back from the right side of her neck, showing Nikki what lay there. Nikki leaned politely and observed a brown circle.

"It's a mole," Nikki declared.

"Hmm," Meg grunted again, twisting her mouth around as she straightened up. She studied her wide-eyed niece. "Ridiculous, isn't it? Mother and her dramatics. I never heard of another initiation like that. She just had to make it hurt," Meg snorted.

"But—the world feels different to me now," Nikki whispered.

"Yes, it's exciting, isn't it?" Meg chuckled softly. Then, pulling her shawl about her and picking up a tiny black bag, she went out.

Nikki turned back to the journal, reflecting on her own relations with men. Men had always seemed inferior to her and quite easy to dominate, just by using a little of her seductive power. She had always been able to land any man she wanted. At least until Philip came along, who somehow threw aside all the ways with men she felt so secure with. Nothing seemed to work with him. As for acquiring special power over men—had her grandmother been speaking of putting spells on men in order to dominate them? That was something Nikki did everyday with the slightest flick of her finger, as second nature. But every woman she knew could do the same if she only wanted...

As it turned out, the old *Cosmopolitan* truism held: It didn't matter whether you were ugly or had a terrible body, you had only to know how to seduce and you could get any man. But all women were not magicians, clearly. Did she have some special power that she had all along been using, wholly unawares? Or was her grandmother referring to something completely different? Perhaps her grandmother had been simply trying to seduce her own daughter into following her? Then for the first time, and not the last, Nikki felt a hesitation about becoming a Cleves herself.

She flipped back to the part where her mother talked about writing her story and read: "By writing you write a story, becoming a character in that story." Reading her mother's story about undergoing an initiation was Nikki's own initiation of sorts, bringing a dawning awareness of herself as a Cleves. She realized with a start that she had been unconsciously putting herself in the place of her mother. That it was her own neck about to get cut with the ritual knife.

She continued reading, heart pounding:

It happened in a second. Mother was on me, Meg holding me by the hair, pulling my head down. They were around me, so that I could not see, as I began to kick and to yell at them. I heard Mother say, "Not to the right—to the left, Meg," then my head was yanked to the right, exposing the left side of my neck.

A flash of pain ran from under my ear down to my shoulder as I began crying, frustrated and hurt. Meg let me go. Mother, meanwhile, was dabbing at the wound with her moist cloth, dipping it in the pan and dabbing again, engrossed in her work. I was dazed and light-headed, crying all the while. I pushed her hand away, and she again stood over us.

"Why her left side?" Meg wanted to know. Touching the wound under my left ear, I felt it not bleeding. It didn't hurt even, though there was a throbbing sensation on the spot. I was crying not so much from pain as from the shock of realizing Mother would intentionally hurt me.

"It is a way of identifying yourselves to your sisters and cousins of the Raven tribe. Right ear, first born; left, second," Mother explained evenly.

"What about for a third or fourth daughter?" Meg asked.

"A cross or v-shape under the right side for the third; for the fourth, under the left."

Nikki reflexively touched underneath her left ear. What was it about the left side of her neck? That was the place where she had always felt most vulnerable, the place where she would have the men kiss her first, which flooded her with sensuous arousal. Once kissed under her left ear, she was lost in a haze of erotic desire, rising up in her like heat. What was the connection? She picked up the thread:

"By means of the potion applied here, the wound will heal, leaving only a small reddish mark," Mother continued. "It is your sign of belonging, hidden under your hair."

"Are we now Ravens?" Meg inquired.

"You have been given your first ritual, the 'Welcoming,' as it is called. So that you can decide whether to go on or not."

"Will you teach us the secret words of the code now?" Meg pressed.

"Not now, but soon. One step at a time."

Meg's face fell.

"Why couldn't we decide before getting cut?" I asked miserably, smearing the tears into my cheeks.

"Because without being wounded first, you would not have the ability to make such a decision. Carol, use what little intelligence you have! In order to decide to join or not, you have to experience firsthand the special powers of magicians and healers, and to understand the meaning of your mother being a Raven. Now you see the choice." Mother looked at Meg, who smiled strangely.

"I could see without the cut," I pouted.

"No, you could not, though you persist in thinking naively. In time you will see."

She was right. After a few months the little cut turned into a mole below my ear, which I have had ever since. It seemed there was magic in it, for whenever I looked in the mirror at it, my head was flooded with all sorts of images and desires. In my mind I saw a great black-winged raven, very noble and flying aloft.

Mother often spoke to Meg and me about the raven, explaining that it is a bird of prophecy, considered in Celtic myth to be one of the oldest animals, and that, above all, the raven is a bird of secrecy and mystery.

"Although the raven is a great healer, its black feathers swallow the light of direct understanding," she warned. "You must come to know the raven only by gliding on its wings. Then you will be able to prophesy and to heal."

It was finally through this wonderful, magical image of the raven that I was reconciled to joining the tribe. I spent time alone in my room looking at that mole, the same room you had, Nikki, and eventually made up my mind really to be a Cleves. You see, that is how it works; you aren't just born to it—you have to make the move yourself. Mother, cruel and cold as she was, knew enough to give Meg and me time to think it over and to come to it ourselves.

Maybe this is why I have waited so long to tell you all this. I have confessed your identity to you in such a way that you will have time to think it over, to consider whether to join me and the long line of women who are your ancestors.

When I did decide to join the tribe, I thought that I should become a member as myself, just as I was. So I would be kind and accommodating and use what came naturally to me—my way of making peace—enhanced by my newfound powers to be all the more of a peacemaker and a caretaker.

I made this decision thinking of Father. The cutting ceremony made me feel a great pang in my heart, as if I were leaving my father. And I had always wanted to live with him forever. So I determined that I would become a Cleves while nevertheless remaining like him. Meg also decided to follow a different path from Mother. Except that Meg decided to go in the other direction from me—to learn and practice all that our mother didn't know.

Once my decision was made, I was ready to become a student of Mother, and I learned nearly as quickly as Meg all the potions and chants and incantations. I went with them to Dogtown to collect roots and berries, learning how to concoct all sorts of medicines.

Meg was always bugging Mother to learn how to brew love potions or revenge spells, but Mother was very firm in what she was willing to teach us. I was never quite sure whether she even knew how to cast spells on people, although I suspect she did know but had made the decision not to—except maybe on our father. If I had learned such spells from her—which I had no desire to learn—I would have put a spell on your father to make him stop drinking.

You see, dear ones, each Cleves meets her limit just by living mortal life, regardless of how much power she may have. That is not the tragedy my sister thinks it is. She is always trying to escape because she finds a rooted life too restrictive, so is always running off to this place and that. I looked for magic in my kitchen—and in my girls. I found it in both places.

It seems we women have a hard time with our mothers and with our daughters, as I'm sure the three of you with daughters of your own understand from both sides. I don't know of a more complicated, difficult relationship. Perhaps the one between a father and son, but I know nothing about that.

What has been personally hard is that I wanted so much for each of you—to live in ways I never could. Every daughter is a branch of her mother and is connected in the deepest way—through her body. Sons wander off and live their own biological lives, but daughters are fated—doomed, you might say on a bad day—to live out in some way the life their mothers lived. When you come of age, you have to face the same problems of gender and procreation. Your body falls into a rhythm with the moon, and you find there is no escaping that rhythm, that it dominates and directs you as surely as any spiritual fate.

That was a scary thing for me to realize. I began menstruating late by today's norms, at fifteen. I think your Aunt Meg began earlier. Mother was very matter-of-fact about our bodies, lacking any feel for the magic and mystery that unfolds in a girl's young body. I had all the typical feelings—fear of the blood, of what was happening to me, and disgust, too. And that soaring sense of spirit you feel when you are taken over by something not outer or foreign to you but something inner, so deep within yourself that it feels like it's happening outside of you.

I was so upset and excited at the same time, but Mother had little patience for either. She gave me all the facts, made sure I knew what was what. I hated her lack of sentimentality, but I had to love her because I was bound to her; she was the only person who could explain the mystery.

But she said something I have never forgotten, which I pass on to you. She told me that beginning my menstrual cycle was what all women experienced, but that it meant something special to a Cleves. By then I had been studying with her, walking the long paths in Dogtown, collecting herbs and making potions and packs, learning to heal myself when I got sick.

"Carol, your connection to the earth is now beginning, and it will last until you die, not ceasing with menopause. Only now will you be able to feel your deepest powers and thereby fully enter into membership in the Raven tribe. Such powers that come from the earth are mantic. You know how to use the earth's plants and animals. Now you will discover your own resources. Your body will mean more now connected to the earth. Men will start to take notice of you, and you will have men if you want. It's the way of the world. But for a Cleves to take a man, she must use her powers sparingly, carefully, in order not to destroy the man in the process.

For we recognize the great power in the body. The body is the physical image of the soul, the material image of spirit, as is all the embodied world. The body manifests the fundamental truth of the Raven clan: periodicity. A single life moves in cycles, individual life but one small part of the greater cycle of life and death. The wings of the raven rise, then fall; together they are one movement. Learn to use that knowledge wisely."

When Mother talked to me like this, I would hold my breath the whole time, understanding about half of what she said. I had no desire for men. Two years before, my father, your grandfather Stephen Keefe, died while serving in World War II...

He had enlisted and sailed off to Europe in 1943. It broke my heart for him to leave, but I was certain he would come back. I spent hours reading books my mother gave me, studying to find spells or incantations to bring him home safely. When I begged my mother to help me, she laughed at me for being such a scaredy-cat.

"Doesn't Father know about our magic?" I asked.

Mother sneered. "He doesn't, and he will never know!" From her look I knew never to say a word to him about it.

The week before Father went off to war, I was so frantic he was leaving that I took over the kitchen. I concocted all sorts of drinks and poultices and plasters for his chest, which he let me rub on him.

I'm sure he thought me a little crazy, but since we were close—and probably because I was crying all the while—he let me have my way. Of course, neither Mother, Meg nor I said anything about our being Cleves magicians.

I sprinkled ground-up bones of certain types of birds mixed with cooked herbs onto the shoulders and chest of his uniform, and I polished his boots with a tarry mass of stuff I made out of rock paste, mud, and slugs.

Really I was trying—and nearly succeeded—to make my father so sick he couldn't leave. He gagged down the potions I made for him, but he was so retiring, such a quiet man, that he never had any reaction to them at all. He just gave me that little half smile of his, his blue eyes twinkling, drinking down the potions, burping a little and covering his mouth, then patting me on the arm.

In the end, nothing worked. When the week was out he dressed—beautiful in his uniform!—and left as planned. I cried and hugged him all the way to the train station, watching the train pull out, thinking my life had ended. At night I had terrible dreams and spent the days alone with Mother and Meg, both of whom hated me and made fun of my broken heart. I could half understand Meg's attitude, but Mother's coldness shocked me. I swore out loud that I would do anything for a man if I loved him, anything at all. This only made them laugh all the more.

Having grown up sailing, Father had joined the navy. They put him on a ship as a supply officer since he had worked as a traveling salesman selling dry goods. He was gone nine months when we received the news that his ship had been torpedoed off the coast of England by a German submarine. No one survived.

It's painful, of course, to remember. When the news came, I fell into a sickness for which all of Mother's power couldn't cure me. I lay in bed for months, numb and deaf to the world. I was dead, in a way, unable to care about anything. The world was a dark shadow, and even when Mother tried to entice me outside, to join her in some activity like gathering herbs or finding certain rocks where spirits were trapped or asleep, I had no interest.

Slowly I came out of the darkest part, since time was passing and I was young. But even though I got out of bed, I moped around the house, didn't go to school, and wore an expression of defeat. My mother and sister were disgusted.

So when two years later I began menstruating, the new life developing within me coupled with Mother's words began to rouse me from my stupor. Listening to her, I felt my spirits rising in spite of myself and for the first time in years felt happiness, now weighted by sadness. For I no longer had a father, except as a spirit. I would always remember, but for now, for life, I had only women around me to support and guide me.

I came to love taking walks in the woods with Mother—the only time she seemed to like me even a little. We walked slowly down the wide rock-strewn roads of Dogtown, past markers where houses had stood in colonial times. Mother knew so much! Just where to find arrowroot and bayberry, under which rock to find a particular kind of slug that, when mashed and boiled with poison ivy, made redbane—a perfectly good antidote for children's burns from hot oil. (It wouldn't work on adults, of course.) She taught me the names of all the plant species we encountered in the woods, the names of the birds and animals, and about their habits.

From her I learned how to use herbs as cures for all sorts of common ailments—easing menstrual cramps, relieving headaches, making blisters and corns disappear. Because Mother believed that vaccinations undermined one's power, Meg and I were never given them. After my sister and I joined the circle, I eventually learned from other members of the Raven tribe that the matter was not as simple as Mother had presented it, so I made sure all you girls were given your shots.

Carefully pointing out the varieties of birds we spotted on our walks, Mother watched my eyes to make sure that I could distinguish between the yellow of the oriole and the yellow of the finch; that I could discern the different reds of the robin, the cardinal, and the red-winged blackbird. Most important, Mother taught me that knowledge of these differences in color and habit was essential for a deeper understanding of the body of the natural world.

This education gave me an appreciation for color and form, which I later learned from my spiritual mother, Rana, how to express in painting. Previously I had never felt a desire to paint or draw, but after the Welcoming ceremony I began to dream much more vividly. Rich colors and forms of all shapes and sizes filled my dreams, so beautiful that I wanted to paint them.

Still, I never asked Mother for paints or said anything to Meg about my new interest; that would have given them another opportunity to make fun of me. Besides, except for the times Meg was directly taught by Mother, she had begun to spend long periods away from home. I never asked where she went, finding out only years later that she had been going to Essex to visit our Aunt Hannah. Sometimes during the nights I could hear Meg and Mother arguing. Meg was now approaching twenty, and she wanted to become a practicing magician in the worst way; she wanted to know all the powerful spells and incantations. Mother refused.

Even though I learned as much of natural magic as I could, when I married I stopped practicing, thinking it was better not to rock the boat. Because your father would have killed me if he had known anything of my hidden powers. Actually, he nearly did when eventually he learned of my Cleves identity. That happened during one of the awful fights he had with your grandmother. He so used to infuriate her that one day she muttered she would have her revenge. When he laughed in her face, she concocted some herbs that she threw at him, causing him to fall down in a faint. I was there, frantic because I didn't want him ever to discover my secret.

After he revived, he was furious with me for weeks.

THAT LAST sentence implied more than it stated, Nikki observed. Her father had beaten her mother, she saw, and her mother had been unwilling to write down the truth. How many times did her mother stand by while the young Nikki was teased mercilessly by her father? How she had hated her mother, bending over her pots, silent, always silent, unwilling to speak up, unwilling to use her power! And now another evasion!

Yet the poor woman was dead. Was it fair to hate the dead? How could you ever overcome hating someone dead? Nikki wondered. They were fixed and unchanging. They couldn't forgive your hating them, and you could so easily become like the dead, fixed in your black hatred. Any possibility of change was on the living.

She sighed and thought of Alice, with whom she had been warring for years. Alice, so unlike her. She remembered Philip once asking her how she would feel if Alice lived the same kind of life Nikki had once lived—what with her lovers, her easy-going ways, her open and spacey manner, her drifting... The question so infuriated her, Nikki replied through clenched teeth, that she would kill Alice if she did half of what her mother had done.

"But that's hypocritical," Philip said simply.

That made her mad, too. "It's the age of AIDS!" she yelled.

"It was when you were being wild, too," he declared.

Was he right? Was AIDS around in the eighties? Yes, it was. But mostly she was over her wild ways by then, she reassured herself. Mostly. Except for a few times with men in bars. Only a few times. All that cocaine...

But Alice—what of Alice? She's so different from me anyway, Nikki told herself. Few boyfriends. Stronger boundaries. She hardly let anyone in. Nikki herself could barely tell her own daughter she loved her. Almost impossible. Yes, but didn't Philip accuse Nikki herself of being exactly what women referred to disparagingly as "a typical male"? A hard shell, born under the sign of the crab. Well, it wasn't her fault if she didn't show her feelings—she took after her father that way. Cold as granite. She was like her father, she considered, finding it hard to express feeling, easy to become emotional.

Or did she more closely resemble her mother, quiet and restrained? After all, it was her father who used to scream. At least you could trust his anger, for it reappeared like clockwork, predictable as the seasons. Such a justification of anger sounding familiar to Nikki, she flipped back through the pages of her mother's journal but found nothing to confirm a similar view.

In any case, Nikki had long thought that growing up with her father's familiar outbursts was how she had come to trust her own anger, as well as other people's anger, as purifying, whole, undiluted, truthful. It seemed axiomatic to her that when you were angry, you spoke the unvarnished truth. She read on.

> Mother became my friend for the first time, though I suppose in part because I was less of the silly little thing. Mother saw that I was becoming a woman, and she was intelligent enough to know what to do about it.
>
> "Carol," she said one day, "you need a man."
>
> When I began to protest, she waved my objections away.
>
> "Granted, there are women who are fine without men, like your Aunt Hannah. Your sister thinks she wants nothing to do with men, but she is simply in the process of discovering for herself how to talk to them. She won't ever marry, but she will have plenty of lovers. Now, you are a different case altogether. You need to marry and continue the Cleves family line. Meg may be twice the Cleves you'll ever be, but she will never produce daughters. That must be your job."
>
> As usual, I was aghast at my mother's frankness. And I had no desire for a man in my life. My father's memories decorated the walls in my bedroom—pictures of him, his navy commission, his diploma. I made a little shrine to him in my room, keeping his picture on a shelf along with his war medal that had come from the War Department in a little green box. I would sit before the shelf night after night and stare at his picture, wishing there were some way that the right incantation could bring him back to life. But mostly I just prayed to him and talked to him every night, relieved and comforted by his spirit for company.
>
> I couldn't see that the three of us needed a man around. My father had left Mother a generous life insurance policy, and the navy paid a stipend. In addition, Mother and Meg grew and sold teas to the local grocer, and

we ate vegetables from our garden. (I had my own garden full of flowers.) Mother went out from time to time to read palms or tea leaves. She was a highly intuitive fortuneteller, imposing in all-black. People were frightened of her, but of course that was good for business.

She insisted I meet a man, and before I knew it there was a young man at our door, Pekka Helmik. He was as handsome a man as my father, I had to admit, even the first time I saw him when I was more apt mentally to compare the two. Your father was a tall and thin young man (I know that surprises you) and had gorgeous blue eyes that pierced me. He was shy, wore a rough coat, and held his hat between his thick hands, twisting the hat out of shape. After taking his hat, Mother introduced the two of us, inviting him to sit down before she quickly left us alone. Meg as usual was out running around somewhere. I was eighteen and dressed in a flowered dress with a lacy collar, and my hair, fair like yours, Cynthia, was done up.

I hadn't the slightest idea of how to talk to a boy. At school I had girlfriends, a few, but mostly I kept to myself. The boys at school seemed very young to me—clumsy and too eager. Besides, I was to graduate in a month.

But after some initial awkwardness, Pekka was easygoing. When Mother returned with tea, I poured and asked him about his family. He was the youngest son of a family of granite cutters, he explained hurriedly; he had no intention of staying in the stonecutting business, even if his brothers seemed happy enough with it. He had very little contact with his family, although he went to see his mother from time to time. I asked him what he intended to do with his life.

As he sipped his tea, a curious look came into his eyes, then a sparkle.

"Marry you," he said matter-of-factly, with a smile so beautiful I nearly fainted. I had no idea what to say.

"You don't know me, Mr. Helmik," I replied, my voice shaking, trying to sound lighthearted. He was scaring me.

"I know you as well as I'll ever know you," he answered, staring into my eyes. I suppose I fell in love with him then. With those words like magic, how could I not? He was so insistent, sure of himself, with such flashing, deep eyes. Who was I to argue? It was as if a spell had been cast over me.

"But I don't know you," I insisted timidly, thinking I should put him off a little for form's sake.

"But you do," he countered, which made me think he might have a bit of the poet in him. Your father used to write such beautiful poems, mostly to me. What turned him to drink was what turns most poets to drink: loss of spirit. Selling insurance. Feeling that they can't reach heaven, or even articulate one-thousandth of the extravagant beauty of life. This was a man none of you ever knew, unless you, Jane, remember your father that far back.

Men can do nothing without women, it's true, even if they must go beyond us and reach for heaven. Women forget that even though their men wander off, in their hearts they cannot live without woman's touch. Perhaps your father's fall had something to do with being surrounded at home by females. After all, he was so threatened by women, poor dear!

Nevertheless, at the time he began courting me, he didn't seem afraid at all. He simply stated that I did know him, and when I demurred, he persisted.

"Look at me, Carol. Listen to my voice. Your intelligence shows on your face. Your deep-set brown eyes, so thoughtful and a little sad. I know from the way you speak that you were close to your father; your mother told me he died in the war. Anyway," he added a little shyly, "I've seen you going to school with your friends, and I've watched you." He blushed.

"I've never seen you—"

"And yet you do know me—don't you?" he stopped, suddenly less sure of himself. It was so terribly charming to see him vulnerable like that, that big man with his large hands and easy ways!

"I—you look somehow familiar…" I responded, reassuring him more out of politeness than truthfulness. Gloucester was such a small place at the time, it was true, I thought I might have seen him down at the docks, perhaps walking with a gang of boys. But I honestly didn't recognize him.

"Ah, that's it, then," he said readily, smiling again that beautiful smile of his and brushing his curly blond hair back. He had a high, proud forehead and a hard flash of light in his eyes. I thought of telling him that I was frightened. I did not, and perhaps that was a mistake.

"Recognition is one of the signs," he remarked brightly, leaning forward to sip his tea. The china cup in his hands looked like it belonged at a doll's tea party. I think that's why your father went for the china first, later when he began to have his fits of anger. It must have enraged him, even then, the delicacy of the cup. But in the beginning I couldn't see any of his temper, so naive was I, so overwhelmed by him.

Nikki sat back, stood stiffly, stretched, then moved slowly to her aunt's hot plate, pouring herself another cup of tea. She turned and regarded the open journal from the sink as she leaned against its side. Her body ached from leaning and concentrating; she pulled at her arms, bending over to stretch her backbone. Something in her felt very low. Where had the feeling come from?

She returned to her seat, propped her head in her hands, and read:

Your father left soon after finishing his tea, and there isn't much more to say about it, other than that we were married six months later. I was sad my father wasn't alive to give me away, but Mother did the honors, then your father and I went off to live in a three-family house down on Rogers Street, not far from the docks.

Although your father worked at first stonecutting with his brothers, soon he got the job selling insurance that he has held ever since. He took over Frank Starr's agency and made it his own, selling insurance to more people in Gloucester than anyone. I was very proud of him—until he began to drink excessively and gain weight.

From the start he drank, going out weekend nights with his brothers to the bars in town, staying out late. But he always came back and sobered up and was fine, and for the first few years he was sober all week long. He wanted to be a writer, but we began having children, and he had to work at night, go out and meet clients, have drinks with them. When we were first married, he wrote long poems and stories about the old days in Gloucester, but as time went on, he was too busy and too tired to write.

Although I said nothing to him about my Cleves ancestry, of course, I thought I might tell him one day, in spite of Mother's insistence we tell no one. I was so close to your father, I wanted to tell him everything, not hide any of myself from him. Feeling that I was betraying him caused me terrible anguish, and that pain is one of the reasons I stopped practicing magic. Years later, when he had become impossible, I often thought of studying again, but by then it was too late—I was too far from it.

Once I began having children I had less time for Mother and Meg, who even though they thought little enough of me were still my main connection to the Cleves. (Other than Rana, my bird-mother, whom I will tell you about.) Meg finally moved down to Salem, and she stayed there. She and Mother had a falling-out, which neither would talk about. I tried for years to reconcile them but finally gave up, instead visiting each of them separately.

We had never had any relatives on our father's side, so when our colorful Aunt Hannah died, no living kin remained outside our immediate family.

It was at this time when you were all little that I made my decision to stop practicing magic—except for the herbal remedies I have always made, which you girls of course remember since you hated most of them. I had no time anyway to go to meetings of the circle, and what would I have said to your father when I had to leave the house at midnight during a full moon, to stay away till dawn? I didn't much miss the meetings because by then I had grown close to Rana, dearer to me than my own mother.

But that was long after I had grown up. As a girl it took me some time first to become reconciled to being a Cleves, then to learn what that meant.

It was about two years after the Welcoming ceremony with Mother at home that Meg and I were initiated into the Raven tribe.

One night very late Mother led us deep into Dogtown. We passed silently down one of the large roads, past the old cellar holes. Under a full moon I could spy shadows deep in the trees to the right and left, my own figure casting a short shadow in front of me. It was nearly as bright as day. We walked farther and deeper into Dogtown than I had ever wandered, even on my own when I used to walk for miles, proceeding singly over meadows high up into the middle of a strange part of the forest.

In the weirdly white moonlight it seemed we had somehow stepped onto the moon herself, though she was all the while shining brightly over our shoulders, walking along with us. I began to imagine that the pines were alien plants, shrubs a hundred feet high, and the granite boulders we passed were really pebbles, that we were wandering into some giant's realm. As we walked single file, I brought up the rear. Mother was walking so quickly, I had to trot from time to time to keep up. Every so often my feet got caught in the hem of my black cape. We were all three wearing black capes that Mother had made.

If my writing has given the impression that Mother was cruel, that is misleading. She was distant and proud, a strong woman, but never unloving. I loved her despite her criticism of me. When I was young it hurt that she was impatient with me and called me a little fool, but once I became a mother I realized that she simply did not understand me. And because I now know that, she is vulnerable in my eyes, and so I can forgive her.

She had problems of her own. She was known in Gloucester as an eccentric old woman, although at that time she would have been only in her mid-forties. But she had always looked old—her hair, although still dark, was losing its youthful luster, her face was jowly and full of wrinkles. Her only friends were others of the Raven clan. I never knew how much of her outcast status was self-imposed and how much she felt was forced on her by circumstances.

Since the Welcoming ceremony I had given little thought to the meaning of my initial wound, as far as its having any effect on me in the everyday world. I thought that being a member of the Raven tribe was some great adventure, a child's dream, nothing more. As we walked silently through the moonscape that night, I had no inkling of what I was about to find out.

After passing through a second and third meadow, wending our way through thick grass that wetted the bottoms of our capes with dew, we ducked into some dense woods smelling strongly of pine. Pine needles covered the floor of the forest, making a soft cushion underfoot. As we began walking steadily downhill, I had the sense we were entering a large round bowl.

The lower we walked the taller and thicker the trees became, until we were walking through pines that must have been hundreds upon hundreds of years old. No night noises sounded, no mourning doves, no nightingales, no owls. Not even a breeze blew, and in the utter stillness I thought I caught glimpses of other black-caped forms moving through the trees. I opened my mouth to say something but thought better of it, the world was so still.

Eventually the ground began to rise and grow stony. In a moment we were standing inside a ring of broken granite, huge old boulders arranged in a circle. Tall pines formed a ring ten steps back from the stones, opening a hole in the sky directly overhead. As the full moon shone down into the clearing, the stones glimmered with an unearthly light.

I became aware of other people, some standing, some sitting on stones, others crouched on the ground. Two or three stood together, their hoods drawn down over their faces, so I could not tell whether they were women or men, whether they were even human.

A chill ran through me. Grateful to be with my mother and sister, I stood close to them for protection. When I bumped into Meg, she shoved me away, so I hovered near Mother and waited.

After a short time one of the female figures, her cape thrown back, walked to the center of the ring and bent down. She waved her hands over the ground as she leaned her head down close; suddenly a flame flickered before her face. I was spellbound, catching a glimpse in the firelight of an old woman with a lined and intelligent, sad face. She stood upright and re-garded the growing flames for a few moments.

Set in a small hole in the ground, I could see by then, a small fire burned steadily. Next to the fire sat a low wooden bench or table on which waited a bowl of water and a stick of burning incense. I learned later that these were the three objects required for Sabbat: fire, a bowl of water, and incense. The incense threw little puffs of smoke into the still air, permeating the space with a musky aroma.

As the priestess stood back and raised her arms slowly, her cape fell back across her shoulders in heavy black drapery, opening to reveal a black dress of velvet with a silver pendant hanging from her neck. As her arms stretched gradually outwards, her hands reached slowly upwards, higher and higher. The figures standing or sitting about came close to form a wide circle around her and the fire. About forty people altogether, deeply hooded similarly in black capes, then stood quietly in the circle.

Almost imperceptibly, so slowly I didn't realize it happening until well under way, all the figures in the circle were raising their arms in unison, arms extended, palms up and thrust out.

Mother had positioned us beforehand such that we three now comprised part of the circle, she in between Meg and me. Standing to Mother's left, I saw that she, too, was raising her arms, as was Meg, so I jerked my arms out and did the same. Not that I knew what we were doing.

Our arms went up and up and up until they stretched out overhead, all forty of us completely silent, the little fire flickering before the priestess of the circle. Now heads leaned back and hoods fell back from faces. I kept my arms overhead and stole glances, noticing that everyone there was a woman: old and young; ugly and beautiful; fat, thin. Some looked intelligent and thoughtful, others hard and brutal and stupid. Several were girls no older than Meg and I.

Soon I realized we were raising our arms to the moon, for everyone was looking at the huge disk riding directly overhead. We stayed that way for a while as the priestess slowly took off her cape and dress, laying her clothes carefully on the ground. When she was naked and white in the moonlight, she again raised her arms to the moon and began a chant. She stood there like a goddess, her long, dark hair roiling at her shoulders as if alive.

"Mother moon, White Goddess, embrace us once again. Mother earth, Great Goddess, raise us once again. Goddess, Great Mother, Eternal Virgin, Enchantress," she sang.

As the priestess continued the chant, everyone joined in at a low murmur, which made an eerie sound in the still forest. When the chant repeated four or five times, I had to struggle to keep up. Suddenly the chant died as the hooded figures dropped their arms. I was relieved, since mine were tired.

"Black Raven, Bird of Prophecy, arrive!" the priestess intoned, as a murmur of assent ran around the circle. Hearing an echoing caw in the distance, I looked up in wonder.

At a signal from the leader, the figures sat down on the ground. Lighting candles, they silently held them forward. Although women in those days did not customarily sit in such unladylike fashion, I had seen Mother do so at home. There was something very natural and, I suppose, freeing to see all those women sitting on the bare ground. So I sucked in my breath, relaxed, and sat down myself.

Mother presented Meg and me with candles to light from hers, and I sat quietly holding mine. All those candles cast a beautifully warm glow in the cold moonlight.

The priestess remained standing and spoke. "Let us welcome with praise the God of the Wood, child of Raven," she nodded toward the woods. I heard a rustle come from somewhere off in the darkness, far away to my right, the sound of something moving around out there.

"Guide us, horned God of the Hunt, Ruler of the Afterworld," the priestess chanted. *"Keeper of the gate into death and rebirth, hover near to protect and guide us."*

The rustle growing louder, my ears pricked up, pointing and straining toward the sound. Something was coming! It was growing nearer, but what? My eyes grew wide waiting, struggling to pierce the dim shadows that hung like velvet curtains in the dark pines.

Sparks of tension chased around our ring like an electric current. Some faces inclined in the direction of the sound, others bent down; all sat waiting. Even Mother barely breathed. My heart pounded. I could hear something in the woods coming toward us swiftly, with purpose and decision. An animal? Some strange god-creature, half human, half—what? Some unknown, altogether different creature was coming, I sensed that—but what?

Hearing it approach behind me, I turned to look, but Mother clamped her hand on my thigh to freeze me in place.

"Something's coming!" I panted. Unable to remain silent, I whispered so only Mother could hear. "Something's coming!" I exclaimed again, my own voice frightening me in the still silence of the moonlit ring.

Nearby, sounds of crashing and splintering, approaching quickly through the trees. Everyone waited, the circle strung now like a high-pitched string.

"*Come, God of the Hunt!*" the priestess exclaimed, throwing her head back and raising her voice and arms. Her voice splintered the night air like a shock, and the sound—as if some great creature were hurtling and stumbling through the trees—grew still louder!

I wanted to throw myself to the ground in terror but was frozen, waiting spellbound for the mystery to reveal itself. Mother clamped my thigh tightly. I clutched both hands around my white candle, the wax bending like paper under my little hands. The thing that was drawing ever nearer was going to shudder me from my bearings on the earth forever. I pressed one hand hard against the ground.

Inside the mounting sound of the approaching thing I heard Mother speak; she was speaking of the sacred hunt:

"*In the hunt we join the animal; the God enters us.*"

The crashing resounded through the ring like a mad spirit; I felt we would all have to rise and flee or remain to be driven crazy.

I ducked my head. The sounds rose to a steady roar as it drew upon us, and in a flash a heavy, thick body, bristly and burning with taut red flashing, leaped over my right shoulder to tear straight to the center of the ring where the priestess stood transfixed, rooted in the ground.

The animal darted straight for her, cruel tusks flashing red in the moonlight, hairy, moist snout erect and snorting, its hard body hugging the ground. I was on the verge of shouting "Watch out!" when at the last second the boar veered right and ran around her, its straight, short legs carrying it past her and darting between two figures sitting huddled on the far side of the ring. Then it was gone, vanishing as quickly as it had flashed into sight, taking with it a retreating sound of thunder chasing lightening.

The rumble faded slowly until at last it was swallowed and, grumbling low, blended into the quiet voices of the night wood.

I sat trembling, heart thudding, head swimming. Was this the God of the Hunt?

For a long time no one uttered a sound as a deep sigh descended on the circle.

After a while the priestess turned to speak, her voice quiet and filled with the hesitation of awe. "Welcome to the circle. Tonight two young ones are to join. Let us welcome them." Her voice grew steadily stronger until she ended with an assured nod, pointing a long arm at my sister and me.

Mother pulled our hoods off our faces and pushed us into the circle. I held back, but Meg walked straight toward the tall, thin woman. When Mother pushed me again, I stumbled to hurry alongside Meg while terrified something terrible was going to happen to us—something far worse than being cut under the ear. Seeing the priestess smiling kindly at us, I relaxed a little, even though I didn't like standing in front of all those hooded figures in black capes.

"I am Celeste," the priestess greeted us, in a voice loud enough for everyone to hear. "As the leader of the circle and your mother's spiritual mother, I am a link to your past—to the history that holds your destiny. Do you wish to join the circle?" she asked us both.

Meg nodded, her eyes narrowing. Sensing her impatience with the ritual, I was embarrassed for her.

"Speak the words," Celeste spoke, to which Meg spoke right up, although how she knew what to say I had no idea.

"I join the circle; it is my wish," Meg intoned in the voice she used for sounding grown up. Immediately taking off all her clothes, Meg stood there naked! I wanted to laugh at her, I was so nervous. Celeste nodded at Meg and turned to me.

When I stammered a few words about wanting to join, trying to sound like Meg, Celeste nodded gravely again. Since they now both waited, with trembling hands I took off my clothes and stood there feeling stupid and vulnerable. Softly putting a hand on each our shoulders, Celeste turned us around the entire circle, slowly. I was so embarrassed! Yet the members of the circle applauded very softly, and the sight of all those women nodding and smiling at us felt warm and wonderful. I could see their hands move, but the sound was like leaves rustling, the applause was so quiet. My eyes filled with tears.

"Sit," pronounced Celeste, her voice like the leaves as well, quiet and firm and certain. Meg took up her clothes and so did I, and we went back to our places and dressed, I more quickly than my sister. More ceremoniously, Celeste put her own robe back on, as if doing something very important.

We all sat on the hard ground. Making a sign, Celeste summoned some of the figures to draw near, whereupon they spread out cloths, laying out cakes, bottles of wine and beer. Celeste took up a knife and cut two slices of one of the cakes, bringing them with a friendly air to Meg and me, then poured and handed us cups of wine. I darted a glance at Mother as I sipped the red wine. It was refreshing with the sweet, dry cake. Now all the women came forward easily, some talking to friends, all greeting us warmly, hugging us or taking our hands, Meg and I rising or remaining seated as the occasion required. The women took wine or beer and cake, returning to their places. I was amazed to see such ease in a solemn place, but I learned later that this is the way of Raven celebrations. Rather than the solemn, serious ceremonies that outsiders might imagine, they are fun, full of gaiety and laughter. There is always food and some alcohol, usually wine, and often music and dancing.

After everyone was fed and had retired to their places, they formed a long line as each woman in turn offered us her own words on becoming members of the Raven tribe. With variations on Celeste's calm, straight-forward manner, they spoke to us on an odd range of subjects. First a short, wiry woman with narrow, concentrated eyes and straight hair cropped short strode quickly up to us, clasping her hands before her as if praying. She must have been about fifty.

"My name is Coral," she introduced herself, smiling seriously. Settling herself a moment, she proceeded. "In joining the circle you join our community, agreeing to abide by the rules of the circle," she paced back and forth in front of us.

"The first rule is secrecy," she continued, stopping to fix her bright, serious eyes on Meg and me. I shifted on the ground. "Each of you must never tell outsiders of the Raven tribe, learning instead to keep your nature to yourself and to your clan. We are here to protect you, but you must first of all protect yourself."

Coral spoke for a long time about the need for secrecy and about the dangers inherent in joining the Raven tribe. Half listening, my mind wandered to Mother mixing herbs and potions. I recalled her words about the secrecy of the Raven. And now as Coral spoke I came to feel danger in being a member of this tribe of Druids, that the people out there, all the teachers and shopkeepers and firemen, the postman and the milkman and the fishermen, even the housewives of Gloucester—as friendly and open and helpful as they appeared to be—could easily turn against Mother, Meg, and me if they knew what we were. The kindly face of my school teacher, Mrs. Franklin, took on a darker look when I imagined her finding out. I grew frightened.

"If you are frightened, you are on the right path," Coral was saying.

"The Bible teaches that fear of the Lord is the beginning of wisdom. The Druid Raven teaches that fear is our first teacher, bringing us into the presence of the Great Spirit."

As I considered her words, my body tensed with fear. The woods all at once felt threatening as this time I imagined the good people of Gloucester rushing out of the dark trees, guns in their hands, pointing them at us, pointing them… I put my head down, covering my eyes.

"Yes, be afraid!" Coral insisted, her voice rising. "Your life is a secret one now and will be forever, even if you renounce your true nature. And being women—bound up in a society in which very different values predominate—it is all the more necessary that you live underground lives. As for those masculine powers that are threatened by us, you must nevertheless overcome their counterthreats by using the fears they provoke in you as guiding spirits—honoring and abiding by these, trusting in them, even cultivating them."

What were we doing? What was I doing here? Sitting around a small fire in the woods in the middle of the night with a group of women, dressed in black capes under the full moon. What was I doing anyway?

I considered that I would have to spend my life hiding just as Mother did, proud and independent as she was. Nowadays, of course, Laurie Cabot and her Wicca kin practice witchcraft openly, without much fear of reprisal. Plenty of Druids meet here and there openly. I wonder what is lost in all this openness, however, for it was critical and essential that I learned as a girl not only to trust my fears—but that it wasn't a lie to keep them secret.

For though it depressed me to think I now had a secret to carry to my grave—unable even to tell girlfriends or my future husband—from that moment on the circle's embrace filled me with a sense of protection and warmth. That feeling of belonging along with Meg to such a community was balm to my soul.

"Those who would harm you convey fear of your power, revealing unwittingly that they recognize it. And your fear of them, in turn, is a way of teaching you at the beginning: Fear and power go hand in hand." Coral stopped and regarded us.

Yes, that was it! With a sudden exaltation I felt protected in the circle by its power, radiating inward, holding me, keeping me safe. A curious feeling, more powerful than any I have felt since. A second awareness accompanied it: The power of people who might kill me for doing magic.

Something shifted in me with the dawning realization: *I will be able to keep the secret because I can look inside and feel my strength and power.* As I looked earnestly into Coral's narrowed eyes, she looked back at both of us, then nodded and, smiling, walked quickly back to her place in the circle.

Our first night in the circle ended exhaustingly late. The moon had long since passed beneath the canopy of trees, some of the women having piled brands on the fire to keep it burning brightly. I was chilled and aching from sitting on the cold ground, overwhelmed listening to the endless stream of people come forward to speak to us—from vague words on ways of hiding to talk on how to open businesses. A tall woman with very straight blond hair spoke to us for a while about anger and its beauties.

Even as my mind was shutting down and I was growing sleepy, Meg seemed as awake as ever, a desert thirsty for more. I began to fall asleep, convinced there was no end to what we were to hear. But in the middle of my stupor, everything grew quiet; I perked up at the sudden stillness.

Celeste came to us bearing a tremendous tome bound in black leather, held together with huge metal clasps.

"This is our Black Book," she announced. "For the Raven tribe, black is not the color of evil but of night and dreams. It is the color of earth spirit deep in the ground. Meg and Carol, if each of you so wishes you may now sign your name in our Black Book—after which for this lifetime you are a clan member, no matter how you conduct your life."

I wondered sleepily whether we had to sign in blood, but absurdly Celeste produced an ordinary fountain pen, then kneeled, opening the great book on her lap before Meg. She handed the pen to Meg, Meg taking it quickly as usual. She leaned over to sign on a page below other names, although in the dim light I couldn't read any of them.

Just as Meg started to bear down, Celeste reached out and touched her hand softly. Meg stopped, raising her eyes.

"You must sign with your Raven name," she instructed.

Suddenly I was frightened. Mother must have neglected to tell us our Raven names, I worried; was she supposed to have done so at our Welcoming? I was glad Meg was going first, although even she was hesitating.

"Think of your Welcoming, of the pain," Celeste suggested evenly.

"It didn't hurt," Meg replied. I felt embarrassed for her bravado.

I expected Celeste to say something like, "Oh, but it did." Instead she merely nodded.

Meg sat still a moment, her face screwed up, then she leaned forward abruptly to *scratch something in the book, pressing down hard. I read the name she had written: "Braise."* It didn't sound like a name. What did it mean?

Now Celeste turned to offer me the book and pen. I panicked. I was suddenly wide awake, although I felt I was simultaneously falling asleep. Or was I asleep already? I couldn't think—what had Celeste said? *"Remember the pain."* I tried to recall the Welcoming—Mother suddenly coming at me with that knife, my sister holding me down—but all I could feel was the panic rise in me. I couldn't breathe. What was I doing? Who were these people? It was all fine to have a wonderful magical evening in the woods, but now the final moment was upon me—there was no turning back. Mother had cut me without asking; now I was asked not only to sign of my own will but to name myself before all those watching hooded faces.

I couldn't do it. Nothing came. I could only think of my own name, and I didn't like it. *"Carol, Carol, Carol"* ran around in my head. I was sweating madly now. The whole circle was waiting. Meg was watching me, the curl of her smile telling me: I know you aren't capable. I didn't see Mother, but I knew I was letting her down every second I hesitated. I glanced at her, only to see her twist up her mouth impatiently, shaking her head critically. I hated her. I hated her; I hated Mother. I saw myself, as if in a dream, lean forward to write in the book, just below that weird name "Braise."

Quickly I scrawled the name *"Redblood,"* my hand shaking. Celeste took the book and handed it to a figure standing close by, then told us to rise. I got up on shaky feet, nearly falling over.

"Here are our sisters," Celeste declared, turning us around to the entire circle as each member in turn looked at us. "Braise and Redblood."

My head swirling, I sat down suddenly, toppling over in a faint from which I didn't wake until the next morning. In my bed, I saw Meg's sarcastic face flitting out of the room as grey dawn blew cool air through the window.

☙

Most of the women in the circle that night told us something of importance about being a member of the Raven clan. Particularly they congratulated Meg and me as direct descendants of Anne Cleves, our Raven clan mother. At the time I thought that each woman present had a predetermined role to play. For instance, Rana talked to us in general terms about herbal remedies and midwifery, so afterward I assumed she was the circle's expert on those subjects. But when I approached her about three months after our initiation to learn more, she directed me to others.

I had gone to see her at her antiques store in Rockport one day. Rana was about fifty, thin and with a spring in her walk, like a young tree. She wore her long grey hair tied back in a long braid; she used to play with its end absently while we had tea or sat together on the tumbled granite boulders that guarded the seaside. She had sharp green eyes and lots of wrinkles.

She greeted me warmly, closed and locked the front door, and led me toward the back. We threaded our way past piles of furniture, old books, records, dusty posters, and dishes. We passed through a curtain, then down a short flight of old and worn stairs.

I followed Rana into a cozy workshop furnished with a long workbench, a high chair, and one or two stools. There were rows of tools hanging along the walls, wood shavings covering the table top and strewn about the floor. It was a nice comfy workshop, but what astonished me were the walls, lined top to bottom on both sides of the long room with little shelves on which perched tiny figures of assorted shapes. I looked closely at these, all carved of wood, some painted, others half painted. There were animals of all sorts—lions sitting next to tigers, armadillos snuggled up to wild boars, giraffes, rabbits, cats, and dogs. There were fantastic creatures as well—griffins, dragons, strange sea creatures with wings and long snouts. On other shelves sat human figures in long robes and ancient costumes—some holding wands; others, tiny crystal balls.

"My other family," Rana introduced them with a smile. Patting a stool for me to sit, she sat on one herself.

I smiled back, conveying how much I liked them. It was like being in a little world, full of people and animals, with no distinction between real and imaginary ones.

Shaking off my wonder and switching to Meg's grown-up voice, I earnestly explained my reason for coming: That in reading recently about childbirth, I wanted to know more about midwifery. Since Rana had been the one to speak to Meg and me about childbirth our first night in the circle, I assumed she would know the answers to my questions.

"Go see Mica about that," she interrupted.

"But aren't you the—expert?" I asked, not sure of the proper term.

"No," Rana laughed. "What makes you think that?"

"But—you were the one who spoke to us our first night about those things," I said.

"I did?" she asked, her eyebrows knotted in thought. "Well, I suppose I did, but really Mica knows far more about midwifery. I may have spoken on those things because no one else had done so up to that point." She shrugged.

I realized then from speaking with Rana, later from others, that our "Grand Welcoming"—as our initiation that night in the circle was called—had been typically special. Instead of the highly organized ritual I had imagined, it was conducted rather spontaneously. While most of the members did present some aspect of the Raven tribe to us, they followed few established procedures and no set order. This surprised and pleased me, for it meant that our Grand Welcoming had been an occasion unique to Meg and me, the events unfolding in a particular way. This Rana verified for me.

"Each Grand Welcoming happens according to the needs of the initiates," she emphasized. "No one seems to speak on the same topic each time. Often we end up not speaking on what we know best. Otherwise, I would have spoken about woodcarving," she said, giving a small smile and pointing with a chisel at her little people.

"We move around in a circle, so you can start anywhere—like life. The important thing is not where to start, but that you start," she pronounced, looking deeply into my eyes in a fashion I was coming to recognize as a Raven quality, which we only reveal when conversing with one another.

"But Coral who spoke first said that fear was the beginning," I wondered aloud.

"That's Coral," Rana said, laughing again. "She likes to go first, feeling strongly that the first person you should meet is your fear."

"So there is a beginning?"

Rana shrugged. "Would it have made a difference if I had begun, insisting that childbirth is the central mystery?"

"Well, midwifery seems less—central, maybe, to being a Raven than learning about fear and power," I answered hesitantly.

"You little philosopher," Rana smiled, patting my hand. She thought a moment. "Let me try this. What if I had been the first to speak and had said, speaking about midwifery, that it represents the central mystery of our Raven tribe—because our central mystery as women is conceiving and bearing children? That our direct participation in this great mystery is the root from which all our power emanates and to which it all returns? What if I had said that the central mystery of being human resides, as many of the poets have celebrated, in our coming forth from the womb, and in our returning to the womb of mother earth?"

"Is that true?" I gasped, suddenly afraid I had gotten it all wrong.

Rana's ringing laughter echoed in the small room. "Oh, my dear! Yes, it is true, in a way! You must remember that all aspects of being move in a circle." She grew more serious. "What I have said just now about midwifery and birth and death is indeed a truth, just as true as Coral's words about power and fear. Each aspect is part of the circle. As to which aspect is the most important," Rana shrugged, "I don't know that. I don't know whether anyone does. Each part has its place in the whole."

I began to see, but it was confusing me. I felt I had lost my bearings, that a small joke had been played on me.

Rana was regarding me closely, seeing my consternation. She leaned and hugged me close to her, and her warmth felt like the sun. She leaned back, still regarding me closely.

"We should talk more about what is most important for you. Your task is to determine which part of being a Raven is most important to you. As a direct descendant of Anne Cleves, you have special work."

"Aren't all the Raven clan members related to Anne?" I asked with surprise.

Rana laughed again. "Spiritually, yes. But you are biologically as well; didn't your mother tell you?" She looked at me curiously. "Do you recall Laura speaking to you at the Grand Welcoming about your new life?"

I nodded vaguely. So much had occurred that night!

"She said that each member is only a part of the great circle of life and death—and that no one's life can encompass the circle entire. That spirit moves us; we each in our own lives live out a smaller circle, echoing the larger one. In relation to this greater circle, each of us must choose which part or parts to play, like a part in a family in which all parts are equally important.

"In time you, too, will choose," she continued. "Some aspect will visit you, sitting with you for so long, like a guest who does not leave, that after a while you will hardly notice her presence. Anne herself may appear to tell you which part you are to play. Or perhaps not an actual ancestor; it doesn't matter. But when—if you listen closely—you awaken to the presence of this spirit as central to your life, you will follow after to learn much from her. She will be your 'familiar,' your guiding spirit."

"And is your familiar these—this—carving?" I asked, stumbling over the thought.

Rana nodded. "I had not one guest arrive to stay but hundreds of tiny ones, who swarmed in and out of my dreams in thousands of shapes that kept shifting and changing. They came to me in a spirit journey; in visions and dreams they took over my hands, guiding me to play with them, turning them over and over. I saw a knife beside them and picked it up, pointing it at their tiny bodies. I was shocked and afraid at first, believing I was about to hurt these beautiful little beings.

"I would awaken from dreams or return from these visions loathing myself for wanting to hurt such creatures. Because when I saw myself holding the sharp knife, pressing it against the bodies of these tiny beings, I could not ignore the delight in my heart."

I stopped breathing, my eyes wide.

"I didn't know what to do—I was confused and sick at heart. Finally I went to Celeste for advice."

"What did she say?"

Rana paused a moment, watching me before speaking as if to gauge my reaction. "She said that delight is holy and must not be interrupted. She asked whether the little creatures were frightened or disturbed by the knife in my hands. It shocked me to be asked that question. I had been considering the matter only from my own viewpoint, assuming I meant the little ones harm. I hadn't thought, in my fear, simply to ask the creatures.

"Celeste wondered aloud whether I was being directed to become a surgeon. So the next time I journeyed, I lifted the knife and, as the creatures drew close, I pressed the knife against the side of one. It lay down immediately, very patient, while I went to work on it, carving tiny details in its body. That was when I realized that they were really just half formed little things, and that my knife served to bring out their forms in ever greater detail. You see, before I cut into them they had only undefined shapes. As I cut, their lines became sharper. They took on actual shapes of animals. They were coming alive."

"So you became a woodcarver!" I exclaimed in wonderment.

"Yes, and the little ones now can enjoy life in the material world—instead of being trapped in my dream body," Rana smiled merrily, eyes narrowing, looking around at her family.

I recalled that she had introduced the figures to me as her other family. It crossed my mind that she considered herself closer to this family than to members of the circle. Suddenly I felt jealous.

"Is this the choice that you made—your part in the circle?"

"Yes," she answered quietly. "What's important is that you learn and listen before choosing. It may take your whole life to choose, and some of us never do. In a curious way, not ever choosing plays a part in the circle as well," she observed, furrowing her brow again. Then she laughed. "I don't know! I'm no good at sustaining deep thought. At your Grand Welcoming I had midwifery on my mind, so when it felt my turn to rise and speak, I spoke on that."

"Simple as that," I offered, smiling shyly.

"Simple as that," she smiled back. We laughed together, and I loved Rana then and for all the time she was on earth.

Actually, there was more to it than that … because later when I did go to Mica to learn about midwifery, she told me that Rana was a midwife!

I was surprised and a little hurt that Rana had played a trick on me. The next time I visited her, I asked about that.

"I talked about matters important to you then," she told me. "You didn't come to me for information about midwifery." And a gleam lit far back in her wise green eyes, green like the sea. She was unmarried and had no children. At first it seemed odd to me that she was a midwife. Later it made sense.

During my second visit to Rana I recalled that the Grand Welcoming ceremony had emphasized the importance for young Ravens of choosing a bird-mother, a sort of godparent who would stand beside us, serving as a mentor.

Rana was watching me through her laughing green eyes. I had begun to laugh along with her, then stopped, thinking of my need for a bird-mother. She stopped suddenly, too, her smile deepening, and she nodded at me.

I burst into tears and threw myself into her arms, and she patted me reassuringly.

"You've got a hard mother, you and Braise," she said softly, stroking my hair. "Maybe your life is harder because Anne is calling you, and there are things expected of you. Braise will be fine—she'll find a mother in one who's even tougher. And she will thrive on it. Me—all my hardness goes into carving. I'm hopeless!" she laughed softly in my ear, and I trembled with love for her, feeling my young heart would burst. I sobbed and clung to her as I never had clung to my mother, for all my life. I would not move out from under Rana's wing, not ever.

Except when you girls were born, it was the sweetest, most unadulterated moment of my life, beyond any in loving your father. Loving your father grew more slowly, even though I was wooed by him. But all in a flash I fell in love with Rana, and I was never the same. She was present at each of your births, you may remember, but because I was in the hospital she wasn't allowed to do the birthing. Rana had such quiet, insistent ways when she wanted to, however, that the doctors let her help. For my part, I made certain she was the first one to touch each of you, so you would have her spirit touching you for your whole lives.

Oddly, we never spoke formally of her becoming my bird-mother. It was understood between us, that was all. I visited her often and spent many days with her; we took trips together to Boston and to Western Massachusetts until I was married, after which I saw less of her.

During those first months I pressed Rana for answers to Raven tribe riddles, though just as she had said she was no good at prolonged analytical discussions on the nature of being a Raven. We would talk for a while, and then when she saw that I was filled up and further talk would be useless, she would put a knife in my hands and a block of wood, teaching me how to carve. I never got much good at it, so I think out of frustration she finally brought me some paints one day—which I really took to.

From then on we would go to the beach and sit on the great granite rocks, Rana pulling out some little pieces of basswood or cherry and a few of her tools wrapped in a soft cloth. She would spread them out and silently get to work. I would set up my easel and canvas, pull out some paints and a brush, and try to render what I saw. Many of the paintings in the house were painted with Rana beside me....

Months after Rana became my bird-mother, I asked her about the Grand Welcoming ceremony, whether she had experienced the same panic I had. She was leaning over her workbench, cutting in very fine details of an armadillo.

"Everyone panics, even Braise," Rana explained without looking up. "That's the reason for the initiation. To bring to a head all one's fears and condense them during that moment of signing one's name."

"But—what if I didn't mean what I wrote? What if the name I wrote wasn't right?"

"You may change your name, if it changes for you," Rana noted, glancing up from her work.

"Just like that?"

"Just like that." She focused again on the little animal.

"But—then why do we sign at all?"

"We sign in a state of exhaustion—emotional, physical, psychological—after the long night has conspired to overwhelm us and put us in a state out of which a meaningful name might arise." She looked up. "Names are powerful things. Knowing one's own name or another's name gives power. But as we change, sometimes our names change. That is why the particular name you give at the Grand Welcoming may not come to hold much power in your life. But most Raven members find that even when they feel at first that the name they signed does not represent their true identity, after a time it does make sense."

"You mean that 'Redblood' might have some meaning for me? I don't even have red hair," I pleaded, pulling at my long brown hair.

"What were you thinking when you signed?" Rana asked, putting her knife down.

I hesitated, for I remembered clearly enough. I had been hating my mother. "Mother," I said finally. "Maybe I was a little mad."

"Anger…frustration…panic." Rana stared past me. "Those are some red-blooded spirits. Anyway," she shrugged, "it's your own depth to plumb."

"You mean—anger at Mother," I whispered.

"The signing became midwife to an essential part of your Raven identity," she observed, making a signing motion with her knife along the well-scarred table top. "You are free to change your name, Redblood, but what you labored to bring forth at your initiation will stay behind, as emotionally bound up and in conflict with you as your identity with your mother."

"But I don't want it to be! I want my own identity! I don't want to be bound to my mother!" I pleaded, nearly crying.

"You may struggle consciously with it or not; your choice. But the fact remains," Rana finished, her voice full of fate.

She went back to work. "You'll discover the alchemical view that the cure lies in the disease. They may be inseparable. Your way to independence will mean working through some powerful blood ties." She frowned.

"There's some value in that, then," I wondered, picking up one of the little figures, a dog.

"There's value in most difficult things and in the things we want to avoid," Rana said evenly. "I had a difficult connection with my mother—I hated her, actually. She hated everything about the Ravens. Refused to help in my initiation. Refused to tell me anything about it."

"So how did you join?" I asked, shocked. Even my mother had at least given me a key.

"Changes started happening to me that I didn't understand. I had a friend—Laura, whose mother was a member. I became initiated through her and her mother." Rana pressed hard into the armadillo's shoulder, peeling away a tiny scrap of wood with the chisel point.

"Your mother didn't belong to the circle?" I asked, unaware that was possible.

"No. Rather, she did long ago, when she was a girl. It happens that way sometimes. Not everyone likes it. You've told me yourself you resented your mother forcing it on you."

"Oh, but I don't now!" I replied quickly.

Rana looked up. "I'm glad, too," she agreed, giving me or the world that half smile I loved.

"And is this all there is to being a member of the Raven tribe? Is there more of an organization to it that I don't know about?"

"There is only a loose organization, which you already know about. We have a community that is very strong, there if one of us needs it, for support and teaching and encouragement. Some of us need a lot, some very little. Most of us go about our everyday lives just as ordinary people do. Just that we—including you—have a secret knowledge of who we are."

"What?" I asked.

"Belonging," Rana answered simply, going back to work.

We had many years together from that small beginning. She was my spiritual mother, and through her I realized that while our biological parents are important, they are not often our spiritual parents. Rana's death was the greatest loss of my life.

And that's everything I have long waited to write to you, my dear girls. I hope these words help you to find yourselves. Please speak with your Aunt Meg and ask her questions. She will help you go further, if you like.

THERE THE WORDS ENDED, Nikki's mother's voice ceasing as abruptly as a quiet motor shut off. Just like her, to end without goodbye, Nikki fretted. So mild—*if you like*. Momentous words!

Nikki sat for a long time in the darkened room, from time to time pierced by Fergus Jr.'s shrieks.

"Ball!" he cried. Nikki felt a heaviness in her pulling her down and down.

5.

THE BURDEN OF PAIN

FOR A LONG TIME Nikki sat, her mind storming and making her head hurt. The whole world was as different as if someone had suddenly died. But someone had died. It was her mother, who had come to life in her long letter as a person radically different from the mother Nikki had known. Only, now that she had arrived as a new person, she left again, a mere ghost presence.

After a while Meg returned in a soft bustle. With a swift glance at her niece, she settled herself and lit a cigarette, observing Nikki through a blue cloud. Nikki's lungs were burning with all the smoke, but for now she didn't mind. She studied her aunt's yellowed fingertips.

"In her own way she was a strong person—and had a kind of independence," Nikki hesitated.

Meg roared with hoarse laughter until the torn tin ceiling shook.

"Second sight! Second sight!" shrieked Fergus Jr. fearfully.

"Strong! Independent!" cried Meg. Tears came into her eyes as her whole body shook, until Nikki, watching, grew impatient and finally offended.

Meg stopped laughing at last, pulled a tattered white lace hankie out of a pocket to wipe her eyes.

"I'm sorry, Nikki, but your mother was weak and not at all independent. No matter how sympathetically she might tell her story. But that's OK," she added, leaning to pat Nikki's hand. Nikki drew her hand away quickly, frowning.

Meg grew serious, though she smiled. "Really, I'm sorry. No harm, I suppose, if you want to think that, but it's far more important to understand the truth, to know," she insisted, emphasizing the last word. "It doesn't matter that your mother wasn't a strong person. Doesn't matter in the least."

Nikki frowned. "Of course it's important."

"To be strong?"

"Of course."

"How do you understand 'strong'?"

"You know—powerful. Independent, courageous, willful. Powerful like a lioness or a goddess."

"Oh—a goddess," Meg echoed, nodding, smiling darkly.

"You're mocking me," Nikki flared.

"A little. I can't help it. Would you call me a strong woman?"

"Yes," Nikki answered in a very soft voice.

"Independent? Courageous?"

"I think—I've always thought you took on that power," she asserted. "I think of you still as powerful."

"I'm also lonely and miserable."

"Maybe loneliness is part of the price," Nikki insisted.

"Oh, don't get romantic on me, Nikki!" Meg retorted, her voice rising. "I'm telling you I'm lonely and tired and full of weakness. That's a fact you'll just have to fit into your definition of power! Your mother, bless her soul, found a voice through writing, finally. That's very good. I have been wondering, these two years she's been gone, whether to speak to any of you about our Cleves heritage. But then I had her letter, telling me to wait. You were the one I thought to speak to—yes, it's true, don't shake your head. False modesty leads nowhere. You are your mother's daughter, in very many ways. But don't be too much like her, Nikki."

"I'm not like her," Nikki argued, raising her head.

"And don't be too much like me, either," Meg murmured. "If you've come to me with questions, you are ready to go on."

"I was told to come—by Rose," Nikki countered.

Meg shrugged. "What did you expect? A thundering voice from the clouds? It's time to go on. But going on requires losing your hesitancy and self-consciousness. Which means recognizing just who you are—and where you are."

Nikki's head was swirling. "I don't know where I am."

Meg watched her niece carefully. "Not yet. I have had my eye on you for years. You're the one most likely to keep the line going. There was a reason why your mother had all those daughters."

"Why do you emphasize daughters? Is the Raven clan solely for women?"

Meg thought a while, smoking. "Not exclusively—it couldn't be, since we don't recognize literal gender."

"What's that mean?"

"Physically, biologically, you are a woman, but what does that mean? Passivity? Emotionality? Or just the opposite? Raven awareness shifts the focus away from arbitrary masculine and feminine categories—to the living spirits and natural powers that give us our changing shapes. Historically, however, the old tradition that Anne comes from is matrilineal—for more than a thousand years, the secret knowledge and arcane powers have been passed down from mother to daughter."

"What makes you think I am the one most likely to carry on the line?"

"Because you've been on a spiritual journey for years, that's been clear. Oh, I know we haven't had much contact, but I've kept in touch with you in other ways." Meg smiled. "It's one of the advantages of being a member of the Raven clan." She nodded toward the front room. "You think that crystal ball is just for show, just a gag, don't you? You don't yet understand, do you?"

Nikki smiled faintly. "The crystal ball is—real?"

"Real enough. What's real, Nikki? Is a story real? It feels real, doesn't it? Do you believe everything your mother wrote?"

"You think she's lying?" Nikki asked, suddenly feeling dizzy. She had indeed at the beginning read her mother's story with incredulity. But by the end she believed it was true. Now she recalled her mother's words about writing a story—that it blurs the line between fact and fiction. That you become a character in your own story.

"No, I think she's written a story—which has magical power. I know when I look into that crystal ball, I fall into a state of intense concentration—imagination, the poets called it—in which I see things that have an uncanny correspondence with the world. That have a truth to them, in other words. A magical occurrence can be dismissed as coincidence or explained as science, depending on the kind of forces you imagine operating when events connect in space and time. Scientists focus on predictable forces to account for an outbreak of fire; the more artistically minded envision a convergence of animating spirits…"

"So Anne Cleves' magic is just—artistic power?" Nikki stared into space. "But it's more than that, isn't it? It's having the strength to influence or control the world around you—even bend things to your will."

"Power, I'm ambivalent about," Meg answered. "When I was young, all I wanted was to have a strong arm, to be able to cast spells, to inflict whatever I wanted without suffering any consequences. I thought that was power."

"Isn't it? Not worrying about the consequences? You said not to hesitate."

"There are always consequences, always karma," Meg spoke sharply. "When I was on the outside, I understood power as something that would enhance me, make me strong. How wrong I was!" Meg laughed hoarsely, coughing.

"But it did make you strong!" Nikki protested.

"Power gave me strength, but the source of that strength belongs to power itself, not to the one who wields it. I didn't understand that until I started exercising my power. Then I realized paradoxically that it demanded a kind of giving myself up to it, the way you have to surrender to love if its force is to infuse you. You let yourself be eclipsed, like the sun by the moon's shadow."

"There's more to it than that," Nikki insisted, lowering her head. There had to be! She suspected that her aunt was doing the same thing to Nikki that Meg's mother had done to Meg herself—withholding crucial information. But she wasn't sure. She would sort it out on her own, she resolved.

"You think I'm not telling you things, but you're wrong," Meg continued. "On the contrary, I have much to pass along to you. You've come to me on your own, so we must talk; now I must give you direction. I will begin by conveying one of the most powerful insights of the Raven tribe. It's deceptively simple: Everything, all the world, is a dream of the dreaming soul, which is held together by the original goddess and god. Magic is possible in reality just as it is in a dream, for the worlds are essentially one and the same. We open our eyes to one in daytime, and to the other at night. We have only to open our eyes."

"I don't follow," Nikki said softly. She was still thinking about power.

Meg got up and went over to a small bookcase tucked in the corner, squinted down the stack of dusty books, finally drawing out a cracked leather-bound tome. Returning to the table, she plunked it down. Reaching for her reading glasses, she threaded them over her head by their red string. Setting the glasses on her wide-bridged nose, she frowned deeply, flipping through the pages.

"This book on paganism is by a man named Sallustius," she explained, looking up over her glasses. "He lived in the fourth century and was a friend of the Emperor Julian. Julian was the leader of the Holy Roman Empire, which was Christian at the time. As in—the great witch burners," Meg snorted, looking back down through her glasses at the pages wrinkled like old skin.

"Julian was one of our friends because he tried to restore the old pagan religion. Early Christians still enacted pagan rituals—it took some time for the Christian rituals to split completely off and develop on their own. At bottom, the present-day Catholic Mass is a pagan ritual, Jesus' death and rebirth another form of the ancient death-rebirth mystery, like the old corn god who dies in order to be reborn every year.

"So, listen to Sallustius: 'One may call the world a myth, in which bodies and things are visible, but souls and minds are hidden.' " Meg looked up. "Understand? The world we know through our senses is not the only world, just the perceptible one."

Nikki was silent, struggling with the implications.

"You're thinking of your mother," Meg remarked matter-of-factly. "It's only natural you would."

"Every true part of her was invisible, it seems," Nikki responded sadly.

"Not every part. Just the part you couldn't see behind the obvious. But maybe you did—don't judge yourself too harshly." Meg gave her niece a sideways glance. "Are you sure you didn't suspect, on some level, that your mother was more than she appeared? Think about it." Meg folded the book closed and shoved it aside.

"There's Irish blood in us, you know. *Keefe.* You think you look so Finnish, like your father. Look again, my dear! Those deep-set eyes with that glint of warmth—that's Irish! The Irish are big believers in having a foot in two worlds. Does that set off any bells?"

Nikki was still, frowning into her tea that was reflecting her eyes. "Is what lies hidden—real?" Nikki asked, her voice quavering.

"Sure! As real as dreams get!"

"I feel like I'm in a dream!" Nikki exclaimed.

Meg winked. "Just keep dreaming. It's taken courage for you to sit here, since you clearly weren't expecting your world to be turned upside down. So I'll give you a few hints. The Raven clan varies too much in belief and practice for any one person to claim possession of the truth. It's in the nature of the Raven clan that everyone practices idiosyncratically, which is why we attract outcasts, subversive thinkers—anyone who finds the predominant Judeo-Christian paradigm unsatisfying. It's not so much that Christianity is wrong as that it's limiting. If you feel left out after taking a hard look at yourself and your life, feeling there's far more to your soul than Jesus can explain, then Anne and her Raven clan may call you. Because Raven truths are variegated and multiple, our members are disgruntled, dissatisfied, cranky, solitary people. Environmentalists and feminists, lesbians and gays. People who feel alienated, but in their hearts are looking for a place to belong.

"It's not really organized as a religion," Meg went on, "say, in the tradition of Christianity—there's no official creed. You'll hear one member say her guiding ethic is not to cause harm, while the next person emphasizes the intimate connection of inner and outer nature. Personally, I think one's view of reality has to give space to the whole gamut of human possibilities. If you join only to shut out the more dangerous aspects of life, such as violence or sex or self-destruction—even that blind impulse we humans seem to carry to destroy the earth—then you risk making the same mistake mass culture makes, of not putting the imagination first."

She puffed thoughtfully on her cigarette.

"But allowing someone who wants to pave the earth over to be a member—doesn't that risk co-opting the Raven clan?"

Meg nodded. "Wanting to do something is different from actually doing it—that's the mistake the Catholics make, and it's what killed your mother in the end."

"Killed her?" Nikki asked, breathless.

"Your mother felt hopelessly guilty for her own unconventional thoughts and desires, and over her lifetime she judged herself as mercilessly as did the old Puritans the witches of Salem and Dogtown. So she kept her religious beliefs from your father, hid her secret heritage—and condemned herself twice for lying to him."

"Wasn't she lying? And wasn't she right to?"

"I can't judge from on high," Meg answered. "I do know all that moral overlay made her conflict worse. If she had stayed true to her Raven roots, which places such value on secrecy, she could have used her secrecy as a lifesaver."

Nikki considered. "But look at someone like Rose Eveless—isn't the developing she's doing—filling in wetlands—wrong?"

"Is it? Don't we need houses? I need one," Meg looked around the shabby room.

"You know what I mean," Nikki insisted seriously.

"Maybe the self-destructiveness of modern life is a matter of degree—we're too silly to know when to stop with the right dosage. So we have to react via extremes; building codes get made into absolutes, and we haven't an idea of how to live in a relationship with the earth. Of course, if you start out thinking of humans as more important than all other living things—than even the earth herself—then you're already in a destructive place...."

Meg stood up, brushed her dress down, and stretched. "Enough philosophy! Tell me about you—what's going on in your life? Still lawyering in Boston?"

Nikki shook her head absently. "That's part of all the changes going on. I quit my job—I just didn't want to be a lawyer anymore. I've had it with that world. I moved back to Gloucester, not really to live in my parents' house but to be near some nature. I got so tired of the city!"

Meg nodded. "So now what?"

"That's exactly the question. Now what? I don't know what to do—about my life, how to think about my mother now.... And I've got Rose breathing down my neck and her son Philip lying nearly dead, imprisoned in his mother's house. I'm so confused—and I guess I'm—scared." She lowered her head.

Meg brightened. "What do you say we look in the ball—or read the tarot—to see what comes up for you?" She smiled playfully at Nikki, and her old leathered face shone with a hard light.

Nikki blanched.

"Cards!" shrieked Fergus Jr.

"You've never had your cards read before?" Meg looked at her in disbelief.

"Of course I have," Nikki straightened herself. "Except not by—"

"By someone with real power?" Meg's eyebrows arched.

"Well, I wouldn't say that...." The words dribbled out of Nikki's mouth.

"Ha!" Meg exclaimed as she rose and ducked through the curtain, returning shortly with a much-used tarot deck. The beaded curtain behind her clicked brightly. Meg handed the cards to Nikki.

"Shuffle," she said, winking. Lighting another Camel with her batwing lighter, she drew deeply, exhaling the smoke in a long blue plume. She looked at the cigarette a moment, picked an imaginary bit of tobacco from her mouth, and set the burning cigarette in the ashtray.

Nikki shuffled slowly and carefully, frowning a bit. Did she want to have her tarot read, just now, with no preliminaries? She was used to being in charge of her life, but lately things had been taking her—people, events, timing. Had it been her decision after all to buy the house and move to Gloucester? She vaguely remembered telling friends a year ago or more that she wanted to move somewhere out of the city. Somewhere north, maybe. But Gloucester? Shuffling absent-mindedly, she saw images of Philip, then Alice, then her mother and father drift past her.

"Trying to rub the pictures off?" Meg teased. Nikki frowned and handed her the cards. She wanted to be serious.

"Hold them for a moment and ask your question out loud."

Nikki hesitated. "I suppose something like, 'What am I to do?' All these crossroads in my life—work, relationships, this strange new way of seeing my mother. I feel like I'm being pushed in a direction but not sure which one, or which is the right one to follow." Nikki handed the cards to her aunt.

Meg held the cards a moment, eyes closed. "The questioner—faced with many changes, many roads before her—asks which direction to take in her life." Opening her eyes, she turned the cards over, one at a time, placing them in the traditional ten-card spread. Nikki watched her aunt's eyes flicker and her own brows jumped.

"ok," Meg announced when she had finished. "Let's start at the beginning." She indicated the center card, on top of which lay a second card perpendicular to the first.

"First position is the King of Wands," Meg explained. "This position indicates who you are, in essence, at this time. Like the lines in the palm of your hand, your self changes over time, and this card in the first position tells us where you are in relation to the world. The King of Wands is a ruler, the one in charge. Power; authority. The tarot presents in images—not as abstract concepts applying out of context. So the kind of power and authority presented here is of the kingly sort, and as such assumes a masculine form."

With a glance at her niece, Meg added, "I'm not at all surprised." A flicker of a smile crossed Nikki's mouth. "Before we go on, let me refresh your memory concerning the various suits," Meg continued.

"*Wands* is a suit that often has to do with career or position in the world. *Swords* has to do with strategies and how to progress, *Cups* with emotions and relationships, and *Pentacles* with money and material wealth. Though that's putting it pretty glibly; there are plenty of overlaps. *Cups*, for example, can often indicate something tangible, some matter in the world. I want to distinguish the suits a bit before we go on because your card, *Card 1*—who you are when you ask your question—is the King of Wands. Male essence, having to do with career. I've found that keeping the cover card in mind throughout the reading can give you a lot of insight into the general trend of the other cards that come up."

"You mean the subject has to do with career?" Nikki asked.

"That career is an important element in everything else that comes up. Doesn't an important aspect of your question—'what to do with your life'—concern which career to choose?" Meg asked.

"Sure," Nikki said. "Have to pay the bills."

"As we all do," Meg agreed. "All right then, *Card 2,* the Empress, crosses you. This is your obstacle, what literally is crossing you, even making you cross."

Nikki started at the connection. Meg glanced at her, continuing. "The Empress is sitting in the field waiting to harvest last year's crop, which is rich and full." She tapped the card with her long fingernail. "The card is about productivity, perhaps connected with the arts. It's a woman who is wonderfully rich and fertile—with ideas, movements, bearing a great harvest. She's what is crossing your path right now; she looms large and carries a great deal of authority."

Nikki stared at the card. "Is that good or bad?"

"Her authority? Depends on whether she's with you or against."

Meg lit up again and set the cigarette in the ashtray. "I remember you as an angry little thing, Nikki. Do you remember the tantrums you used to have? You would fall into them when you were frustrated. This was when you were very young—when your mother used to bring you here often. Before your father decided he hated me and told your mother not to bring you girls to visit."

Meg sat back. Nikki was a little disturbed, as if her aunt were breaking the spell of the reading. But Meg had her own way, always had. Nikki felt a grudging respect for that.

"I don't remember," she answered simply.

"Oh, yes—you had a fit or two right here in the store. One of the most remarkable things I've ever seen—and I've seen a lot. Your little body would get all twisted up, contorted, your face red and screwed up, you would lash out at people, things—we all had to just keep our distance and let you go. The first time it happened—you must have been six or seven—I just watched, amazed. The second time, when I saw your mother wasn't going to do anything, I drew a circle around you, to protect you while you were in that sacred state."

"Sacred!" Nikki snorted.

"Oh, yes—*sacred*," Meg repeated seriously, drawing and exhaling. "You behaved like an old Druid in the middle of a shamanic possession. Or maybe like an ancient Irish warrior—Cúchulainn himself falling into a warp-spasm before going into battle."

"You think I was fighting something?"

"Only you could have told. We were outside looking in. But you were awfully angry. After it passed you actually fell into a faint, and your mother had to carry you out. Later she told me that when your father got a load of you, looking all pale and half-dead as your mother carried you into the house, your long blond hair stringy and dirty, he had a fit of his own. That was when he said you weren't to come here anymore. Thank the moon your mother wasn't a complete mouse! She sneaked you down here several times after that, albeit rarely."

Nikki considered. "I wonder what set me off?"

Meg shrugged. "Your mother blamed it on your stubbornness: You weren't getting your way. Rachel was maybe teasing you, like she used to. But I wonder, too." Meg puffed.

"Whether it was something else?"

"Yes," Meg answered. "It could have been simply a childish tantrum, but it felt different to me. As if all of a sudden you were witnessing something… One time your mother and I were back here talking over tea, you and Rachel out front. I remember the curtain was pulled back on a nail, so I could just make you out through the gap. I couldn't see Rachel. At first you stood there very still—just staring at the books in the bookcase. You were a little thing, long before you grew so tall, and the bookcase was taller than you. With your long blond hair and bright round eyes, you looked like a little magical child—like Alice in Wonderland! Rachel said something to you—teasing you, I'm sure. You coughed once or twice, and then you just started screaming. By the time your mother and I got to you, you were writhing on the floor, practically foaming at the mouth. I thought you were having an epileptic seizure."

"Epileptics were supposed to be holy people," Nikki mused.

"Right. What we think of today as a strange medical condition was once considered a visitation by some god or goddess, which usually meant bad news. Ah, the good old days!"

"And then you drew a circle around me."

"Then I drew a circle."

"What brought it on?"

"I told you what I saw, Nikki," Meg stated. "It's all in you—where it came from, what it means, whether it's something more than a tantrum."

Nikki was silent a few moments, thinking of Rose.

Meg looked at her closely. "So what's made you cross? Your mother's letter? Or something you came in with? Rose Eveless?"

Nikki screwed her mouth up.

Meg continued. "I suspect you are feeling angry because your energy has been misdirected. It's time to bring in some great rich harvest of your own. Something growing in you like a child for a good long season. The card crossing you, the Empress, is only an obstacle if you fight her. Go with it and harvest your crop. Which may mean harvesting your anger, which will be mowed down in turn once your scythes start their work…"

"Maybe you should do what Rose demands: Find the journal. Even if you reap for her," Meg added.

"Is this a tarot reading or therapy?" Nikki asked wryly.

Meg chuckled hoarsely. *"Card 3* is your destination, as far as the question is concerned. Which is a big question."

"It's the High Priestess… Quite amazing. In thousands of readings I've done, I've seen this card come up only once or twice in that position. So I always keep an eye out for anyone receiving it. The High Priestess is intuitive. See the moon at her feet? That's actually a Druid moon, but we'll leave that be for the moment. The High Priestess is in contact with the spirits; she knows things. You are heading in this direction toward understanding, which is like a moon waxing."

"Understand what?"

"A new way of looking at things—or what to do."

"How?"

"Intuitively—you'll just know," Meg shrugged. She waited while Nikki considered. "A High Priestess is present at every initiation," she explained.

She went on. *"Card 4* is your distant past. Something behind you that affects where you are now, and where you are headed. It's the Five of Pentacles, a card of poverty. An old woman with a crippled son following behind her." Meg tapped on the card. "She hasn't the means to take care of her own child, or anyone to help her. She is deprived. Feeling left behind or left out, without help—this is what's behind you. 'Behind you' in multiple senses: in your past; but also behind you, driving you to act out of feelings of impoverishment. Or referring to a state you are leaving behind—possibly feelings of never being good enough, of being a loser… In any case, it's something from long ago that's still at work, pushing you.

"Whereas *Card 4* refers to childhood images still active in the background, *Card 5* has to do with your recent past. Here it is the Four of Pentacles, which is about your distant past. See the man? He's holding tight to the pentacles, directly asserting ownership. They are his, and no mistake about it. He's holding onto something."

"That he's—I'm—supposed to let go of?" Nikki asked suddenly, sitting up straight.

"Depends on the context. Could be something you feel attached to—your old way of life, a habitual way of being—which you're afraid to let go of even though you need to. Or it might be something you should rightfully show ownership of, standing up to say, 'Look, world, this is who I am, and I couldn't care less what you think about it.' Notice the city behind the man? He's making his statement in front of the whole world. That's good if it's something to hold onto and be proud of. More of a problem if you are standing up in front of everyone insisting on some foolishness. Either way, it's being up-front and open about what you possess."

Nikki considered. Of course, there was much to let go of—there always was. She was good at letting go, in fact. But this might be about owning something that was right to own. Taking on her mother's life as a Druid? No—that belonged, if anywhere, to a murky future. Something behind her that she felt strongly identified with. Her power? And was she supposed to let go or hold on tighter? Was that good or bad?

Nikki had a sudden thought. "I've recently lost the good salary I earned for years. I'm letting go of that," she remarked brightly. It was good to let it go, though it scared her.

"That's certainly public," Meg agreed. "This position generally refers to something in the near past, so maybe that's it."

Meg continued. "*Card 6* is what's in front of you—what lies ahead. It is the Three of Swords, and notice the swords are piercing a heart. Also that it's raining." Meg grew quiet and sober. "No getting around it—your future portends a wounded heart. Rain's coming… Are you having a difficult time with Philip?" Meg asked suddenly.

Nikki was caught off guard. "Uh—yes, sort of. Philip is—I have to let go of him, that's for sure. I mean, I want to let go of him, but now there's this matter with Rose… Hard times ahead," she shook her head. "They're pretty hard right now."

"They may get harder yet, and hurt more." Meg looked closely at her niece. "I'm sorry—it may not be as bad as I'm interpreting. Sometimes people go through difficult times without even noticing, for all sorts of reasons. The card could have nothing to do with Philip and you since it refers to your future, and your heartache with Philip is happening now."

"Um," Nikki grunted.

"It could very well be about your relationship with your mother—or your father, for that matter. Something you have loved or felt passionately about, maybe even hated, is about to be pierced. This heart—" she tapped the card where its red heart was punctured by three swords, "might be directed not so much to another person as toward some captivating subject. What sorts of things attract you lately—enough to win your heart?"

"Plenty," Nikki answered, twisting her mouth.

"But that might lead to heartbreak? Or has already started to hurt?"

Nikki was silent. What did she love? Whom did she love? She loved Philip, with a love she had never felt before. He had become the center of her life, but it was killing her, for he kept her away from the center of his own. He said all the words she had been waiting to hear, all those words she always hoped one day a man would say to her, and which she was sure she would laugh at when she did hear them. When he spoke it was already a joke; he was onto it and so it was OK; she could relax and enjoy. But trust? She wouldn't let go of herself to him. Not completely. It was too dangerous. Then, might it be that she, somehow, was keeping him out of the center of her life, in spite of her love for him?

"Let's look at the last four cards," Meg said softly. "*Card 7* is your position relative to the question. It's the King of Swords, which means endurance, firmness, rock-hard resolution. A ruler commands, looms large—queens and kings in the tarot generally indicate large matters. You've got a lot of large cards here, Nikki," Meg laughed lightly. "More, actually, than I've ever seen come up in one reading."

An image of granite cliffs and rain falling flashed before Nikki's inner eye.

"The King of Swords is rock solid, not powerful like the King of Wands but enduring, wielding his own sort of power. Someone powerful and enduring is watching over you. That's good; you'll need a lot of endurance for the journey you are beginning, and this card indicates that you've got just the endurance and determination you'll need. Rose's demand and your own fate are coinciding to send you on a journey. Do you ever study rocks, or collect them?"

Nikki looked up and smiled shyly. "As a matter of fact, I took a seminar in rock reading. I love rocks!" she exclaimed, her face brightening. "I think that's why I came back to Gloucester—for the granite. All those wonderful rocks I used to climb on as a girl, playing games on, seemed like they had spirits or personalities."

Meg studied her niece. "So you've already got a rock nature—that's good news. Keep lots of your rocks around; they'll help. People sometimes think that only animals or disembodied spirits can be familiars, but I think rocks and plants can be too."

Nikki nodded, thinking of the long row of rocks she had set above her headboard. One of the first things she saw when she awoke were her rocks from Alaska, her rocks from Dogtown, from the Southwest. They were like an extended family, speaking to her in their own regional languages.

"*Card 8* is the Queen of Swords—another powerful card! This position has to do with your influence on others, or your position as seen by the people around you. The

Queen is commanding, dominating. Your friends probably see you as domineering, powerful, getting your own way or doing things your own way."

"Makes me sound tyrannical," Nikki snorted.

Meg chuckled throatily. "You said it, not me!" She shook herself. "The card shows that some request you're making is being heard. See how the Queen raises her hand? She is indicating that the subject should rise. The subject could be you or your request, the thing you are looking for. You can read the figures in the cards in terms of the unified person you take yourself to be, but you could just as well understand each as independent forces inside of you—separate feelings, characteristic states, parts of yourself, even autonomous areas of personality beyond your awareness."

"Card 9 is the Knight of Swords. This is astonishing—King, Queen, Knight all in a row! It looks like your kingdom is in Swords these days! The ninth position has to do with your innermost states—instincts, emotions, impulses. The Knight is about aggression. See how he is rushing into battle? Something in you is rushing into the fray—or wants to. You have a desire to grab what matters to you by the teeth, to jump into it with both feet. To take control—that's the sort of person you consider yourself, anyway. But you might also experience it as something rushing into your life from the outside: as a man, a masculine image, an idea that comes waving a sword—daring, brash, presumptuous."

"This news about my mother is breaking into my life," Nikki said uncertainly.

"But the image takes the form of a knight, meaning masculinity…"

"Masculine…" Nikki considered, shaking her head. "Philip? My father?" She looked up.

Meg shrugged. "Your father doesn't seem like a charging force—at least not now in your life."

Nikki considered Philip. Hadn't he in his own way rushed into her life, with his certainty, his presumption of knowing her—? He treated their connection as if it had all been preordained.

"Now for the final card, having to do with what results from your question—from your quest. It is the Ten of Pentacles, which interestingly enough indicates material wealth. The card shows a couple walking in the garden of their estate as an old man looks on from the side. Domestic dogs follow them; the couple is happy and together."

"'Living happily ever after' is the answer to my question?" Nikki asked incredulously.

"Let's just say that the place you're in culminates in something material—in the sense of being real in the world, worldly real…. You said you've been wondering what to do professionally?" Meg asked.

"That's one of the problems I'm facing right now, ever since I quit my job as a lawyer. How am I supposed to earn money? I used all my savings to buy the house… So I suppose material wealth, money, is one of my concerns."

"Sometimes a spiritual path takes a material form. It's just as mistaken to assume that spiritual growth has nothing to do with material wealth as to link the two. All these self-help books with leading promises everywhere you turn: If only you get enlightened enough, you'll become healthy, wealthy, and wise! What a travesty of spirituality! Everyone just feels worse after reading those books and meditating like mad, eating healthy vegetarian, even donating to public radio—and then expecting the dollars to start rolling in."

"Of course, that's a caricature," Nikki protested.

"Of course. But sometimes—sometimes you do get wealthy going on a spiritual journey. No one knows why. Our New Age Calvinism would make a causal connection, as if a rich person is somehow favored by God."

"It's still a curious card to turn up at the very end," Nikki noted.

"I'll say!" Meg acknowledged brightly. She relit her burned-out cigarette, inhaling profoundly. "That will be one million dollars," she declared, holding out an open palm.

Nikki laughed. Was it possible her old aunt was all right? "Thank you," she replied softly.

"You have a lot more questions, dear," Meg observed.

"Why didn't our mother tell us?" Nikki frowned.

Meg tossed up her hand. "Fear, desire to conform... What did she write was the reason for not speaking?"

"The same. I just don't understand. Why tell us at all, then? Why leave something behind that none of us might ever find?"

"Maybe your mother put a spell on her journal to draw you to it."

Nikki looked quickly at her aunt. "Sure."

Meg sat up. "Nikki, do you think there is such a thing as magic?"

"Are you asking whether I think this Cleves story is really true? As more than just a bunch of women out in the woods getting close to nature and worshiping the earth goddess?"

"Yes," Meg answered slowly. "Meaning, what do you make of your mother's secret heritage?"

"I don't know. My mother didn't write anything about magic spells, although she talked about herbal cures and potions."

"Do you believe it's possible to possess special powers, to cast spells and recite incantations to bring about certain effects?"

Nikki hesitated. "I think strange things happen that can't be explained. I'm not sure about magic—I don't know exactly what magic is."

"Your image of magic comes from the Sunday comics."

"I suppose."

"Magic is altogether different, though. Magic can make things happen—I've seen it; hell, I've done magic, the kind I know how. Mine has to do with the crystal ball, seeing things in it. Our ancestor Anne Cleves was supposed to have been a shapeshifter, able to take on the shape of animals."

"To really change," Nikki commented wryly.

"You raise a good question. What does it mean to change into an animal? Does it have to be a material transformation—literally taking on the biology of an animal? Or could it just as well mean assuming an animal's aspect? By putting on the skins of animals—putting on their scents—magicians and shamans 'in a sense' become those animals. It's a matter of degree, I think. If someone looking at you dressed up as a bear sees a bear and not a human, then it seems to me you are a bear, and you've become a bear through magic."

"But the human is still there."

"So is the bear when you look like a human." Meg drew on her Camel and stubbed the butt out. "Let's look at my earlier suggestion: Your mother's spell got you to come here and discover her letter."

"But—considering that Rose's demand I find Anne's journal was what brought me here, Rose herself would somehow have had to be involved in my mother's spell."

"How do you know we aren't all just moving around following the words of some incantation, and that what seem like free will and random acts might not have a deeper purpose and design?"

"Sure, there's fate, I guess. I don't think events happen randomly. But you're suggesting that fate itself is somehow available for individuals to control."

"Forget control."

"My skepticism has to do partly with not understanding why our mother would leave something so important without telling us, relying instead on us to find it."

"You found it."

"But I just happened on it, all because Rose is afraid of getting older."

"Or did you? Nikki, one of your cards, the High Priestess, has to do with psychic powers as well as intuition. She turned up in the third position, which is the destination of your question, and so she should be considered alongside your material wealth card as part of the final outcome. She presides over a certain space. Think of how the old house has been in our family for generations. Feel your way back through it… Lots of ghosts there, presences. Anything odd about the house that might have made you think of coming here?"

"I dream a lot in it—" Nikki began.

"Good, a beginning. Write them down?"

"Yes. Vivid dreams with my parents—I'm just remembering, my father said something about a presence in the house before he died…"

"You mentioned that earlier. He told you directly?"

"Of course not. He told Todd, Cynthia's husband. When Todd was visiting him to take care of the will. Todd told all of us."

"Have you felt anything odd yourself in the house?"

"Something just clicked. When I was cleaning out the basement, I found this old chest with the name 'Cleves' on it. At the time it meant nothing, but now, of course, it makes sense."

"It's like a waking dream, isn't it? When you start the hard work of sorting things out, things in the basement, the box appears and takes you to the next place."

Nikki made a small sound of surprise.

"Except you're leaving out the part of Rose and her demand of me."

"What is it?"

"Philip got hurt—badly. I went to see him, which was when Rose gave me the ultimatum: Find the journal or no Philip."

"And she mentioned me?"

"Indirectly, yes. I didn't believe everything she said, of course."

"So love brought you here?" Meg asked, a wondrous smile lighting her face.

"I—suppose."

Meg paused. "I'll tell you what I see," she said finally. "I believe your mother returned to the Raven tribe before she died, for reasons she took with her. She left me her journal not long before she became ill. Like she knew... Don't look too long exploring the whys," Meg continued. "You could take it just as much a matter of luck as of fate that you found your mother's letter. Though you always were the intuitive one, the one close to nature."

"Oh, that was Rachel—still is!" Nikki insisted.

"She's got her own connection to nature—just not your kind."

"I would think hers would be magical, if anybody's."

"Yours is more complex, I think, having to do with animals and your garden, and the fact that you decided to live close to Dogtown."

Nikki laughed. "It was available."

"How many things have to pile up before there's a tendency? How many coincidences before you call it magic?" Meg demanded.

"That's what magic is?"

"Intuition is magic, in a way. Scientists seek to explain away superstition, but they just keep projecting magic onto smaller and smaller bits—postponing nature's mysteries until they reach subatomic particles. Or they extend their minds outward into space and find magic to dispel in worm holes, alternate universes, black holes... Where does it end? It won't end, because the world is larger than science. How far does science have to go before it admits fully to things unexplainable in its own terms?

"Making magic means trusting that what seems to have no causal connection might have an *acausal* one. So let's just say," she finished, "that although magic is a vast subject, you've got to start somewhere—since you've never practiced." Meg hesitated. "At least, not that I've seen in my ball..."

"No," Nikki admitted.

"You've begun now. Want some advice?" Meg stared at her niece a moment. "Maybe you don't, but here it is anyway. Just go with it. Forces are already leading you. You've got some losses to undergo—the change in you wouldn't be true otherwise. Remember your waking dream—and how one thing leads to another. I'll give you the name of a woman in Rockport to visit. She belongs to the circle in which your mother and I were initiated. The rest is up to you—so they say!" Meg sat back to light another Camel.

"But—I don't really know what I'm doing," Nikki confessed, feeling her head in a daze. "Even whether I want to go further."

Meg nodded and smoked, as curling lines of blue thoughts filled the dark room and ascended to the shadows above.

"I'm sort of scared," Nikki said at last. "Something happened the other night. I think I'm having visions—"

Meg sat up and peered at her. "Yes?"

"The night of the big storm. First I was in the kitchen, where I saw this—thing—face—at the kitchen window."

"Whose?"

"Um—Ernest Eveless," Nikki replied self-consciously.

Meg nodded seriously. "What did he want?"

"I don't know. Did he want something?"

"Ghosts usually do. Blood, or attention—some sacrifice to their memory."

"I was too scared to wonder—even now."

"Go on," Meg exhaled a long plume of thoughtful smoke.

"Then when the storm was going full blast, I suddenly saw Philip on his boat in the storm. I knew it was actually happening, what I was seeing."

Meg chuckled heavily. "And you're not sure you believe in magic! Spirit visitations, second sight—what more magic do you want?" She shook her head. Growing serious, she stood up and disappeared through the curtain, returning shortly bearing the crystal ball in her hands. Setting it on its little black stand between them, she sat down.

"Want to take a look?" she offered her niece.

"OK," Nikki answered in her singsong voice.

"No kidding," Meg frowned, so that Nikki stopped smiling. Meg waved her hand. "Don't listen to an old lady. Maybe you need your girlishness. Anyway, think about Anne Cleves' journal and have a look inside the ball."

As Meg held her outstretched hands over the ball, Nikki stared into it, her mind emptying easily. There was just the ball and a cloudiness of perception.

"See anything?" Meg asked softly.

"I see a cave of some sort—and rocks," Nikki said evenly.

"Go on," Meg prodded, lighting a cigarette and blowing.

"Big trees alongside the cave. Guy is digging in the ground amid mounds of dark dirt... I feel sleepy," Nikki said finally. She looked up. "That's all. Sorry." She smiled hesitantly. "Not much after all."

Meg sat back quietly, smoking. "Not much..." she nodded. "Well!" she blurted, sitting up suddenly. "It's never much—that's the way it works." She tapped cigarette ashes in the ashtray. "But just enough... So you'll have to remember everything you just saw, in as much detail as you can. The whole image."

"Is it important?"

"It might be giving shape to where the journal is. Lots of lore surrounds the journal, including a widespread belief that no one has ever had a vision of its whereabouts."

"What—with so many people looking for it? Doesn't sound possible," Nikki protested.

Meg shrugged. "That's the lore, anyway. All I know is that my own abilities come, like yours, by way of special sight—as visions. Although I've tried to envision the journal's location over the years, nothing has ever come. Whatever images do arise in the ball seem contrived, as if I've made them up. That's why it's important you remember what you've just seen."

Standing abruptly, Meg shuffled over to her little hot plate, reached for a can of lentil soup from the shelf, opened it gruntingly, cigarette in her mouth, and poured the contents into a saucepan.

"Hungry? I am," she muttered around the cigarette. She went to work slicing a loaf of bread she pulled from a dented red-painted box.

"They were a lot alike, you know, your father and grandmother," Meg explained, putting the bread on a plate and setting the plate on the table. She took spoons and a knife, set them out, then fished in a drawer and took out two black linen napkins, which she arranged under the spoons. She dug teabags out of the tin to make tea while the soup heated, then poured. Next she lifted a colorful bowl filled with bruised bananas and red grapes and set it in the middle of the table, then shoved the crystal ball unceremoniously into a corner of the cabinet. When the pan bubbled soft whispers, Meg poured the soup into two bowls, setting one before Nikki, the other in her own spot.

There they sat, door locked against the deepening shadows without, newspapers and plastic shopping bags blowing along the empty block of downtown offices in old Salem. They leaned like conspirators over their steaming bowls, Meg with her ragged dark-red shawl drawn over her shoulders, cigarette balanced in her free hand. Between sips she picked up the thread.

"Your grandmother put some sort of spell on your father, I think, toward your mother."

"To make him marry Mother?" Nikki was shocked.

"Yes. He was a sweet boy at first, handsome and strong. You know the story. I believe my mother was looking for an heir, because she wasn't too happy with either of her daughters as a proper one. I thought she was going beyond the bounds to procure a man for your mother. It was as if he were some sort of daimon of hers, some invisible spirit part of herself that she made manifest in male form in order to beget a granddaughter worthy of her. One day she must have gone down into her workroom in the basement, where she kept stored all her ointments and potions, and decided to create the man your mother would marry. I can see her taking an old broom and dressing it in clothes, putting a hat on his head, and animating it with some spells that she would never teach me." Meg snorted her disgust, slurping soup.

Nikki was appalled by the image.

Meg smiled at her. "It reminds me of the T.S. Eliot poem, *The Four Quartets*. There's a section called "The Dry Salvages," which refers to a group of rocks off the coast of Rockport where young Tom used to spend his summers." Meg looked into the near distance, narrowing her eyes to remember.

" 'The hint half guessed, the gift half received, is incarnation…' " Meg nodded.

Nikki sipped tea and cleared her throat. "Why didn't you have children, if Mother was so against it all? Grandmother must have known my mother was hesitant about joining the Raven circle."

"Sure she knew. But she liked me even less than your mother. She and I used to get into it—because I wasn't afraid of the old hag. You should have heard me, yelling like a banshee all night long! Your mother say anything in her letter about all that? No—? It's a wonder our fights didn't wake up the neighborhood." Meg spooned her soup, ducking her head. " 'Course I wasn't as loud as your father got to be, once he started drinking good, staggering home down Porter Street wailing at the top of his lungs."

Nikki felt her face flush.

Meg took no notice. "No—your grandmother and I fought especially about your mother and father, when they were living down near the docks. Because I knew what she had done to your father, I knew! But she just denied the whole thing, just stood over us with that proud look, always looking down on us from that great height, hard, powerful—that was your grandmother all right!" Meg chuckled. "I was the one who made all the noise screaming at her. She never raised her voice, of course; you weren't worth the trouble. I used to try like hell to get a rise out of her, even though I knew she'd never yell. I wanted a reaction from her. No, she was too civilized, too well-read in all the proper books, carefully spoken, ate only off china and fine silver…" Meg's old eyes drooped and her face sagged.

"What was her problem? My mother wrote that she was hard but not unkind. She certainly seems unkind." Nikki chewed bread.

"Her problem, her *problem*," Meg nodded, emphasizing the word. She shook her spoon at Nikki. "Her problem, my dear, was that appearances mattered most of all to her. Despite the fact that everyone in Gloucester considered her the town weirdo because she dressed in nothing but black and wore exotic silver, she never let on that it made a damn bit of difference to her. Went about with her head up, her husband following behind, carrying her purse. Oh, what she did to her own husband! Always conscious of her special heritage, she was determined to play what she assumed was her proper part in the circle—including producing two fine young Ravens. But I turned out too wild and headstrong even for her; she thought my endless questioning was in bad taste. She told me I was going to become evil if I didn't stop reading old books and visiting the old Druids hereabouts, which of course I did whether she allowed it or not." Meg cackled delightedly. She continued.

"So I turned out crude and rough and headstrong, unwilling to have any children.

At least, not by any ordinary means. I'm a lesbian, did you know?" Meg said, raising her eyes from her bowl. "At least I was, until my body started falling apart." She reflected a moment, drawing on her cigarette. "No—I guess I still am. It must go with the heart, not the body." She nodded. "Yes, that's it." Meg looked at Nikki a little shyly.

"No, I never knew," Nikki whispered, pleased at the confidence.

"That cut me out of the possibility of producing a daughter for your grand-mother. And so your mother was the only one to produce daughters for our mother, who needed a granddaughter since she was so disappointed in her own daughters." Meg nodded grimly.

"Grandmother told you this?"

"Then one day I managed to get a rise out of your grandmother," Meg remarked dryly. "When I finally told her I was a lesbian, she threw the fit I had been waiting for. It was shocking to hear curses from such a well-mannered woman! By my breaking the family tradition of daughters following mothers, she said I was lost to her. That now she had only your mother to bring daughters forth. By which she meant that your mother and I were both lost to her. That's something, huh?" Meg asked softly.

"Something horrible," Nikki commiserated, shaking her head.

"Your poor mother must have died every time she gave birth to yet another daughter! She knew well enough what it meant! She knew all right that her own mother was looking over her shoulder, licking her lips and rubbing her wrinkled old hands, looking at Jane or Cynthia or you, peering into your eyes wondering, waving her wand over your cribs when your mother was out of the room, quietly, secretly. Hoping that this one would be the true Cleves to carry on the line. Always waiting for a real Raven to appear, one she could show off to the circle."

"Is your being—a lesbian—not accepted by the others?"

Meg guffawed. "Of course it is! They couldn't care less! Actually, though, I haven't been to a circle in a decade or more. You might have some Republican mem-bers these days, who knows?" Meg winked.

"It seems so incongruous—your mother seems to have wanted a pagan Druid—with ladylike manners."

"There's something to be said for manners, don't get me wrong," Meg straight-ened her shawl. "And understanding and politeness, well, they make the world go round. But when they become ends in themselves, like for your grandmother.... Always so nervous your mother and I would embarrass her! Always pulling at our clothes, doing our hair, primping us, making us pose in front of her, checking us out before we went anywhere! All that meddling, and for what? So that she could look good, not us! I mean—! If you can't get your hands dirty doing magic—and like it—when can you?"

Meg pulled a cigarette from the crumpled pack and lit up.

"You were saying my father was like Grandmother?" Nikki pursued.

"Like two peas in a pod," Meg nodded. "That's how I think she put a spell on him to fall in love with your mother."

"You don't think my parents loved each other?"

"Of course they did, whatever love is," Meg replied, rolling her eyes. "No, I'm teasing. Of course they *felt* love. What's love, anyway, if not a spell? Only it's usually cast unconsciously, instead of consciously. We say that we *fall* in love; it hits us suddenly." She shrugged. "How are we to know that someone, or some force, isn't outside of us making us fall into love?"

"But what you're talking about is a little different, isn't it? I mean, that Grandmother sort of—forced the situation."

"Maybe she just helped along what was inevitable anyway," Meg mused. "I've never seen a case of a potion working where there was absolutely no attraction between people in the first place. Think about when someone loves you without your knowing it. You've been friends with him but nothing more. Then one day another friend tells you about your secret admirer. What's your reaction?"

"It would make me interested in him," Nikki nodded.

"Right. It's hard to remain indifferent to someone, even if he's nearly a stranger, after learning he has a crush on you. So who did the spell-casting that time? The friend who tells you about your admirer, I think."

Nikki smiled, thinking of Philip. When they were children he had hardly meant anything to her. Or—had he? As she grew up, she'd hear news about him from time to time, and Claire even ran into him once or twice. And then Rose would speak to Nikki of her son, telling her that Philip had inherited his mother's beauty and his father's business sense. So years later whenever his name came up in occasional conversation with Claire or Dawn, Nikki would naturally exclaim what a great guy he was, how much she loved him. Obviously she hadn't meant it romantically, but was that how it all started? Had she cast a spell on herself, as if with her own words? Then—

Her mind shifted back to her parents. What if she did imagine that some cold, selfish woman had used magic to bring Nikki's parents together—? Would that have made any difference in their marriage? But if it had been done through magic, shouldn't there have been no suffering in it? Or did the magic spell in fact make the marriage a bad one?

As Nikki pondered, Philip flashed through her mind again. She heard a conversation between them, one day when she had been trying to break off their affair.

"Whatever you suffer over makes it important," he explained. "That's Rilke."

"You think I should stay with you and suffer, just so you can have what you want," she stormed.

"I think you should do what's good for you—in the deepest sense—and not run from pain just because it hurts."

It was not just what he had said that infuriated her, but how he said it—with that knowing tone that to her sounded oddly paternal, although god knows her father was only condescending and not often wise...

"So my father and my grandmother were alike?" Nikki asked again suddenly.

"Very alike. Both good-looking, liked to present themselves well. Your grandmother was just better at it than your father. Both strong-willed. At first, before all his drinking, your father never used to raise his voice. He thought it was impolite. I used to see them fight—quite a scene. Neither one raising a voice, their voices getting lower and lower as if trying to outdo each other in understatement. She beat him out on that one!" Meg laughed.

"What happened? Mother wrote that she believed he was angry because he was unable to find a place for his creative nature. Though most of the blame she takes on herself."

"That's typical, isn't it?" Meg responded. "Your mother—I wanted to kill her so many times! Aaagh!" she exclaimed, shaking her curled hands as if strangling Nikki's invisible mother. "When your parents first married, they lived in a three-decker down near the docks. After a year or so, your father decided he'd prefer to live rent-free in our house. Since I objected to the entire marriage, I moved out—and not because I was just discovering myself as a lesbian," Meg added, anticipating Nikki's thought. "Why did Mother have to dominate your mother just to get what she wanted?" she wondered aloud.

"A child," Nikki reflected.

"A *girl* child. But the price was high. Little did my mother know that your father would move into the house and start raising a family there, push her into the back room, turn himself into a drunk and go railing around the place smashing the crystal and china. Your father, kind as he was before he became a drunkard, had very little culture, Nikki. Regardless of what he did, he was a peasant stonecutter. Very fine people, the Finns, mystical maybe, but not known for their intellectual capacity."

"I never heard that," Nikki remarked, offended.

"Oh, then it's just me—don't take any notice, dear," Meg replied, patting Nikki's hand again, which Nikki drew away.

"He was handsome," Nikki said, thinking.

"Handsome, yes, and I think he loved Mother because she was dignified and cultured. See, that's what he'd have liked to have been—educated and refined, with real old-world manners. But he had none of that."

"Maybe it was the frustration that started him drinking," Nikki thought out loud. "That he couldn't be like her."

"Maybe it was. I saw it in him when he was young—eager, poetic, earnest. Your mother made sure not to make him feel inferior, though, no matter how much our mother made him feel like a peasant, using words she was certain he didn't know, correcting his grammar."

For one of the few times in her life, Nikki felt a sudden pang of sympathy for her father. She saw Philip in all his European, cultured glory and felt a shiver.

"It was all a power trip between your grandmother and your father. Your mother refused to play. Power!" Meg snorted, lighting another cigarette. "I used to think I was so powerful, dropping by the house unannounced, maybe bringing a girlfriend, just to assert some power over my mother. I wasn't afraid of anything—not of her, not the boys who attacked your mother. Power!" she exclaimed more softly, looking directly at Nikki. "Now I know better."

THEY SAT FAR INTO the night talking and talking, Meg recounting episodes of her life as Nikki sat absorbing it in tides, family stories, like an inlet takes in a bit of the ocean. Quite late, Nikki saw her old aunt was tiring, her voice growing huskier, her shoulders drooping, the old sly smile flattening out.

"It's time to go," Nikki announced, rising.

Meg got up, suddenly fully awake. "I have to give you Clarissa's number in Rockport," she muttered, following Nikki out to the front room and going to the register. Pulling out a creased black leather record book from under the counter, Meg flipped it open, took a scrap of paper and carefully copied out the number, writing down each numeral as if it were a rune, her yellow fingertips trembling over the page. She looked up and handed it to Nikki.

Nikki studied the paper.

"She's the one to help you now," Meg declared.

"To find Anne's journal?"

"To go further. She lives on the other side of Dogtown from you and knows everything about the place."

"*Clarissa Barrow,*" Nikki read, then stopped, a thrill running through her. "Wait a minute! This is the name Philip asked me about!"

"What?"

"Right after his boat wrecked, Philip showed me a note his father left directing him to ask me about a woman named Clarissa Barrow. That she could explain things."

Meg looked at Nikki closely. "You know the name."

"No—I just recognize it. Who is she, Aunt Meg?"

"A strong woman. She—well, I don't know if I should mention this, but I suppose you'll find out anyway. She was Ernest Eveless' longtime lover."

"What!?"

Meg raised both eyebrows. "I don't know what you know about Rose and Ernest—what Philip might have told you.... You'll have to speak with Clarissa to sort it all out, if it's necessary for you."

"*Necessary?* I assumed this woman could help me sort out this mess. She's mixed up in it herself—how could she help?"

"Maybe just because she is involved," Meg said. She shuffled back to the table to light another cigarette.

"I don't know if I should go see her," Nikki paused. "Maybe it's not such a good idea," she added with finality. Her lungs were suddenly burning with all the smoke; her eyes stung. She glanced at the burning cigarette with disgust.

"What are you afraid of?" Meg pressed, studying her niece. "Please spare me the Helmik priggishness!"

"Aunt Meg, Rose was my best friend for years!"

"Was she? Was she a friend, Nikki?"

"You don't have to attack Rose to push me to see your friend. No—I don't think I can betray Rose by going to see this woman." Nikki shook her head.

"You *are* a prig! You!" Meg laughed.

Nikki was gravely offended, which only made Meg laugh louder.

"Hypocrite!" Meg cried, laughing hard. Nikki snatched her purse and turned for the door. Meg hurried after her, grabbing her arm.

"Nikki!" Meg's voice boomed. Stopping, Nikki turned to peer into her aunt's face, which was highlighted in deep shadow. Fergus Jr. screeched from his perch; Nikki felt a sudden jet of fear.

"Now stop that! Just stop it!" Meg demanded, staring up into Nikki's eyes. Nikki was rooted like a tree.

"You'll never take the first step if you proceed only with pudicity."

"Pudicity?" Nikki repeated, dizzied by her aunt's power.

"Virginity of mind!" Meg exclaimed. "Who do you think you are, to risk history for your personal prejudices and your pride?"

"What are you talking about?" Nikki asked, recovering herself. "This is about being true to a friend!" But she felt a quaking in her legs as her voice shook faintly.

"Rose is no true friend, and you know it. Each of you has betrayed the other. You compromised yourself in sleeping with her son. Without hesitating to inflict suffering on both Philip and his wife. You caused everyone pain," Meg said finally.

"That's why I'm stopping it, because it's all wrong—it's too much," Nikki countered flatly.

"Oh, proud! So proud!" Meg cackled, her claw hand gripping Nikki's arm until red welts appeared.

Meg dropped her hand abruptly. "It's too late for pride, my dear—you have already started down this road. It's your choice: Either accept the burden of causing pain—accept being human so you can go on—or deny your part in the whole thing. But you won't get anywhere trying to remain above the problem."

"I thought the Raven clan emphasizes the value of a pure heart—pure intentions, all that?" It was a real question, although Nikki knew she was taunting her aunt with it.

" 'Pure intentions' means being serious about what you are doing. Not wavering in your course. But you want to change course because you can't bear thinking of yourself as a betrayer, a liar, a cheat—someone who puts her own gratification ahead of others. There's a reason, you know, why magicians, seers, and shamans are able to use their healing powers to help people. Because they've first learned how to live out of their own wounds—even from the woundedness that comes from causing others pain."

Nikki bristled. "Well, if that's what you think of me…" She turned to go.

"Are you so weak that a little truth blows you over? Where's your strength for handling life's growing pains?"

"I am—trying—to have strength," Nikki muttered, gritting her teeth. The harsh cigarette smoke was making her eyes start to water, which she resisted with annoyance, rubbing briefly at them.

"That's the wrong kind. You're really being a coward, Nikki, in holding back from your fate. There's nothing wrong, believe me, with admitting human failings."

Nikki stood for a moment collecting her thoughts. "So what are you saying? Forget having a conscience? Forget trying to cut this thing off with Philip? Don't you think the main reason I'm cutting it off is because of the hurt I'm causing his wife?"

Meg regarded her. "That's part of it, but I think you'd like to cut it off because you can't stand seeing yourself for what you are. You want to cut it off because of your pain, not Philip's wife's. How do you know? She might not even be hurting. And look, I'm certainly not saying you should continue in the affair—going from one extreme to the other avoids the problem. What you are trying to do is make it so that it never happened, and that's the thing you can only avoid at your own peril."

"I'm leaving," Nikki said tersely, reaching the door handle.

Meg stopped her once more at the door. "I'll let you go, my dear," she murmured. "But don't be too hard on yourself. No one can live up to her own ideals. That we make mistakes, hurt one another, doesn't make us bad people. It doesn't make you bad any more than it makes Clarissa Barrow bad."

"Hmph," Nikki disagreed. She turned the doorknob.

"Other forces have now been set in motion, other concerns than your narrowly personal ones. Is your pride so great that you can't humble yourself to the necessities of greater powers?"

"What pride?" Nikki burst out, letting go of the doorknob. "What necessities? What are you talking about? You're making no sense at all!"

"All right Nikki," Meg whispered soothingly. "All right. Never mind. Just remember, Anne's journal belongs to all of us, not just to you or to Rose. It means more than our individual lives. You'll need Clarissa to help you, and now you have her number," Meg finished. Grasping the door handle with her yellowed fingertips, she swung the creaky door wide open herself.

Nikki stood swaying, dazed in the doorway. The sodium streetlight poured coldly across the threshold.

"Look!" Meg exclaimed, turning and motioning toward the crystal ball, sitting like a silent ember on the dark cloth in the dim room. Noticing a light flickering deep within it, Meg went over to it and leaned down. She paused, waved her hands over the ball as if soothing it, then closed her eyes and breathed rhythmically.

In spite of herself, Nikki drew closer, looking into the round glass depths. A figure lay in a bed—a man. As the picture cleared she recognized Philip, eyes closed, head bandaged. But he was alive—! Nikki smiled. Then there's no crime, she told herself. No crime.

"See? I'm not guilty like you think," she explained hurriedly to her aunt, but Meg remained silent, hands poised over the ball, eyes closed.

When Nikki looked again, she saw her house. Weird reddish lights flickered in the kitchen. It took her a moment to realize: the light of a fire.

"Oh my god!" she screamed. Meg opened her eyes and blinked.

"My house is on fire!" she yelled, tugging at Meg.

"It's not happening in the present, dear," Meg answered tiredly. She pushed Nikki gently forward, toward the door.

"But—what does it mean?" cried Nikki.

Meg said nothing, simply shuffled Nikki out the door, and then the door was closing behind her and she was alone on the nighttime street. Ghosts of Indians and ancestors thronged the pavement, blowing by her with hurried purpose, like the host of the *sidhe* on its way to terrible deeds.

She ran for her car.

6.

THE VIRGIN QUARRY

NIKKI SLEPT LATE the next day, ignoring the whimpering of Guy as he scratched at her under the covers. When after a time his soft growls modulated into yelps, then into full-fledged barks, she opened her eyes and frowned at him. Too much was pressing on her mind; she had to think; she did not want to think.

She got up heavily, as if hung over. She smelled of Meg's cigarette smoke; her room stank coldly of stale cigarette smoke. She uttered a grunt of disgust as she threw her old clothes in a pile in the corner. In her mind she saw Philip lying in bed in his mother's house under silk coverlets, his head heavily bandaged; bruised and swollen eyes, the gash on his left cheek.

She stumbled through feeding Guy, then took him out into Dogtown for a morning walk. Silk threads of fog hung in the high pines; underfoot, soft needles and green leaves crunched beneath her sneakers. The air was close; it was going to be a hot day, muggy weather; the sea inhabiting the air.

She was angry and frustrated and stimulated—and didn't like it. Of course she would not call Clarissa. That was out of the question. What was she, a traitor to her friend Rose? Besides, what did that say about Philip? Like father, like son. It figured, she thought, kicking the pine needles as Guy nosed about this way and that. Well, she'd find the journal on her own, in spite of what her aunt said. Her mother and grandmother would guide her—somehow.

So Nikki spent the next week poking about with Guy, rambling over hills and burrowing into narrow crags in remote parts of Dogtown. She plunged into the dirt- and grass-filled cellar holes of the old witches who had lived in the houses, now long gone, that lined Dogtown Road. She took along a shovel to dig in desultory fashion but found nothing except a broken bottle and tin cans not thirty years old. She had never been a systematic person; her explorations were random and intuitive, and she found herself going over old ground.

One time she returned home to find a message from Rose on her answering machine. Calmly and quietly, almost in her old friendly, concerned voice, Rose asked how her search was going. Not a word about Philip, though. Nikki angrily pressed the erase button. She was proceeding by her aunt's offhanded remark: Perhaps Nikki was the one meant to find the journal. If so, then she didn't even really have to try; the thing would come to her, as Aunt Meg had implied.

BUT AT THE END of a week wandering all through Dogtown, she had found nothing. One night when the moon was full she wandered the night-dark woods of Dogtown, walking as if in the belly of some great underground cavern down a winding path toward Old Dogtown Road—the same wide, desolate, stony road her mother and grandmother had walked years before. The moon was bright enough to read a book. She breathed in the rich pine and moss of the summer forest air, pulled a paper out of her pocket and read it as she walked, Guy yanking her along.

Clarissa Barrow, 667-9875. Barrow—a strange name, Nikki thought. Didn't it mean a burial mound? No, she wouldn't call.

Nikki rounded a rise and stumbled up a rocky incline, following the path to where it intersected with Dogtown Road. She stopped when she walked out into the middle of the wide road, as wide as a narrow street in Gloucester, and considered her direction. The moon was brighter here, throwing the smallest leaf into sharp definition, leaving pools of midnight shadow on the pale ground. She was looking again for the remains of Anne Cleves' house. Of course the journal was there somewhere, buried beneath layers of dirt, perhaps hidden in a jar or a box.

Who was she fooling? She couldn't find it. Suddenly depressed and angry, she fell down in a pile, pulling angrily at her hair. Guy stopped to stare at her. "Well, it's not here!" she cried. The dog tilted his head at her.

"Don't look at me!" she shrieked, throwing a stick at him. Dodging a shoulder, he stood looking impassively at her.

"What do you want? What?!"

He looked at her.

"Well, I can't go see her, that's all!"

He looked.

She was miserable; the whole thought of finding the journal was hopeless—and what was she doing it for, anyway?

She glanced around the stony roadside, her eyes lighting on a stake, a red strip of dark ribbon dangling from it. The stake stuck a foot above the ground, puncturing the edge of Dogtown Road. What was this?

Getting up slowly, Nikki walked up to the stake to take a closer look. She knew at once what it was; her face went cold. A surveyor's stake, laying out a property line. So she was going ahead with it! How Nikki hated her! Yet—hate the woman she had adored her whole life? She had made herself in Rose's image.

Tears filled Nikki's eyes. She, too, had once been one of those women, and so she could not hate Rose. She, too, had once dressed in leather and permed her hair, softened her eyes and her limbs to offset the hardness and strength of all those successful men, in whose power she glowed like the earth lying burnished beneath the sun.

But lately things were changing; enacting the sort of outer softness that cloaked her own inner hardness—she was not up to these days. The earth now seemed new and tender, no longer felt so much like that earth warmed beneath the golden shower of sunlight. It was a different earth, which somewhere about harbored a secret.

But this portent of the rape of Dogtown—this could not be happening. Dogtown was supposed to be forever, its deep woods inviolate, protected from greedy, groping hands. Without quite knowing what possessed her, Nikki found herself beating the ground with her hands and wailing out loud.

"Nikki!" Hearing a low voice crooning, Nikki whirled around and gaped. Twenty feet away, standing in the shadow of a huge ancient oak, Ernest appeared, eerily white in the moonlight. Nikki stared transfixed.

It was Ernest—it could not be Ernest! The awful figure wavered, its eyes half focused.

"Ernest?" she whispered.

"Love . . . revenge," the figure moaned, its voice full of the disembodied longing of the dead for the living. The spirit pointed a finger at her, then spoke. *"Clarissa,"* it whispered. As Nikki stood riveted, it receded slowly into the deep purple shadows until it was gone. For a long time, in silence, she stared at the spot. An aeon passed. When at last a breeze fluttered her bangs in her eyes, Nikki shook herself and looked down.

The little red ribbon atop the stake flitted playfully.

Shaking in her bones, she picked up Guy's leash in a daze, sticking her hand through the loop, then turned from the path and headed blindly home, breathing hard. She started at a walk, then walked faster, faster, until she was running and stumbling down the moonscape's rocky path, running and running with all her might, until the woods streaked by in a blaze of ghost light. Guy sprinted alongside, his long tongue hanging out, head pointed, the muscles in his haunches tensing and releasing as he galloped beside her.

NIKKI AWOKE feeling sick to her stomach. Though she had cramps, her period was late as usual, coming the way it always did: starting, stopping, flirting with her, making her feel gross and making her wait. Her lower body felt a mess, everything mixed up down there and full of pressure, ready to spill out and down—if only it would! Now her head was beginning to throb. She reached for the sinus capsules nearby and punched a tab out of the aluminum cell, popped a pill in her mouth, then drank from the plastic bottle of lime-flavored spring water. She lay on her side looking at the nightstand where the curled scrap of paper sat with that phone number. She vaguely recalled a dream of having killed her parents. The thought depressed her. She would not think about the other thing she had seen.

Guy was lying with his snout on his paws. Nikki's heart was full of lead; a profound fear had hold of her, the dread that comes with the realization of one's mortality, that awakes when you awake. She rose and called the Dogtown Society, a local group dedicated to the preservation of the forest. Nikki had joined when she moved back to Gloucester. Betsy answered; gruff, good-natured Betsy. Her voice reassured Nikki, but the question spilled out of her with the urgency of a child.

"Hadn't you heard about that?" Betsy asked.

"I saw the marker only last night," Nikki answered. "What are we doing about it?"

"We're dealing with the lawyers those cowards hide behind. Damn moneygrubbers! Rose Eveless in particular, hiding—surprise, surprise—behind the latest tragedies of her husband and her son, both of whom she hated, of course."

"Of course?"

"She's a man-hater," Betsy said simply.

Nikki wiped her brow. "What's going to happen?"

"Who knows? We'll fight, that's for sure."

"We haven't had a meeting in a while."

"Not for three months—guess it's time," Betsy laughed.

Nikki couldn't stand it. "Aren't you afraid—I mean, concerned? They're laying it out already, right there on Dogtown Road!" Nikki cried.

"Doesn't mean squat, Nikki," Betsy replied. "Cleavage Builders was given permission to do that—but no more. The real fight hasn't begun."

"But—why didn't anyone tell me?"

"Don't you read the papers? It's been there for a week. Then we didn't want to bother you since Philip's accident—"

"I'm fine," she responded quickly. She didn't like anyone knowing details about her life, and in tiny Gloucester everyone knew everything as a matter of course. "I read the papers. So what can we do?"

"We'll have a meeting soon. Bob and Terry said they're ready. We've all got some ideas. I'll call you."

"What about right now?"

"There's nothing to do—a hearing before the town is scheduled for October. Even if they got a complete go-ahead, which won't happen, nothing could be done until next spring."

"I have to think about what to do in the meantime."

"Right, you're a lawyer. That's good; we'll need one—again. That Rose—some piece of work, eh?" Betsy finished, voice still smiling.

Nikki could tell Betsy was being careful in her criticism of Rose, well aware of Nikki's strong bond with her. But the woman smiled through the worst crises!

They hung up, Nikki feeling empty. Her stomach settling after a while, she paced back and forth in the kitchen, running her hip into the table from time to time and exclaiming. She didn't want to do lawyering anymore. Besides, what did she know about environmental law? Nothing. Yet she did know people. She made calls and re-established contacts. It was only after three hours of calling that Nikki thought about the curled slip of paper with Clarissa's number. Going to see her Aunt Meg had been easy; she was glad she had gone, even after the way it ended. But Meg was a relative… Nikki remembered Ernest.

Was Clarissa a member of the Raven clan? Maybe she had powers, Nikki considered. Well, why not? What had Meg said about her? That she lived on the other side of Dogtown from Nikki and knew a Dogtown Nikki didn't know. Maybe there wouldn't be any need to bring up the subject of the Eveless family with Clarissa, Nikki reasoned, since she'd be paying a visit to learn more about her own ancestry. Just stick to Dogtown and Anne's journal.

"And another thing," she pointed out to Guy, who stopped as he was settling into his bed near the refrigerator. "Rose seems certain the journal contains some cure for aging. Meg thinks I should find it for the Cleves. Why shouldn't there be something for me in it?" she wondered out loud.

She took up the scrap of paper, set her mouth, and dialed. No, she wouldn't like the woman, but that didn't mean she couldn't use her for help. All right, then.

ALTHOUGH ROCKPORT was not far up the road from Nikki's house, it took her half an hour to find the tiny cottage where Clarissa Barrow lived. After winding her red car endlessly up and down narrow half-paved roads in the backwoods of Rockport, Nikki finally drove into an area more heavily wooded. Pines and maples crowded the road, scraping the low car as Nikki steered hesitantly over holes and around bends, unable to see ahead. The afternoon woods were deeply shadowed. Nikki suspected the area she was in was just as Aunt Meg had said, on the other side of Dogtown from her house.

Clarissa's house must be all alone, she thought. There seemed to be no other houses so far back.

She passed a cracked sign that read:

PRIVATE
NO TRESPASSING
NO HUNTING

Nikki knew she was close, for that was the sign Clarissa had told her to look for. Clarissa's voice on the phone had sounded like an old woman's, with a wistful lilt, full of whimsy and kindly nostalgia yet with depth. So what to expect?

The house—really a cabin, Nikki noted—appeared around the bend, sitting alone against the pines, oaks, and maples, a rusty green Ford sedan parked at its side. The road ended at the house; beyond lay only woods. The cabin slanted badly to the right, its clapboards peeling and cracked. Wicker chairs in a slow process of unraveling sat on a small front porch. Two very large and lean black dogs in the front yard ran up to Nikki's car as she came to a stop.

Delighted with the dogs, she opened her door to let them come close and sniff her. They had remarkably intelligent eyes and inquisitive noses.

"You're wolves!" she exclaimed, even more pleased to find wild things here. Great black monsters, they stood nearly three feet high at the shoulder, with long, pointed snouts and black-tipped ears. They resembled very large German shepherds but moved leanly with a natural gracefulness uncommon in domesticated canines.

The wolves were friendly and aggressive, pressing their snouts against Nikki's hands. She petted them in turn, rubbing her hands over their long, sleek coats. Then she pressed herself out of her car to stand upright before them. The larger of the two immediately raised himself, planting two enormous long paws on Nikki's shoulders, then thumped her nose hard with his long snout. The wolf lowered himself back to all fours, regarding her keenly and expectantly.

Nikki jerked back, her head lowering involuntarily, and grabbed her nose.

A laugh erupted from behind the wolves.

"Timber!" cried a voice Nikki recognized. She shook herself and rubbed her sore nose, regarding the tall woman standing outside the front door of the cabin.

"Don't worry—that's just his way of saying hello," the old woman called out, "and letting you know he's the alpha male here." She laughed again, and it was a light laugh, with much air in it. It floated over to Nikki with a slight echo, as if simultaneously coming off the hills.

Nikki walked toward the woman, who in turn stepped off the porch, extending a hand. She shook hands firmly, looking intently into Nikki's eyes. Just like a man, Nikki thought. *So this is the mistress of—* Instantly an invisible hand covered the mouth of her thought. She could not finish. Nikki was left impressed by the woman's power.

"I'm Clarissa, obviously," she said without ceremony.

"Nikki," Nikki stuttered, fumbling for her name. Something about the woman made her shy. Clarissa was tall, nearly six feet, thin with a face sharply creased and weathered. She had no doubt spent much time out of doors, for her skin looked like tanned leather. She wore jeans and a green cotton blouse with the sleeves rolled up. Her hips were narrow, her legs long. She wore moccasins and was armed with a wide-handled knife set in a sheath at her leather belt. Her hair was grey and straight, cut short around her shapely head, giving her a girlish look. Although she was clearly older than Aunt Meg (around seventy, Nikki figured), she carried herself loosely upright as she led the way with long, even strides into her house.

Noticing Clarissa wore no jewelry, Nikki immediately became aware of her own long silver earrings—the ones with the coyotes—as well as her silver turquoise ring, which she wore on the ring finger of her left hand. Philip had given it to her.

"Amazing animals! They're wolves, aren't they?" Nikki inquired, petting the huge animals who followed along.

Clarissa turned to glance fondly at the two wolves. "Yes—that's Timber, the one who greeted you so forcefully, and his mate, Tara. They're full-blooded wolves; I got them as pups, and now they're family. Do you have a dog?" she asked directly, looking again into Nikki's eyes.

"A mutt," Nikki muttered self-consciously. These were such beautiful animals!

Clarissa gave a little laugh of understanding, which left Nikki uncertain whether it was from condescension or simply joy in animals. "Everyone has a familiar," Clarissa remarked, opening the door for Nikki to enter. With a quick look that Nikki caught, Clarissa directed the wolves to remain outside. Their expectant noses turned down, the pair rambled off across the yard, nipping at each other and growling in play. Nikki entered the living room, which was dim after the bright sunlight, and stood and waited.

"Sit," Clarissa insisted, directing Nikki to a chair. "Not very comfortable, but I don't spend much time here. Even now, old as I am."

Nikki regarded the room hesitantly. The chair she had been invited to sit on was a ramshackle construction of old boards on which a thin, well-worn cushion of some indeterminate color rested. Indeed, the entire room was rough-hewn, rustic, not quite *civilized:* its low ceiling fashioned of worm-eaten beams; walls paneled in cracked planks, as was the floor. A large fireplace stretched along the long wall of the room, the head of a deer mounted in tremendous spectacle above it. Nikki caught her breath at its blank, noble eyes.

With so little inviting or comfortable about the room, the place was more like a cave than a house. Or a camp, perhaps.

"You don't live here year-round?" Nikki asked rhetorically.

This time Clarissa laughed heartily, throwing her head back. Even in the dim interior, Clarissa's hair shone silvery grey, reminding Nikki of someone she had seen before. Perhaps in Gloucester…? She was struck by how green Clarissa's eyes were, as the old woman ended her laugh, gazing at Nikki.

"I do live here year-round, but I'm often in the woods—camping and hunting."

"Hunting!" Nikki exclaimed. The last thing she expected to hear from this woman who lived in the deep woods—and had wolves, for god's sake! Didn't she respect animals—?

"Look behind you," Clarissa gestured. Nikki turned and gasped. Splayed across the rustic wood panels hung an epic bearskin, complete with head and paws.

Nikki jumped up and reached a hand. "Can I touch it?" she asked, turning to Clarissa.

"Of course. That's Maya, a very old and dear friend. Actually, it's not fair to show you Maya after telling you I hunt. I didn't kill her. We were too good of friends for me to want to kill her, even if she was maddening."

"Friends?" Nikki wondered aloud as she rubbed her graceful hands over the soft brown fur. *How wonderful it must feel to wrap yourself in such a fur,* she found herself thinking, to her horror. As a member of PETA, she had herself splashed red paint on some fur coats of women coming out of Filene's one Christmas. A long time ago, true, but still she was opposed on principle to killing animals.

"Not friends in the usual sense—no one is friends with a bear. I say I was her friend. That means she let me draw rather close to her, when she didn't have a cub around, of course. Just sit not far from her, absorbing her presence." Clarissa jumped up.

"Something to drink?" she offered, disappearing into the back room. Nikki knelt on the chair, stroking the rich fur, letting her eyes wander the room. Through the old dripping-glass windows she could see Timber and Tara frisking in the yard, tossing a ball in the air and growling at each other. There were other skins on the wall, further back toward the kitchen, where Nikki could see Clarissa draw her knife from its sheath and slice lemons on a wooden countertop. She proceeded to pour from a pitcher into glasses.

On the wall to the kitchen hung the furs of a rabbit, a fox, and a few other smaller animals Nikki didn't recognize. As her eyes wandered the room, she looked more closely at the deer head, staring out at her. It was a powerful, graceful head, its snout long, delicate, and regal, yet there was something grotesque about it sticking out of the wall, as if its body stood inside.

Nikki wasn't sure whether she liked the woman. She was fascinated by the skins and animal heads and, as always, uncomfortable with her fascination, for it took her outside of herself. Clarissa returned with a tray of two full glasses and a pitcher, setting it down on a coffee table made of planks of worn wood that looked to be two hundred years old. She noticed Nikki looking at it.

"Not very good, but I made it myself," Clarissa apologized.

"It's beautiful," Nikki smiled appreciatively.

Clarissa regarded the table. Lifting the two glasses, she handed one to Nikki. "Not really. But it works."

Nikki took the cold glass feeling the warmth of her compliment abate. Maybe the table wasn't beautiful.

Clarissa swung her glass in a toast toward Nikki as they drank standing. It was lemonade, just barely, tasting mostly of water and a sharp tang. Nikki sat down.

"Did you kill any of these?" she motioned to the animals on the walls.

"Sure," Clarissa replied matter-of-factly. "I killed all of them."

"For sport?" Nikki asked, her voice spiking suddenly. How could she explain this to Claire and her Cambridge women friends?

"Mostly for food." Clarissa looked at the younger woman. "I don't have much money. I hunt for food."

"You're not a vegetarian," Nikki stated.

Clarissa laughed fiercely, baring her teeth with pride. "I eat what I kill. Isn't that what you're supposed to do?"

"What do you hunt with?"

"That," Clarissa answered, pointing to a rifle leaning in the corner. A worn leather satchel lay next to it.

"Not much of a fair fight," Nikki retorted, then regretted being so critical.

"Is it supposed to be fair?" Clarissa asked wholly without guile.

"Isn't it?" Nikki countered.

"I don't know—I haven't thought about it. Other animals are much further along than the human kind. In almost every way. My little popgun—it's a .22—isn't big enough to bring down Buck there—" Clarissa allowed, indicating the deer head.

"Buck?" Nikki inquired. It was coming at her too fast.

"I'm not very original with names. Or with words," Clarissa admitted frankly. "That's the name I gave him before I killed him. Had to get him with a bow. I like the bow," Clarissa licked her lips, then poured herself another glass, splashing the lemonade onto the wide-planked floor. She held the pitcher up to Nikki expectantly, but Nikki shook her head.

Studying Clarissa, Nikki couldn't help reflecting: *She didn't seem to have anything ladylike about her; how could Ernest Eveless have wanted her—?*

Catching herself with such thoughts, Nikki inwardly cringed. Yet her thoughts hurried on like instincts: *Look at her—sitting with her legs uncrossed, like a man. She's obviously not at home indoors, sitting around talking. One minute she sits fidgeting, the next is up pacing, as if sitting still too long is costing her something.*

"It's nice you ask about the animals—I could tell you about them, or I could show you," she offered, walking up and down the room, her softly shod feet soundless on the bare wood floor.

"You mean—in the woods?" Nikki asked.

"Of course. You've never hunted," Clarissa stated.

"No," Nikki answered quickly.

"No shame in that," Clarissa responded. "If you're interested, I can teach you. As far as hunting and fighting fairly, no animal I'm familiar with has any sense of fighting fair. We all use whatever means we have to get what we want."

"Yes, but humans have the means to wipe out all animals."

"Not me," Clarissa proclaimed, as if that settled it. She looked at Nikki a long moment. "Guns don't wipe out animals—humans do."

Nikki was shocked. *Why, she sounds exactly like an* NRA *bumper sticker! Completely not politically correct.*

"You really believe that?"

"It's the truth," Clarissa nodded, sitting and slurping down her lemonade before pouring another. She wiped her mouth with her hand.

"But—handguns and assault rifles, all that—?" Nikki asked.

"Never use them. You don't need to, to hunt. Maybe humans need to use them on each other, and as far as I'm concerned, let them kill each other off. It's actually nature's way."

"Excuse me—it seems kind of cruel, kids getting killed—"

"Oh, don't talk to me about kids!" Clarissa declared, her voice rising. "Children! As if they were somehow more important than adults!"

"Well, they *are* more vulnerable. Aren't they the innocent victims?"

"I don't know. I don't have much use for them, personally," Clarissa remarked,

"Although I do take care of my grandnieces and 'nephews from time to time." She jumped up again. "Shall we go out?"

Nikki rose, flustered. She didn't know what to say to this odd woman. Although she liked the wolves, the stuffed animal heads and furs nailed to the walls were terribly disturbing to her. Clarissa herself seemed awfully—*barbarian,* Nikki thought. *Cold, almost—cruel. And talked almost like a Republican. Guns!* She followed Clarissa back outside, casting a final glance at the rifle in the corner. Timber and Tara came racing up.

Clarissa sat on the porch step with her feet on the dry earth. She bent her head and nuzzled the wolves as if she were one of them. They licked her face when she put it close.

"You're not here for the animals, anyway," Clarissa observed, petting the wolves.

"I don't know—you said on the phone that my aunt called you."

"She told me you were interested in the Gloucester circle—and in Anne Cleves' journal," Clarissa relayed, still giving her attention to the wolves.

"Yes," Nikki responded.

"You're hesitant," Clarissa noted, turning to look in Nikki's eyes. She narrowed her eyes at Nikki, who stood awkwardly on the porch before sitting down a little distance away from Clarissa on the step. When Tara came up to her for petting, she rubbed the wolf's head.

"That's good. Your aunt mentioned your mother's letter. It's fortunate she left you a trail to follow."

Nikki was guarded. "Yes, I am interested in exploring—"

"It's not about wandering in the woods!" Clarissa exploded, her voice suddenly sharp. Nikki drew sharply back, as if she had offended Clarissa.

"You'd better be afraid, or you won't get past step one," Clarissa warned. "Keep your hesitation. Do you think it's the wrong response? It's your instincts speaking up. Follow them—they mark the real trail. Go ahead and mistrust me—or hate me for what you think you know about me."

"I don't hate you—" Nikki began, but Clarissa laughed.

"Yes, but you hate yourself as well."

"What's that supposed to mean?" Nikki stiffened her shoulders.

"What do you know about Ernest Eveless and me?" Clarissa demanded.

Nikki was taken aback by the woman's directness. It seemed a hallmark of hers. "I know... My Aunt Meg told me that you and Ernest Eveless—"

"Were lovers—yes," Clarissa completed the thought, folding her hands across a knee. "And you are a lover of Ernest's son, also a married man. That makes us kind of like sisters. Or rather, you are my daughter-in ... sin?" Clarissa smiled faintly.

Nikki was puzzled. The woman lived in the woods and hunted, yet was acting so cool about the whole thing, so—*sophisticated.* "I don't think of us as related."

"Do you ever think about sisterhood—about what you might be doing to Philip's wife?" Clarissa raised the question.

Nikki's eyebrows shot through the ceiling. "I—think? I—? I think all the time. That's why I want to stop—why I've been trying to end it—" Her voice was rising.

"That's just cowardice," Clarissa returned mildly.

"Cowardice?!" Nikki nearly shouted. She was furious now.

Clarissa remained calm, even leaning toward Nikki a bit. "Yes. It's too late to take back the harm you've done. The work now is to decide whether it's worth it. Are you implying that your love of Philip is so weak, it doesn't justify the pain? That would be like killing when you don't need the food. Killing—or loving—for sport, just to have something to do with your time."

"I—I don't know what to say. It's outrageous, what you're saying. First you insult me asking whether I've ever thought about the pain I've caused the other woman, then you insult my feelings by calling them into question!"

"Is a question an insult?" Clarissa asked reasonably. "Strong feelings, those that lay claim to us by necessity, justify pain. We all need to eat; killing animals for food becomes justifiable when it's necessary. In which case, the burden is on us to sanctify the suffering, to give thanks to the animal and to be in awe of our ability to kill—it's such an awful thing! To recognize that most animals are far nobler than we humans, yet we kill them, and we must be courageous when we do so, else the killing is merely slaughter.

"Can you face up to the other woman's pain without denying the killing you've provoked? Yet without taking refuge in cowardly self-recrimination—using morality to shrink from the spirit's challenge? Can you empathize with her pain enough to honor it, even stand in awe of it and, moreover, in fearful awe of your own destructiveness? And, by the way, can't you speak more directly—say, by actually using the name of Philip's wife, Françoise?"

The two women sat staring at each other, Nikki with daggers and Clarissa careful, watching. For a long time they sat squared off, until at last Clarissa broke the tension by sitting back.

"You've got a whole mess of things stirring inside you right now, Nikki. The work of exploring your heritage is bound up with your feelings about love. Here Meg sent you to a compromised woman—and I seem to you exactly the wrong person to come to for help. What are you looking for? A perfect way out of the mess you yourself have helped create?"

"I—I'm not looking for a perfect way out," Nikki drawled sarcastically. "Those aren't my words."

"All right, you tell me. What are you here for?"

Nikki thought. "First Aunt Meg gave me your name. Then the surveyor's ribbon I found in Dogtown from Rose's company. And there was a note that Philip's father left—"

"Ah…!" Clarissa exclaimed, as a crease of pain flitted across her smiling brow. "What did it say?"

"That Philip should go to you to find out some secret."

"So you're a step ahead of Philip since you now know about the relationship between Ernest and me."

"I don't really know," Nikki muttered sullenly.

"I think you should," Clarissa offered.

"I don't want to know," Nikki countered. "It isn't my business."

"But you are bound up in it."

"Look—I'm here because Meg sent me, because she said you knew Dogtown like no one else, so you might help me find the journal. I think I should leave."

Clarissa said nothing but sat watching Nikki, who remained stationary, stirring only to look as if she were about to rise. Clarissa herself jumped up and went into the house. After a few moments she returned.

"You're still here," she remarked, smiling without recrimination down at Nikki.

Nikki said nothing but would not look at her. She was patting Tara, who nuzzled her.

"You are acting insulted, but it's I who should be, Nikki. You come here to meet having already formed your own judgment, certain it has to do with me rather than yourself. You think I'm bad for having had an affair with Ernest."

"I never said that."

"But you think it, and it's poisoning everything. I understand that Rose is a longtime friend of yours, and I respect your friendship. I have no ill will toward her, only for what she did to Ernest."

"I don't want to hear any of that," Nikki replied quickly.

"Then it can wait. For now, do you want my help or not? Look at me!" Clarissa commanded in a suddenly loud voice, so that Nikki involuntarily raised her eyes.

She met the powerful glow in Clarissa's emerald-green eyes. Her eyes were not unkind, even if demanding.

"In order to learn, you first have to put yourself in the place where you say 'I don't know.' Because you don't, Nikki. Can you say those words without being destroyed?" She smiled her hard smile down at the younger woman.

"I—it's too vulnerable feeling," Nikki replied softly, lowering her gaze from the bright light of Clarissa's eyes. Here was a genuinely powerful woman, she had to admit. She hated Clarissa for breaking the same taboo she had broken, mistrusted her apparent lack of remorse.

Clarissa was watching her think. "Yes, vulnerable. No other way to hunt what is necessary. You have to trust in order to move ahead, which means you can't know ahead of time. One day you may join our circle, like your mother and aunt and the long line of women before you, and come into your own. Keep your hesitation, because that's the surest way to remain both vulnerable and moving."

Nikki was silent a while thinking it over. "Hesitation sounds to me like stopping. I'm still thinking I should leave."

Clarissa nodded. "Yes, but you're not concluding to leave. By not knowing, you clear your mind of its preconceptions."

It was easier to think about Anne Cleves and the Raven clan than to reflect on her own history of relationships, Nikki thought, her mind leaping at the subject. She imagined herself as Clarissa had just implied; a magician at last, full, powerful, unable to be hurt.

"You don't even know in advance what becoming a clan member might mean to you," Clarissa pointed out.

Clarissa's world filled her mind, Nikki was aware—and it felt dangerous. Perhaps not knowing was a form of self-protection. "But if I'm hesitant, I might leave, I might not ever come—"

"To the circle?" Clarissa finished quickly. "Or—might not come soon? Might not find the journal? What does that matter?" she wondered, waving a hand. "Come when it's time. I'll tell you where to go, or you can go with me."

"To one of the *sabbats?*"

"We meet at other times as well—I don't often go anymore, but the others meet."

"It's more a matter of the journal," Nikki realized. "I need to find it."

"To protect Dogtown or yourself?"

"For all your talk of not knowing, you seem to know a lot about the situation."

Clarissa looked up from the wolves. "You're easy to read. Anyway, everyone knows about the journal, as well as about Rose Eveless' plan to build in Dogtown."

"What makes you ask about protecting myself?"

"Because of the way you understand hesitation. Don't get me wrong; self-preservation is fundamental. But you know all about that. Do you want to ask me now about Ernest?"

Again Nikki didn't know what to say. It was too big and complex. "There's no way I can ever see what you did as—OK," she said softly.

"Because of your friendship with Rose," Clarissa guessed.

"That—and other things."

"Because it doesn't seem right."

"Yes," Nikki answered quietly.

"Then nothing I could say would change your mind. Nothing I would say, that is. I make no apologies for my life. Your choice is to use my help or not."

"I'm still here," Nikki uttered almost sarcastically, then regretted it when Clarissa glanced sharply at her.

Nikki was feeling terribly uncomfortable. Still holding her glass, she looked around for a place to put it down, at last setting it beside her. Tara immediately stuck her snout in the glass and slurped. Timber trotted over to investigate.

"You knew my mother," Nikki remarked finally.

"I did know your mother—until she decided that marriage was more important than her life with—us of the circle. Then she lost the way."

"But she left something for her daughters," Nikki insisted, feeling faintly territorial. Clarissa eyed her.

"I said that's good," Clarissa returned a little impatiently.

"What do you remember of her?"

"That she was afraid. At first I hoped she would venture with me into the woods. For a little while she did. She used to come here, back when I was younger and could run fast. We would go off for days together."

"Into the *woods?*" Nikki asked, eyebrows rising. "My mother?"

"She and I and a few of the others. I taught your mother to track and hunt."

"My mother used to hunt?" Nikki's mouth dropped.

"She did—not well, but she tried it. She never gave it time. She was too soft for the Bear clan—us girls from the Raven circle. That was when she was still a girl, of course." Clarissa regarded Nikki playing with the wolves. "They seem to have taken to you. So you never learned to track and hunt as a girl."

"No!" Nikki exclaimed, flabbergasted Clarissa seemed to take these as part of normal learning for a child.

"You look like you've had plenty of men," Clarissa asserted bluntly. "When did that start?"

Nikki flinched. "Uh, what's your question?"

Clarissa nodded. "I bet you started young with the boys. That's the problem—you girls start too young. Your entire family, except your aunt, of course. When did you lose your virginity?"

Nikki was in full flight now. She was suddenly prey pursued by this woman, and the huntress was closing in fast. Even the wolves seemed to sense Nikki's racing heart, her mind running off into the woods for protection. They instinctively sniffed her and retreated to stand near Clarissa, ears pricked, watching Nikki intently.

"Why do you ask?" Nikki panted, breathless.

"Because it's important," Clarissa responded simply, pulling at some grass. "You come to me to introduce you to the circle. You want me to teach you ways to find the journal. You initiate our becoming friends, intrude in my territory, and inquire into what I thought of your mother.

"We are sisters already," she continued, "in that we both fell in love with Eveless men. Illicitly—which means immorally, by the judgment you bring to bear on both of us. Like it or not, that's our first bond—and we can only proceed on that basis. That puts the matter of sex and love right in front of us. You will have to talk to me."

They sat in silence for a long while, as the wolves pattered to and fro. "I was—thirteen," Nikki whispered finally, unable to bear the pressure. *Perhaps it's necessary to speak,* an inner voice suggested. She felt as if she were going to cry. But she would not cry. She had to keep ahead of this huntress.

"That's too young," Clarissa shook her head. "You had no time to be with your girlfriends."

"It was too young," Nikki acknowledged, head sinking, feeling her limbs growing tired. She was tired of running, tired of hiding her life, tired of defending herself.

"You think so?"

"I thought so then, while it was going on. The year before—there was a boy. He was really mad at me. I wouldn't let him. I got poison ivy that lasted a whole summer. I couldn't go out—couldn't go anywhere, do anything." Nikki's breath was heavy in her chest.

"That's good," Clarissa noted. "And now poison ivy is your friend."

"How did you know?" Nikki asked, shooting her a quick glance. "I've never had it since, even though I walk in the woods all the time.

"It was your protection. What happened the next year?"

"It began—he—I got drunk, I guess. Why am I telling you all of this?" Nikki asked out loud.

"Because it's central to the process. Usually clan members are initiated around eight or nine. You are how old?"

"Forty," Nikki replied quickly.

"We have to go back and pick up the trail before going forward."

"Why this subject?"

"So you can feel your virginity again," Clarissa explained flatly, then stood and walked across the yard. The wolves followed her. "Let's go," she announced without turning, striding into the woods.

Nikki jumped up and followed, not knowing where they were going. As the wolves ran ahead down a narrow path, Clarissa plunged in behind them at a slow trot.

Dressed in jeans and sneakers, Nikki was determined to keep up. But it was hard. The wolves disappeared, bounding and yelping off into the deep woods. Although Clarissa was thirty years older than Nikki, she outpaced Nikki from the start and soon was lost ahead.

Nikki broke into a full run. It was a warm, humid New England day in July, the trees in full green bloom, loaded with their dangling freight of leaves. Trees went swirling by as she ran sweating and panting. She thought of Guy and how fast he could run, old as he was. Close hanging branches of oak and maple swatted at her as she passed. Her legs felt heavy and her hips too wide for this kind of running. She stopped finally, panting hard. She had to catch her breath.

Clarissa was beside her in a moment, standing very quietly watching her. She was not even breathing hard.

"Guess I'm not much in shape," Nikki puffed, touching her chest.

"Have to go back to where you grew up," Clarissa declared cryptically.

Nikki nodded, breathing more easily now.

"You ran in these woods," Clarissa stated the question as a fact.

"This is Dogtown?" Nikki asked.

"The other side," Clarissa confirmed.

Nikki looked around, feeling better. "We played all over the place. I've never seen this area before, though. I didn't know it went this far."

"We'll go somewhere you've never seen, deeper in," Clarissa said. "Remember running in the woods?"

Nikki smiled.

"Think about that time," Clarissa directed, turning and running off again, this time at a slower pace. Nikki followed, recalling those days when she was young, running around in Dogtown with Claire and her other girlfriends. For a time the thoughts were clear; she could see herself running and playing. The path was easy, and she could keep up just fine with Clarissa, who did not stop for breath.

From time to time Nikki's thoughts turned to boys, drifting back to the times she took boys in the woods, or they took her. Noticing her breathing become more shallow, she slowed down. And so she learned to keep her thoughts on her younger years, before the boys.

Those years opened up before her like an old book, very slowly, the spine stiff with disuse. Where had that time gone when she had run with Claire, sometimes with Rachel? She saw other old friends, some lost now. Barbara and Dawn and Mary, Peggy and Alex, all of them giggling and laughing. They had a secret place where they all met—Nikki had forgotten all about it, even with her recent walks in Dogtown. It was a little well of land down amid a circle of broken boulders that formed a protective wall. They had called it the Den, where they played at magically transforming into all sorts of characters: animals and witches and married ladies, mothers and members of girl groups. No boys allowed, of course. They would bring their lunches there to eat together, everyone sharing whatever they had brought. The rule was that you had to make the food yourself, plus you had to make up the recipe yourself.

Nikki once brought a sandwich of fried raspberry preserves and cheese with slimy leftover artichokes, and it won the award as the grossest food of all. That meant Nikki got to choose first from the booty scattered around, while everyone else had to eat some of the sickening sandwich.

They hated boys, and even while they whispered stories to one another of what they knew about *the Act*, each made a solemn vow never to engage in anything so disgusting. Their hearts were strong and their limbs were young. After Nikki brought a book to show them all about Indians and how they named themselves, they took animal names for themselves.

Nikki smiled as she ran. She had long forgotten her name. It was *Horse Girl*. Sometimes she called herself *Palomino,* for she loved the color of those horses. Mainly they reminded her of her own hair. Claire was *Shy Squirrel,* and Alex couldn't figure out her name, so together they decided that since she had blue eyes and talked and laughed all the time, she was to be known as *Laughing Jay.* Dawn was *Bone Weasel*—uncanny! How wondrous to recall!

CLARISSA HAD STOPPED, and Nikki drew up behind her. She felt half in a dream, as if her body were filled with smoke. Over Clarissa's shoulder she spied a water-filled quarry.

Clarissa trotted toward the huge slabs of granite that surrounded the quarry, gleaming whitely in the bright sun. Nikki looked at the water, which looked different from usual quarry water—not brackish and scummy from being still so long.

"Is this—" she couldn't articulate her question.

"It's fresh water, not rain," Clarissa called out, making her way easily along the rocks. "There's a spring up top," she explained, indicating a high point where a small waterfall tumbled over a pile of granite boulders to land finally in a fine mist down in the pond.

"That's unusual," Nikki mused, following but still looking at the clear water. "I've never seen this place before."

"It's a secret place. Protected," Clarissa informed her.

Immediately recalling what Meg had said, Nikki stopped in her tracks. *Something about her mother's letter being protected... by a spell!*

Clarissa made her way along the water's edge, climbing up the rocks until she stood where the waterfall began, thirty feet above Nikki.

"Come up," Clarissa called softly, her voice a clear soft bell in the still of the pond.

Nikki complied, wondering where the wolves had gone. When Clarissa disappeared over the rocks, Nikki hurried to follow. Once at the top she turned to look out over the pond. A wall of trees protected the area; Nikki could just see over it into the distance. Everywhere she turned were trees. Overhead the bright afternoon sun was heating the rocks. She felt as if she were no longer in Rockport. Maybe she wasn't.

"Come," Clarissa beckoned. Nikki turned from the view to follow her into the short pines that lined a narrow path running alongside the little brook of spring water. At the end of the path she came upon Clarissa bending down, her face in a small pool of bubbling water. After drinking she stood up.

"Drink," she urged, as Nikki bent and did the same. The water was such a pleasing shock to her lips, she dipped her long hands in the cold, clear water and splashed it on her face. She had never seen or tasted water so clean and clear! It was like a different substance altogether, tasting wholly unlike the bottled spring water she habitually drank.

"Delicious!" she exclaimed, rising, her face wet.

Clarissa laughed at the sight of her, then turned and headed back to the quarry. Clambering halfway back down the cliff of boulders, she stopped on a large flat slab that overhung the water. She stood regarding the pond, then looked up at the afternoon sun. Quickly, so that it surprised Nikki, she pulled her shirt over her head and dropped it. She was wearing no bra, and her small breasts were as tanned as the rest of her body. Pulling off her moccasins and sliding her jeans over her narrow hips, she stood naked in the sunlight a moment.

Nikki inhaled involuntarily. The woman was the most beautiful seventy-year-old she had ever seen: long-limbed and muscular, without a wrinkle anywhere, except on her face. If only she, too, might look like that at seventy! Instead she felt ashamed of her body, so fat and ugly and gross. And with her period!

Right hand on hip, Clarissa paused a moment, breathing easily, then dove off the cliff into the pool twenty feet below.

Following awkwardly, Nikki clambered down the rocks to stand on the slab where Clarissa's clothes lay. She looked down. It looked far. Evidently she was supposed to follow. Even though she was a good swimmer, she had never been much of a diver. Clarissa swam across the pond, calling up to her. Her voice rose in the stillness of the enclosure.

"Remember your girlfriends," she encouraged. At once a memory sprang up in Nikki's mind: Swimming with Claire and the rest of them one late afternoon, in a small pond not far from the Den ... they had splashed naked, playing and laughing, calling out each other's animal names, singing and diving and hiding—until evening came. Sadly they climbed out of the water and drew clothes over their wet bodies, racing one another home in time for dinner.

Looking down a second time into the water, Nikki slowly unbuttoned her shirt and removed her bra. The warm air felt good against her nipples and stomach, in spite of her self-consciousness. Her breasts were white; her stomach stuck out too far. With a sigh she took off her sneakers and socks; next, her jeans and underwear. Clarissa was swimming on the far side of the pond, long, even strokes in the clear water like a naiad. Nikki could see her tanned body beneath the surface.

Twenty feet was a long way down. She looked down. No way she could dive. She leaned over, once, twice. *No use waiting.* She jumped feet first.

Twenty feet *was* a long way down, long enough for Nikki to ask herself why, until a second later her body hit the water and she felt only the blistering cold plunge into the depths.

She rose spluttering, happily triumphant. Clarissa clapped once, yelling something Nikki could not make out. She was in the water with Clarissa; somehow that made them equals. She swam to Clarissa and splashed water at her. But Clarissa was fast, ducking beneath the surface, scattering water so Nikki couldn't see where she went.

The water was so cold! Cold as the Atlantic, yet fresh and infinitely sweet. Nikki kept moving. Where had Clarissa gone? A hand rose up to push her head down under the water, Nikki grabbing a breath just in time. She broke free and came up gasping, splashing as she surfaced at the figure she could barely make out through the haze of water in her eyes. Clarissa splashed her in the face, and the water went down the wrong way.

Nikki coughed but splashed harder, swimming after her prey. Clarissa dodged out of the way, laughing, as the two engaged in a chase around the pond. At first Nikki splashed her way after the older woman, determined to catch her, but gradually fell into a rhythm of strokes, until the two women quieted down, no longer splashing, swimming along evenly.

Nikki drew up beside Clarissa, admiring her strong, supple arms, regretting her own shoulder-length hair getting in her way. The two swam a while matching stroke for stroke. The water was not so cold now, and Nikki felt good in her body, as if years had fallen off. Her breasts felt small and close to her, like when she was ten; her stomach tight and hard. Had the cold water done that?

Clarissa neared a place on the rocks where the waterfall fell into the water. The afternoon sun glistened in the fine mist that wafted onto the rocks. Clarissa climbed out and sat. Nikki swam up and listed herself out of the water as well.

"It's beautiful," Nikki declared, sitting beside Clarissa.

The sun was slanting right into the cubbyhole where the two sat, the little waterfall falling beside them. The air was very still and warm, smelling of pine; soft, undulating rainbows floated at arm's length. Nikki lay back, panting from the exercise, unselfconscious, and dreamed with eyes closed in the sun. It was enough simply to lie there and drift.

Clarissa had other plans.

"Tell about the year before the first boy," she inquired softly.

Nikki opened her eyes with a pang. "Now? Here?" she pleaded.

"You must begin," Clarissa insisted.

"About the poison ivy?" Nikki asked, suddenly feeling she might cry. It was all too beautiful; why bring up such a horrible episode in her life? She felt her body contract.

"To see its importance," Clarissa answered. "That your instincts were right."

"I don't remember how I got it—oh yes, I do," she realized, sitting up. "The boy— we walked into the woods and sat down in the underbrush. He started to pull me down. I didn't want to."

"So you did something," Clarissa prompted.

Oh, why did she feel like she could cry? Why? She hated it … the pleasant mood was getting ruined talking about this stuff.

"I did something," Nikki admitted dully, not certain what she meant.

"You didn't let him do what he wanted. Didn't let him have sex with you."

"No, I didn't."

"Why not?"

Nikki hesitated. "Because I didn't want to. I wasn't ready. It wasn't time."

"And you were right. It was not yet time."

"He was so mad at me," she whispered, her eyes tearing.

"Yes," Clarissa affirmed, looking off into the distance. "They are angry. It doesn't matter."

"It was hard—that he was mad at me," Nikki emphasized, her voice thick.

"So you got sick."

"Poison ivy." Nikki pulled at her wet hair, running her fingers through to dry it. Her body was nearly dry in the sun now.

"And that protected you."

"I didn't see him after that," Nikki disclosed softly, looking down.

"But the next year he was back."

"Oh, no. It was another—older."

"Under the same guise," Clarissa gathered. "And you were afraid of making him angry again."

Nikki stopped. Tears swam into her eyes. Was it that simple? That she was afraid of him being mad at her if she didn't give in? So she had made herself drunk that night at the party—remember? So drunk she could hardly stand. She had thrown up. Claire's parents were having a costume party for Halloween, when they still lived in the old house in Annisquam, and the place was packed.

Nikki went dressed as a mermaid, her hair done up in ringlets. Her mother had set it for her, making it look like waves. She wore a long, slim green dress exposing her young white neck. The dress was glittery satin, very elegant, with a removable tail. In the tradition of Halloween parties, her face was covered with a green glittery mask that highlighted her dramatically outlined eyes. She had felt pretty and magical. Only thirteen, she was nearly as tall as she would ever be, already five-seven. Everyone assumed she was a senior in high school.

Most of the costumed guests wore masks. It was a nice party, Nikki remembered, because there were people of all ages, not just young or old. She danced with men old and young, and she drank punch as the room swirled. Rose did not come, to no one's surprise; parties in Gloucester were too low class for her; she had gone off on the mayor of Boston's yacht for the evening. Nikki's parents came for a little while, her father in a particularly foul mood. He directed his anger at Nikki, muttering his old imprecation that she looked like a whore. He had obviously begun drinking early in the evening. Nikki ignored him as best she could, taking note only that he was dressed very strangely as a bird of some sort, wearing long wings and an avian headdress. Nikki's mother was all in black. Her face painted deathly white, she cowered before the drunken bird-man.

He tottered off across the crowded room for a drink at the bar, where Nikki spotted him standing with a masked devil who seemed somehow familiar. She broke off watching and drew close to her mother. Rachel, dressed as a cowgirl, joined them.

"Mom, you don't look like you want to be here," Nikki remarked.

Her mother shook her head miserably. Nikki sighed and angrily moved away. She never wanted anything to do with her parents' endless fights. Later Rachel whispered to her that their father had insisted their mother go dressed as a witch.

A witch—! Now remembering twenty-seven years later, Nikki was struck by the fact.

Soon after her parents left, the music was changed from Big Band tunes to rock-and-roll so the kids could dance. Although most of the older people took a breather, some of the grownups continued to dance. Woozy with drink by then, Nikki ended up dancing with the devil who had been talking with her father earlier. She detached her mermaid tail when it got in the way of her dancing, leaving a long slit up the side of her dress that showed off a fishnetted leg.

The devil was a little taller than she and lean, dressed all in red with a red cape and a mask that covered his whole face. He still seemed familiar, but so did everyone that night, especially after the rum punch. Claire kept sneaking cups of it for Nikki and herself, which they slurped hurriedly down in the bathroom, giggling and coughing.

Later, Nikki was standing on the balcony at the rear of the house, looking in the moonlight over the railing into the dark woods, her stomach heaving. She bent over the rail, threw up, and came up coughing.

A hairy hand presented her with a handkerchief, which she gratefully took and used to wipe her mouth. All at once the devil's mouth was on hers, and while she inhaled the smell of smoke and alcohol on his breath, he wrapped his red cape around her and pressed her into a corner. Too drunk to move, she was overwhelmed by his pressing into her. With one hand he wrapped her close to him, and with the other he touched her breasts and hips, sliding his hand down her slashed skirt...

Suddenly she was in a car and the devil was driving; she was nearly faint with alcohol. The car seemed to weave and pitch ... she was in a room and the man was on top of her, pushing her dress up. She could hardly breathe. Her mind came and went. He took her and spread her legs, there was terrible pain, and she felt herself bleeding. He moved on top of her, his breath in her face, and when after a while he stopped and moved off her, he became a distant blur. She knew one thing: She was no longer a virgin. From then on she knew firsthand the things her friends bragged about. It took her a little while to figure out they were only bragging—that bragging didn't mean they knew. For a long time she was the only one who knew.

"And it made you separate from your girlfriends," Clarissa observed evenly, puncturing Nikki's thoughts.

Nikki lay down and cried, curling up in a ball. Clarissa sat over her and patted her shoulder. Shudders shook Nikki's body, and she cried full of grief at the loss. She wasn't sure of what—was it of herself or her friends, a direction not taken in her life? All that was dark—an obscure mass heavy in her chest. She felt a great sadness, which overcame her and carried her off, so that she cried as she could not remember ever having cried in her entire life.

Now memories of all her men came back to her, their tremendous weight pressing on her chest, crushing her breath. All the forgotten faces passed before her in dumbshow, as if on display for her memory, and suddenly she could mark every one of them: the ones who had meant something to her; the many more who had not. Faces came and went, unspeaking. She saw the men smiling and frowning, walking and sitting and drinking, she saw them at school and at work, outside and in hotel rooms and along corridors and inside bars across smoke-filled rooms, eager expressions of desire curling their faces. Dimly, in the background, stood Philip, looking steadily at her through gold-flecked eyes that gave voice.

She felt their bodies pressing into her with their insistencies, their needs, their desires that passed through her like a knife. They were endless, this line of men wanting something from her, and they rolled over her like a road. She was bleeding and could feel a trickle of blood move between her legs, down onto the rock.

And she cried from the weight of them all, not out of shame or even regret but simply with the weight of all their beings pressed upon her, pressed into her, spilling their essences into her, flooding her, flooding and flooding until she could contain no more.

"To hunt is to submit to the awful presence of a dead animal," Clarissa declared suddenly, still petting Nikki as if she were a dumb animal. Lying there with her weakness so exposed, she was so ashamed! Yet through her tears she wondered at Clarissa's words. Were these men dead, then, and was she being haunted by the dead?

"Nikki, when you are ready, cleanse yourself under the waterfall. I am going for food and will return shortly. Tara will stay with you," Clarissa finished gently, rising and whistling briefly.

Nikki heard but could not look. Her eyes were swollen shut. Clarissa's voice came to her in a fog; she heard soft retreating footsteps. In her imagination the ghost men overwhelmed her still, their presence too vivid for her to turn away, though she sorely wished to. She writhed on the hard rock, turning her darkened face this way and that, but was met each way by more faces. One by one the men passed, asking something of her, leaving her no choice but to submit to each in turn, passing under each one all over again. Curling herself tighter into a ball; the sun warmed her as she lay in the deep forest; alone, weeping softly, from time to time sobbing or groaning, her body shuddering.

Only after a long while did the faces ebb in her, ceasing their incessant torture. The phantasmagoria dimmed and faded away at last, leaving Nikki empty, utterly emptied out and naked on the slab of white granite in the late afternoon sun.

Above, sitting on a rock of her own, Tara sniffed and kept watch, whimpering from time to time through her long black nose.

IT WAS WHOLLY unlike her, Nikki felt, stretching and opening her puffy eyes at last. Had hours gone by?

She was embarrassed Clarissa had seen her like that. She sat up and looked around, as a small pool of blood underneath her dribbled out. The sun lay low in the sky, just looking over the treetops though still giving warmth.

What had transpired? She exhaled deeply. Something had been taken away from her. She felt thoroughly empty, as if she had been fasting for a week. She nudged closer to the waterfall, reaching a hand into the cold water and drinking from her palm, slurping long and hard, again and again. The water was clean—everything was clean here, she reflected. Her forehead hurt from the cold water and her own crying. Still sitting on the rock and eyeing the freezing water, she ducked her head under it, letting its splashes cascade over her head and down her body. She threw water on the stone to wash the red stain away.

Finding the wetness oddly sensual, she swung her body, which felt light and airy now, close under the fall until the water flowed fast over her limbs and over her breasts, making her nipples harden from the cold. Panting, she turned so that the water fell between her legs and washed her clean, then she leaned back, looking around once to make sure she was alone.

Nikki had never let Philip look, really look, at her body, for she was too self-conscious of her thighs and her stomach. He said they were fine, but she knew better. Only now, sitting with her legs out, the cold water running down between them, she looked at her thighs with a little distance, her mind refreshingly emptied of judgment. What did it matter whether or not her stomach was a little too rounded? Was it, in fact, rounded?

With a mental shrug she gave herself up to the pleasure of the water. Finding it no longer cold, Nikki leaned forward and moved one hand down into her dark pubic hair and began to stroke herself, her legs pulling up as the delicious tension grew in her body. She rubbed herself without stopping, until she came to a climax and, groaning, lay quickly back on the flat, warm slab of granite where the sun was dying.

She lay panting, eyes open wide. Feeling deeply cleaned out, a mere entity lying there naked on her back on the warm rock, she extended her legs, wiggling her toes and giggling as the waterfall splashed over them. "Wow!" she proclaimed a few times.

Although the men still lingered, they were not pressing on her. They were present simply as memories. Nikki was amazed. For years she had forgotten them, had never been able to recall their faces, let alone their names. Until all of them crowded in on her unexpectedly today, in a press, hurting her. Yet now, presenting themselves as remembrances, standing a little away from her, they dared not transgress the space by touching her any longer. From this distance she called their names out in succession. Philip's ghost was no longer present. At first her voice trembled, stuttering unnaturally loud in her ears, as she held each before her eyes to shakily call out his name: "DJ, Robert, Jason…"

Even though shy and frightened to name them, she felt compelled. And as she named each man, his eyes fell and his shade dimmed. So that her courage grew, and as she went on her voice steadied and quieted. More and more softly she called their names, until she was whispering names that were no longer names, only sounds in her mouth, then just the wind moving through her body as she breathed. The shades were gone.

More time passed. Nikki sat up a little unsteadily and scanned her surroundings. The sun had gone down below the trees, the air already growing cooler. Tara was nowhere in sight. Nikki climbed back to where her clothes lay in a warm pile and pulled them slowly on, humming to herself. Drawing a kerchief out of her back pocket, she wound it and lay it in the crotch of her jeans.

She stopped. Something was missing. She had no worries, no voices in her head. She listened. The woods were coming alive with the crepitations of crickets. A bullfrog tronked from below somewhere. A mourning dove hooted softly in the distance. The nearby maple rustled its leaves.

She finished dressing and sat, leaning her head back against a rock and gazing out over the prospect. She had no thoughts, only observations, and the clearing seemed rich and complete. Soon Tara came and lay down beside her while Nikki stroked the fur along the wolf's narrow spine. Her coat felt pleasing to the touch, clean and fresh like Nikki's body but with its own particular animal scent. The sinking sun crayoned rose and orange clouds that splayed across the wide sky like an organ. Soon the orange gave way to steel grey as the sun dimmed.

Tara pricked her pointed ears and started up with a snort of pleasure. From some ways off in the woods a familiar barking rang out. Nikki realized she had been drifting without even wondering about Clarissa or waiting for her return.

Tara raced off into the darkening woods and was lost under the shadowy trees. Nikki stood up and sighed, then frowned worriedly. She knew that bark!

Out from under the trees, down where the granite boulders ringed the edge of the pond, bounded Guy, barking and racing to the water's edge.

"Guy!" Nikki called out, clapping her hands. She was astonished. Where had he come from?

Timber and Tara galloped after Guy, followed by Clarissa walking slowly, leather pouch hanging at her right hip, bearing something draped over her left shoulder while carrying something limp in her left hand, slung low beside her. In the gloaming Nikki could not make out what.

Guy picked his way along the rocks, his tongue lolling, eyes on Nikki. Soon he was at her side, jumping up at her and whimpering happily. Behind him stood Tara and Timber. Nikki leaned down, grabbing Guy's ears and pulling at them.

"Where did you come from?" she greeted him, delighted in turn.

Silently she fretted. Guy was completely unsocialized. Yet here he was, frolicking with two wolves. Nikki wished she had his leash, but he jumped down and barked happily at the two wolves. The three raced off into the woods behind the quarry.

Clarissa came up to Nikki with her hard, assuring smile.

"You brought Guy—?" Nikki asked, brow furrowing. She saw that over Clarissa's left shoulder lay animal furs.

"You weren't going to be home to feed him, so I thought it best," Clarissa replied, as if that explained everything.

"But he's not socialized. How did you—"

"No kidding," Clarissa remarked wryly. "Timber and Tara are good at teaching dogs to be dogs," she declared. "Timber and your dog went at it a bit at first, but then Guy got the hang of being around other canines. He'll be fine with them now."

Clarissa held up her quarry. "Dinner!" she announced. Nikki saw with a shock that it was a lifeless duck, its long, soft neck draped through the huntress's palm.

"Let's go eat where the camping is good. I'm starving!" Clarissa exclaimed. Noting that Nikki was fully dressed, she turned without another word and started down the rocks. Nikki followed, her legs a little shaky.

They embarked on a path that led further from Clarissa's house, as far as Nikki could tell. A neat crescent moon chased the setting sun over the trees like a herald bearing good news. Darkness had already settled beneath the trees, though the fading light allowed the two women to see easily among the shadows. Clarissa trotted ahead with her usual fleetness, but Nikki found it easy to follow. The path was wide and lined with sweet ferns that hugged the trunks of alders and maples. The earthy smell of the forest was warmly welcoming after the cleansing alchemy of stone and spring water and sun.

They sped along for some time, going up hills and down, traversing land Nikki did not recognize at all. If they were still in Dogtown, this was a part she had never explored. Behind them the wolves and Guy came bounding along, stopping to sniff tree roots and underbrush.

When the moon hovered a bit lower, Clarissa drew up to a bubbling stream and stopped.

"This is a good place," she proclaimed, dropping the duck on the ground. When she held up the furs she had been carrying, Nikki was startled to recognize one of them as the bear fur from Clarissa's house called Maya.

Clarissa held Maya out to Nikki, who blanched.

"Take her. It's time you joined the Bear Clan," Clarissa insisted, and there was no humor in her voice.

Nikki reached and took the voluptuous bear fur.

Clarissa stretched her own smaller fur out on the forest floor after unrolling a small pot wrapped inside. Nikki unrolled Maya despite thinking it a shame to lay the gorgeous thing down on the ground.

Noticing the bear looked even larger lying along the ground, Nikki felt an immediate desire to lie down and never get up. The eyes stared coldly out at her, and the two huge paws were mute, but the fur fluttered warmly in the evening breeze. *Bear clan,* Nikki repeated the words to herself.

Clarissa carted the duck carcass to the stream and cleaned it, severing its head and gutting the entrails, afterward carrying the discards downstream and leaving them in a pile. Returning with the cleaned carcass, she handed it to a hesitant Nikki.

"Do you know how to pluck it?" she asked. When Nikki shook her head, Clarissa bent and showed her how to pull the feathers off with quick strokes, beginning at the back. As soon as she saw Nikki getting the hang of it, she turned to making a fire, pulling a single match from her breast pocket and striking it on a rock, then setting fire to a small pile of kindling.

Nikki busied herself with the feathers, rubbing them from her hands as she pulled them off. They insisted on sticking to her palms and then to her jeans where she wiped her hands. The work faintly disgusted her, the soft flesh under the feathers erotic and appalling. Wanting to be done with the mess she was making, she stood up abruptly, scraping the feathers into a pile and carrying them deeper into the woods, where she resumed her work. The duck felt oddly naked in her hand, fleshy and fatty,

cold and dry. Still, the woods smelled fresh and warm, and the sounds of the bubbling stream and young fire crackling made her breathe more easily. More than once
she muttered apologies to the duck, though she was too intimidated by Clarissa to
drop the task and run away. Anyway, she was ravenous herself. By the time she finished and returned, Clarissa had a fire going in a small pit.

Clarissa filled the pot in the stream. She carried it back and set it on heavy logs
on top of the fire, took the duck from Nikki and, unsheathing her knife, cut the
flesh into chunks that she lowered into the water. When nothing more of the fleshy
skeleton was left, she set some small stones against the fire and wedged the remainder of the duck carcass behind them to roast close to the flames.

Clarissa went to wash in the stream, then walked off into the woods. Presently
she returned bearing some leaves, which she broke and sprinkled into the water. She
sat Indian fashion on her skin, across the fire from Nikki, who was already sitting
on Maya and staring at the fire, trying not to watch the simmering chunks of duck
meat.

"You—killed it," Nikki lamented.

"It's dinner," Clarissa declared. "We'll say a prayer over it."

"Where are we?"

"Actually, not far from where the circle meets. There is another spring at the
meeting place, but I didn't want to go there tonight. This is a fine place."

"The woods are very quiet."

"All the animals are leaving," Clarissa explained.

"Isn't that because we're hunting them?"

"No—hunting is natural. Too many humans around. First the animals depart,
because they can uproot themselves more quickly. The forests are nearly empty—you
can feel it. In time the green will follow, just more slowly since it can't run. Then
we'll be left with brown earth, which will be empty."

Filled with melancholy, Nikki glanced across the flames at Clarissa's hard, weathered face. It looked demonic in the flickering flames as bright planes of light played
back and forth across her strong features. Her hard face was not unkind, Nikki reflected, simply rugged from grief.

Still, it felt wrong to eat the duck; she could not remember ever having eaten
duck before. Sometimes three ducks would wander into her yard from the Annisquam
River down the street. They'd come up to the front door for food, driving Guy so
crazy he'd bark like a maniac behind the screen door. They never seemed to mind
his barking—just insisted on being fed, bobbing their feathery heads and quacking.
Nikki threw them all her scraps; loved them like family.

Nikki caressed the soft bear fur. *Dead animals—and I helped kill them,* she
thought. The notion was absurd, of course. *Still.* And something opened in her heart,
a wound that lowered her into a depression.

"It feels so sad," she uttered at last, feeling her heart heavy. "Maya and the duck—
all the animals."

Clarissa looked intently at her. "It *is* sad. You are wounded now—that's good. Maya will care for the wound."

"Maya! She should hate us!" Nikki asserted, her voice rising.

"Why? Because we kill animals? That is a sad necessity, a wound we must inflict. Which in turn leaves us wounded—which is also necessary. Any hunter—any real hunter—carries this wound. No one can stop the killing, but carrying the wound brings hesitation," Clarissa trailed off, nodding severely to herself and looking into the fire.

They were silent a little while.

"Where are the dogs—I mean, Guy and the wolves?"

Clarissa looked up. "Around. Don't you hear them?"

Nikki didn't.

"They'll show up for the duck leftovers. After we're asleep, you'll hear coyotes or foxes going after the entrails downriver."

"Coyotes! I'd love to see coyotes!" Nikki exclaimed, her face brightening. She felt her face flush—felt like a child. She did love coyotes, though, ever since seeing them out on the range in New Mexico in the middle of the night, up in the mountains above Taos.

"I didn't know coyotes lived in New England," she finished.

"Coyotes, deer, foxes, fishers. Lots of birds. Occasionally a wild boar, though not for some time. The bears have gone," Clarissa confirmed, tending the cooking. "Maya told me she was the last." Clarissa studied Maya a moment. She laughed. "Guess she's still here."

The two sat in silence as the duck boiled and fat spattered in the flames. The air was filled with the aroma of boiling duck, which smelled delicious to Nikki.

"Did you bring a knife?" Clarissa asked. Luckily, Nikki had in her pocket her Swiss army knife, which the old Indian in New Mexico had counseled her to always bear. She pulled it out and unfolded it. Clarissa had already poked her own knife into the pan, bringing up a chunk of meat.

"May this duck nourish us and bless us," Clarissa invoked, holding the skewered piece of duck meat pointed upward, like a flag. "Thank you, duck, for sacrificing yourself to keep Nikki and Clarissa alive. May we fly in you to distant moons and settle in friendly ponds."

Clarissa shoved the piece unceremoniously into her mouth and chewed, winking ironically at Nikki, her weathered face creasing.

Nikki hesitated, glancing over at Clarissa. Too shy not to partake, she poked her knife around in the pan until she skewered a piece, lifting it steaming in the cool night air. *Was she supposed to offer in kind a prayer to the duck?*

"This is the first time I've eaten duck," she explained, holding it aloft, the knife wavering in the air. "Thank you, duck spirit. May we become duck-women and have duck in us," Nikki intoned, feeling a little silly, though largely guilty.

"It's we who are inside the duck," Clarissa corrected, poking another piece and filling her mouth. "It's only apparent we're eating duck. It's eating *us,*" she stated, the hot meat muffling her words.

Nikki hemmed, lifting the piece of duck gingerly to her mouth and biting with the edge of her teeth. It tasted good—good enough for her to interpret that as the duck's permission to be eaten. Even if it still felt unnecessary. The leaf flavoring was aromatic, imparting a woodsy herb taste to the fatty game. Nikki wondered distantly about the fat content.

"Is this what it is to be a member of the—tribe?" Nikki asked.

"It's one of the things," Clarissa replied. "At least from where I stand. You have not been initiated, so you can't know yet, of course. But fellowship with women— which is not to say in opposition to men—that's central. Life here in the woods. Another is solitude. That," Clarissa added, throwing up a large hand and indicating the crescent moon, running lower now in the pine trees.

"Hunting," Nikki tried out, savoring the word that was so foreign to her.

"Hunting. One of the original goddesses was a huntress."

"Like you," Nikki smiled.

Clarissa frowned. "I wouldn't mistake one for the other." She leaned back and sighed, putting her knife down and rubbing her head.

The three canines came crashing through the woods, bounding panting up to the fire. Nikki looked at Guy, amazed once again. He had always been wild and antisocial, like her. She smiled at him and rubbed his ears.

With her knife Clarissa expertly edged the duck carcass out of the fire, tossing it to the three, who went at it like siblings.

"What do you mean about us being *inside* the duck?" Nikki asked.

"Have you read *Goddesses In Every Woman?*" Clarissa countered.

Nikki nodded.

"The mistake Bolen makes, wise as she is, is to think that the divine presences— gods and goddesses, whatever you call them—are controlled by ego power." Clarissa laughed lightly. "Ego inflation, we say today—tragic hubris, the Greeks called it. If you reduce the Great Huntress to a power in yourself, then you confuse your human individuality with her divine power. When you're just a mortal."

"What's the difference?"

"Those times when instinctual forces seem to be driving our behavior or overwhelming our thoughts, to the point of making us feel possessed—as if not ourselves— that's the presence of something more powerful. We're not in control—it feels *aweful,*" she finished. Using her knife to skewer more duck, she sat munching.

They ate for a while.

"Oh, these are for you," Clarissa mentioned, digging in her pouch and handing Nikki a bunch of tampons. Nikki took them with a shy smile. She had been aware of the rag getting wet, so she excused herself and went into the woods.

The remainder of the duck Clarissa removed from the pan and wrapped in a piece of leather she carried in her pouch, which she then stuffed under her animal skin. She carried the pan to where the three canines were still wrestling over the duck bones.

The two women lay on their skins across the dying fire from each other. Nikki felt pleasantly sated, comfortable lying on the bearskin under the trees, the evening air full of mourning doves and bug chirps. She stared at the dark canopy overhead, full of thoughts, none of which took form but instead flitted through her like nymphs, inchoate and hidden among the green. She closed her eyes, smelling the burning embers in the night, the wolves and Guy. Her thoughts were green; she saw Clarissa's eyes.

But she was still on guard; after all, nearby lay the woman who had injured Nikki's dear friend Rose. Well, hadn't Clarissa herself insisted hesitation was good—? Yes, she was on guard then, though hardly anxious about it, and so her guardedness was just another tree in the forest of her evening meditations.

Something was entering her this night. Behind her eyelids she spied the crescent moon as it flew under the trees. Close by a circle of darkly hooded figures—the circle somehow open. She saw herself up on the rocks at the quarry, naked under a full moon, yet this time she dove like a comet into the water, and it flooded her heart and brought her body alive. A night breeze stirred her quietly. Was that Maya coming toward her—? The huge bear was alive, walking on her hind legs toward her, a cub bear behind. She came right up to Nikki and spoke to her, saying *"I am your mother."*

Her heart flooded with gratitude, Nikki wanted to weep. She approached Maya, but the bear turned and lumbered off on all fours, her cub following. Nikki sat on the edge of a stony river, looking upriver where Maya fished. Her breasts hurt. What difficulty she had experienced breast-feeding Alice. The doctors had not wanted it, since Alice was premature. She had to take Alice out of her incubator at the hospital and sneak her into the broom closet down the hall, close the door and sit in the stifling dark, the air full of cleaning fluid, ammonia and Ajax. There she had to feel her blouse open, flicking the buttons nervously, then bring tiny Alice up to her nipple, encouraging her to suck. The little thing had responded, her doll mouth finding the hard nipple naturally. Nikki felt her milk flow out of her, the sensuous, erotic feel of the fluid coursing through her and into Alice.

Like an animal she had to keep her ears flicked aware, listening for the sounds of someone approaching. Why should it have been criminal? Once or twice a Latina cleaning woman opened the door, but the cleaning staff had been the ones to tell her where to hide from the doctors. Nikki had not the strength to stand up to the doctors when she was twenty-one and all alone. Alice's father—the seed bearer, as Philip called him—had left her at the hospital. She was feeding Alice as the door opened. Nikki opened her eyes and sat up.

"What animal is underneath me?" she asked the night.

There was no answer. Clarissa slept facing away from her. Nikki looked around in the dark, uncertain whether or not she was dreaming—so strange! The canines had gone off somewhere. She looked up. The sky was grey; nearly dawn.

Nikki stood up without looking at Clarissa. She turned and walked away from the little clearing, wandering into the deeper woods, following her wandering thoughts. There were early morning bird sounds; she felt as if she were awaking from a long, deep dream into a world of dream.

Walking for a time silently, alone with the dawn, Nikki passed a long, low pond on her right where the ground began to rise. She followed it, her footsteps soft. At last her feet brought her to an outcrop of rock that looked out toward the west, still predawn dark, into more trees and a land she didn't recognize.

Absorbed in thought, Nikki sat down and leaned against a tree, her eyes closed. She fell back into a half sleep, images coming and going; were they inside of her, or she inside of them? She tried to remember Clarissa's words. Time drifted; the sounds of the birds were far off and irrelevant.

Suddenly she heard barking. Nikki opened her startled eyes to find Guy standing in front of her, barking furiously, eyes ablaze, mouth full of foam.

She sat bolt upright. Was he rabid? she wondered, feeling afraid yet more concerned for Guy. She reached for him, but he backed off, snarling at her, and from his fangs bubbles of foam dribbled to the ground.

Sensing a stirring all around her, Nikki peered into the dark woods. Something was running. She heard yipping as Guy raced off into the woods, yelping and growling.

Nikki listened, ears aflame, eyes like beacons. Although she could see nothing except shadows, the yipping was resounding loudly in her ears. From all about the woods shadows darted in and out, just outside her line of sight but gradually encircling her.

It began to dawn on her: The restless running came from creatures, the yipping and yelping from animals, moving as if intentionally forming a ring around her.

Suddenly it struck her—coyotes! Coyotes were surrounding her, running in a circle just out of sight, down among the lower branches and behind the trunks of the pines. The morning mist revealed a leg here and there, a sudden haunch, a snout as it raced around and around; Nikki in the middle.

She was bewildered, stunned, amazed. What did it mean, this animal visitation? First the wolves, then coyotes! What was it all about? Nikki strained her mind, desperate for vision, but her thoughts collapsed back, submerged into the morning mist.

Another sound of racing toward her—until Clarissa appeared out of the mist, eyes wide, face concentrated.

"They're coyotes!" she exclaimed.

"Yes," Nikki answered, not understanding what Clarissa meant.

"They're making a circle." Clarissa was breathing hard, peering here and there into the woods. And still the coyotes raced in a circle around Nikki. They ran and leaped over bracken and branch, nostrils snorting, paws dancing along the ground, until the song of the woods itself rang out. Around and around and around and around.

NIKKI AWOKE with the sun streaming down into the pines, not knowing where she was. As Guy sniffed at the sumptuous bearskin, Nikki caught sight of Clarissa carrying wood back to camp, Timber and Tara at her heels.

She sat up and patted Guy, who ran off to be with his new friends.

Approaching, Clarissa unwrapped the cold duck and offered some to Nikki.

Nikki ignored the food for a moment. Something had shifted...

"No—thank you," she managed, waving a hand. "I really don't want to eat duck—anymore," she added deliberately, thinking the words out as she spoke them. She still felt half asleep.

Clarissa stared at her a moment, nodded and withdrew the duck. She took an apple out of her pouch and tossed it to Nikki, who caught it and bit slowly into it.

"Was that a dream? What was it all about?" Nikki asked, sitting cross-legged on the bearskin, chewing.

"Last night? I don't know—do you?" Clarissa munched a piece of duck, tossing the rest to the canines.

"Something powerful..." Nikki began.

Clarissa nodded, stirring the embers. As she leaned and blew on the coals, they flamed into transparent fire. Nikki felt a wave of shallow heat on her face, watching the fire grow as Clarissa added twigs.

"Not many coyotes around here anymore. Didn't know there were so many left. They came for a reason. Did you call them?" Clarissa asked, fixing Nikki with an earnest look.

"Me?" She laughed shortly. "How would I?"

"You were asking to see them last night."

"I was," Nikki mused with some wonderment.

"Coyotes are pretty wild creatures, mostly solitary. Sometimes they go in packs. They were drawing a ring around you."

"A magic ring of power," Nikki declared, thinking out loud.

"Maybe. They may have been familiars."

"You don't know?" Nikki pressed, glancing at Clarissa.

She shook her head, putting water on and crushing some leaves into the pot. The air was soon filled with the aroma of rose hips along with another herbal scent Nikki couldn't make out.

"Why me?"

Clarissa shrugged. "You have some magic in you, maybe."

"Maybe?"

"Your aunt knows more about magic than I do," Clarissa demurred, stirring the tea. "As do many others."

"You bring the animals," Nikki stressed.

"Not like you, though," Clarissa nodded. "Do you think you might be calling the coyotes without knowing it?" She looked straight at Nikki, very serious.

Nikki felt flattered. "I guess so—I—"

Clarissa cut her off with a severe glance. "It's dangerous to bend the unseen, to call animals or people or things to you. It's dangerous to do it consciously. It is far more dangerous to do it unconsciously. Decide."

Nikki sat shocked, as the two fell silent. Her mind was racing. At first flattered, now she felt ashamed, childishly foolish. Too much the sorcerer's apprentice. For Clarissa was fully serious. Nikki peeked at Clarissa's face for a hint of a smile but was confronted instead by hard lines and deep green eyes, as serious as trees.

"What do you mean by 'decide'?"

"What if the coyotes who came were familiars, the guiding animals of—someone else?" Clarissa stopped.

Nikki was waiting for more. There was no more. It was time for her to answer. "Could they have come on their own?" she ventured.

"They did come on their own. Any animal or spirit can refuse you."

"I mean, without my calling them?"

"That is your decision," Clarissa answered simply. She stood up and paced impatiently. Her long legs struck out at the earth, back and forth. Nikki felt afraid of the horribly hard face and the harder eyes directed at her.

"Magic—it seems like a wonderful children's game if you imagine you have nothing to do with it. Things just appear—poof! Animals, spirits, even me with my house and wolves. I see what you think—that I am a wondrous presence appearing magically in your life, in spite of the difficulties I cause for you. But you must decide, Nikki; you cannot go further into your heritage or be welcomed into the clan until you do."

"I don't understand!" Nikki cried out, pressing her hands to her temples. "I don't understand!"

"Breathe," Clarissa counseled, kneeling suddenly by Nikki and touching her shoulder. "Deeply." She held out the pot of tea.

Trembling, Nikki took hold of the pot and drank a few sips. Its heat scalded her lips, but the scalding felt good, for it took her out of her tortured thoughts. She sat back. Clarissa returned to her side of the fire. Nikki began to feel better; the tea did its magic, the aroma filling her lungs and warming her stomach. She breathed.

Clarissa looked hard at Nikki, though her eyes were not unkind. "If you think that magic happens from outside of you, with no active involvement on your part, you remain a child, unconsciously floating in a dream world. The world is a dream, but it is a dream for spirits who have awakened to its dream. The rest—restless spirits looking for home, that's all," Clarissa concluded, making her fingers like small explosions in the air. "An hour on the earth and then gone, nothing advanced, no transformation via the mysteries, no passing on of whatever it is we must pass on. But death demands our participation in the greatest mystery—the great shift in us."

Nikki started at the thought. She exhaled. "What have we to pass on?"

"Whatever is given to you," Clarissa answered simply. "Each of us has something different. I pass on a dance of the dying animals. Your aunt passes on her second sight. Others pass on stories or dance, the art of dressing. Some pass on matters of business—money and enterprise, the law. We pass things on because of each of us nothing remains. All I have to say to you is draped in the gorgeous black and crimson robes of death. All of life is a dance with death, in which death takes the lead. When I kill to live, as we all must do, I keep my dead friends around. I invoke the dying animals and dying world. In the end, perhaps my life as a love of death will pass on to you the death of your innocence about love."

Nikki passed the tea to Clarissa, who drank.

"It depends on what chooses us. If you think you yourself choose what to pass on, you are one of the sleeping ones dangerous to our kind. The benign ones who sleep forget us and forget the great work. That is bad enough. The less benign, sensing something to wake up to but refusing to awaken, sometimes grow to resent those of us awake to the dream and the dance. And they kill us.

"Perhaps that is their own peculiar reminder of death," she ended grimly, setting down the pot and poking the fire with a stick.

Nikki thought of the witch trials. She thought of Anne Cleves. What had Meg said? The story was that Anne was tried as a witch, though she was a Druid by learning.

"What must I decide?" Nikki implored. But something was approaching even as she posed the question. She already knew what it was, and she knew what her decision was, before the last word left her lips. For she saw the answer: A stranger was coming from a distance down the road, coming toward her, walking slowly. The figure of a man—was it her father? She didn't recognize him. He seemed younger than her father, thinner. Someone else was with him, like him and yet different, obscured in shadow. Two men were coming, and they held her answer.

"Did you call the coyotes?" Clarissa asked once more.

"I did call them," Nikki responded, as something shifted in her, as a great weight dropped and could no longer be lifted. Part of her felt silly and sheepish. But the men nodded.

"I feel—silly," Nikki admitted.

"That's in beginning, because you want to laugh like a child in the face of anything serious. When you grow as a child of Anne Cleves, you will be able to laugh with the seriousness of things. Why did you call them?"

Nikki regarded the two men, who were standing close to her now. They did not speak. As she struggled to know herself, she no longer felt wholly certain she had called them.

"I don't know," she uttered at last.

Clarissa nodded. "In time," she acknowledged.

"I don't know that I did," Nikki went on, looking down. She felt a failure.

"How could anyone know completely? It is not for us to know with certainty or even to speak clearly about such shadowy things. But when we stand in the tension between knowing and not knowing, we start to awaken to our responsibility."

"It feels like some awful kind of responsibility to admit or to believe, even for a moment, that I did call them. Oddly enough, it doesn't make me feel good about myself. I mean, I'd have thought calling those magnificent wild coyotes would have made me feel pretty special, like I had done something truly magical. Instead, all I feel is the largeness of the power. As in, what have I done? And that I better find out…"

Nikki thought a moment. "No, not exactly what have I done, but what powers beyond me have I participated in—altering?" she wondered aloud, feeling a strange sensation. The two men were nodding, their grave faces observing her quietly.

"Maybe it's not about me, exactly. Or it is about me, but also about—the coyotes?" Nikki looked hopefully up at Clarissa.

Clarissa smiled her hard smile at Nikki.

"You have taken the first step in becoming a true descendant of Anne Cleves."

7.

IN JOE'S CAVE

After that first night Nikki began to spend more and more time with Clarissa, grudgingly at first and with obvious caution; soon with trust. Clarissa led Nikki on long treks into Dogtown forest, where she showed the younger woman how to recognize animal tracks and scat. They discussed places where the journal might be hidden, although Clarissa seemed uninterested in actually finding it. At the same time, she shared with Nikki all the clues she looked for in detecting signs of human habitation, no matter how old and camouflaged the signs. They began with the cellar holes, roughly circular depressions lined with stones, which were the remains of foundations from the original seventeenth-century houses in Dogtown. The bottom of the stone linings proved soft enough for Clarissa to dig with her toe and unearth what looked at first like more rocks. Upon further inspection these turned out to be shards of pottery, old pieces of iron, and parts of tools encrusted with the decay of centuries.

From the cellar holes along Dogtown Road they ventured deeper into the woods, Clarissa teaching Nikki how to walk the paths with an animal awareness.

"Now we go to where there are no paths, where even the animals don't recognize a trail," she announced one day, leading Nikki into the brush. They circled pools of marshy water, and from time to time Clarissa would kneel suddenly to expose some fragment that looked again to Nikki like mere stone, but which turned out to be a piece of an old plow or the point of a knife.

Slowly Nikki began to catch on, to focus her eyes on those smaller details of the forest that, as is often the way of nature, seemed to hide out in the open. And so the woods' secrets began to open to her. On one of their walks she found an arrowhead, on another a piece of metal that Clarissa explained was part of a mangle, a roller device used to flatten cloth.

"How do you know that?" Nikki asked.

"You extrapolate from what you've got," Clarissa explained, turning over the curved piece of iron in her hand. "I could be wrong, but this is at the least a sure sign of human habitation. I suspect that Anne's cabin—if in fact it was here in Dogtown—would have been left undisturbed after she departed or died. The townspeople would have assumed that she, being a Druid princess, manifested a power that remained bound to her place, protecting it even after she was gone. If so, there's a good chance you'll see other signs of a cabin—a partially buried foundation, implements like this one, even the odd bottle where she kept her herbs and ointments."

So in time Nikki's allegiance shifted slightly toward the older woman and away from Rose, with whom she no longer spoke, ever since the day Rose had given Nikki the ultimatum. For her part, Nikki seemed almost to forget Clarissa had been Ernest's longtime mistress, never broaching the subject with her teacher. She preferred to keep the matter in the background; besides, it had no connection with her visits to Clarissa or with her need for Clarissa's help. Instead, Nikki used what she learned from Clarissa to search for the journal by herself—not that she had come across anything significant so far.

Often Nikki took Guy along on these trips; he and the two wolves would run off into the woods like old friends. Nikki and Clarissa then sat on the porch or went for walks as they conversed. In exploring the woods later on her own, Nikki slowly became familiar with the new paths Clarissa was opening for her. But it had availed her nothing yet; she was not even able to find her way back to the spring-fed pool and granite cliff.

"Think like an animal when you search," Clarissa directed Nikki. "Think like a member of the Raven clan—a descendant of Anne."

"I've always loved animals, but never thought too much about the animals inside of me," Nikki allowed.

"That's the key," Clarissa confirmed. They were sitting on the edge of her sagging porch; Guy was romping with Timber and Tara, growling, nipping, running back and forth in the yard. Nikki squinted in the bright sun. It was late July; she had been searching the woods for weeks on end but had found nothing.

"Instinct," Clarissa underscored. "You'll have to consult Joe on this. He's the one with the long history. Me—I just live here, like them." She pointed with a stick. "I can scratch beneath the surface, but I have a limited knowledge of what I've uncovered." As if to illustrate, Clarissa jumped up and walked a few paces, leaned down to pick something up, which she tossed to Nikki. Nikki looked at it in wonder, brushing off the dirt: an arrowhead!

"Who's Joe?" Nikki inquired, turning over the piece of stone.

"The old man of the wood. A friend of ours; you see him sometimes at our meetings. I know his place in the woods, though it's kept a secret from everyone else—and I don't go there. I can see it, however," Clarissa added, raising her head and staring hard into space.

"His place?"

"Books in a cave. A lantern. The messiness that earth has, its warmth and immediacy. Jumbled old clothes and papers and food scraps. We hunted together in the early days, but now he's so old…" She looked down.

"I'd like to meet him."

"You will, but on his time. He'll know about the journal."

"Is he psychic?"

"No," Clarissa laughed, "just a mole. He wanders about town and hears things. Very long beard; very, very long ears." Clarissa pulled at her own ears, frowning comically.

"Rose wanting to build in Dogtown is not exactly a well-kept secret," Nikki noted.

Clarissa nodded. "Not psychic, just close to the earth. Amazing what you can hear with your ear to the ground."

"I've never seen him."

"He's seen you."

"You know that?" Nikki pressed, turning toward her friend.

She nodded. "All the animals, all the people in the wood have known about you for as long as you have been walking there."

"But—I never noticed you when I was a girl running around out here."

"It's not so mysterious—your mother talked to me about her girls," Clarissa explained. "And Joe has seen you more recently, although he himself isn't much seen."

"He's lived here ever since I was a child?"

"You might recognize him. He didn't always live in the woods. Once he lived in Gloucester. Now he lives among the rocks with his little companion."

"Near where we hiked?"

Clarissa laughed again. "You're trying to get me to tell."

"No—really."

They sat silently watching the wolves and the dog.

"What do you think about the developers?" Nikki asked presently.

"You have taken a lot on, dear," Clarissa commented.

"I love this forest. Someone has to help."

"Listen to your instincts; that is all I can say to you. Isn't it silly, to repeat yourself?"

Nikki felt chastened. "I don't mean to ask the same question over and over."

"Oh, it's a different question—but you're asking the same person. Go walk looking for one thing and find another. Listen to the animals within."

"I know—but what does that mean?"

"Lion heart, bear claws, boar's feet, wolf eyes. Bird mouth. Stomach of a camel and back of the horse. Digestion of a cow and lungs of a fish. Blah, blah, blah. We're all animals inside and out." She smiled at Nikki as if it were all just silly talk.

NIKKI BEGAN by wandering about on walks with Guy, figuring that if she did not look for Joe, she would find him. Without effort: That was the way the books said it must be done. So she tried to have no effort. Letting herself wander, she stumbled over rocks up and down hills, tossing sticks for Guy while looking aimlessly around. At the same time she practiced keeping wide awake and in full awareness, watching the ground for clues.

Mostly they wandered among the moraine, the huge peopled boulders stacked against hillsides or strewn down among the pine and beech groves nestled in the folds of the hills. These were the bones of the earth, sticking out in long columns of vertebrae, winding like a dragon's backbone through the primeval forest. There among the many caves inhabited by badgers and chipmunks, sometimes along a sunny path when the wood suddenly closed in, Nikki would come upon a green snake slithering like spilled mercury into the brush. She wanted to stop it to ask where Joe lived. The toads that Guy turned up were even less helpful. Once she spotted a weasel, but she missed her chance. Everything ran from her. And everywhere the forest seemed so exposed, so fragile! Now the mighty pines and oaks seemed planted shallowly in the rocks, even the muscular rocks were made of papier-mâché, hollow, easily rolled away by menacing plows driven by ash-grey builders come to yank out the trees and flatten the earth.

For days at the end of July Nikki meandered through the forest, expecting at any moment to hear the hungry roar of chainsaws, the sickening thud of the falling giants as they splayed their arms in a death fall against the breast of earth. She had to go talk to Rose. She could not face her—she was afraid. Of what? Of Rose's displeasure with her. The aching for Philip had not subsided. Nikki had not spoken with him since his fall—a month or more. She could only imagine him in his bed, slowly healing, if the doctors were right. What if she could not find the journal? Would she not see Philip again?

Absurd! she answered herself. But—did she want to? She felt herself growing stronger without him, back to her old cavalier self, independent, needing no one to make her whole. Yet his image nagged at her, particularly when she met Claire or Dawn for coffee at the *Glass Sailboat* downtown or wandered across the street into *Dogtown Books*. Rose was too much of a presence in town; everyone knew all about Nikki and Philip. They looked at her, all the faces from her whole life. She could not pass Michelle's hair salon without hurrying past, keeping her head down, not looking in, even though she knew Rose never condescended to come down the hill.

She met Dawn for dinner at *Jalapeño's,* sitting near the window terrified and fascinated lest she be seen. Everyone in the place seemed to shoot glances at her, then whisper. George Starr, Gloucester's mayor whom Nikki knew through Rose, came over to their table and, touching Nikki's shoulder, asked how she was. His doe-eyed look of sympathy, which made Nikki shiver.

"Well, eat!" Nikki exclaimed to a wide-eyed Dawn, after Starr returned to his family. Dawn stared at her, startled, tears filling her eyes. They finished quickly and hurried out.

Even inside her own home she felt unsafe and rather exposed, as if being conscripted to find the journal had unwittingly thrust Nikki into a public role, to her discomfort.

However, when the days passed with no sound of chainsaws, she realized in her lawyer's mind that the permits would take some time. She called City Hall but learned nothing. Rose, Nikki knew, would have made certain the clerks either had no information to give or were told to keep silent. Despite having no news to convey, Betsy kept in touch, annoying Nikki with her good-natured laugh. As if everything would simply turn out all right! As July faded into August, Dogtown filled with steam in the leaves, drooping like green rags in the humid air.

ONE NIGHT Nikki dreamed she was walking in Dogtown, following a narrow path between rocks up- and downhill, finally arriving at a mound in the earth. She knew with a dream's certainty that this was Anne's place—and that somewhere thereabouts lay the hidden journal.

She awoke early, very groggy in the humid summer air, stumbled downstairs and made coffee. She could not wake up, even after two cups. The earth was swimming in watery hot air; her skin felt as if a cloth of warm water lay over it.

She took up Guy's leash, and the two walked desultorily into the forest. She was dreaming as she walked, sunlight pouring down through the tall pines. Guy, too, seemed distracted, wandering off the path, catching himself in brambles. Nikki had to stop from time to time to untangle both of them.

They were wandering along in this way when a rabbit started from under a bush. Guy took off after him, yanking the leash out of Nikki's hand. She woke from her daydream in a flash and was after him, calling out as she ran huffing, threading her way between the stones, up and down the path.

Guy sprinted after the poor rabbit, which veered off the path and ran into the brambles and underbrush. Nikki followed, tripping over stones and catching her ankle in a hollow, calling to the dog, angrily determined to catch him. But Guy ran up over a hill, flashing out of sight, leaving only his bark. Nikki slowed to walk the rest of the way up the hill. Guy stopped barking; Nikki walked over the rise to find him nosing the ground, trotting in wide circles, as if he had lost the scent.

Nikki eyed him.

"Thanks, Guy," she muttered, grabbing his leash. Collapsing in the nook of a granite boulder, she sipped water from her bottle. She was on top of a small rise in the forest, in an area where the trees were far enough apart to see down into the dells and along the tops of the granite-strewn hillsides. A tremendous oak stood not far off, its long branches soaring upright in the forest basilica like the pipes of a grand organ. Nikki observed it curiously. It seemed familiar.

She found the feel of the place immediately to her liking. Sweet grass grew in slender green stalks along the edge of the central mound of earth. Guy had given up the chase of the vanished rabbit and now pulled and gnawed at the straight green threads. Nikki stretched out on a bed of soft caramel pine needles that blanketed the hilltop, brushing up against the few stones crouched there. Trees and hills covered with granite boulders extended as far as she could see, toppling down into deep, shadowy clefts.

She lay down flat on the needles, sighing, then leaned to pour Guy water from her bottle into a cup she carried for him. He took a slurp and resumed circling. The place felt magical and calm to her, although there was something disturbing about being there she couldn't name. Perhaps because she couldn't see the trail from there.

She was very tired; yawning and lying back, she fell asleep in a twinkling. The leash fell from her hand. She dreamed she was walking in the woods, listening to a melodious tiny bell tinkling off in the distance—or was it in her ear? The music was so lovely she wandered up and down hills trying to find the source. No matter how far she walked, the bell sounded no closer, yet always as if in her ear. She began to get frustrated, noticing the sky clouding over. She grew sleepy as she walked, her feet becoming heavier and heavier. She had to get to the bell, she thought, but her body was too heavy to move. She dropped to her knees, trying to keep walking. It was impossible. The bell tinkled in her ear.

Guy was scratching in the needles near Nikki's head. She woke slowly, lying on her back, her eyes slitted open to the sunlight coming through the trees. It was very still, the mist hanging in the trees. Thinking about nothing in particular, she was vaguely annoyed that Guy had chosen to scratch right at her ear. So much for a nap. How long had she been asleep? Her head was groggy.

Guy kept scratching. At last Nikki sighed and turned her head.

"Don't!" she warned, rising up on one arm to frown at Guy. He ignored her as usual and went about his business, scratching a hole in the pine needles, digging his long claws under a rock nearby, and thrusting his long snout into the dirt.

Nikki watched him distractedly. One of Guy's arms went down into a hole he broke through. He pulled quickly to get it out, then stood hesitating, cocking his head at the hole he had made. He growled once.

"Afraid you've dug up a snake, huh?"

But Guy went back to digging. Clearly he sensed something buried he was determined to reach, scrabbling the soft dark earth back and away from the opening. Nikki sat up and watched, frowning.

Moist earth crumbled away from Guy's paws, staining them as if with kohl until he was blackened to his shanks. Still he shoved his paws into the opening to draw the dark earth forward. The opening was a foot across now, Guy whimpering as he dug. Leaning forward, Nikki felt cool stale air flow over her face. She sat back and looked around. The sun shone lightly down through the pines; the hillsides were resting quietly. There was no one about; an air of desolation filled Nikki as she turned back to watch Guy in his digging. The old oak hovered high overhead.

Concluding that Guy was digging into an animal's lair, she leaned forward and pulled worriedly on the dog's leash. Growling, he stuck his nose into the opening. Some large animal, she figured.

Nikki stood up and breathed in the air. There was something new here, yet Guy was not holding back. Why was she? She had an intimation of something large inside the hole, imagining a bear lunging out and swatting Guy's face clean off with one huge hooked paw.

"Guy!" she called sharply, but he wouldn't heed. Only when the hole was big enough for Nikki to crawl through did Guy stop, blackened with wet earth, and turn expectantly to her, panting from the effort.

"What do you want me to do?"

Guy stared at her and cocked his head, tail wagging hesitantly.

"Go in? Something might be living in there. You might have broken into somebody's home."

Guy wagged and waited. Nikki looked around, sighed and dropped to her knees, then peered into the hole. It was deep—completely black. She dug in her jeans and produced a mashed book of cardboard matches from *Club 99,* a bar in downtown Boston. A place far away, she mused, regarding the pack. Four matches left. She tried to remember when she had been there last. Must have been twenty years…

With no wind to douse the flame, Nikki pulled off a paper match and struck it near the hole, holding it partway in. Her hand shook slightly, but what was there to be afraid of? Nothing, she insisted to herself, focusing her gaze on the dark space in front of her.

She could see nothing within. Nothing to do but get down on her belly and crawl in, holding the match before her. The hole sloped down three or four feet before turning sharply upward, running just below ground where it led to the top of the little hill. She pulled herself back out, shaking the match out when it burned her finger. She sat and regarded the hill itself, the one she had just napped on. It was rounded like a flat-topped cone, about twelve feet across, flecked with round granite stones like random thoughts of the earth, coalesced after long rumination into hard certainty.

The hole marked the beginning of a tunnel that led underground to the very top of the hill, Nikki realized. What did it mean?

She stopped. Could this be one of the so-called beehives she had read about— round hillocks that dotted the New England countryside? Their origin and use were much disputed, some historians believing them underground storage containers dug by tribal Indians, used for holding grain and pelts. Others imagined them as barrows like the ancient burial mounds found in England, inside of which were stacked heaps of swords and shields, picks and halberds, quarterstaffs and broadswords of warriors laid to rest. Haunted by barrow wights, these places were to be feared and respected, much as the sacred Indian burial sites.

No conclusive evidence exists of ancient warriors from the white races in America, and only leaf and bark remains from forest rituals are left to mark the lonely burial spots of Indian braves. For the prehistoric weapons of these early Americans were made of wood, leather, feather and bone, which over time rotted into the earth. A few chipped stones carry the entire history of the native hunting tribes downward in time.

In the beehives, however, coins fashioned by Vikings from Norway or Iceland were eventually discovered in the 1980s. And so arose the theory that this was treasure buried by Nordic explorers, warriors who peopled New England as early as the eleventh or twelfth centuries—far earlier than Columbus. As it began to dawn on Nikki she was perhaps standing on such sacred ground, she found herself in awe: Prehistory was alive beneath her feet! Whether the beehives contained artifacts from ancient Indian or from Viking cultures, she reflected, the mound reached far back into the past—half a millennium before the Puritans came.

Nikki leaned down again, struck again for light and drove her arm bravely into the dark. Yes, she concluded, this was a beehive, and she grew excited at the discovery. She entered the low tunnel, leaving Guy whimpering behind her. Crawling along in the semidarkness with the match wavering before her in the dank air, soon she, too, was covered by black earth; her jeans and shirt were wet and blackened, and her face, which she had brushed with her free hand, was now smeared with the underground cosmetic. She probably looked quite a sight, she imagined while grunting along the tunnel. The match went out, though a weak light glowed behind her; she went on, angling down with the tunnel and then up again.

Soon the tunnel widened into a room. Although she could not make out the far side in the dark, she didn't detect any animal scent. She tore off her third match and struck it, the dragging flash of the match echoing in the silence of the underground room.

Nikki pulled herself into a sitting position as Guy, who had crawled along behind her, came in and sniffed around, winking at the bright flame against the blackness. She was in a room whose roof, about five feet above the floor, was rounded like the hill above; floor flat and open with a firepit in the center; sides of the ceiling curving downward. Clearly the room had been fashioned by a human, even though it was not tall enough for Nikki to stand.

She reached for the ceiling, where ribs of thick branches formed rough rafters, rotting thatch twisted in between. Nikki marveled over the strength of the roof. It could not have been more than six inches thick, yet had withstood countless people and animals walking overhead. The curved roof slanted down to walls made of interlocked stones cut flat along the exposed side, held together with flaking mortar. Within small niches stationed along the walls sat boxes and dirt-encrusted bottles of various sizes.

The match burning low by now, Nikki looked hurriedly about. Against the wall lay a twined, foot-long faggot with a blackened end, tied with a cracked leather thong. She reached and touched it with the match, sending a slow flame crawling toward the twig ends and lighting the room with a wavering, lambent light. She stuck it in a cleft in the rock wall.

She slid on her knees to the center of the room, examining the stone-lined firepit. Nothing more there. Nikki edged herself over to one of the boxes, lifted it out of its niche, and set it on the floor: an oblong wooden container with a metal latch and hinges. She coaxed it open slowly, the top complaining loudly of arthritis. Inside were two rows of small brown glass bottles; Nikki lifted one out and peered at it in the dancing light. In wavering flashes she saw it was half filled with dry leaves. A label, much worn, pasted aslant on the side, read ELFHOUND. Nikki gazed at the bottle for a minute, then tucked it back in place beside its brothers. She closed the lid and closed her mouth, thinking. She set the box back in its crevice and glanced around the room. This place must have been dug by Vikings, she concluded.

Pulling another box from its perch, she found folds of stiff cloth inside, which she carefully removed only to uncover a bed of dust and the remains of what looked to be stems of a plant, brown-grey with age. She rewrapped the decayed remains and returned the box to its place. Sitting still, Nikki leaned finally to retrieve the torch, then waved it in long arcs back and forth. Ten, eleven, twelve boxes, in fact, rested in niches or on ledges. She spied, embedded in the wall near where she had come in, a stone cut with marks, and she edged over to it. The marks were letters, she recognized, drawing the torch near the stone to study these. Guy sat watching.

Nikki was able to discern some capital letters: GURYN. Someone's name, no doubt; it sounded vaguely Celtic to her. Perhaps the name of the Viking who built this place. She imagined him scratching his name into this stone long centuries ago. Was this his house? Protection against the elements—or a hiding place? She wished she could take the stone with her but could see it was mortared in place.

She ran her fingers over the stone, inadvertently pressing against it. It was loose! She pressed harder. A half-weight block of granite, six inches square by half as many thick, immediately fell into her hands. For a long moment she gaped at it, then at the wall whence it had come. Tentatively, she reached her right hand inside the cavity. Her fingers made contact with something sharp, catching as she pulled her hand out. In the semidarkness a bit of blood seeped from a long scratch on her middle finger. She sucked on the dirty finger, then moved the torch next to the hole in the wall.

Nikki looked in. The corner of something metal was sticking out of the packed earth. She reached in with her left hand, cautiously working the dirt off the metal object, until she partly uncovered a box. She worked the dirt off the box with her fingers, jamming damp black earth under her nails and pressing the flesh back. The sensation of the ends of her fingers fattening out from the pressure made her think inexplicably of the earth and sky, and she stopped to remember some story she had once read: a creation myth about the earth and sky coming together at the beginning of the world…

The loose earth came away easily. Setting the torch down in a crevice, she reached both hands in and with a crumble of earth pulled out the box, her heart in her throat. But—why was this one hidden? *Because it was Guryn's secret box—!* His weapons were inside, she felt sure. Astounded and out of breath, she sat holding a foot-long box made of hammered metal, rough-hewn and rusted, moldy and ripe with secrets.

Brushing it off, she regarded the lid on which was scratched a rude etching of a dog, lean like a greyhound and turned slightly toward the viewer, almost leaping in a running pose. A hunting dog.

Nikki stuck a fingernail under the rusted catch and pried it upward. Her fingernail breaking, she switched to her injured middle finger and pried again, pulling at the lid until it rose slowly, resisting. She pulled at the top until it screeched open, as if she were prying the secret out of someone very old. At last the catch opened, and she pulled the cover back.

Inside lay a packet that filled the length of the box, half as wide and again as deep. Nikki drew out the bundle, covered with oilcloth that had the feel of old waxed paper but thicker. There were papers inside, old papers, very old. Underneath the packet sat a round of leather thong, about the size of a dog collar. Nikki picked it up and considered it. Perhaps the collar of the dog on the cover, she speculated. Faithful Fido. She turned to the pack of papers.

Nikki opened the packet and lay the papers out on the floor before the wavering torch. The papers were thick, unlike any she had ever seen. Because they were rolled, it was only with difficulty, using both hands, that she was able to view them. The pages were written in a fine, spidery hand that seemed vaguely familiar, the letters looking like a form of Old English. Interspersed throughout appeared odd lines of sticklike figures, simple vertical lines in groups of two, three, or four.

Nikki's heart stopped. She read across the first page:

The Journal of Myselfe,
> by Anne Cleves, Gwern Thornback.

"You are now ready for your journey."

Hearing a whisper from somewhere in the shadows, Nikki spun around. She peered into the faint recesses but saw nothing. Yet unmistakably a woman's voice!

"Good luck, my lost daughter," came the voice again.

Nikki, furiously glancing here and there, caught her eye on the torch: Within the yellow flames flickered a wraith in blue light. She was enshrouded in a flowing blue gown that highlighted her long golden hair. Her left eye was shut, and she smiled out of the bright right one. Nikki looked deeply into it and was wounded to her depths. *The eye! The eye!* she wanted to cry out in longing. But she was dumb and sat in shock, her eyes tearing now from staring into the flames.

SOMETIME LATER Nikki remembered to breathe. She had frozen. She became dimly aware of where she was, still underground, the torch still wavering beside her, Guy still sitting quietly waiting. Except that the pages had rolled themselves back up into a tight scroll, leaving her fingers holding air. Along one finger a line of dried blood throbbed softly.

Nikki came slowly back into herself, shaking off the numbness. She rotated her neck, breathing, blinking, finally humming softly to hear her voice in the eerie stillness.

Slowly and deliberately she wrapped the pages back in the oilcloth, lay the packet carefully inside the box, lowered the lid and bent the arthritic catch back down. She swallowed hard, gave Guy a look, and tucked the box under her arm. After scuttling to the cave's opening, she blew out the torch and crawled back down the tunnel.

Shoving the box out of the hole ahead of herself, she emerged into the late after-noon light, which stung her eyes. Guy followed, shook himself and sneezed. Nikki lifted the box and stood up, staring at it. She sat down again, trying to recall how to breathe. Very cold from being underground, she shivered as she hunched over the treasure in her lap. Leaning in close to it, she breathed steadily, trying to inhale the impossible miracle of the moment, as if the earth itself had tilted slightly toward her. The absolute wonder of it! Guy lay down beside her.

"By what right do you take the journal?" screeched a voice from behind.

Nikki jumped a foot, suddenly standing upright and shaking. She had spun around and now found herself facing a very old man with a long beard whose head wagged with age, seeming about to wag itself right off his neck. He stood at the crest of the mound from which Nikki had emerged. Dressed in ragged clothes of layered motley, his face was lined and his body hunched. His mouth had few teeth, and his eyes though red-rimmed had a bright, hard gleam. Leaning slightly forward, he pointed at Nikki with a cane carved from a stout tree branch. Against his chest dangled a pince-nez on a ragged ribbon. With his long, tangled hair that bore a few stray twigs, he looked like a very skinny mad King Lear. Beside him danced a tiny Pekingese, his shaggy blond head tilted quizzically.

"I—uh," Nikki began.

"By what right?" the old man shrieked again, his voice slow and quivering, seem-ing to measure the words as he spoke. It was not a cruel voice, but it had a shrill edge that pierced her skull. The little dog sat up on his hind legs. Guy whimpered and moved behind Nikki.

"By what right? Um—" she stopped.

"How did you find it?" the man pressed tinnily.

"I—?" Nikki breathed hard. She would not let go of the box. How did he know what she held? She had an impulse to run away, but his glare kept her rooted. A glance behind her at Guy gave her another shock: He was not barking at the intruders.

"Did it call you—? Then it is possible—albeit only *possible*—that it is yours to read, as it was mine." He bowed.

"Yours?" Nikki questioned, completely bewildered.

"Not mine to own, but mine to read. You will find it difficult unless you read Old English. And Ogham. And Celtic. Miss Anne Cleves—Gwern Thornback, as she liked to be called—was not educated at Harvard. By the seven demons I wish I had not been!" the old man cursed loudly, then abruptly chuckled. "She had a far better education than that. The twelve years of the bard," he muttered.

He glared at her. "By what right—?" he shrieked again.

Nikki mastered herself. "I was told to look for it," she explained.

"By whom?"

"By my aunt—and others. I heard a woman's voice inside…"

"Well, perhaps then," the old man nodded, staring at her. His sight wandered high up into the trees, as if he were hearing a far-off call.

"You are Joe, aren't you?" Nikki asked, then shied when he suddenly glanced fiercely at her.

"It's my eyes," Joe nodded, turning away again. "And what is your name, young lady?" He fixed her again with his gaze.

"Nikki. Clarissa said you would find me."

"She did, eh? Then I have found you. You look like a child who has been making mudpies. Didn't your mother teach you to wash?"

Nikki looked down. She was covered with dark, moist earth, her hands were black, and she could feel the dirt on her face. "I was just sitting here thinking," she began, as if that explained it. "But my dog—" Nikki turned, startled to see Guy still hiding behind her, still not barking. "My dog, Guy, was digging. He uncovered the tunnel, and we went in. It really is Anne Cleves' journal?"

"Elfmound," Joe answered, tapping the crest of the hill with his cane.

"What is?" Nikki asked.

"That is, home of the *sidhe,* if you take a look. Opening into the Otherworld, they would say. If you're smart enough to be frightened, which you don't look, by the way. If you don't mind my saying. So. What do *you* think, Peeks?" he inquired of his dog, who looked back noncommittally.

Joe lowered himself onto a rock like a tree about to topple. Even though out of reach, Nikki extended a hand to help him.

"What is there to be frightened of?" Nikki tried to ask politely.

"Indeed," Joe remarked, sadly shaking his head. "She goes to all the trouble to protect the place, casting spells and god knows what else, and you ask what's to fear," he elaborated to his dog, who seemed to understand. Joe stopped to tilt his head at Nikki.

"Who said you were to find it? Who?" he demanded.

"I was sent to find it," Nikki repeated, growing more self-assured.

Joe considered, rubbing his beard melodramatically. "By the story of the golden-haired one, what if—you're the one to arrive? Are you a friend of the *sidhe?* I've never met any fairies, actually." He glanced at Nikki shyly, but Nikki said nothing.

"How about you?" the old man motioned to Guy, who remained behind Nikki.

Joe sighed. "Nor you, either. Dogs never did like me."

"Isn't that a dog?" Nikki queried discreetly, gesturing toward the little Pekingese. Its little tail tied with a blue ribbon, it looked like a pedigree.

"That is Peeks," Joe announced proudly. "Say hello, Your Ankyloseness." The dog sat up again and smiled at Nikki and Guy, tongue dangling in fine dog-friendly fashion.

"My wife—my first wife, that is—had two gargantuan dogs who used to terrorize me," Joe continued mournfully. "Don't know why I ever married that old hag. I mean, she's an old hag now—I suppose." He stroked his grey beard, staring into the blue sky beyond the tree tops. "Or—perhaps I'm the old hag." He chortled. "That's infernality for you," he observed, slapping his thigh, catching Peeks' eye.

"What's that mean?" Nikki inquired respectfully.

"It means that she had two Rottweilers who chased me around the house and nearly ate me alive day after day! It means she had to drag them off me, apologizing. It means I was a fool to think she was my mother, what with her wonderful womb, wide hips—" Joe licked his lips in memory, his red-rimmed eyes widening. "Those huge breasts turned me into an infant all over again. It's what your men are after, at least in the first phase."

"That's what 'infernality' means?" Nikki asked wryly. And she was thinking: *first phase?*

"That and a good deal more, Young Lady Yet-to-Introduce-Herself-Properly. Nikki who, anyway?" he barked peevishly. "Here I'm to protect the journal, and you come to steal it! There's infernality and capricolishness to boot!" he swore, his voice tightening like a steel string.

"Capri— what?"

"Capricolish, capricolish! *Capricolish!* Didn't you study vocabulary when you were a girl? What do they teach you? How to catch a man? How to get the right perm? How to tuck your tummy and lift your sagging buttocks? To inflate your bubble breasts? Impecuniosity!"

Nikki cleared her throat. "'Impecunious' means poor. You're talking about vanity."

"Oh, so she's a bit of a martinet, is she? When I say a word, the whole wood listens and I get no argument! Who are you to come here to my home and explain language to me? *To me!*" Joe looked around, appealing to the trees for their assent. "Capricolish thief!" he snorted, wagging his hoary head in disgust.

"I'm *not* a thief!" Nikki yelled. At once Joe grew still.

"You're not?" he asked quietly, his voice remarkably sane.

"I told you, I was sent here! I never even knew about the journal, and it's been hell trying to find it! It has something to do with my life—and I have no idea what! Something's making me do all this!" Nikki finished, her voice pitching upward toward hysteria.

"All right, all right, my dear," Joe said softly, looking at her wonderingly. "I suppose even thieves have morals." He frowned suddenly. "I'm a poor sentinel at any rate, and we must be careful in these dangerous times. Because you probably would not hand the journal over to its rightful protector, I have no choice but to let you see it. Especially if the blue lady has spoken." He poked an eye at her. "Capricolish thief!" he shrieked in relapse.

His reprimand reminded Nikki of her manners. "I'm sorry not to introduce myself to you properly." She could see that however ragged he might look, he was educated—or at least seemed to be. And had some sense, however fractured, of old-world manners.

"My name is Nikki Helmik. We have a mutual friend, Clarissa Barrow of Rockport. I was born and raised here in Gloucester—"

"We're not in Gloucester," Joe corrected sullenly.

"We're not?" Nikki was genuinely surprised. "Then if this is Rockport, I'm from the next town over, Gloucester, where—"

"This isn't Rockport," Joe interrupted, sticking his beard out and folding his arms tightly against his narrow waistcoat. He rocked and, dropping his cane, nearly fell off his rock perch.

"Cape Ann, then," Nikki guessed more broadly, growing impatient and wondering whether he would actually topple over.

"Not that, either." He righted himself and glared at the rock beneath him.

"Excuse me, then, where are we?"

"In my wood, which I have given its own name," Joe spoke triumphantly.

Nikki was almost afraid to hear the name. But she gritted her teeth, remembering the box under her arm. "What is the name of—your wood?"

" 'Please, sir,' " Joe insisted petulantly.

Nikki groaned. "Please, sir," she imitated in her most sarcastic voice.

"Since you ask so politely, Nikki Helmik of Gloucester-by-the-Sea, I will tell you its name; it has several. And as you are the friend of Clarissa What's-Her-Name, I will reveal to you the secret name of my wood. *My wood.*" Joe twisted his face around.

Nikki waited. Joe glanced around at the trees. "Yes?" she asked finally.

"My wood. Clever, isn't it? A name no one could ever figure out: not all the damn Druid princesses; not those packs of wild children from the useless baby-sitting schools they lead through here—though never, of course, when the hunters are around; not the couples full of dog's love trampling all over the place and having no eyes for the gold and jewels strewn under their feet; not the loners walking their dogs because, too proud, they have no man; not the developers—"

"The developers!" Nikki blurted out. "What do you know about them? Have you seen them?"

Joe jumped up, nearly falling over as he grabbed at his cane. "Seen? I seen them, capricolishly! *With a fundament! Spurious! Eelemosynarily! Completely sangfroidam-errily, with a drub drub drub and a hub-bub-bub! Hotchatoo! Cockatoo! Gang, frang, bang!*"

Nikki watched in amazement as the old man capered about before the rock, was seized by a fit of coughing and hacked bent over, about to collapse, then righted himself and, kicking up his heels, tottered off into the wood without another word, leaning crazily on his twisted cane. All the while little Peeks hovered around him, dancing this way and that out of the stick man's rag-booted feet, then trotted off beside him.

"Wait!" Nikki cried. It was clear the old dear was completely insane. Living alone in the wood, abandoned probably by his wife, or at least one of them, abandoned by his children. It happened all the time. Her heart went out to him. She thought of taking him home to clean him up.

Joe stopped and looked back at Nikki as if seeing her for the first time. He squinted at her. *"Ye—s?"* he asked, drawing out the word while setting upon his nose the absurd pair of pince-nez hanging from their long, ragged twine. He leaned and regarded her through arched eyebrows as if he were in the court of *Louis Quinze.*

Nikki stifled a laugh, smiling twistedly. "I—I'm sorry for being rude, if I was. I was surprised by your sudden appearance, that's all."

"Quite all right. Not everyone is as nimble on their toes as I." As if to punctuate the point Joe leaned on his cane and nearly fell over. Peeks jumped back. Joe's pince-nez fell off his nose and dangled in front of his waistcoat. Nikki laughed out loud, then stopped herself.

"Do you—will I see you again?" she smiled mirthfully.

"You have the journal—you will not return it," he stated, as if that sufficed.

"Yes. I meant to say that I am, or at least I believe I am, a descendant of Anne Cleves."

"But you don't know," Joe quizzed her, frowning like a skeptical judge and, refitting the glasses on his nose with much ado, examining her.

"I was told so by my mother, who had it from her mother."

"Helmik—Cleves: No, they sound like different names to me," Joe concluded, wagging his head.

"Our family name. And the name of the Raven clan. Or something," Nikki finished hesitantly.

"You don't seem much certain about much certain," Joe declared. "Nevertheless!" He raised a long, bony finger with a flourish. The pince-nez fell off. "The Druids are full of nonsense, but they do make a pretty picture from time to time. That is to say, things work. To be quite honest, they have given me food when I was starving. Out of thin air, if I could believe my eyes. And eyes are not for believing, by the way, young lady, and don't you forget it! So if you've found the lost journal, it must be yours. It is no longer lost. It is the found journal. Q.E.D. *Quod erat demonstrandum. Quoque nostrum. Totiosque ecclasiae suae sanctae. Amen."* Joe bowed his head and turned to go.

"Wait!" Nikki yelled, her sharp voice surprising her. "You said something about the language. That I might not understand."

"Do you speak Gaelic with a dash of Celtic and a pebble of Saxon plus a smidgen of Finn and a grain of Mercury, mixing a parcel of Romansh with the leaves of Druid and the branches of Ogham? No—? Then you will need a translator, won't you?

Everyone around me is so smart! I don't understand language, they said. I make up words to mean what I say they mean. You'll see! Capricolishness, that's what you've got, young lady! I've a good mind to turn you over my knee and spank you right here under—" Joe squinted up at the massive oak directly above and stood puzzling a moment, then peering back at Nikki finished with "—under Bartram."

"Bartram?" Nikki was afraid to ask.

"Quite. Now be off before I ask you to conjugate verbs that won't come into existence for a millennium!"

"But the journal!" Nikki blurted out. "I need your help," she pleaded more softly, then stopped. What was she saying? Asking a madman for his help translating a critical document that held secrets from the dark times? Ask *him?* No, she had a friend at the University of Massachusetts; she would call him.

"Then you shall have it," Joe offered graciously, bowing with noble condescension. He proceeded to waltz off into the wood, tiny Peeks scampering after him, the hoary man staggering a bit but walking with arms spread until he was out of sight over the next rise, walking down a red velvet carpet in the court of the Fairy King himself.

Nikki shook her head in wonder. As impossible as she found him, she felt sorry for him and wanted to help. Or was it she who needed *his* help? In a flash it struck her: He knew what was in the box! He spoke as if he already had read the journal!

Nikki pried the box open again, pulled the packet out and looked it over. It showed no signs of having been recently read. The few small tears looked worn; the pages were curled as if they had lain in that position for hundreds of years.

She read the first line:

Is ainm dom Guryn, thrice spieled by awen.

The words were followed by a series of short vertical lines arranged in groups, looking like some sort of stick-man code, after which appeared words in English:

One word to the initiate: The piebald hawk flies over the grey flood to land in the crimson poplar.

Nikki quailed. It meant nothing. She needed help, that was certain. But—Joe's? No matter. She would take it home and think it through.

NIKKI PULLED her little red Miata into the underground parking garage at UMass' urban campus, which lay south of downtown Boston on a spit of land formerly a landfill. Returning to her alma mater now after so many years made her feel as if she were walking around in a dreamscape, even with the school's massive red brick walls and fortress-like buildings. The main plaza stood two stories above ground level and was made of cement flagstones, with but a few scraggly trees planted in huge concrete planters, widely spaced. Low walls surrounding the plaza and the square institutional architecture gave the campus an air of a medieval castle with ramparts. But then commercial jets screamed a mere three hundred feet overhead on their glide path to Logan Airport. The windows of the university were thus sealed to keep the noise out, which in turn created some interesting ventilating problems for the school.

As cold and forbidding as the campus was, Nikki liked it. The site had been conjured up in some mad architect's dream, and she often returned in her own dreams, again to arrive late for classes and to meet old friends. Or a man she had never known personally but whose face her dreams still remembered from the '70s when she was a fellow student: his narrow face stern; blue eyes hard, keeping everyone away; long hair tied back in a ponytail; woven sash for a belt and leather satchel at his side. And the political science professor she had once had a crush on and who had given Nikki her only *B*...

Only thirty years old, the campus was already falling apart. Long cracks raced up the side of the library, and the paving slabs underfoot tilted at odd angles, threatening to give way to the parking garage below.

Dazed, Nikki wandered across the plaza toward the arts and sciences building. The few summer school students taking classes sat on tiny patches of grass reading or talking quietly and coming and going through the heavy glass doors of the red brick buildings. Nikki pulled the thick glass door back, then took an elevator to the fifth floor.

She found Michael Appletree's office and knocked. Hearing a muffled voice, she opened the door and walked in.

Her old friend from her political activist days looked up, his face breaking into a grin.

"Nikki!" he called, rising. He pushed his black-rimmed glasses up on his forehead as he came around his desk toward her. The office was cramped, had no windows, only two cement block walls lined with metal bookcases stuffed with books and papers, a desk with chair and one facing chair.

They hugged. Nikki looked into the dark-brown eyes of the black man, her comrade from the days when Nikki used to picket offices at UMass, making demands for students and working mothers.

"I didn't think you'd come," Michael smiled, motioning her to the extra chair and sitting himself, folding his hands across his scholar's paunch and smiling broadly.

"Nice beard," Nikki complimented him, flicking her head in its direction.

Michael pulled at it, nodding. "Thought it made me look more professorial. Can't be too sure, you know," he chuckled merrily. "It's wonderful to see you. So you're tired of lawyering, eh?"

"Something like that," Nikki mumbled, eyeing the office. Pictures of W.E.B. Du Bois along with one of Eldridge Cleaver, signed, came into view. It seemed dismal, this bunker inside the university.

"How are you doing here?" she asked.

"Good! All right. OK, I guess," he finished, shrugging. "Classes are all right, publishing a bitch—the bitch goddess, you know. I'm the odd boy on the block—scholar of Old and Middle English and black to boot. No one can understand. They assume it's something like a male gynecologist."

"Very funny. What's the political news?"

"Not much. We've all settled down, didn't you hear? I've been co-opted by The Man. The administration treats me very well."

"Yeah, nice office."

"Well. Scholars take a vow of poverty."

"And no nature."

"Of a different order. But you didn't come to badger me about my life or to joust about careers and who's done better."

"I haven't done anything myself. Remember all the things we did in the early days? All the things we did," Nikki reflected wistfully, her eyes revisiting the marches, the strikes, the pickets, the TV appearances. Michael was one of those with whom she had stood side by side; he fought with her for the right of students to welfare as well as day care for their children, even though he had none. Once they had been lovers.

They both sat in silence, remembering, made shy for a moment by their shared history.

Nikki spoke first. "Everything we did, how wonderful it all was."

"How wonderful *you* were," Michael noted.

Nikki eyed him right back, smiling happily, as if she had no reason to hide or to feel self-conscious. And perhaps she did not.

"Still the nymph, eh Nikki?" he prodded gently when she did not reply to his sally, unlocking his hands.

When she said nothing, he continued. "That's all right. I knew from the beginning it wasn't to be between us. You had to wander off. Of course," he laughed abruptly, "I did get hurt, but that was—what? Fifteen years ago? Kids' stuff. *Romance at the barricades!* Glad that's all over," he finished a bit awkwardly. Nikki nodded once and was silent.

"So what's this manuscript you were telling me about on the phone?"

Nikki's eyes came back into focus as she furrowed her brow. She bent her head, pulled the manuscript out of her bag and lay it on the desk close by, within reach of Michael.

"I don't know if you want to look at this. It has to be kept secret, though."

"I haven't forgotten your deal on the phone: I can examine it and help you translate it, but I'm to write no articles about it." Michael pulled on his lower lip and studied the sheaf of papers without picking them up. "Look at this, though!" He reached across the desk to touch the curled pages. "Vellum, perfectly preserved. Some of it appears to be uterine," he observed excitedly, turning the pages carefully.

"Uterine?"

He looked up at her. "Don't worry—nothing personal."

She smirked and nodded.

"OK, OK," he said, giving in. "This is vellum—paper. Not really paper but writing surface made from the skin of calves. What they used in the Middle Ages. Very costly, hard to make. Apparently you had to skin the calf carefully, brush the skin with some sort of special black stone, dry it, then brush it again—a long process," Michael explained, cleaning his glasses. "These pages here—" He pointed with his glasses. "Facing pages are light, then these next two—" Turning the curled pages with a fingertip, he indicated two darker pages. "These are alike. Whoever made this took care to match each set of facing pages by color, depending on whether the piece of hide was from the exposed, darker side of the skin or the light inside." He looked up at her.

"So what's 'uterine'?"

"Some vellum was made from the uterus of the cow, which was especially soft and light in shade. Some of these pages appear to be light enough for that." He turned pages, pointing at one or two. "And I'm to do nothing with these except translate them?" he asked. He sat back and studied her.

"At least for now. It's a family document of sorts that I found in Gloucester— actually a journal left by my great-great-grandmother. From around sixteen ninety-something."

"Your great-great-grandmother at least," Michael emphasized, raising his eyebrows at the manuscript. "May I make a copy?"

"Um—yes, I guess so. Only if you promise—"

"Not to show it to anyone—I know, I know. Nikki, you're awfully protective of this."

"It's—important. But I need help."

"Let me take a look," he countered, reaching for the manuscript.

Nikki handed it over as if she were giving her child away. She leaned forward as Michael took hold of the stack, watching him closely as he set the pages before him and pulled the glasses off his forehead, positioning them on his nose with a frown. Twisting his voluptuous mouth, he examined the pages. Shards of the past tinkled in Nikki's mind as she gazed at Michael's mouth... No, she would not let herself think about that... *How many lovers had there been since Michael*— It wasn't important, she insisted to herself, her eyes growing memory-laden and heavy.

He looked up. "This language isn't anything I recognize, at least not entirely. The pages appear genuine, but they were not written in any single recognizable language. In fact, it's a hodgepodge. Here's Ogham—first case I've ever seen written on anything other than a tree."

"What's that?"

"These—look," he directed, indicating with his glasses several groups of vertical lines. "The vertical lines represent letters—or maybe images. Ogham is called the 'tree alphabet' because, according to our best account, it was originally written on trees. It's a kind of secret language used by the Druids of pre-Christian Ireland to communicate with one another. Apparently the Druids indicated various Ogham letters by pointing to parts of their fingers or hands, like this—" Michael set his glasses down. With his right finger he pointed to the top part of his left index finger. "The joint here would stand for one letter, and so on down the finger, joint by joint."

"And other Druids understood?"

"It was part of their training as poets to learn Ogham and much more," he confirmed.

"I thought Druids were magicians," Nikki frowned.

"As poets they *were* magicians. Recited poetry made the imagination soar, which is the magic all poets practice. And lovers," he finished, attempting to glance into Nikki's eyes.

As she looked down pointedly at the pages, he grunted.

"Was your ancestor a Druid? It would have been unusual for a woman to be one."

"I'm not sure."

"We have various interpretations of Ogham, but nothing definitive—it's too intuitive a language to have single meanings for sounds or words."

Nikki sighed. "I was afraid of that. It's what Joe—" she stopped.

"Joe who?" Michael pounced, astonished as a flash of jealousy flared in his loins. Did these things *never* go away? He thought diffusely of his graduate assistant Gretchen, who always reminded him so much of Nikki, her bed smelling of patchouli, and wondered if he smelled of it himself. He would have to shower before going home to Karen.

"Joe—a man I met I've talked to about the manuscript."

"What's he have to do with this?"

"No questions, remember?"

Michael raised his hands. "OK, no questions. I'll tell you, though, this journal, as you call it, was written by someone who either didn't have the foggiest idea what she was doing, in terms of language, or else was extremely clever—well-versed in several languages of her own time and from ages past." He shook his head in wonder. "I think it's the latter. Look at this," he turned the first page toward her, pointing at certain words with a pen.

"This is Middle English, that is Old. The construction is Middle English, essentially the same as modern syntax. But the vocabulary is all over the map. This word is Celtic, that one is Latin, and the one next to it Greek." Michael tapped the page lightly with the pen. "As for these opening lines—" He read aloud:

One word to the initiate: The piebald hawk flies over the grey flood to land in the crimson poplar.

He probed her face. *"One word—?* It doesn't make sense."

"You mean the words don't fit together? They're nonsense?"

Michael shrugged. "I don't know. The sentence is clearly some sort of poetic language I don't understand. As for the rest, I can't read Greek well enough to translate as I go. The Middle and Old English I understand. The Celtic and Gaelic I can manage. But other words are wholly unrecognizable. Like this one: 'halch.' What does that mean?" He frowned at Nikki.

Nikki shrugged.

"Is it Anglo-Saxon—? Germanic, possibly? That's the problem—I've never seen such a word. Not that *that* means anything…"

"I thought that means everything. You're the expert."

"In some things." Michael took off his glasses and rubbed his face. "Can I show this around? In order to make a fair translation, I'll have to have some help."

Nikki hesitated.

"I understand it's private," Michael allowed, returning his glasses to his forehead.

"Very private, I hope I've made clear."

"Except for this Joe person," Michael inserted wryly.

Nikki inhaled and exhaled deeply. "Except for—not that I know him. I met him—by accident."

"As ever," Michael retorted, immediately regretting he could not refrain from barbs. He returned his attention to the pages.

"He's about eighty years old; we talked a little. He seemed to know all about the manuscript."

"You met him perhaps in a library?" Michael pressed.

"I met him in the woods," Nikki replied simply, as if it meant nothing.

"You met him in the woods. An eighty-year-old man." Michael smiled tightly. "Either I leave off asking a single question more, or else you'd better tell me the whole story."

Nikki shook her head. "Maybe later. I think the manuscript has to do with my family, since it was written by an ancestor. It was buried in the woods near my house. I dug it up—" Nikki's face darkened. "At least, I think I did. I found it—in one of those beehive things."

"Beehive? With bees?" He was smiling his old smile now, seeing clearly the two of them in bed, smiling and listening to Nikki chatter in her lilting child-voice, her dizzy manner, round blue eyes, so expressive, that he wanted to swoon into…. He leaned forward, still grinning, and rested on an elbow. How long had it been since he had felt happy?

"Not *bees,*" Nikki was going on. "You know—those beehive hill things they find all over New England. Where the Indians used to store grain, except some think they were dug by the Vikings, people here way before the Puritans and even the Indians."

"And how did you know to look in the beehive for the manuscript?"

"I didn't!" Nikki huffed, as if unjustly assumed to be speaking gibberish by a dull-witted adult. She bounced up and down on the chair like an impatient child, frustrated. "I found the beehive and climbed inside. My dog, Guy, found it. I climbed in. It was amazing!" she exclaimed, her eyes wide.

"Let me get this straight: You found a beehive mound, your dog did, so you went in. It had a doorway?"

"A tunnel, sort of. You had to climb in."

"And you came to a room of some sort and found the manuscript there."

"That's right!" she exulted triumphantly, bouncing a little and smiling brightly.

The shine of her smile and her deep blue eyes were too much for Michael. "You're beautiful!" he exclaimed.

Suddenly, Nikki wanted to leave. It was clear Michael was the wrong person to help her. He had too much personal stuff involved with the project, she saw right away from his eyes. They were his old eyes, clear as day.

"And then the old man appeared," Michael prodded. He felt her lean away from him as invisibly the old hurt panged in his chest. Nikki's magic was easy to remember; her difficult nature he had forgotten.

"Once I was back outside. He showed up and acted like he knew exactly what I was holding," she recounted guardedly now.

"What did he say?" Michael inquired, feeling sick inside.

"Something about the different languages in the manuscript. Just like you said," she finished softly, looking around the room.

"Why don't you have him translate it, since he already seems to know what it's about?" Michael snapped, feeling frankly jealous. "I don't see what I can do for you." He sat back. Now he was remembering what he had forgotten in the first flush of seeing her again. So beautiful! And so difficult! So unpredictable!

Nikki sat a moment, frowning at Michael. She leaned over and reached for the manuscript. Michael sat forward suddenly and put his hands on it. Very gently she took it out of Michael's hands. He resisted only a second; their hands touched in passing.

Michael felt a shudder pass through him, though he would not let Nikki see it. He knew she saw it. She saw everything about him.

"Well, I don't know if he knows much about it—he's very old and seems a little crazy."

"In that case why not let me have a crack at it?" Michael fairly begged, hope flaring once again in him.

"I think maybe I'm supposed to go back to Joe and see what he has to say," she replied softly. "I mean, there was something about him that was fascinating—so unusual." Nikki looked off. "He treated me like a kid."

"What a surprise," Michael returned, thoroughly miserable now. "What do you mean, 'supposed to'? What's that mean?" he demanded peevishly.

"You know," Nikki answered distantly, looking more beautiful than ever to him. She looked around the room. *"Supposed to.* You know; a feeling you get when something's right."

Michael was trying to gain control of himself, to bear down on the rising desperation in him. How had this happened? He hadn't seen Nikki in years, hardly even thought about her. Until just hours ago, in bed with his student Gretchen, looking at her long legs and for some reason thinking they were Nikki's. Saliva gathered in the corners of his mouth. Then the call from Nikki waiting when he got back to his office. He waking suddenly on her island, as if never having left. And the trees were just as green, the red fruit hanging in rich clusters, air moist and warm. Returning her call excitedly, happy to hear her voice, hurriedly telling her how he had just been thinking about her. How it all made sense, how it all fitted together. How his life could have meaning just like Nikki's seemed to have, at least as she told it, all coincidences and meaningful crosscurrents, as if she swam in a dream of her own making, magical and transcendent. Yes, it could have meaning, too, if she would only—what? He panicked as the full realization of her impossibility, her cruel independence, fell upon him like a slab of granite.

Nikki looked at him and got up. "It's nice to see you, Michael," she muttered, hesitating in the door.

She left when she saw the pain in his eyes.

DRIVING BACK TO Gloucester, Nikki brooded on her meeting with Michael. She liked him so much, after all. But he was still stuck in the past. Years ago, just after they had broken up, they continued to be friends, to march and organize together, leafleting and sitting-in at the governor's office. She introduced him to her new boyfriends, one after the other; through it all Michael was fine, without the two of them becoming lovers again. Why had he been so jealous this time? Had he only pretended, years ago, to accept her independence? Maybe her inkling was true: The journal had some deep connection with her fate. Some strange and wonderful energy was coming into her, and perhaps that was what Michael had sensed.

Why couldn't she just call Philip up and tell him about the journal? He would know what to do with it. She sighed, imagining the look on his face as she told him about the manuscript. At first all full of wonder and excitement, his eyes would soon grow concerned, serious, thoughtful, until his natural competence would burst out of him with some suggestion for the right next move.

Joe could be a good help to her, because at least with him there was no shared past, no sticky disappointments—just the antics of a crazy old man. The rationale did not quite satisfy her. Just why had Michael been so strangely possessive? The usual reason was obvious, but Nikki was beginning to mistrust the obvious. She was even wondering about her reading of the past, which she had thought she understood. A possible new story—Michael jealous and hiding it all that time—was emerging. Just like the way a new story was unfolding of her mother, her aunt and grandmother. Even a new story of her father.

She sat up straighter, careening around traffic, heading up I-93 back to Gloucester. Two in the afternoon and already rush hour had started. She slowed to a crawl at the jammed intersection of 93 North and Route 128.

Joe reminded her of her father, she decided: both unpredictable; both so critical of her. Yet Joe's judgment, even his unpredictability, she would be able to bear. After all, he did not want to swallow her.

GUY MET HER in his new way, without barking, only a few quiet sniffs at her leg. He lay beside her when she sat at the kitchen table looking over the manuscript.

Checking her messages, she found one from Cynthia, asking with her usual matronizing tone how Nikki was doing, since no one had heard from her in a week. Another from Claire, needing advice in dealing with her kids, who wanted to go live with their father. Again.

Nikki drifted back to a conversation with her own father, about a year before.

"There's something in the house," he slurred, thrusting his huge bulk forward in his armchair. His tee shirt was dirty and his face unshaven, a can of beer in his big mitt. Nikki was sitting across from him, out of reach on the couch.

More talk, she had thought. Yet how clean he smelled, for all his mess!

"Spirits?" she asked brightly, looking around for something to straighten up. Eyeing her mother's painting of Halibut Point on the wall across the room, Nikki walked over toward it, taking with her the bottle of white wine she had been pouring. Her milk glass filled with wine sat untasted on an end table.

"*Spirits, spirits!* You and your high ways, you and Rachel, with your spirits! There's no spirit in this family. Know any of the *Saami?*"

Before Nikki could speak, he answered, "No, of course not! Ever hear any yoicking? Finnish ritual chanting—part of your heritage! Spirit! Where's spirit?" His big head wagged and drooped. Seeing that he was about to pass out, Nikki started forward unconsciously, as if to catch him. He roused himself, looking at her out of bloodshot eyes. *"I killed it off."*

It was then that Nikki recollected her father taking off for days at a time, driving the back roads of New Hampshire winding up and down the White Mountains. He would disappear without telling anyone where he was going. How had she learned where he went? As if seeing him fleeing, she saw him riding those narrow, winding roads up the mountains, drunk most likely up there among the clouds, remote, only the swishing of the dense pine forests and the cold air to comfort his tortured soul.

"Why did you drive to the mountains?" she had asked him abruptly then. It was too late for her to worry about being so direct. He couldn't reach her; he was just about out anyway. In the dim twilight between his surly drunkenness and flat-out unconsciousness, sometimes you could get something out of him with the surprise attack of a pointed question—if you were lucky and knew how to ask.

His head jerked upward as if struck. His big, sensuous mouth worked itself around to a dreamy smile. "Driving in the mountains…" he mused. "Who told you that?" he demanded with a startled scowl.

Nikki shrugged. "I just knew. What was it?"

"You know something? There's as much demon-working in the Helmiks as there ever was in the Keefes. Ask your Mummu—your grandmother Nikki."

"She's dead."

"You're Nikki," he smiled foolishly, head rolling. Rousing himself, he glared at her demonically out of bloodshot eyes. "Dead! That never stopped *them*. Damned pagans!" he hissed. "They won't let me go—ask her—" He pointed a shaking finger at the window behind the couch. Nikki turned. There was nothing. "They won't let me go—soon as I get there, I'm trapped! You'll see! *You'll see!*" he cried out in anguish. As his sodden flesh fell back in a heap, his voice bubbled quietly away until he was sleeping, snoring loudly, his mouth a cavern of chaos.

NOW SITTING at the kitchen table replaying the exchange, it was she who was struck: She saw herself a loner like her father, out there on the highway with the wind her only companion. Nikki rested her head in her hands, leaning her elbows on the table. Then, was she so like her father after all? The thought was too painful. She glanced up at the kitchen window.

Nikki turned her attention to the manuscript lying before her. She reread the first page. It was gibberish, a sealed box she had no way of opening. She had no choice: She was being pushed toward Joe. Nikki wondered for a moment whether she should visit Clarissa or call Aunt Meg, but she dismissed both notions with a quick shake. She didn't want to end up in a fight with either of them, not now. For that was what the manuscript seemed to be doing—provoking tensions, as it had with Michael.

How strange: She was beginning to need the help of all sorts of people. To need people… Just to give voice to such a thought felt odd to her, she who had always been the caretaker. Taking care of her daughter, raising her alone. Taking care of Claire during her divorce; taking care of Gerry when she broke up with her lover of five years; taking care of Dawn—Nikki who had always been the rock. What, then, if she now needed help—?

Her whole life seemed changed, utterly. She looked at herself in the vague reflection of the kitchen window and did not recognize herself. With Philip gone life felt like a dream—or a nightmare. She was behaving differently, thinking differently, even Guy was different. He used to be her protection, and now barely barked. Until recently Dogtown had been as familiar as her own house, but how well did she really know either? Her family home was full of ghosts—and Dogtown? Dogtown was inhabited by people who had lived there concurrently with her but whom she had never seen before—not in all the time of growing up and running through the woods. The place felt different, as if coming alive.

She considered calling Clarissa to find out where Joe lived but remembered that was secret knowledge. She would wander through the woods until either she found Joe or he found her. She was confident she would find him somehow. She knew at least that he lived in the rocky area, over in the Rockport section of Dogtown.

Guy stood at the back door wagging his tail.

"Not this time," she smiled, putting the manuscript in a black leather bag and gathering a notebook and a few pens from the scattered table.

Locking the back door behind her and hoisting her satchel, Nikki walked up the hill and down the path deep into Dogtown, trying to focus on where Joe might be. She looked at the trees and thought about words. The trees did not speak in words, but they were eloquent nonetheless. Maybe Clarissa was right that they were like words standing there, like Ogham, and they communicated in the same way, silent as images. Like Guy, who spoke not in words yet expressed so much. Like the flowers in her babel of gardens. Even the rocks she was now climbing over and around, monoliths of grey granite, polished round and worn down by feet and water. Their elegant silence made her feel clumsy. As she slipped on a rock, her ankle was cut by a sharp stone. She leaned to staunch the reddening wound, dabbing at it with a handkerchief. She thought of Anne's writing; there seemed no way to understand— or to be understood. She felt cut off from communicating, and the cut hurt like a wound in her heart. Desire flowed immediately like blood into the fresh wound, so that she suddenly wished for nothing more than to communicate, to speak, to hear and be heard!

Hadn't Alex and Claire even told her she seemed different? Cynthia, too, with her witchy ways knew something was up with Nikki, for she had been repeatedly calling and insisting Nikki call back to tell her what was going on. Funny how families exert subtle pressure on you to remain the same, Nikki thought wryly.

Not only did the journal in her bag not speak to her, she had no words of her own. Her heart fell. She lost her old world when she quit her job at DeVague Insurance, where being a spacey lawyer had been a familiar role. In her work she knew which language to use, which tones and which vocabulary. She knew how to get by.

She knew the vernacular of singles bars, too. When to look shy, when to blush, when to turn away. She knew how to get a man to talk, how to act interested. She knew all that. She knew it. She had been good at it, very good at it. She knew it.

She *had* known it, she thought. Her ankle paining her, she slumped on a table-sized boulder, letting her eyes fall. She *had* known those languages, and she still could lapse effortlessly into street patois. Hadn't she used the old language just that day, with Michael? Her face flushed as she recalled her airy voice, bouncing up and down on the chair before him; it had been for show, for protection. For seduction, finally, she admitted. The thought pained her.

The old words did not work anymore. They did not communicate a deeper truth, which she could discern but not yet articulate. She'd better stop using the old language, for it was causing pain. Like she had hurt Michael....

Then what language was she to speak? She couldn't discern exactly how she was speaking differently, even if friends and family had noticed some sort of change. What did they mean? Which words were different? Or was it a matter of inflection, of differences in intonation? She still managed to communicate—hadn't she eventually called Cynthia back, advised Dawn, continued to counsel Claire? She was making basic sense, somehow. Yet in a deeper sense she was making no sense to herself. She was unable to understand her own language.

And if she could not hear her own language, how was she ever to understand the voice of Anne Cleves? Nikki glanced down at the black bag. The manuscript within, written in a spidery hand on parchment thin as leaves, felt so heavy on her shoulder.

She would never understand. She couldn't. She wasn't worthy of understanding it. It didn't matter that she had found it, didn't matter even that Joe seemed to have gotten there first. She had been harboring the great hope that finding Anne's journal would offer the solution to her life's problems—solve Philip, solve her future, solve her family, even solve Rose.

Now with the consciousness of her hope came the crashing conviction: *It was not to be.* She wasn't up to the task of bearing the burden of Anne's story. Even if she found Joe, which was seeming unlikely—the sun was slanting late afternoon rays through the trees—it wouldn't make any sense to her. She hadn't the ears to hear it. Hadn't Joe already foreseen the tragic irony awaiting her, of finding the great treasure only to be incapable of understanding it—?

Nikki's head bowed; her eyes filled with tears. Of course she had been looking for the manuscript. Of course when she first learned of its legend, she had assumed she was the one to find it and bring it to light. But soon that prospect threatened to weigh her down with responsibility, and so on her walks in the woods she had never really looked for Anne Cleves' cellar hole. Not really—she had only pretended to look, had treated the whole thing as mere fiction, a game.

She had done what her father always did. What she had done her whole life— fallen asleep or turned spacey when something too heavy, too real, came her way. She had always rolled playfully along the ground, lightly assuming life would turn out all right in the end, reassuring herself it was good not to get too intellectual since thinking too much made you separate from things. But life wasn't turning out all right. Those days she had spent with Clarissa, with Meg ... what a fool she must have looked like to them! With her high-pitched little-girl voice, squealing with amazement, wide-eyed with belief.

It was a grim image; her tears stopped. Nikki gritted her teeth. Both Clarissa and Meg had seen what she really was: a little girl playing at being a grownup. Trusting and falling asleep when she should have kept her eyes open.

Her heart flushed with shame, the thought overtook her that she could never see either of them again, at least not without making some sort of recompense, redeeming something. She would aim to be more serious in the future. Although—could you simply resolve such a thing? She felt thoroughly miserable.

Maybe it was her task right now to go off by herself, to take classes and study arcane languages well enough to be able to piece together Anne's story for herself. And only then, after years of work, to bring it out into the community. She felt her age settle upon her like a heavy cloak, bending her head. Forty was getting old—the entrance to old age. The skin on her face felt heavy; the signature Helmik jowls drooped further, giving her face a hangdog sag. Even such a silly picture of herself failed to rouse her now. She would settle lower and lower, down into the dark earth below her feet, where she could at least pull the dirt over herself like a shroud and hide forever.

Her life to this point—what was it? Nothing, really. Not to have accomplished anything, when her heart had always yearned to do something great in the world. When she still carried around stories of having been at Woodstock, of talking with Grace Slick one-on-one through that long wet night before the Airplane went on. Her claim to fame.

Claim to fame! Her body heaved, though her eyes were dry. She looked heavily down at the earth. Philip was a great mistake, and so she had done her best these past weeks to shut him out of her life. Had she in effect pushed him over the cliff—? She had certainly failed him when he wanted to come to her....

And Alice! Alice was now off living with her boyfriend. As for Nikki's few friends—what were they to her? Her life as a lawyer was irrevocably over. She had always believed that something good, something necessary, came out of everything, that everything happened for a reason. It was her eternal optimism, her good-natured spirit that so believed. Where had those reassuring thoughts gone?

A great desert opened up before Nikki, that place of transition where all vegetation had died out but saving rains not yet fallen to renew the land. Dry, airy, sandy; stretching for immeasurable miles. Nikki could not move her head, could barely support it with her hand. She dropped the bag on the ground and sat very still, her thoughts settling as dry leaves settle finally, after a long, slow, circling fall, into winter's stillness.

"If you sit there long enough, you'll lose all sense of belonging altogether!" a voice cried out shrilly in front of her.

Nikki jumped and stood up, panting.

It was Joe, resplendent in his many-layered motley, torn green overcoat over red and blue and plaid shirts, his tangled hair festooned with berries and leaves. Beside him pranced Peeks, perky with a pink ribbon in his tail. Joe's eyes sparkled brightly as he pointed at Nikki with his walking stick, which he began waving around while pulling at his beard with his upper teeth. His hands were garbed in green fingerless woolen gloves, worn out with holes.

"I told you you'd need me, didn't I?" he laughed gaily, capering about as much as his old legs would permit. "Trying to do it all alone, eh?" he cackled.

He turned and walked away as Peeks ran circles around him, hurrying to keep up and then dodging out of the way of his feet.

Nikki sat stunned. Her mind was numb, the heaviness still upon her.

"Wait!" she cried faintly, but her voice would not carry. She took a deep breath and sighed from her chest, falling back onto the rock. She did not have the heart to call out again. Unable to call out, unable to move, she watched Joe rollick down the rocks. She watched him as if she were imprisoned on her rock, her eyes fixed on his retreating form. She could not speak. The desert stretched before her; it was hopeless.

At last, far down the rocks, he halted and turned toward her, his hands waiting melodramatically on his hips. Skipping off the stones, a faint harrumph found its way to Nikki's ears. Then he flapped his arms a few times and trudged laboriously back up to her.

"Lost your voice, eh?" he winked at her, examining her with one eye closed. He lifted his pince-nez, regarding her like a rare artifact.

Nikki gulped, looking back at him. As he stood there her awareness tightened: She was no longer a little girl but a grown woman, old enough to be a grandmother.

"Gee-haw!" Joe yelled abruptly, still staring at her. Nikki flinched, her eyes bouncing in her head.

She panted. "Uh, Alice ... might ... could have a baby." She blinked at him, not understanding what she was saying. "My daughter—Alice." Her voice was husky with the drought.

Joe cocked his head to the side, regarding her like some big, ragged bird. He kept turning his head until he was looking at her upside down. "Repeat after me: 'I am old, Miss Nikki.'"

"I—am old," Nikki muttered. She watched him.

"'I am old, Miss Nikki,'" he piped insistently.

"I am old Miss Nikki," she intoned, her voice out of the earth. She was mortified: Her eyes were tearing now. And they would not stop. He was right—this old madman who lived in the woods. She was old, past her time. All her glories were in the past. It was as clear as muddied water gone calm. She had lived too long in her youth, and her youth had died. And the woe of her great mistake weighed upon her as a loss greater than the loss of her youth. Her tears streamed down to water the land until soon she was sobbing for all the sadness of her life, and for all the sadness in the world. She could not take care that Joe was standing before her. She was lost and little and helpless, and there was no hope anywhere, only life that passed away or vanished from her reach. So her crying went on, even while some inner eye watched in wonder as she cried more tears than she had ever cried before. And the sadness was that all the tears she cried could not bring one small bit of her desert into bloom, for the sand and the desolation were too great, extending beyond her range.

"It's something of my own invention," Joe remarked at last, ignoring the tears coursing down her face.

He waited a bit as Nikki's tears subsided. "A good beginning, what?"

Again she could not speak but only gulp at him out of red-rimmed eyes.

"*I said*—a good beginning, what?" Joe repeated elaborately, waving his arms about like a bird. His pince-nez fell, dangling from its ragged ribbon.

"A good beginning," he continued a bit louder, leaning his head back and speaking at the trees.

Nikki still said nothing, though her tears had stopped altogether in her fascination with the old man.

He fairly yelled at her now, bending down toward her face. "*I said—no voice—a good beginning!!*" His face growing crimson from the effort, he doubled over with a coughing fit. Peeks rapped out a bark at him, jumping backwards.

Gaping at him, Nikki all at once remembered why she was there. Here was her savior, the one who might give her the keys to the dictionary of the new language. *This* man!

Her tears stopped.

"That's it all right. I knew it. No voice. About time," he ended, dropping his stick, folding his arms, and frowning down at her like in every student's worst nightmare.

A smile crept across her face. This old coot was her savior! It was too absurd! What was she doing here in the woods with a madman, seeking help with some lost manuscript that she believed would save her life, would change her forever? What was she doing?

"It's crazy," she concluded quietly, half smiling up at him out of puffy eyes.

"Not crazy—*madness*," Joe corrected, standing erect with pride and glaring at her. "First word—wrong word," he harrumphed, waving a ragged gloved finger reproachfully at her.

"Time for class!" he announced, sweeping up his stick, turning again and scampering down upon the rocks and boulders, followed by Peeks yapping away.

This time Nikki stood up, taking a deep breath. "Then let it be madness," she proclaimed. She picked up her black bag and drew it over her shoulder, following along behind the man of madness and his dog, chuckling and shaking her head. From time to time she laughed outright. Her eyes stung.

IT WAS NOT FAR to Joe's small cave in the rocks. But the place was ingeniously hidden among the larger boulders, its opening a narrow crack down at shin level between two rocks, so that you had to crawl to get inside. Nikki bent down to take a look. She could see the back of the cave clearly enough, only a foot or so deep. She smiled at Joe, her eyes still puffy. She rather liked the post-crying sensation, like she had already learned something. Maybe there was no cave after all—only a madman's crazy dream. With a sigh Nikki stood up straight, waiting.

Joe stood before the opening making elaborate hand gestures as if conferring with invisible spirits. All the while Nikki was unable to keep small snorts and chuckles from escaping. Being a student at her age—! Actually, she had always had the greatest respect for older women who went back to school—

"That's not right," she quietly interrupted her own thoughts, while Joe went on with his gesticulations.

"I respected them, but I never thought their liberal arts studies meant anything in the real world. Or had any real worth in society's eyes…"

"That's honesty," Joe replied, turning quickly to her before sliding on his desiccated butt down through the crack in the rocks. He picked up Peeks and tucked him under his arm.

Bending down to watch him go, Nikki did a double take. A moment before she had seen the rear of the opening but now could see nothing, only the darkness of a hole inside the rock. She could not see how deep it went. Joe slipped nimbly in through the crack and disappeared into the dark. Nikki was astonished, squatting, staring inside and waiting.

"Enter!" commanded the voice from within. Sitting down on the rock and pushing her bag down first, Nikki slipped her legs through the crack. Her feet dangled down into the void, unable to touch any bottom below. Even though she looked over her shoulder and down, she could see no light within. So, taking a breath, she pushed herself forward, shoved her body through, and dropped into the darkness.

She fell only a second before her feet hit soft earth, but the impact took her breath away and left her standing unsteadily. Spotting her bag nearby, she slowly looked around, finding herself in a medium-sized cave whose ceiling disappeared in the shadows overhead. She had landed on a Persian carpet curled at the edges with fringe. Across from her stood Joe at a large oaken desk piled with papers. On it sat a lamp with the shape of a goat's head, shaded in parchment. Next to Joe along the rock wall to the right extended a long row of bookcases merging into the darkness above. To Nikki's left rested a small cot set against the wall, serviced by a small wooden table complete with hot plate, cup and saucer, and a second lamp. A few piles of mismatched clothes drew Nikki's gaze, as did a woman's tortoiseshell comb and brush set sitting incongruously on a shelf. Peeks lay down in front of the cold fireplace and put his head on his paws, greeting the uncommon guest with silent glances.

Although neither lamp was lit, Nikki could see everything by some dim light. She turned around but could no longer discern the opening through which she had come. It was all a rock wall, and she could not even tell how far she had fallen into the cave.

"The light…" she wondered aloud, amazed and puzzled.

Pointing shyly behind him to his left, Joe motioned Nikki closer. Stepping across the thick carpet she discovered a tiny pool of water bubbling in a stone cistern, flowing out through an invisible fissure in the stone. The water glowed and pulsed as alive.

"Phosphorescence!" Nikki whispered, in awe at seeing something so miraculous.

Joe's face was radiant with a fair white light as he, too, leaned over the spring, regarding it with affection. He removed his ragged gloves, reached out a cracked and gnarled hand, and lightly touched the surface of the water, smiling to himself. *"Quickborn,"* he murmured over it, peering into the bubbling water for a time.

He turned toward her. "A good light," he exclaimed softly. Nikki was struck immediately by the change in his voice. She eyed him closely. He had spoken as if sane, without too much unhealthy passion in his voice. He beamed.

"Lucubration needs more light, however!" he pronounced, spinning quickly around and switching on the shaded lamp on his desk. The room was flooded with a warm light, all but the darkest corners of the cave presenting themselves for inspection. Nikki looked in amazement.

"Battery powered," Joe explained absently as he rummaged through the piles of papers on his desk. He stopped to pull up his rusted pince-nez and, after fitting it to his nose with much adjusting and testing, resumed his rummaging. He stopped again to dig around in his pants' pocket with an intent expression, at last triumphantly producing a mashed book of matches, then struck one and held it to a candle in a cracked and much tarnished silver candleholder.

"Sit," he directed Nikki, who stood standing like a colt. He went over to the hearth to light a small fire, which began to leap lightly against the rock as he returned to his desk.

Nikki's eyes followed Joe's cracked hand indicating his cot. Pushing a pile of twisted bedclothes out of the way, she sat down carefully, sensing the bed might give way underneath her at any moment. As soon as she set her bag on the carpet, leaning against her left leg, Peeks came over and snuffled inside.

Joe resumed rummaging, until his head darted forward in surprise. He grabbed a sheaf of papers.

"Eureka!" he cried. He plopped in his chair and turned to her. "That is to say, in the ancient tongue, I have found it."

Nikki waited.

"Greek," he whispered, grinning. His teeth were blackened and cracked. Again Nikki wondered whether he was the right person to help. Or had she wound up after all in the den of a crazy man?

Joe waved the papers in his left hand, shaking them at her, his face aglow. Actually, he was quite beautiful, Nikki observed. Very fine lines stretching from eye to cheekbone disappeared into his tangled grey beard. His eyes were very bright as he observed her intently, like lion's prey.

"See, I wasn't teasing!" he held the papers out again.

"Is that the manuscript?" Nikki inquired.

Joe was already riffling through the torn and dog-eared pages. Reshuffling them he read aloud:

"On that day I died in Paradise to take on fith-fath, at Quickborn when the black sheep is given."

He looked up. "What might that mean, young lady?"

Nikki shrugged. "Are those Anne's words?"

Joe said nothing but continued eyeing his prey.

Nikki made an effort, clearing her throat. "Um, someone died and went to heaven at a place called Quickborn, and a black sheep was given to someone as a gift commemorating the death. Something like that…" She looked at him hopefully.

He shook his head.

"I have already translated the Gaelic and Latin words for you, leaving only the words of poetic sense. But even those you do not understand." His eyes were hard on her.

"No," Nikki admitted simply, feeling her face flush.

"'Fith-fath'—?" Joe pressed, leaning closer and challenging her with a triumphant gleam.

Nikki shook her head. She could not take her eyes from his, much as she wanted to run and hide.

"Fith-fath, fith-fath, fith-fath!" Joe cried, jumping up and capering about. Peeks danced with him and barked.

Nikki stood up too, though she did not caper. Her earlier mood still weighed heavily on her, and as she was taller than Joe by a full head, she towered over him, frowning down in smouldering anger.

"I said I didn't understand!" she cried. "I came to you for help! How do you think *I* feel? I've told you everything—admitted I'd been looking for the manuscript for weeks. And that when I found it, I realized, just like you told me, that I wasn't able to understand a word of it by myself!" She felt tears of frustration coming but managed to hold them back by biting her lip. Her eyes began to sting again.

All this had a miraculous effect on Joe, who stopped and stared at her as if at a curious animal. Sitting down, he carefully folded his hands, waiting for her to continue with the fascinating performance.

"Oh, what do you want?" she cried again, her voice a bellows making the stone walls shudder.

"Sit down," Joe answered carefully. He sighed deeply and paused, averting his gaze out of respect. After a moment Nikki sat down. Now it was her turn to wait. Peeks went back to his place before the fire.

Joe cleared his throat. "It's true I am all that you accuse me of: condescending, misanthropic, judgmental and impatient—"

"I never said—" Nikki began, but Joe held up a hand.

They sat in silence a moment, like old friends, each smiling faintly as if sharing a secret.

At last Nikki spoke. "How did you come here? Do you have family?"

Joe sighed and looked at his candle. Carefully straightening the pile of papers on the desk, he folded his gnarled hands as if praying, set them upon the desk, and spoke to the candle, making the single flame flicker.

"I had a family. Scholar…teacher…Gloucester, it's true. Though I was not born here. Boston. Harvard. Doctor of Humanities, Philosophy. Something or another. I could not heal…could not heal. It was—it was—" his voice caught, and he trembled, eyes filling. His frame shook as he clenched his hands together, fingers writhing like pythons suffocating his sanity.

Nikki half rose to go to him, he seemed to be suffering so. She waited, lips half open, solicitous of the old man who looked frail as wax.

"Is it too much to speak?" she asked gently.

Joe breathed shallowly. "I—moved here in many years before. The time—Gloucester. Very important. Pagans—goddess worship and the entire subculture. You see? They were all wrong, but science—science rules all things now. Even in stories. You see? *You see?*" Joe beseeched, his voice thin. "My mind was the thing, and oh! those books I wrote and wrote, until they came singing out of my ears. And I loved them, the pagans, *you see?* A new study. They had not understood, but that was many years before." He shook his head.

"They would not see, and soon my work, all singing out of my ears, was thrown away. Little by little, you see. Never in a great swallow, for in the university—no! Never in passion, never, never, never. It made me old, my work all thrown away—reviled. You see? I had an idea, and they said it was mad. That these pagans were other." He stopped and bowed his head. "That poetry was truth…"

"When the dark came into me I ran, and I learned to dance. Dancing helped the ineluctable pain. They all left me, Sharon driving away with the little face watching through the glass inside with her. The little face! With her long blond hair, my little Goldilocks!" His voice rose into an arc of pain, then fell. "Then no work, and only my work and research." He shook his head again, remembering.

"The dark time, and then the house door locked, and I shook it and shook it and broke the glass with a stone and ran in fear. No work for me, none. I ran in the dark and the waves and the wind were me and I flew on them into the trees. Dancing I found a place to hide and dancing and running I came here…"

He sat still so long that Nikki nearly spoke again.

"In the dark they found me and wrapped me in the fur cloak, all in black they said when I cried it was the color of death and birth…and then I understood. You see? You see? It—they—found me. Just what I had written: *Not to search only, but to be found by the star you follow.*"

"Who found you?"

"Anne and the others: Mab and Cordelia and Nocticula and Herodias and Diana and Hecate…all of them." He smiled brightly, looking up. "They found me, for my book was alive in them. Don't you see?" he implored, turning all of a sudden to address Nikki. "It was a long night… And even now my brain has a long gash running along it. I have been cleaved." As he bowed his head, Nikki gasped. Down his white scalp, between the thin strands of white hair, lay a long welt of a scar red as a flame.

"What is it?" she gasped. "Are you all right?"

He lifted his face to her. "It is my death. Anne Cleves, *yes?*" he winked. His eyes lit up again as the old madness came into them. Exhaling, Nikki leaned back.

"Can you help me?" she asked softly, trying not to disturb his brain.

"I have long read her book. It is your turn and I will help yes I will yes. As you must help."

"Me—?"

Joe nodded sharply. He stood and walked in his unsteady way to the bookcase, where he thumbed down the spines across a row of books until he stopped at a thin volume, pulling it out. He examined the paper cover briefly, then brought it over and handed it to Nikki.

She looked at it. The bound pages were smeared and dirty, a handwritten title scrawled across the cover: *Dictionary of Poetic Image.* Nikki opened to a page enumerating definitions of words.

"It's something of my own invention," Joe explained proudly.

"I can—take this?"

"To study and learn. I will help and teach you, but you must learn yourself."

Nikki regarded the old man in wonder. Here was the help for her anger and frustration! Joe was handing her the solution to a problem she had been unaware of up until then. For, having to rely on another person, first to translate the story and then to spoon-feed it to her, had undoubtedly been causing her great distress. Maybe with Joe, she now considered, things might be different.

"I can work with you?" she sought assurance.

"Work together," Joe nodded. "But my poor brain is cloven. You must have ... like my hooves!" Joe ended suddenly, guffawing as if at a good joke. Awestruck, Nikki saw the madness again overtake him as he leaped about the cave singing some nonsense rhyme, Peeks yelping in unison:

> *Hey fiddle, fith-fath!*
> *Hey fiddle, dwale,*
> *Pierce athane the mome rath*
> *Gorog, Harog, Dale!*

As Nikki sat listening to the two dance about, singing and barking, she smiled sadly at the old man, recalling the horrible gash along his scalp. He had made enough sense for her to piece together his story: a professor working on a book that had gotten him discredited, that was clear. But how had he come to live in this cave? And how did he manage to *live,* unstable as he was?

Presently Joe sat down, puffing and flushed, growing increasingly shy as he settled down, until he could barely look at his guest.

"Joe," Nikki broke in. "Thank you for your help so far—particularly for lending me your dictionary. I will study it and learn what I can. But do you *want* to help me? Might it be too much of a strain?"

"A strain?" Joe repeated, sitting up stiffly.

"You are very—moody," Nikki ended, not wanting to say "unstable."

"May not madmen have moods, too? Are you frightened of spontaneous exuberance?"

"The life force…" Nikki reflected, catching on.

Joe softened. "Frightened?"

"No—!" Nikki quickly insisted. She backtracked. "Yes."

"Of what?" he asked kindly.

Nikki thought. It was a good question. "Not of you—I don't think. Maybe of your unpredictability."

"I would not translate to make sense," he declaimed.

Nikki nodded, though a sudden fear he would have another episode made her feel low.

Joe grunted. "No promises. But I know—the noggin knows, even a cracked noggin knows. Knuckled nuked niggardly witted noggin knows *nous*," he began, his voice rising. Then he stopped himself and sighed. "The spirits are in me, sure 'n enough now," he broke out in a sudden brogue. "But don't ya be worryin' yer pretty little head about me now," he singsonged, still the leprechaun.

"But will it make sense?" Nikki pressed, her own voice rising.

"Sense—nonsense. Go away so we may begin. To make sense-nonsense. A nonsensical story by one of the old Druid princesses: Ogham. Poetry. Half nonsense already. Lesson one: Learn to see in poetry. One thing as another. No bottom, metaphor. Use the ladder, please," Joe finished, rising and indicating the stone wall where Nikki had descended. His voice sounded suddenly very tired.

Nikki tried to catch his eye, but Joe pushed past her and flopped on his little narrow bed. Pulling the covers over himself, he appeared to fall asleep immediately. Peeks jumped up beside him and followed suit, closing his eyes.

Nikki looked around. Joe began to snore loudly. It was all too much. She went over to the little phosphorescent spring and looked into the clear blue water, the bubbles speaking a language she did not understand. She put her hand out. What word had Joe uttered? Quick-something. Quicktree. She touched the surface of the water, then raised her finger to her mouth. The water was cold and fresh.

She turned back to the room. Joe was out, the ragged covers yanked up to his hooked nose. Peeks snuffled sleepily. At Joe's desk Nikki blew out the candle and switched the lamp off. Once again the cave was filled with the warm, mellow glow from the spring and the flickers of the dying fire.

She stashed the dictionary in her bag, hoisted the bag onto her shoulder, then after a last look at Joe went to the rock wall nearest where she thought she had landed. Footholds appeared that had been invisible just a few feet away, although above all was shadow. Sticking her foot into the first foothold, Nikki pulled herself up, wondering how Joe ever made it out of his cave.

She leaned against the wall, dubious about finding a way out, thinking she would have to awaken Joe at last so he could show her the way. She climbed slowly, though even as her head neared the ceiling she could see no light from outside. Her hands were beginning to get tired.

Soon above her a slit in the rock allowed a shaft of light to enter. She pulled herself up further, using the convenient handholds. The slit proved to be a gap, just large enough for her to get through. She wriggled her head out of the hole, heaving until her body was outside, where she rested for a moment, breathing hard.

The light was failing in the woods: Evening was near. Nikki stood up, pulled her bag onto her shoulder, leaned down and turned to look back into the cave. She saw only the rear of a small, shallow cave two feet deep. It was solid rock.

8.

The Jewel Box Opens

Nikki devoured the dictionary Joe had loaned her with an appetite that surprised her, and she began to visit the old man often to work on translating her ancestor's journal. She checked out from the library all the books she could find on the Celts, then delved into further readings on myth and religion, ancient languages, histories, and old Anglo-Saxon records of spells. These she hurried home and piled in tiered mesas on her kitchen table, leaving a narrow canyon for her stack of papers and Anne's journal. She went online and gathered as much useful information as she could, printing out on the printer beneath the table reams of words and references.

Just what had come over her? she wondered. She had always been a mediocre student, not having a phlegmatic temperament to prefer study over activity. But lately she was filled with excitement pursuing obscure references through stacks of dusty books that, to her joy, would turn out to be kin. She was finding simple pleasure in sounding out the double meanings of words and in trying to hear Anne's voice come alive in her dormant writing.

As the work went on Nikki couldn't avoid asking herself: For whom was she doing this? Surely not for Philip, even if she did feel sick over him. But after she heard through Claire that he was on his way to recovery, she felt no strong impulse to contact him. Which meant she couldn't have been motivated to do all this work primarily because of Rose's demand. Was it for herself, then? No—she had, after all, only a dim idea of who she was and what she was doing.

However, one person did come to mind when Nikki reflected on who was compelling her to work so hard: her mother. As Anne's voice and image began to emerge from Nikki's translation, Anne herself seemed to coalesce with the image Nikki held of her own mother, the way two separate clouds meet and conform one to another. It was her mother speaking to her; surely she was her mother, this woman Anne Cleves. As a result Nikki's lifelong view of her mother was shifting, and with it her own identity as a mother; indeed, her very notion of mothering began to undergo a subtle shift.

Aunt Meg and Clarissa, the two women who had become her guides, were not biological mothers. Yet they were nurturing of her just the same, more like nurses in keeping a small distance between Nikki and themselves, encouraging Nikki to develop away from them. They did not demand fidelity to themselves. Perhaps only to an idea…

And what was that idea? Nikki licked her lips on the edge of the idea, a fragrance she could barely reach. It lay just beyond her ken, centering on goddess worship, an orientation to female values… Such a relief! she felt, finally a means of escape from the horrid patriarchy, of always *men,* men determining all the rules. The way even Philip, just because he was a man, got to set the terms of their relationship.…

In between translating and research she worked on her own journal, writing page by page the story of all that had been happening to her, and it satisfied something deep in her soul to watch the two piles grow up together like new friends. She made meals in the old Radarange and took breaks eating them in the living room, sitting in front of the TV while before her flashed the New England of three hundred years earlier: Through deep forests a tall, light-haired woman walking quietly.… She ate frozen pizza and bowlfuls of soup and salads like a blind person while people confessed the secrets of their hearts in anxious staccato to millions, their taped lives cut into ribbons by commercial breaks.

With a newfound love of all things Celtic, Nikki brought home CDs of Irish music ancient and modern, hung posters of Celtic designs on the walls, filled the house with the rich warmth of Gaelic green. She put up posters of Irish castles and verdant country lanes until the whole house seemed suffused with green light. She danced awkwardly to the Irish tunes, often playing them softly while she read at the kitchen table.

The whispering voices in the house receded upstairs, and when she went to bed they grew quiet, as if conscious of her presence. She barely heard them any more. On the nights she worked at the kitchen table, she saw neither Ernest at the window nor her father in the basement, so that gradually she forgot those earlier horrors. Aside from her work, the only thing she took note of was her back, demanding attention deep down at the base of her spine. She stretched and sat up straighter at the kitchen table, but nothing worked. She did her yoga, sitting cross-legged on the worn living room rug. It was yellow-brown and smelled of must. She stared for hours at the spot where the braid was bulging out of place at the curve at the end of the rug; but it didn't help. Aching had set in; old age, or the scholar's cross; her body suffered. And as July passed into August the heat congealed in the trees like dirty laundry, hanging slack and sticky. She could hear the sea in the distance, faint echoes carried in the hot, damp air.

Somewhere inside her lay an image of Philip convalescing. A curious reluctance had overtaken her. Rose called regularly, in a voice now bitchy and raspy, asking how Nikki was progressing, reminding her of the waiting bulldozers. Nikki hadn't forgotten that if she didn't find the journal, Rose would begin building.

But Nikki did not dare tell Rose of her discovery. What with the new direction her life was taking, she thought the journal all the more in need of protection—especially from Rose. As little as Nikki felt compelled to see Philip, she at least would have liked to tell him about the journal. Nevertheless she was careful not to disclose her find to anyone, not even to Aunt Meg. To reveal this, so her thinking went, would be tantamount to disclosing her own inner journey, which was still too tenuous to expose. When Claire or Dawn called, Nikki took a week to call them back and put off getting together as long as she could. Finally she agreed to meet Claire for a quick coffee at the *Glass Sailboat,* where she sat drumming her long fingers on the table top half listening to her friend go on, all the while staring through the glass to Anne's world. She was jealous of her time, feeling an urgency to finish her work.

Because she continued to feel strongly about protecting Dogtown, she could ill afford to ignore Rose. Yet she was aware of something stronger than Rose's ultimatum driving her work, for Anne's story was opening within Nikki an intimate relationship with her ancestor's woods. The world of Anne the Tree Worshiper was now becoming slowly Nikki's, as if by inheritance she was now "Protector of the Woods, Patroness of Trees." Taking breaks by walking through the pines and maples and oaks, she had begun listening to their rustling talk. But the drama of self-development working within pressured her the more, now that the key seemed shrouded in the occult folds of Anne's journal. For the more closely she examined Anne's words, the more certain she felt Rose was right: The secret of eternal beauty was there inside, perhaps locked away in the journal's strange hieroglyphics, whose mysterious power had already taken hold of Nikki's imagination.

At the outset she had ingenuously flipped through all the pages to locate the secret of eternal beauty in the form Rose seemed to envision, as a kind of recipe for a potion, but she found nothing. Perhaps it was not physical beauty that the potion protected, but beauty of another sort—connected with inevitabilities, finalities. Or did this other, invisible beauty desire to show itself in physical form, as it were? Wasn't the dark, even hollow beauty she was discovering in the trees made apparent by their living shape, their tactile bark and branches? It was a puzzle, this new world; the relation between inner and outer...

Alongside her hesitation over Philip grew up like a second tree the ankylose desire for him. The two thick trunks of her ambivalent soul, hesitation and desire, twisted round about one another until Nikki found it hard to distinguish the two. Was it desire that made her pick up the phone—or hesitation? For, after all, she did not dial. Yet the more she did not actually call, the more often she picked up the phone.

It was better not to call. She had lived her life alone; she did not need a man now. Certainly not one who was already married. Certainly not a man's presence—or any male influence over her life—not while such strong images of women surrounded and bolstered her. Nevertheless she heard Philip's voice in a thousand ways every day: He seemed to hover over her shoulder as she worked; she heard him comment on this passage or that, suggesting alternatives to her renderings of words and passages. Invariably she grew mad and impatient, impulsively swinging around in her chair to confront him but finding only a sleeping Guy and an empty kitchen. On the rare times she went to the supermarket, she heard his voice criticizing her choices of food. Filled with wrath, resenting his presence, she shut him out of her head. But another voice sprang up to haunt her: that of her father. Again and again she tilted her moon face up from the pages of Anne's journal to the back door window, fearful and expectant of her father's appearance. Or was it Ernest she simultaneously feared and looked for repeatedly?

In dreams her father came to her in his younger, fairer guise, all blond curls and rich broad smile, leaving the hovering dove of her dreaming soul confused and flushed by his towering presence. Her young legs twitched with desire and fear.

Meanwhile Ernest's wraith haunted her wherever she went. On walks she often shied sideways, ready to turn and run should she see his ghost again. No—that was not quite true, she had to admit. She took walks half looking for Ernest, hoping that somehow he might help her overcome her present difficulties. What a curious notion! Was she in fact possessed of that vision Meg had hinted at? Or was it possible Ernest was still alive? She had been so certain the coffin was empty… Was that simply her fear and denial? She held Guy on a short leash as she walked in the forest at night, peering about expecting something…

As September arrived, the heat let up some. The leaves began their glorious exhibition, maples outdoing oaks, mystic pines keeping their holy distance from the rampant display. Along with making frequent visits to Joe, Nikki took to visiting Clarissa, listening to her talk of Hecate as the two wandered the woods. Clarissa pointed out healing herbs, showed Nikki how to track animals… Evenings in her wooden living room Clarissa performed prayers to the Triple Goddess, explaining to her student how goddess worship did not exclude men.

Whenever she visited Joe, Nikki brought his dictionary along. It seemed to touch him, even calm him a bit to see her studying it. In addition to classifying words specifically of Druid origin, the reference work included the Ogham alphabet in the back as well as an association of trees with different letter names. Nikki read with fascination how the Druids used their language of rude slashes to communicate with one another secretly, even in the presence of others. The letters were associated not only with trees but with animals, parts of the body, colors and actions, as well as with emotional states and complex poetic descriptions. She felt a kindred spirit with the Druids, what with their synaesthetic connection between letters and things, between sounds, abstract ideas, and concrete objects; that made immediate sense to her. She favored the first of the Ogham letters, the one written with a single downward stroke below a horizontal line, which looked like a modern *T* crossed low. *Glaisium cnis,* it was called, which Joe translated as "fair silver-skinned" and spoke to her familiarly, looking into her eyes, as if that were her name.

"Each thing another thing," Joe explained disjointedly on one of her visits. "Remember!" he shouted. "Shamans—poets! Poets—shamans!"

He was given to shouting this conundrum so often, in fact, that Nikki forgot to listen to its deeper meaning, just sighed and put her hands over her ears. All the while they hovered over the pages of the journal, which lay like a silvery fish upon the desk. From Joe's direction Nikki understood that sometimes images stood for other words, sometimes other letters. But—how was one to know which? He walked her through the opening of the journal, indicating in his fractured way how the words spelled out other words.

"*The piebald hawk flies over the grey flood to land in the crimson poplar,*" he recited, looking directly at her. She stared back blankly. Growing impatient, he tapped a torn-gloved finger at a line in his dictionary, whereupon Nikki read that "piebald" was a color associated with the letter *A*. There were calendrical Ogham alphabets, she learned, in which animals and trees were associated with the seasons and thence with letters of the alphabet. Thus "hawk" indicated the letter *S* and so on, Nikki saw, beginning now to transcribe in front of her teacher. By this painstaking process she finally spelled out the word Anne had indicated for the initiate. The word, as she wrote it, was "ASLFE."

"Is it in another language?" she asked in a hushed voice, half with exhaustion, half impatience. There would never be an end to the work at this rate!

"Latin," Joe answered simply. "Invert, reverse, proverse, subverse," he chanted. "*F* for *V,* and the order out of order as you have written it. *S* and *A;* piebald—hawk, hawk—piebald," he finished, eyeing her.

"All right," she replied slowly, inverting the *S* and the *A,* then substituting a *V* for the *F.* "Now I've got "SALVE." Does that mean something?"

He fixed her with a look, folding his arms around his chest as if he were a wrapped mummy, and harrumphed. "Latin," he repeated after a time, when Nikki remained dense.

Nikki flipped the Latin dictionary she had at hand and quickly found the word. A light came into her eyes. "Greetings—?" She tilted her head toward Joe. *"Greetings!"* she exclaimed softly. "I'm an initiate." She beamed, for the moment happily oblivious of how distant the far shore of true initiation lay.

AS NIKKI WORKED more with Joe she became curious about his life, and on one of her visits to Clarissa she asked the older woman. They sat in late September glory on the granite boulders above the pond, the first maple leaves beginning to flutter down upon the stones. The air was bright and clear that day, and from time to time cackling geese flew low overhead, discussing directions with one another.

"Joe was married twice, as far as I can make out," Clarissa related. "He taught at Harvard, as you've gathered. Got swept up in the '60s revolution, changed his politics, then his whole life. He parted with his wife of twenty years," she added evenly, tossing a stick to the dogs. Down below them, spreading out in a broad blanket, the red-orange trees made a rustling, crayoned bed.

"Oh," Nikki responded, thinking of Philip.

Clarissa turned toward her. "You fault him for hurting his wife." As usual, Clarissa's inquiries emerged as statements of fact.

"I do," Nikki confirmed. "Probably left his wife for a younger woman."

Clarissa was silent.

"Typical male stuff, right?" Nikki gulped, the words catching in her throat. Her Catholic upbringing was suffocating her, constricting her thoughts to Françoise, whom she imagined as she herself would be: terribly hurt and humiliated by Philip's being with another woman.

"I don't know the details," Clarissa said with customary matter-of-factness. "But I have no reason to doubt the story Joe told, that they celebrated their parting with a special ritual."

"They—celebrated?"

Clarissa squinted into the slanting sun. The rocks were very white in the glare of the sun; summer had teasingly returned after hinting of fall over the past few weeks.

"When Joe appeared in the woods, a few of us took care of him. At first he was quite insane, dancing madly and hitting himself. We bound him and fed him and sang over him; later we loosened his bonds and invited him to join us. He continued to dance and sing and play his flute, but by then he seemed better for it. After Peeks found him, together they scouted out the cave, and in time he grew as happy as you see him now."

"What sort of celebration?"

"When Joe and his first wife divorced, they thought it only right to conduct a public ritual witnessed by many of the original wedding guests, among others. So they exchanged the rings each had originally given the other, uttered some parting words, then exited through separate doors." Clarissa tossed another stick.

The scene struck Nikki. "A public divorce—how strange!"

"It makes good sense," Clarissa countered. "As music played, they danced a waltz before parting."

"Wasn't everyone very uncomfortable?"

"Aren't you uncomfortable at weddings?"

"You're supposed to be happy at weddings."

While Clarissa paused to consider her younger friend, an expression passed across her face similar to one Joe had cast Nikki's way, as if contemplating a member of an exotic species. "You're still filled with those girlish spirits."

"Weddings aren't happy?"

"They may be, but I'm speaking of the part that is—strange," Clarissa suggested. "Difficult to know."

Nikki nodded slowly. "When you feel that it might not last, that all the promises could turn out to be hollow." That was certainly familiar terrain—the disappointments of love.

"I believe Joe and his wife had an honest marriage, meaning that once they recognized it was over, they decided it was better to cleave apart as friends, each bearing a share of the pain, rather than breaking up as almost everyone else does: protecting oneself from pain by inflicting it first on the other. Imagine how difficult it must have been for them to dance together a last time, when they still loved each other, and then to part."

"But—if they still loved each other, why split up?"

"Because they had other lives to lead, I imagine," Clarissa offered.

"You make it sound so cold and unfeeling."

"Do I? Well, strength need not be cold—real strength usually isn't, in my experience," she half smiled.

Nikki thought about it. Maybe it wasn't so inexplicable—to go separate ways as friends. She cleared her throat. "It's true, most people end relationships as enemies. As if they wouldn't be able to separate unless they fought hard enough to wind up hating each other." She started to recall her own fights with Philip, then shook herself. An image pressed forward: Joe and a shadowy woman standing on a platform, rows of people before them. Were there flowers? A minister or a priest—? She could imagine well enough Joe, once upon a time a proud, strong gentleman, acting out of principles and honor. But he did go off with another woman—didn't he? That was the grim reality behind the lofty parting ceremony—wasn't it? The same old despicable male behavior—one never enough... Her anger set off in pursuit of Joe. And yet—it wasn't so long ago that she lay warm in Philip's arms, wishing he would leave his wife. Her face flushed.

"Didn't their leave-taking betray the love they had for each other? Isn't it dishonest to part—once you have promised to stay?" Nikki paused to watch the approaching wolves as her strained thoughts darted hurriedly past her various lovers.

Clarissa's voice broke in. "What a peculiar idea."

"What about keeping promises?" Nikki insisted.

Clarissa laughed her short laugh. "We're human!"

"But we at least have to make the effort. Your word...the promises you give...you have to try—" Nikki was struggling out loud.

"Yes, you have to try," Clarissa admitted. "Every move you make better be trying—to reach your lover, to understand, to bear up under the vicissitudes of life. It should be like being on the scent of an animal, I imagine, tracking your thoughts, watching your heart, examining yourself for motives. Observing the flickers of hatred and disgust that every lover is ashamed to admit she feels for her beloved. Feelings we don't understand, but which we need to note and follow to their source. Even in the middle of a fight with your lover, you should be watching and seeking, asking 'Am I wrong?' When the blood is flying you need to have all your wits about you, your mind aflame, trying to pierce the veil of confusion." Clarissa tossed a stick absently, almost angrily. "Even if we can never really understand the why of love."

"Then, it's not our fault—love simply fails? What about responsibility?"

"The ancient classics and even today's silly self-help books tell us: Love doesn't last."

"No love—?"

"None." Clarissa thought a moment. "The most difficult task, I think, is to have enough faith to follow love's winding ways. Its winding ways, not ours. What did Wallace Stevens say—? 'The path through life is more difficult than the path beyond it'? Probably murdering his exact words..."

They sat in silence a while.

Hesitant to broach the subject, Nikki swallowed. "I've been wanting to ask—about you and—Ernest," she stuttered.

Clarissa looked almost bemused. "You—actually asking?" She observed Nikki more closely. "Some great change has come over you, dear!"

"It doesn't mean I like it—your life," Nikki hurried on.

"But you'd be interested to hear about Ernest and me."

Nikki sat up. "You so often talk about love, yet you're all alone here in the woods. Or so it seems. As if you're happy to live alone."

"I am," Clarissa acknowledged. "I've got the woods and my wolves—and this sky!" she exclaimed. Then, still smiling, she went on. "And I've got a broken heart and a wound that stretches across this sky." The smile that lit up her face turned wistful.

Nikki was speechless. Never had anyone described a heartbreak like that to her. Sure, when she used to joke with friends about her old fool of a father, she knew it was in part to cover the hurt. But never over a guy had her heart been broken. It had always been easier to break it off with them first.

"Ernest and I met a long time ago, before he was married. I was a help to him with fishing."

"You know about fishing?"

Clarissa laughed. "Ernest had a well-earned reputation as a great fisherman, but I was the one who advised him where and when to fish. I don't know how I knew, I just did, and he was smart enough to come to me. He had a rich love of the sea and its creatures; I was a better huntress. We became lovers."

"Before or after he married?" Nikki tossed the bait.

Clarissa wasn't about to bite. "No—it's too easy for you to take at a distance."

"At a distance?"

"You're far too ready to cast my life—and your own—in moral terms: 'This is right; that's wrong.'" She made chopping motions with her right hand. "I live life close up; it's useless to moralize when you've got your face in something. Whether you're being attacked or actually attracted, you don't have time to judge the morality of your actions. You just act."

"Are you trying to control what I think?" Nikki demanded, suddenly feeling that Clarissa was imposing her own notions on Nikki.

Clarissa laughed lightly. "You don't know whose side to take—mine or Rose's. As if there were sides."

"Didn't you side against Rose as soon as you let yourself get involved with her husband?" Nikki pressed.

"What did my loving Ernest have to do with Rose?"

"Because Ernest, then, had to love you as a—" she broke off.

"Go on, dear. As a mistress. Is 'mistress' always a term of disapprobation? I know a married woman who jokes that she'd rather her husband see her as a mistress than a wife. A wise woman."

"Sounds sad to me."

"That's you, not her," Clarissa said a little impatiently. "Your sadness at losing your innocence—your innocent notion of love. You're still a virgin! Nothing wrong with that—just that mature people get into trouble still trying to love with the starry-eyed views of a ten-year-old."

Now Nikki was angry and insulted. Clarissa felt it and stood up, walking up and down on the rocks. She whistled to the wolves, who came romping.

"So you continued to carry on your affair by convincing yourself you weren't hurting Rose?"

"I knew it hurt Rose," Clarissa allowed, looking after the dogs. "I loved Ernest—and our love was good. It was not a marriage; Ernest married the person he should have married." She motioned to herself. "Look at me! I would have made a terrible wife."

The memory of fleet-footed Clarissa running through the woods flashed through Nikki's mind. "So being a mistress was your consolation prize? To be second best?" Nikki cried out the injustice.

Clarissa shook her head. "I don't understand your hierarchy; I wasn't comparing."

"But you couldn't go out in public with Ernest; the world didn't recognize you two as a legitimate couple..."

Clarissa grew thoughtful, tossing sticks down the granite boulders, which the dogs galloped after.

"If social respectability is what you want, go get it. You're stuck on hating Philip for being married instead of trying to figure out why you've taken this path. You're making such an issue out of being married—why?" Twisting her mouth in exasperation, Clarissa turned to face Nikki. "If you think adultery is so wrong, don't do it. You're acting like a naughty ten-year-old."

Nikki was on fire now. "I got involved without thinking about it, all right? I admit to doing something wrong that I'm ashamed of—is that what you want to hear? That I hate myself for what I've done?" She was nearly shouting.

Clarissa replied calmly. "What does hating yourself have to do with anything? It's the goddess of love who's distraught here."

Clarissa tilted her head, pensive. "There is great value in having children and growing old together—and, yes, social recognition. Ernest and I never went out together in public, it's true."

"Because he controlled the relationship, determining when he would see you!" Nikki insisted acidly.

"Control—?" Clarissa drew out the word, genuinely puzzled.

"It's what I hope Anne Cleves can give me—more control—power."

"Over what?"

"This mess. Myself."

Clarissa stood silently for some time, her brow furrowed. "I don't know about control," she pronounced finally.

"You mean all this—magic—has nothing to do with power?"

"Power—of a sort, I suppose... Oh, as in spells and potions!" Clarissa smiled.

"Yes—"

"You need to exercise immense caution to cast a spell—responsibly."

"Spells are what affect matters—bridging the outer and inner worlds," Nikki stressed.

"Are you asking whether being of the Raven clan made a difference in my affair with Ernest?"

"I suppose I am—I didn't mean to be so direct," Nikki answered, taken aback by Clarissa's directness.

"To the extent that it gave me self-respect—yes."

"Having an affair with a married man," Nikki declared mordantly.

"Self-respect in the sense of understanding the parts of my life as part of a whole—instead of mistakes I was the victim of," Clarissa replied sincerely, her impatience a touch higher again. "Because I accepted the limitations of our involvement, I never felt Ernest and I had to hide. Because I accepted the inner constraints—my own desires and his—I didn't need to feel society was imposing them. Every love has a particular shape, which gives it rules it must follow and which can narrow it—sometimes marriages especially. Is social recognition so important if the marriage is all routine, each taking the other for granted, a long, tired march tied together toward old age and death? This culturally reinforced compulsion to marry seems so often due to people's desperate need for protection—from their own fundamental sense of aloneness. After they marry and find themselves still feeling alone—sometimes all the more in the company of another—then the trouble starts. The blame and awful fights—or the boredom and routine."

"Then something was wrong with them to begin with. You're using the worst examples to make your case."

"You seem to think that gaining entry to the occult mysteries of your ancestor will somehow transform you into a superwoman, empowering you with mastery over the sufferings of life."

"So instead you say it made you happy to be a mistress," Nikki countered sarcastically.

"Not happy—trusting that something about our affair, exactly as it was, made sense, and so had intrinsic value regardless of our desires. That it had its own reasons. I trusted that even the shortcomings pointed to something valuable in each of us, and that the failure was in my inability to see their value, not in the relationship itself. Knowing that made it hurt less."

"So you think it's fine for me to be involved with Philip?" Nikki asked rhetorically.

"I never said that. The Raven clan gave me the sense to see my life in its particular granularity and against a larger background. We don't just live our separate lives cut off from the rest of the world. That's one of Anne and the Raven clan's teachings. All that we do affects the wider world. I am first interested in examining small clues for meaning, not in making sweeping moral judgments and giving generalized advice. My own life is enough of a struggle to understand. I can't tell what's good for you but can only pass along an insight, which is to observe your particular conflicts. And, yes, there were times when Ernest's being with his wife and not with me hurt me deeply."

"And hurt Rose."

"And hurt Rose. In loving Ernest I betrayed her and caused her pain, for which I took responsibility. I did not compound the pain by threatening Ernest or manipulating him to leave his wife. I accepted my fate and bore it as bravely as I could—which wasn't always bravely, I can tell you! Instead of making Ernest suffer, I thought about what powerful force in myself wanted to continue something so difficult."

"Why not have stopped altogether and ended the hurt?" Nikki demanded. "It's what I—am trying to do—with Philip. Because it's wrong."

"Hurt is neither wrong nor avoidable, Nikki. I could argue that Ernest would have fallen in love with another, less thoughtful woman, which could have made matters for him and Rose worse. I could argue that I never tried to break up the marriage, to make him choose. But you'll probably respond that I was being agreeable and complacent, only enabling Ernest's immoral behavior. I could counter that suffering is good for the soul, but I've lived long enough to learn that plenty of suffering is not good for the soul. All I can say is that I am human; lonely at times, wanting love, appreciating another human and, I admit, thinking of myself sometimes before someone else. No one likes to cause pain, and I am too wary of letting myself off the hook to rationalize that it was good for Rose. Besides, I have no idea what it did or didn't do for her," Clarissa ended.

"Rose knew the whole time?"

"She did know."

"So that explains why Philip insinuated she had lovers. I couldn't believe it. Now I know why he said it."

"Why?"

"To get back at his mother." She considered further. "Unless—suppose it's true. Didn't she have just cause?"

"I didn't get involved in their relationship," Clarissa shook her head.

"Well—did she have affairs?" Nikki demanded.

"I don't know," Clarissa uttered quickly, which sounded like lying to Nikki.

Clarissa went back to another trail. "I suppose my self-justification is to believe I gave Ernest something that no one, neither Rose nor anyone else, could ever have given him, which he needed."

"As a lover," Nikki intoned like a judge.

"Yes, as a lover, this time, with this man." She threw another stick. "You know, our culture thinks of itself as socially liberal, but we won't even consider anything other than complete fidelity to monogamy."

"It's the worst thing for love," Nikki persisted stubbornly, "because it destroys the love. You won't indoctrinate me into your way of thinking, Clarissa, so if that's what the Raven clan is all about, I'm not interested."

"See? We can't even discuss it without hysteria breaking in, absolute statements. I'm not saying it's all right. Just trying to open the door to other possibilities, sometimes, for some people."

Nikki's mind flashed to the conversation at her party that had so inflamed her. "Don't tell me you were one of those supposed feminists who defended Clinton," Nikki taunted.

"Why does the subject still rankle? I always thought he showed remarkable restraint…"

Nikki shook her head, smiling sarcastically, and the women fell silent.

"What can I say to justify myself, Nikki?" Clarissa asked at last. She threw up her hands. "Ordinarily I wouldn't feel the need to. It's just that—you are important to me, and I can't pretend your judgment doesn't affect me. I spent thirty years with Ernest and never once felt the need to explain myself." She laughed lightly. "Now he's dead all the uncertainty comes to the surface. I fell in love; that filled me with certainty but also doubt, as I believe any love contains doubts. Love is a difficult hunt, all right," she concluded grimly.

Clarissa looked out into the sky for a time. "Actually, my work cultivating the invisible spirits has helped in a critical way. Studying the Raven ways led me to reflect on how a word—this word 'love'—becomes incarnate, the word become flesh, as the New Testament says. You love someone; that's a spiritual emotion, so to speak. You can't touch it, and yet you die if you can't touch your lover, be in his presence. It's as if the image of Raven that we honor is at one and the same time an invisible and a visible presence. 'Raven'—'love'—any powerful word can be a seed that impregnates you. And I am glad to death I loved Ernest! Anyway," she finished, "my time in this drama is over now. Ernest has died, and I no longer have to carry the burden of knowing I am causing hurt. Which really means I am no longer in the business of loving."

"Do you seriously think all love must hurt?"

"Yes, I do," Clarissa replied evenly. "Because it is a fact."

"Then how do you know what is a good love and what is a bad one?"

Clarissa exhaled. "Let's get down to specifics. You say you never intended to get involved with Philip."

"I didn't."

Clarissa laughed out loud. "So, you were duped by yourself?"

"I wasn't duped. It turned into something bigger than I thought—"

"And did you think of the hurt you were causing Philip's wife when you took Philip to bed?"

"It wasn't serious that first night."

"You mean, your intentions weren't serious. Nikki, you aren't taking responsibility for your own actions. You are dangerous, because you are using your own unconsciousness as a cover for irresponsible behavior. How do you know that casually sleeping with some woman's husband might not cause her every bit as much pain as your having a loving relationship with him? You conveniently cite moral concern for the wife when it coincides with your own interests. But as soon as the hypocrisy is exposed, it makes you crazy."

"I'm not hypocritical!" Nikki cried. "I made a mistake, and now I'm trying to rectify it!"

"Do you not love Philip?"

"I'm—I don't think it's right to, since it hurts his wife—and me. Which I wouldn't want another woman doing to me."

Clarissa paused. "I think that's laudable—"

"Thanks," Nikki interrupted sarcastically.

Clarissa regarded her younger friend. "Except for two matters that I can see."

"What's that?" Nikki asked miserably.

"One, I think you do love him, which means it's not so easy to throw overboard. Maybe you can, but at great peril to your soul. You'll find another married man to get involved with, then begin hating yourself, or him, all over again. Two, you're forgetting the original idea that drove you to fall in love with Philip in the first place."

"I didn't have an idea," Nikki protested.

Clarissa ignored her. "Imagine that our souls call us to certain people. It's what Anne Cleves imagined—and long before her, Diotima. That we are attracted to certain soul mates, people who have something to do with our fate, who change the current in our lives. And that even though this love brings pain and suffering, it has its own necessity: to make us aware of death and limitation."

"Death—?"

"Becoming involved with Philip is asking for rejection, in one way or another. Rejection brings a little death, brings us up against the limits of life. Maybe this suffering comes to teach you about your own limits. You can't love with abandon, you know. Even if you have until now assumed you could love with no thought of the consequences."

This time Nikki ignored the criticism. Aunt Meg's words about how we all give and receive pain gonged in her. "Are you saying I shouldn't think about the pain I'm—I was—causing Philip's wife?"

"Of course you should. I don't know whether this newfound love is important for your soul, but consider: Philip is Rose's son, and your life has changed as a result of loving him. Through him you've discovered Anne Cleves—and me."

"Philip—? What's he got to do with my ancestor?"

Clarissa laughed. "Do you think Rose set you on this path wholly out of fear of losing her beauty? She's out for revenge."

Nikki was stunned. True, she had been lately trying to deal with the new Rose—the cold and demanding one, whose voice froze her answering machine.

"She's—out to get me?" Nikki asked slowly.

"This situation is more dangerous than you think." Clarissa walked away up the cliff and disappeared though soon returned, wiping water from her face. Crouching down beside Nikki, she spoke in a low voice.

"We're at a break in the trail, Nikki. Both Joe and I are now highly compromised in your moral scheme, yet we are the two who can help with the journal. Maybe Rose could help, but you said you haven't told her you found the journal, which tells me you don't trust her fully."

"Not necessarily," Nikki countered quickly.

"You think about it. Because you now have to decide which way to turn. In the world that Rose inhabits, she rules by way of her beauty—as do you. But there is another kind of beauty that she lacks. That's why she is looking desperately for the journal."

"What is the beauty you and Rose keep hinting at?" Nikki asked straight-forwardly.

"I guess you could say it's invisible, but that doesn't get to it."

"If you know all about it, why doesn't Rose just ask you? Why all this energy spent on the journal?"

"One answer is that Rose sees me as her rival. There are other reasons why she won't come and ask. One of them is that I haven't got it."

"But you seem familiar with it."

"All of us are interested in the journal. Rose figures to outwit time by means of a potion. She won't."

"How do you know?"

Clarissa shot her a glance. "I don't."

Giving Nikki a quick hug, Clarissa whistled once, then trotted off with Tara and Timber bounding at her heels. Guy followed them out of sight into the darkening trees and returned a few minutes later, nosing about distractedly as if hesitant to disturb Nikki, still sitting staring into the spinning web.

AFTER A LONG WHILE Nikki stood up and stretched, then wandered home, feeling smothered under an avalanche of necessity. Everyone was crowding her: Rose; Clarissa; even Philip, whom she obscurely felt she had wronged. The thought of him lying in his sumptuous bedroom inside his mother's mansion made Nikki suddenly aware of money worries. Precious little remained of her separation package from DeVague Insurance; soon she would have to make some decisions. What to do? She paced the house and worked diligently on the translation. Her laptop glowed blue on the edge of the table. The Internet gave her more information than she needed, and so after a brief attempt at using this library of the universe to help with the translation, Nikki resumed working by hand, using Joe's dictionary as a guide.

In the evenings she detected strange whispers coming from upstairs. Her ears pricked up to sounds coming from the woods, and she thought she already could hear bulldozers plowing over trees—the long, heavy groan as they toppled and crashed.

It was a terrible strain, adjusting to her old friend Rose in new garb. The kindly mentor had devolved into a monster who was keeping her from Philip. Well, Nikki did not want to see Philip anyway; she had to stop thinking of him. Even so, did Rose's hatefulness excuse Clarissa's affair with Ernest? Nikki could not altogether renounce her loyalty to Rose for the sake of Clarissa, but her new friend was right: Nikki needed Clarissa and Joe.

As the pressure increased Nikki visited Joe more often, happy to descend into his safe cave, descend into his timeless madness where bulldozers and life were held at bay. By working assiduously, Nikki found Anne Cleves' labyrinthine language slowly unwinding its secrets. Through the rest of September she worked her way along the tortuous sentences, unpacking the metaphors, deciphering the Druid code words and Ogham scratches, asking for help from Joe with this word and that, listening to his long, twisting disquisitions on the nature of language and the connections between Anglo-Saxon and Gaelic, between Provençal and Latin, on the origins of Ogham and the ways in which the old language for which there was no name (unless it be Poetry) rose from deep springs hidden within the primordial rock of human consciousness and, once bifurcating, formed the eddies and swirls of all living languages, all the while maintaining its underground voice, an ocean current all its own.

Yet all these poetic images and cross references, the secret code of Ogham, all of it seemed to be a language that sprang from the very source of human culture, its roots still clumped with the dirt of the first mothers and fathers who fashioned sounds into words and then into poetry, transforming the world in the process. Words themselves carried magic within them, which meant no words were to be taken at face value, literally, but rather as images, as fleeting and varied as the thousand shifting facets of a cut diamond. The same word could mean two, five, ten different things, depending on context and subtext.

Ogham scratches on trees not only symbolized simultaneously a tree, a bird, a color, but were also the tree itself; the tree speaking; humans speaking in Tree, those vegetable presences most like humans. At this immediacy, image, idea, and speech echoing from a shaped letter were no more separate from the tree than that end of a branch humans called "leaf."

"Joe, is there is a connection between the poetry of the old bards—those like the Druids who spoke the ancient language—and their practice of magic?" Nikki asked one night as she sat on Joe's dirty old cot riffling through papers. He had a fire going that warmed the place, from time to time sending little spurts of smoke through the cave. Sitting at his wide, dark-oak desk Joe observed his student intently, bushy grey eyebrows dancing, eyes rolling in his head, arms and legs twitching. Peeks lay sleeping near the fire, snoozing adenoidally through his pug nose.

"Yes, yes, yes!" he exclaimed, jumping up. "Poetry—spells—metaphor!" He clapped his hands in glee. Peeks hopped up, ready for another dance.

It was coming clear to her: Making magic exactly paralleled making poetry, in which life itself was bent or shaped through words.

"The power of words!" Nikki exclaimed, a light dawning in her face. "The magical power of words! Why, that's spell-casting!"

Joe gazed at her curiously.

"No, really, do you understand? The more I work on the journal, the more I feel like—sort of like—I'm made of the same stuff as the world. The words change shape, and then, oddly, so do I. I become somehow different—to myself—and, there's something else," she offered shyly. He waited as she went on. "Well—I've always had these—visions, I guess you'd call them. My Aunt Meg told me maybe it runs in the family..."

Again Joe clapped his wrinkled hands. "Meg!" he cried. "All the pictures in her glass!"

"Yes, and the more I work on the journal, even though it's frustrating, the more the world...Dogtown...the forest...seems—" she stuttered on the thought.

"Magic," Joe nodded, bending his head.

Her eyes stared through him. "In a way. When I work, I have vivid images of Anne looking at me. Particularly when I walk in the woods she seems present. Usually I recite pieces of Anne's work as I walk, to remind myself. I'm trying to commit to memory all the cross references I've learned—which trees are associated with which letters and which colors, to begin with. As I walk along with Guy reciting softly, it seems I'm no longer walking in the woods of today but in those of Anne's day..." Nikki stopped, fingering her chin. "Her time is more real than mine—does that make sense?"

"Every word bend, especially that tricky one," Joe cocked his head.

"I'm beginning to love the trickiness of the words, to love Anne's words. It drives me crazy not being able to hold their meanings down, but when I let them go and take on the many things they are, they seem just that more colorful—and real."

"Love alters when it alteration finds," Joe misquoted.

"Anne's journal is a love story, isn't it?" Nikki mused, smiling distantly, no longer worried about direct answers. Her brow darkened. "But it's *her* love story."

"Hers, mine, ours," Joe recited, shrugging. "One net catches all fish." He smiled as a wisp of spittle collected on his lower lip. "These are not our woods," he quoted again, more obscurely.

Catching his gaze nonetheless, Nikki returned it in kind. He understood. She sat back and considered. All the while they spoke, a kind of word magic was working its spell. A spell of words, more subliminal and more substantial, maybe even longer lasting, than an everyday spell for money or healing. Anne's words were transfiguring the woods, touching the delicate falling leaves with the rose edge of spirit, so that Nikki felt as if she were walking through a poem.

NIKKI WORKED AT her kitchen table late into the lengthening nights, neglecting to return phone calls from friends, even from Betsy at the Dogtown Committee. Papers were strewn all about the table and floor near her seat: full sheets on which she was writing out her version of Anne's journal and small scraps scribbled with various words and word usage. She was not an organized scholar. Guy would sometimes kick the sheets and send them skittering across the linoleum floor. Although her laptop lay ready at hand, she preferred writing out in longhand.

It was difficult enough to translate the Celtic and Latin into English, but once in English the words often made little sense, seeming no more than a series of nouns strung together as in: "oak-interpretation-dreaming-elder-raven-three days." Other times Nikki managed to improvise a more or less grammatically coherent sentence from the material, but the words themselves were obviously symbols, the divining of which required deep knowledge of the secrets of Druidism. Their meaning lay beyond, but in which direction?

Frustrated at times to tears by her inability to learn the language of Anne Cleves, Nikki would drink herself into a stupor of Sauvignon Blanc and pass out, head down among the scribbled sheets, her last thought a flung hope that perhaps by sleeping on the words, her poor muddled head might absorb their meaning via osmosis.

"I CAN'T understand it!" she cried to Joe, when the earth was settling into October. The warm weather of summer tarrying late into September gave way at last to early fall. In the evenings the air cleared and felt crisp and light, good air for thinking. Wrapping herself in a sweater to walk in the woods, Nikki still moved cautiously about, as if half expecting to see Ernest; but she saw no one.

Working hard, she again and again brought pages of her translation to Joe only to watch him put on his bent-frame glasses, read the page, shake his head, furrow his brow, turn the page upside down, then try to read it upside down. All the while Nikki sat, impatient, waiting, holding her breath. She felt like a student—no, she had never been a student like this before, having to endure feeling an utter failure before a teacher.

Sometimes after studying one of her pages a long while, Joe would finally set it afire in a nearby candle and hand it back to her, half in flames. The first time Nikki rushed to smother the flame. By the tenth such episode she merely sighed, carried the page to the fire, dropped it in—the two of them watching it blacken as Nikki's face burned hot with embarrassment.

"I can't make any sense of it!" she cried, turning back. "Every time I get a few words along, I have to stop to ask you what some damn word is. It's not fair!" Pacing the cave, she caught her sneakered foot on the Persian rug and yanked it loose.

"Not to make sense," Joe replied quietly. Nikki turned to hear him out. "Not a language. Properly speaking." He cleared his throat. "You try too hard with sand filtering through. Anne—" He looked into the cave's shadows overhead as a glow came over his face. "Make magic in language ... reveal and conceal, yes?" he asked brightly, intertwining his fingers. He splayed the fingers of both hands so that they crossed at right angles, forming a small checkerboard. He held them up floating, then suddenly shoved them right up to her face, absurdly close so that she backed off. She smiled, though, recognizing the last of the Ogham letters—actually the last of the additional five letters, the one called "Emancoll" that designated the witch hazel or beech tree. His fingers a screen; behind the screen, what? He was making a joke, and Nikki laughed a moment, realizing she got it. For a moment they were two Druids in the dark cave, communicating silently in the secret, age-old language of Ogham, old as the trees it was rooted in.

Still, she shook her head. "I understand *that*—but I still can't get the full sense of Anne's words. I thought at first if I studied I might be able to do it, but it's no use. I might as well use your translation."

Joe tsked and snorted peevishly through his narrow proboscis, then folded his thin arms tightly against his chest. "Impatient, are we? Then we shall have no tea and cakes, shall we? No, we shan't."

Nikki smiled in spite of herself and shook her head. Plopping down on the cot, she leaned back against the cold stone wall. "Well, what am I to do? I want to read the damn thing!"

"Soon, soon," he encouraged, leaning and patting her knee. The capricious display of a sane and sympathetic heart in the old wreck moved Nikki unexpectedly.

"All the languages sing in me," he chanted. *"Birds of all feathers flocking and flying. I am a capricolish treadmill,"* he singsonged. He seemed to drift off but came back and regarded her, the old gleam of life again shining out of his deeply wrinkled eyes. Nikki smiled sadly.

"It is no language, Cleves. Cloven, as I have said—galloping hooves. Too many secrets. Secrets for two reasons," he instructed, lifting three fingers. "First," he intoned, ticking two fingers down at once, "protection. A powerful sorceress needs protection," he grimaced. Turning down his third finger, he concluded. "Four, initiate."

"Because she was an initiate?" Nikki shook her head impatiently.

"*For* initiate. Learning the straight way does not teach. Too sane. She knew. Confusion secrets keeps outsiders' fingers on the door. They never enter," he shook his head, pursing his lips. "The door in many places. Each one opens the room ... together they open the room. Impossible, eh? Too many doors, eh?" Joe chuckled. "Impossible to understand!"

"Well, let me look at your translation," Nikki insisted.

Lifting a pile of papers from his desk he proffered them to Nikki. Nikki began to reach for them, but a certain expression in Joe's eyes made her stop.

"No—" she sighed, dropping her hand. "I can't." They exchanged glances. "So you say I can't learn the language because there are too many of them all jumbled together. You've said that, right?"

Joe set the pages down and nodded as if his head were on a spring, smiling with an idiot's delight.

"Do I have to ask you every word?"

Still smiling, Joe tilted his head to the side, like a bird hearkening to a song. He sifted through his papers with a bony, rag-gloved hand, plucking a page from his translation. Clearing his throat theatrically, he boomed: "Translate! *'On that day I died in Paradise to take on fith-fath, at Quickborn when the black sheep is given.'"* Joe set the page down and studied her, intertwining his fingers across his layered chest as if the checkerboard were now a barrier Nikki had to cross.

Nikki sat stunned. Here was the same sentence Joe had read to her all those weeks ago, which made no sense then. Now she understood it!

"Wait a minute—*wait a minute.*" The little hairs on the back of her neck stood on end, and her eyes watered; she leaned quickly forward, peering inwardly into her catalogue of knowledge. Peeks woke and trotted over to her, looking up. "Wait a minute!" A smile crept over her face. "I know what it means," she exclaimed in wonder. "I know what it means. I understand—I think I understand. It means—it means—that on some day, I don't know which, Anne was—*initiated*—that's what 'die' means—initiated into fith-fath. That's *shape-shifting!*" Nikki marveled at her own illumination. "Anne was initiated as a *shape-shifter.* In *Paradise*—that would be some sacred grove—of trees. At *Quickborn*—the fountain of life, a sacred fountain. I know that word because I looked it up in your dictionary after the first time I was here. I remembered you calling your spring 'Quickborn.'" She pointed to the little bubbling spring in the corner, glowing with life. "The fountain of life." Nikki smiled. "Maybe it's your Fountain of Youth."

Joe nodded his rotten-toothed grin at her.

She furrowed her brow. "Then Anne refers to the 'black sheep.' I learned they are sacrificed at Samhain—All Souls' Day on the first of November. So the entire sentence means that in a sacred grove at the fountain, Anne was initiated into shape-shifting during the festival of Samhain." She looked at Joe in awe as a light infused her face and eyes, her whole being radiant.

"I understand! I understand!" she nearly shouted. Peeks barked. Nikki's eyes were wide. "I can hear the words—I know what they mean!"

Joe jumped up and cavorted about the room, this time Nikki joining him as the two danced about in a strange jig that the old gods would have recognized as the *Dance of Understanding.* Peeks danced between their legs, barking sharply. Joe pulled a wooden flute out of a cracked brown leather bag slung over the back of his chair, put it to his lips and played a real Irish jig, the three frolicking about like dancing sprites.

"Fith-fath! Fith-fath!" Nikki sang as she danced, circling around and around, bouncing from foot to foot. All her life she had felt too clumsy, too Finnish and thick-skinned to dance. Her legs, which she had always thought too fat, and her hips, which she had always hated for their breadth, now felt light as air. Today in the cave she was the ballerina she had never dared dream of being as a little girl.

"Fith-fath!" she cried out again and again, tilting her head back and singing at the ceiling to Joe's mad flute playing. "I understand! I understand!" She was filled with the madness of knowing, the ecstasy of the shaman and the poet. She was free, possessed by the spirit and utterly free.

Round and round and round they danced, Peeks' whole body barking as the flute played on and on, until the rocks rang, laughing along with their mirth and joy, and still they danced and played and sang. After a time they were out of breath and so stopped, laughing, eyes tearing; then still laughing Joe put his flute to his lips once again and they danced some more.

The sight of Joe with flute pressed to his lips flashed before Nikki as she whirled around and around, but even in the passing frenzy she caught a look that startled her. His eyes were no longer the eyes of a madman, the wreck of a powerful intellect. Calm and clear and knowing, they smiled shrewdly at Nikki above the curved horizon of the wooden flute, as if to say: *I know, I know, Welcome; I know.*

And Nikki danced and swirled until she went mad herself, and they did not stop for a long, long time.

AFTER THAT EVENING in early October Nikki felt renewed determination and energy. Anne's words were beginning to open for her—and when they did not, Nikki would put her pen down and think of Joe, rising finally to dance a little. First she lowered the shades, humming along to a CD of Irish jigs. She danced more quietly and, oddly, with more self-consciousness when she was alone with only Guy to look on, puzzled, from his bed near the back door. After one or two jigs she would sit down, able to work again. She learned to leap over the words she could make no sense of and to dance with the ones she could, drawing their meaning out slowly. In time the ancestral journal opened its pages to her, the story of her distant great-grandmother rubbing along her ankles like a cat.

Her work was in the depths; Nikki spent the tunneling days at her kitchen table; deep-cave nights lying under the dome of her bed, spangled with starry insight in diamond words she had chiseled as if from stone. She lay immersed in the forest of books covering the history of Druids, Celts, and European witches. The leafed books fluttered onto her bed and lay, spines open, like huge white flakes, floated to the floor and piled up in masses like the leaves against her house. Nikki poked around in them, looking down through reading glasses perched on the end of her nose, a frown settled on her brow. Anne used names for the old gods and goddesses that had been lost to history, Nikki discovered by accident—after she came across a dusty reference tucked away in the forgotten footnote of a large, crinkle-leafed book bound in calf, which she first had to go to Boston to track down.

The advice Joe had given her earlier turned out to be true: She had to proceed through many doors to arrive at any real understanding of the journal. Anne's language purposely seemed to distort and confuse, it dawned on Nikki; her grand ancestor had written in riddles only the elect or the intuitive could fully decipher. Nikki was not an initiate, but she could limp along. In addition, the narrative was interspersed with charms and spells written in obscure verse, such as healing for water-elf disease—which she eventually discovered was smallpox.

Finally Nikki happened upon the spells and learned to perform them, albeit with great self-doubt and clumsiness. Her first spell was to make the Druid wind blow. She sat at her back door one night looking out into the night-dark yard, chanting softly the requisite poetic words from Anne's journal while the proper herbs burned in a stone bowl at her feet. She grew very sleepy and dull-eyed as the world swirled slowly around her. After spending what seemed to her hours repeating the words over and over and over, she realized with a start that she had fallen into a half sleep. She snapped her eyes open and felt a breeze blowing against her face, warm with a deep fragrance of far-off lands. She closed her mouth and held her breath, and the wind blew steadily for a long time.

"Joe!" she yelled the next day, jumping down into his cave. "I've learned to cast a spell!" The old man was sitting at the fire with Peeks, looking a little sad. He turned to her; she grew hesitant at his gaze. Was she wrong to want to make magic?

"Did—you learn to cast spells?" she asked quietly.

Gaping at her with a half-witted smile, he pinched a hair from his beard and threw it into the fire, which instantly roared in a deep guttural voice words that Nikki did not understand, but which frightened her to the bone. She jumped back. Joe turned to her and shrugged, and Nikki had to concede: *Indeed, why should he?* Sitting down beside Joe, Nikki engaged him in her latest difficulties with Anne's language. The two settled down to work.

Although the journal was written mostly in an ancient form of Gaelic, interspersed with an arcane mixture of languages, the story, once Nikki had most of it sorted out, was simple, straightforward, and remarkably frank. A story of love and magic stretched far back to the days when Gloucester—as all of New England—had been forests of animals and silent Indians. Where the natives could be glimpsed as free and wild as the animals, yet like all humans feared or loved. It was a story of the witch trials Anne Cleves had witnessed, the torture and the hangings. Even so, the story Anne told was a tale of love, Nikki recognized, though how exactly love was central to the life of a powerful Druid, she had to puzzle long over.

Spells aplenty embellished the manuscript—instructions detailing which little bottles to use and how to mix the concoctions, under which moon and in what kind of bowl. As a book of healing, the journal contained remedies for ailments—from tea made of cowslip for nervous conditions to mugwort for hemorrhoids. For along with the journal Nikki had brought Anne's bottles back, setting them in a row on the window sill in the kitchen. These were so many, they overflowed onto the counter and filled a small shelf.

One evening in late October while Nikki sat impatiently pondering the final twenty pages of the journal, her phone rang. She was nearing the end; she could feel the momentum build as her heart pounded. Absently she lifted the receiver, remembering too late she didn't want to speak with anyone.

"Hello, Nikki? It's Betsy. Time to move, hon. Things are heating up. What have you been doing all this time?"

Nikki shook her head. "Nothing—stuff."

"You never answer your phone anymore—guess you know you missed the last meeting of our Dogtown Committee. Get my newsletter? Cleavage Builders is moving ahead, now that they've got the first stage of approval from the town. Might be time for us to lie down in front of the bulldozers," Betsy laughed good-naturedly.

"What—? Developers?" Fully aware now, Nikki was brought back with a jolt to Rose. Rose! How many weeks had passed while Nikki had been too involved in Anne's story to think about the outer world?

"Haven't you been following the news? It's happening—if we don't move immediately."

"Where—when?"

"We're meeting tomorrow. Coming?"

"Uh—yes, of course."

"Good! High times!" Betsy cried, hanging up.

Nikki set the phone slowly into its cradle, looked longingly at the manuscript, then at the clock. Eight in the evening: long since dark. Although October thirtieth by the calendar, Indian summer was lingering, a warm breeze blowing the curtains. She took coffee from the freezer and put water on to boil. She had to finish that very night. Even if she had slept only three hours the night before and felt woozy already—she had to finish. She slid the emerald brooch out of its leather pouch, turning it over and over. It was quite beautiful, she mused—how unfortunate it was broken... She thought of Philip.

The phone rang again; Nikki nearly ignored it. It was probably Philip, she thought; coincidences like that never really surprised her. She was exhausted, having slept less and less recently as the story and its people had grown more and more vivid. The whispers had started up again in the house, but Nikki by this time felt used to them.

Anne's life now seemed more real to Nikki than her own. Anne was a living presence whom she half expected to meet in the woods. When she did take breaks from translating to walk Guy through the woods, her surroundings looked altogether different, transfigured, the fall sunlight clear as crystal, hollow with meaning like a bell tolling. The rustle of the wind was not the rustle of the common wind but the herald of another world. Piles of leaves were not simply leaves but flakes of poetry that Nikki turned over and over in her amazed hand, wondering at their endless variations in color and texture. Gorgeous red and gold leaves flooded the paths that Nikki and Guy swished through like waves. At every turn Nikki expected to meet Anne Cleves' teacher, the old Druid Ganieda, leaning on his stick, or Nanepa, perhaps, the ancient Indian squaw.

Yes, she smiled in reverie, this is the magic of poetry, why the Druid shamans were at root poets—because poetry creates the world. It startled her to realize, for the first time, the meaning of Joe's conundrum: poets, shamans; shamans, poets.

She reached distractedly for the burbling phone.

"Nikki? You haven't been to the spring in days and days," Clarissa stated in her usual matter-of-fact way.

"Busy translating, you know."

"Yes. And it's nearly done."

"Nearly. I'm exhausted." Nikki was too tired to ask Clarissa how she knew.

"Any further visitations from your father?" Clarissa probed.

"No," Nikki sighed.

"That's too bad."

"Hah!" Nikki laughed. "He's really the one I want to see when I'm just about home free."

"But he is, isn't he?" Clarissa continued.

Nikki felt herself hunker down, waiting. She rubbed her forehead.

"Doesn't Anne say that her big dream is to find her father?" the older woman half stated.

"Glad to see everyone has already read the journal."

Clarissa laughed. "Joe told me that, dear. Just because he's read it doesn't mean it wasn't yours to find."

"Except that someone else found it first—and translated it," Nikki retorted. The water began to boil, and she got up and poured it into the filter. "I mean, what am I doing? Making a translation that is already made. Sitting at home for weeks and weeks going crazy, for what? I found Anne's potion for eternal beauty, but it mustn't be used."

"No," Clarissa agreed quietly.

"No. So you already knew. Why didn't you and Joe just tell me?"

"Do you regret the work?"

"No—I don't think so," Nikki hesitated. "It's not that. I'm sure it's done something for me. But what then?"

"You mean, for who else? For your father."

"What has my father to do with all this? Yeah, so Anne searches for her father. She has a great father. Nothing like mine."

"Did you know your father and Ernest were friends?" Clarissa queried.

"I'm not surprised," Nikki replied dully. She poured herself a cup of coffee and sat down, sipping and blowing. "Why didn't you tell me?" she added as an afterthought.

"You didn't ask. Haven't you wondered why Ernest left that note for Philip? He left one for me, too."

"Yes, I wondered," Nikki stated evenly. "Why haven't you ever said anything about that?"

"You never asked."

They were silent.

"You are unbelievable, Nikki! The whole thing is sitting there right out in the open for you to grasp, but you won't reach. Why not? Does it cost too much?"

"I want to know," Nikki insisted quietly. "I didn't ask before because—I figured if you wanted to talk about it, you would."

"Is this what today passes for communication skills?"

"What do you want?" Nikki countered peevishly. "I'm overtired and stressed out from working on Anne's journal. My back hurts, my head hurts, my stomach is in knots over Rose and Philip. I won't have enough money to pay the mortgage in a few months because I've been spending my time translating a journal that's already translated instead of finding a job. I want to finish—I'm going to finish, so I can move on with my life."

"Are you still hoping Anne's journal will give you an answer?"

"To what?"

"To your problems, as you once conveyed to me."

"Yes—and you told me I was a fool for thinking that way."

"Don't put words in my mouth," Clarissa declared quietly but firmly.

"All right!" Nikki blurted. "I am still looking for some sort of answer... to help ... to be free of all this mess in my life—"

"You mean, Philip."

"That—and other things. I want to feel at home. I want to rest. I want not to have to struggle all the time. You don't know what it's like, being single—"

A laugh came softly from the other end of the phone.

"Well, you don't seem to mind it. And you don't know what it's like today—for professional women of my generation. There's a social stigma around being single. You're not supposed to be—and one by one your friends get married. The men left over are all jokes."

"So you don't want to be married."

"I want it not to matter!" Nikki shrieked. Her hand shaking the coffee, she set the cup down. "It doesn't seem to matter to Anne or to you or even to Aunt Meg! Why should it matter so much to me? Where are the men?"

"You know, I used to wonder—still do wonder—whether I fell in love with Ernest exactly because he couldn't help me out of my loneliness."

"That again!" Nikki exhaled tiredly.

"I don't have an answer for loneliness, Nikki. A female folk singer from Rockport used to sing a song wondering where all the cowboys have gone. Men wonder the same thing about women."

"Yeah, well—it's not a stigma for men to be single."

Clarissa paused. "Why don't I tell you about your father and Ernest."

"Can't wait," Nikki gulped coffee, burning her mouth.

"Nikki, what stands out for you in what Anne, your Aunt Meg, and I each have to say?"

"You all have—a different orientation from the usual male-dominated patriarchy. Earth goddess worship . . . you know."

"Been dreaming about your father?" Clarissa wondered as if aloud.

"How did you know—?" The question caught her off guard.

Clarissa laughed lightly. "If you think what's going on in contemporary culture is predominantly the patriarchy, you're not seeing much."

"Yes, I know. Goddess worship like Anne's recognizes the feminine."

"As already basic to our cultural tradition," Clarissa emphasized. "Your struggle is the same one in your outer and inner lives, you see."

"Which means?" Nikki asked rotely, yawning suddenly. Her head was sagging and her eyes closing; the coffee wasn't working yet. She glanced at the pot. Hadn't she made it strong enough?

"Your personal struggle with Philip is part of your larger struggle to find a place for men within your feminist vision. It's no good trying to make them into second-class citizens. I've seen enough of women's condescension toward men to know that that's no solution," Clarissa insisted.

"You were going to say something about my father and Ernest," Nikki yawned again. At once she sprang up, staring at the back door window. Was that passing shadow there—her father? Blindingly, she was seized with terror: He was out there! Wasn't that shimmer of light off the glass her father? She strained her eyes, slowly realizing she wanted to see her father's face there. How strange!

"Yes," came Clarissa's reply. And with a shock Nikki realized that Clarissa had worked some magic. Nikki felt a cloud descending around her that filled her with deep longing.

"Tell me—about my father," Nikki spoke softly from within the cloud, quiet and hollowed out as a shell.

When in a very low voice Clarissa began to speak, it sounded to Nikki like a chant coming from far off. She pressed her ear into the phone until it hurt.

"Ernest and your father were friends. They first met when they discovered they each liked to drink at the old Towline Bar downtown in Gloucester. They were both businessmen who liked a good deal. Your father sold insurance to Ernest; Ernest rented his New Hampshire mountain cabin to your father. Also, they were connected because of you."

"Through Rose and me," Nikki nodded. Her heart was beginning to pound. She felt something coming that terrified her. What was it? As she stared at the window her eyes teared. She sipped coffee, hoping warmth would reassure her.

"Yes. Even then, thirty years ago, Rose was after the journal. She had told Ernest of your ancestry, and Ernest, in turn, brought it up one night with his friend Pekka Helmik, assuming he knew."

"So my father did know all those years."

"Yes, though apparently your father was furious, because until that moment with Ernest he hadn't known about Anne Cleves and the journal. All at once he became aware of what his wife was, and it angered and frustrated him. He planned his revenge like a bully, focusing on you—as the youngest and most like your mother. He was determined to get revenge . . . by having you seduced."

"What?!" Nikki shouted, her heart leaping into her throat. She set her cup down, hand violently shaking. The cloud dispersed; the overhead light suddenly shone harshly.

"Nikki—the older man—was Ernest," Clarissa whispered.

"What older man?" Nikki demanded, but she already knew.

"Your older man."

"Ernest Eveless—?" Nikki mumbled, shocked. Her heart roaring in her ears made her voice sound far off, as if muffled in cotton.

"He was put up to it by your father."

"Ernest—told you this?" she panted.

"In the note he left me."

Nikki was straining to listen to her heart. She could barely hear over the roar.

"It was what had to happen, Nikki," Clarissa declared more firmly.

"What—? Didn't you say when we first met—that when it happened—it was too early?" Nikki's head was reeling. The noise was deafening.

"Yes, but also that it was necessary."

"I hate you!" she screamed over the howling storm.

"Well," Clarissa intoned sadly. "I don't bring happy news."

"You knew . . . this . . . the whole time . . . you were talking to me, making me feel horrible—so then you could make me feel better!" Nikki stuttered, the old anger rising in her as the words dribbled out.

"Yes, I knew. I know now that Ernest killed himself as recompense, in some way. He could not live with what he had done."

"And you dare to call to tell me it was necessary?" Acid trickled from Nikki's voice. Her heart was subsiding now, but a cold fury was taking over. Though her ears were ringing, she was on the moon, where it was cold and white and dead all around her.

"It doesn't matter," Clarissa said softly.

"Well, I think it does matter! You sit up there in the woods and coolly say I have to learn how to keep the men inside of me? When you knew that I was raped as a little girl? By the man who made you his mistress—after he did that to me?" Now the cloud descending over her was of ice, and crystals tinkled sharply in her voice.

"There's nothing I could say, Nikki. He was drunk—you said yourself—and so were you."

"He was older, too—remember you saying that?"

"Your—long journey—would not be possible without—such a beginning."

"Oh, how nice to have your blessing! I hate your magic, if this is what it gives people! Your detachment, unfeeling coldness toward people! Your callous immorality. You made me feel like a slut, forcing me to relive all those men, and I went through it because I trusted you. It was hell for me to go through again—"

"And did it help?" Clarissa cut in.

"Yes! But so what? It doesn't help now! It hurts worse now! Now it's all a sham—all your words, the supposed healing! I feel like the worst kind of fool right now! You know what word is screaming in my head right now? 'Whore, whore, whore'!" Nikki bellowed.

"What has changed?" Clarissa asked softly.

"All the goddam awareness you've forced on me!" Nikki screamed. Her voice percussing in her ears made them hurt. Everything hurt. "I don't want to talk anymore," she finished, abruptly quiet, and set the phone down on its hook.

Nikki picked up Anne's journal and shook it until the tears came, but she would not cry. She was far too angry. She would throw the journal away. She would burn it into blackened ash and cinders and blow it away into the rising wind. What did it matter now? She sat for a long while glaring at the journal, staring at nothing, seeing the devil in his red cape all those years ago, remembering the excitement, loathing her complacency, loathing herself for having loved the excitement. Yet even in her red anger she knew it somehow made sense—that in some way maybe she had known … and not known. Even back then she had felt the man's power, behind the mask.

The hurt went very deep indeed. The shock engulfed her spirit and dragged her with an iron weight into the black pit. She had been used, victimized by her own father—why? Because she had been secretly aligned from an early age with her mother's ancestral power? Had she somehow, by some visible mark on her, displayed this very connection? Was there a connection between her sexual desire and the journal? What had she been desiring with the red devil? With all the men? It had brought down her father's wrath on her.

Full of disgust, Nikki hurried upstairs and took a shower that lasted as long as the hot water held out, pouring hot water all over herself, soaking her spirit as deeply as she could, letting the rain fall and fall and fall, the weight of the water washing the stain of her mortal flesh away, pounding her with its drowning heat, scalding her and scalding her arms and stomach and back, burning her so that her rotted and charred flesh fell off in flakes and swirled down the drain and away into the dark underground. As she stood with head bowed under the showerhead peering down into the drain, the water fell like hot blood, her own blood coursing down the drain and away from her. She was suffocating in her anger and humiliation and could not think, standing and steadying herself against the ugly lime tiles. For there before her, no matter which way she wagged her soaking head, the figure of the red devil leered over her as she lay on the motel bed…

A long while afterward she sat, towel wrapped around her on the edge of the bathtub, head bowed, hair dripping absently onto the cracked tiles. Guy entered and sat on the rug by her feet without looking at her. She was aware of his presence the way an artist is aware of an element in a painting, as part of the gestalt. The room was just a room, the tiles neither more nor less ugly than they had ever been. She was wet, as she was supposed to be, and did not care that water pooled at her feet. Vaguely she heard her father yelling at her for dripping on the floor. The frosted glass light over the old porcelain sink stark and glaring.

At last she went back to the kitchen, a new resolve entering her cold heart. No, she determined, she would not destroy the journal, eyeing it enthroned like a mute sibyl on the table. Clarissa was right about one thing; this was about more than Nikki alone. The journal—her seduction—stood between Rose and herself. Now how did she feel about Rose? Was Clarissa right about Rose wanting to destroy Nikki? It made sense . . . if Rose had known all these years about Ernest and Nikki. If she had known about that night after the party in the motel. Nikki sat before the journal wrapped in her robe, hair in a towel, and began to plot inside the icy darkness.

Just let Rose try to take revenge on her—the woman would see what kind of person she had to reckon with now, Nikki thought grimly. For Nikki by her own labor had gained a powerful ally. Right there before her, speaking with the authority of the dead, was her patroness and protector Anne, guarding Nikki against all the men and women who had abused her. It seemed they were all out to get her. Every one of them. Well, let them try to make her suffer now.

The threat to her from Rose: She had to think this through. What would it be, exactly? Was there some spell around the journal? Not that she could see as yet. Was Rose going to kill her once Nikki dutifully handed over the journal? Certainly Rose was expecting the compliant, obedient, awestruck good daughter Nikki of old, willing to do anything for Rose, to be like Rose. To be liked by Rose.

Although exhausted, she got up and flicked on the gas to the coffee, the new reality settling in. She had been abandoned and betrayed by everyone and everything, only to be left—ironically—with the hard truth she had always known: life as warfare; human relationships as a perpetual struggle for power. She smiled darkly as she waited for the coffee to heat, then poured herself a boiling cup.

Yes, power. Aunt Meg had been wrong to minimize it. Nikki was in the middle of a great struggle here, much like the heroic battles Anne Cleves had fought. Real battles for her soul, for her self. She drank black coffee; the caffeine and the courage melded inside her and swirled in her soul; she felt like a woman warrior. She would finish the work and then have done with it, without turning it over to Rose. Never again would she speak to Clarissa, damn her! As for what to do with the translation, the journal itself would guide her, she concluded, turning to view it straight on.

Inside lay the secret, she thought with a smile. Not just of beauty, but of power and strength. And maybe, after all, that was the secret of everlasting beauty—the beauty of war and power. Hadn't Clarissa herself said that love didn't last? What did, then? Power, certainly. The journal held magic that would be hers when she finished. Which she would use to overcome all the pain inflicted on her by the likes of Philip and Ernest, by Clarissa and Rose. Maybe she would leave Gloucester, take the journal on the road, give worldwide talks on it, become famous and rich and live far away from Gloucester. Yes, she would do just that... But first she would exact her revenge using the new power Anne had given her—the power of doing magic.

Nikki looked up to behold Ernest looking in at her from the window. This time she did not flinch but stared stonily at her enemy. All these weeks of half searching for him in Dogtown, hoping to find his comforting ghost presence blessing her. All that was destroyed—this was war. On the other side of the glass lurked the specter who had murdered her soul, and she tasted the blood in her teeth, as if she could kill him, ghost that he was. For a long time she stared back with hate at the damned vision ... until it held up an apple cut through the core, its pentacle seeds glistening like dark-brown jewels in the white flesh of the apple. And at that the vision faded. For a long time Nikki sat, full of rage and loathing, until she grew exhausted from the effort, tired as she already was.

It was just a ghost after all, she told herself; more haunting presences than Ernest's, deeper even than that of her father, beckoned her henceforth. She now carried within her the immortal seed of Anne Cleves, which was beginning to make her feel powerful indeed.

"I'm a ghost, too!" Nikki shouted impulsively at the empty kitchen window. She stopped and heard what she had said. "I'm a ghost," she murmured, looking back at the journal. There was much still to do, so little time left. The thirtieth of October: one day until her own initiation. She half wondered what she might have meant.

Guy darted from his bed and whimpered at her feet. She took note of him, went upstairs to dress, returned and clipped on his leash. They stepped through the door into the warm night air—too warm for October. Down the three cracked cement stairs stained with the faded red paint, up the short hill and through the fallen leaves into Dogtown. The forest was alive this night, limbs swaying, breeze murmuring. Nikki's head was full of Anne. She had walked in these very woods! She was walking here still! For a time the two walked quietly, Guy padding along, Nikki setting one foot in front of the other in expectant awe, peering around every tree for a glimpse of her ancestor in long black cloak, chanting spells over a fire, her hair twisted into snakes of magic. I am a ghost, she echoed, over and over. *I have become one of those old women I used to long for, when I was a girl playing in their cellar holes.*

The wind came up strong and good and tossed her soul about, filling Nikki with a high and indomitable spirit. She was close to the end—and then they would see! She would have her revenge! From a distance she heard police sirens and smiled twistedly at the thought that they were for her. *Beware!* the sirens cried out. *Power unleashed!*

Back home noticing the light flashing on the answering machine, she absently pressed the button as she poured herself a glass of Sauvignon Blanc.

"Nikki, this is Rose. I'm sorry to have to tell you this, but as I haven't heard from you in all this time, I'm going ahead with the project I discussed with you. I have heard gossip about you having actually found the journal—and that you've been hiding yourself away translating it. Is that true? I hope it's not, my dear. I trust you would have let me know if you had found it. Your task was just to find it, not work on it. I have people much more suited to that task. Since I know you wouldn't deceive me, I'm forced to proceed with the plan. Call me if you'd like to talk," she finished.

Fury overcame Nikki, shaking her hand around the wine glass. *Soon, soon!* she promised.

Breathing deeply, she took up her pen. Rose would have to wait. Despite her nagging fear, Nikki shoved the problem of Rose over the horizon of her mind and set to work. From time to time she glanced at the window in the back door, one ear hearkening for the phone. Nothing intruded; even the whispering voices were still. She made more coffee and drank from the endless black river.

The phone did ring finally, startling Nikki out of her absorption in Anne's story. She picked it up, setting her jaw.

"Nikki, it's Claire. Did you hear? Rose wrecked her Mercedes."

"Good for her," Nikki replied, disappointed.

"You don't know then," Claire continued. Nikki was silent. "It was around the corner from your house—she ran off the road and into a ditch. John told me."

John Cummings, young officer on the Gloucester police force, was Claire's latest boyfriend. "And—?" Nikki waited.

"And she had her pistol on the front seat. Nikki, she was heading for your house!" Claire gasped.

"Well, she didn't get here," Nikki observed. She shooed Claire off the phone. Her lip curling with satisfaction, she considered. "I'm protected," she explained to Guy, then returned to Anne's journal.

Nikki slowly climbed up into the work as the night chariot drove on, wrestling with the words when they would not yield readily to her pen, scribbling frantically various possible meanings. The proper names she now knew, so she did not bother with those. She felt good and loose and full of knowing. The language came easily, as if another mind than hers were inhabiting her head, directing her pen and her thoughts. As the sand ran out, it ran more quickly. Anne's story in drawing to a close ran along such smooth paths that Nikki barely had to pause to understand. The knowing was upon her as she flowed downstream rapidly now, the fluidity of a running coyote pacing her, her limbs stretching and flexing without effort. Sentence after sentence streamed out of her pen. The story was rushing toward its end.

The rest of the long night passed in outer silence, until after many hours of coasting along Nikki came to the last words of Anne's story, her fingers trembling in the dawn light as she held the final page of the manuscript. Sweat beaded on her upper lip, her heart pounding from the caffeine, yet she was exhausted and triumphant. She had copied out the story, and it made sense. It had Joe's marks on it, but it had hers, too. The fluid running in her heart all night wound slowly to a stop, slowing and slowing as she regained herself and the knowing mind left hers. She was left with an exhaustion far deeper than she had ever known, greater than when she had birthed Alice. For the moment her hatred and anger had dissipated, and she was as empty as a bellows. She sat silently regarding the pages piled before her, then picked up the broken brooch again, now understanding that it had been deliberately broken. Still, she wondered how it was that Philip had come by the broken piece, even if now she had a hint from Anne.

The jewel box of Anne Cleves' journal had opened at last.

9,

GURYN'S TALE

WELCOME by my two names. My Druid name is Guryn Thornback; my English, Anne Cleves. I have lived long enough to write down all in this Journal, recorded in the year 1753 of the Common Era. This is my story of one new world and many old, full of spells and incantations of the three styles: *Imbas Forosnai,* by word of mouth; *Tenm Laida,* the shining; and *Dechetal do Chennaib,* the headship of wisdom and of divination by touch.

My story must be believed so that the Wheel of the Year may be turned. The Gods cast into darkness by Patrick of Eire live in the new land, even as that descendant of Patrick known as Mather would condemn the Gods and fairies to a dark hell not of the Otherworld. Queen Aine presiding over the fairies in her shining blue has whispered such to me, for she does not wish for the heaven of Patrick; nor do I. All matters will be told.

For whom is the word? Not hard. A younger one must read and understand, stand in the sacred grove, chant to the Gods and Goddesses, and hunt the sacred boar. Through the tumultuous years, I am last in the line of queens who since dim times have ruled over our tribe of the Raven. Another must follow. A woman of golden hair must come forth to stand upright before the Great Oak where I and others have stood, and must reach up and turn the wheel with one arm of life, the other of death, reaching into the darkness and believing without faith. So that the magic may live and life may go on.

You will read and go into the grove, turn the wheel and tell the story. Else all is lost, we fall into utter darkness, and the sun will not rise in the sky again from the sleeping time.

Long is the dark time wherein the English Patricks hunt us in the woods and seek to find me again, though once I defeated them in battle. I write alone under the tent pole of the stars in the short time of night. For I am too old to hunt or to climb the Pole of the World, and Richard has gone into the wide world following upon my only daughter Diana. So do I sit and chant: *May Wolf come, may I run with her, though my limbs be ancient.*

I have been dead; I have been reborn. We the children of Bile, God of the Dead, die to be reborn. The time is very dark. They come for me even as they have broken the Faery *sidh,* cut down the Oak of the World, and defiled the Elfmound. I gather my strength and chant spells upon this land that the Saxon again seeks to take by force. Imbas speaks. My store of *awen* flows in midnight's stony dark. Then hear my story:

WHENCE CAME WE? Not hard. My forebears sailed to this new world from the old country of Eire whence we were clan of Druids of the Old Order. Our lineage reaches far back into the dim ages when the Gods and Goddesses were awake and alive in Cruithne and walked the earth.

Many are the stories my father told me of the shadowy beginnings of our people, who traveled from our land to the Far Reaches to learn the secrets from the wise women and men: of the circularity of life, extending from the Great Womb and returning thence; and of the everlasting soul's return in animal and plant. The weary travelers returned to Gaul to teach the ragged tribes the ancient ways. From Gaul our Druid ancestors migrated to Britannia in Roman times long before Caesar, then to the land of Eire whence our tribe grew in Connachta, on the plains of the Raven.

Caesar's Roman legions came as conquerors to our fair Isle, imprisoning and executing my people. Thenceforth our old ones went into hiding and so remained invisible, they and their descendants, for generations to come. During the dark time—lasting centuries—some of us became necromancers and workers of the dark spirits, at home in the occult. For there was little light. They forbade us to sacrifice at the sacred Oak, they forbade us to pray at the circle of stones of the turning stars; we could neither sing under the open sky nor read from the Black Book.

In time the Romans departed our green land, leaving their garrisons unmanned, their centurions recalled to Rome, their tax gatherers vanished like the wind of the *sidhe* on a dark night. Thence came the Normans and the Saxons, they of the matted hair and fierce mien, whereupon uneasy truces were made between my people and theirs for many years—until the Normans invaded our lands, taking our women and our horses for their own.

There followed much bloodshed and many great feats of arms, but my people were beaten as the invader ravaged our country and forbade our old ways. Like unto the Fomorians of old were they in the devastation they wrought. Because our bards were forbidden at the courts, their sacred learning of the Twelve Years' Poetry was lost to the darkness. The poetry chair of Ceridwen was vacated, the schools closed. Few were left to remember the Three Hundred and Fifty Tales, the grammars, and the myths. Thus did the ancient learning pass to the Druid priests, known forever after as the *Fili,* the poets. From these poet magicians was my tribe of Raven descended.

My grandfather Cuipre, chief bard at the court of Connachta, was exiled. With the men and women of the Raven tribe he sailed from Eire, across the Fountain of Venus, to the strange new paradise in the West. With them came varied workers of the Old Arts and those who remembered the lore. Under cover of night we sailed, guided by the stars shining in a clear sky: the Court of Arianrhod and Arthur's Plow Tail; and the smaller Plow Tail turning about the Pole of the Universe. As we sailed through the nights all the jewels of Neifion's Court lay under the breast of our boat, while we bowed our uncovered heads before the stars of the Court of Gwydion, flung from horizon to horizon like the glittering seed of men.

Gwydion's star, shining brightly in clear skies, steered our passage. "A good omen," our pilot declared: a portent that the trees in the new land would give us a home. For Gwydion had enchanted the trees to life, that they would thereby fight for him. Our seers consulted their charm stones and foretold that our way was clear.

After the pilot read the stars, my grandfather whispered to my father, then a boy.

"Behold the enchantment of poetry, my son. The sacred words bring the trees to life."

"Are the trees not alive before?" asked my young father.

"Alive, but unmoved until the poet speaks his *awen*—the true words—and writes the sacred Ogham upon their barks."

"What words are they?"

"Why, the secret words of poetry!" my grandfather winked.

Thus came the Raven tribe of two hundred Druid exiles to the New World in the year 1446 C.E. I was at that time a cock caged with the hens, left on deck for air along with the horses and cattle. I ducked my red-cocked head and sniffed, raising my head sharply so my hens would see I was their master, trimmed my beak and waited, keeping an eye on my brood. It was a fertile breeding time on the long trip while my feathers grew long with progeny. My hens produced many eggs and hatchlings.

We landed on the rocky coast of the New World where a swollen river we named the Boyne flowed out to sea. There Cuipre himself with his much-honed *athane,* whose bone handle was fashioned from the Brown Bull of Connachta, held me upright by the neck before the people. With one draw of his sacred knife my neck was hewn as I was sacrificed to Ler, God of the Sea, in thanksgiving for a safe journey. My blood became a proud fountain cascading over my people, anointing them with life.

This memory returned only much later, long after I was a grown woman, during my initiation with the old Druid Ganieda. It was then, when I gazed into the Boyne, that a vision of the past swam to the surface:

How high I held my head even as I saw the gleam of the knife edge, unafraid to pass through the darkness. Into the smoke of the sacrificial fire where I lay burning a small girl stuck her head, and I entered her womb.

As our Raven tribe sailed up the Boyne we hearkened closely to the voices of the land, uncertain whether our Gods and Goddesses would speak to us so far from our home in Eire. Oaks and rowan trees grew thick as flies along the bank, come to watch us pass in our boat.

Along the riverbank we spied a raven of prodigious size and noble manner, who sat preening his sable feathers and eyeing us. He called to us in a voice so musical that we thought he was the great bard Taliesin in one of his hundred guises. The seers cast him bread that he ate, after which we dropped our sails to wait until our wise ones could journey to the raven to speak with him in his own tongue. The huge bird flew toward us and landed on the gunwales in a flutter of feathers; we held our breaths and waited. For days Ganieda, the oldest and most honored of our Druids, lay motionless on deck, bound and watched over that he not roll onto his side. He lay utterly still until shaken out of his trance after the prescribed three days. Nor all that time did the raven take flight but kept watch on deck, shifting from one clawed foot to the other.

When he could speak again, Ganieda reported that he had followed behind the raven as he had been instructed, spreading his wings and flying into a new land. Below him glistened fields of crops and a small town, smoke rising from chimneys. There the raven settled into an age-old Oak tree. Ganieda's vision ended as a dark cloud rose from the south, unquiet spirits stirring in its fearsome depths. The sight had terrified the old Druid.

We waited and watched the raven as day passed into evening. When at dusk he rose into the sky and winged his way up the river, we followed, raising our sails and tacking as best we could up current, always keeping the great bird within our sights. At a bend in the river he lighted upon an Oak tall as a mountain, which stood alone commanding the prospect up- and downriver. As this king of trees was filled with singing and screeching birds day and night, all agreed that beneath it we would build our new settlement, to be called Ravenoak.

We made our own stone circles, lit sacred fires, and chanted prayers under the clear skies: to Danu for the land's blessings; to the Dagda for justice; to Lugh for bravery and protection; to Diancecht for safety and health. Above all, we prayed to Brigit of the triple mien that we be made fertile and wise. From their journeys our bards brought good news back: Our Gods had come with us to the new land; they blessed it.

And so we multiplied, telling stories and working our magic. Children and crops grew as if inspired by the magic of the old Druids. For, indeed, we had cast powerful spells over the fields to ensure the grain. The land was rich with oaks and pines, and so we were happy. The woods were full of coneys and deer; there were eagles and many ravens at Ravenoak. We honored the ravens by leaving bread upon the broad stone that we had carved and set beneath the Great Oak. From time to time we saw swans floating along the Boyne and with happy shouts sent our greetings to the children of Ler, still under the enchantment of Aeife, that their return to the land of men be swift.

Peering into the Otherworld, our seers saw that the people of Faery lived in this land, too. They spied tiny lights in the trees and along the ground at night in the great forest that stretched on forever. *Sidh* mounds, home of the fairies and Gods, we found in the deep forests. We marveled to discover that these were already old;

perhaps some older Gods inhabited this land. When many years later the great sickness came and I fled the Blackcoats, I took refuge in such a fairy *sidh*.

Our bards, my grandfather among them, by singing the old songs taught the young ones the Art, for the chants of the seers and magicians protected the little settlement from dark visitations. The bravest of us ventured into the wood to cut trees and build houses. Ganieda, feeling his years, retired deep into the forest to the north, there to build himself a cabin. Each year on Beltaine the old man, already ancient when we sailed from Eire, visited Ravenoak to give his blessing, and by sticking his thumb in his mouth he foretold matters for us by means of *Imbas Forosnai*.

Dark creatures moved about in the woods, some like the boar and the stag visiting us. Snakes slithered on the forest floor while birds of many colors startled us overhead, strange birds whose names and tongues I did not know.

One day three red tribesmen, dressed in the hides of deer and bear, came to meet with us. They sat at the central fire while by gestures and looks our bards conversed with them, the poets twisting their tongues around the words the Indians spoke. The red people became our friends, teaching us the many ways of the new land—how to hunt the deer and the rabbit, how to become invisible among the oaks and maples. They respected the Otherworld and feared it as do we; their stories of the spirits of the ancestors were not unlike our own. Often would the red ones visit to trade and eat with us, some of our people traveling in turn to their wigwams to bring back their native knowledge of these New World woods, of their animals and the spirits of their ancestors who roamed like our heroes, ever on the hunt. We adopted them as our Fenians, respecting and fearing their arts in the hunt and in war. They were kindly presences who comforted us against the darkness of the night and the endless depth of the forest.

As the land would have it, the dark things came not from the woods but from our own people. For generations we lived and prospered in Ravenoak until, as the story goes, at the feast of Samhain two of our strongest men came to blows over a woman. That provoked the weaker, Bran Dark Brow, to depart Ravenoak with his companions, leaving us his curses. Into the dark wood to the west they moved, and we heard no more of them for many years—until one day on a hunt some of our men were attacked by unknown white men resembling those from the breakaway tribe, bearing lances and shields similar to our own.

Waging fierce battle against this tribe—who called themselves the Branna after their leader Bran—many of our heroes were slain, even more wounded. Although the enemy was beaten back by our tribe, neither the herbs and waters of our healers could make our men whole, nor the chants of the Druids cure them. From time to time through the years the Branna made raids on our cattle and goats; the bitterness of strife thus tinged this sacred land.

Many were the times, I still recall, when my father would saddle his horse Grey, shoulder his leather shield embossed with the carmine eagle and, raising his double-pointed spear, ride into battle at the head of his men. How I cried as a young girl to watch him go, uncertain whether he would return! My mother the queen would send me stern looks, warning me to comport myself in the proper manner of a Druid princess.

When I was still very young, a peace was forged at last between the Branna and my people of Ravenoak, and children from each tribe exchanged as honor prices and as surety. For some years we lived in peace, and only when again the peace was destroyed did Ravenoak suffer the wrongs of the Branna.

I SIT NOW writing as an old woman living far from Ravenoak, in Gloucester, longing for my old home. It is many years since Ravenoak was destroyed by war and by the Christians. Some time after I found refuge here as a young woman, I returned to the ruins at Ravenoak by ten days' journey and found the stones and mounds by the years grown over with moss and weeds, deep in the woods as they are. Because there were Christian Blackcoats nearby, I did not venture within sight but hid myself in a cloud of my making, shape-shifting into wolf.

Our tribe's numbers have thinned until I alone am left of the line of Druids. My daughter Diana fled long ago to escape the hangings in Salem. Those cursed trials happened when I was old even by Druid years. Many times have I gone by fith-fath into wolf shape to look for Diana, roaming the woods and hills far from Gloucester. Whether running along the water and sniffing for food or searching further inland, deep in the woods, I never smelled her scent or heard anything of her from my sisters. I have never been able to learn anything of her whereabouts. That is another matter.

My family name was not Cleves; that was a Saxon name I took early on, in the Druid tradition of taking a name for protection. For the black-coated Saxon Christians have love neither of beauty nor of animals; neither do they know of the Wood Gods nor of Faery—or only enough to be mistaken and afraid, like untutored children.

Although Ganieda taught me about the old Druids of Eire, I have never met up with any who came also to these shores from Eire. Having studied our traditions over a lifetime, I am well versed in ancestral knowledge. Over the same years I have witnessed as well the disappearance of the old ways—and even I do not know all of the old spells. They are forgotten in these woods, remembered only by the Oak who does not speak. Perhaps they are remembered by our sisters and brothers in Britannia. I do not know. I pray there remains a place where the lore is not lost; where it can still live.

My mother Gwyn—*White-Breast*—was the daughter of the first queen of Ravenoak, whose mother and mother's mother in turn had been queen of the Raven tribe in the old land. When each woman married her husband became king, back through preceding generations of the queen's maternal line. Descended from an old line of Raven magicians, my mother had been instructed in all the arts of healing and steeped in the lore of wood and stream, knowing the uses of plant and animal, herb and fruit. She was very fair, with hair of gold, her skin like unstirred milk.

Like her mother and mother's mother, she wore the Raven emblem of queenship. Of ageless antiquity, it was an emerald five-pointed star chased in gold, ritually fastened over the left breast. From my earliest childhood my eyes were fixed upon this star, bound by its spell.

When I was nine my mother took me one spring day to greet the sacred Salmon of Wisdom that swam like silky gold in the freezing upland waters of the Boyne. She bade me pray to the Goddess Boann for inspiration as she chanted herself a long while over me. I grew sleepy as the magic cloud enveloped me in blue light, and as I peered into the water over which hung the sacred hazel, I saw nine hazelnuts drop one by one into the water. Each of the nine salmon consumed a nut, the sacred fish dancing below the water in sunlight flashing amidst the rocks.

My mother instructed me to become like the bear and pull from the cold water such salmon who swam near me. As I was within the magic circle of her making, I was easily able to put my hand in and catch one. I ate and licked the slippery fish taste from my fingers, savoring the embodied spirit of the fish. Then praying as I looked at my fingers, I beheld the first of my poetic visions through *Dechetal do Chennaib,* divining by finger ends, speaking a poem of vision. The vision was childish and dim; I spoke what I saw, of a great calamity I could not discern. Yet I have always remembered this vision, which occurred long before my years of training with Ganieda.

"I see a land by the sea, an angry place of woods, granite cliffs, and waves," I intoned from a half sleep. As soon as I came back to myself I turned self-conscious, licking my fingers again and giving a little laugh.

My mother, of stern and serious disposition, did not laugh.

"That is the place where you will go someday, for it matches your anger," she explained. There was a dark aspect to her I did not understand; she was determined and proud. I did not like that she would tell me with such certainly what would happen in my own life, and so I turned from her. She caught the gesture of my averted head, however, and afterward smiled tightly, observing that I was made like her—proud and hard. Seeing that I could be molded into a Druid princess, she bade me follow, that she might instruct me in the mysteries of birth and death.

Visiting the pigs on that same spring day, we saw a sow giving birth, then stopped to watch a cat birth her kittens. My mother talked to me of my body's mystery and of the ways of men. As we walked by the pig sties I listened to their grunting and snuffling.

"Fear them, mistrust them—their desire when they are near, their sudden distance," my mother warned, as we continued our walk in the woods. "Within a man's penis is the white seed of heaven, and within you, when your time comes to have the moon-blood, the red vessel of earth. A man desires nothing more than to lie with a woman—there," she said, poking at my legs with the stick she was carrying. "Between your legs, in your soft, open place."

My face was hot; I had no words. The mystery was closed to me, still a young girl. I turned back to look at the pigs. The sun was very hot overhead, and I felt uncomfortable in my woven tunic. My mother always spoke frankly, as if there were no mysteries.

"I do not understand," I replied softly, not looking at her. Suddenly a line from an old Druid poem came to mind:

Thighs shining with vetiver, tacky with blood.

Mysterious words spoken by the fairy Ailinn to her lover, which once had meant nothing, now frightened me.

"Nor would you, child, until it is yours to live and to bear children. When you are some years older, each moon will usher forth from you a cycle of blood flow—a sign of the fertile moon's waxing. You must heed that blood, for a circle drawn in blood is the crux of life and death, marking the movement of the Great Cycle. Hearken to my words! Choose the man who will press himself into you. Choose carefully! And be fair warned of his going, for he will go. That, too, is part of the circle." She turned away with a grave look.

"Will my husband leave, then?" I asked, following after her into the fields behind our house.

"Afterward, yes," she insisted.

"My father will never leave," I replied, certain of myself. I preferred my father's strong presence in the flesh to any girlish daydreams of far-off lovers—visions that had never captivated me anyway.

"Your father leaves often," she continued. "My sight shows me he leaves again with you, never to return."

Even though I quailed at her words, I kept quiet, certain that my mother's visions had nothing to do with my own father. Nevertheless I knew in one regard she had simply spoken the truth, for my father often traveled by himself into the deep wood, staying away for many days. Whither he went we never knew and did not ask, for he was a proud king and a fierce warrior.

My father was named Engan—*Talon*—and by marriage to my mother was king of Ravenoak. He was tall with dark hair and brown eyes, his face looking carved from stone, so beautiful was he! He knew some of the old Druid arts and could speak poetry with the best of our bards, reciting at length the poems of Taliesin and Talhearn. Like all bards he boasted of having spoken with Ceridwen herself once, deep in the wood where he often hunted. When he drank beer he could be a jolly fellow, hearty and full of stories and poems. Although he was as proud as my mother, in his more light-hearted moments a small smile of mischief often flickered across his face, especially when he looked at me.

At other times my father fell into deep brooding and could not be reached. Never have I forgotten the day I approached him when he swatted me away with his sword, leaving a purple welt on my arm that remained for nine days. I learned then how little I knew about my father, which made me love him all the more with girlish devotion. How I longed to save him from his demons, which darkened his brow like shadows on the Boyne. As soon as the welt healed, I again approached him, wanting a lasting scar by which to remember him. Trembling with love I stepped up to him, startling him out of his brooding one night as he sat in the wood, alone by a small fire. He drew his sword and slashed at me before he fully saw who stood before him. Although I was young and quick, his eagle's talon caught my shoulder at a glance as I dodged away, cutting it deeply albeit not reaching the bone. Since the pain was of my own doing, I did not cry. Even as I heard my father's cries for me, I fled further into the woods, staying there for three days, filling the wound with leaves so that a scar would form. To this day my left shoulder, marked by the wound, is where I carry my father, the powerful, beautiful King Engan.

From my father came my voice; from my mother the wisdom to use my voice. My hair was golden like my mother's. The eyes I grew were given to me at the transformation by Wolf, which was why I did not recognize her at first—she who became my spirit shape and guide.

As a girl I often played along the banks of the sacred Boyne, watching the swans float upon her breast while I breathed the air of the Otherworld, childish visions of which came to me when I stared into the waters. Long hours I passed gazing at the flapping butterflies, the winged souls of my ancestors flying around my head in orange and yellow rays, having returned to go with me through my *tuirgen,* my circuit of birth and death and rebirth. We of the Raven tribe had gone far from the old land, but our ancestors came with us. As I prayed to the butterflies for protection, I fancied that I saw on their small heads tiny birch-bark hats, the signature of the dead. As a Druid I understood death as marking the beginning of life, just as the birch is the oldest of the trees and hence the first letter in the Ogham alphabet, so my mother taught me. I would spend days wandering in the deep woods and along the banks of the Boyne, preferring to be alone.

At night when I lay on my cot watching the candle, listening to the sounds of the woods and the voices of the men as they told tales by the village fire, I kept an eye on the moths that touched the flame—for they, too, were my ancestors, come to bring me good dreams in the night.

The good people of Ravenoak either farmed the fields they cleared or moved deeper into the woods, and so I did not see them often together. Our family lived in the Great House of Ravenoak, which contained a hall for feasts. The royal fire burned at one end in a large carved-stone hearth. Each year when Beltaine came, as the earth awakened and the land grew warm, the people of Ravenoak would let their hearth fires go out and come to rekindle them through the ritual fire of our hearth. Afterward everyone gathered to feast under the stars at tables set beneath the spreading Great Oak. I would stand proudly with my mother and father, awed by the long line of people coming by one's and two's, dipping their brands in the flame and bowing, carrying the renewed fire with them back to their houses.

We celebrated Beltaine with feasting and music, storytelling and sacrifices to

Bile, the God of the Dead and our first ancestor. The Beltaine I remember most took place when I was nine years old, after I had tasted the Salmon of Wisdom.

After the people returned in the evening for the feast, eating and drinking went on far into the warm night around a bonfire set outside before the hall, under the stars. Everyone could smell summer coming, so felt happy. Tremendous sparks leaped and burst in the air, the fire popping and talking to us, telling stories of heat and light. The long table in front of the fire was set for my parents and our kin. All the people of Ravenoak, having come to drink and eat and be merry, filled the other tables arranged beneath the Great Oak. Through huge old branches the moon shone down on us.

Good food in abundance beckoned all to eat—even a wild boar roasting on a spit! Servers brought out puddings in tremendous iron kettles and set out bread and dried fruits, porridge and rabbit stews upon the long boards.

After a time the Wheel of the Year was brought forth, which my mother turned slowly while uttering a prayer to the Goddess Eriu: *May the seasons follow in due course as you watch over us. May Brigit offer us her protection as well.*

More eating and revelry followed until the bards came forward and sang, outdoing one another composing poems before the fire. My mother watched it all, unsmiling but with warmth in her dark eyes, which I glanced at from time to time; my heart felt troubled though I did not know why.

Full of beer, my father joined in the contests, jumping over the table and standing before the fire, howling out lines to rival the other bards. He boasted and danced with the other poets, gauging by the cheers of the people who had extemporized the best lines.

Next the musicians brought out harps, flutes and drums, joining the bards in singing merry drinking songs and songs of secret lust. I rose with my friends, the other girls of the tribe with whom I played at calixte twigs, as we chanted at length to the beat of drums accompanied by flute and harp. I can hear us still, singing a young women's chorus that made fun of the boys, secretly fearful of the men they would become when we became women. We sang in high, pure tones, ever faster to the beat of the drum, to Bile and to the reawakening year. I was shy to stand barefoot before the crowd and sing, but I was proud, too, for all knew whose daughter I was.

Afterward I crept beneath the table where my parents sat feasting, clinging to my father's leg as I listened to the music fill the air with enchantment, loving especially the sound of the flute. Only now do I see the fatefulness of my heart's desire, for Richard wooed me with his flute playing.

When at last the bards tuned their harps for storytelling—my favorite part of the evening—I stole away from my parents to sit down close to the fire. I wanted to catch every word the bards sang, so huddled alone lest any of my childhood friends whisper in my ear while the bards recited.

I heard that night, as I had each year, legends from the old land: of Tara and Connachta; then, going back to the very early days, of Ler, the Dagda and Madb;

of the Fomorians and how Eire came to be named. Glorious scenes of men fighting bravely, of men and women loving truly and untruly, of curses cast by jealous Goddesses lasting nine hundred years.

The chief bard stepped forward, an old man named Cormac who wobbled as he spoke. I did not much like him, but he had the true *imbas* and could improvise poetry for any occasion. People loved and feared him for his ability to make satire that had the power to destroy someone's reputation. On that night he stood to recite the *Colloquy of the Two Sages,* the story of the poetic contest between Ferchertne and Nede, two great poets of the old land. The story so made me shiver, transporting me back to the green hills whence I lived centuries ago in the old land, that some elf pulled at my heart, leaning close to whisper in my ear that one day I might make poetry as well. But when I once expressed this desire to my mother, I recalled, how she had scoffed and said it was men's work!

Still, my longing was true, for I could see the same longing in the eyes of others—the way the old ones listening to the bards grew quiet and thoughtful, leaning over their mugs of beer with queer, faraway looks. One or two of them glanced at my parents to see whether there was a chance we might return to our homeland. At the sight of that wish so evident on their faces, I realized then the terrible homesickness that we of Ravenoak carry within; our longing for the old land, for the old ways. That was my first taste of longing, and it was bitter.

Too soon the stories ended; the spell broken, most of the old ones simply shrugged and grinned at one another or pursed their lips while staring into the night-blackened woods, perhaps searching out some animal hovering near or unwilling for anyone to look deeply into their eyes. Even as a child I could see why.

At last my mother stood up very straight, her golden hair long and her gaze commanding. How I wished my own golden hair might one day shine like hers, as if lit with the fires of the sun! I could not yet see the pain that shining with the sun's light might bring.

"Good people!" she began. "The stories of Eire are noble stories, making our hearts long for our old land. Yet there is another story to tell: how we were forced to leave our homeland to settle in a new land. For the black-hearted invaders had commanded that our bards be silent, and they killed many of our Druids, forbidding us the old practices."

"You are not our true queen!" shouted a voice out of the dark night. All turned to see who had spoken, even though we already knew: Finn Green-Eye, so named because he had one brown eye and one green in his head. Some said that was what made him so troublesome, full of lies and mischief. Others insisted he had true visions.

"We have heard your nonsense before, Green-Eye," my mother answered, fire in her eyes. The villagers waited quietly as the old rumors about their queen returned like a whiff of rotting apples. I had heard the stories questioning my mother's lineage but had never believed them. That she was not fully Gaelic. That she had a blemish making her unfit to be queen, just as any blemish makes a woman or man unfit to rule.

"You know it is not nonsense, Queen Stern-Eyes," Finn retorted, provoking some titters.

"The story you tell is an old one, Finn," my mother answered, sitting down abruptly on her high-backed chair, resting her arms on its arms, giant carved raven wings. When she resumed, I watched entranced. "In ancient times barbarians invaded Eire—the Vikings, whom we called the Fomorians. Who were those people? They came and—"

"And had your great-grandmother and all her bastard children!" Finn blurted out in drunkenness. We still could not make him out in the dark, for he was sitting far back, away from the fire's light.

Hearing someone gasp, I turned. There beside the fire, near me, sat Finn himself, smiling and nodding at everyone. He rolled over in a drunken heap.

Then—whose voice had shouted from the back, near the woods?

The clang of drawn swords rang out as I turned to see my father, his own sword drawn, leap over the table, overturning cups and plates, and dart into the darkness. Others joined him, racing off into the woods. As the rest of us sat frozen, the men remaining made a circle around us, brandishing their swords, their hard faces trying to penetrate the dark. From the dark woods erupted shouts and cries, then a clamor of animal calls, which soon grew fainter. Unspoken on everyone's lips was the question: Whose was the voice that had mimicked Finn's?

After some time my father returned running, his men behind, their swords still drawn.

"Blood on the feast of Bile!" my father panted, sitting down next to my mother and touching her arm reassuringly. The other men fell back in their former places, keeping their swords drawn by their sides. Eventually my father dismissed the ring of guards, who broke and rejoined the feast. The musicians tuned their harps again and gave us music. Gradually the festivities resumed although a weight hung in the air, for the voice remained a mystery. Whenever a bird cried or the sidhe softly rustled the leaves in the stately ring of trees nearby, faces turned toward the dark forest with questions.

I huddled at my father's knee, under the table listening as he whispered to my mother.

"The damned Branna!" he hissed, while I imagined my mother's nodding frown.

"They will have the crown if you are not more careful!" my mother said openly.

"They are cursed!" my father spat. When the silence held between them, I could sense even from my hiding place my mother's scorn of him.

Still the music went on along with drinking and storytelling well into the night, until at last the exhausted dancers and musicians grew quiet. We were waiting for the old Druid Ganieda's yearly appearance in Ravenoak, during which he sat in judgment on matters too difficult for my parents to decide. He would stay for many days, and our people were happy to have him amongst us—even though he was a cross old man whose immense knowledge and power many feared. It was said that in his cottage in the deep wood he possessed a cauldron made from the first poet Ceridwen's own, which conferred youth upon the aged. I did not believe such stories, for why would Ganieda not turn himself into a handsome youth, had he such power?

Ganieda's visit culminated with the feast of Beltaine, whereupon he would utter a prophecy for the coming year before retiring. Every year we waited anxiously for his poem of prophecy, for he often predicted the harvest, warned of enemies arriving, and gave cures for illnesses that had not yet broken out among us.

Many faggots were heaped upon the dying fire so that soon it roared into new life, the flames springing wildly upward searching out the old magician. All our faces waited to hear the omens.

Ganieda finally hobbled forward, his wagging beard brushing against his heavy cloak. While he leaned on his staff over the fire, staring into the flames with his one good eye as large as an eagle's, the flames leaped in his face. Looking like an aged CúChulainn in war-fury, he began to chant prophecies for the coming year.

"Good people," he muttered, his voice gaining strength, "I speak in honor of Tlachtga, Goddess of the Druids and Bringer of Inspiration. She has spoken to me thus." He put his thumb in his mouth for a time, then withdrew it:

> Two hundred dead, many harvests in one year;
> A child of mine, golden queen of the dark.
> Not of Ravenoak; lost in the sidh.
> Bloodshed under the Oak, a new king;
> He drinks of the horse broth.
> The black foreigner comes in multitudes.
> A maid on the end of a rope.
> The Black Book hidden in the ground;
> A far descendant, Guryn, and a war.
> The black foreigner comes again.

After Ganieda finished he stood, silent, slightly rocking before the leaping flames. I sat stricken, my hand frozen against my mouth. Spitting into my palm as my mother had taught me and smearing my spittle, I looked into the crevasses of knowledge. In the flickers of firelight I was very still, limning the place of granite and sea I had seen in my first vision with my mother. Then I understood that Ganieda's vision was pointing to me and that I would someday, as my mother had foretold, travel to this place by the sea. Suddenly my heart ached for Ravenoak.

"Come, Ganieda—what do you see?" one of the young men called out, which shook me out of my vision. This time we could all see the speaker, and we laughed, for Ganieda had been like this since everyone could remember: droopy and pessimistic even on the eve of summer, or else speaking his prophecies in such a way that few could understand.

Except my mother, who always seemed to understand everything. I glanced at her; I still recall the look she returned, a signal that my life would change from that moment. In an instant I saw that my life running in the woods with my rabbits and playing with the goats and sheep was at an end; other tasks awaited me. I knew it and I did not like it, because like Ganieda I felt a powerful darkness rise and hover over the fire. The shadows playing along the trees moved in to surround the fire, making the flames flicker weakly against an endless darkness.

Dumbstruck like the others, my father studied me, his brow furrowed as if seeing something that he, too, did not like. Never before had he looked at me—the jewel of his eye—that way. Ganieda, of course, did not answer the plea to explain his prophecy but doddered off tapping his stick, soon vanishing into the dark woods. Until another year would pass he was headed back to his hut far from Ravenoak, where he lived with his pigs and his spells.

In time the people roused themselves from the long feasting tables, yawning and stretching. Leftover food was gathered up and taken to be thrown to the pigs and cattle; my father carried me to bed while I dozed, happy I was still the fair young one he held in his arms. Even so my dreams that night, more dark inklings, dispelled any lingering illusions of my future.

The following day my mother summoned me to confirm what I already knew. Tilting her head a bit while observing me closely, a hard half-smile wrinkled her face.

"You will go live and study with Ganieda, there to come to your strengths."

I nodded, trying to hold back tears. My life was vanishing before me; those warm days in the woods and the fields... I recalled the day I first found the fairies playing in the wood, though when I raced after them they disappeared, leaving me with the fairy-longing my mother had warned me about. The children who had been companions in my games gone to stay with uncles, aunts, and teachers, some of whom had sailed back to Eire, never to be heard of again. My first kitten, Aengus, black as the hearth and quick as fire—long dead and buried behind the Great House, out in the field where the wheat grew.

No one left, it seemed: neither my goats nor the rabbits nor Aengus; all a dream already passing into the Otherworld, leaving me with a great store of longing. Longing and loss, then, were to be my companions, which I would have to accept as always present. For longing and loss had shadowed my family going back ages, I gathered from pieces of stories my mother relayed. Although she had never revealed the full story of her great-grandmother, she too bore a loss. As for the longing I observed in my father's eyes, already I could anticipate his expression when he arrived to take me to Ganieda.

No, I would not cry before my mother the queen. I left quickly to fill my sack with clothes and to dress for the journey.

The prospect of my first journey opened up a wider world for discovery. Never before had I visited Ganieda in his cabin; no one in the tribe had ever visited him other than my mother, who went to learn spells from him. As queen she was chief among the magicians of our tribe. My mother had taken me to the enchanted circles deep in the wood where the Raven shamans prayed and sacrificed, but I was not yet old enough for initiation.

After saddling Grey, my father belted his purple cloak, fastened at the shoulder with a majestical gold brooch. Glimpsing that sadness in his blue eyes I could not bear to witness, I watched instead while he slung his sword and shield across Grey's back, calling me to mount in front of him. With only a small bag I mounted with my father's help, then turned to bid farewell to my mother and kin, and to those of our tribe who had come to see me off. My mother looked hard at me, lest anyone see the slightest blemish on her face. From then on, I carried that hard look in her eyes with me always.

In full view of everyone present, she spoke to me in a commanding voice:

"One day you will return to become queen, and the man you take shall rule as king of Ravenoak."

I looked at her with a question, for I knew as well as she that I would never become queen of Ravenoak. My certainty stemmed from a childish vision more vivid than any I had yet beheld. I saw myself riding to Ganieda's, saw the war with the Blackcoats; indeed, I saw in my own way all that Ganieda had prophesied. I saw that I would never rule as queen in Ravenoak. Why, then, had she spoken such words?

"Take the talisman of the queen," she added, coming swiftly toward me as she removed the emerald star from her breast, fastening it upon my shoulder. It was a fey gesture, which made me tremble for Ravenoak, for my mother, and for what my future with Ganieda held. As soon as she nodded once at my father and me, my father chucked Grey, and without looking back we plunged into the forest.

AFTER I BECAME accustomed to leaving Ravenoak, I chattered away like any child, asking question upon question, to which my father answered in his strong, clear voice. So happy was I to ride with him, I wished for us to meet Niamh on our path. She would take us into the Otherworld so that the journey would last all our days, neither of us ever growing older. There my father and I would eat beside a warm fire, hunting and riding through the Faery wood forever. A child's dream.

A full day we journeyed before making camp, whereupon we built a fire beside a huge fallen log not far from a stream. My father pulled a skin of beer and another of bread and cheese from Grey's saddle while I fetched water from the stream. As we sat eating and smiling at each other, my father told stories I had heard many times before, heroic stories of the noble warriors CúChulainn and MacRoith, Fergus, Angus, and Finn.

I asked him to tell me stories of animals, for I especially loved those. At home I had kept a deer as well as my favorite animal, a small wolf. Often, wandering in the woods I would hide behind a tree until a boar or a floating eagle passed close enough for me to venture out, that we might converse.

My father began with a story of the Brown Bull Donn of Cuailnge and the Cattle-Raid before turning to tales of Ysgithrwyn Chief-Boar, whom Arthur himself hunted, and of the despoiling of the lands by Twrch Trwyth, which frightened me. Then he spoke of Aife, turned into a crane by the sorceress Iuchra because of jealousy, who gave her skin to make the first crane-bag—the poet's repository of wisdom.

"Ganieda will give you a crane-bag," my father promised, looking straight into my eyes before quickly turning away.

"Not you?" I asked, preferring to receive the bag from my father.

"It is not mine to give, Little Tree," he replied, calling me by the meaning of my name Gwern. I had been called that ever since I sprouted tall as a sapling, certain to grow tall like my mother.

I looked around into the dark woods, where the waxing moon shone brightly through the trees. Watching a branch glow silvery in the moonlight, I thought of my animals and of what was to come from Ganieda; I began to pass into sleep.

"The apple!" I heard my father call out behind me as I dozed sitting against the log. Idly wondering at his words, I heard a strange swooshing as I was flung to the ground on my side, my eyes wide open and my heart suddenly pounding. Passing over my shoulder flapped the wings of some gigantic bird. I leaped up to follow its flight, assuming an owl had knocked me to the ground.

"Hsst!" my father whispered, glaring at me to keep down and to follow instead with my eyes. Crouching alongside him behind the huge log, I saw that it was my father himself who had pushed me down; I wondered at that. As the bird alighted in a clearing visible through the trees, I caught a glimpse of him in the dusky light. In the silvery moon shadow upon a branch sat an owl much larger than any I had ever seen. Already well north of Ravenoak, we were traversing woods no longer familiar to me.

My father stood up and, breaking off a stout piece of straight branch, strode quietly toward the figure without taking his weapons, which I thought curious. I jumped up and followed until we reached the moonlit clearing, where we waited in the shadows. Looking high up into an oak tree, I marked crouching on a branch a man-bird figure. Although he was covered by a hooded cloak so that I could not discern his face, I could make out that he clenched a salmon in his mouth. In one hand he was holding an apple that he proceeded to split in two, dropping one half to the ground. My father and I stayed hidden under the dark shadows of the trees at the edge of the clearing, watching.

"Who is it?" I whispered, prompting my father to jab my ribs with his stick. He then planted the stick firmly in the ground and closed his eyes. I learned later that he was divining by means of *Teinm Laida,* using the stick as a wand to see.

Looking down the tree, I saw a many-antlered stag pawing at the base, chewing on the apple half the man-bird had dropped. The animal was in its prime, royal of limb and proud of head; it took no notice of my father and me. Finishing the apple, the stag passed silently into the woods, walking with long, determined strides.

My father strode manfully to the center of the clearing; beneath the white moon he planted his stick once again in the ground before speaking:

> *I behold a wondrous bird, owl,*
> *Sitting in the ancient Oak.*
> *What is the vision of the mighty owl?*

Out of an ensuing silence I heard a high-pitched voice coming from up in the tree, though the words were lost on me, spoken in a language I did not yet understand. Later my father translated the man-bird's reply:

> *I see a child-woman, queen of no throne;*
> *Thrice blessed, thrice cursed.*
> *Generations pass, all is darkness.*

My father raised his voice in response:

> *The child is mine, Great Derg,*
> *Lord of the Animals.*
> *Is there an end of darkness?*

The creature answered:

> *Thrice-three generations*
> *The sidh dug up, all in ruins.*
> *Her crown gleams darkly for her daughter.*

Dropping my gaze, I spied a narrow-haunched wolf nuzzling the bole of the oak. When I looked up again, the man-bird had flown away; I saw only wide wings against the moon before he disappeared.

Suddenly frightened and cold, I ran into my father's arms. He carried me back to the fire and lay me down under many skins, rubbing my arms and shoulders as he looked seriously into my eyes. He got up to throw more wood on the fire, then returned to my side.

"Who was the creature?" I asked from under the skins.

"The great prophet Derg, Lord of Animals. He knows of your journey to Ganieda's and came to speak to me."

"Why could I not see his face?"

"Because you are not yet an initiate into the mysteries as I am. That I was able to see his face clearly and look into his eyes is a good omen. And yet—" he broke off.

Silent, I lay breathing in the musky air of the bear and wolf in whose skins I was tightly wrapped. I asked my father to tell me what Derg had prophesied.

"I couldn't understand, but I'm very afraid," I confessed.

"Derg appears on the Tree of the World, the Great Pole," he began, looking off into the dark as if reciting a lesson, trying not to answer plainly. "He carries in his mouth the Salmon of Wisdom, through whom he speaks. The apple is sacred to us, for within its cut half lies the sacred pentacle—like the five-pointed jewel your mother gave you," he said, pointing to my wrapped breast. "That was his stag who came and ate. And the wolf was—"

"The wolf is my spirit," I interrupted, pushing the skins away from my mouth.

My father looked gravely at me. "Yes, though it is not a happy spirit. Nor, according to our reckoning, is the wolf one of the oldest animals. Boar or horse would have suited you better, or even eagle—all ancient animals."

"As your guide is the eagle," I added. "And Mother's is the horse."

He nodded.

"The prophecy sounds very dim," I worried.

"It is a hard hazelnut you must crack, Little Tree," he replied, forcing a smile. I could see he was frightened himself, powerful warrior though he was. Many times I had heard the stories of his exploits against the red-browed Branna from the west—how my father single-handedly had kept their hordes from the gates of Ravenoak. But now he bent his head and would not look me in the eye.

THE DAY DAWNED full of fog with no sun, yet I awoke with a smile. Then the vision of Derg and his prophecy returned. Already awake and saddling Grey, my father motioned me to mount. He had put out the fire, scattered the ashes and stones, and was standing silently, looking with furrowed brow to the west, still dawn-dark.

Sensing that he smelled the Branna nearby, I quickly rolled up the skins and mounted, for we were in danger. As soon as I settled into the arms of my waiting father, Grey bounded forward without a word, knowing full well how fast he had to run.

Through the oaks and pines we galloped, up and down hills, Grey scattering the fog with his hooves. My father, ducking branches, had to push these out of our way, so eager were the mischievous tree spirits to snatch us off Grey. My father leaned his mouth to my ear.

"They are close by."

I nodded.

"They have found you out, Little Tree of Great Price," he warned.

I frowned at that. Of what use was I to the Branna? Reading my thought, my father spoke.

"Remember your mother's parting words: Because you are the queen's only daughter, the man who marries you will rule as king of Ravenoak. Bran's heir, Cian Redmane, has bruited it about that he will take you for his wife, thereby to rejoin our sundered tribes as one kingdom. What say you to that, Little Tree?" he laughed grimly, raising his voice above the thundering of Grey's hooves.

I shuddered, envisioning a rough-clad man on horseback leering and snorting at me, his mane of red hair flowing like a river of blood.

"You will be safe with Ganieda, for he protects his borders with powerful spells," my father reassured me. Even so, he donned his helmet from a pouch while we rode like spirits in the wind, as if we were the passing Sidhe. My heart pounded, for I did not understand. I was far from awakening to love and conquest; the travails of war were exciting stories to my young heart. Something thrilled in me and I felt years older, riding snugly in the arms of my father.

As we raced deeper into the endless woods, I still felt safe. When I felt my father stiffen, however, I sat up straighter so as not to burden him while he rode. He turned his head to listen; I heard the sound at the same time.

Horses were pursuing us, mounted warriors were coming! With wild eyes I looked up at my father, and he looked down gravely before settling into the saddle, tightening one arm around me. He spurred Grey on until the trees became a passing blur. The sun rising to our right could barely keep up with Grey, so swift was his pace.

All the while the horses were coming closer!

When my father sang out in a bright voice to Grey in a language I did not understand, the huge horse leaped forward, nearly pulling us off the saddle. I wanted to turn around to look behind us, but my father held me too tightly.

"Ya-hi! Ya-hi!" cried my father, drawing his sword as we dashed ahead, the silver gleam catching the morning sun and ringing out, high-spirited at smelling blood.

I knew my father's thought: We would not escape. And his next: We had to hide or else be caught. He glanced from side to side as we rode over flat ground, the pine trees spaced like sentinels. Spying in the distance a deer bounding through the wood, I pointed him out to my father, who turned Grey to follow. As soon as we drew near, I saw with amazement the deer was pure white with red horns. Off through the pine wood he ran as we raced behind, until we both spotted a mound some distance off to our right. The deer bounded toward it as Grey followed, throwing up boulders of dewy mud in our wake, making the earth thunder, as if it were hollow in this place.

Looking back at the woods whence we had come, now I could see. There in the morning sun gleamed ten riders in red—dark, determined men riding with lances and swords, their horses galloping with eyes of fire, nostrils flaring breath like steaming caves. Turning back around, I caught sight of the deer up ahead leap as if into the mound itself—and disappear! The mound was the size of a small hill in the forest, no taller than Grey and no longer than the feasting table in Ravenoak. It contained no opening, no way to follow the magical animal. Dashing toward the hillock, around and around it we rode, Grey rearing up before it, my father chanting in a loud voice:

Morrigan, we beseech you, open!
The blood of my child, open!

All the while that we were galloping in circles I was unable to see clearly, though my eyes were open wide and I could hear my father panting above me. When in a tremendous thundering of hooves the riders were upon us, my father forsook the mound and turned Grey toward them. Swinging, cutting and slashing, his sword all aglow, he drove Grey straight into them as I huddled down inside his cloak. Several warriors fell screaming before his furious onslaught, even as the others managed to pull their horses away.

"Cian, you will not have her by force!" my father shouted, his voice resounding like a horn through the woods. I peeked out for a sight of the man who would wed me and make himself king of Ravenoak in my father's place. As my father rode toward him, I could see that he was young and dark-eyed, red hair flowing down onto his shoulders. In a visionary moment I caught his story: A mere boy had once sat drunkenly around a fire with friends, boasting that one day he would take me and become king. A boy now caught by his words like poetry come [for its] due, compelled to prove the worth of his words by deed.

When he raised his sword a mighty clash resounded as he and my father struck one another with blow after blow, Cian always falling back before my father and Grey.

"Nuada's sword!" I heard the Branna cry out, fearfully pulling their horses back amidst yells of frustration and dismay. Taking no notice, Cian and my father fiercely threw themselves against each other, Grey bumping the broad flank of Cian's roan. Again and again their swords clanged in the misty woods, until with a mighty swing of his arm my father struck a blow on Cian's shield that splintered it in twain. Glancing off, it slashed Cian's cheek and drew a long gash along his forearm. Red blood leaped like an eager fountain from his left cheek and forearm.

At the sight of his wounded arm, Cian was seized with a blood-madness like CúChulainn in the throes of his warp-spasm. Fire blazing in his glaring eyes, his red hair standing on end and entire body contorted with rage, he charged at my father with a bloody cry. Clenching his sword and wielding it high with both hands, he brought it down so mightily that it glanced off my father's helmet and sank itself into his shoulder. My father uttered a great gasp as his body pitched forward over me, the hot blood pouring down over my head, blinding me in my right eye.

In utter terror I turned to the mound, frantically praying without knowing for what. Looking out of my left eye through tears of panic and pain, I spied a narrow gap in the mound that hinted at a doorway. Grabbing the loosened reins, I pulled Grey to face it, my father slumping over me, barely able to hold himself upright. I looked back to catch sight of Cian, his arm a bloody mass, sword raised over my father's head for the killing blow.

Gritting my teeth, I turned to face my enemy and, recalling all my mother had taught me, began to chant. At once a wind sprang up that blew dust in Cian's face and in the faces of his men, who had begun riding back into the fray upon seeing my father nearly dead. While I chanted and sang the wind blew fiercely, forcing Cian to wave his sword blindly—only to throw it down at last, spur his horse close to Grey, and reach out for me with blood-soaked fingers. As I chanted the spell of protection and fear, Cian suddenly drew his arm back with a loud cry of pain.

Knowing nevertheless the incantation could not save my father and me from harm, I turned again toward the mound. Though the cleft was too small for the horse to pass through, I tugged the reins and called out sharply to Grey. For one long moment he hesitated, his body tensed in fear, Cian and the others closing in behind us. The wind was dying down; my powers were not yet strong. Again I shouted to Grey: *Go!* And with a single, grand, arching leap he plunged us forward into the mound's shadowy cleft, as all the world went dark.

10.

The shape-shifter

ON A SUNNY HILLSIDE I woke from a dream of another sun and a happier time. When I came to my senses fully, I saw that it was no ordinary sun but a bright purple ball hanging like a lantern in the noon sky. I looked about in wonder, finding myself in a forest of purple trees shimmering with leaves of gold that were showering their goods to the earth in endless flakes. Leaping to my feet, I spied my father not far off. Yet there was something wrong with my sight! My right eye was dim. I closed the left—the right could see only as you see in the dark.

My father was deep in conversation with a tall woman dressed entirely in red, her hair red flames tied in two braids twisting down the front of her dress. She had wide, high cheekbones, very white skin, and eyes that flashed green. I had never seen a more beautiful woman in my life. As I drew near my father turned his cleft brow instinctively to me, blue eyes piercing me to see whether I was whole. Noticing his shoulder wrapped in white linen, I knew then that the strange woman had nursed him.

"You slept long," my father commented.

I stared at the woman.

"Come closer, child," the woman insisted. "You know who I am."

I shuddered. "The Morrigan," I answered, my eyes dropping from her sharpened emerald eyes that hurt to look in.

"This is my *sidh,* where you and your father are welcome." Although smooth and pure, her voice had an unshakeable authority, possessed of a timeless knowledge of life and death.

I bowed my thanks but remained speechless before this powerful magician, the Goddess of War. What could she want with me—or my father?

"My shoulder is badly wounded," my father announced, touching it with his right hand. "Deformed as I am, I shall never rule again."

"Does it hurt?" I asked, aware of my voice trembling as the Morrigan took the measure of me.

"Your father is healed by my magic," she replied for him. Touching his shoulder with her long-fingered hand, the bandages dropped away to reveal pink and whole flesh, wholly unscarred. "He is now whole."

The Morrigan spoke softly, though the tenor of her voice was as unrelenting and full of pride as war itself. I saw all at once that she had cast a spell on my father. Only if he remained in the Morrigan's sidh for all time would he stay young and whole. But if like Ossian he were to leave his fair Niamh's abode and set foot on earthly soil, he would once more suffer from his old wound, no matter the span of time passed. Time would overtake him with a vengeance; from the strong king who stood before us in his prime he would be transformed into an old man and just as swiftly into a doddering half-corpse, a sack of sagging skin filled with dried bones.

My father smiled gravely, touching his shoulder anew at the spot. His eyes said that though his shoulder was whole, he carried another wound I could but dimly see. At that moment I learned a powerful lesson about mortals and Gods and the love between the two. One glance at the expression with which my father beheld the Morrigan made me despair of his ever leaving the sidh with me. Already strained with longing, my heart grew years older.

I cleared my throat, speaking in a strong voice. "I am thankful to the Morrigan for healing my father, and I shall honor her name ever after. But what is to become of me—and can you not heal my eye?"

The Morrigan's laugh lit her fiery eyes. "The girl speaks bravely—"

"Little Tree! Mind your tongue!" my father admonished me, frowning. "It is not for us to ask favors. Yet—is your eye injured?"

"Let her speak," the Goddess commanded, not taking her proud eyes from me.

"My right eye is dim. Into it dropped the mixed blood of Cian Redmane and you, Father."

"It is your sight coming," the Morrigan declared simply, nodding.

"Can my daughter be healed?" my father beseeched her.

Now it was my turn to be angry.

"You see yourself she does not wish my healing. Do you want to lose your second sight, Little Tree?" she demanded.

Despite anger that an unfamiliar should call me by that name, I had to stop and think. Although I did not understand what the Morrigan meant, all my young life I had wished for that other kind of knowing, which my mother had promised would come to me in time. Yet never had she instructed that it would come as a wound! Confused, I nevertheless mustered my strength.

"I see but little, yet I see well enough," I muttered, staring hard at her.

"She speaks like a sorcerer already!" the Morrigan laughed, now with a glint in her eye meant only for me. And, indeed, I did see that she would not joust with me, small as I was—and mortal besides.

"Little Tree!" my father cried in a pained voice. "The Morrigan is our hostess. Mind your manners."

"You surely know that I am on my way to Ganieda the Druid's abode," I explained to the Morrigan, ignoring my father. The matter lay between the two of us, and I felt almost a woman. "Shall I be allowed to continue?" I asked her plainly.

My father's eyes widened in shame at my talk, his cheek coloring.

"You may—and you may take Grey with you," she replied. I did not like her, it was true, but I knew enough not to anger her.

So: There was to be no fight for my father; he would remain in her sidh forevermore. Nevertheless, I swore a silent oath that I would return to him, for my heart was leaden with grief at the thought of leaving him. Already I felt much older—as is often the way when one meets the Morrigan, so I had heard.

"Shall my father not leave with me?" I could not refrain from asking, hating myself for not holding my girlish tongue. I gritted my teeth as I spoke. Even though my heart was breaking, I did not wish the tears to show.

"Will you have him alive or dead?" she demanded simply.

I bowed before her and turned to my father. I could not help hating him then, too, for his weakness before her. At the same time, I knew my father was not CúChulainn to be able to withstand her.

"I would have him as he was before," I whispered.

"That is not in your power—at least not yet, Little Tree," the Morrigan proclaimed.

I challenged her with a hard stare. It hurt to look into her hard-sparkling eyes.

Grey at my side nuzzled my arm, lifting it to his bridle. I sighed and grasped it; although the day before I was too small to leap onto his back unaided, this day I turned and was on his back in a moment.

As soon as the Morrigan looked into Grey's eyes, he flicked his head, listening to her silent directions, then turned to go.

"Father!" I cried as he walked toward me, his eyes narrowed in pain. When he patted my leg I bent and kissed his cheek, wetting it with my tears of anger and frustration.

"You will grow strong and well," he prophesied. "You will become a powerful queen. I charge you to use your power to forgive all men what you have seen today."

"You lay a heavy burden on me," I retorted angrily. Now I would certainly not let him see further tears. Cry for him? Not I!

"It is yours to carry," he insisted sadly. "Let us not part in anger." He looked into my eyes; my little heart broke. Was he weak? Strong—? Bowing under his loss, he bore his fate nobly and firmly, I realized, for he, too, was suffering greatly. Never again would he look upon my mother, neither would he rule in Ravenoak nor dance and make poetry before the great fire. He would dance and sing only with the fairies and the spirits. Whether he would see his daughter again, I could not bear to think of then…rather that he taught me in that parting how to carry my life willingly and with love, and not to call it hard names. And so in learning that final lesson from him, I could not hate him. And yet I did hate him.…

Never in all my life since has such a leave-taking been more bitter, not even my daughter's, not even Richard's when he went away. Still, in that moment I foresaw many things: I saw myself as a woman, journeying to the Otherworld to find my father. Undertaking that heroic deed, which I might accomplish for my people of Ravenoak, would be my life's work. The sight was blinding to my good eye—and the face of Ganieda, his brow furrowed, arose as a warning. I shook off the vision.

I leaned again to hug my father, until he pulled away from me. I sat upright, no longer caring that the Morrigan see me so weak. As my hands touched the saddle, they felt the hilt of my father's sword, in its scabbard lashed to the saddle. On an impulse I drew it forth.

"I shall return for my father!" I sang out in a voice as loud as I could muster.

The Morrigan peered into my eyes. "The strongest foes in war are those wounded in love," she spoke in a voice kinder than I had yet heard from her. "Your wound is your sight. Use it."

Through my tears I recognized that my rival had a heart, albeit the fierce heart befitting a Goddess of War. Grey turned and cantered away through the trees as I rode, an absurd little girl of nine barely able to hold her father's great sword aloft. All the same, I held it aloft until certain I was out of sight of my father and the Morrigan, my pitiful arm sagging under the tremendous weight of the weapon.

I RODE GREY for what seemed like hours, letting him take the lead, for I did not know the way to Ganieda's house. Obscured behind layers of thick clouds that floated far above the trees, the sun was no help. I sat as if dead upon Grey's broad back, uncaring whether we should ever find Ganieda. Up and down hills we went, so many that after a time I was uncertain whether we were still within the bounds of the Morrigan's sidh or had instead become lost in the deep wood north of Ravenoak. I did not care. Gone was my father the king, and I was unable to rule myself. Still, I was restless in spirit, for already my small body was possessed by the angry demon who would drive me henceforth for revenge against the Morrigan and Cian Redmane. I was wholly resolute that all I might learn from Ganieda should serve this single purpose.

When after a time we came to a rude cottage I knew immediately it was Ganieda's, for all about the sagging little house danced the tiny blue lights of the fairies, as if hovering about waiting for the wizard to emerge and play with them. The lights gave me a flicker of joy before I dismounted with a heavy heart and stood long before the door, silent and sad. At last I sighed and knocked, my heart feeling like a block of dry wood. Little did I know then how quick to burn such a dry, scorched heart could be!

Presently Ganieda opened and with a nod led me inside. In appearance he was unchanged from the way he had looked for years: grey, grizzled beard in tangles down to his chest, dressed in a long, dark-blue gown decorated with a ragged fringe of tapestry lining the bottom hem, through which (it was said) ran a thread of pure gold. His one good eye leering at me out of sunken cheeks reflected the hungry and eager way he looked upon the world. What did he see to assume that expression? I wondered. His mouth was sensuous, the lips long and well-formed, full of thought; pursed as if about to speak. His brow was like two knobby cliffs overhanging cavern eyes.

At his urging I entered into the strangest room I have ever known, to this day, a world teeming with pictures and instruments and books of all sizes and shapes. A large black dog lying on the hearth where, though the day was warm, a fire blazed. And what a fire it was! Flames of all colors of the rainbow danced and twined themselves like imps at play. Truly a Druid fire! Over the flames was slung a black cauldron; I thought of the stories that said Druids brewed their magic in the cauldrons of rebirth. For all of the fifteen years I was to remain with Ganieda, I never saw the fire go out or even burn low. And always the cauldron hovered over the fire, the old magician forever breaking herbs and leaves into the cauldron and spooning potions out. Little wonder that my long apprenticeship with Ganieda would pass like magic....

I spied a small weasel curled asleep in a ball on a chair, next to a table strewn with papers and more books. Never had I seen such books! Large, heavy volumes bound in cracked red and black leather, closed with massive brass clasps: I was to read deeply in these. A raven hopped from desk to chair and back, cocking an eye at me. I bowed to him as protector of our tribe.

Strangest of all in this strange room was the sight of a giant Indian sitting cross-legged next to the dog before the fire, quietly smoking a long-stemmed pipe. Slowly he turned and regarded me silently with a look that frightened me more than the look of my new teacher.

"Enter, child," urged Ganieda in a voice grating and full of curiosity, which surprised me. It sounded altogether human, simply the greeting of an old man rather than that of an aged magician of immense power. As the Indian rose I marked that he was indeed of prodigious size, his head nearly scraping the blackened beams of the low ceiling. The bones of his cheeks protruded like lance points. His eyes nearly black looked at me with the distance of many years, so still were they. His mouth was set in a deep frown, his brow furrowed by a single line that ran from his black hairline straight down to his brow. He wore his long hair braided down the back.

"This is Oroonca Tall-Bear, medicine man of the Nipmuc tribe dwelling in the hills to the north," the old magician explained.

Bowing my head, I stood awkwardly in the middle of the room. I wished they would leave me there to myself for a time, that I might investigate all the books and instruments. Ganieda spoke.

"Well, we won't go away, since this is our place," he admonished. Blushing, I resolved forthwith to harbor my thoughts closely when near the old man. Pointing, he continued. "That is my dog Burna—and sleeping at my desk is Hella, a tiny weasel who came to stay. Gern the Raven is resident poet, our protector and deliverer of oracles. They are your friends now. You are very young, and though the daughter of a queen, you know nothing. You have much to learn. You will begin by keeping the pigs."

My eyebrows shot up as anger took hold of me. Pigs? That was peasant work! I knew enough about pigs from life at home, where from time to time I used to visit Diarmat, keeper of my mother's pigs. A hunched-over old man who knew everything about his charges, he was rich in stories. Even so, already I knew some Druid spells my mother had taught me; surely I was above such work as feeding pigs! Indignation flared in me, and in my queenly pride I sneered at the old man. Old man—! The man who was to become my wise, my greatest teacher!

"Nevertheless!" remonstrated Ganieda more forcefully, eyeing me as if he had caught the thoughts playing across my face. Again my face grew red; I would have to learn quickly not to give myself away. "You will begin at once. The pigs are descendants of Annwn, whom Pwyll brought from Wales. Do you understand, child?" he challenged, glaring at me out of his good eye.

When I did not answer he waved me away, disgusted. I knew he had been waiting for me to acknowledge the story. Although I loved the stories the poets used to tell at fireside, this story I had not heard. In the years to come I was to learn all the Three Hundred and Fifty Tales, to learn the many ways into and out of the Otherworld, the danger mortals invited in going there. I was to learn to use fairy thimble to avoid the wasting sickness that often comes upon those who have ventured into the Otherworld and thereby been touched by the fairies.

"They are in the back," Ganieda waved again impatiently, spitting into the fire before turning to his friend, leaving me standing.

Angry and embarrassed, I flushed for some minutes, then left the little house and wandered around to the back, where I found pigs foraging in a pen. Familiar with the chore, I lifted the bucket from the hook and began to slop the animals, my heart sinking. I had lost mother and father; my heart was desolate. Now I was to be enslaved to the crotchety old Ganieda! I mumbled smokily through my labors like a prisoner.

Set against a low cliff that ran downhill from the cottage, the well was built of stones closely fitted and forming a semicircle. I spied a small house further down a path, but the well drew my attention. For above the rim of the well against the cliff, set within a high niche, peered a large human skull—too large, I first thought, to be a man's. But it could be nothing else, and I marveled at its black eye sockets and dented forehead. Was it by this head that Ganieda spoke with the spirits of the dead? Beside the well resting on a slab of stone sat a small silver bowl, held fast by a finely wrought silver chain that was, in turn, bound by a staple of rusted iron set deep in the stone.

I shivered as I raised water, glancing up at the fearsome head leering down at me. Would I one day learn to hear the head speak?

Back to the despised pigs I trudged, dumping a bucketful into their trough. As they squealed and nudged one another for space, a demon of hate who wished to kill the pigs and run away suddenly flooded me. My nose felt foreign, like an unfamiliar protrusion. What was happening to me? Standing very still, I impulsively dropped to all fours, snarling at the pigs. They scurried away, squealing in fright and huddling together on the far edge of their pen.

What was this erupting? To my astonishment I was no longer a girl but some creature snarling with fevered eyes, licking my chops at the pigs, pacing back and forth in front of the pen, snapping and growling. I could have torn their flesh and devoured them, relishing the blood dripping over my teeth. Panting and racing back and forth, back and forth, I stared at my prey through eyes of blood. Back and forth I ran, the demon pressing my limbs, until after a time I began to weaken. I felt the demon leave me as the fit passed, and I collapsed in exhaustion on the ground, hot tears starting out of my eyes. For a long time I lay shuddering with cold, lost, shaking, until my breath slowed and my tears dried, leaving my cheeks stinging.

Although I did not know it at the time, that was my first experience of fith-fath, or shape-shifting. I had turned into an animal that for years afterward I could not name, knowing only that it ran on all fours and frightened the pigs. At last I was strong enough to stand and brush off my skirt. I was determined to find out which animal had so fiercely overtaken me, as if lurking near to spring upon my native anger. Much more study lay ahead of me before I could hope to know. Still, I never again hated tending the pigs, instead approaching them with proper caution. They, in turn, regarded me thereafter with sideways looks of mistrust.

SO BEGAN my studies with Ganieda as I sat by the master's side at his oaken desk, listening to him read from his magical books—primarily from the *Grimoire: The Book of Spells,* a huge book too heavy for me to lift, bound in black bull's hide, dusty with pages that smelled of old men. Curiously printed with elaborately painted lettering, the book contained intricate drawings of plants and animals as well as notes scribbled in the margins by Ganieda's own hand. Because I could not yet read when I first arrived, Ganieda taught me slowly, until in time the book opened its secrets to me.

In addition Ganieda read from the *Clavicule,* the master reference by Solomon of old that contained the names of all the demons in this world and the Otherworld, accompanied by lists of their habitats and habits, advice on how to avoid their spells, and how to cure those possessed by demons. Ganieda forbade me even to look inside this book until I was far along in my studies.

Thus did the years pass, as many a long and sleepy hour we two spent side by side studying those works! Sometimes I drowsed while listening to Ganieda's tireless, unhurried voice, curiously high-pitched. Often imagining in my half sleep an old aunt speaking to me, I nodded and smiled stupidly to be near her warmth. From time to time Ganieda would switch my sagging shoulder with a thin rod he kept at his side, making me start awake and rub my eyes. At first I was certain I was not disciplined enough to become a magician or seer, for all the learning made me sleepy. Then one day Ganieda explained that the state of half sleep was a way for the arcane knowledge to enter.

"I only wake you when you fall too deeply into sleep, Little Tree," he said, having adopted the name my father used for me.

On our long walks in the woods I learned properties of the plants for healing and spell-making that even my mother had not known. We traveled to a secret place where the little people lived; it was there that I lost all hope of my right eye healing. Although it had been dim ever since my awakening in the Morrigan's sidh, always I had held a secret hope it would heal, in spite of what the Morrigan had foretold.

On this day, however, Ganieda and I were walking in the dim woods, Ganieda poking the ground with his stick. By then I stood nearly eye-level with him; I walked alongside him that I might see from his perspective. Frustrated by my bad eye, which ached mightily, I kicked the ground and shooed my dog Fern, whelp of Burna, away from my side. Fern looked at me quizzically and trotted away, then returned.

"Bad eye! Bad eye!" chanted Ganieda teasingly, provoking a look from me. Could he be smiling—? He was! I was so surprised to catch his half-toothed grin that I stopped.

"Yes, but why does it not heal?" I demanded, irritated.

"All your herb cures have come to naught?" Ganieda asked.

For months I had been applying every bit of herb lore I learned to the task of finding a potion to restore full sight to my right eye. Late at night after Ganieda fell asleep I brewed potions in a small pot and stole away to my little room behind the house, where I would plaster these, still steaming, onto my bad eye. Nearly shrieking from the pain, I kept quiet as my good eye flooded with tears; I was certain that in the morning my eye would be clear. Yet each morning I awakened with a right eye that saw only shadows and dim light.

I shook my head.

"You must play, you know. How else do you think you will see the fairies? A serious heart cannot begin to see them. Have you no joy, Little Tree?" he tsked. "Such a serious young thing!"

"I have been made serious," I retorted sternly. At that Ganieda laughed outright.

I was offended, but he tsked again until I relented.

"I wish to learn the art of war," I insisted. "I have a score to settle with the Morrigan."

"Oh-ho! Little Tree will go to war!" he cackled. "Out of vengeance against the Goddess for loving her father!"

"Yes—to avenge a great wrong," I maintained. "I must learn the art of war so as to engage her."

"You will lose," Ganieda replied simply, stopping to stroke his chin with a serious air.

"Nevertheless!" I exclaimed. "I have no fear."

"Indeed, you have none," he intoned mournfully, wagging his head.

"Is it proper to fear?" I demanded. "I was taught otherwise," I added haughtily.

"First you will have to learn to dance," he nodded, a twinkle in his eye.

"Dance?"

"Of course. Any warrior who would learn the art of war must begin by dancing. You may begin with the fairies—if they will teach you. In time we shall see whether your way is the warrior's."

Fairies? I wondered, pricking up my ears and looking about. Ganieda's way was to lead me by suggestion in a new direction, then to sit back and watch whether my good eye opened in wonder. That approach seemed always to give him pleasure. I smiled to think of his silly tricks, recalling the time he had stood over me while I mixed herbs, then asked before walking away, "What do you think would happen if you mixed something altogether different into your concoction?" Pausing, I sorted through my herbs and plants and on a whim pulled out fairy thimble, which I mixed in. The result was a wondrous salve for a burn I had been suffering from.

Now, to meet the fairies! Only once, as a little girl, did I think I had seen them, flitting like butterflies back into their sidh before I could draw close…

"Do you think they like to be looked at directly, through two good eyes?" Ganieda twitted. Noticing he was peering into the wood off to our left with his one good eye cocked, I turned to look, too. Flickering amidst the boles of old rotted oaks, a scatter of tiny blue lights danced lightly.

As Ganieda murmured a chant in the secret language he had taught me, I fell into rhythm with a song of honor to the fairies:

> *Old ones, entrance to the Otherworld,*
> *Kindly spirits of the blue flame.*
> *May the eye be blessed upon seeing you,*
> *May the heart be comforted.*
> *Full of holes! Full of holes!*
> *The earth is your wicker basket*
> *Of flickering light through our blindness.*

Ganieda and I chanted together—this children's song that had seemed so silly when he first taught it to me. He began to move his narrow body this way and that when we had been singing for a time. I followed clumsily.

The little lights began to shine more clearly, and as we two danced our slow dance near, winged shapes showed themselves for a moment—then were gone.

"Their world is fleeting," I observed, a little sadly.

Ganieda eyed me. "It is our own world that flees. Your good eye is the blind one," he grunted. "Which would you have?"

I paused, my breath trapped in my lungs like a stopped bellows. Life is choosing, Ganieda had taught me; now the choice wavered before me. All the world lay still, as if waiting for my answer. I looked into the Otherworld with my blind eye…and in an instant I decided. After all my longing to have my sight back, at that moment it became easy to give up the hope. I knew from then on I would never again brew a potion secretly, sneaking like a thief in the night—while Ganieda slept—to repossess what I had already sacrificed. As I turned my head to look once more at the fairies, my right eye dimmed further...until winking out.... And ever since I have been half-blind.

Then how brightly sparkled the little blue lights! What a marvel as all the earth was a-chatter with the airy, slight, half-silly sounds of fairy song! Ganieda and I sang softly along, dancing all the while through the deep wood, the blue lights dancing around us, fleeing this way and that. I could only glimpse them barely, like the most fleeting of feelings, but it was enough, and so we danced and my heart was lighter than I could remember. It seemed we danced for hours as the blue lights played, into the wee hour of the morning, which brought its own yellow light. Tiny wings and lighthearted sounds flickered into thin air and were gone....

Ganieda and I stopped.

"On Samhain we shall return, when the barrier between the worlds opens," Ganieda promised, as I well knew. For each year on Samhain as the leaves showered us in waterfalls of red and gold fire, we children used to creep into the woods by night, behind the adults, in search of fairy knolls. Lights I had seen—but never a fairy. Some of the adults, however, would be gone for days, only to return haggard and heartbroken with stories of having wooed fairies deep in the wood. The tales always ended the same: some misfortune falling on the head of the poor man or woman, despite using fairy thimble to ward off the deep longing that can kill mortal life. As we walked back to the cottage, I wondered whether finding the fairies was such a pot of gold. Already the longing for the magic of the Otherworld made me ache.

FROM THE OLD DRUID I learned many things: the lore of the ancient times; why milk is white and the wife loving; why the goat is bearded and the wheel round; learned of the dry-craeft and the other sacred mysteries. The thousand and one secret spells to chant over potions and herbs I learned by heart, listening to Ganieda's voice crackle like dry leaves in the wind, his knobby hand beating time with a stick while he spoke. Else while he beat time I recited, always in poetic form, the many spells and incantations he taught me: to bend fire and make the Druid wind blow; cause the cat to rise in the air and hover there; and make the door open and close to fan itself...

All these I learned as the years passed, yet they were mere knowledge until my initiation, until they became blood-knowing. For with my initiation I died and returned in the required way, so that I knew both death and birth and saw each place in the circle. It was then that I learned to speak the truth of the collar and to hide what must remain hidden.

"The fundamental truth, Little Tree," explained Ganieda one day, when I had grown taller than he, "is that with our limited horizon we see only a part of the great circle. In the way of the earth, the circle bends to connect itself. But we, traveling the surface like ants, see only a small part of the circle; our own life followed by death appears as a straight line. We cannot see as a whole the circle bending under the earth, do not see that we meet our own existence again."

These were fateful words that I did not understand for a long time.

DURING THOSE rich fifteen years I stayed with Ganieda, sleeping in my little loft at the back of the cottage, I grew into a young woman. Many times I was angry and cursed the old man; many more times I would have fallen at his feet had he allowed me. The moon-blood began in my sixth year as a student of Ganieda, as my mother had prophesied. Remembering her words I made a prayer to the blood, for I feared at first my life was slipping out of me in the night. Though I never spoke to Ganieda about it, I noticed he was kinder to me during the full moon, once touching my stomach with his scratchy fingers in silent acknowledgment. Because the mystery set me apart from him, I consulted instead with the cow and the pigs, having no mother to ask. Strange to feel currents moving in me like hands making the shapes of waves!

Grey grew old and died finally, after a long time spent merely standing in his stall and munching hay, in spite of Ganieda's complaints that he was eating too much. He was my last living link to my father, and I loved remembering my father still astride him. Burna, Ganieda's black dog, died, too, as did the raven and the weasel Hella. Ganieda had given me one of Burna's pups, and this was my dog Fern. We slept together in the straw bed, he never leaving my side.

"How old are you, Ganieda?" I once asked, feeling sad over Grey's death. Ganieda seemed always to have been old.

"Six hundred years and then again threescore," he declared without glancing up from reading the *Clavicule*.

"Is it true you were on board ship when we came to this land, many, many years ago?"

Now he looked up. "I was on the ship, guiding it as we sailed across the Plow Tail. As a boy I studied at the knee of Ban Buannan, the Long-Lived Lady."

"Who was she?"

"From the dim times, she was my teacher. I do not know whether she lives yet, but if she does she is seven times seventy my age."

"Will I grow as old as you and become like Brigit Greyhair, who mutters and drools as she walks the paths of Ravenoak?"

Ganieda considered. "Time shortens as the world grows older. Perhaps for centuries nothing happened during the very old times, but now that many changes occur, time babbles along more swiftly—and so do our lives. I do not know the answer," he finished.

IT WAS TRUE that Ganieda's cottage was protected by strong spells, for though I wandered in the woods gathering herbs and berries to make medicines and magic potions, never did I come to any harm. We saw the Branna ride by from time to time peering through the woods at us, but it was as if an invisible hand kept them some distance away. Once I caught sight of Cian Redmane himself, who seemed to have grown into a serious-faced man, his red hair flowing down his back and a frightening dark scar slanting across his face—the mark of the wound my father had given him.

I was alone with my herb basket and Fern, who growled and would have rushed at Cian had I not stayed him. Cian, too, was alone, though I could hear other voices some ways off. Reining his horse, he stared at me, eyes large with fury. He dismounted in a storm and made to rush at me, but stopped, his face slanting as if from a blow. I stood very still, trusting that a spell from Ganieda held Cian away from me. I, too, was possessed by a fury for revenge against Cian, against the Morrigan, against the whole world—for taking my father from me.

Other sensations, however, took my attention. Ever since my dim right eye passed into blindness, the sight in my left eye had grown sharper. Now as I looked at Cian, I sensed the stirring of hidden life. And may the fire consume me, I wished to kill this warrior; to embrace this warrior. In deep shame I hurried away, my thighs shaking. One day I would wrestle with him, my enemy.

Rushing from him as he stood there glowering, I renewed my vow: All my studies with Ganieda were wholly in the service of avenging my father. I would use the powers Ganieda taught me and return first to the Morrigan, then to Cian.

IN TIME I became friends with Oroonca, who took me to visit his family in the long house of his clan, the Bear tribe. So it was that I learned to speak his language, just as Ganieda had done. His mother was a beautiful old woman named Nanepa Sharp-Moon who had a head like a brown nut, a face etched by fine lines, and a clear, sharp, watchful look. So unlike her son's eyes, which outwardly were dull and seemed to see nothing! Her nose was a long, narrow hook like a crescent moon. Her speech I could scarcely understand, for she was toothless and mumbled. A powerful sorceress in the tribe, she showed me some of her secrets and gave me a blue healing stone that I kept in my crane-bag. She had kind words, too, for my moon-blood.

A bad spirit hovered about the one or two white men trading for furs at Oroonca's village, I sensed, so I avoided them. Oroonca told me they were from the seashore, coming at times through the woods to find Indians with whom to trade.

"Do you trust them?" I asked.

"They worship a God not of the deer and the oak," he replied, leaving me to puzzle over that. In Ravenoak we heard tell of other peoples who had sailed, like us, across the seas to the new land, then built houses and villages along the coast wherein they were thriving. Even in remote Ravenoak, we feared lest they be Britons come again to subdue our Druids and poets. But as a young girl I paid little heed to such matters, for no strangers other than the Indians came to Ravenoak.

By means of signs and gestures Nanepa encouraged me to meet the other girls my age, who played in a circle by the center of the village and were often together laughing and singing. So I joined other girls of the Bear clan on journeys into the woods to camp, where we would sing and dance around the fire we built. With no elders and no boys, only ten or twelve girls my age or a bit younger, it was much like singing in the chorus with the other girls of Ravenoak on Beltaine, gathering around the kindling fire. I was very happy playing amongst the children of the Bear clan—a kindly, fierce red tribe. For years afterward I had visions of their deaths—but who needs second sight to see what the white Englishmen have done to the red people?

From my Bear clan sisters I learned about being a woman. Sharing the arrival of our moon-blood, we would rush in secret far upstream to wash and giggle and talk quietly. Even as I watched my sisters go off with boys from the tribe, whenever a brave approached me I swatted at him and drove him away. For I was a queen, I reminded myself: of a different rank from a common mortal, no matter how beautiful the boy! My sisters thought me foolish to resist a boy's advances but left me to my own ways. Soon I found myself alone in the woods beside our campfire, my sisters having gone with the boys into deeper woods than I knew how to track at the time. Yet I did not fret; I was the proud daughter of a proud mother and naturally kept myself apart from the rest.

Just as Ganieda taught me all the secrets he knew of medicine and magic, so Oroonca instructed me in his Indian shaman ways. Taking me along on many hunts, he taught me how to make traps and how to put on the guise of deer or rabbits so they would not suspect me. From him I learned how to run through the forest at great speed without tiring; how to read the clouds and smell humans in the air; how to distinguish the tracks of the fox from those of the coyote; how to determine which animal had broken a twig and whether it had been hurrying or slowing down, foraging or looking for a mate.

I drank in all that Oroonca and Ganieda had to teach me, always keeping before my mind's eye my cold desire for revenge against Cian and the Morrigan. That desire imparted to all my studies the salty taste of blood.

One day Oroonca led me deep in the woods to a sacred place of his people. As I held onto his large hand, we entered a cave through a large-mouthed opening. He kindled a torch and carried it lightly in his free hand. Down a long, rough corridor we walked slowly, the walls narrowing on us. Eventually the ceiling became so low we had to crouch to go on, although before long we seemed to reach the end of the tunnel.

Oroonca in the lead grunted as he confronted a large stone lodged at the end of the tunnel. He had never said anything about this place before, though that was not unusual for him. I assumed we were simply exploring a new cave. Thrusting the torch into my hand, he pulled mightily at the stone until with a single strong grunt he dislodged it. Pressing his elongated body through the small opening, he reached back to take the torch and motioned me to follow.

Crawling in after him, I felt the passageway become so narrow that the walls pressed in on all sides, and I wondered how Oroonca managed to struggle through the space. I felt as though I might suffocate, but still we crawled on. Life was nothing but *this,* I thought darkly—crawling endlessly through a tunnel barely large enough to squeeze through—and I feared the earth might press in upon us until we merged finally with the rock.

At last the tunnel ended, opening into a cavernous room. I stood up, brushing myself off while looking up at the lofty ceiling, made of stone that flickered slickly in the torchlight. A soft tinkle brought my eyes down. In the middle of the tilted stone floor gurgled a spring. After fastening the torch in a niche in the rock, Oroonca knelt before the spring and chanted some Indian words unfamiliar to me, then cupped his hands in the water and drank. He turned and bade me do likewise.

"What is the prayer?" I asked, my hushed voice echoing in the still, sacred place.

"I have chanted for you. You are welcome to our mother," he whispered, unsmiling in his usual way. I reached my hands into the cold water and slurped water down my chin.

I regarded the room more thoroughly, following the curling smoke from the torch as it wafted toward the ceiling. "Look—paintings!" I exclaimed more loudly, pointing upward. Along the curved ceiling, higher than a woman or man could possibly reach, were scenes painted in reds and browns and blues: hunters pursuing prey and engaging in ritual sacrifices; a shaman dancing on one leg in a sacred circle, spirit animals hovering around him....

Oroonca nodded, looking up. "Very old," he explained. "From the early times before our knowing."

We stayed long in the cavern, Oroonca teaching me all he knew of the paintings and about his people's dreaming time. I left knowing I would return.

"YOU WILL BE FIRST of our clan both a Celtic shaman and an Indian shaman," Ganieda smiled one evening many years later, when I had reached womanhood. We were sitting on stools outside the door, Fern beside me, looking up at the stars on a cloudless night. It was fifteen years since I had left the Morrigan's sidh and arrived at Ganieda's door.

Having studied hard and long through those years, I was able to cast spells of protection, to make myself invisible, and to concoct the thousand and one cures Ganieda had taught me. I could make the pine wither or prosper, and I knew the uses of claw and fang and fir in all the incantations. Looking glimmeringly into the future, I could foretell small events, especially those having to do with our animals.

I knew when a pig was to produce a litter before she herself knew, and I foresaw in dreams a goat grow ill or escape by jumping the fence.

On this night blue lights danced in the great oak trees, and a light singing seemed to come from far off, far over the sea that sent no smell this far from shore, far away from olden times. Or was it the wind?

Fifteen years! Even if Ganieda did insist, with an old man's sense of time, that I had been his student but eight. The warmth of summer hid like a secret within the cool evening air, for winter was coming.

Now that I was taller than Ganieda and nearly as tall as Oroonca, they had taken to calling me Tall Tree. Ganieda was pointing out the various stars, explaining to me for the hundredth time the meaning of their constellations. And, as with all he imparted to me, I still recall everything, even to the smells of clean pine and moss and the scent of that night air, when I close my eyes.

"The time has come for your journey to find your spirit animal," Ganieda announced, shifting direction as we sat brooding beneath the stars.

"I know my guide is the wolf," I replied easily. After so many years, I was quite comfortable with the old magician. Indeed, I had come to love him.

He glanced quickly at me with those sharp, overgrown eyebrows, stroking his beard. With his high-pitched, old-woman's voice, he shot back, "Indeed? Then what need have you of me?"

I quickly demurred.

"Has the wolf come to you, then?"

"In a dream," I replied more softly.

"Come to stay?" he continued, peering again at the stars.

I had nothing to say, not understanding what he meant. A wolf had appeared to me in several dreams.

"In a dream a running she-wolf was bearing children as she ran. From her belly emerged a wolf pup and I together, then we both ran off in different directions," I recited, breathless. "When angry I have fallen into an animal on all fours. For years I did not know which animal, until she appeared in this dream."

Ganieda shook his head slowly, squinting upward. Distractedly I, too, gazed upward, wishing I could see what Ganieda beheld there.

"Tomorrow Oroonca will come, whereupon you will make your first true journey into fith-fath. This shape-shifting is different from dreams and the same. You will learn your spirit animal—perhaps of more than one. Then you will see. It is the nature of humans to desire to know everything, and to believe that we do know. The secret of the shaman I can teach you in a few words: It consists in not knowing. Once you focus your mind on setting it free to roam, knowing neither what will come nor why nor how, you make a connection with the Otherworld where reside the fairies and heroes, the ancestors and the animal helpers. Where the stories are kept, where the secret knowledge is protected. Some reach that place through anger, some through fear, just as the Morrigan's sidh opened once you, in a moment of terror, leaped. It was your jump—without knowing what would come or why or how—that opened the door. Which is all the more puzzling, considering our aim is to be as alive and awake as possible."

"Then it is a matter of knowing, in a way?" I ventured.

"Our learning is essential—no one enters the Otherworld and receives its gifts out of ignorance or childlike trust, even if those states might lead us to the door."

"Then why not leave off learning before the knowledge of root and branch and the lives of the world, which you have taught me? Of what purpose are they?"

He turned back to me, his eye fierce and glowing. Long as I had been with him, I still feared that look and trembled. "If you enter the Otherworld in ignorance, you will emerge more ignorant! Being lost is a dangerous path, Tall Tree—beware! You have seen the Senchan? He wanders about Ravenoak in rags, tongue hanging out, spittle draining down his chin, eyes vacant in his head."

I remembered the old fool whom many revered as touched by the Gods. He spent his days meandering through Ravenoak's farms, receiving food from each family he called upon. Some sought out his prophecies, though I found in his mutterings only nonsense.

"He was indeed touched, but he has nothing to tell us of his touching," Ganieda continued. "He entered the Otherworld unprepared and so was driven mad. It can be just as dangerous to journey into that strange land too well-prepared and armed. There is a narrow crack through which we must slip—between all things set in motion by the Gods and all things set in motion by mortal man....

Put all your knowing, so dear to you now, aside tomorrow when you journey. Let it bear you up, if it will. You have learned much, Tall Tree, but you must not make the fatal error of believing that you are your knowledge. Do not be too quick to reach for your learning, as if it were a weapon to protect yourself against the fear that will surely come. For the Otherworld is a fearful place! Let yourself be taken, only sparingly—*sparingly!* I would not have my work go to waste, nor would Oroonca be pleased, to see you reduced to a babbling idiot—or else to a useless, vain thing, hoarding your experience like a miser. Worse yet are those for whom knowledge of the Otherworld kindles an immense greed for power. Thus evil enters the world!"

Ganieda fell silent. Never in all my years with him had I heard him speak so many words at one time. His wide mouth pursing, his good eye on the stars, he had more.

"Have you no fear, Tall Tree?"

He waited, expecting an answer.

"I have fear. I have much fear."

He regarded me closely. "In these eight years, I have never seen you afraid. Were you afraid when you awoke in the sidh?"

I thought back to that hateful time. "I was angry."

"In the stories you have learned of lovers' souls, the *riocht*—the soul journey of a lover—is always bent on finding her mate. It is ever so."

"Is my initiation bound to love?" I asked with a smirk, feeling a growing strength. I knew full well what initiation would consist of, and even though I was hesitant and shy to make my first journey, I was not afraid. I knew I would gain many powers.

Ganieda glared at me. "You are a proud one, young thing! You have learned nothing! *Nothing!*" He stood and tottered off into the dark woods, chanting some words lost to the trees. The blue lights flickered and flew off as a cool night descended on us. I sighed and walked slowly after the old man. I shook my head at him, for I was now full of disdain as well as pride, thinking the old magician was merely cranky as usual.

When I caught up to him I fell into silent step beside him.

He spoke to the trees. "What do you know of love, child? Or of beauty?"

I spoke from rote memory, my voice a monotone. How well I knew whither he was leading! "I know of the seven types of loves: the love of the child for the mother; the love of the father for his children; the love of two who share their hearts—"

"Enough!" he cried, waving his hands, his voice making the trees ring. "You know nothing! It was wrong to have kept you cooped up here with an old man. Did you not fall in love with a young brave from Oroonca's tribe? Have you not had your heart broken when I was not looking? Did you never run off into the dark night, while I studied or slept, to meet a lover under the Great Oak, heart pounding in your mouth with anticipation and fear and longing?"

I was silent for a time. There had been no brave, only silly boys sidling up to us girls of the Bear clan whom I shoved away. Taller than any of them, I had been proud and embarrassed. Cian Redmane and his vow to have me leaped like a stag into my thoughts, but I hurried away from his image.

"Ah yes, Cian Redmane the reprobate!" Ganieda cackled, licking his lips. "He's not for you—you know that, don't you?"

Suddenly Cian's face came to mind again, and this time, to spite the old man, I smiled inwardly at the younger man.

"But perhaps, perhaps it's enough. Child, a wizard is a lover in another guise. You cannot become a wizard without learning the ways of love. Leave off your pride! The preaching of the Blackcoats in the name of their God that love driveth out fear is a lie. Love brings fear, and without fear to guide you, you will be lost tomorrow. Approach your birthright with certain pride, and you will fail. Tomorrow, tomorrow…" he muttered, meandering off through the trees again.

I caught up to him again. "Think of your father tomorrow," he said, a little sadly.

"I have long sworn to find my father," I countered.

Ganieda turned toward me but suddenly began to walk quickly back to the cottage, whereupon he flung the heavy door open. Striding to his scholar's chair at the desk, he plunked himself down, studying me carefully.

"You may believe so, but beware of not giving suffering its due," he instructed.

"What suffering is that?" I asked cautiously. Though he was still angry and impatient, the atmosphere had loosened enough for me to sit down beside him. It was my right as his heir.

"There was once a king who lost his throne. His children took everything he had, leaving him but a pittance. The poor king was forced to decide which child to live with. When his firstborn offered him little, in anger he declined and petitioned the second. The second child offered even less, so the king, being mortal, returned to the first. His firstborn offered him less than the second, and so the king, bargaining against his own suffering, lost all."

"Am I to suffer pain?" I pursued slowly, brushing an invisible mote from my leg.

"We all suffer pain—it is the way of life!" he snorted, reaching down a tome from the high shelf and setting it on the desk.

"And there is a deeper pain," I nodded, following his thought. I overlooked his shoulder as he scanned the book.

Peering closely at the torn, stiff pages, he flipped through them slowly, then continued. "You suffer over your father, which makes you stern and wary, but all pain contains a deeper pain. Be wary of bargaining with pain."

"All pain?" I demanded, unbelieving.

Evidently he found what he had sought, for he looked up at me directly, his long, bony finger pressing against a spot on the page. I arched my eyebrows to make out what he indicated. "Remember on your journey: There is a place more terrible than the painful spot that grips you, and there you must go in order to be free, washed clean, and ready for your life. Our period together is finished, as each in turn must be. Another begins."

I was dazed by these words, though I have remembered them clearly all my life. Only when Richard came to me did I learn where my true journey led. Then was it that I lost my pride fully, for only then did I love fully. All my learning came to life once I came to understand: Divining by means of fingertips was inseparable from touching Richard.

Richard came years later; on that evening I was but twenty-four and had other things to think about. Right then my future was more dim to me than ever. Ganieda was mumbling as he continued to scan the book. He tapped his finger and poked me again.

"Beauty—you have not answered my question concerning beauty." He waited.

Taking a breath I recited again for my teacher. "Beauty resides in all things and draws them together; it is the sun rising and the moon setting, is—"

"Enough!" he cried, holding his hands over his ears. "This is more nonsense, worse than before!" He pressed me onto my stool with two hard, powerful arms. Shuffling meditatively to the fire, he reached down his wand of many colors, pointing it at the fire and swirling it abstractedly as he spoke.

"Beauty is the deep soul of the world, which anyone with any sense longs after.

Beware those who mistake the things that shine for the essence. You have learned that beauty is always half hidden, half revealed. I have taught you everything I know but one thing, which I have been saving for the eve of your initiation. The book there—" he turned, shaking a finger at the book before my eyes, "shows the correct incantation for invoking the Spell of Eternal Beauty. Yet the spell must remain a secret and never be cast."

I read the strange incantation written in the book before me, the letters seeming to dance on the page. Then I watched the back of my old master, who had already returned to the fire and seemed again sunk in thought. "Why never cast it if it is written down, and we possess it?"

"Can you tell me where lie the roots of eternal beauty, Tall Tree? For they lie deep, as do the roots of all created things." He turned, his eyes bearing down on me.

I thought hard. "In a lover's eyes—?" When he did not answer, I tried again. "Or heart?"

"Yes and yes, but they are rooted deeper than that, for the beauty in a lover's eyes and in one's own heart are themselves rooted in these. I have taught you to hide your soul for protection, in the Druid way—which is but a reflection of nature's ways. Beauty hides in the Otherworld, where its roots lie. Do you understand then why its spell must never be invoked?"

"Because it is death to invoke it," I concluded, seeing with Ganieda's eye.

"Good. Now you are ready to learn the spell."

"But—why learn it if it is never to be cast?" Not having heard my own answer, I was growing impatient.

"Beauty casts its own spell; it does not need us to cast it. Beauty's roots lie, for mortals, in death and transformation. To learn the words of the spell is to possess the knowledge that to cast it means certain death. We keep the written record of the spell to remind us of this; knowing that the humble words on a page make present the invisible treasure of beauty. The words tease us to recite them and cast the spell, but we must not, for this is the essence of the secret: to have and not be able to use. This awakens us again and again to the awareness that we do not so much shift the shape of things as we ourselves are shaped by them—by the world, by beauty, by love—and that we stand as mortals with one foot in the Otherworld. Beauty, then, need not be invoked, for it resides always within us: the beauty of our own deaths. Therefore study the words and know that you are peering into the pit of darkness and mystery."

"Then we are…we already possess—" I was thinking out loud, "—eternal beauty?"

Ganieda smiled. We two proceeded with studying the spell.

After several hours I left Ganieda and wandered to the back of the cottage, opening the rutted plank door to my loft as images and fears dragged on my soul like a plow heavy with spring mud. Fern whimpered at my side. He had become an old limping dog, by now more blind than I. The pigs were quiet, one or two snuffling along the ground in search of food. I absently lifted the bucket and tossed a few grains into the pen, the pigs still regarding me, despite so many years, with distrust. At the prospect of the next day, my heart fluttered. I was aware that I might be looking at the pigs for the last time. Indeed, with *that* eye it was the last time. I bent down to talk to Fern.

"Old boy, do you possess this beauty, too? Am I only now catching up to you?" As I patted his head, he smiled in answer and nuzzled me with his cool, wet nose. He shivered like an old man. I stood up with a deep sigh, feeling like Fern—*old, old, too soon old.*

THE FOLLOWING MORNING I performed my chores as usual, then waited quietly near Ganieda's desk until he finished his reading in the *Clavicule*. A strange odor hung in the air, one I had never smelled before from any of Ganieda's potions boiling in the cauldron. It was a smell of overturned moss and something darker, reminiscent of the female body—an old smell, as if musty from cold water seeping through the wet earth.

I knew the book Ganieda was reading was the one he had made special effort to teach me: *Solomon's Key, the Clavicule.* It contained numerous chants and spells and the names of all the demons, as the wise King Solomon himself had set down.

Ganieda motioned toward the fire. "Drink that," he directed, pointing a bony finger not at the cauldron but at the kettle steaming near the fire. Pouring a cup, I drank the hot broth, burning my mouth in haste before turning back to Ganieda.

He came close and peered at me. "You have grown into a woman, Tall Tree. We shall soon call you by a new name. There is much to be done today."

As he was speaking Oroonca opened the door, ducking his head under the lintel.

"The Little Tree has become a strong oak," the Indian intoned solemnly. "Today she will be hewn for a canoe," he nodded, his heavy-lidded eyes unsmiling. I glanced at Ganieda. It was Samhain (October thirty-one, by the Christian reckoning); I thought of Ravenoak. Winter had yet to arrive, and the air was still light and dry. I had not returned home in my fifteen years with Ganieda, although Ganieda himself returned annually on Beltaine. He used to return with little news, other than to confirm yearly that my mother still lived and ruled as queen. That was of little consequence to me, since there was never any news of my father.

"You can advance no further in learning until you have undergone the proper initiation," Ganieda explained in his usual half-distracted way. As he spoke he moved about, drawing on his ritualistic bull hide and his *encennach*—this last a wondrous motley headdress of bird feathers falling in a rainbow cascade about his shoulders. The feathers were surmounted by a tremendous pair of many-pointed deer antlers. Watching closely, Oroonca grunted his approval before unraveling a heavy bearskin cloak of his own that he threw over his massive shoulders. Ganieda went about gathering herbs and shoving these into his pockets. He unwound from a long twist of leather a miraculous silver branch, and holding it aloft he regarded me. I knew, of course, what was to come. That on that day I died in Paradise to take on fith-fath, at Quickborn when the black sheep is given.

First Ganieda made an incantation, during which he bade me sit off in the corner while Oroonca sat before the fire, Indian fashion. Drawing from the pot a piece of meat, Ganieda chewed this very slowly and thoughtfully, looking at neither of us. Dressed so splendidly, he looked like some weird God—a colorful, fearsome sight. Already I could feel the potion stirring my eyesight, giving the world the air of a dream. I sat waiting, silent.

Ganieda removed the chewed piece of meat from his mouth and set it upon the flagstone outside the closed door. He pronounced an invocation over this offering to his spirits. Then sitting in his chair he closed his heavy-lidded eyes and, holding his hands aloft, chanted anew a low song. He laid his palms on his cheeks, continuing his chant. His voice, steady and low at first, soon subsided to a murmur, from there to a mumble, quieter and quieter, until I could make out no words, until only his smooth lips moved in time, and before long he sat very still, whether in trance or sleep I could not tell. I, too, must have followed him into trance.

I was witnessing *Imbas Forosnai,* the divination by tradition. I knew it had something to do with my initiation, but what I could not discern. A fog clouded the room, and my limbs felt heavy as lead.

For as long as it took for the sun to set Ganieda remained completely still, until with a small start he opened his eyes and looked about, lowering his hands. He bade me go to him, speaking in a droning voice as if asleep. I moved toward him slowly, walking in the same dream.

"Ravenoak—many years since you have seen it," his voice quavered. "I have seen much befall it. The cattle do not produce, and the grain fails."

"Why?" I asked, my voice coming from far away.

"It is said that the queen is besmirched with deformity, and the king held captive by the Branna. Some whisper that your mother the queen has done away with your father." His eyes pleaded with me.

"My father lives still in the Morrigan's sidh," I replied sadly. "I have heard the accusations; they are false."

"Go to Ravenoak, child, and find the cure. The Branna are coming!" he whispered heavily, the urgency of his voice shivering me. Immediately he stood up, shaking himself and grunting.

"Come, Little Tree," he directed, his voice sounding like the old Ganieda again. Dazed, I followed. Oroonca joined us, we three stepping carefully outdoors over the meat on the cottage threshold.

Ganieda and Oroonca on each side led me behind the cottage past the pigs to the well, where the ancient skull towered over me, grinning horribly. Feeling the potion more intensely, I felt I would fall if Ganieda and Oroonca did not hold me up, their hands under my arms. My head was beginning to loll. I stared at the skull curiously, seeing it alive. Its eye sockets glowed dully red with fire.

"Who is that?" I asked, my voice becoming a blur.

"That is Fiann, the hero of the Old World, whom I have brought to our new land," responded Ganieda. "He lived many long ages ago. Soon you will fall into the dark world and hear him speak."

"What will he say?" I queried stupidly, unable to restrain my tongue rolling around in my head.

Ganieda did not reply directly. "Take the bowl," he ordered, handing it to me after dipping it into a bucket of water.

"Pour it out onto the stone when you are ready," he gestured at the stone slab. "Turn your thoughts to Ravenoak and its coming troubles. Your work lies partly there."

I stood a moment staring at the strange head before pouring the water upon the flat stone. Hearing a distant rumbling like thunder, in my half stupor I wondered whether a storm might be approaching. Another part of me knew better.

"Now sit on this blanket, and let us wrap you up. After a while we shall take you to the hot room to begin your journey." Ganieda pressed down on my shoulders.

I sat down like a stone, crossing my legs as I had learned from Oroonca. The earth felt warm. As the two wrapped my shoulders in Oroonca's bear cloak, I inhaled the Indian's deep earth scent as if it were my own. When Ganieda set his headdress upon my head, it too felt heavy as a stone.

"Look at Fiann," Ganieda indicated. As I did, at once all my senses sharpened, although I could no longer speak. My breath came in white clouds; I smelled Oroonca and even Ganieda standing off, his old magician's smell of brimstone and herbs. I could hear the pigs behind me snuffling and snorting on the ground; I seemed to hear Hella with her tiny, light voice snoring by the fire inside, though she was years dead. I sensed Fern's presence even though he had been made to sit some ways off.

As a cloud enveloped the world, Fiann floated above me in silent and terrible splendor. Again I waited, my breathing sounding like that of a fish underwater.

It struck me that I had been listening to a voice, deep and resonant, speaking to me for some time.

I recognized with a shock the voice of my father. Although my heart leaped, my body stayed calm, seated upright. For another thought followed close behind: My father was speaking to me from the Otherworld…my father, then, was dead…. I did not move. I was beyond moving now. His voice sounded clearly in my ears while my eye remained on the age-whitened skull of Fiann. I stared deep into its black, empty sockets and at its leering teeth that seemed to smile in victory over me. The bones at the nose were withered and rotted to translucent stems. All was fading. I had shrunk to a tiny, rolled-up weasel and could only gape at the awesome thing, ghastly white against the black rock.

"AGES AGO," spoke my father's voice, "Vikings conducted raids on Eire, pillaging and sacking wherever they pleased, even invading the great seat of Emain Macha. On one of those forays ventured a strong Viking from Lapland named Hessa Goldhair, chief of a band of fierce bearskin-clad soldiers whose helmets were adorned with the antlers of the deer that roamed their land.

"Clad all in white, his long golden hair tied back with a red band, Hessa wore a helmet embossed with silver and crowned with a tremendous set of many-pointed antlers. His white cloak was held at the left shoulder by a brooch of red-gold fashioned in the shape of a wolf, and though fair to look upon, his eyes sparkled with anger. In his left hand he carried a silver-embossed shield and in his right an ivory-hilted sword.

"Hessa and his band advanced on Eire, cutting down the native warriors like so many shafts of wheat in the wind. The great heroes CúChulainn and Fergus, Ailill and MacRoith had long since fallen; all-powerful Conchobor already lay in his sidh a hundred years. No heroes strong enough to resist Hessa Goldhair remained alive.

"After reaching the castle at Connachta and engaging in lengthy, single-handed combat to defeat the king, Hessa mounted the walls despite a serious wound to his shoulder. For now that the native heroes had been slain along with the king and the soldiers sent into rout, Hessa claimed the castle as his own. Weary from long days of war, he barged into the royal household demanding refreshment.

" 'Water!' Hessa commanded the newly bereft Queen Emer, from the family of Cuipre that had long reigned in Connacht. Bowing her head, the queen dispatched her daughter Ailinn Dark-Hair to fetch it. Ailinn returned bearing water in a silver bowl.

" 'That vessel is too good for this dying barbarian,' Emer shouted at her daughter, striking her and sending the silver bowl flying to the floor. Weakened from bleeding, Hessa fainted in the commotion as Emer stormed out of the room.

"Ailinn was left to tend to the injuries of her father's murderer, now her mortal enemy. Dripping herb mixtures into his gashes, she toiled to heal the wounded warrior. Four days Hessa remained in a stupor while Ailinn watched over him in the nights, studying the strong face with its broad brow, large-lidded eyes, and outthrust chin. His golden hair lay across his shoulder. But though she found him beautiful, she felt a dark hatred for him—he who had killed the one man she loved most, her father the king. Nevertheless, she was drawn strangely to his face.

"As Ailinn's medicines worked their magic, Hessa recovered. The world returned to him in the form of the lovely Ailinn, bending over him with care on her brow. Thus did he in turn find her blue eyes and clear brow beautiful. When after some days Emer returned, she saw at once what was afoot and cursed Hessa, sending Ailinn away. Emer no longer ruled in Connacht, however. So it was that Hessa had the queen bound and sent into exile, and she was heard from no more.

"Certain of having his way with the young princess who now provoked him with a burning lust, Hessa summoned Ailinn to the royal chamber. When she arrived she at once asked for her mother.

"'I have sent her away,' proclaimed the proud new king.

"'Then I have another reason to hate you,' Ailinn replied, whereupon Hessa snatched her in his powerful arms and lay upon her. Although she cried with all her might and tried to fight him off, still he entered her until the spasm was nearly upon him. When he found himself looking into Ailinn's proud and defiant eyes, he thought to withdraw in shame. Yet when he looked again into her eyes he could not withdraw, and he felt the spasm take his seed until it was over. He left the bed in haste, ashamed of his wicked deed.

"Hessa withdrew from Connacht with his troops and sailed from Eire; Ailinn heard no more of him. In nine months' time she gave birth to a golden-haired daughter whom she named Niamh: your great ancestor. Ever after have the daughters of Ailinn been golden-haired, even unto your mother Gwyn and you yourself, Guryn."

I ADDRESSED THE HEAD who spoke in my father's voice. "What of Hessa?"

"HESSA WAS NOT SEEN in Eire until many years later. A ragged wanderer, face much worn and lined with age though body still strong of limb, landed on our shores and made his way to Connacht dressed in the garments of a traveling bard. He wore strange foreign skins and carried a small bag wherein he kept his poet's stone and his animal of inspiration's bone. Arriving at court on Beltaine, he requested entrance to the feast. When asked what he could do, he replied that he was a poet.

"'We have a poet,' the guards replied.

"'Not one who knows "The Lay of Ailinn Dark-Hair,"' replied the poet, his white hair closely cropped and flecked with grey.

"Since the guards had never heard this tale of their beloved queen, they sent word to the feast, and the bard was admitted. As the bard approached the royal table he spied Queen Ailinn and at her side her daughter Niamh, grown into a woman of twenty. Beside Niamh sat a young man, tall and dark-haired. When the bard gazed upon Ailinn, longing overflowed into his heart, though he spoke not. However, as he beheld Niamh he felt he would faint, for in her beauty lay the commingled flesh of Ailinn and Hessa, a miraculous beauty smiling secretly at the strange foreign bard come to play.

"The bard bowed and requested allowance to play for the queen.

"'What is that lay unbeknownst to us?' Ailinn demanded, frowning and setting her cup down.

"'How your child was born of the God,' the bard answered bravely, in a loud voice.

"A gasp ran through the hall. All Connacht knew the birth of Niamh was never to be spoken of. Twenty years before Ailinn had given birth in secret, swearing her nurses to silence on pain of death. So of Niamh Golden-Hair was it said that she had arisen from the sidh, one day to rule Connacht.

"'Sing, then, and hope to save yourself from dying,' Ailinn commanded.

"The bard tuned his harp, fashioned from the reindeer's breastbone, and sang in a clear voice:

> Ailinn Dark-Hair traveled in the night,
> Looking for her mother who had gone before.
> She came to a river, bloody red,
> And there she shed many tears.
>
> Upon the land lay a terrible curse,
> Invaders from the Northlands all about.
> The king killed and the invader on the throne,
> And the queen exiled wrongly.
>
> Ailinn cried in the night until the stones yielded,
> And opened the sidh before her.
> Into it she ventured, seeking her mother,
> She found instead a great warrior.
>
> 'I will take you from this place to make you my queen,'
> Said the warrior, his white hair burning in her eyes.
> Beautiful to look upon, Ailinn trembled in fear,
> Of her own forbidden desire.
>
> It was CúChulainn himself, proud and strong,
> Who took her in his arms.
> There they lay four days and nights,
> And in the end Ailinn lost her fear.
>
> 'You will be queen and your daughter to follow,
> Henceforth a new line of queens,'
> CúChulainn spoke, then disappeared,
> As fearless Ailinn left the sidh.

"The bard finished his song and stopped. Silence reigned until Ailinn spoke.

"'You have found the death you were seeking, foolish bard,' she proclaimed haughtily, then had him bound and carried off.

"In the days following the feast of Beltaine Ailinn could not bring herself to have the bard killed, though he had made the queen look the fool. She forbade anyone to see him.

"Niamh's heart was moved by the poor haggard bard, however, for she had felt a spirit move between them. When she went to him and saw that the guards had beaten him, she ministered to his wounds; he smiled at her through his wrinkles. Niamh poured her medicines into his wounds, and he thanked her, thinking of another age when another woman had done the same.

"'My mother is a proud woman. The story of my birth was never to be voiced; did you not know?' Niamh whispered.

"'I speak of what I know, Golden-Hair,' his battered voice croaked. 'Your line is strong and noble. Find a suitable mate, strong like yourself.'

"Niamh blushed, turning her head to recall the young warrior who had sat beside her at the feast.

"'Not that one,' the bard shook his head.

"In a day or two Niamh loosened his bonds and set him free by nightfall. When Ailinn learned the bard had left the land, she was greatly angered, reviling and punishing her daughter for her love of the bard. But soon the queen fell into a waking dream of longing from which she could not awake, wherein she saw the Lapland king in all his youthful splendor lying upon her. Thus was she stung by an old wound, fretting and pacing. She could not sleep, she ate not and grew thin, spending her days on the ramparts at the high tower looking out over Connacht, looking always to the north."

THE VOICE OF THE HEAD—or was it that of my father?—fell silent. My face was full of tears. Night had fallen, but my eye focused still on the ghostly skull. What did the tale mean? This was not the time for understanding, even if my heart hurt mightily trying to comprehend my father dead. Dead! I had lived so many years alongside Ganieda with the hope of returning to the Morrigan's sidh, whereby I might fulfill my vow to take my father back to Ravenoak. It was not to be....

I fell down, my heart bursting. Ganieda and Oroonca carried me senseless into the small house down the path. After building a fire to heat some stones, they threw water upon the stone. As thick steam arose they left me in the dark, swaddled in Oroonca's blanket.

How I sweated and rolled in the dense cloud of steam! My mind was boiled into a living flame, flickering without intent and burning brightly in an immense darkness.

Down, down the well I felt myself pulled, until I fell into a dim land that looked much like the forest above. Thudding sounds pounded close to the ground... A grey wolf appeared before me and bade me follow. In a twinkling I became that selfsame wolf as we ranged far through the woods, stopping for water, hunting down a rabbit, howling at the moon when it rose full in my long-snouted face.

My skin was grey fur, my limbs powerful and lean. My tail was a blazon in the night as I moved like silence and death between the trees. I could smell animals on the other side of the forest while I watched how they moved and for what purpose. When hunger gnawed I sniffed the night air for squirrel or rabbit and followed the trail of scent, plain as a wavering line of smoke in the air.

After many days I could feel the heat rising in my body, and I wanted a mate. I knew my scent was abroad in the forest. Before long a grey wolf came running lean-limbed through the trees, his glowing eyes narrowly focused on me as if he would penetrate me. I could feel the dark urge and warm presence of his seed hanging down between his legs like ripe fruit. I nosed and barked at him, bit his ear and leaped upon him, as did he upon me. But it was too soon for my womb; I ran off with him nipping my heels. I was the faster runner and felt the warm tension of my muscles contracting, waiting, keeping him at bay until the madness was upon him. Almost as soon it was upon me; turning at the crest of a hill I snarled at him when he ran up to me, so that he backed away. I lunged at him and bit deeply into his flank as he howled mightily, tearing himself from me.

Crouching, we circled one another. He leaped upon me; I wrested from him only to back into him, pressing my heated legs against his belly. He howled with high-spirited exultation as I pressed further into him, the tremendous pressure of his member thrust into me like living fire, swollen and bloody, until we moved as one.

For hours I panted before him, still now and receiving his thrusts. Many days we were as one, every stagger of my hind legs met by one of his. He bit my ears and nuzzled my neck. Still I pressed into him, until at last I felt the spurt of his seed. We were locked still…until at length it was over, and I eased myself from him, turning and eyeing him. Rapidly the strength was returning to my limbs as I shuddered and breathed deeply, snorting once at him.

Suddenly I turned and was off, and he was gone, leaving my belly full.

In time I gave birth to four pups under a ragged cedar twisted by the years, watching over and suckling my young until they were strong enough to roam on their own. One was carried off by an eagle and another mauled by a bear when it ventured too close to her cub, meaning only to play. The other two grew to adulthood at last and strayed into parts of the forest even I did not know.

Long I adventured and traveled far, meeting other wolves and running in packs over and under hills and deep into the endless forest, even into the frozen north, leaping over fields of strewn boulders like grey mounds, howling at the moon when it tortured us with its endlessly pale light.

In my wanderings I reached the settlement of Ravenoak, peering through the trees at its people. The sun was leaving as I arrived, the Great Oak already in deep shadow. I sniffed the air, cocked my ears, and waited. With my sharpened senses I could discern what was happening all about, affecting even the things I could not see. The crops were failing just as Ganieda had foretold; I could detect the presence of much human suffering. One sniff in the direction of the main cattle pen told me that the bulls were impotent and the calves barren. The little group of humans had shrunk, and the people remaining walked about with suspicious eyes and hunched shoulders, each worried about his own. Knowing that humans fought amongst themselves, I gathered that the heroes had gone off to fight the Branna.

Even as a wolf I felt a distant loyalty to these humans, that I had to help them if I could. And so after sitting all night in the shadow of the forest to consider, I trotted off in the direction of the smell of human blood, coming at last upon a field to the north where men in warrior dress did battle. Recognizing at once the scent of the enemy, I leaped from the forest and with a great howl threw myself into the thickest of the fray. Some of the men's faces I found familiar: a man with red hair who glanced wildly in my direction, fear in his eyes. I left him to the humans while I rent and tore at the other enemy throats, driving back the charging warriors until they fled in terror before this Druid wolf.

Catching a whiff of a fierce storm coming on, I knew the rout would be complete when the black clouds threatened overhead, for the Branna would believe I had summoned them. And, indeed, when the storm came they fled to their home, leaving the wounded men of Ravenoak the victors despite the many who had died.

Swiftly I fled back into the deep wood and there lived many years alone, taking a mate when my body so instructed, chasing the forest floor mice for my food.

I grew old and was killed by a panther finally and taken into his belly. Thereafter I lived as a panther for years, in black awareness of the night, always watching and purring in slow rhythms, my yellow eyes opening and closing on the world.

Many times I died and was reborn, and so came to know the mystery of the passing and returning. When I was wolf in the vicious teeth of the panther, I felt the spirit shudder in my body, my eyes look sharply upward into his, feeling love for the panther, then the throttle and surging, sighing release. I watched and felt as my breath choked in my body; I witnessed as from outside the deep purple of the soul pass across my face and with a sigh spread into the vastness. The dark that many fear I saw was no dark but a luminosity glowing all around me, until the shimmering that was all of me there was left shimmered like a wind-blown lake, shimmering and shimmering until I, my soul, was utterly, utterly of the world's essence.

In a timeless time I hovered in that nether world before coming to myself as the panther, awake to another way of seeing. Only in time to die again at last, to relearn the tearing shudder and shimmering of the soul rent from its own flesh. I saw that it was the same for all creatures, the passing and the returning.

After that I was born as a horse, then as a stag, a boar, eagle and a salmon, until I was on board the ship to the new land as a rooster. It was then I saw my mother and father as little children. I passed that life, too, and many others, until I found myself as a mere human again, now wrapped in Oroonca's blanket, bound tightly and lying on my side in the open air near Ganieda's well.

Again I passed into the Otherworld as a vision of a man sitting in a tree overcame me. Walking into a deep wood by the light of a full moon, I came to a clearing I recognized. In an aged oak high amidst the lightest branches crouched a man-creature, a cowl covering his face but for his mouth, which held a salmon clenched between his teeth. He sat cracking nuts and dropping these to the ground. At the base of the tree stood a magnificent many-pointed buck with monumental horns, pawing and feeding on the nuts. Drawing near, I looked up.

"Where has my father gone?" I asked the man-creature. "Ravenoak has need of him."

As his cowl fell back, I saw that he was Lord of the Beasts.

"You know this," the man-creature replied, and went on cracking nuts.

"What is my duty?" I asked after a long pause.

"Go to Ravenoak and follow the funnel of the dark cloud," the creature ordered. He turned toward me.

My eyesight grew dim, then brightened, and when the haze cleared altogether I came to myself once again on the ground, wrapped in Oroonca's blanket. Gradually I realized I had been speaking with Ganieda himself, he looking no older than the day I had embarked on my journey through death and rebirth. He stood above regarding me closely with his one good eye. I lay beneath the tall pines as a fresh breeze blew. I was wrapped tightly and could not move, though my body felt sore from exertion.

Ganieda nodded. "It is well—the light is in her." Oroonca bent over me closely, staring into my face but a finger's length from his. Grunting, he began to unwind me from the blanket. When I was freed he helped me sit up and brought a bowl of water to my lips. I drank as if I had gone years without water.

"What news?" Ganieda inquired, his voice a harsh guttural. I turned to him and took a deep breath.

"The wolves are wandering eastward," I replied without thinking.

At once I began to chant, much the way Ganieda had done at the feasts in Ravenoak:

> Wolves wandering eastward,
> A dark cloud over Ravenoak,
> Many troubles, and a wandering time.
> The people scattered like leaves;
> No queen will reign again in Ravenoak.
> A rock in the forest, the sound of the sea;
> A girl child, men in high hats and dark looks.
> A broken brooch—my fate in love.

It was my first prophecy, simple as it was. My life as a seer had begun.

Ganieda nodded and grew thoughtful. He wandered back to the cabin as Oroonca helped me to my feet. I tottered after the Indian, around to the front of the cabin where I paused in the dark doorway a long moment, as if returning from a journey of many years. Yet there lay the piece of chewed meat on the same boot-scarred threshold my toes now touched. As I stood regarding it, I knew I would leave very soon, that my life henceforth was to be that of a wanderer. No place ever again—no matter how long I might stay—would be home. A cramp of sadness gripped my belly.

That night we three sat before the fire talking as equals. Relations among us had altered irrevocably; sometimes I spoke while they, listening, nodded at my advice.

When I described the various animal lives I had lived, Ganieda stepped in. "That is *tuirgen,* the circular birth. You have been spun upon the gyre that directs us all." He grimaced through his wrinkles, half for me, half for his own work.

How I cherished Ganieda's presence that night! So hard, so demanding, so little affection! He had grown as dear to me as my own father, whose image burned in me like a magic candle that never burns out, keeping a steady flame.

"It is time to go," I spoke softly. "I dreamed of finding my father, and on the path to him found you. Although my father is gone and I will never reach him, my promise to him entails a promise to Ravenoak. I must return. Trouble rises there I can see only dimly."

"As can I," agreed Ganieda.

"As can I," echoed Oroonca. Oroonca and Ganieda were sharing a pipe, and the curls of smoke hesitated, listening at our heads.

"I doubt whether I can stem the evil that comes. But there is a task I must undertake before Ravenoak disperses. Only in dreaming shall I ever see either of you again."

Never had I thought I could speak with that spirit in me, but there it was! A new voice—older, calmer, speaking from a deeper source without fear. No—I spoke with fear, for I felt much fear. But that night I drew from a well of quiet courage so unlike the childlike boldness that had possessed me hitherto, when my younger soul took life wholly at extremes and found death a distant story. Now I knew the in-between places where life is lived....

Still, strong feelings shook me, for was I not descended from a ravished queen? Whose blood had mixed with the royal shamans of Lapland? That ragged bard in the story, once a king, was my ancestor; Niamh Golden-Hair, a hovering spirit guiding me. Oh, how much I knew already! And yet how frightened I was—and am still! For with the new power of visions came feelings deeper and more fraught, piercing me like knives. Joy and anger and ignorance would henceforth visit as powerful spirits to carry me away. My soul was now indeed a wanderer, my heart light and transparent. Any spirit could whisk me away, I feared.

"Therefore, you must learn one more art: to hide your soul in many places, as I have hidden mine," Ganieda explained, studying my face on which he still could too easily read my thoughts.

Oroonca stood up to leave, embracing me in the doorway.

"Tall Tree," he grunted, pulling from his medicine bag three leaves. "One, goodness; two, poison; three, knowing." He tucked them into my crane-bag, then unstrapped the hunting knife from his waist, handing it to me.

"No," I stammered, my eyes wide. He pushed it on me, and so I received his gift in awe. It was heavy, its handle made from a white bone.

Oroonca tapped the handle. "Leg of the wolf," he stated. The hair rose on the back of my neck as I wrapped its leather strap around my waist and tied the knife securely.

When I looked up, Oroonca was gone.

I sat with Ganieda before the fire, the air heavy with leaving. It was now clear to me that I had to leave the following evening, which made me sad. Neither of us spoke for a while. My thoughts turned to my mother who still reigned in Ravenoak, for all I knew, then to my father. Again I felt the pang of deserting him.

"I have failed my father," I bit my lip.

"What if we are but leaves blowing in the wind?" Ganieda asked, his eye twinkling at mine.

"Just as we do not make the world," he continued, "we do not make our burdens. They come to us bidden by greater spirits than ourselves. And all necessary."

"Then am I to forsake my father, lay aside blame and responsibility?"

"Blame and responsibility take separate paths. Blame leads us away from responsibility. We seek to respond. Life comes as a man, a woman, a cow, a wind. It comes as a song, a dance, a hope. Each comes only because it is ours to bear."

"Do we not then shape our lives?"

"How could we?" Ganieda asked the fire. "We are not Gods who create. We are the workers, we humans. Or players. A song comes, and we sing. That is good. A war comes, and we fight. A lover comes, and we love. To know what the spirit wants takes rare wisdom."

I thought of my wolf spirit. How wondrous to have been in her skin for a time, traveling with her instinctive knowing, without doubt! That was living as Ganieda described—by responding. She moved at all times in unison with the world, as if spirit and body were one, blade and handle.

THE FOLLOWING afternoon Ganieda and I walked in the woods once more. He showed me by incantations and spells good places to disperse my spirit and hide it, so that no one might steal it from me.

"Not even a lover, if you love wisely," he smiled, then bethought himself. "At first your lover will take all—but will give it back if he is kindly. That is how you can recognize one learned in that most sacred and difficult of arts."

"Why do you speak so much of love?" I asked him.

"It is the greatest power," he replied, laughing lightly. "It is a power we can never wield but rather, are subject to. Our highest goal is to learn by love that exerting power over another—and calling that love—is one thing; loving as two equally subject to the power, quite another." He patted my hand and pointed to a little cairn of rocks. "Another good place for an airy part of your spirit to hide," he instructed. As Ganieda waved his arm, sparks flew from his right hand to the pile of rocks and made them glisten, forming a halo of gold light about the cairn.

"Why the airy part? Why not the part that is like rock?"

"You must learn to cheat and trick and lie," he explained. "That is the way of the lover. Anyone looking to steal your spirit would look first in the rocks to find your hardness. Use your imagination! Hide it elsewhere!"

"In a tree, perhaps?" I asked.

"No, no! Don't name the place!" he shrieked, putting his hands over his ears. We meandered back to the cottage as the light of the day was dying.

We sat together that last evening by the fire, where it seemed we had been sitting since time began. Ganieda's head rolled as he mumbled something unintelligible. I stared at the motley shapes of his Druid fire: small tornadoes of crimson and gold; funnels of green and amber; miniature trees of blue and red. Though my heart was heavy as lead, I smiled at the pain. What a wonder to be mortal! What a wonder even to feel my heart even like an ingot bearing me down! I whispered a Druid blessing to Ganieda, to his teaching, his cottage, the warm fire...

Had I been speaking aloud? A wind blew against the door, letting out a creak. Suddenly feeling Oroonca's absence, I stood and stretched, leaving Ganieda sleeping to return to my little loft at the rear of the cabin. Fern limped along with me as usual. I smelled the heavy musk of the animals in my room as I gathered my few things from behind the straw bed. From a leather bag I pulled out the emerald five-pointed star brooch my mother had given me so long ago and pinned it on my cape. Digging under the bed I drew out a long object wrapped in many rags and unwound the cloth. Inside lay my father's sword in its scabbard, which I drew and raised in the dim light. I had not unsheathed it since coming to Ganieda's cottage though I slept beside it, each night feeling its hard coldness against my side, like a dead lover. Carrying the bare sword outside, I bathed it in moonlight until it gleamed quietly, like a panther on guard in the forest.

I looked in the pen at the pigs and the cow, stroking and whispering to my favorites as they grunted in return. Why were the rest no longer wary of me? The moon had risen large amidst the high pines, and the wind was growing. I drew my cloak about me and, carrying my small bag and the sheathed sword, returned to the cabin, Fern at my heels.

Ganieda still sat before the fire but now was quite awake, making yellow and red smoke curls rise from his pipe as he leaned forward on his stick. Staring into the fire as if carved of stone. Even now I see him before the fire stroking the tiny black, shiny head of the child of the child of the weasel Hella, whom long before I had buried in the back beneath a standing stone. I entered and sat down again next to Ganieda, my cloak fastened at the neck with the star brooch.

"How can I say my thanks?" I whispered, wanting so deeply to stay. I did not want to go to Ravenoak.

Ganieda turned toward me. "Only a fool says there are no leave-takings, that we are all together in the spirit world!" he exclaimed bitterly, glaring at me with a hurt expression.

Shocked, I drew back. Often he had been vehement, even angry, but always because I had not learned a lesson well or when a spell of his had failed.

"Our bond is timeless. I shall remember always and move in the Otherworld with you," I replied, touching the gnarled hands resting atop the knob of his stick.

"Bah!" he barked, as a bit of spittle gathered at his lower lip. Pulling his hands away, he poked at the fire with his stick. I was stunned to see him behaving like a petulant child—or like a lover I was leaving behind. Or, perhaps, like a father?

"I am old; you are stronger than I. A good student," he added wistfully. This time I was astonished to hear a compliment from him—he who had rarely spoken a kind word to me.

"Show me some magic!" he exclaimed brightly, smiling suddenly. By now wholly taken aback, I sat a few moments without responding, wondering what he meant. Then I stared into the fire and looked into my heart. Within was Ganieda's chamber, like and unlike the room the two of us now sat in. On each of the shelves that lined the walls lay boxes. Each box contained many bottles of herbs and distillates. From one I selected several leaves and a pinch of bee pollen.

Standing near Ganieda, I uttered words of incantation in a loud voice. When the circle was fashioned about me—I moving on the circle and the power flowing through me—I extended my hand through the circle and back into the world where Ganieda sat quietly by the fire, not looking at me. I waved my hand at the fire. Blue lights danced in the flames. With a slow shudder the fire quieted, flickering lower and lower until it flickered out altogether.

Performing a second gesture and uttering words of incantation, I brought the fire back while Ganieda gazed into the flames. I made the great pot hanging from the hook over the fire lift itself and settle upon the hearth. The child of Hella sprang up and ran into a corner, squealing. Turning to Ganieda, I enchanted his cloak to wrap closely about him, as if embracing him.

I sat down again, returning to my small place on the great circle. All was quiet. When I glanced at Ganieda to glean what he thought of my magic, he nodded once.

"Golden one-eyed woman! Tall Tree!" he exclaimed. Did he mean those names to refer to my long blond hair and my stature—or to my magic? I could not tell. He continued. "The Otherworld is an island where we go at death. The island is connected to the mainland of our lives; thus we return on the great circle. Your work is to feel longing for this world until it breaks you and makes you transparent. To know this world and only be able to touch it as you touched the Morrigan's sidh, which left you full of longing. Now you long for this world. Remember your longing when it comes time to understand. Farewell!"

I stood up quickly, as if a hand had raised me. Surely Ganieda was working his spell on me, making me rise! I moved back a step, feeling the invisible hand press against my chest. With an effort I stopped, bending down close to the old man, my master, to kiss his forehead, dry as leaves. Even though the invisible hand pressed all the harder against me as I drew near Ganieda, I resisted its pressure while I touched his forehead with my lips. I was thrown back staggering but undaunted made my way to the door, whither the hand was pressing me. Picking up my bag and my father's sword I regarded again the room, that strange room full of instruments and books, where bunches of herbs and leaves hung all about the eaves, the roaring fire bellowing colorfully.

"Here I was concocted," I prayed out loud, though the old man did not turn. Opening the door, I let the wind pull Fern and me out, leaving the room a tableau for all time emblazoned in my heart; and the fire, Ganieda meditating before the fire, lost among faraway lands speaking strange unheard words, smoke wreathing colorfully from his pipe, the flickering lights. All a dream! And oh, how right he was! The longing that set upon me, making of me a wandering wraith, half on and half off the great circle of life and death for all my days upon the earth!

AND SO I stepped into the dark night, a long journey before me with no Grey to ride on. Not for the first time, I realized that to be a worker in the invisible world was to be a lover, for my heart was broken a second time. Once again I was alone, wandering, with but a faint wavering light as my heart's guide.

Slinging my bag over one shoulder, I leaned my father's sword against the other and touched Oroonca's knife in its sheath, then trod quietly down the hill. In spite of my long absence from Ravenoak, I knew the way as water remembers to run downhill. My skin bristled for fear of what awaited me in Ravenoak, which already I could sniff like a wolf. I felt her guidance as I padded quietly across pine needles, passing like a slender shadow through the cloudy night, Fern trotting alongside.

Although it was a walk of two days to reach Ravenoak, long before arriving at my old home I could smell the fires. *But what fires!* I worried as I hurried on, hearing screams muffled through the trees. When the warm day sent thicker smoke to my nose, I began to run, Fern alternately galloping and limping beside me.

The trees thinned until at last I came to Ravenoak, back in my childhood home. Everywhere I found people running while riders bore down on them with raised swords. Screams of women rent the air, and the wails of little children tore my ears. When plumes of thick smoke burned my eye, I stopped to look into the dim world to see what was happening. I could see plainly that the riders attacking Ravenoak were indeed the Branna. Round and round the Great Oak they rode, hacking and killing, and when the outnumbered and surprised men of Ravenoak mounted against them, they slew the defenders, crushing them from their horses onto the ground.

I rushed through the clearing toward the Great House to look for my mother. Now I knew why neither Ganieda nor Oroonca nor I had been able to scry Ravenoak with any clarity from afar, for strong defensive spells had been cast over the land—cast by my mother's own hand to protect the village from attack. Alas, her magic had worked to thwart those come to help, rather than the invaders determined to destroy.

I gritted my teeth as I ran. Not only had my mother's spells not been strong enough, neither had the victory I helped gain in my vision-life as a wolf... My melancholy musing proved short-lived, for just then a horse thundered behind me; a rough hand grabbed at my cloak and tried to pull me up. As I twisted myself free, Fern nipped at the heels of the horse and sent it flying. While running for the house I unsheathed my father's sword and saw it gleam in the sun, eager for battle.

Through the broken door I sped, toward the interior rooms. Down a long corridor full of smoke, shouting all the while for my mother, I barged through her door with outstretched sword, Fern near. The chamber was choked with smoke; I heard my mother coughing. I coughed, too, squinting my left eye to discern her form, finally finding her lying on a pile of skins.

"Mother!" I cried, rushing over to her.

She looked at me out of wild eyes. To witness such fear in her—that was my homecoming!

"Get out!" she hissed, baring her teeth like a cat.

I started to draw back, then regarded her more closely. Her long dress, smeared with blood, was torn nearly off her, her greying hair was tangled and matted, her legs twisted beneath her. Anguish flooded my heart! My proud, strong mother! Whose image I carried always with me, whose anger and pride I grew into, like a dress she had bequeathed me. A terrible ache clutched my heart for all the years lost from her. So angry did I feel, my heart split between care and disdain at her final weakness; I did not know whether to sneer or fall into the tears I had never shed. To come home, only to find her dying!

"The old ways are upon us," she croaked pitifully. "The golden-haired king of Lapland has come round again," she moaned, her eyes rolling in her head. "I bear the seed unto death," she grimaced in pain.

I started at her words, calling me back to my initiation, the tale the skull had recited: a blond-haired king invading Eire, the love and devastation that followed; the new queen lost on the ramparts, leaving her daughter, the daughter of the blond-haired king... The circle turning!

My mother's side was slashed and bleeding freely, a long gash running from breast to thigh. I drew my crane-bag open and knelt beside her, unstopping a bottle of healing potion and touching it with shaking fingers to her lips.

"I need no medicines," she croaked harshly, pushing the vial away. I pressed it closer.

"What is upon us?" I asked faintly, my voice failing me.

As her eyes glittered at me, I glimpsed the still beautiful, still regal face of the old proud woman. The realization that I was not yet her equal made me angry. I wanted to shout at her that I loved her, that she was acting a fool. My heart beat furiously.

"Did that old fool of a Druid teach you to see only the upper arc of the great circle and not the lower?" she smirked. "Are you blind to what lies before your human eye?"

Biting my lip, I pressed the liquid on her so that she drank. Crushing a few bella-donna leaves into a mixture of water from a cracked dish I found lying nearby, I rubbed the tincture onto her soot-smeared forehead, all the while peering into the dim.

"The Branna have attacked," I whispered.

"Can you guess why, O Seer?" she taunted cruelly.

I did not see why. "For—Ravenoak," I answered, hesitant.

My mother reached her hand out roughly and caught me between my thighs, laughing coarsely. "Ganieda taught you precious little!"

I started back. She looked at that moment so like a crone from the nether re-gions, I let hatred course through me. Nevertheless, I held my tongue—if only from love in equal measure to hate!

"On account of you, Little Tree grown so tall and golden!" she cried. "No mat-ter my dried-up womb, they have raped me. What do the cursed Branna care! You were the one they were looking for—you know that, don't you? Despite your wolf guise, they knew you that day on the field of battle. You were not clever enough to hide from the Redmane's eye! You made them suffer that day—all Ravenoak knows the tale! And now they want you! You entered the darkness blindly believing you could make spells and cure evils, but failed to see... the visible and invisible are on the same circle." She stopped and coughed at length.

"Alas, my daughter!" she continued more softly. "The world alters with you, and each second sight for good is met by another for ill." She coughed again, blood drool-ing from her slack mouth, though she kept her lizard eye on me.

"Then Cian has the sight—? Did they know I was coming?" I asked quickly, frightened.

"They knew... they knew," my mother moaned, her head sagging, her eyes clouding. "They will take you, too. It is our story. The old way... the old way," she murmured.

Watching her closely, I saw her eye change, looking at me with a sadness I had never seen there before. Her loose mouth formed a grim smile.

"Mother!" I cried, clinging to her. She did not answer, only raised a shaking hand to give my bowed head a single pat. Weakly pressing her hand to raise my chin, she touched the five-pointed brooch she had given me so long ago. Now my tears came.

I gathered the bed skins and swaddled her in them, washed her face with the tincture and set aside the bowl, then listened to the wails coming from outside as I counted her heartbeats falling away like a passing rain, my cheeks wet.

All the years lost! I touched her face softly. When soon my mother's spirit passed to the hidden arc, I closed my eyes to witness the beautiful shimmering of her jour-neying spirit, beautiful even in torment. I pressed her eyes closed.

Stiffly I rose. Leaving my crane-bag and satchel behind while taking my father's sword, I turned to go. Grave, back down the hall I walked, Fern by my side. Out into the bright midday sun to meet the screams and the smoke. I murmured a chant, and as a riderless horse galloped toward me, I mounted. Raising my father's sword, I rode into battle.

Round the Great Oak I, too, now raced, taking my place beside fellow warriors, wielding the sword as lightly as a pine bough. The sword possessed a magic I had only to direct, cleaving helmet and shield, throwing down warrior after warrior. Even so, I was wounded in the arm and side, the blood soon covering my brown cloak. Through the mist I spied Cian ride to the aid of his fellows, now falling back before our men.

As he rode into the fray, I took note of the scar running like the sign of the bastard across his cheek, permanently purple against his fair skin. His red hair blew wild in the wind. One exchange of glances and we knew each other, our swords clashing like claps of thunder over our heads. Fire spurted from my eye while I murmured spells against him, even as I marveled at his beauty and strength. He was fully grown with the beard of a man, his eye having gained the mature look of chieftain and father. I knew he had taken a wife and fathered a child. I pressed harder against him until I pushed him back, his horse neighing uncertainly, harried by Fern at his heels.

Again and again I beat down on his sword and shield, ducking and swinging while murmuring under my breath for the help of the Invisibles. But my woman's muscles were no match for his, and my arm grew weak; he overtook me at last and drove me back. Pulling my horse away from his and raising my sword for a final swing, I spurred toward him at a furious gallop.

When our swords met in another tremendous clash, mine was splintered to bits, his bursting the haft from my hand.

"Mine!" he thundered, as I leaped from my horse and raced back to the Great House, Cian in pursuit, while his men rejoined the fray. Hearing a yelp, I turned and saw Fern trampled by a horse. He raised his poor black head as the hooves passed, looked at me with longing, and fell to the earth. Heart of a lion! Courageous friend! How I wanted to stop and grieve over my poor friend, but the terror was great and Fern's voice from the distance called out "Run!" I turned away and ran through the doorway.

Down the hall I raced again, into the smoky back room, shape-shifting into a murderous raven and flying out a window. Cian spotted me; no sooner did I fly off than he turned himself into a soaring lark, flying after me in pursuit. High I flew, as fast and high as a raven might, but always Cian flapped behind me. Down, down into the deep forest I swept, shifting again into haunched wolf as I reached the ground, then darted through the trees and tangled brambles where no bird could fly.

Cian changed into a wolf and pursued. For a time I became a horse snorting steam and galloped away from him, until Cian in horse guise stampeded close behind. Reaching the Boyne I leaped in, fluidly becoming a red-eyed salmon. Swimming deeper with all my strength, I thought I could elude him, but again he mirrored me as a salmon, as silvery red as I.

Long and hard I swam only to circle back to Ravenoak, whereupon I leaped onto dry ground and ran as myself back to the Great House, dashing breathlessly into my mother's dark chamber.

Behind me in an instant, Cian grabbed my shoulders, throwing me down on the bed beside my mother so that my head touched hers. Pressing himself upon me, he drew his dagger and held it up before my eye.

"Mine!" he hissed, leaning and tearing my gown down the front, leaving me lying exposed before him. He stood and looked down at me. "Thy beauty is mine by right," he growled hoarsely, shrugging off his shirt as his long mane of red hair swept over his shoulders. I shuddered at the sight of his wild, exalted eyes, of his body and his member, which pointed at me. Suddenly he was upon me, sending a sharp pain shooting through my body as he entered.

I dug claws into him and rose as he rose, my mother's blood mixing with my own and with Cian's. He bore upon me like a living stone... And never since have I known such union of fire, not even with Richard. I grasped his red hair and pulled hard, bit his cheek until the blood ran over my face and he screamed in agony, yet still he bore upon me—until I felt his lust crest and overturn deep within me, and then a spurt of silver thread.

A tiny crystal began to glisten in my womb, and an unbearably sad stillness in the darkness reigned.

Cian lay in a stupor on top of me. I pushed him away and drew the remnant of my dress about me. Slowly I drew Oroonca's bone-handled knife and pressed it against Cian's throat.

"I am not your woman," I croaked.

He said nothing but opened his eyes slowly. "My seed," he muttered, swallowing hard.

"You know what I am," I replied.

"A powerful magician, we have learned. Do you need a lowly knife to kill me? Are not your spells not powerful enough?"

I bore down on my anger, then withdrew the knife; this man would not direct my vengeance. Yet as I sheathed my knife, my own behavior bewildered me. Was not herewith the revenge I had longed for year after year? There he lay, willing that I should kill him—and no less beautiful for that. This was not vengeance.

"You know nothing of Druid matters," I insisted. "Spells are those spoken as truth visible, not wished."

"And what truth is visible, O Queen of Ravenoak?" he smiled twistedly, sitting up and pulling on his shirt while keeping his watchful eyes on me.

"That neither you nor I shall rule in Ravenoak. That your race is dying. That is what I see."

"You dare curse me!"

I turned toward him, searching his face for something I could recognize and remember. Already as his seed swirled within me I saw the young girl of flaming hair, my daughter. Might I one day see her father in her? Or must he, too, be a stranger to my spirit?

"I see a daughter you will never know," I proclaimed, my voice low as I rose.

"You see nothing!" he hissed, coming near me. Tall as I am, we stood eye to eye. "You have embraced your fate." I turned away.

"Then stab me now, Little Tree, Guryn Golden-Hair! Whom only have I loved my whole life!"

"You with wife and child," I smiled.

He hesitated, his shoulders sagging. "Then kill me," he repeated.

Thus was my enemy defeated.

Another truth stared me in the face. Although I bore his seed, Cian was not of my race. I made a pact in the silence to be true to my fate and to bear it, as my father had taught me, with a glad heart, and not to call it hard names as Cian now did his.

"You have not yet lived; you may not die ere you do," I nodded soberly, and taking my crane-bag and satchel departed that tomb.

Slowly I walked down the hall and out the front of the Great House. Three horsemen charged up to me, swords drawn, though halted when they saw I made no move to run or protect myself.

"Go back; it is finished," I murmured, raising the knife I clutched like iron.

"Your life will pay if you have done aught to Cian," one said, dismounting and approaching.

I chanted until the world grew dim and a great wind swirled up from behind me, sweeping along the ground and into the warrior's face. Five paces from me he stopped, ducking his head, covering his eyes now filled with dust. He turned to his fellows, but their horses were neighing loudly as the mounts struggled to hold them. The wind blew mightily. Bravely turning back to me, he raised his sword yet did not swing, finally letting it fall at his side, again covering his eyes as the wind moaned without cease.

"Crone of the sidh!" he spat, turning and with difficulty remounting.

"Your tribe is now withered," I proclaimed in a loud voice. As the Druid wind took up my words and flung them in their faces, the three drew back in horror. "I bear the new life." I hardly knew what I was saying, only that I felt the coldness of power pass through me, dizzying me. I knew the curse would work because I spoke the truth. Sheathing my *athane,* I walked through them. As the wind poured into their faces, blowing clouds of dust high in the air, they scattered like leaves.

RAVENOAK LAY conquered and ravaged. Many days passed before the destruction was cleared away, the fire rekindled, the dead buried and the corpses of the enemy given grudging burial under the stern eye of our conquerors. Word spread that I was the daughter of the murdered queen returned from study with Ganieda. The people thought it a matter of course that somehow I would defeat the Branna and come to rule in my mother's place. I knew that was not to be. I found myself a ruined hut away from the tumult and there bided my days, repairing the roof and sweeping out the mice.

A different sort of shape-shifting began to alter me without my bidding. Deeply I fell into an unfamiliar blackness, pacing the earthen floor in my cottage, back and forth, hardly knowing whence or whither. A fierce dragon of hate writhed and wrapped its scaly body about my soul and would not free it.

My eye red with hatred and blood in my teeth, I relived again and again Cian's violation of me, even as I sat, head bowed, weaving out of rope the *sianchrios,* the belt of pregnancy, to protect my daughter. Rage and shame coiled in me like demons; I wrestled with them unceasingly, until my soul fragmented and wandered off into the world.

Thus did I suffer the first of my soul losses, dwelling long in that dark place, lost. My hatred terrified me lest it eat away the life growing in my womb.

The dark despair taught me about the black soul bequeathed me as my mother's daughter. From then on I knew that some measure of black hatred would cling to me for all time, and I began to understand why the wolf is black coated. That even hatred has a place on the Great Circle and must be honored.

The people of Ravenoak, my kin, likewise were suffering soul fragmentation and wandered about aimlessly, unable for a long time to sow and tend the fields, to husband and protect the stock.

I sat long in my hut with hooded eyes, remembering that Ganieda had kept his soul hidden in many places lest it be discovered and taken from him. How proud I had been to keep mine in the temple of my flesh! Henceforth would I, too, secrete my soul in many places: within the leg of the table; in the cry of my sister wolves when I heard them in the forest; even in the Morrigan's sidh, now that I recognized as kindred spirits the passion and hatred that were her province as Goddess of War.

In time I healed sufficiently to walk about and breathe more easily, though now carrying my newly fragmented soul only partly within. I stood under the Great Oak and addressed the people, old friends grown mature and young ones I had never met.

"Good people, have I an imperfection?"

"No!" they cried, relief on their faces. "Lead us!"

"Have I a mate?"

"Death to Cian and the Branna!" they shouted.

I knew my presence before the people would rub raw the collective wound of Ravenoak's conquest. For just days after the onslaught Cian Redmane had returned surrounded by his soldiers and the Druids of his tribe, who thereon camped beneath the Great Oak and set about preparing the King's Feast. The finest horse, a white stallion, was slaughtered and cut into gobbets of flesh that were tossed into the Dagda's cauldron, standing shoulder high at its rim. Beneath the cauldron was set a roaring fire tended by the Druids. The people of Ravenoak had come to watch the old ritual of the arrival of the new king, though their hearts were as angry as mine; I watched partially hidden in the surrounding wood.

When the flesh of the horse was fully cooked, Cian removed his clothes, stepped into the hot broth and, following tribal custom, drank some of the broth. Afterward he bade his subjects do the same. First came the Druids, three stern men in long cloaks bearing bowls of silver that they dipped and drank from, then retired. Next the soldiers advanced, surrounding the cauldron and dipping into the broth with wooden bowls or, if they had no bowls, catching the liquid on the edge of their knives or with dirty hands.

Cian raised his voice. "Good people of Ravenoak! I bid you drink! From this day forward we are kin like in the old days, never to be sundered again. There is goodness in the Cauldron of Warmth. Let our differences be healed!"

No one of Ravenoak came forward to drink excepting the mad Senchan, who approached like a kicked dog, nearly shaking to pieces from spasms of pain. He was an ancient bundle of rags dragging himself to the cauldron's lip, babbling all the while. He dug a claw into the recesses of his rags and produced a cracked wooden bowl. Jabbering in a mystic tongue, he dipped the bowl as Cian stared in wide-eyed horror. For this was a bad sign, that the first of Ravenoak to drink be a madman. By all rights it should have been the queen. But my feet were stone. The Senchan drank, the broth dribbling down his idiot chin, after which the soldiers carried him roughly away. I withdrew, knowing that no others of our tribe would drink.

And so after a fashion Cian established himself as king of Ravenoak. Following the humiliation over the broth he departed to his own village, leaving many soldiers to watch over his subdued flock.

Now, months later, as I spoke under the same Oak to a crowd of my people, I spied Cian Redmane's soldiers leaning on their lances, standing at some distance keeping their eyes on me. The story of my Druid wind had spread among them. They were openly afraid of me, which was of some use.

"You are kind to proclaim me free of blemish and fit to rule, but consider: Your king is consort to a woman of another tribe; my right eye is blind," I replied plainly. "Although my mother ruled long and well as the descendant of queens, mine is a different task. Ravenoak must yet defeat the Branna and establish her own queen and king." I knew well enough I was leading my people in a futile dream, but I had learned from Ganieda that words may be used falsely in good cause. Thence did I learn the usefulness of sly language when it might give people heart. I remembered clearly that Ganieda had conjoined love and words; I was using crooked words out of love.

I called to Conaire, an old man I knew from girlhood as trusted minister to my father and mother, and bade him lead our tribe. The people quickly gave their consent and dispersed, for all were afraid of the Branna soldiers. I walked with Conaire past the Great Oak, down lanes where people were busy rebuilding their houses and still mourning their dead with sprinkled offerings. They greeted us kindly as we passed.

"What will you do, Guryn?" he asked. It pleased me to hear my Celtic name again.

"Begin my life as healer and seer," I replied firmly.

"The wheel is turning for Ravenoak," he shook his head. "Cian Redmane I think means to devastate us."

"I think not," I countered. "He is benign, in his way, and would have Ravenoak for his own without further war if he could."

"Our people will not know which of us to follow. And I am no leader."

I stopped to regard Conaire Grey-Hair in his prime, his blue eyes bright. He spoke the truth, and I could only nod.

"A new presence goes among us," he continued. "A solemn man from a settlement to the south who speaks our language. He comes cloaked in black, wears the sign of the Christian cross around his neck, and does not smile. Each day under the Oak he preaches, proclaiming to bring the good news of his One True God. I fear the old story comes round again. Invasion and death," he finished sadly.

I shuddered, for I knew as well as he the old stories of Patrick and his Christian brethren, who had brought their God of hate and death in the name of love to our beautiful land of Eire. I felt a deep sickening in my heart, even as the life stirred in my womb. The sad story returned to mind of the blond invader from the Northlands, which the skull had told in my father's voice during my initiation. Conaire was right; the old stories traveled the Great Circle, too, visiting us again and again!

"Even here, so far from the old land, we meet them," I sighed.

"He goes by the name of John Stewart," Conaire explained. "A Saxon name."

"The Saxons," I grunted. "Who take life at a distance."

"Shall we send him away? Already some listen to him and begin to cast aside the old ways. Your mother was ready to banish the man before the Branna fell upon us."

I reflected. Our people's beliefs were their own concern. Some worshiped one God, others another; some prayed to two Gods, many to several. Together we gathered on the great feast days—Beltaine, Samhain, Imbolc, and Lughnasa. All knew the old stories and loved them. And when we made friends with the red people, their stories became ours, and ours, theirs. We, too, learned to honor the Old Woman of the North who had brought grain to the two starving red hunters, remembering her in our prayers at Samhain when the fairy knolls opened.

My mother had taught me about the black-cloaked strangers who worshiped the God named the One True God, having brought that God's intolerance and wrath with them from the old land. The Romans in ancient times had killed some of our people, but that was for political domination after we rose up against them to regain Eire for our own. The black-coated Christians, however, seemed to kill out of vengeance when by their judgment the heathen had angered the One True God—usually by doing nothing more than listening to wondrous stories and longing to live amongst the fairies. Why were different beliefs and practices from theirs so wrong to them?

That was when it struck me that my fate would be tied to these Christians, for my heart still longed terribly to return to the fairy world, the source of those magic blue lights! To walk with my father in the Morrigan's sidh! To sing the old songs and dance and tell the stories, to listen to the stories of the Gods and Goddesses and heroes and so abide with them for a time....

To fulfill such desires required respect for spells and shape-shifting. Yet the magic of spell-making and the profundity of shape-shifting evoked those very powers the Christians feared and hated. I did not understand at the time why the Christians considered not believing in their creed as blasphemy, only saw that it was so, which troubled me deeply.

"I must meet with John Stewart the Christian," I declared at last. "We send no foreigner away who is willing to live among us in peace. Others have come to stay in peace."

"Beware his tongue," Conaire warned simply, as I nodded and left him.

THE SHORT TIME I lived in Ravenoak was bittersweet. I did not see Ganieda and knew not to expect him, for I had already spent Beltaine that year with Oroonca and him. I lived in the small house I rebuilt on the edge of the wood, away from the Great House in which I had lived as a child, and collected herbs and plants for my potions. I chanted, sucked my thumb, and used second sight to offer healing words to people who came for help or advice. Out gathering herbs in the woods one day I found another dog, black like Fern; I named him "Fern" in memory.

Still a young woman, I felt the young life in my body stirring. My maternal soul sought to live in Ravenoak the rest of my life, there to raise my daughter, but a deeper voice told me that was not to be.

Cian returned after several more months away. While I did not avoid seeing him—indeed, watched from my window as he passed with his wife and child, accompanied by soldiers— nevertheless he did not come to me. As my belly grew I made no secret of who had fathered the child. Some of the people were sympathetic; others spat and scorned me as I passed. I could not hate them for that, however, and instead vehemently urged the people to throw off the rule of the Branna. Those who had seen me kill some of the Branna and fight against Cian himself held out hope I might become a warrior again and lead the people into battle.

Nor was that to be, I knew. For a time I was content to make my way as a healer and storyteller. My father had taught me poetry, so I was able to teach some of the young children the old stories in verse—in particular, of the three Cauldrons of Warmth, Vocation, and Wisdom and how to use them.

With increasing stridency John Stewart the Blackcoat preached his Christian message under the Great Oak, although I quailed to think of him as our enemy. Even so, there was no avoiding him or his mission. Some in our hard-pressed tribe were beginning to believe that those who followed the God of Charity would have easier lives. Much impoverishment had fallen on Ravenoak since being conquered; we were a fallen people. John Stewart promised that his God would raise us up through acts of Christian love. Yet Stewart did not act full of love.

When one day I walked past him as he stood preaching on a rock to dozens of people, he called out to me. He was a young man, perhaps no more than thirty, with thin arms, pale face, and glaring, frightened eyes sunken in his skull. His arms raised, he held in his left hand a black book he seemed to have always with him, which I assumed was his book of spells.

"Guryn Thornback!" he called out in a ringing voice. I stopped, shifting my basket across my round belly as Fern turned to regard the stranger. Because I had never married and I lived alone, those who mistrusted me called me "Thornback"—*old maid*—rather than "Guryn." It was customary for all young women to marry, else to become healers or prostitutes to survive. I had responded by taking their taunt as my family name, so now all knew me by that.

I moved to the back of the crowd and waited.

"Some say you practice the dark arts," John Stewart shouted.

I remained silent.

"Have you nothing to say in your defense?" he persisted, eyes widening. I did not understand his question.

"What are the dark arts?" I asked.

"They are—*eh-hem!* They are those arts that the Devil himself, Lucifer, practices: necromancy; chiromancy; the mantic arts. Summoning forth and speaking with demons!" he cried, waving his arms. "May the Lord Jesus save and protect us from such foulness!"

I stared at this man, at his narrow, sagging shoulders and conical hat, his pale, pasty skin and hard eyes. He looked like a piece of dried meat, devoid of blood. All the same, I deliberated how to respond, since many people had turned to look at me.

"Demons inhabit this world and the Otherworld, that I know," I replied evenly. "I have learned their names in Solomon's *Clavicule* and in the Lesser Key, the *Lamegeton*. I do not summon them—only a fool would do so."

"So you know their names!" he cried triumphantly. "By what authority have you learned them?"

I considered silently. "By my own," I answered at last.

"It is said, Guryn Thornback, that you prophesy the future and see into the dark world. Is this so?" he asked.

"I practice *Imbas Forosnai*," I replied. "I have seen the Salmon of Wisdom and have spoken with the fairies. I have walked as wolf and died and been reborn many times."

"The Lord God commands that none may prophesy without His consent. Do you pray to Jesus Christ, Guryn? Are you a believer?" he snapped.

"I believe all that exists."

"You practice the dark arts, Guryn. You are a witch, admit it."

"I am not a witch," I answered quite easily, for I was not. I recalled Ganieda teaching me about the witches of Europe, of Wicca and the fivefold path. "They are our sisters and brothers, but of another order," Ganieda had instructed.

"I am a worker in the invisible world," I explained to Stewart. "Are you not such yourself?" I challenged him.

"Then you are in league with the Devil and must repent! You must ask forgiveness of the Lord!" John Stewart declaimed, falling to his knees on the stone, hands raised to the sky. "Lord, look down upon this poor, wretched sinner and make a believer of her! Show her the error of her ways! Raise her up out of the darkness in which her poor pagan heart struggles, ignorant of Thy light and glory!"

At this I turned and left. His prayers seemed full of rage and hatred, like curses directed at me. It was bad to remain close to him, so I went to the woods, turning over his words. I understood little of their meaning, nor who could be the God he spoke of. Gathering the herbs of protection I needed, I returned to my cottage.

As soon as I opened the door, Fern rushed in and snarled at the intruder who was studying my few possessions. John Stewart turned.

"Guryn Thornback, I have come to offer you a chance at life," he said, his voice soft as he held forward his black book of spells.

"You are welcome in my house so long as you place no spells. I have already protected my home by means of a sacred circle," I explained calmly, though my heart raced.

"What—with this?" he sneered, snatching a bunch of tied herbs hanging from a beam. He shook the bundle in my face, his eyes ablaze. "In Europe they are burning women for offenses far less than those you commit openly here! Do you understand?"

"I have seen the burning in my visions," I replied slowly. "I am protected."

He laughed scornfully. "You? You are not protected! The good people of Ravenoak are hearkening to my words; they cleave unto the Lord thy God. You will pay the price for your heathen ways if you persist. I give you good warning, as I am a God-fearing man," he remonstrated. He threw the bundle to the floor and pressed a black boot into the herbs, grinding them to dust.

"Here is how God punishes the worshipers of Satan," he snarled. Suddenly I saw the angry panther that had overtaken him. His was a hatred that would burn forever, bubbling and boiling without relief, for it was ashamed of itself. I saw this difference between us: My hate was not shameful to me, and so it had the chance to cleanse.

"You will leave now," I commanded. He looked surprised.

"I have stronger protections," he countered, his voice low and threatening. "I know who you people are—renegades from Ireland, pagan worshipers who would not submit to Saint Patrick's holy ways. You have run far, but now the Lord has found you out, as He said he would. 'I am with you even unto the consummation of the world,' so saith the Lord."

I began to chant, a stream of words issuing unbidden from my mouth. My good eye grew dim, and in the half-light I saw John Stewart grow wide-eyed in fear, then rush out.

In the days that followed I could find no peace in my cottage. I saw in visions all that was passing in Ravenoak, the great upheaval. Cian Redmane now professed the new faith that the Lord God was the only true God, renouncing all belief in the older pantheon of Gods. John Stewart poured water over the king's head and gave Cian the new name of Paul. Sometimes when I wandered the town and watched from the rear of the crowd, I saw Cian's face growing as pale and colorless as John Stewart's. And I realized he was no longer king, that a new spirit had taken rule of him. I wondered whether he knew there was a new king in Ravenoak.

Cian began to use violence against the people in ways he had never used before outside of wartime. I sensed his heart was sad to forego the tribal feasts and singing of the old stories around the fire, now that John Stewart had forbidden true Christians from heathen celebrations—by which meant any occasions not centered around prayer. Even as my round belly protected the growing life inside me, the swelling tension of my surroundings was unsettling: I knew of no magic powerful enough to shield us from the coming dangers. Incantations made of words were no match against strong-armed believers on a mission.

I avoided John Stewart afterward, contenting myself with the company of the few people who still came to see me, healing them by the old ways.

As John Stewart's black-coated friends started to settle in Ravenoak, I noticed their half-veiled glances at my belly whenever they passed me—judgmental looks from a people who felt themselves forever watched over by a judging God.

When summer came around more Blackcoats arrived from the sea to the east, many sailing up the Boyne in tall-masted ships. Whole families in black dress came to live among us that season, the women not speaking and humble before the men, their men grim and determined. They set about building houses of wood rather than with wattles and clay, cutting down scores of trees and wasting many more by setting huge unbanked fires for no apparent purpose. They built a large church wherein they shut themselves up to worship their God and trembled like lambs as John Stewart preached from his black book, admonishing them lest they stray from the true path. Before long Ravenoak bustled with more of them and fewer of us. We descendants of Druids were the old ones in this new land—and I but twenty-three!

Though I kept mostly to myself, the Blackcoats began to whisper audibly as they passed, shunning me entirely at last. The harvest came in as the trees began to shower gold and orange leaves upon the forest floor; the festival of Samhain was coming on. Those of us unconverted to the One True God were busy preparing for the night when the two worlds would be open to each other.

Two days before the feast day Cian came to me. "You must leave Ravenoak immediately," he commanded, avoiding my eye as he spoke. Wearing a cross pendant tied around his neck with a leather thong, he was changed in manner and yet not changed. He was cowed and overly polite, but a strange, unhealthy anger glowed far back in his eyes as he touched the cross at his chest.

"There is shame upon you?" I asked, touching my womb.

"Word goes about that you invoke spells on behalf of those still unbelieving—"

"Say rather, those who still believe the old ways," I interrupted.

He nodded sharply. "As you will. I care nought for my shame. I forgive you—"

"You forgive me?" I cried out. "By what right do you speak thus?"

"All this is—from a time past," he muttered wearily, waving his hand vaguely in the direction of my womb. He could scarce stand to look there.

"A time past!" I stressed, my anger rising, thinking of my time coming.

"Yes, for the Blackcoats bring us God's love and healing," he continued hurriedly.

"God's resentment," I laughed scornfully. "Days ago I anticipated your visit, Cian Redmane—never "Paul" to me! Your noble anger, your warlike nature, even your overpowering of me—these I might have loved for the sake of your child. But not the whimpering, cowardly, scowling ways you have taken on in the name of your God."

"This is a powerful God, Guryn," he replied softly, still bowing his head, so that I knew not whether to strike him, to curse him, or to touch his head softly as once I did, for a moment...

Finally he faced me, sensing my confusion. "You must leave Ravenoak—before they come for you. They are powerful now, the Christians."

"You have forfeited them your power," I countered. "You no longer seek out your wise healers and seers for guidance. I see clearly that you think to consolidate your power by acceding to their God. It will end badly, for you and for Ravenoak."

"I dare not," he whispered, hanging his head. "Others have become the healers—only those men called by God to minister. And prophecy is blasphemy."

"Only men may heal? Do they know herb and root as do we who are steeped in the lore? Speak! Are you not still king?"

"A higher King who lives in heaven rules us all. Praised be His name." He touched his cross again.

"My prophecy so soon has come to pass: You no longer rule Ravenoak. When these days I put my thumb in my mouth, visions of the new king appear before me—but they are dark visions. The red people have warned us of the white man come to drive them off their land—if he does not kill them first. Is it out of your new King's love that I am being driven out of my home, along with our friends?"

"It is for your safety!" he growled through clenched teeth. "I am in danger even coming to warn you."

"The real king is now John Stewart," I observed bleakly. As Cian made haste to leave, I felt the world too heavy to bear, the weight in my belly a sickness I had best be rid of.

The following day Fern and I returned from the wood to find our cottage burned to the ground, reduced to smouldering ash.

"Guryn, they look for you even now, to take you to the Oak for trial," a woman whispered, hurrying by as I stood dumbstruck before my razed house.

"Tried for what?"

"Witchcraft," she explained. "The Blackcoats proclaim witchcraft a burning offense against God," she finished and scurried away, throwing her cowl over her head.

Feeling for Oroonca's blade strapped to my side, I hailed Fern away from snuffling the ashes and wrapped my cloak about me. I had no food but did not bother about that. I would be able to find food in the woods, for Oroonca had taught me well. Before setting out for Ganieda's cottage, I passed hastily by the Great Oak to leave a token there that might protect the spirit of Ravenoak from the Blackcoats. Afterward I searched out Conaire at his cottage, finding him agitated.

"Guryn! You must flee!" he gasped when he saw me. "I can do nothing for you, and Cian will not. Soon they will come for me," he finished mournfully, collapsing on his pallet.

"They are themselves the very demons they claim to fight," I snapped, my heart hardening in my chest. "I am going to Ganieda's—come with me!" I tried to raise him, but his thin arm fell back when I pulled.

Conaire shook his head. "I am not as young as you. Ganieda knows me only in passing—and perhaps there is still time to restrain the Christians from their evil intentions."

"Under the Oak at the meeting rock I have left a token for John Stewart to find," I explained. "Thus will he learn of our power."

"What have you done?" Conaire shrieked. "It will but fuel their fires of fear and hate—they already call upon their God to bring damnation down on us!"

Although I trembled, I set my mouth firm of purpose. "Part of my spirit will remain behind after I depart. When you see a lone she-wolf stand by the Oak, you will recognize me. Protect her, good Conaire!" I begged, and turned to go, making my way by a circular route into the wood.

As I passed the last house two horsemen rode up from behind, calling out "Halt!" I kept walking, drawing up the Druid wind behind me with a word of incantation. Swirls of dust blinded the riders while I disappeared into the forest.

Evening fell as I walked; it was Samhain. Already I had walked far from Ravenoak when I heard horses thundering through the wood and knew at once they were pursuing me. I knelt down to Fern.

"Go quickly, little one—save yourself. They will leave you alone, so perhaps you will divert them from me." I patted his head, and he ran off in a different direction. By now the horses were close enough to view plainly through the darkening trees. John Stewart rather than Cian rode at the head of a troop of armed and helmeted soldiers, thrusting out a cross before him like an amulet, as if to light up the gloaming.

I stood next to a tree, whispering an incantation beseeching it to hide me inside. Leaning against the trunk I stood very still, breathing deeply of the tree's spirit. The horses halted in a shamble of hooves and neighs as their riders reined them in, the men casting looks all about them.

"Her tracks lead here and stop," a rider called out, pointing to the damp ground.

"Then she is close by, the witch!" Stewart swore softly. "We shall catch her yet—and child or no, she will burn!" He gestured to his men. "Some go that way, some this. I will drive straight on."

As the others spurred away into the growing darkness, Stewart chucked his horse forward at a slow gait.

I looked around. Blue lights danced in the distance—a fairy knoll! I moved toward the lights, chanting the song Ganieda and I had sung years before when last we saw the fairies. No longer concerned with Stewart and his soldiers, I continued walking, certain I would find protection in the sidh.

When I drew closer to the lights, I discerned a fire glowing fantastically at the center of a ring of tall rocks, where a group of beautiful Little People were dancing slowly and gaily about to the music of soft bells. Within the circle of rocks presided strange and beautiful purple trees. I prayed and crouched, waiting that the dancers might call out to me; I was certain they knew of my presence, for fairies can sense all nearby spirits. All the same it is not possible even for one who knows their ways to draw near unless they allow it. A dark-haired tiny woman, radiant in a golden gown, beckoned me forward. I stood up and entered the ring of rocks.

"Welcome, Guryn," she sang, her voice like snow falling in the wood. She held out her hand, and I smiled in relief.

A clap of thunder roared behind me, inducing the dancers to stop and wait. I turned to catch John Stewart dismounting and coming forward, grim and fierce, brandishing his cross before him like a sword unsheathed. As more thunder shook the earth the rest of the soldiers appeared, reining in and waiting in the near distance.

"In the name of the Heavenly Father, come out of your demon circle!" Stewart demanded of me. "You have much to answer for, Guryn," he insisted, pulling from his pocket and shaking at me the token of bundled herbs tied with red ribbon that I had left beneath the Oak. "This is some of your devil-witching!"

"Will you not greet our hosts?" I asked mildly, gesturing about.

"Are you mad? Which hosts are those?" he snickered, looking all about.

I saw that he was blind to the fairies, seeing nought but a poor woman heavy with child standing in the middle of a ring of stones, alone in the nighttime wood. But I also saw that he feared some invisible demon might be present, giving me protection. I was jolted to realize it was this fear that gave him false visions of evil.

"By the power of God, I cast out your demons and summon you hither!" he cried, flinging down my token and holding the cross out before him, his hand shaking.

I looked at the beautiful woman for a sign. Regarding Stewart calmly as simply a boy possessed himself by a demon, she held out her hands to him with an accepting smile. Her face glowed like moon crystal. I looked back at Stewart.

Still holding the outstretched cross, he stared agape over my shoulder at the fairy woman. Evidently she had allowed him to see her. His arm finally slackening, the cross fell to his side, his eyes all the while never leaving the woman's face. He knelt slowly, transfixed by the sight. A long while he knelt thus, hunched shoulders contorted, struggling with himself as if deep in tormented adoration. For a moment he seemed to master himself and straighten up. I glanced at the fair woman to see whether she might be torturing Stewart, but from her serene eyes I knew she was not, that Stewart himself was causing his own torture. With one part of him he would adore and praise the fairy princess forever and ever, yet with another part hate himself for that. At last he shrieked loudly, covering his eyes with his hands until these, too, wavered and fell. Tears streaming down his enraptured face, he could do nothing but look upon the fairy princess, his expression contorted with grimaces and sudden smiles of transfiguration.

At the sight of their leader's weakened condition his men advanced and dragged him away, searching with terrified eyes for the cause. Unable to see the fairies, they lifted Stewart onto his horse, leaving his cross and my token behind, and with backward glances rode off into the night.

I knelt before the tiny lady, who bade me rise.

"You may continue on your way; it is a fine night for walking in the wood. No harm can come to the fairies' friend traveling in the company of the little one." She called Fern's name; he was there in a twinkle, panting and smiling.

"But before embarking on your journey wherein much sadness awaits, you are invited to join our Samhain feast," the lady indicated with a wave of her hand. As I looked behind me I saw a long table spread with plates and cups and food. She sat down at the head, and I beside her; the little people gathered around and with much musical laughter ate and drank, as did I. Even Fern ate from his bowl beside me on the ground. And for hours, it seemed, we breathed in the clear night air of the fairy mound, which enlivened my drooping spirit like a tonic.

When at last I drained my cup I asked the lady's leave, thanking her and all the fairy folk for their hospitality. The food I ate was manna and the drink magical mead, and thence soon I would be marked with wasting sickness, I knew; any more of the fairies' kindness would be death to a longing heart. For their manna was heartbreaking, and their mead left an ache. Still, I was filled with calm while with them. Happily, the lady bestowed her blessing on my visit to Ganieda, friend of the fairies, whereupon I rose and kissed her hand. As Fern and I left the circle I resumed the chant to the fairies, my heart uplifted albeit sore from the parting. We two travelers made our way down paths lit by the moon and by blue lights that flitted through the trees as the night wore on...

In two days I reached the land of rolling hills where Ganieda's cottage lay, the sight of smoke wreathing from the chimney making my heart leap. Strong indeed were the spells the old Druid had cast, to leave him safe from the Blackcoats!

I knocked and opened the door to find Ganieda stretched out upon his straw bed in the far corner. I went quickly to him; something was wrong. His wasted body panted as his good eye stared upward. Cratered pustules, erupted and emitting a foul odor, streamed ichor down his cheeks and across his chest where his nightshirt lay open.

"Ganieda!" I whispered, horrified.

He twisted his head to look at me. "Be gone! No spells are powerful enough to protect you from this evil!" he croaked in a voice that wrung tears from me. Dropping my bag I shooed Fern over to the fire, which I built up hurriedly until a lively blaze leaped in the hearth. I turned back to aid my master.

I drew water from the spring at the back of the cottage, glancing up darkly at the skull glowering fatefully, then returned to heat the water over the fire. I broke herbs from my crane-bag into the hot water and bathed Ganieda's head and shoulders, chest and arms with the soothing liquid. The aromatic steam made my heart rise, and I smiled at him. Soon Ganieda seemed in less pain, for his face relaxed and he returned a cracked smile.

"You must not stay. The spirit will enter you and your child," he mumbled.

"This is the water elf disease," I spoke aloud, confirming the sickness.

"Some far worse demon than that," he croaked.

I touched my womb. Of all the spells I had concocted, the most powerful were for protection of my child, to ensure that no evil could touch her. My guiding wolf snarled at the prospect of danger.

"More powerful than any," he replied ominously. "The Blackcoats have brought smallpox in blankets to Oroonca's people. Soon I will die, but you must go at once to find Oroonca. Fighting rages with the Britons from the coast; I fear for his people."

"The Blackcoats have taken over Ravenoak," I murmured, continuing to bathe his wounds.

Ganieda nodded. "Heed the words of Oroonca. 'When the snow falls, the wise animal burrows.' You must find your burrow, Little Tree," he insisted softly, and I smiled to hear my old name; it seemed so long ago. "A place of anger and love; your heart inside out."

"I will go to Oroonca's village," I assured him.

"No!" Ganieda growled. "There the disease took me, when I sought to help Oroonca's sick people. Oroonca himself suffers—"

"His mother, Nanepa—is she sick, too?"

"I do not know. She was abroad when last I visited the tribe. All my work come to nought," he finished sadly. "They die like leaves, our friends..."

For two days I watched over Ganieda, sleeping little, bathing him with potions, applying Oroonca's leaves. And when the great sigh escaped him as the spirit left his body, I closed his eyes. What to do next was clear. So after packing the *Clavicule* and some smaller books in Ganieda's leather bag, I shooed Fern outside and set about to burn the cottage.

Hastening to the back of the cottage, I set the pigs and the cow free, then returning inside I took a torch from the fire and shut the door firmly. I walked around the cottage chanting spells of protection for Ganieda's spirit, touching the torch to the old cabin. Soon the flames roared and wrestled with the dry wood, blackening it and torturing the timbers into cinders. Backing away with Fern, I stood with heated face and heart, watching the last of my old life being consumed. Fingering the extinguished torch and smudging its black ash on my face, I smeared my cheeks until I knew I was as dark as Ganieda.

I kept vigil, crouched under a nearby oak, until the cabin collapsed in embers and the flames flickered away into the air. Shouldering my heavier pack, I turned my face to Oroonca's village.

IN ONE DAY I reached the village, only to find utter desolation. Everywhere lay corpses or else too many dying, people's faces full of the horrible bursting pustules that streamed with so foul a stench. The ravaging sickness was already too pervasive and too severe for me to help. Hurrying away, I made camp that night in the crook of a sturdy old Oak who seemed to care nothing for the sufferings of humans. I lit a small fire, poked at it with a stick, and chewed the dried bread I had brought, seeing into the dark. No visions came, however, not even when I thrust my thumb into the fire, then sucked it for relief.

That night I dreamed Oroonca was leading me down a long wooded path. Lights flickered in the trees, and in the distance hunters pursued a hind.

I awoke understanding whither I had to go. After wandering in the wood following Fern's nose, we came upon the mouth of the ancient cave Oroonca had once led me through. In the dark, without a torch, I found the stone and unrolled it. Asking my child's forgiveness, I lay down on my belly and crawled into the dark suffocation. Fern crawled along behind, whimpering.

The blackness was deep; I trembled and halted. Fear had entered me, and it was unfamiliar. Not since first arriving at Ganieda's cottage had I felt afraid; my willfulness always overpowered any fears. True, Ganieda had taught me the importance of fear, but my pride and will to follow after my mother refused me any sign of hesitation or weakness.

Now the words of the old Druid sprang to life: Fear moves like a wolf; to ignore fearfulness would mean not to heed the wisdom of my spirit animal. The day John Stewart had broken in with his threats, I was inwardly afraid not for myself but for the fledgling life inside of me. Was it possible that as the child grew in my womb, fear grew beside her like a dark twin? The thought haunted me as I crawled in the darkness, making the darkness weigh more heavily upon me with each push through the low passageway. When after a while the tunnel constricted to its narrowest, I was forced to stop. Even if I had wanted to run from the fear pursuing me, I no longer had a choice: I was nearly pinned in place, panting in the dark.

All was silence. Where was I going? What was I doing? A dream had brought me there without my understanding why. Had not the dreams of magicians sometimes driven them to their deaths? Ganieda, I felt certain, foresaw his fate in going to Oroonca's village—and yet he went. Had he, too, been inwardly fearful, an old man living alone in the deep woods? Now I had joined him, I realized; now I was his equal; now I was afraid.

My belly ached mightily even though the birth was still far off. Now that I had cracked a door to meet with fear, my sense of discomfort filled the tunnel like a plenum: All of a sudden I feared what lurked in the cavern room. Was Oroonca there, as the dream had hinted? Sick? Might my child become sick? I felt myself squeezed in the middle, barely able to breathe, trapped in the tension between a desire to go forward and an impulse to flee in panic. The running began far back in my soul. Yet I lay still, panting now in the spirit of wolf, who suddenly was with me. The vision was dizzying...

I saw her clearly: lean and black like my face and heart, eyes narrowed—was she looking at me? Standing on a hillside, sniffing the air once, nostrils flaring. She, too, carried young in her womb. I sensed her ready to run at the slightest unfriendly sound from the wood. She loped off, knowing instinctively which way to move—why, then, my own dreadful uncertainty?

She turned and trotted away, leaving me in the black tunnel. The vision had lasted only a moment, but tears streamed down my cheeks. She had left me! *Help me!* I cried out to her. She turned once and stared into my eyes. I heard her speak for the first time.

"No," she replied evenly, and trotted off. I observed her moving in an expansive arc to circle around behind me. Though I could no longer see her, I knew she was not far off—somewhere behind me, in fact, hovering and watching.

I wiped my eyes and crawled on, grunting and struggling. Only after a long time did the tunnel open into the cavern.

Within, a torch burned dimly. As my eyes adjusted to the light, I saw with sudden joy Nanepa crouched beside a small fire, turning a piece of meat on a stick! She turned slowly toward me as I rose unsteadily to my feet.

"Nanepa!" I gasped, going over to her and kneeling at her side. Now the tears came in earnest, as my mother's voice of derision passed through me like a chill wind for which I was nevertheless grateful.

Pressing my head against her withered breast, she patted me while I clung to her tightly, sobbing and shuddering.

"I do not wish this life, Nanepa," I muttered bleakly after a long time, speaking her tongue haltingly.

She whinnied a high-pitched laugh and raised my head, pressing a bowl to my lips. The hot porridge warmed me.

She clucked and regarded me. "Nor do I, young mother," she chuckled, smiling her toothless smile. "But how am I to eat this meat without teeth?" she asked.

"Nanepa, Ganieda is dead. Where is Oroonca?" I trembled, still clinging to her.

She straightened herself and pointed. I followed her gaze to a dim corner where Fern sat quietly, having drunk his fill from the cave's spring. He seemed to be standing guard over the huge form of Oroonca, who lay asleep or in a swoon. Or was he—

"Dead?" I gasped.

"Dead two days. Last of my children. My magic is no good," she finished sadly, though she was smiling strangely.

"Oroonca! Gone to the spirits!" I wailed, rising and going over to him. Kneeling beside him, I took in his ravaged face, still proud and strong in spite of the sickness. His features in repose called up the time he taught me hunting: his mouth set in concentration, corners turned inward revealing little; his jaw still firm and unspeaking, as it so often was in life.

I murmured a prayer of farewell to Oroonca, the second of my two friends and teachers now gone. Shakily returning to Nanepa, I sat down across the fire from her. She gave me more porridge, but I pushed it back at her. She passed me the meat.

"I see now why I cooked it," she explained, smiling. With her child dead but ten paces from her!

"I am not hungry," I replied, miserable.

"Eat!" she fairly screamed, jolting me backwards. She nudged the piece of meat toward me. "You are hungry, and so is your child. Eat!"

With a trembling hand I took the meat and sat back. It smelled good, and my empty stomach craved it. Giving Nanepa a glance, I chewed slowly. I was ravenous.

"What shall we do? Where shall we go to be safe?" I asked, now hungrily chewing on the horseflesh. My *geis* prohibited only my eating of wolf meat. The food was tough but nourished the child and me. I took spirit and dried my eyes.

Nanepa regarded me with a twinkle. "I know of a place where my sisters live," she stated simply.

"Will you take me with you there?" I asked, rubbing the grease from my mouth.

"No, but I will allow you to take me there," she smiled gleefully. "You think I am able to walk to the moon rise? I am too old and will need your strength."

I began to cry again. This time I faced Nanepa and let the tears run.

"Less proud is good," she nodded, still smiling as if holding a secret. "The land we go to is ten days' walk, to the great-water-without-another-side. Gloucester."

I gasped. "Gloucester—? But that is where the Blackcoats live!" Yet even as I spoke a girlhood memory leaped to the fore, and I knew that was the place of my first vision.

"Not with them but with our sisters."

We sat and ate for a time, and even though my heart was full, I was uncannily full of longing, and my heart hurt; it hurt for the fairies, for I had the fairy-longing in me now. Even for Cian my heart hurt, for I longed for love and comfort. Already I knew this place, Gloucester; angry like me, as Ganieda had said. And within the anger, love.

While we slept Oroonca stood guard over our spirits, Fern with his head on his paws. In the morning we gathered sticks and formed a burial mound for Nanepa's noble son, chanting prayers over him that his spirit be released. Then, gathering our bags and crawling down the long passageway to the mouth of the cave, we stood blinking in the sunlight. I sniffed a cold wind blowing from the direction of Nanepa's village.

"Why did we not sicken—or will I?" I asked Nanepa, again seized with fear. She patted my arm, then gripped it.

"You had no visions in the night," she answered, staring into my eye.

And so we journeyed, the four of us, along trails foreign to me, for ten days toward the rising sun and moon as Nanepa guided us. Nanepa babbled like a lunatic, singing snatches of song and chanting bits of Indian magic in language I did not understand. My heart was bursting with loneliness and loss; many ghosts I carried within, all crouched beside my child.

11,

ÐIVINING BY TOUCH

Ten days of walking uphill and down brought us to the colony of Massachusetts on the promontory of Gloucester, where the people fished and grew corn. Throughout our long journey I half carried Nanepa as she mumbled directions and half followed after her, rushing to gather our few blankets on the mornings she would suddenly start up out of sleep and begin walking without a word. At times she staggered and tottered as if she would die on the next step. Fern did his best to herd her along, but neither he nor I knew whither she was taking us.

That was not altogether so; for, lying under my thin blanket in the dim woods at night, I recollected my vision of long ago as a girl at my mother's side: a town on the seashore, all of granite, surrounded by ragged woods of pine and oak. An angry place; a place fit for me, my mother had stated with her usual certainty. We were now headed there.

I grew to love the old Indian woman. By our fires she unfolded the secrets of her magical arts, matters Oroonca never taught me because he did not know them himself, according to his mother.

From her I learned cunning, something I had never valued even after growing to understand Ganieda's tricky ways and Oroonca's wily silence. Nanepa scoffed to hear that my spirit animal was the wolf, as we sat by our meager fire one night.

"You? Who has named you so?" she demanded, incredulous, tossing a scrap of old bread to Fern. He trotted off into the wood to find fresh food.

"I found wolf in my initiation vision," I answered.

"Guryn Newborn Wolf, then, you shall be," Nanepa pronounced flatly, "although a newborn wolf knows more about wiles than you. Have you ever enticed a man? Concocted a political scheme? Arranged to intersect lovers—or bring them together? Brought yourself some small goodness through a sideways chant?"

"What is a sideways chant?" I inquired.

Nanepa cocked an eye. "You know of the evil eye—yet know nothing of love?" she laughed, looking at my belly. "What is that?"

"I know—some matters," I stammered.

"Your mother hated men," she mused, as if she saw it all.

354

"But my father was a good and wise man, a bard and the king of—"

"I do not speak of kings, Newborn," she broke in, adopting the name she called me often thereafter. "Rather, men—*men!* Oh, men!" She reached over and patted my belly, to which my daughter replied with a quiver. Taking my face in her hard, bony hands with those crooked fingers, she held it tight while looking in my eye—studying my soul, it seemed. It was not an evil eye Nanepa cast, albeit a searching one nevertheless. She gave me a look more penetrating than any lover's, and no less threatening. Yet without guilt or guile she held me long. I looked down at last.

"It was done to you—or so you think," she declared, tilting her head. "So you deny your own wiles. Not a good practice," she finished, turning to the porridge I had cooked over our small fire.

"What have you to teach me?" I erupted, hesitant and angry, my face flushed. Suddenly I wanted to learn nothing from the old crone!

Nanepa—bless her!—ignored my outburst and chattered away. "Oh, many things about men, blessed men!"

"What about women, blessed women?" I parried slyly. Though I was asking in earnest.

"Get a man to teach you those things," she replied without blinking, slurping porridge out of our wooden bowl. "About men I know much, not least that thither lies magic! You are entering a time when a man shall be important—and love!"

I touched my belly. "My daughter and I need no man—"

"Oh, yes, you do! I need a man, too, though no man knows it, what with my poor husband dead. Do you wish a mate for life?" she wheezed, licking her lips deliciously. For Nanepa even the meanest of soups was a feast.

"I do not know what that means," I answered. "Besides, the life of a Druid queen in exile is not one for settled family life with children and a husband to hunt."

"Oh, but it is! My brave, Pauwa Sharp-Tooth, became my husband who brought me four children, many skins, and much meat. Am I not a medicine woman?" she demanded.

"You are a medicine woman," I admitted. "However, I am of a different sort."

She snorted, porridge drooling down her chin. "A woman wastes herself without a man."

Such talk confused me; I did not know how to answer. These were matters I would have to consider, which I began to do as we walked, ever toward the sea. My heart sank to think that each step was bringing us closer to the Blackcoats—those from whom I most wanted to run.

AT LAST we did reach Gloucester, the angry granite ground. My first view of the town was from a distance and by the light of a waning moon.

We emerged from the forest as evening fell. Nanepa stopped and pointed to the south, whereupon we spied dark houses with smoke rising and some few scattered lights in windows. In another village, the lights would have been inviting at journey's end. Instead, I shivered to think of the Blackcoats living within...

"Are we going into town?" I whispered.

"We stay north of it in this very wood, where my sisters live," Nanepa croaked. She led the way down a pile of boulders to the darkening water. Then down along the thundering sea we walked, boulder waves falling like avalanches upon the white sands. I stopped to watch. *Falling like a lover,* a voice whispered in my ear. Startled, I glanced quickly at Nanepa to see if she had heard the voice. I looked back at the waves. Wave after wave receded with a long, low rattle in the throat—this, too, like the rhythm of a lover, leaving inevitably, invariably, a catch of regret in his voice and arms...

How strange! To stand ashore as the moon rose over the water, dreaming of a man's arms around me! As Fern sniffed uncertainly at my heels, I pulled away and knelt beside him, ruffling his ears. I rose and hurried after Nanepa's receding form.

Up and over enormous boulders thrown down by giants we climbed. At a signal from Nanepa we turned inland, passing through low pine trees stunted by salt air and never-ending winds. Deeper still we ventured into the wood, the land rising all the while. Up and down hill and dale we traveled, in time arriving at a place where tall pines and oaks grew in abundance. Passing a clear stream as the moon settled down among the trees, Nanepa stopped in a grassy clearing.

"This is our new home," she declared simply.

I looked about. Nothing was there—neither friends nor sisters of Nanepa as she had promised. I wondered what foolishness had brought us here.

"Sit down and rest," Nanepa insisted, pressing her hard hands on my shoulders. I did as she commanded. She sat beside me, at ease and seemingly unconcerned we might be surrounded by the enemy in the middle of the nighttime woods.

A path ran from north to south through the clearing; approaching from the east, we had not seen it. Stuffing her roll under her head, Nanepa curled up in a ball and in no time fell asleep. I watched as the moon swung low in the trees and shivered under the stars. Fern nosed off into the woods to find his own dinner. My stomach growled. Sore and tired from walking, I did not bother with a fire; we had no food anyway. Trying not to feel hunger, I chanted softly, patting my belly to soothe the fledgling raven-child within. I drowsed in the dim light and leaned against a rock.

After a long while I was roused by voices. I shook Nanepa until she sat up, her old head rolling.

"Men!" I hissed. She looked north where the path disappeared into the trees.

When I started to rise, Nanepa pulled me back. Suddenly three men emerged around the bend, laughing and drinking and singing.

When they discovered two women huddled against the cool night, they stopped.

"Pretty mistresses—" began a young man, lifting his cap. An older, bearded one hushed him.

"Just a couple of old Indian squaws," he pointed out, shaking his head in disappointment.

"Haven't you two had enough for one night?" put in the third, a thin old thing. He tugged at his companions, but they shook him off, hovering over us. Their breath heavy with liquor, they swayed in the moonlight.

"Come along with us, squaws," slurred the bearded one. "We'll back to town and have us a party."

"Back to Sara's?" asked the thin one, scratching his chin and shaking his head.

"Oh, let's have a little fun with them before bed," proposed the bearded one. The young one frowned, then drunkenly broke out in a smile.

"Sure, fun!" he guffawed, clapping his hands.

"Get up, squaws!" bellowed the bearded one, pulling me to my feet. "Now, this one is something to look at. Why, you're no Indian! What are you?" he demanded.

They spoke English, which Ganieda had taught me. I looked at Nanepa, whose shrewd eyes told me she understood more than she revealed.

"No Indian I ever seen had blond hair," coughed the sickly one, coming closer and twitching my hair. I glared at him, so he backed away. "Maybe they's witches," he mumbled, glancing nervously at his fellows.

"Witches! So ain't Sara!" scoffed the bearded one. "Them witches with their broomsticks and spells—lot of good that does her! Can't even get herself food enough, has to entertain!" He turned back to us, rocking slightly and bearing down with his eyes.

"Now, what makes you ladies sit here in the dark? Waitin' for customers?" he taunted, laughing again and pawing at me. He made to throw off my shawl, but I caught his hand tightly and held it. His glassy eyes narrowed and cleared as the smile fell off his face.

"Oh, a mean one, eh?" he poked. "Come with me!" he yelled, yanking on my arm. He pulled me away from Nanepa as the younger one grabbed my other arm.

"She's a beauty!" he whispered as I struggled.

"We'll be back in no time!" the bearded one cried out to the third, who stood guard over Nanepa. The old woman stood and fixed him with a searing eye; he backed away, hesitant.

The other two shoved me into some nearby bushes and began to undo their belts. I lay crumpled on the ground, too stunned and weary to recover myself sufficiently to work my magic. As my thoughts cleared and I reached to unsheathe my *athane,* I heard the miraculous sound of a woman's singing piercing the night. I looked back down the path at Nanepa, but she was standing entirely still. The voice grew closer; the men heard it now, too, and stopped. The young one shot a stricken look at his friend.

"Sara!" he gasped hoarsely, his voice thrilling. Rebuckling his breeches, he darted off into the darkness, stumbling and scrambling over leaves and through the trees.

"*Th' divil—!*" swore the bearded one, catching sight of the older one scampering southward down the path after his young friend. The bearded one glared down at me, his eyes dark. "I'll be back for you, my pretty mistress!" he snarled, kicking my foot with his boot before stalking off down the path.

Now the voice rang out from the shadows, singing a ballad:

> *Hey, derry-down-doe,*
> *Merrily we go,*
> *Tonny-tonny-town-row*
> *Derry-derry-down.*

Staggering to my feet, I watched in the moonlight as a tall figure appeared from around the corner. Dressed like a man in leggings and a leather blouse, wide-belted at the waist, the woman wore high leather boots that tramped as she walked and sported a soft leather hat, its long red feather sticking out from behind. She was taller than I by a full head, her long chestnut hair flying out around her having caught in the trees a passing spirit, the waning moon gleaming off it.

Stopping when she spied her old friend, she let out a wild howl of delight and with a broad smile strode to Nanepa and embraced her, lifting her bodily up in the air. The old woman screeched, and the two proceeded to jabber in a tongue I did not understand. I approached.

Nanepa turned to introduce me.

"Sara Topping, at your service!" the woman cried out in a voice that boomed through the trees. Bowing low like a man and sweeping off her feathered hat, she stood upright with hands on hips, grinning at me as if there were some joke I did not understand. Perhaps the same joke Nanepa had laughed at when she looked at me in the cave... Sara's brow was broad and clear, her nose upturned and rounded, her cheeks round like apples, and her chin, though outthrust with determination, was alike rounded. She appeared to be about ten years or so older than I. Her broad smile revealed very white teeth, like trophies. Her eyes were soft brown like leaves and without any more guile. It seemed to me she was made of the stuff of trees and leaves.

She led us back up the path, Nanepa hobbling along while I, nearly falling down asleep, tottered behind. When I whistled softly, Fern joined us. Without a word about the men, Sara strutted along the path to her house as if she owned the wood.

In short order we came upon a rude cabin in the woods to which Sara welcomed us. She had built it herself of pine trees that she had hewn and split. Part of a circle of women healers and midwives, Sara long ago had traveled to Nanepa's village to learn the Nipmuc arts, whereupon she and Nanepa became fast friends.

Built upon a rock and set on its back like a whale swimming in the earth, Sara's cabin had three rooms, two on the lower floor, one a kitchen. A narrow stair fashioned of rough pine wound upwards to a sleeping loft. As the stone fireplace roared with good cheer, I looked about at the many skins, colored pictures, and shelves holding colored bits of glass, which the firelight touched and set aglow like lively elves.

These pieces of glass were very delicate and broken. Nearby, a diminutive white cat arched her fine back and circled her bowl.

"Pearl," Sara introduced as she observed the cat and me exchange a shy glance. I was struck that so strong and willful a woman would be taken by such delicate, womanly things of beauty.

"Out walking to shake out the seed!" Sara guffawed, breaking into gales of laughter. I sat wide-eyed as Nanepa nodded with a thin, cracked smile and rocked in the rocker. Sara gave us water followed by mead that she poured from a stone bottle, and already in this strange house I was beginning to feel safe. I found it curious how quiet Nanepa became, looking weary and old after just minutes in the snug abode. Her drooping eyes and shoulders were showing all the weight she had carried so lightly over the previous days, now that she was safe under Sara's wing.

With few words Nanepa told our story. Sara glanced at me, shaking her finger once or twice and winking broadly, conveying the same attitude that had disarmed me so at the moment of meeting her: as if all the travails of life—including my own!—were some secret joke. At first I took offense, until I reminded myself that a good guest must soften her contours to blend with those of her host. So, swallowing hard, I listened as Sara explained that she labored as a prostitute to supplement her meager income as a healer. She noted in passing how little effect such work had on her spirit.

"May you find a home here," she prayed, raising a cup of mead to me. "You are home when you sink into our midst, for you will find life very different from Ravenoak." Her voice was kind, and her brown eyes soft.

"You know of Ravenoak?" I asked with a surprised smile.

"In time you will hear my story—why I am one of the few familiar with your childhood home of Ravenoak."

Although I pressed her for details, she instead inquired after Nanepa, wishing to hear her sad story. As the fire burned down, I felt as if we three had sat for years conversing—and that we would be sitting so before a dying fire long into the future. A darkness over Ravenoak was distant, so I paid it little heed. Yet how I longed to see my home again! I promised silently that I would journey to the Otherworld to find a cure for Ravenoak's ills.

WITH FALL coming on, Sara prepared to bring in her small harvest. As the wind increased and the leaves blew about the woods, we three settled in to await my daughter's birth. I discovered that Sara Topping led an unusual life indeed in the hills outside Gloucester. Known by locals as a healer and apothecary, she was visited by villagers for the herbs and potions by which she cured all manner of ailments: headache, earache, and toothaches; water-elf disease, bleeding, and swelling. Her pantry shelves were chock-full of concoctions marked variously for treating the four hundred conditions, mixtures from which Sara dispensed precise dosages to her patients, explaining their particular usages and the requisite charms to utter with each.

The jars were labeled thus: shivering fits, swelling, dwarf, fever, flying venom; blains, St. Columkill's circle, whitlow, pocks; as well as big-with-child troubles. For treatment of this last, Sara brewed a potion for me when my time came that marvelously reduced the birth cramps. Although hundreds of small jars and boxes sat jumbled on the shelves, she always seemed to know where to put her hands on a particular herb. When villagers in need of her medicine came, Sara would take their hands and invite them to speak of their pains, all the while listening twice over: one ear cocked to the sufferer's voice, the other to the ailment's particular landscape. After a time even the shyest ones unburdened themselves.

Thus did I learn from Sara's patients the multitudinous shapes of suffering, as well as from Sara how to hear the wide variety of ways people use to tell their stories. I learned how someone will be kind to another in order to hide a greater unkindness; how a man will wander from home to follow a woman or a dream, that he might feel more strongly the chain of guilt around him—by way of backache. I learned how a child comes to bear the passions of her parents in her little body, suffering fits and becoming hateful, when it is her father and mother who hate each other. Above all I saw firsthand, just as Ganieda had taught, that each condition of the body has its correspondence in the mind, and these in turn their correspondence in the land or the weather or in a favorite animal.

Most people were too poor to pay Sara with more than a bit of broken glass or a ribband; those of means brought a chicken or goose that we then feasted on for several nights. Although Sara tended a small garden, the soil was too rocky for an abundant harvest. And so at times we went without, for all that winter we three ate the food Sara had grown for herself only.

Because Sara, Nanepa, and I were each adept in the midwife's art, from time to time we walked through the woods to the house of a woman quickening, there to help her child into the world and take in a few coins.

Sometimes Sara brought a man to the cabin, whereupon upstairs they climbed, shutting the small door to the loft. Nanepa and I sat below by the fire, as if waiting. True, I was startled the first time and my heart embittered, but life is a large cauldron that encompasses all the little we throw into it, as the sea swallows a pebble with a momentary ripple and soon smooths over. Even so, many times I felt compelled to leave the house when one of Sara's men appeared, especially any of the three who had menaced Nanepa and me in the wood. From their hesitant glances I knew they remembered me, though they said nothing.

I left the cabin then and stalked the bare trees as if trapped in a prison, snatching a long stick and swatting down the winter-dry shoots of undergrowth like so many men, finally trotting away alone down the long paths, heavy with child though I was.

Sara seemed unmindful of any awkwardness, welcoming the gifts of good food or few extra coins her patrons would provide. Disappearing into the deep wood, strutting along and singing at the top of her lungs for all the world to hear, stamping her fine long legs like a stallion, thereby to shake the seed out of her...

Afterward she used to dress herself up in heavy furs and go into town, to return with flour and grain, molasses and even an egg or two. Then we would make a feast, which though somehow melancholy for me would have a lively effect on Sara and Nanepa: Nanepa rocking back and forth laughing while Sara told wild stories by the blazing fire.

As the fine snow melted and the breezes began to blow from the south, I felt my time coming; my daughter had grown full in me. We three spent evenings gathered around the stone fireplace, Nanepa smoking her pipe and rocking slightly, staring into the fire, thinking no doubt of her Pauwa and Oroonca. The years sat upon her like stone, her back and her very bones having grown hard as an old gnarled tree. Sara, however, never sat still for long but rattled on, looking alternately at each of us or into the fire while recounting marvelous stories of her adventures, waving her large, graceful hands before the flickers so that they danced like puppets and dazed me. She spoke breathlessly, eyes dancing, as if the circle of time were still not enough to tell all she had to tell. For though far younger than Nanepa, Sara had already seen much in life.

"The gloomy ones are coming again, I can see it!" she exclaimed one night; even Nanepa turned to her.

"What do you mean?" I asked, touching my belly.

"Those who call themselves 'Puritans' and 'men of science' come to stoke people's fears, for their own are endless!" she declared. Suddenly her face took on the aspect of a snake: darting eyes at the fire, ready to strike.

"Who are they?" I asked warily.

"Have you not heard? The ones who charge that our healing does the handiwork of their Devil. You have seen them in the village—those men and women who go about with downcast eyes and wear black, grim faces with clenched teeth. They like their beer, but they like their praying more."

Reminded of the Blackcoats who had spread their fear to Ravenoak, I bristled to think of them still in that hallowed place.

"They are evil, and they do evil," Sara cursed, thrusting a stick into the fire and rising. "Bad enough they mutter maliciously about us behind our backs. But when they convince the people that our remedies bear the mark of their devil… What have we to do with their demon?" Sara cried, her voice booming in the low-raftered room.

"By their science these men would drive us out of the healing arts. They claim even birthing as their province, seeking to usurp our midwifery."

"Midwifery and healing have ever been women's work," I replied. Nanepa, who by this time had learned enough English to join in, spoke up.

Her voice croaking like an old frog, she addressed Sara. "They mean to leave us no work—except the foul sort you do."

My face went red for our host, who was a kind and generous woman. For a moment Sara glowered at Nanepa, then laughed grimly. "It keeps food on our table, old one," she drawled, her voice softer and a little sad. "None of us is rich, so we each must make shift to find our way."

Sitting between the two headstrong women, one old and the other in her haughty prime, I did not know what to think. Of course, like Nanepa I was ashamed for Sara. But Sara for her part did not seem to find selling her body shameful. In Ravenoak those who did such things were rarely spoken of, and though I noticed them slinking darkly along the paths, avoiding my eye as they passed, I had never spoken to them. With their greasy, stringy hair and their wasted bodies, I had thought them servants of the Morrigan: Death come to haunt the paths of Ravenoak, lovemaking as a war in which both sides paid dearly. It was bad luck to pass one of them, especially at night.

Sara, however, had kept the child in my womb alive by dint of her courageous heart. Even though men used her, she was by far the stronger and could have at any moment broken their necks, had she so pleased. Perhaps this was a wish on my part… For all that, after overcoming my initial reserve toward Sara I loved her dearly and used to follow after her into the woods to gather herbs. Wearing leather leggings and leather tunic open at the throat, her feathered hat waving in the breeze, she was a marvel to look upon, having the stride of a queen. It took time to accustom myself to seeing her form, with its large, broad hips and long legs, clothed in the manner of a man.

"Why do you wear men's clothes?" I asked her one day as we tramped through the wood. She had stopped to let me catch up, for the baby was nearly upon me.

She twitched a slender branch from a tree, switched the air. The buds were tight on the fingertips of the branches. "Because it feels good," she replied simply.

"Are you not afraid of what the villagers think?"

"Are they thinking?" she asked, her mouth curling.

"I am a healer and a whore, and that should give them enough to think about to leave me alone the rest of the time," she continued walking, her long chestnut hair flying behind her like a flag.

I gave birth in Sara's cabin where the girl came with ease, for Sara and Nanepa helped. Still, she arrived with a piercing scream, which startled us. Lifting my daughter up in her strong arms, Sara wrapped her in a lamb's skin while Nanepa walked thrice around the baby with the fire *deosil*. They cut the navel string and took up the afterbirth, part of which Sara buried in the earth; the rest she kept as a cure for women unable to bear children.

Afterward my child was lustrated nine times in the milk of goats, that she might receive many gifts, but again the little one screamed upon immersion in the milk. Nanepa shook telling bones over her, Sara laid out tarot cards and cast her chart, and by these it was foretold: My daughter would follow me as a great and wise shaman, traveling further than I in the world.

Diana, where are you? I am grown old and weak…and can no longer go with the wolves searching for you. I shall bury these words in the fairy mound and protect them with strong spells, so that you may find the journal one day when you return. Herewith I pass on to you, as Ganieda and Oroonca and Nanepa and Sara have given unto me, the sum of all my lore.

SO MY DAUGHTER grew, and I became strong again. Sara and I found a ruined cottage deeper in the wood, not far off, with an old well in the back that we cleared of stones. Together we raised a new roof and thatched it, swept the place out, and hung a door of planks. There I moved with my daughter and Fern. After some years Fern died; when soon after an old dog wandered up to the door of our cottage, I named him Finn; he slept the rest of his life away by the fire. I told fortunes, gave salves and potions to the ailing, kept pigs and even a cow after some years. Diana grew up playing with the animals and running in the woods, and I seemed content.

Diana's early years were marked by the King Philip War during which the Blackcoat women warned us to fear for our lives, for the raging Indians were coming to inflict terror, to burn out and scalp those few of us living in the deep woods outside the safety of Gloucester. When I related to Nanepa the ill tidings, she cackled and spit into the fire, rocking in her chair and uttering curses I could not understand.

"Those are my people," she grunted. "We are protected." So we were, and I thought no more of the warnings. One day when three of the Nipmuc tribe came to my house, I led them to Sara's cabin, whereupon they greeted Nanepa with great respect and honor.

Beyond our homes, however, mayhem was breaking out: Shots rang in the wood. Smoke drifted over from the woods near Gloucester, and we heard rumors of outlying farms burned by the Indians.

"Why do they fight?" I asked Nanepa.

"Because the Blackcoats have killed off all the game, leaving my people nothing to hunt," she answered, spitting into the fire.

I stared at her, at which she stared back. "Nothing left to hunt but Blackcoats!" she cackled. However, when I sought news from Sara about the skirmishes we daily heard tell from the villagers, she shook her head.

"This is the end of the red people," she muttered sadly. "Nanepa talks proudly, but she knows the British Blackcoats have the guns and the bloodlust. They betray the red man who has befriended them, then justify the slaughter of Indians and the plunder of tribal lands in the name of their God!"

I saw the fear in the eyes of the people who still came to me for cures. For long stretches none of the villagers visited the deep wood, out of fear of suffering the very havoc they had provoked by making war on the Indian.

Months after the visit from the Nipmuc tribesmen, word reached us: The Blackcoats had lured Chief Metacomet into a trap and killed him, selling his family into slavery. Thereafter we saw no more of the red people in the wood; Nanepa had to hide from marauding Blackcoats, who now streamed through the woods looking to kill any Natives they found.

Eventually the Blackcoats returned to Gloucester, leaving those few of us still living in the deep wood at peace. I prayed to Brigid to watch over my endeavors and went about practicing my arts. Villagers once again came to me for healing. In the back of my cottage by the well I dug a large pit to make a room for steam, after the beehive mounds my people had always made. Digging deep into the rocky soil, I stacked the excavated stones in a circle and upon this foundation built walls, leaving space for a short passageway into the room. At the top of the structure I left a small opening for the airs to escape. Following the tradition my mother had passed to me from her own mother, after heating stones in the cottage fireplace I would place these in the beehive, cover with herbs and douse with water, thereby sending scented steam through the room. Thus by the room's beneficent air was I able to treat countless people.

When my time comes to die, I shall bury this record within the walls of the beehive: May the Goddess watch over it. For in writing my story I have brought healing upon myself, after the horrors of Salem.

DIANA WAS A strange little girl with red hair and a disposition to fit. Wild from the start, she would let no one near her but me, suffering Sara's and Nanepa's presence only occasionally even though she loved them deeply. Although she let few near, those she allowed she loved with unwavering devotion. As a little girl she was always wandering off into the deep wood, but whenever I grew frantic enough to follow her tracks she would greet me with anger for not leaving her in peace, even if she had strayed into brambles and seemed unable to free her little body. From the start she was beyond me, and I was both proud of and fearful for her—fearful of her—for never was a child more of a born magician.

Living with Sara, Nanepa told fortunes herself and wandered in the woods gathering plants to make strange teas. Often while I walked the moonlit nights I would happen upon the old Indian standing stiffly upon a huge block of stone looking out to sea, swaying gently and chanting, her lilting voice haunting like a nightingale. The voice followed me through the wood, hovering over my shoulder as I bent to pick the mushrooms that only grew at night. Nanepa's chants were laments for her lost man and children and, as she told me one night, for all the Indians killed to glut the white man's anger. I did not grieve for those whom I had lost. It was better, now that the child was born, to face that which I had to do to keep us both alive.

Yet I did journey back to Ravenoak in search of my father several times in those early years by the sea. As the settlement of Ravenoak grew into a town, the Blackcoats took over entirely, renaming it Innocence. I hid inside a Druid cloud or, disguising myself as a man, wandered about the town as a wayfarer; other times I shifted into wolf and ranged widely through the woods. The fairy mound where my father, Grey and I had been given protection was gone altogether, and the mice and squirrels who inhabited the ruins of Ganieda's cottage would give me no news, skittering about and talking only nonsense.

Although I searched at length for the Morrigan's sidh, I could find no trace. Long hours I sat chanting and casting spells in the forest, conjuring the Morrigan. When Beltaine came around, I chanted and burned herbs under a full moon. Wrapping myself in a heavy cloak and drinking a potion, I lay against a giant oak and fell into a trance.

Some time later I stood and looked about. In the distance appeared a little man no larger than my hand, beckoning me to follow. Up and down hills he raced as I hurried after, the colors of the trees all the while changing to purple. Spying a castle in the distance, I hurried after the little man up to the entrance gate, whereupon he disappeared. Into the Great House I pursued him until I found myself in a long hall, whereat a table stretching end to end all sorts of people were seated. At the head sat the Morrigan—and at her side my father, looking just as I had left him so long ago. Gaiety and music filled the room where hundreds drank and feasted. I waited, my heart in my mouth.

"You have returned for a favor," the Morrigan addressed me as I bowed low, unable to tear my eyes from my father. He looked at me kindly but made no move to greet me. I trembled with a lifetime of longing for him.

"You have stood at my side in war," I answered, "for which I thank you, powerful Goddess. I come seeking a cure for Ravenoak, to undo what has transpired and restore the old order."

The Morrigan smiled; there was blood in her teeth. "Even I cannot change fate. Still, I shall give you a gift to help with your task." She raised a crystal goblet and proffered it to me. It was of the finest work, marked with a blood-red vein that wound through the glass like a wound of passion. Bowing my gratitude, I accepted the goblet from her outstretched hand, then asked permission to speak with my father. She nodded.

"You have grown tall and patient," the Morrigan observed, but I knew better.

Walking outside with my father in a grove of purple trees, I touched him at last, and in a stroke my entire life was lightened.

"My father, may I come live with you?" I begged. Gravely, he shook his head.

"You would first have to die," he spoke in a voice that made me tremble anew, for it came from under the mountains. "I can never leave. Depart bearing the Morrigan's goblet, and let that heal Ravenoak."

"How might it help?" I asked.

"Give it to the one you tell the story of your journey," he responded. "For you cannot help Ravenoak until you are wounded in love—until you have told the story."

With that he was gone from my side as I awoke, still wound tightly in my cloak against the giant oak. When I stood and drew up my hand, my fingers were clasping the crystal goblet.

And so I returned to my friends in the wood by the sea, contenting myself with raising Diana. But my heart thought always of the crystal goblet, which I showed to no one, and of Ravenoak. Thus was I left to puzzle: How could this goblet rid Ravenoak of the Blackcoats and restore the old age, recover the worship of the earth and sky?

ONE EVENING when Diana was still a baby in the cradle, Nanepa and Sara visited and bade me follow them.

"And the child?" I asked.

"She will be protected," Sara stated. Nevertheless I swaddled my baby, lifted her against my shoulder, and without another word from Sara followed them into the deep wood.

We walked a long while, venturing into a part of the forest I had never been. Beltaine had arrived and the air was warm; already I had celebrated by dancing and singing beneath the Oak that stood outside my door, swaying with Diana in my arms. The moon rose large over the trees and looked over our shoulders as if curious, we four walking in a line, the towering Sara leading the limping Nanepa leading me carrying Diana.

After a time I heard chanting as we came to a clearing, in the middle of which blazed a snapping fire. Around the fire stood a ring of naked women, arms raised upwards directing their voices, throats stretched to the black heavens. They chanted in a language I did not know; Sara halted us at the circle's edge and waited. Women of all ages were gathered: maidens whose small cupped breasts glowed white in the moonlight and whose hair glittered like golden down; an old woman whose upraised arms and jaw shook, her stomach lined and paunched, hair stringy and grey against her moon-blanched skin. Light from the flames cast flickering shadows across her body, as if her younger soul were dancing across her aged skin. A bark-brown woman whose skin gleamed darkly swayed from side to side, eyes closed. In all I counted twelve, including at the edge of the circle a woman with long black hair holding a tremendous book bound in black leather, its massive gold clasp hanging loose.

Their voices rising and falling in the night were so sweet that tears came as I thought of Ravenoak and my mother. For when I left Ravenoak to study with Ganieda, I had been too young to be initiated into my mother's Druid circle... As Diana stirred I held her close, feeling again that my life was to be one of wandering, and again I felt the pain of loneliness. I hugged my daughter, for she was with me, and she was all I had. All at once I was young again and had learned nothing, did not know whether the world was kindly or hurtful... My eyes darting from side to side, I watched full of fear, ready to run. With my free hand I felt for my *athane,* strapped as always to my side.

The chanting went on, until from inside that well of singing I began to breathe more easily, and my hand dropped. *I was not alone, not here,* a voice whispered, though these women were strangers to me.

The chanting ceased, the black-haired woman closed the huge tome, setting it on a rock, then nodded toward us. Sara stepped forward.

"Welcome to our sisters," intoned the woman, and her voice was deep and strong.

Sara unbuckled her belt, lowered and stepped out of her breeches, then removed her jerkin and all of her undergarments, after which she, too, stood naked. When she in turn nodded to us, I set Diana down and undressed, as did Nanepa, and we three stood waiting. The warm night air felt close to my body, and I thought distantly that I had never been much aware of it, other than as a sheath for my soul. Now I felt the hair stir between my legs, the hair down my back tickle my shoulder blades, teasing me to come out... For the first time in my life I began to think with pleasure of a man touching me. As I remembered Cian Redmane softly, hesitantly, a vision of his fate passed before me: Coming to his senses at last, he had fought the Blackcoats—too late. With the few men still loyal to him, he attacked but was driven back—to fall at last under the sword of John Stewart himself. So...Cian was gone to the Otherworld...I could desire him without constraint now.... Yet to be touched as the light breeze touched me—!

I lifted Diana and held her close as the leader bade us enter the circle.

"Sister Madness is welcome," she looked at Sara, who smiled in acknowledgement around the circle.

"I bring Sharp Moon, whom you know," Sara declared, touching Nanepa's shoulder. "And a new sister, to be initiated tonight."

"Does she have a name?" the leader asked, looking directly at me.

"'Beloved,'" I replied without thinking. Too late I realized what I had done. Abashed at being henceforth known as a soft woman, my face flushed; anger followed close behind. I caught Sara eye me with surprise as Nanepa nodded her old head, as if she had known all along. My heart beat against my ribs.

"Beloved, we have heard well of you and welcome you as a powerful seer into our circle. *May we give much to you; may you give much to us,*" she chanted, approaching with a silver bowl and bidding me drink. With my left hand I lifted the bowl to my lips, finding the water refreshingly cool. When Nanepa took the bowl, I dipped my fingers in the water and splashed a few drops on Diana, who wriggled and screamed, spirited as ever.

As laughter ran around the circle, Nanepa and Sara drank in turn.

Many ceremonies of welcome and magic continued into the night, Diana by then sleeping through them all like lullabies sung just for her. Setting her down in a warm nook in a rock, I joined the others in singing and talk, raising spirits and communing, happy to feel the warm fire in my face. After inscribing my name in the Black Book of initiates, I was admitted to the secrets of the circle and given instruction in its practices and beliefs. I saw how similar the teachings of these healers were to those I had learned from my mother and from Ganieda—that the roots of Druid knowledge and this circle wound underground to the same Oak.

After that evening members of the circle from neighboring villages visited often, bringing food and gossip. Years passed in this way, Diana growing into a lively sprite who wandered the woods freely. At times my sisters brought with their gossip dark stories of the burnings in Europe, just as John Stewart had warned, confirming my worst fears of the narrow, hard-hearted Puritans living in the village of Gloucester. For a long while the Puritans did not bother those of us in the deep wood, though well they knew of the loose community of healers and seekers living thereabouts; they even came for our herbs. Little by little, however, fear cast its wing over the kindly wood, as if some dark bird had flown up from the south. Stories of Salem began to reach us: of women who lived alone accused of practicing witchcraft, widows sent to the stake or hung—ofttimes because children attempting to steal their widowed mothers' thirds had leveled charges against them. A mother's own children!

Women of all sorts were being arrested: independent women of means who had thrived in Boston's bustling commerce to the south; ones who had attained political power. Even respected judges' wives who had spoken their minds too freely had been charged with the wicked crime of witchcraft. High-spirited maidens who had been spied dancing in the woods were brought before stone-faced magistrates to explain themselves. Dancing—! Nothing seemed more innocent to me, for as the years passed my little Diana had become a fierce dancer. With her flaming red hair and bright eyes she spun round and round under the mighty oaks, crying out in all sorts of made-up languages—how she made me laugh!

Although this atmosphere of distrust was not new to me, I found it incomprehensible women were singled out as the source of a new fear. For a woman to speak her mind or to do the bidding of her guiding spirits seemed only natural to me, just as a man had to follow his Gods. Being a healer was sacred work, partaking of ancient wisdom; why should it suddenly have become a crime? No, we of our circle in the wood were not witches. Some were healers and seers, even if not of the Druid Oak as I, yet we were all equally vulnerable!

From the lore of my Raven tribe I knew that ever since the time of Patrick, being called a witch was to be called evil. Slowly I came to understand that fearful men were charging with witchcraft any woman who stood in their way. What did they want so badly from women, or what did they so fear, that made them lash out in such anger and hate? I recalled the face of John Stewart and shuddered at the fury in his mad eyes. For the time being, Diana and I, Sara and Nanepa were safe in the deep wood, for I had drawn powerful Druid circles around our cottage, working my magic on Sara's cottage as well. But sensing that our days of finding refuge in the wood were passing swiftly, I felt increasingly frightened and alone, even with powerful Sara and wise Nanepa close at hand. My Diana, meantime, growing daily into a fine little girl, remained as untamed as a mountain cat.

Eventually several healers from our wood were taken away by the Puritans, who came in force to their houses to arrest them. One of the married women was accused of causing the death of a goat that had wandered into her garden. The goat had beforehand eaten poison sumac in the wood and died soon after. When the goat's owner, a narrow, hard old man, remembered Ruth muttering as she drove the goat away from her vegetables, he accused her in court, and she was arrested.

Then Patience Lawton was arrested. The oldest of our circle, she lived alone on a hillside that was good grazing for cattle, though she owned none herself. Despite the curses of nearby farmers eager for the land, she refused to sell and instead responded with curses of her own, being a sturdy dame. When one of the farmers fell and broke his leg, she was immediately arrested. Even as I chanted and fasted, making potions to protect my daughter and friends, I began to wonder openly if we should leave our homes.

"Do you not think they will find us wherever we go? Did the Blackcoats not go even to Ravenoak years ago?" Sara was pacing furiously in her cottage as Nanepa sat rocking, silent.

"No! I say we must fight their evil!" Sara shook her finger at Diana, who was teasing the cat in the corner.

"For the little one! For our way of life!"

"But they are many, and our magic does not have their devil's power as they think," I argued wearily. "I tried to fight them directly and lost; I was saved only by the fairies. I do not know what magic the fairies could invoke against so many Blackcoats."

"Our darkness began long ago," Nanepa put in, wrapping her shawl around her. "Now it quickens."

Sara shook her head and stormed out as Diana, watching her, followed; to her it was a game. I did not know whether to laugh or cry.

But for all my worry, the time moved slowly in our wood by the sea, and even times of trouble we grow accustomed to. Daily life weighs on us, so powerful and real is its dream. The thousand and one colors and shapes, the duties and the tendings-to that are necessary with each day we rise—all these absorbed my waking attention.

At night I dreamed of the Blackcoats coming up from the south amidst a huge cloud, as Ganieda had prophesied. I saw Diana, a grown woman, screaming at me in hatred before turning herself into a tremendous cat, then skitter into the wood, my heart sinking.

Of all the dreams that came so thick and full in those days, none disturbed me so much as one: a man, dark-haired with curls, who lounged on a stick and looked at me without speaking, a secret smile on his face and a companion nearby in shadow. When I inquired of this man why he had come, he never would answer. For the dream came often, although each time I responded differently to his silence. Sometimes I yelled at him; other times I walked away without turning around. Or else I threw myself into his arms and felt as blissfully safe as inside the fairy circle. When a blue light enveloped us and the rocks about us glowed with streaming colors, I saw through his eyes into a deeper world of knowledge and mystery…and felt upon waking as if all my years of study counted for nothing.

One dream was particularly curious. Again the dark-haired man silently met and held my gaze. Yet as I drew near him, I saw such depth of sadness in his eyes that I put my arms around him. Suddenly he shape-shifted into a swan, thence into a fish, a horse, an eagle and, last, a wolf; all the while I held each form fast in my arms. Finally he turned into himself again, falling against me in an agony of exhaustion; long I held him silently.

To my blind eye the dreams were so vivid that they set me wandering in wolf guise through the deep wood, or else I found myself pacing in my little cottage as if caged.

NOT LONG AFTER those dreams, I was walking through the market in Gloucester with Diana when a large group of men passed, all dressed in scholars' robes and talking amongst themselves. Some were arguing, a few haranguing one another, still others punching and joking with their fellows. While Diana and I stood aside along with others to let them pass, I heard it whispered that Mather himself marched at the head of this group of students, who had come from Harvard after graduating and were now on holiday together.

I watched the faces at first idly and saw many young, a few older, and the grim faces of Mather and his lieutenants at the head. Soon I found myself searching among the passing faces as if seeking someone, though whom I could not tell. With a start I recognized a curly-haired man walking amidst the crowd. His face full of light and smiles, he was nodding in understanding as a friend who stood behind him out of my sight talked animatedly.

My heart racing, I clutched Diana's little hand.

"In time, Mother," she answered, as I glanced to frown at her and her knowing ways. When I looked up, he was gone. I returned home shaken and brewed a potion for the quivers.

THEN RICHARD APPEARED. One day as I worked in the garden I heard a voice singing up the path. Raising my head, I felt a sinking in my chest without knowing why. People came from time to time to ask advice or to receive my healing; more often than not, I could sense someone approaching or hear a sound in advance. And sometimes little Diana, who had a healer's sixth sense even as a sprite, would come dashing breathlessly into the house to tell me of a man or woman nearing, describing the person in colorful detail.

One hour later, perhaps two, the person would appear invariably as Diana had foretold. Off she would gallop into the woods, there to speak in tongues even I could not understand with her squirrels and with the cow or the chicken, even with the ravens, and to grow angry and impatient with me if I should interfere or call her to return.

This time, though, my little girl came skipping up the hill and stopped beneath the oak, leaning against its trunk and eyeing me carefully. I raised my head from the garden and took note of her but could not guess what she had in mind. Then from down the path sauntered a man, singing a ballad with gusto. His hair was dark and full of curls, his eyes blue like the sea and as piercing. Dressed in leather, he carried a musket on his right shoulder and a bag over his left, as if traveling. When I saw by his eye he was learned, I felt oddly shy. My fear proved well-founded, I was soon to learn, though not for the reason I thought. For my impression was that he was a Christian from Gloucester, come to arrest me for witchcraft.

Though now he is gone, I still see his eyes…and what he did next. Walking over to Diana he crouched before her, setting his gun and bag on the ground and reaching for her. And to my amazement she went to him, whereupon he lifted her up and set her on his shoulders.

"Look at me! Look at me!" Diana cried, clapping her hands while I stood staring in astonishment. Richard danced around the old Oak with her, and no sooner had they passed under the lower branches than Diana broke off a narrow branch and beat upon his back.

"Faster! Faster!" she commanded, at which I went over to them.

"Diana! Our guest is not a horse!" I exclaimed.

Richard laughed loudly, continuing to run rings around the tree with Diana, then winked at me as he passed. Only, it was strange: As he winked with his left eye, he kept that eye closed. Could he have known of my blindness—? Surely not.

At last they finished their game as Richard, puffing, set Diana down.

"More!" she demanded, insistent as ever. Richard, still catching his breath, only smiled at her.

"Later, if your mother is willing," he promised, patting her head. She twisted away from him, swatting him with her little switch before running off into the wood. Knowing it was useless to call out, I turned to our visitor.

"You are welcome," I murmured.

He held out his hand, which I accepted carefully. I felt a competence and knowing in him. He was a craftsman—of what, I could not see, but I sensed it. And he had studied. His eyes, set close together, looked at me like he was studying an old book.

"Sara gave me the way," he explained, smiling again.

"You are friends?"

"For many years!" he effused. "Did she not tell you—of how we met in Boston? Many years ago now! Many!" he exclaimed, his blue eyes lighting up as if it were a wondrous thing, the passing of years. Though I could not see the story behind the two, I felt a pang in my chest, a flicker of regret at missing out on their times together in Boston. And why had Sara said nothing to me about this handsome man! Another pang creased my brow: Could this man have been one of Sara's—patrons?

"Have you come with an ailment?" I asked to disperse the thought, opening my door to him. He stepped in.

"None except life," he replied, his voice warm and resonant. A musician, I realized, though of what sort, again I could not tell.

"This is a fine house," he nodded, looking around. I knew he was sincere, so why I nevertheless mistrusted him I could not tell. Perhaps because he was a man. Finn raised his head from the hearth, regarded the stranger, and fell back asleep. Richard crouched near him and patted his head.

"If not for healing, then why have you come?" I asked.

"To speak with you. Oh—" he stopped, "I have not told my name. It is Richard Youngworth, of Boston and the world."

"I am Anne Cleves, of this small cottage," I replied in turn.

He started at my archness, a smile dawning on his face. "I have deserved your disapprobation," he admitted. Then, his face turning serious, he proclaimed, "Your left eye is blind!"

I drew back. No one excepting Nanepa and Sara knew of my blindness. I had always been proud that those knowing nothing of the ways of Druid poets were unable to detect my blindness.

"Will you have something to eat or drink?" I offered, taking two cups down from the cupboard.

"Is your blindness that of *Imbas Forosnai?*" he asked frankly. "And your star brooch—reflects the five sacred points of Druids, does it not?" he continued eagerly.

I turned back to him and regarded him long. "What do you know of such things? You are not from the old land, surely."

"Only a scholar who has read many books. I have come to learn the secrets of your order."

"If you know even a little, you know such secrets are not divulged," I retorted, pouring water from a ewer and handing him a cup. I was not certain I liked him. A boar spirit who ruled over him raced forward heedlessly, trampling any gate and bracken that stood in his way.

Accepting the water, he slurped it noisily. That, too, I did not like. How unlike my father, how common; a mere mortal next to the memory of my father.

"Forgive me," he begged, not taking his eyes from mine—and looking into both of them. He set the cup down hurriedly. "I am being rude in your home. Allow me to explain: I have traveled widely in the New World, speaking with the Red people, learning their languages and listening to their stories, which I have written down in a book—" He turned around as if looking for something, raised his eyebrows and dashed outside, returning in a moment with his leather satchel. Kneeling beside it, he drew open the leather thong and pulled out a few possessions, namely, a wooden flute and a large book bound in brown leather. Greeting the book with a smile, he sat down cross-legged on the floor. Stopping to set a pair of spectacles carefully upon his nose, he opened the book and began to peruse a page, scanning it all over greedily.

Like a child, all at once he became completely absorbed and apparently oblivious to my presence. Slowly he pursed his lips and looked up.

"These are wonderful stories!" Abruptly he removed his spectacles and leaped up so that I started at his quickness—and balance.

"We still have not met," he apologized, extending his hand. "I know your name by way of Sara—and from your brief introduction—but you must give it to me yourself in truth." He waited as I remained silent. "If at all," he finished, his voice falling a little.

"I have made a bad impression," he fretted, frowning deeply.

I laughed out loud. He looked puzzled, then broke into a smile, until we laughed in unison. As water splashed from the cup I held, I bit my lip, eyes watering, and tried to steady the cup. He seemed so comical, I could not refrain from laughing, like watching a puppet come alive; jumping up, then falling down; one moment a sad frown in despair, the next full of mischief and trickery and an arched eye. When he saw my water splash, he raised his cup and splashed some of his own onto the floor as well, so that we two laughed again. My eye caught a little figure peering through the crack in the door. So she had come to see for herself—! What a wonder!

Soon we stopped laughing at this silliness, and I took his hand. "In these parts I go by the name of Anne Cleves. My Celtic name is Guryn, but I do not use it here amongst the Saxons. It is my experience that the Saxon bears no love for my people."

He took my hand, after which we two sat down.

"I know of your people—I have traveled to Eire and spoken with the old bards." He replaced his glasses and riffled through his book, looking down again.

"The old bards!" I marveled.

He looked up nearsightedly. "I have their poems here, at least those I learned by heart and later wrote down."

Twisting my head to look more closely at the curious book, I could see the lines of poetry. "But why—?"

"I am looking for a cure," he replied. "I was not altogether honest earlier, when you asked why I had come."

"For what disease?" I inquired, feeling serious and older suddenly.

"The heart's longing," he replied softly, and I saw he was in earnest.

"There is no cure for that, if you are one of the wanderers," I whispered, looking aside.

"Then you recognize me," he stated.

"I, too—am a wanderer. The Otherworld is so close—" I turned to catch my little Diana dart from the door, "that when a mortal looks into it—"

"As you have," he uttered flatly.

"You presume much," I answered, turning back to throw him a challenging glare.

"I know," he confessed, bending his head long enough for me to spot flecks of grey in his hair. He was not a young man—perhaps ten years older than I.

"I presume not carelessly," he hastened to add. "I pray you not mistake my clumsiness for carelessness. For I long to know that world whence, as a Saxon, I am shut," he ended forlornly.

"No one is shut out," I demurred.

"But you are an initiate."

"How come you by your learning?" I countered.

"I have studied at Harvard College in Cambridge."

"Such a place holds the books of old lore?"

He smiled wryly. "It does not; rather, the keys to where those books might be found. The academy shuts out the dark world, for it favors science over the magic arts, clear-eyed sight over the dim second-sight. But because it prides itself on classifying all teachings under the sun, it studies those areas of learning to which its method would never submit."

"And you are such a scholar."

"I am a scholar," he admitted, his face flushing. "I have taken pride in knowing by the light of reason. But as my heart is a poet's, I spent my years at Harvard searching out the ways to the Otherworld."

"One does not simply go to the Otherworld—there lies death."

He hesitated. "Perhaps I speak incorrectly. I mean to say, I seek those places of which the poets speak."

"They are here before you."

"The other world! The invisible one!" he cried, his voice rising passionately. "That is what I seek!"

"Then find it and cease this long dirge," I finished, rising.

He looked up at me as if stricken.

"Richard Youngworth, I have nothing to give you. You say you have come for the secret knowledge, but the lore I know, I have spent many years studying and practicing. That cannot be grasped as so much theory. You wish to find the other world, then perceive it! You will not find it here," I shook my head, returning the cups to the board, where I dipped them in water and rubbed them dry on my apron.

He rose silently, placing his book, flute, and spectacles in his bag, and left. I felt very angry without knowing why—which disturbed me in turn.

For a long while I stood, silent, looking into the Otherworld for a vision. I saw Richard walk sadly away down the path, his face burning and his heart broken, and only then did I see his intent in coming. The realization of his desire for me made me tremble. I saw as well that his nature would not leave him in despair for long, that a renewing spirit would soon enough take hold of him...and therefore I did not regret speaking harshly to him. I saw him return, saw the two of us speaking, saw there was to be life between us, much life—and the vision made my breath catch in my chest.

In a heartbeat I found myself with Ailinn, queen of the fairies, who was dressed in that radiant blue in the sidh where she had protected me from the Blackcoats. Again I felt the same hurt in my heart as after that beautiful vision departed, leaving me alone deep in the woods on the hillside, alone under the stars, safe from Stewart and the Blackcoats, but alone. I understood Richard's desire, and that I had to call him back. But the vision went its own way: I saw him walk with lowered shoulders back to the village, back to his small room in a rambling house built over the water in Gloucester Harbor, back to his books and his flute. I saw him take up his flute and, looking out over the moon-sprinkled water, pipe a sad air to the night. I heard his longing for me and Diana, heard his desire to return. So even as he went away, I called him back...and felt certain of his return.

AND YET his return did not come for a long time. That I could not move Richard in my customary ways was a hard lesson for me, bringing back Ganieda's words about love's power and the limitations of magic. When Richard did not come after I summoned him in trance, I resorted to drinking potions and spreading an herbal salve on the cup from which he had drunk. Diana watched me curiously, her eyes mocking my every move, until I lost patience and chased the little demon outside.

"Not that way!" she screamed, eluding my grasping fingers and running down the path. She stopped and, seeing me watch her from the door, performed a little pantomime: Pretending to throw a satchel over her shoulder, she lifted an imaginary musket from the ground and with downcast eyes glanced back at me, shrugged and trudged down the path, looking for all the world as if her little heart had broken.

"Imp of the sidh!" I cried out after her mockery of my heart, flinging a stick at her—which, of course, she saw coming through eyes in the back of her head and dodged easily, disappearing into her beloved wood. Diana and Richard were much alike! Much alike!

I returned to the empty cottage. Finn raised his shaggy head once, eyed me with a sleepy look, and fell asleep again. Many days had passed since Richard had come and gone. I wanted to ask Sara for news of him, but pride held my tongue. Besides, was I not a powerful magician? For Ganieda had taught me many ways to make a visitor appear. So settling down before a raging fire, I mixed the secret herbs Ganieda had once given me with one of the leaves from Oroonca (the one named "Goodness"), and I stirred the potion while chanting the ancient tongue.

Hours I sat breathing in the wondrous vapor, until fantastical shapes of demons and spirits from the sidh appeared before me. As I summoned forth with all my strength the ghosts of ancestors and heroes, smoky forms of red and blue floated past, overawing me. Spirits of the earth and sky I invoked, beseeching that they bring about Richard's return.

Even so, the shapes were mute and flickering in the haze, dissolving at last without a word into the Otherworld whence they had emerged. I was left exhausted and heavy with the black lead of my exertions. My blind eye aching mightily, I rocked back and forth in the failing light, perplexed and hurt. Out of the hurt I shifted into wolf and wandered heavily in the night forest for days, sniffing at the cold trail of my discontent.

Why had the spells not worked? Could Richard himself be a Druid of the old order, hiding his powers for some secret reason? Yet he had behaved like nothing so much as an overgrown child; even if he knew the old lore, it seemed lost on him. No—I would make him come.

In the end, however, I determined to travel by foot to Gloucester, down to the busy harbor to seek him out. I told Diana as well as myself that I was in need of a few threads and such. Diana, now seven, looked at me blankly, as usual her expression saying all. I left her with Sara, certain that the tale of Richard's visit and my long search for him would be told on little legs.

The town bustled: fishermen on the docks unloading their catches; women with baskets strolling along Market Street pinching the fruits and vegetables for purchase; enormous piles of crossed rolls beckoning from carts; delectable ginger and marzipan sweets set on little silver trays. Recognizing the many Puritans by their stark, lined faces and black clothes, I took care to keep my presence shadowy to them. I did not feel safe in their midst.

Guided by my vision after Richard's departure, I came upon a large boarding house suspended over the water by means of poles set below the splashing waves. With its many windows—some cracked, others patched with strips of cloth or heavy paper—the structure sagged heavily to the right, giving an impression of being close to collapse; I feared for anyone living in so ramshackle and run-down a place. In the entranceway sat a heavy woman wearing a kerchief and dirty apron, peeling onions. Possessed of few teeth but massive jowls, she bent over several times to take hearty bites from an onion, then gulped water from a cracked pitcher at her feet. The onion rinds she flung to some chickens penned behind a low wooden fence, who pecked uncertainly at the shards.

"Good woman, I beg your pardon," I began hesitantly. "I am looking for Richard Youngworth."

She regarded me suspiciously; her thoughts were clear enough. For rather than follow the custom of Puritan women to bind their tresses under widows' caps of muslin, I let my long locks fall freely down my back.

"Ye'll be missin' yer pay, Irish lassy," she sneered. My lilting mother tongue was noticeable, no doubt.

"Does Richard Youngworth live here?" I pursued, ignoring her insulting presumption I had come for money.

"Did at that. Wandered off again." Finished sizing me up, she returned her attention to the onions.

"When will he return?" I asked.

"Th' divil knows, Mistress Ireland."

Turning away from the hag, I wandered the streets of the harbor town. How different was this village from Ravenoak! Here the people were all in a hurry; solemn, downcast looks and hard faces met me everywhere I turned. A bell tolled in the distance, sounding as mournful as the Boyne though the sky was bright and cheery and robins chirped in the trees.

Finally exhausted from fruitless walking, I returned for Diana, who did not hesitate to make me feel foolish by her sly look. Sara also regarded me closely. Sitting before the hearth, Nanepa smiled toothlessly and cackled with glee, her eyes full of light.

For some days afterward the world seemed to have gone dull and lifeless, and I wandered dreamlike through life, worried my soul had been stolen. I trotted off as wolf through the forest and howled at the moon, letting the wound open in my chest. When I returned I could dispense no healing and barely spoke to Diana, who was just as content to be left to herself amongst her animal friends. Catching sight of myself in a bit of cracked looking glass, I feared I had become old like that hag.

"And why would he want to come to you?" I asked my haggard reflection. "You are an old dried-out stick." Although unlike me to fret so over my face, yet I did, studying my eyes, the lines in my forehead, and the arch of my eyebrow. True, I was no longer a young woman, but I had some beauty left me. Taking up my hairbrush, which I used mostly for Diana, I drew it slowly through my hair and gave myself up to desire: each stroke a chant to draw Richard to me. I found my blond hair darkening, the darker layers lying beneath the lighter like petals of a flower. At night I prayed in despair to Brigit that she make me beautiful to Richard. I was nearly thirty; I had crossed a divide; never before had my longing settled on a man, nor had I wanted to radiate some small part of the beauty of the world, enough that he might find me comely as a rose.

This I prayed without daring to hope—for what sort of chant was this? Nothing I had ever learned from Ganieda. Casting aside tradition and lore, moved rather by the ache in my heart, I murmured the words as they formed on my lips. I gave myself up to recalling each of his features, from the crow's feet at the corners of his blue eyes to the small scar along the edge of his mouth, down to his crooked smile and the uneven line of his chin. I did not need second sight to see Richard vividly, for he was real to me.

WHEN, DAYS LATER, I had all but given up waiting, laughter reached me from the yard. I looked out to find Richard galloping around the oak with Diana on his shoulders, as if he had never left. Even as my heart leaped, I pulled back on the reins. Had it cost him to return? Had I not sent him away? Still, I could not resist standing in the doorway.

Richard spied me immediately and stopped, his face flushed from exertion—or was it shyness?

He bowed stiffly, careful to hold onto Diana.

"More!" she commanded, but Richard very seriously set her down. She swatted him with her crop and raced off, giving me a look of disdain.

"Welcome, Richard Youngworth," I greeted him, my voice quavering.

"That is my hope," he replied, coming up to me.

"Have you been traveling?"

"I went to the northlands in search of my Indian friends. I have copied down—" he broke off.

"—stories?" I finished, smiling wryly and inviting him to enter.

"Yes—I wish to apologize for my bad behavior."

I blinked at him in surprise. "Your behavior has no need of apology in my home; rather has mine," I replied, not looking at him.

"I accept, if in return you will accept mine." He extended his hand. I took his wide-palmed hand in mine, its warmth reminding me of my father's hands. I nodded my assent.

"Good! Then that's done!" he exclaimed, smiling broadly and relaxing his face. "Long ago I came to you with questions—"

"Ask them again," I interrupted softly, handing him a cup of water.

With a glance at me, he took the cup. "No—that is, my questions were rudely put; I am a clumsy man. But my interest is sincere."

"That much I never doubted," I replied.

"Then—it is a matter of manners," he explained, shaking his head. "I am able to converse patiently with the Indians according to their formality, sitting still and silent for hours if need be. But some contrary spirit entered me when I entered your house that day...no...before that, when I was outside—"

I laughed. "That was my daughter Diana's spirit. She will bewitch you if you are not careful!"

"That is what I came for!" he whispered, impassioned.

This was a strange man! Never had I heard anyone speak in such a manner—so seemingly on the knife edge between buffoonery and deep feeling. As I began to wonder whether there lay sincerity, a vision of the two of us lying in embrace flitted before my eye. Quickly I hushed it to sleep like a bothersome child, expelling a quick breath.

"You have come to ask me questions, Richard Youngworth," I prompted.

"So I once thought. Rather, I have returned to speak with you."

"Then, let us speak," I declared, feeling on my cheeks the warmth of his presence, the strong glow of his aura. Bidding him sit near the fire, I sat down opposite.

And so we sat long while Richard unfolded stories of his travels, eventually pulling out his treasured book to read aloud. He relayed versions of stories of the Red people familiar to me from Oroonca and Nanepa and from gatherings around the fire with the Bear clan: stories of the creation of the world, of the cultivation of grain, and of the heroic hunts. Stories of the white man, thrown up from the sea wielding long sticks of deadly fire. I relived the sight of Nanepa's village, people everywhere dying from infected blankets, saw myself that first time in the cave with Oroonca, then with Nanepa while Oroonca slept at her back...

I encouraged Richard to tell aloud those stories he had half learned by heart from the old bards of Eire, even though I knew them well. After quietly holding Raven lore for so long without a tribe, able to share tales only with Diana and Sara, I was relieved to hear these spoken again in the open.

"Where is Diana's father?" Richard asked after a time, as the sun drifted into the trees and the light grew dim.

"He is dead, so I have seen with my mind's eye," I explained. "It is a long and bloody story—and unkind."

"You must tell it," he insisted, looking directly at me.

"Must I?" I mused. "I am no *seanchai;* not a storyteller but a healer. Taletelling is for others—such as you."

"You read and write; why not transcribe your life's story? Many would benefit."

"I would not do so for the wind's reason but for such task that directed me," I answered. "What is your book for but to satisfy idle curiosity or to entertain those who would spy? Are you any more than a spy and a thief, stealing by the charm of night into our hearts to take what is not yours?" I asked, wishing with all my heart he would answer otherwise.

Richard lowered his head. "To deny I have been a spy, stealing stories for my work…would be a lie." When he raised his face it was old with grief. "As you say, for idle curiosity or for scholars to trample. God knows how they can trample upon the flowers, cutting them to fit their dried-out theories!"

"I see that fearfulness in the sickness the Blackcoats spread. Their God's judgment makes them afraid, which instead of inspiring them with courage sets them in judgment of us all. Or is their God yours too?" I provoked.

"He is not my God. Oh, Anne! I am not only a spy, and perhaps not primarily one. You know why I have traveled, and why I come to you now!" His eyes beseeched my understanding.

"Why are you here?" I inquired.

"Because of—your company," he replied haltingly. "I care nought for those stories—no, that is not true, either! I do care, but not idly—because I care more for being here with you, playing with Diana around the Oak, and…" he stopped, looking miserable.

"You love the stories and, perhaps, me for holding them." I smiled, even as my heart hurt. "I would not deny you the stories—nor, then, my company, because they are wedded."

"Yes, that's it!" he enthused, eyes widening. "You have expressed it perfectly! I wish neither to gain advantage by your people—nor by you. May not each of us be a path to a greater truth—as well as to a higher life?"

Now I laughed boldly outright, hearing my voice ring from the cottage beams. "My old Druid teacher Ganieda once spoke similar words to me. 'Love people,' he taught me, 'both for themselves and for what they may give you. Loving them inherently humbles you before the larger world, which flies beyond your ken. Choose them for what they may give you, that thereby might you know of a larger world. Love always above yourself.'" I looked past him.

"So neither giving nor receiving is for oneself alone," Richard nodded, continuing Ganieda's thought.

"Yes—rather, for the Gods and Goddesses. For the stories we have to live are laid down long before our birth—"

"Yet ours is a land that insists on starting anew: that we must each make our own way in the world. I have heard it go about that settlers in the New World soon will no longer recognize the divine presence everywhere—even that of the angry God whose worshipers you fear."

"What God shall take that God's place?" I wondered aloud.

"The God of science."

I recalled Sara's words about the new sort of doctors, men of science all, with their scorn for healing lore. "The men of science do not seem so different from those Christian Blackcoats who hang witches."

"Whereas the Puritans worship the God who makes miracles and delivers devils amongst us, the men of science like Mather—who is himself a minister—nevertheless regard Reason as divinely given," Richard answered. "Mather has voiced doubt that witchcraft is possession by the Devil; instead he thinks the beliefs and practices of witchery may be a physical malady of the brain."

"He would not damn the poor women, but would imprison them even so in his reason," I replied.

"He was once my teacher," Richard explained, smiling hesitantly. "And no longer is."

I rekindled the fire until it blazed in the hearth, throwing leaping shadows across the room and over Richard's face. His eyes followed me as I moved to the window. "I have met the Blackcoats before. After the Branna—" I turned back to him.

"It has become one of the stories, which now I will pass along to you."

"And one day you will write it," he nodded solemnly.

With my left hand I touched the first joint of the middle finger on my right hand—*alder,* as it is known in the Ogham.

"That is Ogham!" Richard cried, like a child proud of his learning.

"The Ogham is the way I learned by heart and head the Three Hundred and Fifty Tales. Each finger—moreover, each joint of each finger—holds a different story. The story of Ravenoak took place after my learning, so I have set it here."

Richard became quiet, whereupon I fell into the reciting trance of *Dechetal do Chennaib* and relayed the unhappy history of Ravenoak, describing its devastation by the Blackcoats following its destruction by the Branna. However, I told the story as if I had not lived it, for I nowhere appeared in the story I told.

Hours later I grew still. Richard's face was white, and for a time we were quiet.

"By the power of...I shall kill the Blackcoats!" he swore through clenched teeth. I stood up stiffly and went to the window.

"The hour grows late," I sighed, peering into the darkness. "You will sup with us—although often that means only dinner by myself."

"And your daughter?" he inquired.

"She often returns after dark," I replied, a shiver passing through me. Richard stood and came near.

"I shall go find her."

I half smiled. "She will not come."

He smiled in return, his eyes sparkling. "Yes, she will." He went out into the gloaming, and I watched his dim figure retreat into the wood while he called Diana's name softly, as if she were a cat. And perhaps she was.

After stoking the fire, I set about making a stew in the pot above the flames. I was well into the preparations, the broth steaming, when I sensed something.

Faint sounds of Diana's bright, high-spirited laughter tinkling through the wood grew louder. At last the door flung open to reveal my daughter perched on Richard's shoulders, her red hair mimicking the firelight. He ducked low, and she touched the top of the lintel in delight as they passed under. I shook my head in amazement, wondering what sort of magic Richard possessed that seemed to sit so lightly on him.

Taking hold of Diana, I set her down with a groan. "Heavy as a stone!" I puffed, as she squirmed out of my reach.

After I ladled stew into three bowls, we three sat down at the board as if we were a family. Reaching into the cupboard to take down cups for water, I found my hand touching something unfamiliar. Curious, I pulled the object out to discover with a start the crystal goblet. For a long moment I stood there gazing, meditating on the red vein that ran through the fine-bubbled glass.

"What is that beautiful glass?" asked my little imp.

"It is Richard's goblet," I replied, setting it before him. He regarded it with raised eyebrows and shot a glance at me. I sucked in my breath and turned to sit.

For all that, the meal turned out to be a merry one, Richard and Diana chattering away like magpies, teasing one another while playing with their food. After a few words of warning I saw it was no use. As Richard raised his goblet, pausing to peer in the firelight at the ruby cut winding through the crystal, I caught the hurt reflected in his eyes.

"May all that quenches me be you," he toasted simply, drinking without waiting for us to join him. I was stunned into silence.

"Richard, will you tell me a story?" Diana interrupted soon enough, tugging at his free hand until he lowered the goblet in his other.

"Don't be bold," I admonished her, rising from the table as the three of us broke to clear away the dishes.

With a sheepish smile Richard allowed Diana to lead him into her small room at the back. She could not shut the door without showing her serious face in the crack, her dark eyes meeting my stare. The spirit of my mother lived in that child, no doubt! So proud, headstrong, stubborn. Perhaps she was a true queen, destined to escape her mother's fate of wandering as a queen without a realm. Perhaps she would have a domain to rule. I thought of Ravenoak, for I was full of my home with the telling; again I promised to return and reclaim it. Perhaps for Diana.

But I shivered before the fire, haunted by the Blackcoats.

In a little while Richard stepped through Diana's doorway and closed her door carefully.

"She has taken to you," I murmured. "Beware the burden."

He laughed softly, sitting down beside me before the fire. "Is she a burden?" he returned, his eyes glistening and teasing.

"Do you think she is not?"

"Your daughter weighs, it's true," he admitted, smiling ruefully and rubbing his shoulder. "Not that I pretend to understand her. A magical sprite!" he finished.

"You have not answered my question."

"Do you imply that in concerning myself with her, I take on a responsibility? If so, then I accept that burden, whether light or no. At the moment it seems light as air, for Diana seems as if made of air."

My mother's heart was touched; how could it not be? Diana's father—gone away forever. Did it matter to her that she would never know him? Did she miss him in a secret chamber of her heart through which she never spoke? For she had never asked about her father, as if she already knew. My own father—how large in my life he loomed still! Diana Red-Hair: as wild as her own father, as powerful as the urge that conceived her, as stubborn and violent. And perhaps a cruelty driving her as well, for I had witnessed her impatiently slashing the plants and hitting the animals from time to time with her switch. I was afraid of her.

Yet how differently she behaved with this stranger! My vision could not penetrate the mystery.

"Why do you smile?" he asked.

"You do not feel the burden as a burden. That is a kind of magic," I explained.

"Your daughter may not be a burden to me," he replied.

"Indeed!" I laughed. "There is time to tell. Do all burdens sit lightly on you?"

He jumped up and pranced about, then pulled the flute from his bag, raising it crosswise to his lips and blowing softly so that delicate, sad strands floated in the air. But his eyes were bright, and the music sweet. Noticing Diana's door open a crack, I knew she sat there listening; eventually she would fall asleep again on the floor behind the door.

Sitting down beside me again, he continued playing a bit before setting the flute aside.

"Will you tell me the rest of your story?" he pressed.

I looked at him quizzically. "I have told you my story."

"You have given me the history but not your part in it."

"It would hurt you to know." I turned away.

"Yes," he said. "But I want to hear it."

"What do you know of the Blackcoats?" I asked, looking at him closely.

His face changing, he drew near. "I have long ears and am at home with townsfolk rich and poor. I banter with the laborers like a fellow worker, I know how to use chisel and mallet and saw, know the difference between a purlin and a kingpost. I converse with scholars concerning planetary motions—you saw me with the scholars of Harvard, Sara has told me. My father was a judge in Boston; I grew up playing on the lap of the governor. I can speak the language of political expedience." He shook his head. "Dangerous times are upon us. The religious tumult that has shaken Europe has traveled here, as you well know from your own village."

"What news have you?"

"In Salem there are trials underway. Do you know the women?"

"I have heard tell—some of them are my…sisters," I hesitated.

"Members of your circle?" he asked matter-of-factly.

I eyed him in surprise. "Are you a wizard?"

He laughed. "I am too awkward—or too much in love with playing the fool." He studied the fire. "Or too much in love with love."

"In my tradition we imagine fate as a cauldron. Each cauldron begins upside down and thus empty. It is set upright by the taking up of one's fate and filled thereby. We speak of cauldrons for the various aspects of one's life—love, calling, duty. The cauldron of vocation is set upright either by sorrow or by joy. It seems mine holds sorrow; yours, joy." I could see it pained him for me to name a difference between us. He faced me in earnest.

"Does a cloud hang over our souls?" he wondered, eyes misting.

I patted his shoulder, for I saw the boy. "All our comings and goings are shadowed by the Otherworld."

"Must it always be so? You are a seer—say what you see!"

"Sometimes it is better not to speak but to let time tell," I replied, hurting. Although I sat at Richard's side, my heart longed all the more for that which I would never have. I saw then that every love, like every life, fails at last. That my longing for Richard was kin to my longing for Faery. And that yes, I loved him.

"Maybe," I added softly, "in every cauldron joy and sorrow commingle… I know little of love, after all." My pride was pricked at speaking thus openly, but an imp had hold of my tongue!

"Tell me your story!" he implored, penetrating my eye with the depth of a lover. A lover who will pierce his heart upon the point of your life because it is different from his; because he and you can never be one. This mystery of men I learned from Richard and from Cian—they so longed for another that death seemed sweet compared with the exile that bearing separate souls entails. Yet feeling separated from their beloved—from me—they had no choice but to immerse themselves in the particulars of my life—particulars that only made the separation that much more final and hence deadly for them. Their proximity to this death makes of men monsters that sometimes kill and sometimes are killed. I wondered whether every woman, then, bore death for every man who loved. I heard Richard's silent answer to my thought: "Let it kill me then."

"I was raped by Diana's father, Cian Redmane of the Branna, the usurper-king of Ravenoak," I whispered, not daring to look at him. "No—that is not altogether the truth. I would not have it that I was a lamb before that lion; rather that only by such violation might I have borne Diana. So do I understand what had to be, and I do not curse my fate."

"Such a past bears no shame," Richard murmured, touching my arm, though his hand trembled.

"Of shame I do not speak, sir, rather of that deeper, more difficult work: to understand the place so monstrous a deed holds on the circle of my life. To accept the violation of my body and soul as—perhaps that of a virgin's fate."

"You are a noble woman!" he exclaimed softly, bowing his head.

I laughed briefly. "I am of a noble tribe whose people, both men and women, have suffered countless cruelties reaching back across the generations. As such, I am a queen without a realm—else these woods are mine to rule." When I looked again at him, the curve of his jawline and the crease that ran down between his eyes seemed familiar, like an old friend come to visit.

"And what of you, Richard Youngworth?" I asked.

"Restlessness is my curse," he gritted, his voice touched with melancholy—though not self-pity.

"Years ago I was married in Boston. I have not seen my wife in a very long time. The wandering spirit overtook me, and I could not stay."

"Have you any children?" I pursued, my voice shaking a little.

"None," he replied, not without a little sadness.

I nodded in relief. "My mother, the queen of our tribe and a great healer, taught me to be wary of men. 'Beware their going, for they will take their leave, afterwards,' she warned. What have you to say of that?" I asked plainly.

"None more than I," he countered.

"Yet—you come to me in want."

"I want—*yes*. With deep desire I come to you."

"To be taught—" My voice sounded harder than I felt.

He stood up. "To be taught—to love, to live, to experience, to teach. Yes, *yes!*" he cried impatiently, pacing before the fire like a goat on a short leash. "All those! For each of those—and many more!—this demiurge sends me seeking. You—" he pointed a dark finger at me as the flames cast his face in shadow, "you are in grave danger, Anne. They are coming for you soon, and you will be unable to protect yourself. You were once violated; it could happen again." He wrung his hands in anguish. "Except that it *must not* happen again... There must be a way to break the chain of repetition—to stop the story from repeating!" He turned sharply away, only to swing around and peer into my face.

He spoke again. "Here we sit exchanging histories, distinguishing between our higher and our lower selves. Your suffering, my sufferings; my shortcomings! Yes, I am not worthy of you! Yes, I am not your kin! Yes, I should not be here; I should be searching for the wife I left years ago! Yes, I long to call your little one 'daughter'...and wish that her life might renew mine! Yes, I am dangerous and restless and untrustworthy, a thief and a liar and a cheat! Yes, yes, all wrong, Anne, all wrong!"

He cast himself down upon the floor and groaned, his body writhing as if tortured by invisible daimons. I sat straight as stone.

He looked up out of red eyes. "I hereby commit the grievous crime. I place myself before you as worthy, daring to affirm *yes,* it is I who have come to beseech you." Raising himself on a knee, he drew near and took my hand. "I say *yes,* Guryn, I love you; this power far greater than I is tearing my heart to shreds." He stopped and looked away, dropping my hands.

I was touched he used my Celtic name; I had not heard it in so long; had not heard it spoken so tenderly.

Richard spoke again. "So if you would still send me away, do it now—do it quickly! My life is a shadow; you are a light—oh! I do not yet adore you, nor call you goddess! You are a woman to me of flesh and blood: strong and beautiful; able and wise. You now bear my heart; bear it carefully," he finished.

For some time I sat quite still, gazing not at him but into the fire. From the flames came my answer. In their crackling I could hear the echo of him speaking my name, and it was sweet.

"You have many words, Richard," I sighed, then suddenly was laughing. As I turned toward him, he looked back at me in surprise, eyes puffy with tears. "Now look at you!" I exclaimed softly. "Something has surely become a burden!" I touched his shoulder, feeling the spark run between us, feeling like a young girl, the years and the griefs gone off to the edge of my soul. I could not keep from smiling, and the smile lit my soul's torch. In the cracked glass I caught a glimpse of a girl with two good eyes and upright breasts.

He reached for me.

"What am I to do with a soul like yours?" I asked gently, as we touched softly. His lips were like pillows, and my tired head rested near them that night; all night Richard whispered in my left ear, *"Guryn, Guryn, Guryn."* He stayed that night and many nights thereafter. And so I learned what it meant to be touched as the waves touch the shore, the sands giving always up to them, over and over and over.

SO IT WAS that Richard danced into my life and made himself at home, taking Diana as his own, much to her delight, and spending long periods with us in our little cottage in the wood. He could not live with us, for the woods, deep as they were, had ears and eyes; to provoke the Blackcoats' disapprobation had become too dangerous for me to risk. Nevertheless each day and again each night Richard returned, and the three of us became a family.

The joy we felt in those early days together was too much for the little house to contain. We began leaving the door open to dance and sing under the oak, Richard playing his flute, Diana and I calling out nonsense syllables during the leafy summer days. Richard and Diana went on long walks in the wood, returning with armfuls of fragrant blooms in hues of purple and scarlet and rose. In the nights Richard and I forged our own intimate language, whispering sacred words of mystery to one another by firelight.

Half forgetting my old spells and incantations, I learned new ones by way of touching with my fingertips. In my studies with Ganieda I had never truly mastered *Dechtel do chennaib*—divining by touch—using the ends of the fingers, for I could not feel their power. Now that my fingers were on fire, I felt a knowing spirit come to inhabit them when I pressed fingertips against Richard's chest or touched his locks as he slept beside me. Whispering a prayer that our world endure through the great circle, my heart beat with a rapture that lightened my step and turned life almost unbearably sweet.

Happy to share my learning, I gave Richard instruction in spell-casting and incantation, teaching him the particular use of each of my vials and packets of herb and root, tooth and dried organ. Often he bade me sit before the fire and float small circling stars above the flames or make colorful smoke rings rise from his pipe. I concocted for him all the potions I knew, revealing even the secret recipe for making the greatest and most potent of potions, that of eternal beauty.

"Let us imbibe the potion and live forever!" he cried after I had brought it forth, albeit cautiously and with trepidation, for it is a powerful potion indeed.

"That would mean death—do you not see?" I asked, startled and suddenly afraid. "We must not bend fate for our own ends."

"Then what good is the magic?" he frowned.

"For the good of others; for its own good; for the good of the world. Richard, you have taught me the most precious of all the magician's secrets, which even old Ganieda was not able to teach me."

"What is that?"

"That our love makes the magic thrive. After the first night you stayed, I sat alone in the woods behind the cottage and chanted. Up until then, I had never been able to perform much magic."

"You?" he puzzled.

I nodded. "Before then I had been too strong and proud. Love now makes me less so, and at the same time more confused and startled. Once I gave up my life to you, the Otherworld reached back to me—and only thenceforth has the magic flourished. And so have I come to understand: It is not I who makes these colorful rings but the spirit that moves me—which you have sparked."

"I still do not understand," he replied.

"Nor I fully, yet I feel that it is so. Love infuses me with a spirit that flows out into the world, infusing the world in turn with love. Magic is a way of reaching a world that is aflame and hence malleable, touching and caressing its spirit. With care and knowing."

He spoke hesitantly. "Then why not use such magic to protect the three of us? Why not make us immortal, as you assert this potion of eternal beauty has the power to do, by uttering the proper incantation while we imbibe it?"

"That would be death, both to us and to our love," I answered simply. "It cannot be."

"Then why keep the secret and pass it down? Why was such a potion ever devised if you cannot use it?"

"Richard, can you not see?" I smiled at him, throwing my arms around his neck. "The magic works through us *now*. Eternal beauty, eternal life! Have we not attained it by way of our love?" Lowering my arms, I grew serious. "Were you to leave and never return, our love lives on as an immortal spirit that neither of us can alter. Is that not the face of eternal beauty?"

"That beauty is a strange, otherworldly beauty!" he whispered cautiously.

"Indeed, beauty steeps in the Otherworld. Just as our life together is rooted in death, my love."

Richard was not satisfied, and from time to time he would return to the subject of eternal beauty. With crystal goblet raised, it seemed, he was daring me to fill it with the enticing potion. As if we were not already happy as larks, sailing our way against that summer's darker clouds!

Even as we strove to ignore the looming cloud, however, its shadow showed as the worried look on Richard's face, which no degree of comforting embrace could dispel. From town he returned with news of more women arrested and, ominously, word that official hangings were to take place in Salem.

"Powerful spells are protecting us," I insisted.

"Not strong enough, if the past be our guide!" he answered, wringing his hands. He played the flute less and moped about more, waiting for disaster to befall us.

"That is not your thought," I said quietly.

"No—?" he looked at me in feigned surprise.

"You are hurt by my life," I declared.

"As you are by mine," he retorted, jutting his chin at me, his eyes growing hard.

"No—not in the same way. I am pierced by you, not by what you have done. By the look in your eyes these days, it is clear: My life is too different from yours for you to bear—"

"Oh, Guryn! Do not speak so! Think you so little of me to believe that?"

"On the contrary, Richard. I know you are strong—enough to hide what pains you. My very life is a threat to you in some way—which you can no more bear than I can change. Your lowered spirits betray you and hasten your footsteps from me."

"If I fail you, the fault lies in my nature as a man," he replied. "Perhaps in time, should you come to write your story, you will understand me better. As for the present, far more pressing dangers beset us, Guryn," he warned.

"Lovers are protected," I insisted quietly.

"Your name has been mentioned in the General Court," he responded, his face blanching.

I thought long on how unable Richard was to name directly what disturbed him so. In the end I decided to heed his warning, though the menace of the Blackcoats seemed small compared to Richard leaving. "Will they come to arrest me?" I asked finally.

"I do not know. Among the officials are friends I might persuade to avert such disaster. Meantime the hysteria grows daily. Fear grips the souls of the townspeople, speaking through their eyes; even children sneak down paths with glances left and right, afraid to gather in the sunshine. It is a dark time.

"What is more," he continued, "the accursed doctors of science, envying you and your sisters your powers of healing, seek to ban the magic arts from legitimate medical practice. Something else I do not understand," he wondered.

"Speak openly," I asked of him.

"Why should the learned ones want to hang women who do them no harm, after all? Can they not practice their own science of doctoring and ignore you and your sisters?"

"They, too, are afraid."

"Are you not afraid?" Richard asked.

I looked at him evenly. "In truth I am more afraid of the spirit driving you away, Richard."

He protested. "But I have no desire to—"

"Oh yes you have!" I smiled, though it hurt. "Do you think I who love you need special vision to see into your heart?"

"But I love you!" he exclaimed passionately. And in truth I loved to hear him say so.

"As I love you, sweet Richard," I replied. "Yet that pacing panther by your side pulls you away to roam the forest deep…"

He was quiet. "We have much to ready. You and Diana must come away with me, far from Gloucester. We shall start a new life together."

"That is not the truth," I murmured.

"You must come!" he insisted.

"You must go, if it comes to that," I declared.

"Why are you so stubborn?" he pleaded, desperate.

"Was I stubborn in loving you? I think not."

"You do not love me if you refuse to come with me," he insisted.

"The talk of a child is beneath you," I replied.

"Haughty! The queen emerges!" he proclaimed unkindly. "I plead not only for your own safety but for Diana's. Guryn—you must agree it is far too dangerous to remain."

"I am not certain that is your real purpose."

"What mean you by that?" he countered warily.

"You insist we depart, knowing full well that I would leave only at the spirit's urging. You stress our immediate danger so that you are forced to leave alone if not with the two of us—thereby going clear of conscience that you tried as best you could to reason with a witch."

Scarcely could I believe my own words, so harsh were they! But I was desperate to keep him with me and, for all my pride, fearful that I could not live without him.

All that I wished to say, I could not! To rail against the panther driving him to roam, who would ever be driving him away! How I longed to press him to me and make him stay, seduce him with my body into staying, cajole or shame him with hard words, even cast a spell on him! Even as I knew I would do none of those, it was my own conscience that nagged: Was I wiling him into doing what in fact I wished?

He had fallen quiet though his face burned darkly. "You are very cruel, Guryn," he muttered at last. "I will not leave. You are right about the restless beast ruling me. How I hate him right now—that animal quick to make me bolt. But without you I cannot leave; if you stay so be it, I stay as well." He folded his arms.

I remained silent. That night there was a space between us as we lay in bed. The cloud was hovering close. What had I to do with witch trials and arrests? I brooded; I am a lover, not a witch! But I knew with another mind such airs were foolish. I could not avoid my *tuirgen.* Then why not flee with Richard? Whither, though? The Blackcoats held sway in Ravenoak as well. They were everywhere. Had I not seen the visions? The time was at hand for us healers, seers, Druids, and magicians—we keepers of the ancient lore in the new land—to enter into darkness, just as our ancestors had done centuries before.

Nevertheless I would not flee. And yet how fair was that to Diana? Richard had brought news of children arrested and tried for witchcraft, and if ever there breathed a child of magic, it was Diana. I shuddered to imagine her brazenness before the authorities—a far cry from the way I would behave.

At last I slept, but restlessly. I held Richard close, trying to stretch the silk of the night, wrapped with him inside a cocoon of timelessness. After a while he stirred and turned to hold me, and I wept in his arms for all the grief that I saw would surely come to pass, and soon.

THE END OF MY STORY nears, and I must tarry no longer. I have at long last decided to leave Gloucester—this cabin where I have lived for more than sixty years—to seek out Ganieda's old home in the deep wood to the north, there to rebuild his ruin. There to end my days with the mice and the eagles, close by the fairies and the sidh where my father lives yet as a king in his prime, feasting and telling stories beside the terrible, beautiful Morrigan. When I finish my story I will go.

Richard's prod so long ago to write my story, I have come to realize, has proven a prophetic gift. One day my descendant will return to these haunts and, piecing together my mother's treasure, no longer wander lost in some shape yet dim. Then might the power of the old Gods, celebrated anew through our stories, again gladden the heart of the old earth.

Richard went back and forth to town, bringing news, and all the while we heard soldiers marching through the wood, passing at a little distance. One day when Diana and I visited Sara and Nanepa, Sara proudly displayed her matchlock and shot pouch.

"Is your magic not strong enough?" I half teased her.

"Fight fire with fire," she glowered, shaking the weapon at me.

I knelt before Nanepa rocking by the fire. By now ancient as dust, she rarely spoke. It was unfair she should undergo more troubles. Diana snuggled up to her, patting her head kindly.

Nanepa looked at me through lowered lids; words seemed written all over her lined face. "You will survive," she prophesied, voice croaking.

"And you, little one," she addressed Diana. "What mischief have you planned for the black demons?"

Never one to reveal her secrets, Diana shied away with a strange smile. Although I had wondered myself, I knew well enough to leave her to herself, trusting in her own wisdom. But ten years old, already she possessed the education of a full-grown woman, so roundly had I instructed her. As for tribal lore, she had learned much from Sara and Nanepa. She was ready to undergo full initiation, that the secrets be revealed at their source, but there was no Ganieda to send her off for study. In recent years our circle gathered infrequently, for many participants had either moved deeper into the woods or been taken away. And so I taught her all I knew even while she listened yawning, as if the old, old stories were already old to her. Now I felt I had nothing to teach her she did not in some uncanny way know.

I stood up to speak quietly with Sara. "Have you not thought of leaving? Richard has said—"

"Richard!" Sara scoffed. "Yes, to go away, I know. He warned me as well, vowing to take all of us with him. Such noble condescension! My home is here—so my fight is here!" she fairly shouted, setting her matchlock down with a bang.

Why did I think she would leave any more than I? I realized. Even so, I had been harboring some hope she might decide to flee, taking Diana and Nanepa with her.

"You know we cannot win this fight," I admitted.

"We can win," she insisted. "Even if we must become invisible or turn ourselves into animals."

"Look at the ravens," I replied, motioning toward the window. For, indeed, Sara's yard was full of those harbingers of death fluttering and cawing, their black wings dipped in death's waters.

ONE DAY soon after when Richard and Diana had gone to town for supplies, Sara's words returned to mind as the Blackcoats arrived. They came in a mass, the stern leader reinforced by musket-wielding soldiers. Spotting them through the window, I went out to meet them.

"Anne Cleves?" the commander inquired. I nodded.

"We come in the name of His Excellency the Royal Governor of Massachusetts Bay, Sir William Phips, and the ministers of Gloucester and Salem. It is reported that you practice healing by means of the Devil's potions," he recited, as if by rote.

"I know nothing of your devil," I answered. "I give herb and root to those who suffer, that their pains be eased."

"That you chant heathen prayers on behalf of the townspeople, uttering incantations and casting spells," he continued.

I explained. "The cures will not work without the proper words—"

"Anne Cleves! No one may heal without the blessing of our Lord God—and He curses witches!" the man spat. A collective murmur of assent rose up from the soldiers.

"Have you come to arrest me?" I asked plainly.

"Not at this time—we have no warrant. I have been commissioned by the good people of Gloucester to order you to cease your practice of the dark arts. Should you not desist forthwith, you shall be arrested, then condemned and punished should you not recant."

"For your concern I am grateful, friend," I replied, turning to reenter my house. While I stood meditating on which spells I might cast anew to protect the cottage from intruders, the sound of rocks banging against the cottage walls followed by retreating curses reached my ears. One such rock broke the window beside the door, which I set to patching with a bit of cloth.

Richard was desperate upon hearing of the incident, staring at the broken window with a stricken expression. Diana listened from the corner.

"Now you must listen!" he growled, his eyes flaming.

"The spirits have spoken nary a word," I answered.

"And what of her?" Richard pointed to Diana, noticeably taller in recent days. Like a cat waiting for a bird, she looked curiously at me.

"Diana is old enough to make her own decision," I pronounced, although I had my doubts. "However, it is my wish that you not take her with you when you go," I added, bowing my head.

Diana spoke in her grave little girl's voice. "I shall go in my own way and time," she explained.

"Oh! I am surrounded by mules!" Richard threw his hands in the air. He set his booted foot on the hob, stirring the ashes with a stick.

With that Diana went skipping out the door.

"You and I meet in portentous times—for my own fate, a time of convergence," I stated. "Through my love for you, Richard, I see that my fateful fight is not yours. After all, the Blackcoats are your people. I can no longer turn my eye from that truth, and so..." I turned away from him to address the broken window. "And so I ask...that you leave without me," I finished.

"Guryn!" Richard exclaimed, turning from the fire, eyes all pain.

My heart was heavy, for the moment of reckoning had struck all at once. A door opened in my heart, and I saw that my life with Richard was but one part of my soul's journey. I had received from him the strength to face the Blackcoats.

"I do not speak to hurt you, my dear heart," I whispered, turning back as he drew near me. Together we sat as he took my hands. I spoke as he stroked my hair, all the while tears coming down his cheeks.

"You have been my teacher of love…and I have been a good student. I who have taken so much from you must now go on without you, for you have taught me just that. Until I learned to love you, never would I have had the heart to face the Blackcoats. At first I did not understand your ways; now I do. With your courage I will stand straight when they come and not falter in my speech. With your lightness of heart I will silently deny their danger—and thereby overcome it. With your trickery and wiles I will not consider it beneath me to escape when the time comes. In meeting them with your fairness I will judge them as fellow travelers, perhaps even finding some measure of compassion for the regrets they might yet suffer."

Turning away from me, Richard kept silent, tears skittering like fairies down his shadowed face. I reached for his face, but he pushed my hand away.

"You must go tonight, Richard. They are very close; for you to put your life in jeopardy here is more than I can bear. I give you my heart to take. Never have I loved another as I have loved you. How else could I have received so much from you? And in return I leave you all my treasures—save Diana. She may yet find you in the wide world, for in troth you are her father."

For a long while Richard sat unable to speak. When he did turn to me he kept his eyes averted and spoke in a voice heavy with grief.

"You are forever my only beloved, Guryn. All that you profess to have gained from me has long belonged to your selfsame spirit. What you see in me is but a lesser reflection of your own great soul. I will go if you ask me, though you must tell me again and again this evening. I will go—but I will return, as you know."

I nodded, touching his shoulder. "You are always welcome at my hearth."

"May I prove myself worthy of all the gifts you have given me. As for your daughter, though I do love her as my own, as strange and wild as she is, I shall not steal her away as my own. My bond with her, no less than that with you, is already forged to last a lifetime." Finally he looked in my eyes. "May I not stay the night?"

My heart turned to lead in my chest. I shook my head.

"Oh! May I not stay?" he begged again, his eyes wild with loss. I shook my head once and turned away.

"Very well," he heaved a sigh, rising as stiffly as an old man.

Terrible the time ticking as he gathered his belongings, stowing them in his sailor's sack, wrapping his flute and placing it in the knitted bag I had made. I touched it just before it disappeared. How much music was leaving with Richard!

He touched his lips to mine, and I sucked in the air from his soul as he stood in the doorway on that moonless night.

He shot a glance at me, then down at my gleaming brooch. A wild look came into his eye. Impetuously, he grasped the star roughly and broke off a point, shoving the fragment into his pocket. I was stunned into silence. Without a word he broke away, hurrying down the three wooden steps, past the oak where we had danced, beyond the small clearing, until he became all but invisible to mortal eyes in the dark. My fingers moving to my stinging chest, I looked down long enough to wonder at the broken jewel dangling from my garment. With my thoughts swirling around Richard, my blind eye caught him up as he walked, watching him remove the jewel from his pocket and savor its touch with his fingertips. Pausing at Sara's doorstep as if in search of solace, he hesitated a moment before walking on, his rounded shoulders betraying what he so sorely believed just then, that never again would he play his flute…. Watching from the dark corner of an oak, Diana muttered a spell over him, I saw, half out of anger and half in love, no doubt.

For a time that night I wandered as wolf through the wood, pausing to howl, my long snout pointed at the treetops whereto my soul could not fly. When I nosed out sleeping squirrels and a badger, in my anguish I tore their throats out—until, covered in blood and exhausted, I staggered home.

That night Diana did not return, and in the morning the Blackcoats came. Riding in a rough cart alongside them stood my own Sara, bound and gagged. Her hair was in a fury and her eyes were fire. Despite the dirty scarf binding her mouth that blocked her from speaking, her look told me all. Beside her I saw clearly her *riocht*: unbound, hair streaming, sitting leisurely on the edge of the cart and taking little notice of anything. So real did the spirit seem, appearing precisely in contour and dress so like Sara, that my mouth fell open. Knowing it was death to look directly into the spirit's eyes—for it had turned to look at me—I quickly averted my gaze. A shudder thrilled my soul. I knew what that meant: It was finished; Sara's hour was near.

Scanning the mob of ministers and soldiers, I spied toward the rear two men bound in bloody bandages; the result of Sara's gun, I was certain. I saw that fever would overtake them and they would die in a fortnight.

I stood straight in the doorway. Perhaps I might have fought…but I had no weapon, and all my spells were useless. The powerful spells I had cast to protect our cottage worked for a long time, until they were overmatched by the matchlocks of the Blackcoats.

In a loud voice, the commander addressed me. "Anne Cleves, you are hereby charged with the crime of witchcraft. You must submit at once, else we shall take you by force same as your sister witch Sara Topping."

"I will go with you," I sighed, stepping down. My eye was searching hastily for Diana, but I could not see her. My daughter had gone far away, and I could not penetrate the mist.

The men took hold of me roughly. "Who shall feed the pigs and cow?" I inquired.

"They are confiscated to pay for your imprisonment," the commander answered, as two soldiers tramped to the back of the cottage to seize my animals. Pushed into the cart alongside Sara, I sought to console her. With her hands bound she could only stiffly communicate in Ogham, yet she managed to convey that Nanepa had hidden when the Blackcoats broke in; she knew nothing more.

The wooden cart jolted us down the rough paths to Gloucester and from there to Salem, whither we arrived to much fanfare in the evening. Led by the Blackcoats in charge, we were paraded past a throng of whooping and howling townspeople. Torches blazed all around us, as if we were in a nightmare of the Christian Devil's own making. Monstrously glowering faces jumped out of the dark at us, spitting and hurling curses and rocks. I moved close to Sara, who stood defiantly before the mob while stones pelted us. At the Salem jail the cart came to a halt.

Sara was thrown into one cell, I into another, in a long, low, wooden building with bars built into the windows and straw covering the floor; no fire burned to warm the night. Food was a crust of green bread accompanied by a cracked bowl of dirty water, from which I drank greedily.

For eight days I was imprisoned in that cell with little food or water, and no sun. I passed the time in meditation, constantly striving to reach Diana's spirit. Often I thought of Richard, reconsidering my rash refusal to leave Gloucester. But each time my thoughts turned to whither I might have fled, the memory of Ravenoak overrun with Blackcoats returned to mind, so I sat still to bear my fate. I stayed because the time had come to face it.

Sara was tried but would not recant, as I knew she would not. Looking into the mist, I witnessed her in the dock cursing her judges and the stupidity of the people. She was hung the following morning—and I was alone.

At last I was led into open court before the stone-faced judges in their black robes, Cotton Mather himself sitting at their head beside the lieutenant governor. The spectators filling the benches looked frightened and stupid, assuming the gaping expression of those fearful of everything. The trial was a miscarriage. I was allowed no witnesses to speak on my behalf, only a final opportunity to defend myself. I rose when summoned to speak.

"The many young girls who stand before you accused of witchcraft have done nothing; they are worthy neither in name nor by practice of the charges against them. I beg you not commit the injustice of confusing the true practitioners of poetic magic and healing with those poor children whose hysteria is nothing more than buoyant spirits, which thankfully uplift us in the new land. You who have landed here from across the seas, leaving ancestors and traditions behind, now find yourselves in the position of children throughout the whole of your lives—high-spirited, yes, but ignorant and frightened. That is the fate awaiting settlers upon these shores. Whereas we who practice healing by herb and prayer and root come by a different inheritance, for we have brought our old ways along with us; our Gods and Goddesses have accompanied us."

"Heathen!" erupted cries from the crowd. "Infidel!" "Burn the witch!"

Judge Hathorn looked down upon me. "By your own voice you stand condemned, Anne Cleves. As earthly guardian of Our Father's wrathful justice, this Court demands you answer: Do you recant your dark practices, which the Good Book condemns clearly as the way of the Arch-Usurper?"

"I know nothing of your devil, aside from those injustices I see wrought here. What have I to recant but all the learning sacred to my tribe, for which healing ministrations your townspeople seek me out?"

"She does not recant; she remains intransigent!" Mather proclaimed in a piping voice, whereupon a clamor rose up again in the courthouse.

After sentence was pronounced, I was taken away and thrown back into my cell to await hanging in the morning.

That evening proved an unexpectedly lightsome one as with a gay heart I mused on the whole of my mortal life. Now that I was about to pass on, a Latin phrase Ganieda once taught me came to mind: *Ars longa, vita brevis est.* Always I had understood by it that art endures while mortal life does not, but sitting there I saw something more: that a single mortal life is too brief for the great work. Thus was I content to have lived a flaming arc of mortal existence before passing once again into the circle's shadow.

As I sat in meditation I heard a scratching at the barred window, which admitted the only light in my dark cell. The window looked out on the woods nearby. As soon as I rose I beheld the face of my daughter peering in at me, calm and serious. Her face was dirty and her red hair tangled with twigs. Utter joy! Another moment, and my broad smile gave way to a perplexed frown: Why had I not foreseen her coming? She had become more powerful than I!

"*Hst!* You are in danger!" I whispered.

"I am outside the prison," she replied matter-of-factly. Hearing whimpering over her shoulder, I peered out into the darkness. Four wolves were pacing about, huge females with rippling haunches who stopped to stare with dark, knowing eyes through the window. Diana had brought my sisters!

Diana slung ropes through the bars and, murmuring a prayer, withdrew. As the wolves snarled and snapped, the ropes grew taut, until with a crash the bars flew from the window frame, taking loose stones with them. Diana reappeared.

"*Now,* Mother!" she commanded, helping me out through the opening. Suddenly I was standing freely in the open air, the wolves swarming around my legs like a black sea, the wind blowing my tangled hair. Diana motioned me to hurry into the wood nearby. "A friend," she tossed over her shoulder before racing ahead.

Stepping quickly to follow, I heard a shout behind me. From around the corner of the prison bounded a guard, who with pointed musket was now raising the alarm.

"Stop or I shoot!" he yelled. I turned to look. Another and then another soldier rounded the corner and raised muskets. One pointed his weapon at me, the others at the wolves, who in turn darted into the wood. In an instant I was left their sole target.

All at once from the wood behind me a flash exploded with a loud report. A guard fell dead. Another bursting flash—and Richard himself leaped from the darkness, grabbing my arm. "Run!" he cried, shoving me out of the way and into the wood. More shots fired as Richard sped behind me, the soldiers in close pursuit. Like spirits gathering in the dark, several wolves rapidly encircled and attacked the soldiers. The howls of the men, their shadows glinting off the trees, tore the air as my sisters rent their flesh, snarling and snapping in their fury.

Richard by then reached my side, a great wave of fullness embracing me. While hurrying us along he shortly returned my smile, looking repeatedly over his shoulder, for from the growing clamor ringing through the wood it was clear a larger band of soldiers was now in pursuit. Our hearts leaped into each other's breast, and I was flooded with his joy as if we lay together.

The soldiers drew nearer. Carrying a second musket, Richard stopped and knelt, then fired. Another guard dropped. Whereupon the men fired more shots and balls whished through the night, tearing leaves and thudding into trees. As I ran I heard Richard fall with a groan. I hurried back to him, but he pushed me angrily away. His leg was bleeding badly.

"Go on!" he spat, rising and limping slowly after me.

Dragging him into the hollow of a dead oak, I chanted softly. "Get on my back and ride!" I whispered, having shape-shifted into wolf. Nuzzling his tottering body so that he slumped across my back, I groaned with the weight but bore him up, trotting away through the wood.

"*Guryn!*" I heard him whisper desperately in my left ear, and again his love flooded me, urging me on.

Still the soldiers came after us, closer and closer. More shots were fired, followed by the wrenching cries of my sisters as they fell. With Richard barely able to hold on, I was forced to slow down. Soon the soldiers surrounded us, poking and tearing at my flanks. Shrugging Richard from me, I snapped and tore at them with bared teeth.

"It's the witch!" yelled one. "A man on her back—that is no wolf! Get her!"

Grabbing me with their huge paws, they clamped heavy boots against my sides and beat me with iron cudgels until I squealed with pain and snarled at the blood running down my flanks. Again and again I tore and snapped at their hands, driving them back; again and again they seized hold of my long black fur, pounding me with their clubs. So many soldiers were assaulting me that I grew exhausted, close to collapse under the weight of their blows.

Out of the corner of my eye I spied Richard being dragged off into the dark; I looked about but could not see him. The loss of him triggered the black of the wolf's fury and hatred, as a deeper and more violent shape-shift than any I had known overtook me. I sensed my soul plunge to the depths. My eyes widening and my teeth elongating, I warped into a beast of pure hatred and seismic wrath. Expanding in a rush to four times my size, I felt my eyes turn around in my head, my head rear backwards, my backbone arch, until I bellowed forth so horribly that the few remaining men who did not fall back at once raced further into the wood, panic-stricken by the demon before them.

"*The Devil! The Devil!*" they screamed.

Breaking free of the circle, I turned upon the men and rent and tore them, biting into their flanks and tossing them like pebbles into the air. Though shots rang in my ears as many a ball sank into my flesh, these struck with no more impact than flies landing on a horse, and still my fury did not abate. Finally I raced like fire driven by a howling wind, running and running with the blood in my eyes, shots coming at me from all sides. A man came across my path; I leaped upon him and tore his throat out with a single snap of my ferocious jaw, his blood gushing into my eyes and splashing hotly over my face. A second, a third I charged after in that dark wood, killing each in the spasm of hatred. Even as I left many corpses strewn about the wood, more and more men bearing arms continued to spring up, the balls flying thick around me. Seizing a moment to break clear, I dashed away from the fiendish Blackcoats.

Up and down hills I sped, my lungs bursting as I ran feverishly, possessed by the weird of the wolf. When after a little while the shooting faded into the distance, my war fury began to lessen and I could breathe more easily. But I dared not stop, for the demons were surely pursuing me. And so all through that long, cursed night I ran, crying for Diana and for Richard, crying for Sara and Nanepa, cursing and wailing at the moon that she help me avenge the bloodshed. Long and long I ran, until the sky at last paled and I fell bloodied and exhausted in a heap at the foot of a gnarled oak standing at the edge of a swamp, where I lay as if dead.

FOR MANY NIGHTS after returning to my cottage I roamed the woods as wolf, searching for Diana and Richard, finding only Blackcoat prey. By then my sight had so deepened that I could sense humans for miles around. I knew when the Blackcoats would be searching the woods, smelled their fear and determination; I could perceive which young men out of brave folly were on my trail. Some of the youths, seeking to save their fellows, had taken on the heroic task of searching out and killing the "demon wolf," as they now called the witch in their midst.

Nonetheless all my powers were of no avail in tracking Diana, and I discovered myself utterly alone. In Sara's old cottage I found Nanepa in a heap of woe, her little brown body crumpled at the foot of her rocking chair. After hitting her over the head, the Blackcoats had left her on the floor. I buried her properly, that her spirit might find her people's hunting grounds and be free.

The men of Gloucester and Salem trembled as they walked the nighttime paths lest the demon-wolf, springing suddenly upon them, rend them lifeless in a heartbeat. But no matter how much during that dark time I glutted the maw of death with Blackcoat corpses, my hatred could not be sated. Even to my sisters I became a creature too wild to approach, and they left me to the madness. Five times the moon waxed before my rapacious eyes, and every night I returned to wolf shape to wander and kill.

One day as I lay in a sickened stupor before the fire, two young women approached the cottage, hesitating on the stoop before peering in. I recognized them at once as healers of some power. Thus it happened on a sunny morning that two young ones entered and took me under their care, singing soft songs of healing over me, burning herbs and laying me on my bed, washing my wounds with their healing salves.

After they departed, the madness that had held me in so deep a blackness refused to loosen its grip. Not until I reached for some clean pages of soft vellum that Richard had left me and, dipping a pen, began to write the story you now hold. For in recounting my life I discovered I had to relive that life, and hence in this after-time have come to know myself as a spirit in a story.

So I wrote until the madness left me, gradually feeling my wolf shape diminish as I became more human. As wolf I had barely felt my wounds, but as I became increasingly mortal I realized how deeply I was hurt. It hurts my hand to write this; the deep wound in my rear flank left me with a bad limp. And even as I looked at myself in the cracked glass and witnessed a woman reappearing, I had to face a hard truth: Not only had Diana and Richard disappeared but all traces of my beauty and youth. Over time my face shifted so completely that an old woman came to greet me in the glass, and I could not avoid noticing that a once proudly erect woman was carrying her losses on her back like a sack of bricks.

Yet there was work to do, and so I went on until an enduring old woman took shape, thanking my daughters and sending them away with gifts.

I knew that the madness of the Blackcoats, still raging through Gloucester, would relent no more sensibly than had my own. Prolonged battle had only sharpened the men's animal fears, teaching them how to track far and wide the one who was hounding them. Hence I turned my attention to preparing incantations, casting spells, and shaking sticks around my cottage. All the enchantments in my power I chanted under the moon before the oak, while around the pole of heaven I tethered my little shelter, that the Blackcoats be turned back from my home. Even so I feared them, for with my strength mostly gone I could not easily shape-shift into wolf. Instead, whenever I summoned my animal spirit I suffered much weakness, wandering in a dark mist.

In the end it was the fairies who saved me from the Blackcoats—but that story must remain hidden. Of my long journey in the Otherworld for Richard, I cannot yet write. I may have to leave that story unfinished because its strength extends far past my own life. Suffice it to say that, lonely for him, I used my powers to seek him throughout the wide world and beneath, despairing of ever finding him. I found him in the one place I could not see. And that when love lived again, so did beauty…

Of Diana I have had no news these sixty years. The crystal goblet was gone when I returned to my cottage; only Diana and Richard knew where it was hidden. I believe Diana claimed it.

For a long time I fretted over my daughter and for a long time cried for her, then for just as long cursed her for wandering and ignoring me. The years have brought some peace. Perhaps she has from time to time returned to hide herself behind the oak outside the cottage door—perhaps hides there now—since she has long held the power to keep me from knowing whether she is near. More stubborn than I ever was, she now walks in her own *tuirgen,* preferring her way to remain a mystery to me. So be it.

For sixty years the people of Gloucester and Salem have left me alone—left me to live shunned by all but my own pigs. Now the time comes round to journey back to Ganieda's land, seeking out along the way the Morrigan's sidh. For I have killed enough and hated enough to be kin to her. My soul—dispersed to Diana and to Richard, to Ganieda and Oroonca, to my father—is hidden away in enough places that it can never be lost again. When on that day I first met Richard, only to send him away so quickly after, I feared he might steal my soul. A proud woman, I held back from him. Over the long years I have learned that one whom you love enough to entrust with your soul can never steal it. Rather, to give part of yourself to a beloved is a Druid way to hide your soul—and thereby protect it. Whether or no Richard and I meet again, as long as he carries a piece of my brooch, he carries my soul. I know that he protects it unto death.

A WORD TO YOU for whom I have written—you for whom the presence of the Otherworld has lit the path to my journal. Use the record herein to take another step on your *tuirgen,* mindful always that the spells and chants, the recipes and charms by themselves are nothing: Only your own power can make them work. Yet until you understand that all you feel and know has been felt and known before in different guises, your singular efforts will be for nought. Unless you are humbled before the circle of life and death, you will be unable to summon spirits or see in the dark, nor to enter fith-fath. We live not for ourselves alone, but for the Goddesses and Gods. In my long life I have seen enough use of the reason that our men of science promulgate to fear its fruits into the future: that women and men will come to forget their deeper natures altogether and in their stead fight futile wars for domination. Whereas the souls of women and men are but branches of the same Oak.

The eternal beauty that all people seek lies at the bottom of the cauldron. True, use fairy thimble for the wasting sickness, but above all endure that wasting sickness of age and decay wherein lies our portion of beauty. Just as the Morrigan's beauty takes nourishment from her war wounds, we mortals must take nourishment from our own, else our very life spirit suffers. The wasting sickness of my beauty that Richard so loved, my blind eye and stubborn ways, even the thorns I put in Richard's way: Out of what was apportioned me I concocted my potion. Take up your beauty and use it well, for to attract and to endure is our destiny.

Only by loving—by longing for my father and for Richard, for Diana, Nanepa, Sara, Cian, and even the Morrigan—have I become a shaman, so protected by my wounds that the Blackcoats can no longer touch me. For I move at last upon the entire circle of life and death, seeing them whole. Half in, half out of life, my voice whispers like a ghost in your ears, *Do not forget, Do not forget,* like the whippoorwill or the mourning dove you hearken to in the far forest.

Daughter of the future, I hover over you...and who knows? Perhaps part of your soul lies hidden away within my spirit, which long after I am gone will breathe still in these Gloucester woods, whispering to you from the half-world where your left foot is planted. May it be planted deeply.

12.

NIKKI THE SHAPE-SHIFTER

NIKKI SAT IN STUNNED SILENCE, the softly curled leaves of Anne's journal open before her, its fine, spidery hand dancing before her blurred eyes. Her head ached from fatigue and too much concentration, and her arms were someone else's. The coffee boiled in her stomach like acid.

"Cleves," she murmured as the late afternoon sun slanted dustily through the curtains, meditating on the curled red linoleum. A thrumming echoed in Nikki as if from a far-off lute, a melody faintly familiar she could not quite make out. Smelling white wine, she thought of Philip, recalling a conversation between them one Sunday in late spring as they lay about the house, morning papers spread out on the floor and Guy asleep on his end of the couch. Coltrane played softly on the CD, and the sun shone in. She looked up from an article she had been reading on the ever-increasing speed of life as the millennium approached.

"How do we slow down?" she had asked Philip, lying on the living room rug absorbed in a book review. He turned toward her, his eyes momentarily out of focus in diverted attention. Straightening his glasses, he smiled.

"Indeed," he replied in his Euro-voice, as she called it, the seemingly sophisticated, slightly British-accented manner that charmed her and made her mad, it could sound so pretentious. He sat up and crossed his long legs, resting chin in hand. "That's the big question, isn't it? How to live in time—if it's even real."

"Time? I think it is. Everyone believes it is."

"Well, belief is one thing."

"I have my own sense of time," Nikki remarked.

"As we know," he smiled wryly, touching on Nikki's habitual lateness. "But isn't that the point? That time is relative, flowing faster or slower—"

"Or backward," she continued. "Why not remember the future?"

"Right!" He sat up straighter, warming to the topic. "Exactly—isn't that poetic intuition? It seems that American culture especially has lost a sense of seasons. Didn't we once have more awareness of them?"

"Instead everyone wonders when the stock market will crash," she observed.

"Precisely! We all know it's inevitable. Cycles."

"Women know about those."

He eyed her. Was she being territorial—? But the sun was kind, and he didn't have the heart for a fight over gender superiority. "Yes, cycles are both external events and internal rhythms. But the issue has to do with thinking in terms of them—"

"Which is why the patriarchy has to go," she stressed.

"Men are not somehow compelled to think linearly."

"No, but women are by nature attuned to cycles."

"Then why aren't you attuned to men's cycles?" he challenged her suddenly. Silence settled in the room, broken only by the distant horn of Coltrane softly wailing "My Favorite Things."

"You pull me toward you like the moon, then you go into eclipse and shut me out in the dark. And back again."

She studied him. Each of them knew that to refer to their periodic fights was itself tempting a fight. But she didn't feel like fighting either.

"If those are the natural phases of the moon, what else can you do but accommodate yourself to them?"

"You lay claim to the moon for womankind," he plowed ahead, too annoyed to heed the danger. "You aren't the moon—you aren't as predictable as the moon. I forget all the cruelties as soon as you start waxing. You're the kind, fruitful earth, bestowing summer sunshine and flowers. Flower child. I know full well you'll go into eclipse—but when?"

"You're like primitive man before he understood the seasons," she laughed. "If there was ever such a time." She grew serious. "At least you know it's coming."

NOW SITTING IN her kitchen six months later, Nikki recalled the way she had felt her lip curl with superiority, remembering the stricken look in Philip's eyes. He had risen smoothly and gone over to her, whispering soothing words and kissing her neck, until they moved upstairs to forget and pretend. Although she had won then, she didn't want to win any longer. She rubbed her aching temples, trying to wipe the sinus headache away. It didn't work; the throbbing intensified.

Nikki glanced outside. A warm October thirty-first, though the sun was fading fast this Halloween. She stood up stiffly and looked at the clock. Five thirty. Pouring herself a glass of Sauvignon Blanc from the refrigerator, she sat again, flipping idly through the pages of her translation, pondering cycles and power. She felt a heaviness accompanying the growing recognition: No longer could she revel in exercising power over Philip. Not when he lay hurt... She missed him.

The name "Cleves" kept resounding in her like waves pounding the shore. A splitting and a conjoining, a word containing its opposite.... Just like the way she and Philip connected—and split. It even had a cyclical connotation, in Anne's sense of a natural process. Or was Nikki's presumption of women's natural connection with circularity at the heart of her troubles?

Was it she, not Philip, who had been imposing a cyclical pattern...or maybe just a repetitive one? Was she the one who had been unable to bear patiently the natural course of their relationship, allowing its seasons to unfold in their own time rather than forcing them?

She caught herself humming the Birds' song "Turn! Turn! Turn!" as she washed out her glass. When the phone rang, she hesitated as she turned to stare at it in the living room. Waiting for the answering machine, Nikki heard not Rose's voice, as she had feared, but Clarissa's.

"Nikki?" came the full-throated voice, resonating even electronically. Nikki shivered without moving to the phone. She listened. "It's All Hallow's Eve, as you know. Your Aunt Meg was going to make this call, but even though we're in a fight of sorts, I wanted to do it. Now that you have finished the journal, you are ready for initiation—if you're still willing. We meet by the apple tree at midnight. All your friends will be present to welcome you into the circle of magic. Please don't let what has passed between us stand in your way. Let Guy lead you near the clearing where we camped that first night. The final secret will be yours tonight." Nikki stood watching as the click of the phone gave way to a buzz.

Samhain, she thought absently...*Samhain!*

"On that day I died, in the sacred grove at Quickborn, when the black sheep is given," she recited, startled to find Anne's words—prophetic! "To hell with Clarissa and all of them. This is my night," she resolved, suddenly determined to be initiated. After all, Clarissa didn't own the circle.... And once initiated, Nikki concluded, she could go her own way at last, untrammeled by Philip or her own sad history. "My way is opening into a new life, Guy," she explained to the dog, who raised his sad eyes from the mat. "A new life!" she exclaimed, kneeling beside him and rubbing his ears.

Seeking to clear her raging headache, Nikki jumped up abruptly, threw on her coat and left the house. It was a clear October evening, the sky's blues just darkening in the west out beyond the Annisquam River. The air felt light and limpid, as if nothing ballasted the old earth ship on this night, no barrier between the heavy earth and the boundless deep of the heavens. She breathed deeply, striking out toward the town center and the waterfront.

Here and there small groups of children ran about shouting in costume. Nikki wondered vaguely what she should wear to the midnight meeting. Black, of course. One of the children who spied her broke away from his group, running up to Nikki.

"Trick or treat!" he cried. Nikki stopped. Dressed in heavy pants and black boots, the boy carried a long, evil-looking hooked hammer over his narrow shoulder. His face was scarred dramatically, and his little nose painted red. He carried a plastic bottle taped with handwritten paper that read: GIN.

"What a great costume! What's the bottle for?" Nikki asked.

"I'm a drunken Finnish stonecutter from Gloucester!" he squealed, opening his bag in expectation.

She shuddered while absently poking in her bag, not taking her eyes off the homunculus. He cavorted before her, tilting the bottle to his mouth, dropping it, wiping his lips and smacking them, leering at Nikki through darkened eyes and snickering wickedly. He finished by swinging his hammer at the level of her crotch. Nikki jumped back, dropping her purse. As she stooped to retrieve it, all the children, smelling a quick touch, ran over and clamored about her with open bags.

"Trick or treat! Trick or treat! Trick or treat!" they screamed, their little high-pitched squeals like banshees racketing inside her aching head. Though her head hurt too much to see straight, she managed to make out a little ballerina, an American Indian, Zorro, a king, and Madonna. Their faces were leering and contorted with greed as they pressed in around her like beggars for treasure.

"I—don't—have—any—candy—" she stuttered, which only brought sharper screams.

"Money! Money! Money!" they screeched so that at last Nikki turned and bolted, running down and up streets until the little voices echoed far behind. She stopped under a tree and sat down on the grass, waiting while her heart quieted. For what seemed to her a long time she sat quietly, the world growing dim and calm once again. She stood up and walked toward the sea.

The sloping streets rounded corners and finally planed out to the sea, lying flat beneath a crepuscular sky. Behind her the heavy sun pressing into the dark hills was leaving its hammered work on the sea, which gleamed in the evening blue and grey and green, nacreous and mystic. Resplendent clouds shot streams backward from the sun, where just above the houses to the west they glowed orange as lilies, then faded into bluebells and nightshade over the sullen sea. Groups of children romped and darted past in the gloaming, but they were far-off now, making the earlier incident seem absurd and even embarrassing. Nikki pressed it out of her mind, like putting the cat out for the night.

SUNSET. Lines of clouds glowed bright orange against a deepening sky, nearest where the sun had disappeared. Overhead sailed a few leftover clumps of fleecy nimbus, steel gray underneath and blue at the edges where the memory of the sun still touched them.

How rare were such sunsets in the city! And no one stopping to watch except Nikki, looking back over the city to the west. The whole was like a vast composition behind which loomed no God to thank, only the earth and sky; nature quite alive, yet its design unconsciously conscious. Nor fathered by a distant king, staring with a telescope eye from the super-distance of Jupiter; not a vector but a circle.

It was a painting, a landscape, a skyscape, the sun resting under the earth, the bright glowing marmalade streaks, cerulean at the horizon, and above the renegade nimbus loose puffs, silhouetted by a charcoal sky. And to the east out over the water, already drawing on its night-black cape, the saturnine blue of dusky night settled in. Everything in its place.

Nikki walked on, peering into the windows of the bars lining Commercial Street where lumbering fishermen, their moves heavy as sea swells, sat trying to drink up the sea. From inside the dark bars of her past their lined faces and barnacled hands twitched expectantly, as if still reaching to grab hold of the tarry sheets, the flying shrouds, the day's slippery, slimy catch. All their days their hands remembered. A lost memory of Ernest and his fleet found its way back to Nikki's mind. These days as the catch hid further down in the ocean deep, sonar blips on board fishing vessels echoed mournfully back to hopeful sailors: *No fish today. No fish.*

All those times her father had taken her to his favorite bar, the *Towline,* she mused. He was proud of his young daughter for knowing all the batting averages of the Red Sox, all their stats even better than the men at the bar. They always greeted him as king of the bar, calling out from the packed line of hunched shoulders. The one everyone jokingly called *Uncle Dickie,* with his sparse thatch of hair, blunt nose, and dull, watery eyes. He was a stonecutter with hands of horn; Nikki squirmed when he patted her. She was afraid to look in his eyes, for in them she saw a lost man.

And Mr. Symmes the accountant, whose office was in the same one-story building as her father's: a sandy-haired, balding man, fat like a woman around the waist yet with spindly legs. He had a huge nose and a little moustache stuffed under it, twinkly eyes and lines in his forehead. He was perpetually frightened and predictably cautious, repeating his words in a soft voice. He appeared to worship her father, who dominated him in turn—which depending on Nikki's mood left her either admiring her father or despising Mr. Symmes.

The man known as *Old Curley…* A bald, hunched-over old twig of a sailor with a wild look in his eye, he was full of stories of the sea that Nikki listened to with a grain of salt. He drank Irish whiskey, curling his hand around the glass to hold it from the far side before pouring the drink down his crow's neck. Afterward he would smack his lips, wipe them with the dirty sleeve of his coat, and open his toothless mouth in a wide grin that terrified Nikki.

This was her father's court, and they always kept a seat in the center of the bar for him, freeing an extra for her whenever she came along. So Nikki would sit, legs dangling, sipping a bar coke, from time to time answering a challenge from one of the men to recite Yaz's average or Williams' hits. At her success her father would beam with pride while she would feel wonderful and warm, giggling behind a cupped hand when inevitably one of the men roared that someone should buy her a drink.…

When later as a young woman she went to bars on her own (never to the *Towline,* though), she met all sorts of men—sailors and students and businessmen, sad men who gave her a bit of adventure and a sense of risk. Claire and Nikki teasingly provoked one another into ever-wilder exploits: who could pick up a man in the shorter time; who could land the cuter guy. Nikki always did. Who would go further… How was she to know that Claire was lying about what she knew, just to brag? How was Nikki to know that Claire thought Nikki was the one bragging—?

Her face burning with recollections, Nikki hurried past the dark wood bars, head lowered. She heard Philip whispering in her ear like a ghost and wondered absently, through her raging headache, whether he had died. It was the night for spirits to speak.

"It's your past that hurts me," he uttered.

"It's the past," she insisted. "It's dead."

"Not for me. Nor should it be for you. You are your past. If you've lost your past, who is left in the present?"

No, he was wrong! Unfairly wrong! She had changed, she knew it! She hadn't gone to bars for years now. Years! He used her past against her like a fulcrum to push himself away from her. Which only put her more on guard that confiding in anyone—a man, especially—was always a mistake. They never understood.

She cut across the bars on Commercial Street to expansive Causeway Boulevard, head aching, by now in a fog. There were no buildings and no people to come between her and the sea, and the air was better. Cars flicked headlights on and drifted by absently, as if thinking of something other than driving. Out on the wide stretch of road that curved alongside the sea she found walkers and joggers about, scattered lovers and loners.

She stopped to lean on the metal railing that overlooked the beach a few steps below. Watching the surf thump whitely on the strand, in the dark she could make out three thin white lines of breakers hurrying for the shore. Drifting back to thoughts of Anne, Nikki envisioned her ancestor standing a short distance away in a long Druid cloak. Like the tall, blond-haired woman standing below on the beach, head bowed, a cloak draped over her shoulders. Nikki stood at the railing, musing over the figure of woman at the edge of the sea. From time to time the woman looked out at the darkling sea, then down again, as if a weight were pressing her head back down.

Philip was speaking in her head again. "You've spent your life chasing men, all the while despising them. Look at how you view me—I'm either everything good and beautiful to you, or suddenly I've become a monster. There's no in-between with you."

No in-between.

"I don't think you love me as an actual person."

"But I do love you for the person you are!" she spoke out loud to the beach. "I love your kind and loving self, not that wandering, stubborn man of mystery! I love the Philip who is with me, who stays with me, not that man who is in thrall to some dark god I don't understand!" Her father came immediately to mind, though she could only think about him as she always did: in flashes, never sustained. His image was overpowering, too large for her to face all at once. She lowered her head. Wasn't there some spell she could use to look at just a part of him at a time? Something that could help reduce him to human size?

The woman on the beach turned and began walking toward Nikki, who stared back at her with a rising thrill. With her chalk-white face, black circles rimming her eyes...*Anne!* gasped Nikki, panting from the shock and clutching at the cold railing as the woman drew near. She walked up the stairs where Nikki stood and at the moment their paths crossed met Nikki's gaze. Nikki regarded her spellbound, starkly conscious of facing an ancestor come eerily to life. For she trod with the assurance of the dead, this ghostly woman garbed in black, her sunken black eyes fixing Nikki with the deafening silence of death.

Nikki held herself steady against the railing, heart thumping wildly until the figure passed. For a moment the barrier between the worlds opened, then snapped closed. Her mind struggling hurriedly to make sense, soon with an enormous sigh of relief Nikki concluded, "That must be one of the members of the circle I'll meet tonight! Yes, yes, *of course—!*"

The sky had grown dusky by then, a soft, inky radiance glimmering on the sea's face. Again the question pestered Nikki: How could she withstand the wrathful Rose demanding her due? Nikki would have to admit to Rose that she had indeed translated the journal and, yes, had discovered within the secret of eternal beauty, vague that it was.

Discordant strands were coming together in a vast orchestra of mounting pressure: her mother's letter; her budding identity as a Druid magician in her own right; Rose; Philip.... Yet the composition was building toward a climax that felt out of her hands. Was she the conductor or merely a player? Either way, she had yet to learn the music; she knew something was expected of her, without knowing what. Her headache pervaded her entire body now—back, head, arms, everywhere aching from all that sitting. Was it her period? She couldn't think straight to figure it out. She only knew she felt a mass of symptoms, had in fact every right to forego the initiation. Nikki reached in her bag and took two sinus pills.

She stopped. *All right, she was afraid.* The fear that had been gathering in her for a long time, fear that she had always fought off with anger or determination, now lay upon her like a weasel, fastening its jaws on her heart, and could not be shaken off. She shivered and looked around abstractedly, then walked quickly away from the water and back down Commercial Street.

At the first bar she came to, the *Buoy,* she pushed through the door and stood still, letting her eyes accustom themselves to the murky light. From the long bar across the room several men turned hunched shoulders and pale faces to peer at her in the gloom. She sat down at a small round table as far from the bar as possible. The men turned back to watch a flickering TV. There was very little conversation. Soon the bartender called out.

"Get you something?"

Rummaging through her bag for money, Nikki looked up. She pulled out some rolled dollar bills and waved them vaguely in the air. "White wine," her voice croaked in the smoky light. Through the cocktail of beer and antiseptic, the air smelled heavily of salt and oil, an odor of corruption that made her stomach turn. She pressed a comb quickly through her tangled hair. The bartender brought a spilling glass of white wine and set it on a coaster in front of her. Nikki nodded.

"You haven't been here before," he observed. As Nikki looked up, he gave her a smile. Twenty years younger than she, he sported lovely long blond hair that curved around a square jaw and inviting, easy dark-brown eyes. A manly, meaty, good-natured face. Not like Philip's face, so narrow and intense and *vulnerable*, Nikki considered. He wore a dark-brown cape draped about his shoulders over a medieval-style breastplate. At his side tinked a long sword tied to his waist by a leather thong. Nikki returned his smile, shaking her head, as he sat down across from her.

"Harry," he introduced himself, extending a large hand. *Big hands—!* Nikki briefly gripped his hand, shaking her bangs like a pony. She could feel the warmth of his hand in the back of her head; she wanted to forget.

"I'm off in two minutes—my replacement should have been here a half-hour ago. Mind if I join you?" He sat back and shucked a cigarette out, lit and leaned his chair back, blowing the smoke away. Although Nikki had quit smoking when pregnant with Alice, she waved two fingers in the air in a vague gesture of desire. He leaned forward quickly and stuck a second cigarette in his mouth, lit it and handed it to her. She took a long drag.

"Sweet costume," Nikki remarked. The smoke was raw and good.

"Like it? I'm looking for damsels in distress," he smiled rakishly.

Obvious, she thought, replying out loud, "This humid weather. My aching head." She rubbed her forehead.

"Yeah, it's a drag," he agreed. "It's a drag, whoever you are." He grinned wryly at her. They smoked. Nikki said nothing, staring into space and sipping her drink. Framing his hands like a movie director sizing up a scene, he regarded her.

"Let's see—that's not a hippie costume, exactly. With your hair, I'd say a princess of some sort, though the jeans don't go. I've got it!" he cried. "Part saint, part—well…" he broke off with a light-hearted laugh. They were silent. "So OK, I'm only a knight, not a psychic," he pleaded.

"Oh! I'm sorry. I'm Nikki." She raised her glass and drank off half the contents. Though the acid burned her throat, she could feel the wine's warm plume as it hit her stomach.

"You're going to want another," he observed, at which she pushed dollars at him.

"I'm a knight, remember?" he replied, ignoring the money and getting up. Returning to his post, he joked with a few of the men while handing them fresh draughts of beer. When one of the men said something low he chuckled and blushed, glancing quickly over at Nikki.

It was so charming! Nikki thought, catching his eye. A dark-haired older man came through the door, going behind the bar as Harry nodded to him. The two men shook hands, and Harry slapped him on the shoulder. Slurred greetings issued from the men at the bar, followed by a few loud guffaws at a joke Nikki could not hear over the din of the television. The older man stood back to admire Harry's costume, making another joke.

Harry returned to Nikki with another glass of wine, along with a mug of beer for himself.

"Here you go, cure for any headache in the world. The finest vintage," he joked. He had good teeth.

Nikki smiled back twistedly. "Not just head—back, shoulders, everything."

Harry scooted his chair around near hers and turned Nikki halfway around. She gulped at the second glass of wine. "What are you doing?"

"Massage, my specialty," he explained. "Look at these hands—they're made for more than popping tops off beers or building houses—or killing dragons." He held them up as if they weren't his, then set them on her shoulders, beginning to massage. She turned back to relax.

It was like a dream... Nikki nearly fell asleep from the wondrous feel of the slow working of his fingers against her shoulders. Her shoulders were concrete, the movement of his hands warm currents of water, gently nudging her muscles to loosen, whispering to her that she must do something. She closed her eyes and moaned softly. More talk and laughter wafted over from the bar, but Nikki was by then too deeply transported to care. The wine was working in her now, the sinus pills doing their subterranean work on her head. She breathed deeply, imagining the knight had a horse tied up outside. She took one more deep drag from her cigarette before stubbing it out.

"So this is what you do?" she asked, opening her eyes, leaning and finishing the wine. She closed them again. Harry leaped up and returned with replenishment before she could reach again for the glass. She gulped greedily at her third.

"You guessed it—I'm not really a bartender in a broken-down bar full of deadbeat men." He pulled his chair closer and straddled one leg on either side of her chair, speaking softly into her right ear. "And I'm only a knight on special occasions. For my daily grind I'm a concert pianist. You're experiencing million-dollar hands right now," he whispered, leaning close to her ear. His voice was like silk. She was getting drunk.

"I believe it," she replied dreamily. With one part of her mind she marveled at how easy it all was—and how much she remembered. How to carry on a casual conversation about nothing, all jokes, no meaning except the hidden one, poised shyly there like a young girl in a very short dress. He crooned over her and breathed onto her neck with jagged breaths.

"What do you do?" he asked familiarly.

"I was a lawyer, but I quit. Now I walk my dog in Dogtown."

"Dogtown! I go there all the time on my mountain bike—eh, horse. Great trails."

"Yeah. Except they're trying to develop it."

"Is that right?" he asked casually. He went on rubbing, and she wanted to stop her life right there amidst this sea of pleasure, his hands like reeds waving in the sea currents, softly playing soft underwater music.

She reached and drank more, having lost track of when Harry last refreshed her glass. Or was she still drinking the same one? The glass looked the same, had the same droplets of water clinging to it and the yellowish wine like a globe inside. She drank until her head rose softly into a cloud. She could smell his body behind her, rich with musk and man-sweat, carrying her off into a different world.

"Should we leave?" he murmured in her ear in a way that worked like a charm. She had been waiting for something endearing from him, and there it was—seduction in the form of a question asked uncertainly, sweet with hesitation. Nikki gathered up her bag and drained her glass, rising unsteadily.

"I can do better for you at my place, if you want," he offered, smiling uncertainly. As if he had never done this before!

That was the trick, uttered a voice deep below as she rocked on the surface. To believe this was the first time…

She stopped. Here was something new. To be aware of another voice, even inside her drunkenness. Never before had she experienced that. Always she had gotten drunk and that had been that. No voices talking to her. Just silence and alcohol. Wake up the next day beside a stranger. And this voice was a woman's voice, not Philip's—nor her father's. A clear woman's voice! Rapt, she stopped in her tracks, wanting to hear more. There was no more.

They stepped outside to a Gloucester evening in full bloom, the wind blowing gently toward the sea as if dying to be under sail. The air had warmed—or was it she? Nikki let her coat fall open. *Take me, take me,* the wind soughed through the streets, seeking its way onto the cradle of the sea. *Take me too!* Nikki wanted to sing to the dark sea, somewhere out there whither the wind swept. Somewhere out there waited Ernest…and Philip!

Breathing deeply in the dark, she gazed about, feeling the pull of some fate. But whither? Which way should she hurry? Harry put his arm around her, turning her away from the sea up the street inland. He nuzzled her, the scratchiness of his chin exciting and reassuring her. He smelled faintly of beer and mouthwash, a hint of cologne. She forgot the sea, bidding her mind be like the night breeze and not tarry, for he was handsome enough and tall. A thought of Philip flickered, torturing her mind.

Do not tarry! Do not tarry! whistled the wind, sweeping about them in gusts as Harry slitted his eyes against the blowing dust. She angled her face up to his and they kissed, as Nikki glanced over his shoulder down the narrow street and out toward the black sea. *Take me! Take me!* the wind begged in reply to the sea's beckoning. Over the water the harvest moon rose full and silent as an egg, hanging pregnant in the low sky.

"Take me too," Nikki murmured, her voice full of despair.

Nikki turned away from the moon and let herself sag onto Harry's shoulder. The wind died down; the voices grew silent. Blessed silence! As one shape they staggered down the street, Nikki's heart pounding. Harry's big arm around her waist and her head gone, her heart gave up the struggle. She was being led like a lamb, and the lights were going dim. *Away! Come away!* cooed the wind, racing out to the warm, waiting sea under the kindly eye of the moon....

As the two rounded a corner they were caught up short, bumping into an old bearded man. As if a troll had materialized in their path demanding a toll, he planted himself before them.

"Here!" cried the hunched old man in a piping voice. Dressed in many layers of coats, his beard long and straggly, he leered at the couple salaciously out of rheumy eyes. Between the wine and her headache Nikki found herself standing face-to-face with a gargoyle.

She gasped. Standing before her seemingly forbidding passage stirred old Joe, his arms folded in a tight grip across his narrow chest.

"Joe!" Nikki exclaimed, awake in an instant. Her face went red as the night breeze succumbed into stillness.

He did an unexpected thing then, reaching out to take her by the arm. "Coming with me!" he insisted like a father. He shot her a look that told her he understood everything, as if he had been spying through the barroom window the whole time.

Harry was abashed and fell back. Nikki turned to peer at him but was no more able to break Joe's grasp than had it been forged across the aeons of stone. Inevitabilities were taking hold, she could feel even through the shimmer of wine. Harry stepped back into the night and was swept away by an ebbing tide. As the surge of her libido rolled back like a wave, Nikki was startled to discover herself alone with Joe, standing on a night-lit street in Gloucester, soft breezes springing up around her.

"Coming with me?" he inquired, and this time his words were an open question. Or were they so the first time—? Nikki wondered. She looked around in amazement. No Harry!

Joe held her arm, hurrying her along as they turned corners and crossed streets. They came to the waterfront at last, open streets full of shadows and the dark sea beyond. The breeze wafted freely, stirring the neighborhood to life. *Everything come alive!* marveled Nikki as Joe quickened the pace like a man fleeing the tax collector. People in costume passed, raging and flying in colors of gory and glory and black: devils, gypsies, and princesses, strong men and fairy godmothers. All part of the grand game of playacting on this night of Samhain, when you passed back and forth easily from this world to the next.

Couples in costume dashed past, ducking their heads into a stiffening wind all of a sudden putting their capes and trains to the test. The wind was toying with Nikki's hair like a child. *Warm...and again Philip's fingers played in her hair. What was that man's name in the bar? Why had he run away like that?*

She shook herself, keeping up with Joe, still in a daze. The sound of crickets chirping; arguing voices of a man and a woman fell from an upper story as Nikki and Joe passed, the man frantic and weak behind his cruel, defensive insistence, the woman determined and unpredictable as lava underneath her pleading. The same old story—except this time Nikki could hear right through their words to the tones as if listening through a tuning funnel. A bell clanged impatiently in the distance—a fire engine? She stopped. Behind all those sounds the steady hiss of surf meeting the beach. Traffic whooshing along the highway not half a mile off. The smell of still-warm pavement in the evening pulsing underfoot with the day's life, while far off the dying year curved its passage over the horizon. The earth itself leaning into the sun like a lover drifting closer with winter, a lover's cold embrace. Cars streaming past Nikki stealthily carrying secrets, looking out of the corners of their eyes.

Nikki halted suddenly, Joe stopped as well, just as a black limousine passed like a hearse. Three roaring motorcycles escorted the limousine, helmeted police riding dressed for battle. Nikki glimpsed Rose's face darkly in the passing window, impassively staring out behind the tinted glass; evidently she did not see Nikki in return. The unexpected sight of Rose's mask-like face frightened her. Or—was that actually Rose inside? Nikki began to doubt. But those policemen sidling along like rats brushing table legs—weren't they the giveaway henchmen? Exhaustion fell over Nikki like a tidal wave.

"I have finished the journal, Joe," Nikki turned to the old man, not expecting him to respond with any sense.

"Your Druid nature!" he exclaimed vehemently.

Nikki was taken aback. Was that it? Was her very work as a translator—a writer, in fact, of Anne's story—her Druid inheritance? Anne was a shape-shifter; Clarissa lived the life of the woods; Meg found magic in her ball; and she—?

"Joe, remember we talked about shamans and poets?"

Now his head was bobbing, and she felt their thoughts run along parallel grooves. "Maybe that's the only magic I have," she said. "If that is magic—?"

"Make sure we are alive!" he exclaimed, his face a broad smile.

All at once gathering clouds blocked Joe's gleaming smile.

"Peeks is gone!" he exploded piteously, eyes tearing.

Nikki didn't know what to say. "He—got lost?" she asked softly. But now the old man was sobbing, eyes pouring, snot running down his nose. He wiped it with a filthy sleeve.

"We'll find him—"

"You will!" he exclaimed, flashing her an agitated look, then abruptly hurrying off. It broke her heart to see him limp away so very alone, tapping his walking stick against the curb like a blind man. A jet of fear flared in Nikki: Had Rose something to do with the dog's disappearance? She brushed it off. With a shiver she hurried up and down the close-lidded, dark streets that wound to her house. Late groups of children were dashing home too, their costumes blown about by the rude winds now snarling and snapping like dogs.

Her house loomed up in the dark like a great yellow cat sitting on its haunches, a blinking sphinx in the growing wind. Nikki's head swam, headache back in force sparring with her lower back for attention. The wine was dying away like an echo in her stomach. She was parched.

She climbed the back stairs slowly, squinting in the yellow light of the back porch. Something was not right, she sensed. She pulled out the key, but her hand fell; the lock was broken, the door casing splintered. She froze, heart in her throat. Vigilant, gingerly pushing open the back door, she called out softly in the dark for Guy. Always he met her at the door, barking his silly head off with delight at her return. The house was quiet.

"Guy?" her voice quavered as she reached a shaking hand inside to flick on the overhead light. Pushing the back door closed behind her as she entered, she felt the handle fall to the floor with a thump.

Guy stood motionless in the doorway to the dining room, silently staring at her, fear in his eyes. He backed into the dining room, snarling when she reached for him.

"What is it?" Nikki whispered, although she noticed as soon as she spoke. The round kitchen table, which she had left earlier buried beneath the journal and her translation, was bare. All the papers were gone, her reference books scattered about the floor. Anne's journal was gone; Nikki's translation was gone, as was her own journal. The only thing on the table was a longish bundle little larger than a breadbox.

Nikki stood very still. "Anyone there?" she called again shakily, though she sensed no one else. For a long time she stood rooted, wondering dully who had broken in even as she suspected. A rising shock of violation seized her, leaving her quaking with anger, shot through with vulnerability. Pushing a chair against the back door, she jammed a broom handle under the stem of the broken knob, her hands shaking with rage and shame. She turned back to the table.

"Guy, it's OK," she leaned over to reassure him, but he snarled and backed away again. Better leave him be for now, she decided. Taking a breath, she let her purse fall and went over to the table. She reached to pick up the bundle, then hesitated as her fingers touched the cloth. A chill ran through her, making her eyes tear. Her stomach felt sick, knowing what was there. She folded back the stiff cloth to expose the head of Peeks. Animals must have souls, for we know when they are dead. Peeks' soul was gone. Nikki raised the little one and caressed him, moaning a little. Quietly Guy approached, sniffing and glancing up at what she held. She lay the burden back down on the table, not having the heart to pull the cloth away. He was already wound in a winding sheet.

She was enraged. Was it Rose? It must have been. Or Philip, somehow? Had he grown all too willing to do his mother's bidding? Her head reeled, encircling the possibilities and making her dizzy. The phone rang, freezing her thoughts. Nikki waited and listened to the answering machine.

"Nikki, this is Betsy. I'm sorry about how I sounded in our last conversation—I must be more upset and frightened than I act. Anyway, I really hope you will join us tomorrow—nine o'clock at the west gate to Dogtown. We're going to lie down in front of the backhoes…"

How was she supposed to argue with apologies? Nikki thought irritably. In any case, she felt certain Rose would not begin breaking ground—now that she possessed the journal. But—how had she found out about the journal? Was it in fact Rose? Yes, it must have been. Rose knew everything that went on in Gloucester: the family secrets and illicit affairs, the heroin addictions, gambling debts, cosmetic surgeries.... How often had she heard Rose go on about the assorted failings of "the little people" of Gloucester? It always used to make Nikki sick; now it made her livid—and afraid.

While she was absorbed in the translation she had more or less forgotten about Rose. But the time of reckoning was at hand. What of the actual formula Anne had written down for the potion of eternal beauty? For Anne had interspersed numerous spells and potions throughout her journal that Nikki had yet to translate. She meant to get to them later, after she finished working through Anne's narrative. Now there would be no later, she considered sadly, her anger flaring anew at the thought of the theft.

Nikki rechecked the collection of vials and jars she had taken from Anne's cave, discovering at a glance several missing. It struck her that she had never even considered concocting the potion for herself. Ganieda as well as Anne had been adamant that it was never to be drunk by a mortal being, on certainty of death. Could it actually kill you—? That the secret of eternal beauty lay not in physical beauty had seemed clear to Nikki during her work on the journal. Now she was confused. Could Rose actually *use* the potion, assuming she could ever decipher Anne's language? Nikki felt protective of Anne's secret; the potion was Nikki's own family secret, never intended for Rose. The potion, like the journal, belonged to Nikki by right of inheritance.

And perhaps, Nikki thought, she had already imbibed the potion....

Nikki gritted her teeth. She and Rose were headed for a showdown; she would have to face Rose alone, just as she had always done. Anyway, there was no one who could help. Joe was crazy; Clarissa thought Nikki should learn to suffer and enjoy it; Claire was out of town; Meg, too disinterested.

Philip? She leaned toward the phone. No. She would not call. Besides, what if Peeks' death had been his doing? She gathered up the melancholy bundle and carried Peeks to the back yard, brought a shovel from under the stairs and dug him a grave, her heart beating hard all the while. The old anger was stirring inside like an evil brew. Guy sat like a sentinel, unspeaking.

Back in the living room, Nikki collapsed in her father's chair. Her head was a locomotive. She looked at her shaking hands, smeared with dark dirt. Guy eyed her strangely. She leaned back, closed her eyes, and...on a carousel she was riding a pink pony that rose and fell. Round and round she turned, the colored lights flashing. Exhausted down in her bones and unable to open her eyes, Nikki watched electric sparks flicker against the dark. It was all too much, the spinning out of control, the noise, the lights! She would fail everyone and everything. Figures floated up and down on the merry-go-round: knights on horseback with lances raised, mounted mysteries floating past in the spinning mist. Elves and fairies darting in and out of the rising and falling horses, promising no good; witches riding broomsticks; and everywhere the weird figures turning to her and staring as they passed, silent laughter streaming out of cavern mouths, yawning chaos in her brain. Horrified by the madcap antics but too dizzy and exhausted to pull away, she watched the demons glare at her as they spun round and round. Everywhere she turned she encountered demonic eyes, all watching, waiting, taunting her. The eyes, the eyes! Glaring as they passed, boring into her, asking, prodding, demanding!

Out of time Nikki sat thus, eyes closed, head spinning, vertiginous visions circling and recircling, creatures of her imagination run amok in dumbshow. She writhed in her father's chair like a dervish. At last as her eyelids fluttered open, she spied Guy still watching her curiously. How long had it been? She craned her neck to glimpse the kitchen clock. Eleven-thirty. With a groan she sat up, forcing her eyes to stay open. Her stomach was churning slowly, mixing a load of rocks and concrete. Her head felt cloudier yet. An hour of frantic sleep was worse than none.

She staggered to the kitchen, pulled a crushed box of fat-free pizza from the freezer, and plopped one frozen rectangle in the Radarange. Then she flew as fast as her head would allow upstairs to her bedroom and began flinging clothes around trying to focus on what to wear. Her sinuses full and aching like pudding shoved under her cheeks, she bent to peer out the little window by the bedside. Clouds were scudding past the moon. Some storm must be blowing in, she imagined, rubbing her temples. Suddenly struck white with fear, she spun around.

Yet there it sat, glistening quietly on the dresser. Surprised and vastly relieved, she hurried to dress. Soon she stood in a long black skirt, black leather boots and black sweater before the mirror, gazing at her shining blond hair while tying a black cape over her shoulders. Her hair shimmered platinum against the black cape, falling in writhing chiaroscuro to her shoulders. On a whim she picked up Anne's broken brooch and pinned it to her cape. It felt heavy against her left shoulder, like a war medal. Her head still reeling, she remembered the pizza as the aroma crept up the stairs like a forgotten dinner guest.

"I look like Anne," she whispered in wonderment, touching her cheek in wide-eyed shock.

"I am Anne's heir. I am the one." Her body tingled.

She became mesmerized by the epiphany, staring into her own eyes in the mirror like a cobra at the mouth of a flute. She would fall in and never come out. But those red-rimmed eyes! Pulling herself away at last, she hurried downstairs and wolfed the pizza, burning her mouth, then gulped down a glass of wine to cool it. She stood up. The room was pitching and rolling.

Come away! Come away! the night was calling. When on that night the barrier between the worlds opens and one passes between, the dream becomes real, Nikki reflected. She wanted to go down to the sea as she had gone so often when young, at this very hour, to bathe by herself after lying with a boy in the back of his car. Picking her way across the boulders to walk slowly into the nighttide, breakers laving her cold feet, the ocean as eternal and cold as outer space. Then at length, by degrees, kneeling down in her clothes, the salt water swarming up to her and over her shoulders like a mass of little children. There she washed herself clean, rubbing her body in the cold surf and once taking off all her clothes to feel the earth and the sea clean on her skin.

Now in her kitchen on Halloween, decades later, she felt too old and too tired and achy to go bathe in the sea. Maybe after the initiation.

Guy was at her side whimpering.

"Not tonight, Guy," she replied, but at once reconsidered. "Why not?" she shrugged, snapping his leash on as Guy smiled from ear to ear, panting in anticipation. She edged them both out the back, pulling the door closed as best she could.

They picked their way uphill behind the house to stand a moment on the edge of Dogtown. Nikki held tight on the leash, as if about to fall. Her heart heavy, she was afraid of the dark this night, it was so wild. The wind was high, clouds obscuring the moon, racing around up there like madmen. The woods were alive with the scent of an approaching storm. Wind through the blowing branches, whiffs of pine and salt, like a body pressed against her! Out of every tree a spirit was leaping, curling around her, blowing her hair, plucking at her cape, nudging her forward with invisible, demon-tiny hands. Surrounded by presences, she felt nervous and elated, plunging into the dark wood as Guy pulled her along, taut on his leash.

Down the old pebbled path they stumbled, past the rough stone cellar holes of the old witches of Dogtown. Tonight their spirits were abroad, the wind whistling through the holes roaring out as woman and dog passed. *Who are you? Who are you?* the voices taunted her, blowing her skirt into Möbius curls and swatting her hair. *Come with us!* they tempted. *Come away! Come away!*

She quickened their pace even though it made her dizzy, the new wine exulting in her blood, shoved along by the wind. Soon coming to a crossroads, she stopped to consider. For the first time she felt seriously afraid of the voices howling through the half-bare trees, gusting winds hurtling loose leaves and bending even the larger branches, tearing up the earth. Guy chose their path, pulling her along as she scrambled behind. Up and down thickly wooded hills they raced as voices in the driving wind chased after them, demanding *Who? Which one are you?* Before long the path thinned out, then disappeared altogether, overrun by thick undergrowth and narrow tree branches that caught in Nikki's hair and grabbed at her clothes.

"Good job," she called out dryly to Guy, picking off a thorny twig from her sleeve. Yanking all the more tightly on the leash, Guy pulled her tripping through brambles and scrub pines. Eventually the ground changed, until before long they reached an area that in the moonlight seemed familiar to Nikki. Yes—she recalled it from her walks. Why, it was not very deep into Dogtown after all! Not two hundred feet off to the right lay a parking lot she could have driven to. Guy waded casually through a bubbling, dark stream that she stepped over; it looked to be the same one Clarissa had led her to when they camped. The meeting place had to be near.... But how her head ached! And how tired she was!

Standing very still, Nikki listened and sniffed the air, rubbing her poor forehead. From a distance she heard the snap of a fire, then smelled smoke. She followed the scent, wending her way through the trees, Guy at her side, until she spied a fire splintering shadows in the distance. The wind blowing her along, she soon found herself on the perimeter of a clearing. At the center stood an apple tree pregnant with fruit, shoulders sagging under its scorched load; nearby a bonfire roared angrily, snapping and lashing the black night with long curling arms.

Encircling the fire stood ten or fifteen black-cloaked figures. Tying Guy to a tree and patting his head absently, Nikki approached the circle while the wind roared behind her. Scudding clouds brindled the moon, flicking the shapes on and off like lights, one moment standing before Nikki, the next disappearing in shadow.

When some of the figures turned toward her, Nikki regarded with a shock the planes of faces pale as death. Deep, gleaming eyes peered intently from hooded faces. They came to her as a group, silently taking her hands and leading her to the presiding figure, alike dressed in black and hooded.

Invited to join the circle around the fire, Nikki in a stupor sat down alongside the others. The leader opened a leather-bound tome and intoned some words, but the wind was too high for Nikki to hear, or else she was still too drunk. As the wind quieted, the voice grew stronger. It was a woman's voice.

"...the barrier between this world and the Otherworld lies open. Though spirits visit us, and we may enter their realm, the danger is great that we mortal travelers not return. As our mother the Triple Goddess opens her arms of bounty and terror to us on this night, we sense her power beneath our feet, in our blood, and within our wombs. We pray to her, calling out to her by many names—Hecate, Persephone, Hestia, Brigid, Isis, Diana. In fear and love we invoke her. Our bodies, female and male, enact her deep truths.

"So do we pray to and invoke her consort, the Great God whom we know as well by many names—Hunter, the Horned God, Osiris, Father Pan, Dionysus. We honor death just as we honor life on this night of ending and beginning, recognizing death as but birth into another life and life as the beginning of death, each circling upon the great mystical wheel of existence.

"The time is at hand to honor our dead," she pronounced. As everyone settled into yoga sitting posture, she produced a massive goblet of ornately wrought silver from which each was to drink in turn. Hand to hand the goblet was passed ritually around the circle.

Taking the cup with shaking fingers, Nikki drank from it like a desert before passing the drink on and sitting like the others, silent and meditative. After a time she felt a stirring in her blood, sensing the presence of a drug. Her eyes felt glowing, even as she closed and reopened them, and her breath echoed in her ears. All of her senses were pricked up: The wind crooned; the crackling fire licked itself like a cat. Although Nikki's head began to swim, a certain clarity of the spirit began opening to her.

"Let us each in one's own way call forth our dead, that we might speak with them," the leader directed, whereupon a deep silence took root in the circle. The wind died down, and the moon settled into a calm white light over their heads.

Nikki swayed with closed eyes, her head lolling. In the suchness of the moment a profound feeling of oneness enveloped her; was her. Whole mountain ranges were coming to birth inside of her, and the earth shook with each of her heartbeats.

Her thoughts racing, Nikki felt herself pulled back and down through the funnel of time. Before her appeared no other than Anne in cape and black dress, walking silently through the purple forest of the elfmound picking herbs and putting them in her basket, Fern sniffing at her side. The sorceress raised her head and peered nearsightedly in Nikki's direction. Rapt and frightened, longing to call out to the beautiful Druid magician, her ancestor, her mother, Nikki opened her mouth to beckon the womb of all being. She wanted to cling to Anne and weep and be safe in her strong arms, to live out her embryo existence forevermore in that protecting embrace.

But the magical Anne turned her head and walked slowly away, as if Nikki were not real enough to catch her eye. A profound depression descended on Nikki; she felt herself sinking slowly down a deep, cold well, her body weighted with lead. The water rose as she was submerged, until it was suffocating her; the weight made it impossible to lift her lungs to breathe. She wanted desperately to cry out. For a few moments she struggled in near panic, then gave up, exhausted. Anne had vanished along with the purple woods. She had not drowned; she was still alive, but it was difficult to fill her lungs. Persisting, she sighed finally into one breath, one jagged breath following upon another, enacting the very essence of life. She dragged her eyes open.

She stared dully at the leader, who was standing with one robed arm draped over something in her left hand.

"The mystery of the great circle of time," the leader chanted, raising her right hand to uncover an ear of corn, its long, pointed leaves huddling against yellow fruit gleaming like a studded sun.

Nikki watched the ear of corn glow and pulse as if it were a chronometer of the universe. What did it mean? Her eyes clouded; all the world swirled. Shapeless lights flashing before her closed eyes gave her a sensation of hallucinating; the whisper of the wind and echoes of coughing reverberated in the hollows. The lights went low.

For a time Nikki kept her heavy eyelids closed, hearing only the softening breeze and the crackle of the fire burning low. Behind her somewhere Guy whimpered, paced at the end of his leash and lay down; that was all vaguely visible to her. She felt lulled.

"Nikki!" a voice bellowed in her ear, as she jumped.

Her father paced in front of her. Nikki was sitting in his chair. *"I am the Life!"* he thundered, reaching for her. She shrank from him deeper into the chair, the smells of his body and alcohol filling her face. Her breathing grew labored. His hand was a paw of some sort—or no, it was a hoof cloven down the middle, which he extended with a leer, shaking it in her face.

"I am the Life!" again he howled, his face contorted with a fever that writhed itself into a wolf, baying at her out of blazingly maddened eyes.

Now the eyes were alive and glimmering like the eyes of a cobra, like jewels piercing her soul. Her father was not a wolf; he was a cobra. She could not look away: The hooded, reptilian face grew larger until it filled all of her existence. The green-gold eyes silently spoke to her, this father-snake not her father. Drawing her downward after them, the eyes catapulted far and away and down, drawing her down upon them, until father and daughter passed under the earth. She followed tethered, inevitably, unable to struggle or resist.

Distantly Nikki felt her eyes flip in their sockets, pressing against her forehead from gravity. She sensed herself standing on her head, the stink of her own body rising in her nostrils and making her gag. Her mother stood before her leering, waving at her a massive erection that protruded from her winding cloth. *"You are less real because you are dead,"* she cackled. *"Take dick-tation!"* she then demanded, splintering the thick air with peals of ghoulish laughter, her eyes bright and merry and mad. Nikki was shaken to the core.

"Wait! Wait!" she wanted to shout, but she was rooted in place like Lot's wife, half turned in longing memory.

Father cobra bored his jewel-eyes into her with diabolical patience, all of time at a stop. His seduction would writhe its way into her, she knew, no matter how long she resisted, for it would outwait her. The demon shape-shifted into her own father, horribly naked before her. Witnessing him, she was filled with a wrathful and destructive terror that lifted her chest with the force of a gale. Her eyes glowing like coals, she reached to her side instinctively, withdrew her *athane* and plunged it into her father's breast. His steaming red blood gushed like the fountain of life over her, bursting forth in tremendous shooting gusts that drowned her.

Nikki felt a blow to her heart like she had been physically struck, and she toppled over, unconscious.

THE HOODED FIGURES were bent over ministering to her as Nikki came to herself, slowly. Looking up from twitching eyes, she recognized the hooded form of Clarissa and beside her Joe, also hooded. An acute sense of shame overspread her, weighing on her chest as she looked from one to the other, certain that Joe had told Clarissa about the bartender. Aware of her face deeply flushing, she turned away to shelter her shame. The fate of poor Peeks came back to her. *No,* her mind wailed, *that was only part of me!*

But Clarissa was kind, sponging Nikki's face with water from a silver bowl that Meg brought over, who in turn smiled down at her niece. Behind Nikki the fire snapped familiarly, its heat warming her. Holding her head, Joe raised a silver goblet to her lips while quietly prodding her to drink. The expression of deep concentration on his face touched her; she caught the sad sanity in his eyes. Did he know about

Peeks—? She could not be the one to tell him, although looking more closely into his eyes she guessed he already knew; his eyes appeared clouded with grief.

She lay unmoving, moaning when one of the others gathered around her pressed a pomegranate to her lips. Still, she nibbled with relief the tangy-sweet, scarlet-coated seeds. It was the bright seed of creation she ate, the seed of death.

Utterly spent and only half-conscious, she felt she lay upon her deathbed. Perhaps she was already dead, surrounded by darkness and wind and black-robed silent figures. Into and out of her view they drifted…one wearing massive antlers bowed over her, face too deeply installed inside its cowl to see. *Man or woman…human or animal…demon or angel?* she wondered floatingly. A half-bird figure regarded her impassively, holding up a split apple to display its pentacle of seeds. The figure passed slowly out of her vision.

Nikki was paralyzed by a planetary depression that had spread through her body like infected blood. It seemed hours passed before chanting commenced, softly, by celebrants hypnotically caught up in the ritual of the dying year. A treasure trove of grand-sounding words and names reached her—Hecate…Great Circle…Renewal—but these fell out of her consciousness like pearls come unstrung, scattering across the forest floor.

Nikki lay deathly still, blinking in the dark trying to consider what had just transpired, feeling more alone than she had ever felt. Above, the dark outlines of trees shifted uneasily. The moon by then had floated out of sight behind thick clouds. She could make no sense of what she had experienced. More than that: She lacked the ability to categorize it. She knew only that she was frightened and alone. She felt dirty, violated, as if thirty years had passed in a day, taking with them the last vestiges of her youthful beauty.

Her thoughts returned to Ernest and memories of that hateful night so long ago, when her death began. She raised a trembling hand to touch her face; her fingertips needed no special sensitivity to feel her sagging skin and wrinkles, her watery eyes and drooping eyelids. And her slackening mouth, devoid of that youthful suppleness by which she had always been able to manage any difficulty—simply by showing her girlish smile. Her girlish smile—that, too, was gone; she could feel it.

"We are all the walking dead," rattled a voice inside, to which she nodded with the sadness of infinity in her lungs. What did it matter? Her resourcefulness in buying the house of her youth, her return to Gloucester, then finding her ancestor's journal, all the work to translate and understand it—what did it matter? What could possibly justify the perishable value of any of that, make sense of the whole or redeem the price? Her foolish desires, her even more foolish insecurities over Philip—what did they matter?

"We are the eternal beauty," the voice within proclaimed. Nikki nodded.

Nevertheless she could see clearly the whole of her life, for lying on her deathbed gave her a raven's eye view: refusing to understand, to believe in her own death, clinging always to transient and insubstantial pursuits while beneath her feet lay the invisible inevitabilities. Beneath her feet, down under the earth lay the bones of everyone she loved, her mother and father… For she could manage to feel, if not love, then forgiveness, now that it did not matter and her father could not hurt her. Below the earth lay Anne and the sum of her world. Even Philip carried his death knotted around his neck like those arresting neckties he sometimes wore. Did he know—?

Nikki blinked: She could see everyone's death, she slowly realized. Wanting to flex her new sight as if a new muscle, she sat up hesitantly on both elbows. The figures were sitting unhooded now in a semicircle before the fire, some still with eyes closed. Clarissa, sitting in the dim firelight: Her death was gentle and smooth as a dove in flight; she carried it round-bellied, floating below her chest. Joe, nodding distractedly: From the branch of a mighty oak hung his death, entangled around and through every part of his body, sticking its spiny fingers out from his two mad eyes. Meg sat amidst the others huddled in her dark cloak, watching the fire with a low smile. Hers hung about her neck like balls of dust and jewels interspersed, tinkling like bells whenever she shifted position.

Nikki wished for a mirror to see her own death, now that at last she could see the invisible.

As if the circle's psyche had read her mind, the chanting slowed to a stop; again the silver bowl was brought before her. She peered in, looking for herself. In the dark water shimmered broken reflections of firelight and night clouds. But—where was it? All she saw was a jowly face whose broken eyes gazed back steadily, equally interested in looking up at her. Slowly the watery face tilted slightly, its knowing eyes beneath the water acknowledging her. Nikki's heart leaped at the reflection, for it seemed to move on its own. Yet—who was the reflection?

They took the bowl away while she watched in horrified fascination, feeling as insubstantial as a fall breeze moving dead leaves, as if they were taking away in the bowl her original, more fluid soul. She reached out an arm in a futile gesture to grasp it.

Her mind lingered in reflection. Was that not the great wisdom of the ancients: the intuition of death? Treading softly on the earth hollow with the land of the dead; the dead walking with their feet planted on the soles of the feet of the living; life inverted. It began to make sense to her, Ganieda's and Anne's insistence that death was but one point on the circle of death and rebirth. Something gave in her heart like a blood vessel giving way under pressure, and insights flowed in like loosened blood.

Rising, the leader addressed her. "Nikki Helmik, you have come for your initiation?"

Nikki looked up and nodded.

"Stand," the voice bade, as everyone rose. Nikki stood uncertainly, her legs new and untested. While the members turned their backs to her, the leader approached and, pulling gently at Nikki's cape, removed it. As the rising wind blew her about like a wand, Nikki quickly turned cold.

Turning back around, the others formed a semicircle in front of the initiate. She felt abysmally uncomfortable.

"Nikki, you have translated Anne Cleves' journal," the leader began.

"Yes," she heard herself whisper. "Yes," she repeated in a stronger voice.

"What have you to tell us of the journal?"

What had she learned? What—? She made herself answer—something, anything.

"Love—stories. Old stories. The Otherworld. Death. Writing."

"What have you written?" the leader asked.

In her confusion, Nikki wanted to say that she had written the journal, for it had felt so much like hers. *But it was not hers; no, it was not,* she knew in her depths. She had botched the job of translating it; there was no magic in her understanding. She had nothing to give.

Then there is nothing to lose, came a voice that seemed outside of her.

"I have written the journal of Anne Cleves," Nikki stated bluntly, her eyes watering.

Silence followed. "Well done," the leader responded. "You have given us much; you are not alone. Henceforth we shall name you "Storyteller." A name of your choosing you will sign for yourself."

A figure brought forward the great book, bound in black leather with huge dull brass hinges and clasp. The book was opened and held before her, a pen put in her hand, the figures gathering around as she raised her shaking hand in the dim moonlight to write.

She hesitated. *What to write? What—? Who! Who to write!* Her fingers trembling, a name bobbed to the surface that she had long coveted as a secret name: Grace. A name she had wished for herself ever since a little girl, begging her mother for a middle name. Wanting to glide through life with real grace, she now realized, she instead had worn veils to distract from her clumsy inadequacy. No, her habitual floating was not grace. Grace meant gravity because grace implied weight like courage implied fear. The weight of death. So she wrote with trembling letters: *Grace.* And felt a fool.

Nikki looked up to find the others having thrown back their hoods. She saw openly the faces of Clarissa and Joe and Meg, some others vaguely familiar, women from Gloucester and Rockport—Cape Ann was such a small place, you got to know pretty much all the faces. Regarding the thoughtful, kindly faces, Nikki felt again the sting of her misdirected life. What had she been doing all her life, while these people practiced seeing into the Otherworld? She would not forget this salty lesson.

Remorse was returning, regrets and recriminations crowded around her again like unhappy trick-or-treaters come back for more, beginning to play tricks on her imagination: Back of the circle, silent and watchful, stood Philip, looking very much like his mother...

With a start Nikki realized she was looking at Rose in the flesh. She jumped.

Brandishing a vial, Rose gestured wildly from the edge of the circle. *"I've got it! I've got it!"* she shrieked, her black hair writhing and hissing in the moonlight like Medusa's snakes. Everything froze. The banshee Rose was dressed in black, high heels unintimidated by the woods. Her makeup was heavy and ghastly in the moonlight, her lips a vivid smear of red.

"Don't take it, Rose!" Nikki cried out.

Rose turned to her, her face twisted in rage.

"Don't take the potion—it'll kill you," Nikki repeated tremblingly, averting her gaze.

"This is yours," Rose slurred by way of reply, holding out the journal before dropping it to the ground. "I've got what I wanted."

"Did you read Anne's journal?" Nikki pressed. Rose had been drinking, Nikki could tell. She knew her well enough, remembering all the times Rose had come home late from a party, Nikki waiting in her bedroom to help her undress and to listen to her. Often falling asleep in Rose's chair by the open balcony, Nikki always woke with a start when the bustling, noisy, self-absorbed Rose threw the door open and yelled out what a triumph her evening had been, which prominent man she had held in the palm of her hand.

Yet Rose's eyes glowed strangely now, her head tilting as if facing a too-bright light.

"Did you read the journal, Rose?" Nikki pursued.

"I read enough," Rose smirked. "I found what I wanted—what you agreed to get for me. You went back on your end of our bargain, Nikki. I warned you what would happen if you did."

"Don't take the potion, Rose," Nikki insisted. *"Don't."*

"You dare talk to me like that? Know what you've done, little whore? Ingrate! You've ruined my life—almost. Bitch!" she spat. "First my husband, then Philip, now me. Know what? Ernest is back—yes! Can you imagine? Back in my house—comes in at night and wanders the halls, just like a real ghost. Scaring the hell out of me!" Rose glared at Nikki. "And you're the source of it, *yes!* I know you're behind this! With your witch friends and potions. You loved him—and learned how to bring him back, just so he could torture me as punishment! *You!"* she screamed.

Nikki was thinking furiously. *Then—she hadn't been the only one to see Ernest...*

"I've had nothing to do with that," Nikki insisted. "Please listen to me—"

Rose grew quiet. "I took out my little gun and for the past few nights I've been conducting target practice in my house. Target practice at the ghost you've conjured!"

"If you've read the journal, then you know: The warning that the potion is deadly comes from Anne Cleves herself," Nikki persisted.

In response Rose tucked the vial in her bosom, drew a small pistol out of her black handbag as easily as if it were a compact, and waved the gun around.

"You want the potion for yourself, Nikki? Of course you do—you're no fool. You always wanted everything that was mine!"

Clarissa stepped out of the shadow of the circle. "Hello, Rose," she greeted the madwoman calmly. Rose started, then pointed the gun at Clarissa.

"So, here's the other whore!" Rose roared. "I should kill both of you. Haven't I earned the right of revenge? Haven't I?"

"You've got the money, the power, and the beauty, Rose. What would you get for your revenge?" Clarissa demanded evenly.

"He killed himself because of you—you or the other whore!" Rose charged.

"No, he didn't," Clarissa rejoined. "He killed himself because he was subject to the same forces we all are. It's a sad business. You're only making it sadder," Clarissa stated, turning away from the pointed gun.

"You wait until I've dismissed you!" Rose yelled, shaking the gun at Clarissa's back.

Time slowed down for Nikki—even as her heart raced. She considered Clarissa's words. *Everyone* a victim? Her mind began to wrestle with the notion. But spotting Rose's finger tightening on the trigger, she opened her mouth to yell—when a booming voice from the far end of the circle interceded.

"Rose!" it thundered. Out from the shadows stepped Ernest, his face ashen and his long arm pointing an accusing finger at her. Transfixed as Nikki was by the sight, a sequence of eruptions seized her attention, for in rapid succession came a scream, a jolting explosion, followed by a second.

The first was Rose's gun going off at Ernest, whom Nikki saw crumple like a dried flower.

The second was an explosion of blue light and smoke in the center of the circle, shooting wild streams of sparks and rockets through the moonlit air. The force of the blast threw Rose backwards, knocking the gun out of her hand. Nikki, too, was shoved back, but something braced her against a fall. Looking down at her shaking hand, she realized with a shock: She had reached into her shallow pocket and, chanting a quick incantation, thrown a handful of Anne's herbs on the fire. She was the one who had caused the explosion.

Before the smoke finished clearing, members of the circle were restraining Rose, Nikki noted as she ran over to Ernest. Clarissa already knelt beside him.

"You're alive!" Nikki whispered thrillingly. Raising Ernest's bony head in her sinewy hands, Clarissa gently lay his head in her lap, stroking his hair. At the spot where blood poured from his stomach, Clarissa pressed her hand against the wound.

His voice was reduced to a croak. "I had to make amends," he explained, looking from one woman to the other. "Rose—couldn't go on bleeding the world. I thought I had it in me—forgive me," he whispered, gazing up out of bloodshot eyes at Clarissa and Nikki.

"Oh no," Clarissa murmured back, shaking her head and leaning close to him. "Nothing to forgive."

Nikki drew back, observing. Something in her, an incorrigible memory, kept her insulted and infuriated still. The image of a devil and herself lying on a bed and loving it refused to die. Ernest waved Nikki to come close.

"Please—" he smiled wanly at Clarissa, who immediately stood up and retired. His stomach began to ooze red, pulsing with each jagged breath.

Nikki knelt down a little away.

"Nearer," Ernest pressed. "You once liked being near."

"A lot has happened," Nikki clenched her teeth, trying not to look at him. Raging with hatred and anger and anguish, her heart was about to splinter under the pressure.

"So you know," Ernest nodded. Grabbing her black sleeve with a determined claw, he pulled her close with the irresistible strength of the dying. "I have tried to make amends. Loving your beauty too much, as I loved Rose's—I am guilty. I gave my life once for her beauty, a second time for yours. I once did you an unspeakable wrong, and I lived as long as I could with the burden—until your father died. All the weight once shared bore down on me alone after that. Rose hated me, and you—were so vulnerable. You remember that night!" he cried softly, his hoarse voice strained with passion.

Nikki nodded, her eyes tearing.

"After she learned about it from your aunt who had foreseen it in her ball, Clarissa warned me of Rose's declaration of war against you. So I made a plan to live as your guardian. From death I have hovered over you, watching and protecting. When Rose arranged to have you attacked in the forest, I thwarted the danger. When she drove to your house to kill you, I sabotaged her car. I saw you and my son—"

Nikki shot Ernest a darting glance. He nodded at her. "I cannot judge. I would be proud to call you—daughter."

Nikki turned away.

"Wait!" Ernest pleaded. "I do not ask your forgiveness, but for you to know...I have tried to make amends. I have tried to make amends—" his voice trailed off, hand dropping from her sleeve. Nikki motioned to Clarissa, who was at his side in an instant.

Nikki stood up, watching Clarissa hold Ernest's head and bathe it with a white cloth she dipped in the silver bowl. In the ripples Nikki glimpsed her own face, set and unkind, her mind fixed on that night long ago. She was ashamed... But now the image was weak and already fading like the sparks in the air, falling like the moon out of the sky, until it was gone, taking with it her shame and desire, for it was only a ghost.

"No, nothing to forgive," she mumbled, nodding at Ernest. Ernest closed his eyes.

Nikki sighed deeply and turned to Rose, who was screaming like a child. She lay writhing on the ground as Joe sat on top of her. Nikki smiled darkly, going over to the pair and looking down at Rose, who glared madly up at her.

"Is he dead for good?" she hissed. "I'm not finished with you, Nikki."

"But you are," Nikki answered wearily. "Because I'm no longer in thrall to you. You can let her up, Joe. She's a worse menace to herself than to any of us."

Rose jerked herself free of Joe, who stumbled and moved shakily away from her.

"Peeks," he muttered, sniveling and turning this way and that. As the others in the circle gathered around, Meg came forward.

"You will have to answer for that—as well as for Ernest," Meg stonily assured Rose.

Rose spat at that and lunged, but two members of the circle grabbed her arms.

"All right! *All right! Let me go!*" she screamed, until they released her after a nod from Meg.

Her face twisted and eyes glaring, Rose turned her wrath on Nikki. "What is it that makes you so destructive?" she seethed.

"*Me—?*" Nikki blurted, breathless with astonishment.

"You know it's the truth, Nikki, my little beauty. All those years of devotion at my side, willingly—only to betray me in the end. *Hah!*" she let loose, as Nikki blinked, stung by the charge. "I should have expected it—you acted just like I would have. No loyalty, except to yourself! And damn the consequences!" she yelled.

"I'm not like you," Nikki countered quietly.

"Oh yes you are," Rose insisted, her voice dropping. "I'm your real mother, you know. The one you've taken on—and taken after."

"My spiritual mother is Anne," Nikki declared softly.

"You're far more destructive than she ever was," Rose replied. "You destroyed my family, though for what reason I don't know—just because you could."

"I—I've been destructive," Nikki admitted. "I don't pretend to be as—advanced as Anne. But I'm trying to make amends by warning you about the potion. I've been studying the journal, practicing the magic. I understand things now I didn't. You can't take the potion of eternal beauty—because no one can," Nikki finished.

"Look at her!" Rose sneered. "So innocent of blame, so well-meaning! Her only wish is to keep me alive!" She stopped. "When we know you relish watching me become old and decrepit. When we both know your plot to steal away my beauty for yourself!"

"That vial holds a deathly beauty. Drink it and you will become as beautiful as everlasting marble," Nikki gave up tiredly.

Rose spun around and was gone. The members of the circle watched in silence as she roared off in her black Mercedes.

"Think she'll take it?" Meg asked Nikki. Nikki shook her head, then turned to Ernest. Clarissa sat rocking him slowly in her arms, crying softly over him. Two members of the circle hovering nearby had finished quietly bandaging Ernest, trying to staunch the bleeding.

"I think we'd better leave them their last minutes," Meg muttered sadly, leading Nikki away.

IN NIKKI'S KITCHEN at three in the morning, Meg petted Guy and sipped her tea; Nikki did not touch her own cup. They sat like exhausted statues. Before them on the table lay Anne's journal in a rough pile, next to it Nikki's translation and her own journal. Scattered on top of the pile of papers was a layer of the daily mail. A white envelope in Philip's handwriting rested on top, which Nikki was staring at.

"This place has held up pretty well," Meg observed quietly, seeming a little awed to be back in the house she had grown up in. "Any sugar?" she inquired, glancing cautiously around the kitchen and out toward the adjoining rooms. Nikki stood and pulled down her mother's white ceramic sugar bowl, its lid and one handle still missing, and set it before Meg, who spooned and stirred thoughtfully.

"He was watching over me," Nikki remarked vaguely, eyeing Philip's letter.

Moving into the doorway to the dining room, rubbing her neck, Meg nodded soberly.

Nikki touched the envelope with leaden fingers. "I have to pay another visit to the mansion."

"Philip?" Meg inquired, turning back. Nikki raised her head.

"What are you going to say?"

"Things are too confused and shadowy," Nikki replied after an extended pause. "I have no idea…"

"That's a change from ambivalent—for the better," Meg noted, sitting back down heavily.

"What?"

"Even though all your life you've blown hot and cold, you've always been so certain of whichever side becomes your current ally. I don't think I've ever heard you say you don't know—and just sit with the uncertainty. A good sign," Meg offered, patting her niece's hand.

"Doesn't help resolve matters," Nikki remarked, not taking her hand away.

"Most difficulties don't get resolved," Meg observed. "I had a close friend who died of AIDS years ago—one of the first to get it, one of the first to go. When he was first diagnosed and told me, I burst into tears and hugged him, then asked, 'What are we going to do?' He gave me that warm and wistful expression of his and quietly replied, 'Oh, we'll muddle through.' What do you think of that?" Meg looked up sadly.

"'Muddle through'…" Nikki echoed. "Has a kind of sweet and sad ring."

"Like life," Meg nodded.

"I'm not sure what I need—want—from Philip. Not sure even why I got involved with him."

"Was it to feel rejected?"

Nikki winced, sitting up straight. She started to react but, too tired, instead breathed deeply, letting the now-familiar heaviness in her settle. When she answered, her voice was low and slightly quavering. "Maybe that—and to get mad at him."

"For being married," Meg called the spade.

"Hmh!" Nikki shook her head, a mordant smile breaking through.

"Our friend Clarissa is full of stories about unconventional lives," Meg pointed out.

Nikki was quiet, her eyes sad. Meg pressed on.

"It's important not to live according to the way you think society says you should. Where would I be if I thought that way—? A neurotic mess," Meg chuckled with her deep-throated, heavy laugh. "Mind if I smoke?" she asked, fidgeting.

"Go ahead," Nikki returned, bemused.

"I'm neurotic regardless, come to think of it," Meg continued. "The socially-approved way, however, would make it much worse. That's one path you can freely choose *not* to follow."

"Rules?"

"Why not make them up as you go along?"

"Anything goes—?" Nikki sighed.

"So long as it's not a neurotic compulsion," Meg muttered through cupped hands, striking her cigarette. She drew deeply, exhaling with great satisfaction.

Nikki rubbed her forehead. Her headache was nearly gone, and the wind had died down. Looking out the kitchen window and recollecting the vision of Ernest, she shook her head thoughtfully, then spoke. "I remember Philip saying that the dead have to learn to be dead.… I can see his eyes and his hands, hear the tone of his voice," she admitted, closing her eyes and laying her head on the table.

Meg absently twirled her spoon, lifting a spoonful of sugar from the bowl, pouring it slowly back. "Granulated consciousness."

"What—" Nikki looked up sleepily.

"Understanding in bits, small insights…"

"It does come gradually, doesn't it?" Nikki reflected, raising her heavy head.

"And we've got to be like misers counting every penny of it, telling the little gold coins through our fingers, greedily savoring the details of life." Meg leaned back and smiled expansively at her niece. "You're becoming quite human, you know? I believe I'm proud to say I'm related."

Smiling shyly, Nikki went on. "That moment tonight when poor Clarissa assured Ernest he was not to blame.…" She hesitated. "I guess she really loved him," she admitted very quietly.

"Clarissa is a woman of integrity," Meg pronounced simply, waving smoke away from the table. Guy got up from his bed by the refrigerator and, trotting into the living room, jumped stiffly onto the couch and circled himself into a sleeping icon.

Nikki regarded her old aunt. "I used to argue with Philip about him getting his cake and eating it."

"Jesus! Would you want to try keeping up two relationships at once?"

"I suddenly felt a pang of pity for him."

"Pity—a good place to start, I suppose," Meg mumbled through her cigarette. "Or—compassion for a fellow sufferer on the road."

"I guess…yes," Nikki answered vaguely. "A *fellow* sufferer—?"

"No hierarchy," Meg spoke into her tea.

Nikki stared past Meg. "Then, I'm in the same—" She paused. "That explosion

I set off tonight—you'd think it would have left me charged. You know—*power.* It didn't...." Nikki sipped her lukewarm tea. "Do you think Rose will take the potion?"

Meg shrugged. "She's not stupid—just unbelievably vain. And frightened, of course, like all women in a society so lacking in breadth of imagination. She's fixed on her idea of beauty. But you couldn't have done anything to stop her if she's possessed by such a powerful death wish. Apparently Ernest imbibed it himself, in his own way...." Meg thought out loud, looking away.

Nikki considered Ernest's fate, but her mind was on Rose. "I feel sorry for her," Nikki declared. "She seems so powerless."

"That's the spirit moving you," Meg commented. "Everyone has power—it's our birthright. Some of us are more aware of it than others, that's all. I think those like Rose who don't know this prefer to be stuck in worrying about themselves. Something in them knows what they'd have to give up if they felt genuine power."

"Give up what?" Nikki poured them both more tea.

"Oscillating between feeling like a victim—and lording it over others. Or both at once! Playing the power game, wielding power like a muscle over others, worrying about protecting yourself all the time. Whereas if you have any sense you'll laugh at yourself—because the truest thing about life is that the joke's on us."

"I feel like I've been through a round of this before—with Philip," Nikki heaved another sigh.

"You have," Meg confirmed mildly.

"It's exhausting."

"Remember y2k!" Meg exploded, as Nikki raised an eyebrow. "Don't you remember? Going forward exposed the common worry—not that anyone will admit to it now—that we might be going back. The sense of time as circular is no idle abstraction once you realize how much...we just keep doing the same things over and over and over."

"That's a depressing thought."

"Not as an image. People's anxiety at the turn of the second Christian millennium was a kind of recognition of what the Druids knew long ago. We feared our computers would return us to 1900, and with that all the cars would revert to horse-drawn carriages. It was too wonderful!"

"Silly fears," Nikki waved a hand tiredly.

"Yes, but fears reveal something meaningful."

"That time goes in a circle," Nikki's head bobbed.

"A good joke, huh?"

"It's still depressing."

"It is, in a sense. It forces the issue—do you love Philip enough to bless a reality in which the two of you always go around and around and around?"

"Isn't that what you just warned was neurotic compulsion?"

"Not if you learn each time, and so shift it a little here and there."

Nikki thought on that, drawing out her words. "Something has shifted…in me."

"That's all you can hope for; true power is the ability to change. Life is worth it—and the last time I checked, so is love."

"Even if we just go around and around?"

"Maybe the trick is to enjoy the ride."

Nikki looked at Meg blankly. "I'm sorry, Auntie, I'm way too exhausted to understand. What's with you? You seem to get more energy the later it gets. Are you staying over tonight?"

Meg stopped twirling the spoon in her tea.

Nikki smiled. "I'd like it very much if you did—there's plenty of room. You might even come for visits. You know, your place in Salem seems a little—sad. Maybe you'd want to live with me. It's your house, after all."

Meg's eyes misted; she drew out a handkerchief.

Nikki regarded her old aunt in wonder.

Meg reached over and patted her niece's hand. "That's real kindness. You know, Sweetie, even I'm getting choked up thinking about you and Philip. As for enjoying the ride… What if much of your suffering over Philip stemmed from considering the rhythm between you two—being together and apart—as something inherently wrong? Rather than a fluctuation fundamental and beautiful, like the cyclical movement of the seasons?" Meg's eyes were clear now as she regarded Nikki closely.

"Seasons?" Nikki gasped, glancing up at the kitchen window. Spotting a figure dart across the other side of the glass, she felt a momentary flare of fear. But no—it was not Ernest, not her father; only a raven, rustling and dipping its black head on the sill. *Only—!* her mind marveled. Anne!

She stood as if an invisible hand had pressed into the small of her back, lifted by an invisible hand pressing into her lower back, pressing her on her way, her apprenticeship finished.

Walking toward the kitchen window, Nikki caught sight of the raven flying away, cawing once. She stood at the window, gazing out at the clearing sky. The stars were out, the moon was gone, and Mercury was hurrying stealthily past in the black deep. Her headache was gone; her sinuses as empty as a cave. Reflexively, Nikki touched the left shoulder of her cape, aware of the weight there. Her long fingers played softly over the broken brooch; she recalled that Philip had the missing piece.

It was not a sad time, she said to herself; *yes, it was a sad time*, her heart replied. She was ready to find Philip for them to talk together, now that she was whole. Now that she had lost herself in a thousand fragments. She found it easier to breathe and to think, easier to sink down and consider just what she actually did feel about him. Yes, she loved him, and wanted to tell him how he had changed her life. Maybe she wanted simply to see him looking back at her with recognition, with that warm, clear light in his eyes. Yes, she wanted him connected to her. But how?

"Maybe that's the muddling through," Nikki turned and spoke to her aunt.

"That's life," Meg responded hopefully, blowing a plume of smoke out into the kitchen air, which as Nikki watched changed into a cloud of swirling colors, forming itself into rings and floating around the room. Meg cocked an eye at Nikki, her mouth shaping an *O,* holding back the half smile forming on her face.

Nikki cast a sideways glance at her Aunt Meg, and the two burst out laughing. Guy raised his head at the new sound in the old house, then went back to sleep.